FATE'S FAVOR

FATE'S FAVOR

BOOK TWO IN THE
FRAYED THREADS SERIES

JADE NIOMA

Phoenix's
Fate
publishing

Content Warning:

Fate's Favor is an adult fantasy novel with darker themes, and is not suitable for those under the age of 18. This is not a dark romance novel. Please be advised of the following:

This book contains domestic violence/abusive relationships, swearing, substance use, blood and gore, violence and death, explicit consensual sex, mentions of sexual assault (no graphic on-page depictions), abduction, sexism and misogyny, mentions of suicidal thoughts, and mental health topics such as panic attacks, cPTSD, and depression.

This book contains many graphic depictions of fantasy violence, dipping into the realm of body horror during later chapters. There are depictions of physical transformations and mutations of the human body. There are also scenes involving descriptions of organs and corpses.

Name Pronunciation Guide
(Hierarcby Chart & Glossary of terms in the back of the book)

Eternal Kingdom
The Divinity
Alala *(Ah-lah-lah)* - action, passion, impulse
Alena *(Ah-lehn-ah)* - leadership, growth, vibrancy
Alessa *(Ah-less-ah)* - protection, defense, vulnerability
Astraea *(Ah-stray-ah)* - balance, justice, truth
Celestia *(Cell-ehs-tee-ah)* - spirit, intuition, unknown
Demi *(Dehm-ee)* - communication, wisdom, duality
Fay *(Fae)* - illumination, discovery, hope
Fria *(Free-ah)* - stability, teaching, guidance
Keres *(Care-ez)* - pain, rebirth, metamorphosis
Telma *(Tell-muh)* - expansion, freedom, innovation
Thera *(There-ah)* - creation, fertility, details
Sevasti *(Sev-ahs-tee)* - order, authority, power

Sacred Twelve
Sostene *(Sohs-teen)*
Amadeo *(Ah-muh-day-oh)*
Alvize *(Ahl-veez)*
Aurelio *(Owl-rehl-ee-oh)*
Brio *(Bree-oh)*
Carmine *(Car-mine)*
Dario *(Dahr-ee-oh)*
Giancarlo *(Gee-ahn-car-loh)*
Matteo *(Muh-tay-oh)*
Nicolo *(Neek-ah-loh)*
Terzo *(Tehr-zoh)*
Vincenzo *(Vin-CHen-zoh)*

Trine Scouts
Aether *(Aye-thur)*
Earnest *(Earn-est)*
Elara *(Eh-lar-ah)*
Horacio *(Or-ah-see-oh)*
Merit *(Mare-it)*
Michi *(Mee-chee)*
Nariah *(Nuh-rye-uh)*
Pollux *(Pohl-ux)*

Gods
Bendis *(Behn-dees)*
Domani *(Doh-mahn-ee)*
Luciano *(Lew-see-ahn-oh)*

Misc.
Hirtia *(Her-shuh)*
Yeyhara *(Yay-har-uh)*

Other Worlds
Haelos *(hay-lohs)* - Aurelio's planet
Alma *(Ahl-mah)*
Aspasia *(Ahs-pay-zee-ah)*
Calix *(Kay-licks)*
Eeda *(Ee-duh)*
Erelya *(Eh-rell-yah)*
Grimaldo *(Grim-ahl-doh)*
Itana *(Eye-tahn-uh)*
Monte *(Mohn-tee)*
Odilia *(Oh-dill-uh)*
Santoro *(San-tohr-oh)*
Tasia *(Tay-zee-ah)*
Yadira *(Yuh-deer-uh)*
Yensa *(Yehn-sah)*

Paiturn *(Pie-turn)* - Carmine's planet
Riejj *(Reeg)* - City on Paiturn
Delmira (Dehl-meer-ah)
Ezekiel (Eh-zeek-ee-ehl)
Letika (Let-ih-kah)
Jasira (Jah-seer-ah)
Zadkiel (Zad-key-ehl)

Yaailo *(Y-eye-loh)* - Dario's planet
Dileyna (Dill-ehn-yah)
Prai *(Pry)*
Saya *(Say-uh)*

Unknown Origin
Isolde *(eye-zowl-duh)*
Johanna *(Joe-han-uh)*

For the ones kissed by stardust.

Your empathetic heart is your superpower.

Author's Note

Fate's Favor contains domestic violence, which may be unsuitable for some readers. This series was written with the purpose of educating and raising awareness about the impact of abuse on survivors. Although this novel is a work of fiction, every day in our world, those who are meant to love and protect subject their victims to horrible treatment. Intimate partner violence is isolating, traumatic, and extremely dangerous.

As a survivor of an abusive relationship, it was vital to me that my main character's story didn't end when she escaped. I wanted these books to be about her journey toward freedom as she works toward healing all the trauma she carries with her and about learning to trust again after so much heartbreak. These novels follow Cosima through all the ups and downs and I don't shy away from showing all of the messy, complicated emotions. Survivors are not perfect victims, they are real people coping with the unthinkable.

If you know someone that has experienced DV, I hope this series can provide you with perspective on the inner struggle people go through both during and after abuse. If you find that you relate to Cosima's story, even if you wouldn't classify your situation as abuse, I want you to know that I see you and your pain is valid.

If you are a victim of domestic violence, help is available. You are not alone. There is no world in which you deserve to be treated with disrespect, or mental, physical, or emotional abuse. You deserve to be treated with softness and care. You deserve to find a loving relationship where your safety is prioritized. You deserve your peace. You are strong, you are capable, and your story is not over. In the US the National Domestic Violence Hotline is 800-799-7233.

$1 from every sale of this novel will be donated to "Control Alt Delete LLC", an organization that helps survivors flee abusive relationships. It is located in the Phoenix, AZ area. As per their website, they provide "emergency cab rides, hotel accommodations, home security, lock change assistance, meals, storage, and assistance with moving expenses". My hope is to expand these donations to more organizations with time. Thank you for helping me donate to a cause that means so much to me.

The Misjudged

When you sit at the feet of the Source of your
existence, bearing your fragile, impossibly
imperfect soul,

Will you turn away as your decisions are
dissected?

Will you wonder if your Creator is capable of
loving a child drenched with madness?

With the path, as you walked it, on full
display—the inescapable evidence of your
authentic nature and endless stumbling staring you
down—will you tremble beneath its weight, or will
you hold your head high?

Can you bear to be loved? Can you stand to
watch as your sins are washed away?

Or will you be the last to deny your soul the
mercy of being understood?

Chapter 1

Cosima

From dust and cosmic breath came squirming souls.
From wisdom and trials came our destined roles.

Cosima Aphelion had encountered the words on numerous occasions. They were inscribed on the frames of paintings and, at times like this, at the bottom of every important document that came her way. It had been nearly eighty empty days since she had left her home planet, Haelos, for the enigmatic Eternal Kingdom, and she had little to show for her time. She sighed as she ran her eyes over the paper on the desk once more.

The trance of time is the universe's poem. One sharp and one endless, the needle and thread are the universe's totem.

She rubbed her eyes, unsure if she would ever understand why the language used in the Kingdom's communication had to be so complex. It had not been her choice to arrive in the Ethereal Realm; she had been summoned by the twelve governing Goddesses, aptly referred to as 'the Divinity'. Cosima's former husband, Aurelio, had forced her to disrupt the delicate Fate threads to carry out his demented desire. This left her with no option but to await the judgment of this realm's Most High as she completed their busy work. They kept her occupied with pointless paragraphs filled with flowery words, requiring her to recite what she understood of it at the end of each session in order to move on to the next.

"I know it's quite boring, but at least finish this one so you can be done for the day," her Trine Scout said.

Trine Scouts were multi-faceted guardians for the Eternal Kingdom. More durable than Rani with a wider range of abilities, the Scouts were fit to trek across the many universes to hunt down criminals, find resources, and keep track of the creations placed by the Divinity. Cosima's assigned Scout was Nariah.

Cosima reluctantly met her gaze. Nariah was heartbreakingly beautiful. Warm wisteria eyes hid beneath her long, sweeping lashes. The way her mouth sat gave her a perpetual pout, and a lush pink sprouted from the center of her bottom lip from constant nervous chewing. Her ears resembled the wings of a faerie, the edges fanning outward with delicate ripples. Her white hair was tied behind her in an elegant bun, held together by decorative hairpins. Streams of it hung loosely, framing her face.

"This one is about the High Priestesses," Sima said with her head in her hands. "Something about the way they create and why."

Nariah frowned. "Wrong."

Sima threw her hands up. "I don't know then. I am tired. Can we please pick this back up tomorrow?"

The Scout crossed her arms. "No, Cosima. You must finish this by the end of today."

"I don't understand the point of this."

"Look, you are required to receive a trial in front of the twelve High Priestesses. The Divinity needs to make sure you are capable of taking the stand and have a minimum level of knowledge about the Kingdom in order to move forward. They cannot decide your future if you cannot comprehend how the court works."

Sima rested her forehead against the wooden table covered in shooting star-like patterns. She thought of Vincenzo and sent a silent prayer that he was faring well, despite the fact that they hadn't seen each other in months. Thinking of him brought her a drop of energy, enough to push forward. She took a deep breath and sat up. "Fine. I'll read it again."

None may unravel what has already come; only a Fated hand may reverse what is done. To withstand the wavering Weave, a thread must be divided thrice.

"I think this is about the three sisters I read about last week. The women who are above even the Divinity."

Nariah smiled. "Correct. Tell me one fact about the way their magic works, and I will let you return to your room to rest. In private."

At that, Sima raised a brow. Nariah was required to keep a near-constant eye on Cosima, as she was considered to be a dangerous criminal. She would not turn down a moment of solitude. "One is capable of creating new threads, one can sever them, and one can manipulate existing strings."

"Very good," Nariah said. She pulled Sima's document over and signed the bottom of the page before passing it back. "Add your signature and you can have two hours by yourself."

She did as she was told and rose to her feet. "What are you going to do?"

"Aether is coming by. Some movement is happening in the Kingdom, nothing to be worried about, but they're doubling up on Scouts for the evening. She and I will probably chat for a while."

Sima shuffled into her room, thankful to be able to shut the door behind her. Her accommodations included a fabulously decorated bedroom chamber with one extravagant bathroom, as well as a living area with a small kitchen. In her room, silk fabric sheets and soft, fuzzy blankets bloomed across the mattress, the gentle purple hue reminding her of rosemary flowers. From the ceiling, airy violet curtains tumbled to the floor, encapsulating her sleeping area in a quiet, false sense of privacy. The living area carried on the purple palette with a moody twist—sangria painted walls with plum couches adorned with periwinkle pillows.

Despite the beauty, Sima resided in a sick reality where she escaped her confinement inside the palace with Aurelio, only to end up in a frustratingly similar living arrangement. Every immaculate detail was a painful reminder she remained a captive, even after she had killed her previous captor. It was not that she would prefer to be living in squalor, but it drove her mad that her physical reality seemed to echo none of the pain she had been through, as if it had all been a dream.

With every day that passed, Sima only seemed to grow more homesick for her home, Haelos. She missed Ivo and Yadira, the two friends who had gotten her through her nightmare life with their love and support. There were times when she missed those she met in Ombra, too, including Calix, Monte, and Alma. Would she ever have the chance to see the creature-fighting trio again? Would she be granted one final chance to thank them and tell them how she admired them all, or would the High Priestesses erase them all with a snap of their fingers?

Cosima sat on the edge of her bed. She had known it was risky to alter the threads of Fate, but with her former husband's toxic demands, complying meant staying alive. At the yearly Giving ceremony on Haelos, Aurelio had recited the commandments, meaning Cosima could not claim she was unaware of the risks. Opposing the natural order of the universe put in place by the Kingdom would be met with divine retribution. Shame coiled inside her like a snake. It was because of her Aurelio had managed to stay in power for long, and it was because of her changes to Fate that her entire planet was at risk. It was clear that if she could not convince them otherwise, Haelos would be wiped from existence in the name of balance.

She squeezed her eyes shut and focused on breathing. Although it seemed like an impossible task, Sima searched her mind for faith—for a morsel of hope large enough to fuel her through the doubts. Her mind could be a wicked place to be lost in, but she could not give up with so much at stake. She lay down and curled into a ball as she allowed herself to find peace.

She thought of Vincenzo again—the depth of his emerald gaze and the way it held a near infinite amount of devotion within. The fullness of his lips and the soft way they brushed against her skin. Somewhere inside, he had created a sanctuary of safety for her, a place full of unshakable warmth. She could feel almost as good as she did in his presence so long as she immersed herself in the reminders of his love.

When the ache in her heart finally subsided, she wiped away the tiny tears at the corners of her eyes. Cosima had many questions that still required answers, and she was motivated to resolve them. A significant portion of her memories had been stripped from her or manipulated by Aurelio and Vincenzo's mother, Ehses. The Spirit Goddess was formerly a High Priestess before it was discovered that she had birthed her twelve sons in an attempt to overthrow the Kingdom. Cosima did not know why the Goddess had targeted her, but it left her with no recollection of her previous life and no family to return to.

"I will find where I belong," Sima whispered.

A knock sounded upon the door, and Sima dragged herself from the bed. She opened it and found two Scouts waiting for her. Beside Nariah was Aether, a Scout with curly red hair and a dual-toned gaze with one blue and one hazel eye. She grinned at Sima as she waved.

"You're being granted twenty minutes beneath the sun." Aether reached in and pulled her forward. "Don't waste it."

Sima followed the Scouts out of the exterior door to her chambers and into the main hallway. Although Cosima was a prisoner, she and the other less lethal captives were kept in a holding facility just outside of the court where the High Priestesses resided. What she had experienced of the Kingdom had been irritatingly minimal; however, she found herself looking forward to recreational time outdoors.

The hallways were made of incredibly high-quality druzy agate slabs covered with a clear hardening material meant to preserve the elaborate stones as people walked across them. It was obvious to her now where Aurelio had drawn inspiration for his remodeling of the Archipelago on Haelos—however, his crystal palace failed to compare to the real thing.

The Kingdom breathed quartz and agate crystals into every nook, creating a dazzling display, no matter where her eyes fell.

The white marble walls on either side of the hallway were lined with artwork capable of moving and recreating sound. Each offered a glimpse into other worlds as well as depicted the rich history of how the Eternal Kingdom came to be. Her eyes sank into the magnetizing artwork as she drank in as much of the novelty as she could before they reached the end of the exit.

She kept her hands folded in front of her as she walked, her dress and cape dragging behind her. The mossy green outfit perfectly complemented the elaborate gold belt fashioned around her waist. The belt was composed of carved disks bearing suns, crescent moons, and a series of unrecognizable planets. A long, delicate chain fell down the middle, ending near her knees. The cape, with its hand-stitched patterns and gold thread, further elevated her look. Her fingers aimlessly dragged up and down the fine yellow stars on the sleeve as they exited the holding chambers and stepped outside.

Though Cosima's clothing appeared luxurious to her, the ensemble was nothing compared to what the others wore. The Scout's iridescent metal glinted with the sun, creating tiny rainbows in their shadows. Nariah carried out a hushed conversation with Aether as Sima watched the sunlight dance off her armor. Wrapped around Nariah's shoulders was the carving of a Vinet. It was similar to a viper, except it had no eyes and its fangs hung below its bottom jaw. The craftsmanship made the Scout's undeniably elegant, mirroring the same sophistication the Eternal Kingdom radiated.

Cosima drank in the giant cherry blossom trees outside of the holding chambers that lined the long bridge, connecting their floating cloud island to the main spiral in the center of the Kingdom. At the very top sat a lotus flower tower. When she had arrived with the Trine Scouts through the portal, the lotus flower had been one of the first things that caught her attention.

As she stared up at it now, her heart skipped. She paused, and the Scouts turned toward her. "Do you think I will ever get to go back home, Nariah?"

"Only time will tell," she replied. Nariah revealed her wings, which were nearly translucent with a shimmering rainbow of color spread across them. Despite being shaped like delicate butterfly wings, they were surprisingly firm as they nudged Sima forward. "We aren't allowed to stop here. Let's keep moving."

When they reached the tiny outdoor courtyard where Cosima was allowed to spend time outdoors, she wasted no time finding a patch of sunlight to lie in. She plopped onto the clover and sighed as her skin began to warm beneath the amber rays. The courtyard itself sat between two tall buildings made from gray and yellow stone with a magnolia tree at the center.

Aether and Nariah slid onto a matching stone bench to the left of Sima. A tiny blue butterfly floated over to the red-haired Scout and landed on her fingertip. Aether laughed as she placed it on Nariah's shoulder. Nariah smiled and let the tiny insect crawl onto her hand. It flew off and circled around Sima a few times before it wandered off.

"Cosima, I must admit something to you," Nariah said, her expression soft. "I have spent an unruly amount of time pondering your situation, and though I have spent centuries as a Scout, never have I come across a story such as yours. Here in the holding chambers, we spend more time worrying about subduing the angry or unstable criminals. With you, it has been about reflection and growth and…"

Sima cocked her head to the side. "And?"

"I never thought I would care so much. I was told to be impartial, to not care for what those accused have to say. To wait for justice to enact its desired retribution, never interfering. However, I have come to realize you are not like the others in any sense. We see violent, despicable people here. You are anything but that."

Aether nodded. "Nariah and I have discussed your case on a few occasions, and I can't say I have seen signs of malice."

Sima's brows furrowed. "If only your Kingdom could see that as well. I almost wonder if they are ignoring me out of spite. Shouldn't this matter to them?"

Nariah's lip twitched. "It does matter to them."

Aether leaned forward slightly. "There is a lot that goes into managing the greater part of a realm, Cosima. Much goes wayward in the pursuit of boundless creation and sustainable balance."

"It is further complicated because of the Spirit Goddess's interference," Nariah said. "I can't reveal everything, but capturing Ehses and her sons is high on the list of priorities for this Kingdom. The Divinity will restore harmony in time. The reason Aether and I are telling you this is we need you to not give up. It is a great mystery of the universe what has turned Ehses and her sons into this, but have faith and trust. We shall find out why in due time. The Kingdom is not ignoring you. You are not the only case of chaos in the cosmos."

Aether crossed her ankles and chewed her cheek. "We are trying to gain you more recreation, and we've requested that you be allowed to visit with Vincenzo."

Sima sat straighter as she blinked a few times in a row. "Really? You did that for me? But I thought you hated him because of his relation to the Sacred Twelve."

A flicker of emotion made Nariah's nose and brows twitch lightly. "You should not depend on anyone else. Especially not men like him. However, we acknowledge that this man has some meaning to you, and we would like to raise your spirits."

"Thank you," Sima breathed. "When can I see him?"

"Tomorrow morning," Aether said.

"Listen, I've met a few of the Sacred Twelve before," Nariah bit out. "They are all the same, whether he shows it to you or not. You cannot be sure of anything he says or has planned. He will reveal his wicked ways in time. All I ask is that you be careful, even if you continue to pursue your relationship."

Cosima tilted her head to view the open sky between the bumblebee jasper buildings and took a deep breath. It was the warmth of the daylight or maybe the scent of the trees that made Sima more optimistic than she had been since her arrival. "Vincenzo has shown me nothing but softness and care. I know it doesn't make sense, but I don't feel afraid of him. A deep piece of me feels we are entwined somehow. Trust the weaving, isn't that right, Nariah?"

Nariah sighed. "Do not mock my devotion to the path laid before us."

"I am following where the wind guides me." Cosima smiled and let herself fall backward into the clover. She let its soft scent fill her, and music echoed in her mind, like it did each time she thought the pain of missing him would devour her.

"Save the lectures for another time," Aether said. "Let her enjoy her last couple of minutes before we take her back to her room."

Sima's eyes fluttered shut, and a gentle memory washed on the shore of her consciousness. She indulged a habit she had grown attached to since the first batches of her once hidden memories became decipherable. It had taken her mind quite some time to adjust to the flood, but every once in a while, it presented her with a gift.

"That boy," Cosima hissed. She was crouched around the bottom of a statue of High Priestess Alala with her bow and arrow pointed toward the rising sun on the horizon. "How does he always manage to sneak off?"

Watching the split-haired boy had become a favorite pastime of hers, especially since she had never met anyone quite like him. She frowned. Not that she had actually met him either, but she knew his name was Vincenzo and that he was a Rani Guardian, and that, along with his rampant good deeds, was enough for her to be enamored.

Massive trees rained pink and blue flowers over her head as she scurried along the outer rim of the Kingdom. She knew better than to go beyond the gates, as she was forbidden from exploring the remainder of the Ethereal Realm; however, she did not plan to actually leave. Instead, she used a branch hanging over the wall to pull herself up onto the ledge. From there, she scanned her surroundings.

"Ha, found you," she whispered. She made herself comfortable on the edge of the wall and continued to watch him. "What could you possibly be up to today?"

Vincenzo glanced around with a deep grimace, creating lines in his cheeks. It amused Sima to watch him be so careful when he had yet to spot her trailing him. She wasn't sure why exactly she followed him the first time, but now she was in too deep to stop. Other immortals wasted their time or treated each other in demeaning ways, but he never did.

Once he was sure the coast was clear, Sima watched as he stepped outside of the open gate, his feet landing on the hard dirt of the Ethereal Realm. He tipped his head back and whistled. A low rumbling came from somewhere in the distance, growing closer until it came to a sudden halt. A cloud of dust hid Vincenzo and a massive, shadowed figure from view.

As it settled, Sima strained her eyes to see what was happening. She could not tell what the black furred creature was, but it had long floppy ears, a giant, almost boxy shape to its body, and sad eyes. Vincenzo patted the creature on its back before he pulled out a thin glass tube from a holster on his hip. He pulled off the cap and poured it into its mouth.

The creature shook its head as it swallowed, and within seconds, it transformed. Already twice Vincenzo's size, the being seemed to expand, growing taller and wider. Where she believed she had seen black fur, there was now brilliant dark purple hair with a healthy shine. Its sad eyes were replaced with what Sima could only describe as a gaze filled with gratitude.

It licked at his chin, and Vincenzo laughed, taking a step back. After one last nuzzle of its nose against Vincenzo's Rani uniform, it turned and walked away, just out of Sima's sight. Vincenzo waved it goodbye, dusted himself off, and ventured back into the territory of the Eternal Kingdom.

"What a strange one you are," Sima whispered to herself. "A dangerously kind man."

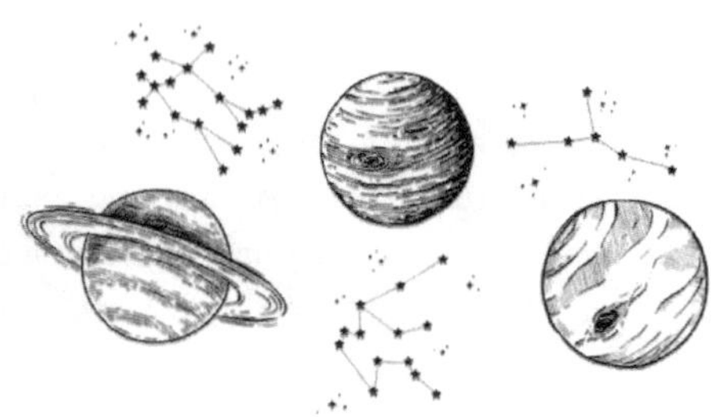

Chapter 2

Vincenzo

Vincenzo pried his eyes open at the first sound of footsteps down the hallway outside. His breathing stalled, and he waited for confirmation of his suspicions. From where he lay tangled in his pine green sheets, Merit, his Trine Scout, was visible through the crack Enzo left in his bedroom door. He watched as Merit unlocked the front entrance and spoke to someone, taking it as all the initiative he needed to spring from the bed.

Conversation flowed easily in the living area as he pulled on a black undershirt and pants. He frowned at himself in the mirror, finding he could think only of Cosima. What bothered him about his appearance was not the distinct lack of armor he grew accustomed to wearing since his birth, but the hauntingly empty space beside him. What would she think of him in this state? It was a new vulnerability—to be outside of Haelos but still at a distance from one another. His body was on alert constantly, as if every piece of him recognized her absence and searched for her continuously. He shook his head and attempted to straighten the locks of white and black hair, which had entangled themselves into a desperate mess.

"Vincenzo," Merit called. "Where are you?"

He sighed, exiting the wardrobe to meet his Scout.

"Here." Enzo's voice was rough enough to make him wince. The long weeks spent without speaking wore on his vocal cords. He rubbed his throat and coughed. "Who's here?"

He did not respond, but Merit's nose wrinkled as he took in Vincenzo. Something like disgust, or something like supreme apathy. Enzo was never sure which emotion described Merit's strange demeanor. The Scout wore his tan uniformed armor with a long olive cape swaying behind his kneecaps and brushed a hand through his short navy hair as he rolled his eyes.

"What? Do I still smell like my feathered brothers, even after all these weeks?"

Merit's mouth twisted. "Something like that."

"Who's here?"

"A friend."

"Of yours or mine?" Vincenzo swayed on his feet with unease. *Could this be it?*

"Yours," Merit said. He left the room, returning a moment later with another Scout. She was tall, with long arms and legs. Her purple eyes narrowed, and she scrunched up her face as she flicked her ivory hair over her shoulder.

"Opposite of a friend," Vincenzo said, with a grimace. "Still. Seeing you here could only mean one thing."

Nariah folded her arms in front of her chest. "At least you are wise enough to know I do not think fondly of you. But yes, it is time."

His heart squeezed in his chest, but he cooled his face into a neutral expression. *I wish I spent more time getting ready.* Enzo smoothed his hair down with his hands before he tugged on his boots and followed the Scouts, endless thoughts of Cosima drifting through his mind like soft snowfall in the heart of winter. This would be their first reunion since being separated upon arrival to the Eternal Kingdom. Every second without her tormented him, and now his heart pounded as if it could break through his chest and land directly in her lap.

I only just found you. It will never be enough; I could never have enough of you.

Merit and Nariah chatted as the three of them walked out of the chamber and into the hallway. Although it had only been a few months, Nariah moved as though she were uncomfortable without Cosima by her side. The Scouts took their positions seriously, but something about the persistent scowl on Nariah's face convinced him that she cared for Sima, at least to some degree, beyond mere obligation.

Their footsteps echoed as they turned a corner, his jaw grinding his teeth tightly. The extravagance of his home irritated him, and though it was aesthetic, the mere sight of crystals reignited the flame of protective anger within. The opulent displays did not infuriate him prior to Haelos, but his brother ruined the sparkling stones for Enzo permanently. Now he only associated them with despair and unending stress headaches. At minimum, the gems in this realm were inert, or so the Kingdom claimed.

Hallways he had never seen before emulated the same overly decadent displays of fine artwork, hand-carved baseboards, and expert crown molding. The many tiny details in this Kingdom intrigued him once before, but lately, it was all unimpressive. Now that he knew he would see her soon, he cocked his head to the side, examining the small constellations, wondering what Cosima thought the first time she experienced the craftsmanship of the center of the universe. A string in his heart tugged, and without thinking, he sent beams of comforting embrace toward her, hoping she could feel it. Her shielding made much of his magic ineffective, but he sent her as much peace as he could manage.

"How long do they have?" Merit picked at his teeth with a fingernail.

"Bendis gave them an hour, despite general objections from the Priestesses."

Vincenzo's brows lifted. *Bendis.* Goddess of the hunt, second in command to High Priestess, Alala. While not a member of the Divinity herself, it was her tenacious spirit that led to the expansion of the universe, to the change and ascension of their society. It was clear Bendis carried influence in this realm. *Why has she favored us?*

Merit chuckled. "Better than nothing. Are we on the whole time?"

Nariah shook her head, and he dodged the strands of her white hair that flicked toward his face. Vincenzo scowled. "We are granted two nights of restoration. Pollux has them for now, then Michi will reside with her."

"Pollux, huh?" Merit peered over his shoulder. Vincenzo shot him a sharp gaze, causing him to huff. "I wish him luck. I tell ya, I need this break more than you know."

Vincenzo bit down his desire to bite Merit's head off and instead focused on the internal tug vying for his attention. Cosima was near. He could feel her, could sense her. Her magic was powerful, but her presence alone was enough to make him weak in the knees. His feet would bring him to her whether he commanded them forward or not. Their reunion was inevitable the moment he became aware of her.

"Through here, feathers." Merit grinned at him, clearly pleased to be rid of him for some time.

Nariah held open a thick stone door the color of pearls. Her nose twitched as he passed, and his lip curled upward. He was delighted to be able to make her as uncomfortable as she made him, though it was ultimately a hollow win. Nariah was not mean out of spite, she merely viewed him as an outlier in the greater plan set forth by the Divinity. He stood between her and the pristine existence she imagined this realm deserved, if only because he was alive at all. His mother's creation of him and his brothers unraveled a host of permeating disruptions throughout galaxies and sprouted chaos that would be solved best with their swift deaths.

He walked through the door and spotted the solitary golden bench beneath a full magnolia tree. It was empty. "Where is she?" He spun, scanning their faces for any hint of deception.

"Relax," Nariah growled. "She's only a minute behind us."

"Why are you not with her?" His fingers curled into a fist. The rational side of him preached patience as he pulled himself out of anger.

"We know better than to leave her alone," Nariah said, adding emphasis with dramatic blinks, providing attitude through eyelashes.

"Michi needed an introduction to her routine. Go take a seat," Merit commanded.

Vincenzo stared at her for a moment before his eyes flicked to Merit. Like a storm cloud, his power shadowed over him, plummeting him into a deep desire to kill anyone who came between him and Cosima. It was what he should have done the first moment he saw her on Haelos, instead of being a coward. Guilt rattled him, and he averted his eyes.

The Trine Scouts left him, and emptiness personified itself in the suffocating silence in the courtyard. Surrounded on all sides by walls, he had no choice but to feel trapped. The open sky above him taunted him, toying with every bit of logic ingrained in him about this kingdom. Invisible restraints coated the nonexistent ceiling, keeping him contained, for now. Freedom was so close and yet wholly unachievable without excessive force.

The sound of a door opening had him on his feet. Time slowed the moment his eyes fell on her. Cosima knocked the breath from his lungs, and the words he rehearsed slipped from his mind. There was only her— beautiful, irreplaceable her. No worries, no fears, only devotion and untamed love surged from him, his soul in pure recognition of hers. Before him stood the greatest relief he had ever been granted, the only true divinity he believed in.

He took in her captivating aura, her beauty reaping straight ecstasy from his longing heart. Every agonizing drop of untethered rage vanished, raising his vibration to match the magic that was Cosima. He could never forget her, and he read her features like the pages of his favorite book. Her expression almost broke him, his stomach twisting in response to the pain dripping off her as if she were soaked in it. They rushed toward each other, a broken sob escaping her lips as he wrapped his arms around her.

Enzo held his breath as if she might slip through his grasp until the warmth of her body bled into his. He broke, breathing her scent deep as it reminded him why he had bothered to live at all, why he held on for so long. She smelled sweet like blooms from forbidden gardens, beckoning him to pull her even tighter against him. He was whole again as long as she was here. His undying adoration for her gripped him as he peppered gentle kisses along her shoulder and neck. The sensation of her skin against his lips and the scent of her hair ravaged a blissful destruction through him.

Home. You are my home.

He resisted the urge to keep her close as she twisted free and met his gaze. Her warm brown eyes spoke of the experiences weighing on her, reminding him once again, they were not free. The truth was palpable in the furious thud of his heart—he could not live inside his delusion. They were shackled perhaps more than ever before, and with no word on their futures, he had no tangible hope to cling to—beyond the spark in her eye and the burning in his soul for her.

Enzo scooped her face in his hands and kissed her with the fury of every unjust moment they had spent apart. She threaded her arms around him, encouraging him to kiss her deeper and more desperately. Only when Pollux arrived, clearing his throat audibly, did their passion wane, and Enzo reluctantly pressed his lips just one more time on hers before pulling away.

"I love you." The words tumbled through his lips, the only ones that made sense to say. His voice lowered enough for Pollux to be unable to hear him—the Scout's presence was intrusion enough. "If there is any mercy in this endless universe, it is everything you are. Being yours has irrevocably changed me, and I could not be more willing to prove how worthy I am of your grace. Nothing has been the same without you."

Her expression softened, and he thought the mere sight of it might do him in completely. "I love you, Enzo," she whispered, the words like a prophetic vision of freedom. Her voice was velvet, smooth in ways that had him begging for more of it. "I feel like I've finally stopped running, like I've been searching for you everywhere."

"I'm here, my love," he whispered. "They could never keep me from you. Even in death, my soul is bound to yours." He held her at arm's length and inspected her closely, his eyes covering every inch of her from head to toe. "How are you? How have you been? Are you eating enough? Do you like what they feed you?"

She averted her eyes but did not pull away. "I have been well enough... And you? Where do they have you? Have they hurt you?"

"No," he said, adding a small laugh. "No one has hurt me. Don't turn this back on me. Tell me the truth." When she frowned, he raised his hand and gently brushed it against her cheek. "I wish I could take it all away. I wish I could mend every pain."

Sima sighed. "I haven't heard anything about what the High Priestesses think of us or of Haelos. I thought they would help us or…care, at least. How much longer will we be forced to wait for them to deem us worthy of their attention?"

The little bit of fire in her had a smile forming across his face. "Haelos is one of billions causing trouble. Perhaps it is a good sign we are not the ones they are most concerned with."

"I thought his death…"

Aurelio. The mention of him opened a wicked, sprawling wound that survived purely on spite and blinding wrath. "You thought his death would signal some level of urgency to them, especially after they witnessed what occurred?"

She nodded. "The waiting is eroding my confidence. What about your other brothers? What about your mother and the crystals?"

He'd spent his time dwelling on the same questions in captivity as well. It frightened him, the possibility they would be killed for the sake of simplicity, treated with not even a drop of mercy. "What about us?" His fingers found hers in a loving embrace, and the effortless act of holding hands made him brave enough to push further. "Have you thought about what you want after this? If they allow us to be free, I will take you anywhere you want to go."

"How can you focus on something that might never happen?"

"Quite the pessimist."

She smiled, and his eyes locked onto it.

"What is out there for me? I have a family, I think, but Nariah told me they have no idea who I am. Who am I supposed to be?"

Vincenzo's lip twitched. "Only you can answer that."

She pouted her lips in a way that enamored him as she considered his words and ran her fingers up and down his arm. He allowed the feeling of her touch to comfort the pitifully dark pieces of himself and imagined the woman she could become someday with a future untapped. An image of her dressed as elegantly as a Celestial Empress popped into his mind. The intrusion was unnerving as he craved an easy life by her side. Yet her character, her drive, her kind-heartedness, all reminded him of her strength as a leader. Someone like Cosima would transform a Kingdom as impractically callous as this.

"The first thing I want to do is find my real family, whoever they are. I think all decisions depend on that."

"We will find them," he promised. "I will do whatever it takes to give you the life you desire."

She relented a small grin. "I remembered something." Her voice was low, secretive, or perhaps she was nervous.

"That's good," he whispered. "What happened?"

She giggled, and the sound of it was music after an eternity of silence. "It was about us. We strolled through a market, buying anything we did not recognize. We spent the entire day laughing and eating."

He smiled. He knew that day well; the memory of their innocent beginning was enough to make his chest ache. "Yes, we ventured outside the Kingdom, into the greater parts of this realm. We went without permission, and would you believe me if I told you that you talked me into it?"

She held him tighter, sniffling. "I didn't remember that part."

"It will all come back in time."

"Enzo?" she asked, her honey brown eyes wide as she looked at him. "We will get out of here one day, won't we? What if the Eternal Kingdom chooses to lock me up and throw away the key? What if they decide to kill me for what Aurelio made me do?"

Vincenzo's breath caught as rage flooded through him, reddening his cheeks. "I promise I will protect you. I wouldn't let them lock you away forever, nor would I let them lay a hand on you."

The sound of the stone door opening behind him brought waves of hopeless dread. He was not ready to leave her. He could never be ready. Pollux and a Scout, whom he assumed was Michi, arrived, based on the two sets of footsteps that entered.

Michi's sash was plum purple and adorned with many medals. Each star and planet arrangement depicted a different achievement. A sudden wind blew her shoulder-length midnight blue hair across her face. Her hand reflexively adjusted it as her sharp nose tilted upward with disapproval. For the first time, Enzo got a proper look at Pollux. He had medium-length wavy blond hair and a casual demeanor, giving him the appearance of a permanently relaxed traveler on the coast world's away, instead of an expertly trained Scout.

"Time to go," Michi said, her voice flat.

"You, as well," Pollux said, jerking a thumb over his shoulder. "Get a move on."

Cosima turned to him, her eyes pleading for more time, and he hated that he could not give it to her. "We were supposed to have an hour," he grumbled. Part of him felt like a child having to ask for what was rightfully his.

Michi glared at him. "Don't care. Time to go."

"I don't want to go," Sima whispered.

Enzo pulled her hand into his and gazed into her eyes. "I am always with you. There is nothing anyone can do to keep me from you."

A sharp stabbing pain targeted his heart—the words were truer than she knew, but for now, he would keep himself in line. He pulled her into another embrace, tighter than before. Enzo breathed her in and whispered that he loved her. Her face was blank, covered in a foreign and ghostly expression, as a tear slipped down her cheek. She stepped out of his arms and whispered a miserably short goodbye.

Before he could object, Cosima and Michi departed, and his reality became grim and incomplete once again. He blinked, dismayed at how quickly she vanished from his sight. The internal tether between them was taut, heavy with their mutual grief. He could not explain the connection between them, or even discern whether it truly existed in the way he imagined it did. Either way, he sent all the love his broken heart could muster through, hoping to give her whatever strength he had left.

Sleep came in fits for Enzo ever since his arrival in the Eternal Kingdom. Despite how he longed for a night of continuous sleep, that was evidently too much for him to ask of the universe. As his heavy eyelids teetered shut, his mind flared with terrifying truths and haunting hints at a future of eternal suffering.

His dream overtook him at last, smothering his body's fear response to the horrid scenes that gripped his unconscious mind. He found himself running through a black void, explosions of fervent screams and harrowing utterances of unimaginable pain pelting his mind. Everywhere he looked, he only found more emptiness and a never-ending supply of all-consuming dread. He wondered if there was something chasing him, if he should stop running and fight instead, but he could not get his legs to stop moving.

When at last he toppled to his knees, the shadows dissipated, showing him the horror he had created. He had not been running from someone, desperate to save his own life. Instead, his dreams were a twisted rendition of everything he feared—that the entire time he was running from himself and his actions.

All around him lay death and devastation, blood running rivers off the edges of the sky. He saw the Eternal Kingdom in shattered pieces, the people, the Divinity, the Caelari, all dead because of him. Their torment echoed in the air around him, suffocating him on his own misdeeds. The dream made one thing, above all else, abundantly clear.

This is the price to pay if you lose control.

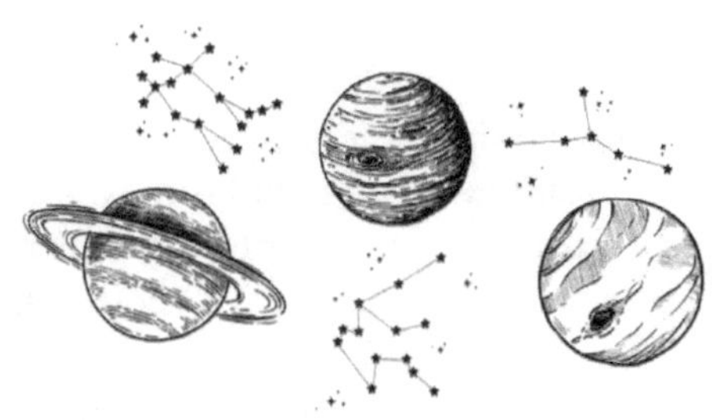

Chapter 3

Cosima

Obnoxiously bright lights snaked across Cosima's bed and barreled straight through the thin skin of her eyelids, startling her awake. She rubbed the sleep from her eyes with the back of her hands and found Michi standing above her. She screamed, and Michi's palm clamped tightly over her mouth.

"Do not," Michi growled. The dark circles planted firmly on her face spoke of her energy level, accompanied by dried drool crusted to the side of her mouth. "I am exhausted and displeased about this situation enough as it is. There is somewhere we must go."

"Where?" Her mind swam with deliriously frightful scenarios.

Why couldn't they have assigned me anyone else in Nariah's absence? Sima thought as she sat up. *Why not Aether? Or that one I met in passing, Elara? Why Michi?*

The Scout tugged her from the bed with a tight grip around her wrist. With her free hand, Sima snagged a silky lilac robe discarded on an armchair and slipped it on. Once Michi released her, she tied the garment shut, relieving her of the worry that others would catch a glimpse of her body through her nightgown. The mere idea of anyone besides Vincenzo looking at her in that way made her uncomfortable.

She squinted her eyes against the blinding hallway lights and followed the Scout barefoot to their mystery destination. She debated pressing Michi for more information, but as far as Cosima was concerned, the Scout was a stranger and apparently did not take kindly to being woken up at an early hour. Instead, Sima resigned to half-asleep patience as the cold floor bit at her toes. The early hour meant every twist and turn was met with lingering quiet, and the emptiness became more unsettling the further they traveled.

Michi came to a sudden halt and turned. The colorful, flowery trim on the white stone door drew in Cosima's attention, only for it to be ripped open by the grumpy Scout, who waved Cosima in with a thick scowl. Her head peered around the corner, taking in the dimly lit room. Inside, a single light orb hung from the ceiling above a black oak table, complete with two matching chairs with worn red cushions. The bare room sent warning bells through her gut, but before she could reject, Michi shoved her inside, and the door latched behind her.

Cosima stumbled forward, nearly colliding with the table. The room was claustrophobic and threatened to collapse in on her with every fast breath she took. She banged her fists against the door, the sweltering grip of panic hot against the nape of her neck.

"Please," she cried. "Please, Michi. Why am I in here?"

She beat against the door until her hands grew sore and heavy. When it was clear she would not be let out, she began inspecting the limited furniture for something to pick the lock. As if manufactured with magic and not conventional means, the chairs bore no loose metal or screws. She hissed with frustration and stood. Her brain rambled through potential reasons Michi discarded her in such a dreary room, questioning everything from being left for dead to torturous interrogations. She slid her palms against the walls, hoping to uncover a way out. It was then that the door opened.

Cosima snapped into a neutral position with her hands at her sides to not give the impression she was attempting to escape. Her heartbeat hammered in her ears as a woman stepped inside the room. Even as the door shut behind her, Cosima did not move a muscle. She was frozen, unsure if her eyes were deceiving her, or if she was truly face to face with someone she'd seen only in contorted memories.

Kismet.

The energy vibrating from the deity was enough to bring Cosima to her knees, unable to resist the demanding urge to repent and swear her loyalty. It was heavy and squeezed her like a hand to the throat, choking the life from her body. The solitary glance at the mythical woman brought fiery illumination to every dark crevice of Cosima's soul, making it impossible to hide her shadows. Kismet's hair flowed like galaxies, the midnight black as deep as space itself, hiding infinite creation within. Her eyes were gray and white, marbled like smoke rising to kiss the clouds.

Kismet's beauty was incomparable, cosmic. Intricate like the vast universe, delicate like a fawn hidden in the grass, and harsh like tsunamis and natural destruction. Her heart-shaped face was the perfect canvas for her prominent high cheekbones, plump lips, and sculpted, full brows. Her grassy green gown flooded at her feet, spilling onto the floor. The medium-length train featured tiny, fragile flowers as if they fell across the back of her dress while she swept through the forest.

"Hello." Her voice was angelic, and most confusing of all, sorrowful.

Cosima straightened her back. She remained on her knees before Kismet, unsure of the proper manner to address a deity of magnificent proportions. Her mouth opened, and no words came out.

"Come, little diamond. Rise." Kismet swept over to the table and took a seat, as if it were normal for someone of her stature to sit in a room completely beneath her. The room was a grim recreation of misery, and Kismet was a thunderous force, powerful enough to command more than Cosima could conceptualize. The entire setting seemed so out of place that it only added to her rising anxiety.

Hesitantly, Sima rose to her feet. Her knees wobbled and threatened to give out, but she walked to the table and took the remaining open seat. She commanded calm from within and hoped it reflected outwardly. She could not allow herself to be a coward. Yet, it was impossible to meet Kismet's eyes, to take in her smoky gaze, and each time Sima tried, she lost confidence before succeeding. Kismet sat statuesque, seemingly unaware that Cosima struggled to acclimate to the weight of the woman's aura.

Is this how it feels to be near the only entity the Gods themselves fear?

"I can sense you are wondering why I chose to bring you here and why our meeting must take place in a setting such as this," Kismet said with measured speed. The deity of predestination, the one who appointed the stars in the sky, the one who laid destiny for all, spoke with immeasurable delicacy in every word. "The High Priestesses decided against this vehemently; however, I am not someone who accepts 'no' as a deterrent. Instead, it makes me hungry. It makes me pursue my path with spite and fervor. Each day, my threads grow weaker, but I have not relinquished my power yet."

Cosima smiled, and a hand floated up to touch her lips. Her own expression was somewhat unexpected, given her prior fear and desire to grovel at Kismet's feet, but something about the deity felt familiar. This was the woman Cosima suspected she might be related to, to some degree. "I suppose I can understand that."

Kismet's lips tugged upward, though her expression remained too melancholic to convey happiness. It unlocked something within Cosima—a desire to comfort the mysterious deity, rebounded only by the woman's intimidating presence.

A single clear drop of Kismet's sadness slid down her cheek and dove from her chin to the chilly floor. "You are striking. When they first described you to me, I predicted deception. But no, you look exactly like her."

"Like whom?"

"My daughter."

Cosima swallowed stiffly, her mouth suddenly dry. "Your daughter?"

Could it be?

"She has been missing for quite some time. Many decades, though the wound is just as fresh as the day she vanished. I had heard the whispers about disappearances occurring in our realm, but never once did I believe my own family would fall victim. The grief has driven me to insanity, or at least the others believe so, but I still have hope." Kismet turned her head toward the empty wall and her eyes scanned it aimlessly, mind riddled with unspoken thoughts and anguish. "I thought perhaps you were her from the descriptions the Trine Scouts brought me. However, now that you are in front of me, I can see I was mistaken. You resemble my daughter, but my soul does not recognize you."

Disappointment saturated Sima's skin. In a few, too-short seconds, she'd grown painfully hopeful someone recognized her at last. Yet, the universe would not grant her this relief, and instead, plummeted her into further darkness and despair.

"Oh." She briefly considered explaining the memories she had, alluding to some relation between the two, but it was pointless. If Cosima had ever known mercy, she might have believed this was simply a hiccup in the greater journey home to herself. Instead, she knew the key to her past would not manifest so simply, at least not here.

Kismet's slender fingers drummed on the table with an almost vacant expression. "Under usual circumstances, my powers catalog each life I connect with. It appears we have not met before; otherwise, perhaps I would have been able to discern your heritage. As it stands, no one is aware of where you come from. That fact alone is what drove me here tonight, desperate to know once and for all if you were her. You share such a striking resemblance to my daughter, Moira, that before I took a closer glance at your features, I wondered if my magic had somehow deceived me." Kismet shook her head. "But despite the similarities, you are not her. I am sorry I am not able to offer you the answers to questions that must trouble you deeply."

Cosima nodded slowly. She often carried the invisible weight of her grief. More time without answers, while difficult, was not enough to stop her completely. It was foolish to dare assume she was worthy enough to be Kismet's daughter, but Sima did not know how else to interpret the memories—if not fraudulent altogether, they perhaps misrepresented Cosima's true origins. How was she to know which memories to trust? "Can you tell me about Moira?"

Kismet's mouth dropped open, appearing as though she were unaccustomed to being asked about the missing piece of her heart. The deity's eyes were hazy, as if her mind was dazed by the rushing current of emotions Cosima imagined Kismet was experiencing. Her chin dropped a fraction, and her full lips trembled. The air grew thicker, harder to breathe, and Cosima knew it was Kismet's power blanketing the room in its suffocating embrace. This was nothing short of torture for both of them.

"She was the hum of night, the empty silence where sleep steals us off to imaginary lands. She was every star, in its full, incomprehensible brilliance. Even without inheriting my abilities, she was the light of my life, and sometimes I think…" Her throat bobbed, and another tear slid from her cloudy eyes. "I think she became my reason for existence, the muse behind my creation. In the sprawling of our worlds, it was the connection to my child that tethered me to life with undying devotion. I knew love existed because there was no other word to describe what I felt for her."

Tears somersaulted from Cosima's face like graceful performers as Kismet spoke, tumbling one after another in measured chaos. The years spent beneath an abuser never numbed the inner burning to be loved, to be cherished. Aurelio could take away her sanity, but he could never demolish the little girl within, reaching toward the sky, expecting a motherly touch to clean her of her troubles. The loneliness had never been quite so palpable, and she stared down at her open palms in her lap.

"Thank you for sharing that with me. I can't imagine the immensity of your pain, but in some small ways I relate. I long to be with my family, but I can't remember who they are. My memories were…altered by Ehses, and the unraveling of her work has left me with a confusing, unclear puzzle."

Kismet sniffed softly, dabbing at the inner corners of her eye with the fleshy pads of her fingertips. It took only a steadying breath before she was the picture of refined sophistication once more. "Ah, that I can understand," Kismet said. "I struggle with my memory as of late. Grief can make the weight of the past too grand to cope with. There are dozens of items I have misplaced, even some of my most treasured pieces that reminded me of Moira. I wonder at times if my jewels have up and flown away." The deity tilted her head. "How much of your memories do you retain?"

Sima laced her fingers together. "A pitiful amount. The recollection comes out of nowhere and strikes me, often leaving me dazed afterward. Without proper context, I see faces and hear snippets of conversation, but not enough to ground me."

Kismet gave her a sad smile. "You may not be my daughter, but your loved ones are out there. I am confident there are people who miss you. Don't give up hope."

At that, Sima's heart squeezed. "Thank you, Empress. What becomes of me after this?" Sima asked.

"The High Priestesses shall send for you when the time is right. There is no telling what conclusion they will come to, though, I will request extensive deliberation before any rulings are enacted."

"Apologies if this is an inappropriate question, but I find myself with no knowledge of how this realm functions. Are you a Goddess or something… greater?" Cosima resisted the urge to cringe at the discomfort probing Kismet brought.

A ghostly smile marked her lips. "Ah. Yes. I believe the term you are looking for is Celestial Empress. That is my official title. There are three of us who command, perched atop the hierarchy, I suppose. Lethe and Nyssa are my sisters in spirit. We share no common blood, but we are the hierophants of destiny."

"I have not heard of them before."

"They are quite wrapped in their roles. Life and Death require precision balance."

That caught Cosima's attention. Her brows flew upward as the words settled. *Life? Death?*

Reading her confused expression, Kismet laughed. It was empty, forced. "There are legends, you know, about the Weave. The Weave is where all Fated strings originate, where our decisions are enacted. Nyssa prepares the strings and begins the inevitable cycle of birth for each soul. I prepare their allotment and apportion their paths. When the story reaches its finality, it is Lethe who welcomes them home. There they shall slumber, rest, replenish, until it is once again time for refinement. In time, these souls eventually become Caelari—powerful Gods and Goddesses in our realm—or they become one of the other three immortal types, like the Ambrosi or Rani."

The Drago, the gigantic, scaled creature from the In-Between, appeared behind her eyelids. With every blink, her mind pelted with reminders that it was Cosima who changed the decisions put forth by Kismet.

"How do you decide their Fate?" she asked, too terrified to keep quiet. There was no telling if Kismet was aware of Cosima's ability to alter predetermined lives.

What would it take to balance what I have disrupted?

Kismet cocked her head to the side, weighing her question carefully. "It is not me who decides, little diamond. Their souls communicate their needs and desires, and I pull the strings necessary to achieve it. It is a nuanced occupation. While not every moment is decided, it can be for some. Others have freedom that creates ripple effects."

"Freedom?"

"Some would view it as an unfortunate side effect of destiny, but yes, each life has varying degrees of freedom, ultimately. Only those with cosmic greatness are born unbound by Fate, as they must cultivate a strong connection to the weave in order to walk without snapping threads." Kismet stood, rising with supernatural ease. "Thank you for allowing me to bring some semblance of peace to my wicked, ruminating mind. Each false alarm leads me closer to the day my daughter is in my arms again. I wish you the best of luck on your journey."

Before she could protest, Kismet made for the door, and after one last joining of their eyes, the deity disappeared. Immediately, Cosima gasped for air, the room finally free of the Celestial Empress's aura. Michi emerged with the same scowl and under-eye bags as the last time she saw her. Without needing to be told, she rose and followed Michi through the mind-numbing puzzle of hallways back toward her room. Her Scout was silent, leaving her to only her cluttered, shock-filled thoughts.

The Kingdom is aware of my powers to some degree, but I should still keep them to myself as best I can.

Once in her rooms, Michi held open the door with an exasperated sigh. Sima wandered into her bathing chamber and shut the door firmly behind her. This was the one room where she was granted true privacy, but with a time limit. Soon, Michi would bang on the door and demand she exit, but until then, Cosima wanted only one thing. She peeled off her robe and nightgown, letting them collect on the floor around her feet. Steam toiled from the hot water inside the tub as she stepped inside, hissing as the heat pricked her ice-cold toes.

Behind closed eyes, images danced and twirled with merriment. Images of Cosima somewhere she couldn't name, spinning to music she couldn't hear. A lighter, easier moment in time, pieced together from broken memories in a traumatized brain. She sealed out the emotions too heavy to carry and let the bath drown her heart's hopeless homesickness in a watery grave.

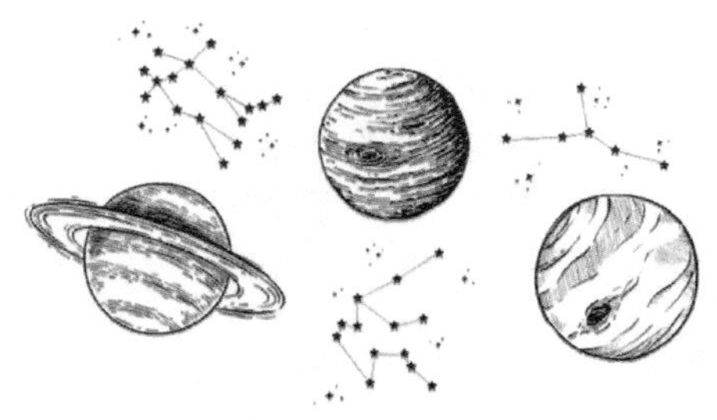

Chapter 4

Vincenzo

Vincenzo rolled his neck, achy rivers of pain cruising through his being in response to the motion. He cushioned his chin in his bound hands, and blood dribbled across his knuckles onto the floor. He smirked and spat scarlet saliva onto the nearest Scout's shiny boots.

"For the last time, that is absolutely everything I know."

"I don't believe him," one of the three Scouts murmured. "Hit him again, Cino."

He grunted as another punch reverberated through his skull and blurred his vision. He took the battery well. Fighting was his life. Every minute since his conception, he had been tossed around, roughed up, and left for the vultures to pick at. In the present moment, the interrogations had become similarly routine. Merit would snatch Vincenzo sometime in the night, drag him down a maze, and purposefully retracing steps to confuse him. After that, he'd get knocked around for a while, and when they exhausted themselves, Merit would babysit him back in his rooms.

"How many of your brothers are still alive?" Cino demanded.

"Four, as far as I know. The same answer I've given twenty-seven times in a row."

"Twenty-eight," Asella corrected. Her auburn hair was tied back in a thick braid, and it resembled a whip with the fierce way she commanded herself. "Are you losing touch now, Vincenzo?"

He shook his head. "Twenty-eight, *sorry.*"

Her fist barreled into his jaw, and the chair they'd strapped him to tipped, sending his head straight into the unforgiving floor. "Rude to do that to someone who can't catch himself," he wheezed.

"You're right, it's not even a fair fight." Cino gave a hearty laugh before picking Vincenzo up with one hand and setting him upright. He had short black hair from a recently shaved head, arms as large as Vincenzo's legs, and a lick of malevolence in his eyes. "All we want are some answers, and you've got 'em."

He resisted the urge to spit in the man's face and instead met his smug gaze. "Oh, you're right. After nearly thirty days of this, I've suddenly remembered everything! Joy is upon us at last."

That earned him another strike to the face, this time from Cino's burly arm. His hits carried a stronger bite, but still nothing he couldn't handle. The pain they caused him was abysmal in comparison to the aching madness of his pent-up magic. His skin felt tight, as if the accumulated power would burst through his tissue if it meant finding a way out of his body. Enzo had found ways to burn tiny, insignificant amounts, but it was not enough. It was never enough.

"Smart-ass," Cino snarled.

"You spent half a century trapped on a planet with your brother. You expect me to believe you know nothing about his operations?" Asella's auburn braid narrowly missed him as she spun around like a python ready for another attack.

"I explained to you how he destroyed the planet, what he did to others, and how he died. That is all I know. My mother abandoned me with the Guardians before my brain could comprehend I was a living, breathing entity. You think she made sure to tell me she loved me and would be back one day? I don't even remember the last time I saw her. I spent my time training in the Eternal Kingdom before I received an assignment to Haelos. If she had some grander plan for me, I'm sure she would have interfered by now. In fact, where is my dear ol' mom? Why don't you ask her where her sons are?"

Asella narrowed her eyes at him. "How do you know she's missing?"

Vincenzo smiled, ignoring the taste of iron on his tongue. "Best guess. I mean, you *are* going through all this trouble. Unless you truly have nothing better to do, and this is how you get your rocks off, I'd say you're scrambling."

The redhead gripped his chin in her hand, squeezing until pain dampened his skin with his tears. When her toxic eyes looked into his, he knew he was beginning to win. She was far angrier than he'd ever seen her. The Trine Scouts on his duty were always well versed in shielding techniques to deflect his mind manipulation, but what could not be won with magic could be tempered with charisma and games. Plain and simple, he waged a war to get beneath their skin, to force them into his territory with rampaging emotions. One where they might put their guard down, might tear through their restraint.

"How much can you beat me before it just becomes bullying?"

She threw his face, and four gleaming scratches oozed more of his blood onto his cheek.

"Enough, Asella." He'd been quiet for most of their questioning, but now, Surano looked ready to separate Vincenzo's head from his body. "I know what you're doing, feathered rat." His eyes were pale blue like a frosted lake. His cool demeanor reflected a man used to weathering the raging storms.

"Come on now, I'm getting bored. What else is a man to do when he's spilled his guts, and you beg him to regurgitate more? I'll spew acid from my stomach before any more useful information for you lovely three."

Cino growled, reminding him of an unleashed canine stalking small kids down the street.

The sight of the Scout two steps from feral made Vincenzo chuckle. "Down, boy." When it earned him a wrathful kick from Asella and sent him cascading onto the floor, Enzo couldn't help but take a bigger bite. "My apologies for offending your dog."

"I said, *enough*, Asella." Surano snatched her firmly by the shoulder and shoved her backward. It pleased Vincenzo. Surano never wanted to play any of his games. Up until now, he'd sat quietly, observing each interrogation like a brain-dead bystander. His stoic mask was cracking. "You've answered all their questions, but none of mine. Let's change that, shall we?"

"I'm up for anything," Vincenzo grinned. "I *am* parched, though. Cino and Asella," he said their names with a mockery of Surano's deeply serious voice, "Be good dogs and fetch us some refreshments immediately. Leave the big boys to play."

Surano scowled but waved them off. Vincenzo waved his bound hands in farewell. Cino huffed before slamming the door shut behind him.

"Explain to me your relationship to the woman brought in with you."

Vincenzo ground his teeth at the mention of Cosima. This was not the direction he expected the conversation to pivot to. He would allow no one, not even a cocky Scout, to come anywhere near her. Enzo had made his share of mistakes, but he was wise enough to learn from them. It had only been a matter of time before the questions about Cosima began, and at the very least, he could lead them astray. He took a slow breath and recalled the pain in the ass attitude he'd come in with.

"She is a friend of mine. We had the same prerogative—eliminate Aurelio."

"That's not what Pollux tells us. You were granted a special recreational reunion with her, and according to him, you two are involved too intimately to be friends. You did little to hide your mutual affection, so why lie to me now?"

"Why are you asking me if you already know the answer?"

"I am simply attempting to discern if she is involved with the murderous cult you call your family tree." His tongue slid over his teeth with an expression of disgust. "Though, I'm not sure what would draw her to you all. Ambrosi are hardly born with wings, and yet when they are, people act like you're special. In your bloodline, I see it for what it really is—a defect that should have been extinguished in the womb."

Enzo rolled his neck, remembering that it was not yet widespread knowledge that he and his brothers were not Ambrosi at all, they were Caelari—Gods. The lie manufactured by his mother, Ehses, seemed to have taken root among the immortals. "I didn't peg you for a purist, Surano."

"Guardians are shipped off to other planets because they are not worthy of defending our kingdom or the lives inside it. Trine Scouts are authentic incarnations of what your winged brothers are fooled into believing they are. No matter how you try to scrub it off you, I can smell the undeserving odor emanating from your weak little soul. You are the biggest shame of all your brothers, and perhaps that is the only reason you are still alive."

Vincenzo scoffed. "I don't fear being underestimated. I fear not being able to stop myself once the rampage begins." His gaze darkened as he glared at Surano. "Perhaps it is you who is lucky I have mastered restraint."

"Restraint? Or are you crippled by doubt? You cannot compare to your brothers if you were truly raised as a Guardian. Your brothers are capable of monumental levels of destruction, and you want me to believe you simply choose to not wreak havoc?"

Enzo laughed, amused by the Trine Scout's attitude. Scouts, while stronger than Ambrosi and Rani, were still beneath Caelari. "Precisely. I wasn't raised to be bloodthirsty like the good-for-nothing men I share a mother with. They know only how to take, break, and abandon. I am capable of expansion and creation. You seem to forget that my brothers and I are not mere Ambrosi."

Confusion twisted Surano's face.

"My mother is Ehses, a Goddess. Do you know my sire shares full God-blood as well?"

Surano blanched. "Impossible. How could she hide the birth of twelve new Caelari? It would have been felt, noticed by others. How could the Divinity have missed it? If you were truly a God, why have you not escaped?"

The Divinity are not as tapped in as you believe, Enzo thought. *My unrestricted power is evidence of that. Still, I stay in line.*

Vincenzo blew a lock of white hair from his face. His mind flicked to

Cosima. She did not want to run. She wanted to find her family and learn her history. He would not be the one to damn those dreams, but he could also not live without her. No amount of freedom was worth leaving her behind, and no escape could bring her happiness. His throat bobbed, and he shook his head lightly. "We are innocent, and I will wait for justice and time to vindicate me. I fear no retribution for my hands are clean."

Surano shot him an incredulous look and scoffed. Just when Vincenzo thought he had properly diverted the conversation, the Scout pressed further. "What are her powers? Give me all of them."

"Her powers?"

"We have no information on her beyond her ability to touch the Weave. It's like she materialized out of thin air. She can't truly be Ambrosi, not with Fate capabilities. So, what is she?"

Vincenzo bit the inside of his cheek and pondered the question. "No clue."

"Fine. Describe her magic to me, in detail, then."

He weighed his options. On one hand, they might already know her full range of power. Alternatively, if they truly did not, revealing it could damn her. *How would the Kingdom respond if they knew she could not only touch the Weave, but command as though born from it?* He couldn't imagine they would respond positively, especially with the way the Trine's devoted themselves to the High Priestesses—and to Kismet's will above all others. Any unapproved alterations brought chaos, and Trine Scouts were one piece in the greater mission toward balance.

"Obviously, you are aware of her minor Fate-altering abilities." The words crawled from his lips slowly. He knew better than to reveal her shielding, especially if the Kingdom found a way to use it against her. "Self-restorative capabilities and minor slows on time."

"Is that all?"

"Yes."

"Interesting," Surano said. "My next question is about you."

Vincenzo sighed, welcoming any discussion that steered them away from discussing Cosima. His heart longed to take her far from a reality where others were committed to misunderstanding her. She was not capable of colluding with evil. She was an unfortunate casualty in a war of control.

"The interpretation of the Sacred Twelves' prophecy is that the final living brother shall receive a highly esteemed position with the Divinity. You seem attached to survival. What are your plans if you remain the only brother alive?"

Rage speared a hole in the curtain of calm he manifested, and a snarl escaped his lips. "I am not interested in leading anything. What does no one understand about this? I am not a king, a priest, or an emperor. I am a man desperate to experience my existence. I was birthed into this life, and now

I have to live it, one way or another. I cannot do it the way others think I should, because ultimately it is about what I want. And it cannot be about what I want if I am crowned."

Surano cocked a brow and crossed his arms in front of his chest. "Like I said, weak-willed. You know you aren't man enough to command eternity. You can hardly care for yourself. You will always be bird-shit ruining someone's day, and never will others obey you."

Vincenzo'd had enough. Surano's flimsy shield wavered, and with the speed of a hawk, Enzo swooped beyond it and seized the Scout's mind. His power surged, grateful for the chance to burn off what he had been forced to accumulate during his captivity. As he cut off Surano's air and blurred his mind with horrific visions, Enzo rolled his neck, his body overcome with genuine relief as the perpetual ache began to subside.

He poured as much of his magic from himself as he could physically manage without creating a crater in the center of the Eternal Kingdom—and without triggering his curse. With the restrictions on his usage, Enzo had to come up with creative ways to keep his own energy from devouring him. But now, he opened the floodgates a fraction, allowing himself to burn off steam until he could think clearly once more.

As Surano lay choking and twitching on the floor before him, the thought of *her* entered his mind with an urgency he could not ignore. He glanced down, knowing if he let his furious storm continue, he could never take it back.

I can't. Not yet. Not without her.

Enzo sighed, his hair falling over his face as he hung his head. Resigned to his current Fate, he ended the flow of his magic, despite how his body protested. He wiped Surano's recent memories and released his grip. He intended to toy with the Scout to keep himself entertained, to continue to pass the time. Yet, the interaction soured quickly, and he no longer found the idea of torturing Surano appealing.

For you, I will wait.

The only resource he had to quell his anger was music, and the notes hummed inside his skull as Enzo took slow breaths over Scout's unconscious body. He wiped his memory, but the Surano was injured enough that the other Scouts were bound to notice. However, he held no fear of repercussions. When the others returned, he hardly noticed them approaching. The song he often sent Cosima at the lowest of times soothed out the noise of the Trine Scouts battering his body into a collage of bruises and broken, bent limbs. The notes of the melody kissed away his bleeding, mangled heart and replaced it with the honey-sweet memories of her. For her, he would wait.

When the Trine Scouts were finished with him, they dumped him back in his rooms. He vaguely recalled washing his blood off himself in the bathing chamber before he crawled into bed. Though he desperately wanted to sleep, the magic build-up inside him was impossible to ignore.

It doesn't have to be like this, whispered the darkness within.

It was a voice that Enzo had grown quite accustomed to hearing. The first time he heard it whisper to him was after his fight with Aurelio, where he had nearly died. Something had broken open inside him, refusing to let him fade away into nothing. He had fought to stay alive, and his power had fought to revitalize his body.

However, it had come with a cost. Now the voice haunted him, begged him to do evil and horrid things. He considered the voice to be his curse, to be a dreary sign that he might be beyond saving. It made him believe he was all the awful things he knew his brothers to be, because they must have had the same voice inside their minds, too, manipulating them into destruction.

But Enzo was different. He would not give in.

He groaned as his magic permeated through his tissue, healing him with efficiency as he tried without much success to force himself to fall asleep. The longer he went with the disruptions in his rest, the more he thought he might truly go insane.

Why are you still here? His curse was growing louder. *These walls cannot stop you. These Scouts cannot kill you. Why do you obey their rules?*

A growl of frustration left his lips as he curled his fists. "I will not give in," he whispered to himself. "No matter what it says to me, I will not give in. I am stronger. I will not fail as my brothers have."

Eventually, his muscles and mind relaxed enough to allow him to drift off to sleep, only for him to be met with more raging nightmares. This time, however, the dreams were centered around the only woman he had ever loved. She did not gaze at him with love or gentle curiosity. Instead, her eyes were pools overflowing with fear and panic. She refused to come near him, refused to listen to his pleas.

"You're a monster," dream Sima shouted as she backed away. "Leave me alone. I never want to see you again."

"Please," he whispered. "I can't do this without you. You know me, Sima. You know who I am."

"No, I don't," she shouted back, causing him to flinch. "I thought I knew you, but I would have never fallen in love with you if I knew your heart was tainted black. I wish I had never loved you."

The pain of her words was too great, forcing him awake to end the nightmare. As he curled into a ball in his bed, the sheets and pillows tossed onto the floor, he attempted to soothe his furious thoughts.

I won't let anyone hurt her, not even me. I will outlast this awful power for eternity, if it means keeping her safe.

Chapter 5

Cosima

Cosima's nose twitched as she hunched forward to better examine her face in the mirror. Her skin was smooth like still water and pale like the moon. With so much time spent indoors, her solitude reflected in her dull-gray features and near-permanent heavy purple eye bags. The pads of her ring fingers slid across her eyebrows in an effort to refine their shape. When it did nothing to quell her dissatisfaction, she sighed and turned to Nariah, who stood behind her, rocking on her heels.

"Do you have to breathe down my neck, or do you just enjoy watching me all day long?"

The remark earned a sly smile from Nariah. She tipped her nose into the air, shutting her eyes and crossing her arms. "What more is there for me to do? This is precisely where the Divinity believes my abilities are best utilized, and I will not be the one to reject the assignment. Besides, you're more pleasant than most of those detained by the Kingdom. At best, *you* are my entertainment."

Cosima glared at Nariah. The eternally loyal characteristic ran thickly in Trine Scout blood, more abundant and more crucial than any nutrient. Perhaps, in another life, she would not find her Scout's devotion so grating, but Sima's irritation equally felt clumsy and ill-fitting. Nariah was complex, enigmatic. The Scout's words often harshly contradicted her actions, and yet, she was still Cosima's only form of companion, for now. "I am no one's entertainment."

Nariah shrugged. "So you say. You are the one who enacted the connection between realms, displaying the death of a Sacred Brother."

"I thought it would vindicate me."

"It might," Nariah said slowly, tapping a finger against her chin. "That is still yet to be decided."

Familiar melancholic woes crept under her skin like hundreds of tiny insects. The sensation unnerved her, yet she made no efforts to shake away the building emotion. She'd spent decades subjecting herself to the mercy of her feelings, fighting to change them, hide them, or erase them. What did she have to show for it now? Tattered pride and oscillating emotional volatility. She'd expected her anger to dissolve with Aurelio's death, but instead, the scent of her rage clung to her, tainting every breath with its sour burn. She could not escape the ruins he'd left her in.

"What are you thinking about?" Nariah asked.

Cosima shook off the haze of thoughts and cleared her throat. "Is there any chance I can live a normal life? If they allow me to survive, do I return to Haelos? Stay here?"

The Scout sighed and paced back and forth as Cosima resumed mulling over her appearance in the mirror. "No one knows who you are, and your memories are unhelpful. This is certainly an unexpected outcome, but the Kingdom deals with erroneous situations frequently enough; I should think there is someone with the proper answers."

"Like whom?"

Nariah sighed and chewed on her lip. She tucked a snowy lock of hair behind her magnificent wing-like ears before an expression of inspiration flooded her face. "When it is time for your hearing, you will meet the twelve High Priestesses. There is one Goddess in particular, I think, who shall be partial to your suffering. Her name is Demi, and she is the Goddess of wisdom, communication, and negotiation. She prefers to know every morsel of information before making any final decisions, and often, her meticulous curiosity slows the process as a whole."

Cosima brightened at the mention of a potential ally. "Will I have the opportunity to speak for myself?"

"Yes, of course. However, not until after a presentation of all collected evidence and recreation of events is performed by those who work beneath Goddess Astraea. She governs balance, justice, and truth. Unfortunately, Astraea is decisive and stubborn. If her division detects anything suspicious, she has been known to sway the opinion of the others. They will scrutinize you, and for your sake, I hope there is nothing they will unearth."

Cosima shook her head, but internally, fear flickered like a reignited flame. It was impossible to recall in detail the changes she had made for Aurelio across the fifty years of her captivity. *How much can they uncover of my past transgressions? Will I ever know freedom if the truth is worse than I can recall?*

A knock sounded from the front room. Nariah immediately turned in the direction of the door and left Cosima to her thoughts. The clanking of plates and utensils signaled it was their nightly meal delivery. For what it was worth, the Kingdom fed her well, and beyond the maddening isolation, left her untouched and unharmed. It left her confused about her true feelings surrounding her mandatory seclusion. In some ways, it was cruel and unjust in her mind. On the opposite side of the scale, it was what she deserved for operating beneath the embodiment of poisonous intention that was Aurelio.

Nariah's voice carried in from the front room, "Aether, good to see you."

Aether spoke softly, but Sima could just make out the words, "you'll wish you hadn't…"

A dizzy wave made her knees buckle, and she steadied herself against the wall. Her hand cradled her forehead as she fought through the blinding pain that ambushed her. Just as she thought she would lose consciousness, a memory overtook her vision and demanded her attention.

Buttery streams of silk fabric adorned the lush field of densely packed, low-lying shrubbery. Steel blue, bright yellow, and burnt sienna cloth raced through the open expanse of land, building pathways in all directions. In the far distance, the intimidating lotus at the center of the Eternal Kingdom breathed. Its delicate blush pink petals danced with the wind, swaying up and down as the air pulsed with cooling gusts. Night kissed the edges of the sky, warning the populace of the still metamorphosis soon to overtake their slumbering beings.

Insects with glowing abdomens floated in the sky like stars she could almost touch. In the wispy tree branches hung brilliant recreations of space, all crafted from glorious blends of crystals. Without conscious effort, her hand floated up, her skin desperate to collide with the magnetizing stones. It felt like the vast universe was a carefully curated collection, doted on and displayed with pride. In the reflection of a dusty red and orange orb, a smaller, tender version of herself tumbled into view. She was boisterous, youthful. So full of life, she radiated blissful creation from her pores, as if the oils of her skin built the cosmos themselves.

A rustling in the trees to her left startled her, and she snapped her focus toward the approaching group. Several Ambrosi women wandered through the field, picking flowers and chattering about expansions to the Kingdom. Two broke off from the others, growing closer to where she stood. Once they passed, Cosima trailed behind them.

"I hear they are entering the next phase soon. The number of souls reaching the first level of maturity is growing at an optimal pace." The woman slid a baby pink rose behind her ear. "Do you ever wonder what it's like to be out there, somewhere, experiencing the mysterious planets alongside the creations?"

A strawberry blonde looped her arm through the other woman's arm as she grimaced. "We are eternal servants to our Kingdom, and yet, I find myself grateful I devote my time here instead of growing up on a planet swirling helplessly in the universe. Especially with a planet full of fresh souls. The chaos it must inspire."

"Don't say that, Delilah," her friend scolded. "We were once new."

Delilah scoffed. "If the Divinity wanted me to remain humble, they would not wipe my past life memories. I live forevermore in this vessel, and I wonder at times if the never-ending journey is a curse. Why are we not enough to become one of them? They are calling the winged Ambrosi brothers the Sacred Twelve. I will not be surprised when they are granted closer access to the Divinity."

"The High Priestesses are always in need of skilled Ambrosi. We are the only support the Goddesses have in maintaining and operating this Kingdom. The Caelari are divinely powerful, but they are not nearly as steady as we are. We are everything. There could be nothing without us, Delilah."

"If every move of mine is supposedly written in the stars, if every decision is pre-written, then I was born to resist the hierarchy I was born within. Either I was crafted from a broken mold, or they designed me to despise them. Why create me capable of envy if I am supposed to be pure, sure, never questioning? Why give me imperfections if I am not meant to be flawed?"

"It is our uniqueness that is the purpose of the universe. There is no greater mission than to exist simply as an expression of the many sides of the Divinity."

Delilah tugged herself free. "Why are so many disappearing from the Kingdom then? If we are so special, why does the Divinity fail to investigate those who vanish?"

"You don't know they are truly missing. Plenty have chosen to abandon their positions throughout history. Some buckle beneath responsibility. That is not an indication of a greater injustice."

As the memory faded, and she absorbed back into her conscious body, light stung her eyes. She blinked rapidly, finding herself on the floor of her bathing chamber in the same position she had collapsed in.

Cosima considered the puzzling conversation as the memory dispersed. Flashbacks made her ache for more, desperate to solve the mystery of her past, of her heritage. It was impossible to tell what triggered the event to resurface, but she was able to discern one thing—Cosima was not the only missing person. Even the Celestial Empress had mentioned whispers of people vanishing. Where were the missing immortals from the Eternal Kingdom? In the time since the memory, had the mystery of their disappearances been solved?

"Are you coming or not?" Nariah called from the dining table in the living area.

She rubbed her eyes and pulled herself off the floor. She left her bedroom and stumbled to the table, greeted by roasted fish and steamed vegetables in a garlicky sauce. Nariah eyed her suspiciously, and she pretended not to notice, sliding into her seat with a wince of exhaustion.

"Are you… perishing?"

Cosima lifted her head and rolled her eyes. "Not quite yet." She rubbed her forehead. "Nariah, how are the High Priestesses chosen?"

Nariah took a slim bite of her fish. "Only Goddesses may be selected. Each of them rules as long as the general public approves of their reign."

"When was the last time there was a change?"

Nariah shifted in her chair restlessly. "A bit ago. Hard to tell you precisely."

"It was the Spirit Goddess, right?"

The Scout met her gaze with a cold and steady look. "Yes. Which is precisely why I do not trust Vincenzo, or any of his brothers for that matter."

"Does anyone trust them?"

Nariah opened her mouth, but promptly slammed it shut again. She stayed quiet for a moment, chewing on her words before continuing. "Some believe the brothers offered positive utility to the Kingdom, and while there are rumors of their supposed shared destiny, Kismet and her sisters have yet to confirm or deny this. In fact, no one can confirm where the rumor originated. In my opinion, they created it themselves to appear powerful or to play into some hidden tactics by the Spirit Goddess."

"Is nothing being done about them?"

"The Divinity can be slow to action, you know this firsthand. It is hard to say what they will decide. I am not high enough ranking to know more than I have already shared with you. While I am devoted to this Kingdom, I was blessed with discernment, the ability to detect things others cannot. Because of this, I make my own decisions regarding others. I must if I wish to fulfill my duties as a protector of this Kingdom and the will of the Divine."

"And your abilities detect something off about Vincenzo?"

Nariah blew on a morsel of fish. Her eyes were heavy with disdain. "I suppose you could say that."

"Then tell me what's so wrong about him and let me decide for myself."

The Scout rolled her eyes. "Settle down, Sima."

"Whatever you suspect is enough to make you pester me to not trust him every chance you get. If you're not willing to tell me, then how can I make a proper decision?"

Nariah raised a brow, but her expression was strange, too sad to fit the conversation. "I don't know exactly what it is that I am sensing, but there is just something not right with him. I also don't agree with the Divinity deciding to hide their true heritage from the Kingdom. Enzo is not a regular immortal, Sima. The Caelari can be incredibly powerful, as they help sustain the expansion across galaxies, but they can be a force for evil, as well, given their heightened abilities. I told the Divinity about the other members of the Sacred Twelve that I've encountered—they are hiding something awful within, a twisted, infected energy. Whatever it is, it is only strengthened by their God-blood. I think it is a mistake that the Divinity has yet to formally announce the true origin of the Sacred Brothers."

Sima frowned. "I believe you're right about the others, but not about Vincenzo. He is nothing like Aurelio."

"As far as you know."

Nariah's comment made Sima's stomach lurch with uncertainty. To save herself, Sima pivoted the conversation. "How have you come in contact with his other brothers?"

"They're arrogant criminals, most of them were bound to end up caught red-handed. The Kingdom has put several to death already, despite the ambiguity around their prophecy. It was simply too much of a risk to keep them alive any longer. There was one brother who poked his nose around here, sucking up to every immortal and Goddess until he made acquaintance with the High Priestesses."

"What happened to him? Surely, they did not trust him?"

"He stopped coming around after a while. Many other Scouts, and myself, are vehemently against all the Sacred Twelve—whether they can sense the malice within like I can is another story. Either way," Nariah said, blowing on another bite of food, "just try to keep your distance from Vincenzo as best you can."

Cosima could not imagine keeping herself away from the one person who had made themselves a safe place for her. "Do you know what I really want out of life?"

"What's that?" the Scout asked.

"To stop listening to the plans others have for me. To not be swayed by the opinions of others, but to follow the guidance from within my soul, wherever it leads me."

Nariah wrinkled her nose but took the hint and dropped her attempts at persuasion. Sima ate the rest of her meal in silence, debating internally how Nariah's distrust of Vincenzo made her feel. She was certain the Scout had her best interests in mind, and she trusted her opinion, but Nariah did not know Enzo the way Sima did. Still, doubt surfaced, and she was quick to shove it away. She chewed as though it did not continue to linger in the back of her mind.

"By the way," Nariah said casually, "Aether brought a message with the food. For better or for worse, things are about to change."

A pearl-white card slid across the table. She picked it up and read the swirled, elegant handwriting.

Tomorrow marks day one of justice apportioning. Prepare for the investigation into your case to begin promptly at sunrise.

With the day nearly over, Vincenzo was reaching intolerable levels of magic accumulation. He only needed to wait long enough for his Trine Scout, Merit, to fall asleep. Merit was a somewhat skilled Scout, capable of monitoring and shielding certain aspects of Enzo's abilities, but he was rendered inert when asleep. This allowed Enzo to blow off a bit of steam without risking being seen.

Normally, he would expel energy by crafting tiny things in his rooms before destroying them to leave behind no trace. Sometimes he would only create a cube or sphere of matter—such as marble or gray stone, which were the simplest—and other times, he would create small figurines of animals or people. He only refrained from making ones of Sima, as he knew he'd never be able to crush the recreation of her beauty, and he did not want to be caught. However, he knew tonight, he would need a large expulsion, or his mental state would begin to deteriorate from the excessive magic.

His arms trembled as jolts of electricity shot through his muscles. His skin felt tight, as though it might burst from the weight of his magic. The sensation grew more bothersome as the minutes passed, but Merit was still awake and walking around Enzo's chambers. Although the Scout primarily stuck to the main living area, his footsteps were loud enough to remind Enzo he was never alone. Thankfully, after a few more minutes, the walking ceased, and Merit's snores were audible even with the door to his room firmly shut.

He wasted no time and got to work on burning as much magic as he could in bursts. At first, he created hundreds of small, solid iron cubes. They covered every inch of the floor before Enzo snapped his fingers, and they turned to ash, vanishing seconds after. He moved on to creating mini homes out of wood and stone, mapping an entire artificial city at his feet.

Enzo waved his hand in front of him, and it vanished, leaving him with another blank slate. He continued this repeating pattern of creating and erasing, eventually reaching a point where he hardly paid attention to what he created in front of him. He nearly forgot he was creating matter from nothing as his mind grew distracted.

Thoughts of his time in Ombra led him down the same path as always—a sobering recognition of his own cowardice. Prior to the snap that awakened his curse, Enzo lived each day in fear of his brothers. He hated to admit it, but there was no use in hiding the way he felt utterly useless, forcing Sima to endure half a century worth of pain and trauma.

All because I was too weak to save her. I knew it was her, I knew I loved her, and I did nothing.

A fire broke out among a miniature forest he'd created, and Enzo stomped his feet on the flames to put it out. He sighed and sank to the floor. Perhaps the only thing he hated more than his lack of bravery was his family. He had been raised in the brutal way of life that was normal to the Rani Guardians, but had never quite fit in, even amongst a group that was itself avoided by the other immortals in the Eternal Kingdom. If they were outcasts, then Enzo was the twice-overlooked shadow of exiles—unworthy of even the smallest sliver of grace from the Caelari and Ambrosi.

Their abuse, their neglect, their ignorance, may have hurt him, covered him in invisible scars, but it never broke him entirely. It had never changed his heart. He helped others without second thought, not because he expected praise or fame, but because he truly wanted to be kind.

Kindness is nothing when the universe demands savagery to survive.

None of his good deeds were enough to undo the damage that the Sacred Twelve prophecy caused him when he learned of it. He remembered the day he uncovered his true heritage as if it were burned into the backs of his eyelids.

Knowing what he did now, he wished he could go back to when that mysterious letter appeared atop his belongings without a trace of who left it. He would have ripped it up, never daring to read the words inside. The letter had been left by his brother, Alvize, and its contents confessed the sins of their shared mother and revealed the blood Enzo shared with his unique sire, Domani.

This sole difference between him and his brothers gave Enzo a small ember of hope that he was somehow unlike them. That he was somehow insulated from their cosmic consequences. However, the curse that now thumped within him seemed to be proof of the opposite. He was as damned as they were.

Alvize had continued leaving behind notes for him, whether to taunt him or to save him, Enzo was unsure. It took time to verify, but every piece of information his brother provided him proved to be true. In fact, it was only five years prior to Enzo meeting Sima that Alvize revealed the biggest piece of the prophecy.

"A full-blood daughter of Kismet, without a sire, will be born with no destiny of her own, her enigmatic soul powerful and vast. The brother who remains will be tethered to this heir of Fate's Hand for eternity. Time will bend around their union, creating a holy sanctuary from harm. This daughter will cleanse the sole Sacred One of his poison, ushering in a new era. The Realm will restructure beneath their rule, the land unrecognizable but tilled for seasons to come."

At the time, Enzo had been primarily focused on the insinuation that whoever survived until the end would be forced to irrevocably change and then rule the Eternal Kingdom. It was a confusing, out-of-place fact that haunted him as he could think of no Fate worse than being forced to command others when he could not trust a single decision he made for himself.

He lived his Guardian life convinced that each day would be his last. In his mind, it was only a matter of time before one of his brothers hunted him down. It wasn't until Enzo fell helplessly in love with Cosima that he began picturing a future for himself. He was not privy to her powers prior to Haelos, but once he was aware, he had spiraled, wondering if she could be the daughter of Fate's Hand that the prophecy spoke of.

Enzo wholeheartedly believed that fact now, even if Sima retained her doubts. Aurelio was attached to her, in some ways, for her power and the control he had over her, but Enzo had always suspected that it was also because of her true heritage, as well.

Vincenzo's bond to her was unmistakable, strong in ways even he could not understand. Could he ever allow himself to believe it was because he was the one destined to survive? "Forgive me, Sima," Enzo whispered. "Forgive me for not being the man I should have been for you. I won't make that mistake again."

If Enzo could outlast his brothers, the love he and Sima shared had the opportunity to be powerful enough to reshape life as they all knew it in this Kingdom. His stomach dropped. In the many years since he learned of his potential destiny, it only grew more ill-fitting for him. He could not see himself becoming a leader, especially not one who led beside the heir of Kismet. Despite his doubts, an irritatingly familiar voice echoed inside his head.

You will have the last laugh, his curse whispered. *Show them why you were chosen by the cosmos.*

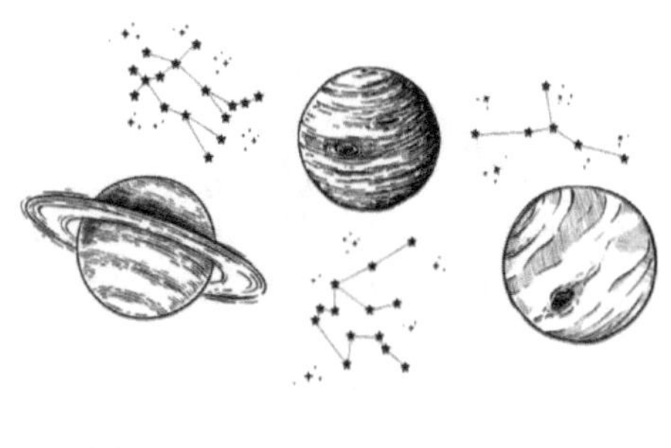

Chapter 6

Cosima

As she brushed her onyx black hair away from her face, Cosima wondered where her soul might go if let loose from this dimension. If her tether snapped and she were sent adrift in the silky embrace of the veil until she reached the Valley of the Dead, would she know it? Would the silence and empty waiting be madness? How badly would it hurt to die?

She shifted in her shoes, the material slippery on the smooth floors. A meeting with the High Priestesses of this realm meant the Scouts aimed to make Sima inert—incapable of manifesting into a threat to the most powerful and revered Goddesses of this realm, and thus chose each detail, down to her clothes and gliding footwear.

Her body was covered in a soft taupe-colored dress that fell down to her feet, thankfully covering the stress rash that had broken out across her entire midsection and back. At the top, a silk jacket with elegant red adornments shielded her shoulders and arms in an outfit fit to honor the twelve women who would determine her future. A lump rose in her throat. She would wear any outfit they demanded if it meant the people of Haelos might live. Their Fate rested in her hands, in her ability to beg for benevolence.

The Eternal Kingdom, stuffed to the brim with mystical, awe-inspiring, magical High Priestesses, who were regarded as the very top of society, maintained order across the many realms. Beneath them, immortals contributed in varying degrees, but were not individually vital to running the Kingdom, ultimately. It would be up to her to sway the tides of the cosmos in her favor. Cosima would seize this chance to save her beloved planet, and everyone who lived on it, even if their future seemed murky and unattainable.

Before she could wallow any further, someone knocked on her bedroom door. She flinched, but relaxed at the sight of Nariah, who wore a bright expression.

"Cosima, it is nice to see you again," she chirped. "Today is your day."

"So it seems."

She slid her sweaty palms against her skirts and followed the Scout, ready for her opportunity to declare her innocence. Nariah's dreamy, long locks of hair swished behind her as she strutted, annoying Sima with her carefree attitude. It opposed the reality of the situation—in mere moments, she would become no more than an insignificant insect, subject to the whims of the universe's highest court. Nariah was relaxed while Sima wondered how long she had left to live. Had she come this far for it to be the end already?

The path to the Ecliptic Court was purposefully obscured by Nariah through meaningless turns, but it didn't matter. Cosima's mind reached a speed at which the thoughts became background noise to the inner patter of her racing heart. There could only be so much rehearsal of her lines, so much preparation, before there was nothing left but to face the consequences of her actions. She would confess like a sinner on his knees, she would beg until her tears ran dry. Haelos demanded it of her, and she would not let them down.

When Nariah seemed satiated in her desires to properly confuse Sima, they stopped outside of two grand doors. The doors, a twin set of brilliant peach stone slabs that shimmered effortlessly, bore two enormous golden handles. The elaborate carvings depicted eons of history she was unfamiliar with and spanned upward, with the metal encompassing nearly half of both doors. Her head cocked to the side as she felt it.

The power.

The transcendent power was of a magnitude only equivalent to her meeting with Kismet. This time, however, she could discern the presence of many entities inside. The hair on her body raised with fear, and she took several stumbling steps backward. Involuntarily, her head shook back and forth, communicating the refusal to enter the room that her mouth could not form. Whatever awaited her within was of incomparable intensity, and Sima couldn't deny the way it made her feel small and insignificant, and she had not even laid eyes on the High Priestesses yet.

Nariah, to her credit, softened to her hesitation. "You must journey forward. There is nothing in the past for you. On the other side of that door is the only opportunity at a future you have. Seize it, before your time runs out. You are not a gruesome criminal, but they do not know that yet. You have to show them."

Cosima met her gaze slowly. Her bottom lip trembled, and she sank her top teeth into it to hold it still. She gave a small nod and called forth courage from every dusty corner of her inner being and awoke the strength that slumbered within for decades. She had proved she could be brave, that she could grow from the torrential rain instead of drowning in its puddles. It nourished her, washed her clean of her sins, and she had been born anew. She would not give over this new lease on life easily.

The doors opened silently, and the previous bustle of noise halted entirely. She dragged her eyes from the floor and met the gaze of a Priestess with a golden wing on each of her temples, seated on a tall platform against the back wall. She was the only Priestess seated, leaving to question when the others would arrive. The Goddess's eyes flamed with a molten vermilion against her smooth, pale skin. Ribbons of wavy crimson hair sat in voluminous bundles over the Goddess's shoulder, and her hand lazily toyed with the white billowed fabrics of her dress as she quietly inspected Sima.

"That is High Priestess Alala," Nariah whispered. "Goddess of action, passion, and impulse."

Sima broke the stare, unable to endure it any longer, and ignored the amused smile from the Priestess. Only then did she realize the room was neatly packed with hundreds of immortals, all watching her with unreadable, blank expressions. The majority of her audience were Caelari, unmistakable in their ethereal greatness, which stood in great contrast to the aura of what she assumed were immortals along one of the walls, though she could not be certain. She faced forward, and she kept her eyes on the back of Nariah's cape as she was directed to her proper seat.

Nariah whispered a wish of luck to Sima before she departed, leaving her alone with the crowd. If the first Priestess' energy was any indication, she would crumble before them once all had arrived. Sima slid into the soft magenta armchair and folded her hands in front of her on the short, rectangular table. A small card sat in front of her, ominously declaring her name for all to see. She imagined she was a strange item on display, advertised by its precariously violent and disruptive past.

The few Ambrosi in front of her held various administrative duties to aid the High Priestesses during Cosima's harrowing judgment day, dutifully scribbling on forms beside each Divine member of the council's designated seat. They each wore sandy dresses hovering just a hair above their ankles. Over their heads were forest green hoods, adorned with golden jewelry, the thin metal chains trailing down their backs.

The atmosphere was thick, and Cosima's nostrils flared widely with each inhale. No breath was enough; she could not quell her body's demand for more air. The door behind her opened once more, Sima's ears barely registering the sound before she felt it.

A second High Priestess had arrived.

The attention of the attending immortals shifted as a grounding wave of energy emanated into the room. The sensation of the new High Priestess's power reminded Sima of the safety she felt inside Vincenzo's embrace. Her power was calming, in an almost demanding way. An entourage of Ambrosi swept into the Courtroom, all fussing about one thing or another, as the Goddess strutted in behind them. Her hazel hair touched her hips as if it were a partner in a performance, intimate affection and intention laced into the movement around her elegant, flowing skirts. Her skin was bronze and dewy, and her eyes were a piercing light green that went nowhere near Cosima as she ascended the steps to her dedicated seat.

Cosima avoided gawking by leaning forward and pressing her fingertips to the underside of her chin. She propped her elbows on the table as another wave of energy slid into the room. The next Priestess's power came in waves, pulsing inward until Sima was breathless, before it was replaced by a light and airy sensation. The Priestess's curly black hair was braided back, perfectly adorned with gold clips and charms. Her ensemble was composed of scale-like patterns of gold and rich red-hued fabric. Its fierceness easily complemented her feminine, pointed nose and plump lips. Aether, who was escorting the Goddess, flashed Sima a small smile as the two walked right toward her. Unlike the other two Priestesses, this Goddess came to a stop just beside her. The crowd held its breath.

Sima swallowed the lump in her throat and tilted her head until their eyes met.

"I am High Priestess Demi," she said matter-of-factly. She studied Sima's shocked expression for a moment before a smile broke across her face. "Welcome to the unrivaled Ecliptic Court, the supreme arbiter of justice. Bring me facts today, little one, and you will have nothing to fear. Tell me your story however you must, but do not lie to me. I can be convincing, but only of the truth."

Her head bobbed in understanding. Cosima was half-frozen in awe of the Goddess, who smiled as if she stood to gain something from her success. Nariah had mentioned Demi would be inclined to help her, and their brief interaction confirmed it to be so. With a nod, High Priestess Demi left with Aether by her side and found her seat. As the Goddess began conversing with her Ambrosi aide, the crowd relaxed, the low murmur of conversation floating toward Sima's seat.

Sweat prickled along her temples, dampening her coal black hair. The room was a comfortable temperature, but nine seats remained, and Cosima's faith in her ability to convince the Divinity to spare her wavered. The sound of delicate musical chimes echoed through the hall, marking the arrival of the remaining Goddesses.

The High Priestesses swept into the room quickly, their grace unparalleled. Their steps seemed to hover above the ground, as if they walked in a different dimension. Sima couldn't take her eyes off them. The first wore an elaborate headdress of blue and purple flowers and golden jewelry. Her indigo dress hid beneath a deep ocean blue shawl, adorned with petals in shapes of hearts. She shot Cosima one deathly glare as she walked past, a finger flicking across her perfect nose in dismissal.

Then came a warrior woman with white doves seated on her shoulders. Gold leaf armbands matched the crown nestled in her distractingly luminous blond curls. Her hair mirrored the extravagance of the previous Goddess's headdress, and the crowd began to glow under her energy. She worked the audience magnanimously, stealing every ounce of attention with bright smiles. By the time Sima pulled her eyes off the Priestess, the others had found their seats, and the Ecliptic Court erupted with whispers from behind. Some of the Caelari were loud enough that Sima could discern that they were whispering about her.

Ignore them, she told herself. *They have no clue who I am. I know the truth.*

"Move it before I start plucking feathers," groaned Merit, shoving the tip of his boot into the back of Vincenzo's thigh, causing him to stumble. "We're already late as it is."

Vincenzo huffed, shaking off Merit's usual overly grumpy attitude. Today would be day one in front of the High Priestesses, and if he was lucky, he would be able to see Cosima again. Whenever he was near her, his perilous ruminating ceased, allowing his mind to rest—he desperately sought that sanctuary now. He wasn't sure the opening comments would be very telling of the way the judgment would unfold, but nevertheless, he found himself wishing for the best. For the mercy of the Priestesses to be bestowed upon them. For the women so high above him to consider him and Cosima as more than inter-dimensional pests.

They were not far from the room where the hearing would unfold. Enzo mitigated the heavy wave of powerful auras with a dull supply of his power. It was enough to take the edge off without having to apply much concentration to the flow, allowing him to remain alert.

He pondered it for a moment. The absurdity of it all.

In minutes, he would sit in a courtroom full of immeasurably powerful Caelari, some of whom he and his brothers were sinfully created to murder. His mother's convoluted plots concerned him little. Like the woman he loved, Enzo was uninterested in being a pawn for others. There was no throne he craved, no position of high stature that would fill an ache within. All he desired was freedom, despite his haunting fear that surviving the prophecy would require commanding a Kingdom. His future was his own, and he would listen to no instruction; he would bend to no one's will.

Unless, of course, it was Cosima who called upon him.

Merit slowed to a stop just outside the imposing doors of the Ecliptic Court. He crossed his arms in front of his chest and rolled his eyes. "Do *not* act out. We are to sit in the back until we are called upon. You will not go near her, and you will not talk to her."

How dare he reprimand you like a child? Kill him, his curse commanded.

Enzo pushed it aside before he locked eyes with Merit and weighed how much patience he had today. Lately, it had been wearing thin, but this was also not the place to draw more attention. He relented a single half-nod, which was enough for the Trine Scout to turn around and wrench a heavy door open.

A couple of the deities in the crowd deigned him a curious glance, but most were fixated on the High Priestesses seated on the platform in the front of the room as they spoke. He spotted Cosima within seconds, relieved that she at least appeared unharmed, despite her long expression. His heart tugged, and twinges of his power reached toward her with comforting pulses, like water lapping against the shore. He tore his eyes away from her, hating how grim the world seemed when he wasn't looking in her direction.

"This way," whispered Merit harshly.

He led Vincenzo to a section of the courtroom with open spots on a wooden bench for them to sit. The bench was uncomfortable, and his wings interfered with his ability to sit without putting feathers in the face of the person behind him. Trine Scouts could make their wings disappear on command, and so could he. However, doing so would raise more questions about the Sacred Twelve. The common rumor placed the Sacred Twelve in the category of extraordinary Ambrosi—few knew the truth of the full God blood that ran through their veins.

They keep you a secret because they fear you, his curse sang.

A hierarchy existed in this realm. Creations on planets—fresh souls, not yet refined—were at the bottom. Just above them, Rani Guardians, followed by Trine Scouts and Ambrosi, all servants ultimately. At the top, the births of Caelari were celebrated, written about in history books. The energy shift in the realm was spectacular during their first breaths, enough that all in the Ethereal Realm could feel the change. However she had done it, his mother, Ehses, had concealed the birth of not just one God, but twelve.

Now he was damned to a life of hiding his true identity at every miserable turn. *Will it ever end?*

He allowed himself to take in his surroundings and noticed several familiar forms in the crowd. Other Guardians from Haelos stood along the side wall, encountering the same problem with their wings as Vincenzo. There were over fifty residents of Haelos seated in the room, but Vincenzo could only identify a few of them.

What method did they use to pick these citizens? Hardly anyone involved is actually here, he grumbled internally.

He pretended to stretch his back and swiveled to search for a face he recognized. Grimaldo and Odilia stood on the opposite side of the courtroom, the two Rani Guardian friends who had aided him in running the Depths. Grimaldo was holding Odilia's hand tightly, and they appeared nervous. Habit encouraged him to speak to his friends through the telepathic bond Guardians shared, one Enzo himself tapped into with his mental manipulation abilities, but the smothering power of the High Priestesses would likely not allow his message to make it. More troublesome than their dampening auras was the fact that Enzo knew using his power in this manner was extremely risky. While he retained the ability to break through the weight of their auras, the High Priestesses would likely sense the signature of his energy before it got close enough to deliver messages or persuade a Goddess into ruling in favor of Sima. He would need to be more careful than that.

Enzo's eyes slid over to Aspasia, Tasia's sister from the Fae kingdom. She was alone, nervously twirling her hair much like her sister did. He expected to spot Calix's red hair, Monte's Viipir wings, or Alma's braids, but the trio was not here today. His stomach sank at the realization. Those most aware of Aurelio's crimes on their planet were not present.

A strange man with an unpleasant demeanor approached the council of women. Although he could not see Sima from where he sat in the crowd of Caelari, he could sense her almost numb discomfort, as if she had to disassociate to survive the Divinity's oppressive auras. He attempted to lift the heavy weight off her, though he was limited as her shields kept him almost entirely at bay. All except for their bond. Through it, he could make a little go a long way, and Enzo was thankful this shade of his power remained undetectable by others.

"Yes, Mr. Fallone?" asked High Priestess Sevasti. She regarded the man with a raised brow and tight frown.

"We are prepared to begin, High Priestesses," said Fallone, with a deep, folded bow. "For our highest good, we bring a call to action upon this council to declare judgment on the accused. We intend to bring before the Divinity a declaration of misdeeds, evidence collected during the post-discovery phase, and our recommended consequences."

Sevasti nodded. "Please confirm who you've brought before the council."

Fallone cleared his throat. "Cosima Aphelion from Haelos."

Vincenzo's muscles went rigid and fastened in place, his body perceiving the threat immediately. This was not a regulatory hearing where they intended to discern if Haelos deserved to remain. It was a hunt—a sloppy, cheap execution of pinning all Aurelio's crimes on Cosima.

You bastards.

His jaw tightened, and his teeth ground into each other as his ears rang. He should have known better. They were not interested in the truth, only naming someone the villain in order to cleanly sweep it under the rug. There had been something off about the High Priestesses, and he sensed it when he walked in. However, he could not have imagined he would be validated this way.

Remove every last one of the Divinity from rule, his curse snapped. *Only then can Cosima be free.*

Enzo took a breath, his thoughts reeling. The threat to Cosima was not one he took lightly, but he willed himself to remain in control, to not make decisions he might regret. He quieted the parts of him that craved destruction. *I won't give in. There has to be another way out of this.*

Chapter 7

Cosima

"Verify your identity," commanded Astraea.

Sima blinked, realizing she had not been paying attention to her surroundings. She fought off the urge to vomit and did her best to hold her chin high. "I am Cosima Aphelion, from planet Haelos."

"Thank you, Miss Aphelion," Astraea said. An Ambrosi aide stopped at each of the Priestesses and handed them a thick stack of papers. "Please read the summary provided at the top of page one before we start, sisters."

A headache pulsed with pain as Cosima attempted to acclimate to the weight of their auras. The musical chimes resonated once again, evoking a hushed wince from her. *Why does the air feel so thick? I can hardly breathe,* Sima thought. At the sound of High Priestess Alala's voice, her head snapped up.

"Justice apportioning is beginning," Alala commanded the attention of the room nearly as well as the Priestess with the doves. The crowd sat at attention, prepared to dive into every detail. Cosima shifted. "As we all are aware, there was a disturbance on a faraway planet called Haelos. It is highly unusual to hear from our planets directly, so the community experienced heavy confusion when word spread about the recreated reality of violent scenes unfolding. As such, we are here today to investigate each and every crime committed. Please remain seated during the opening comments from both sides."

Both sides? Have I missed something? Cosima turned her head for the first time to her left and paled when she realized there was a table with two men seated behind it. Cosima could not sense their auras over the intensity of the High Priestesses', meaning they were likely immortals, not Caelari. Neither turned toward her, as if her presence was irrelevant when it came to their plans for the day. One with a relaxed olive pantsuit and a satin burgundy tie stood, folding with a bow of respect before the Divinity.

"For our highest good, High Priestess Alala," he said by way of greeting. "We would appreciate it if the first round of witnesses could be present for the opening comments today."

Alala glanced to the side, reading the eyes of the others before responding. A Priestess with slick black hair and bright, flushed cheeks nodded her approval. Her hooded eyes were accentuated with black lines from the corners, giving her a cat-eye appearance.

"I will grant your request, Mr. Vallone. While this occurs…" A Priestess locked eyes with Cosima as the men scurried from the room to retrieve their witnesses. "You, small one, know none of our council. You may be suspicious in the eyes of our Kingdom, but I wish to grant you the opportunity to know the women who will be deciding your future. While our individual identities are perhaps not vital to remember, I hope you can gain some understanding of the way we think. I am High Priestess Thera, Goddess of new creation, fertility, and cosmic details."

She pointed to the Goddess with light green eyes from earlier. "Fria—stability, teaching, guidance." Then, she pointed to the flowered headdress of the Priestess, "Alessa—protection, defense, and vulnerability. Beside her is Alena—leadership, growth, vibrancy."

Alena grinned, once again ensnaring Cosima's attention with her beauty and shiny locks of hair. Thera pointed to a deity with thin black brows, a small, round nose, and heart-shaped lips. "This is Telma—Goddess of expansion, freedom, and innovation."

Telma dipped her chin in acknowledgment. The Priestess wore a crown shaped like an exquisite dragon, its mouth open on top of her head. The dragon's scales were made of glimmering diamonds and emeralds, entrancing enough to make Sima wish she could reach out and touch them.

"Astraea is the Goddess of balance, justice, *truth*," Thera said with a sly smile as she turned to her left.

She followed Thera's gaze and found a Priestess clad entirely in silky gold and red fabric with massive earrings adorning her ears. Her brown skin was radiant beneath her accessories, visible along her upper chest, arms, and stomach. It was a mesmerizing display, and it took Sima a moment to register the furious look on the Goddess's face.

"Yes, she is," Demi growled. "Do not intimidate the accused. Astraea seeks harmony and retribution." Demi gestured to Cosima. "She may very well prove to need justice as much as our Kingdom does."

Accused?

A Priestess with a frightful bone crown barked with laughter.

"Something to say, Keres?" Astraea asked. "Speak your disagreements respectfully."

High Priestess Keres sat forward. Her essence was shadowy and reminded Sima of the void. Her features were sharp like the edges of a blade, matching her jarring appearance. The Goddess's demeanor set Cosima on edge.

"I don't know why we bother," Keres droned. "We already know enough about what transpired on that disgusting planet. Let me wipe it clean, and we can consider it resolved."

"We do *not* know all of the facts," Demi countered. "Hasty decisions leave room for destruction we cannot undo. It is in our best interests to learn what transpired before—"

"Who cares?" interrupted Keres. "This is the same woman who altered Fate on a *planet*—a small, insignificant planet. If our Celestial Empress were not fatigued with grief, she would punish her to the fullest extent."

Sima resisted the urge to whine in response to the High Priestess' criticisms. Cosima's mind emptied, and in place of thoughts, she found only unrelenting shame.

Demi laughed. "Kismet does not act without forethought, sister. She would hear the story to its completion."

"Then she is a fo—"

"Enough." The order came from a different Goddess.

Cosima waited for the discussion to continue, but it ceased entirely. Every Priestess, including the bright and all-encompassing Alena, shrank slightly as they stared at the speaker. The voice came from a woman with thick black braids and glowing amethyst eyes. She was magnificent, and her gentle, doe-like beauty complemented her determined authority. This Goddess appeared higher on the chain of command, and it took little for her to control the other deities.

"Apologies, Sevasti," Demi said coolly. "Keres and I can get carried away. How shall we proceed?"

Sevasti's eyes illuminated a brighter purple than before. "High Priestess Keres. You were forged to lead us through the metamorphosis of death and rebirth, and it appears your expertise has become your own blindfold. You cannot clearly interpret the situation before us. We will reserve our judgment until the discovery portion is completed."

Astraea nodded her approval. "Thank you, High Priestess Sevasti."

"Apologies, Sevasti," Keres drawled as Mr. Vallone and his assistant from the opposing table returned to their seats.

Though she could hear footsteps behind her, Cosima kept herself from turning to the witnesses. What could people from the Eternal Kingdom have to say? She imagined those who witnessed the replicated reality from Haelos the night she killed Aurelio might possess a less-than-ideal image of her in their minds.

"If I may, sisters…" a Goddess with white hair like delicate flower petals interjected. "Uh, Miss Cosima Aphelion." Metal armor adorned her body atop her lengthy moss green dress. She ran her finger along the sheet handed to her by an aide. "I am High Priestess Fay. It is up to me to ensure our Kingdom's residents are properly supported, and to illuminate paths for those who lose their way. That being said, I have approved your council."

The chair beside Sima squealed as it departed, and in its place sat an entity made of space itself. She smiled, her luxuriously enigmatic skin swirling purples, blues, pinks. Constellations illuminated patterns and covered every inch of her body in starlight. Her eyes were a soft, glowing blue, and Cosima's head involuntarily cocked to the side.

"Who are—you are a—" Cosima stuttered.

"I am High Priestess Celestia." She grinned, and it was like watching shooting stars in the night sky. "I am your council, darling."

Sevasti cleared her throat. "Yes, Miss Aphelion. Celestia has not completed all initiations into the Divinity. Therefore, she is permitted to act as representation for the accused."

Cosima nodded slowly, unwilling to deny the help. Celestia, while the most striking and unique entity Cosima had ever met, had an aura that was soft and welcoming. She immediately began sorting through a folder full of papers, occasionally sliding a few in front of Cosima as Mr. Vallone and his assistant militarily sorted through their files.

"Well, with that being settled, I feel we can now move forward." High Priestess Astraea leaned back in her seat. "Opening comments will begin from the representation for the Eternal Kingdom. Please, Mr. Pietro Vallone. The floor is now yours."

Fighting through the haze, she glanced down and attempted to read.

It was the witness list.

The witnesses, she realized, were from *Haelos.*

Vincenzo

Enzo's heart was in his throat. Cosima's fear had been palpable in the warble of her voice as she spoke. A pulse of his power found its way toward her again in encouragement. He could never be sure what made it beyond her shielding, but he always tried anyway. If he were next to her, he would have found a way to remind her she was strong and that she could do anything. If this council could not see her worth as easily as he did, he would find a way to get her out of here and away from their prying eyes.

Enzo's curse demanded his attention. *None of them deserve their power. There are a poisonous few among them. If they haven't seen it, they are already too far gone.*

At that, his eyes bounced from Goddess to Goddess, scrutinizing the Divinity for outward signs of corruption or malice. He frowned, doubting it would be that easy to find proof of wayward intentions. However, his mother had been a conniving, wicked woman. He did not doubt the possibility that her toxic influence still lingered.

Vallone waddled around his table with a file in hand. "On behalf of the Eternal Kingdom, we bring the following violations before the council: unauthorized manipulation of Fate on a stage four planet, tampering with soul paths during refinement, aiding in the overthrow of an Archipelago on a stage four planet, misuse of an Archipelago's power level four and above. Furthermore, violations of the commandments include murder of multiple citizens under sworn protection, murder of the reigning King, destruction of a planet's natural resources, harm and suffering caused to citizens under sworn protection, conspiring with rebellions against the Archipelago, conspiring against the Eternal Kingdom, concealment of crimes committed in the queen's presence..."

Mr. Fallone coughed, needing to grab a glass of water to hydrate his throat before he finished. Vincenzo realized he was sitting on the edge of his seat, fists balled in fury. None of the listed crimes had any context added to them. They were claiming she conspired to harm the Eternal Kingdom. If the council found those claims substantial, they would order Cosima to be put to death.

"Where were we... Ah, yes," Fallone continued. "Disrupting the peace, inciting panic, failure to report offenses to the Eternal Kingdom, and disaster incitement with the use of uncontrolled magic abilities."

Enzo craned to get a better look at Cosima, to see how she was responding to the list of offenses they claimed she'd committed. The only view he could manage was one of her hanging her head in resignation. How else was she to respond to a Kingdom immeasurably more powerful than her deciding she was a criminal?

"Very well," said Sevasti slowly. "This is a troublesome list of your misdeeds, Miss Aphelion. You may have a few moments to confer with your council before it is time for your side's opening comments. We are going to take a brief reprieve. Everyone, report back in twenty minutes."

The High Priestesses left one by one, relieving the strain on his magic to block out their heavy auras. Soon, he saw a moment of opportunity. Vincenzo stood abruptly, causing Merit, who had been slumbering in the seat next to him, to jolt awake. "Hey, where do you think you're going?"

Vincenzo ignored him, pushing himself free from the sprawl of benches before he jogged down the aisle toward the front of the room where she sat. Deities all around them shot him incredulous looks as he broke from the crowd and approached her.

She didn't notice him at first. Cosima faintly nodded to the words whispered to her by High Priestess Celestia as she sat with her hair covering her face. He reached out for her, adding to his rising impulsiveness. "Cosima," he half-whispered. She turned to him, and without thinking, he crouched down, bringing himself eye-level with her. Sima's unspoken grief was trapped in her honey brown irises, and he wished he could erase it.

"Enzo," she breathed, pummeling her body into his in an embrace.

"My sweet Sima," Vincenzo said, breathing in her scent. He pulled back to see the tears she was desperately trying to hold back.

"They said—"

"I heard," he said, wrapping her hand in his. "It will be alright. They are trying to blame you for the entirety of Aurelio's crimes. Whatever you complied with, whatever rules you broke, we will show them he forced you to do those things."

"I'm not villainous, Enzo. They think the worst, I am some sort of criminal. Is it me against *all* of them?" She gestured behind them toward the sea of witnesses. "I didn't know they were bringing people from Haelos here."

"Yes, I am surprised as well. I have spotted a few friends of ours among the witnesses. There are people I don't know as well, but don't give up hope yet. We don't know what they are going to say, and maybe they will be on your side."

She attempted a small smile, and the radiance of it was enough to fuel him—enough to make him fight harder for the future Cosima deserved. Enzo's mind raced with a thousand half-finished thoughts on how to ensure *no one* stood in the way of her happiness. The justice apportioning would unfold across several weeks, if they truly gave them a chance to provide evidence in favor of Sima, and Enzo assured himself he would manifest a plan when the time was right.

"Excuse me." The voice came from High Priestess Celestia.

"My apologies, High Priestess," Vincenzo said.

"You are a brother of the Sacred Twelve, aren't you? You were discovered by the Trine Scouts on the same planet as Aurelio."

Her swirling galaxy skin was enough to make him dizzy, so he turned his attention back to Cosima's hand in his. "Yes, that's me."

"Hmm, interesting," she said simply, turning back to study the papers before her.

Vincenzo gave the Priestess an awkward smile. The last he was aware, one Sacred brother had conned and manipulated their way into being useful for the Kingdom through errands and allegiances. It was frightening that any of the Goddesses would trust them to be so close, and Enzo wondered if the Divinity kept their true origins under wraps out of fear of backlash. The rest of his siblings were somewhere off in the universe, leaching their toxic influence onto unsuspecting planets, wreaking havoc for havoc's sake. Due to the Sacred Twelve prophecy, he was restricted, confined to only two options—become the Kingdom's puppet, or take his chances out in the universe alone until one day everything he ran from caught up to him.

The sound of people arguing in the back caused the three of them to snap quickly to the source of the commotion. A set of ominous, fully black wings came into view above the heads of Trine Scouts near the back entrance. He blinked, and the wings were gone.

Vincenzo shook his head.

Cosima and Celestia showed no sign of witnessing the same auspicious display he did, and Vincenzo wondered if he had actually seen those wings at all. There were more Guardians around than usual. Perhaps there was a particularly large Guardian that caught his eye, and Enzo's nerves were just simply on edge.

He did, however, spot Merit. Fumes emanated from the Scout's head as he approached, his cheeks pink with anger. Two other Scouts trailed behind Merit in an attempt to intimidate Enzo. He chuckled to himself. "How can I help you?"

"Back to your seat, bird-bitch," Merit snarled.

Celestia swiveled to meet Merit's eyes. The Scout paled and shrank back slightly, realizing the enormity of his mistake. Knowing better, Enzo kept the satisfied smirk off his face as Merit approached and snagged his arm.

"My deepest apologies," Merit said with a sugary tone. "He is not permitted to be down here, and if the council were to see him when they returned…"

Celestia tilted her head to the side. "You are a much opinionated Scout. I will see to it that something is done about that." Her eyes spun daggers toward Merit, but nevertheless, the now-sweating Scout pulled Vincenzo back toward their seats.

Enzo's hand slid from Cosima's, and he planted a quick kiss on the top of her head before the distance once again grew between them. His world grew colder as her energy slipped farther from his reach. He pushed his mind back to the objective ahead.

Once again fidgeting in his seat to find a comfortable position for his wings, Vincenzo noted the way the room grew hot and the air grew thick as the Divinity instructed the proceedings to resume. It would be time for Celestia to give the opening comments for Cosima, and he hoped she was a kind and merciful Goddess. He could never forgive the High Priestess if she failed this task before them.

He glued his attention to what he could see of Cosima, his knee bouncing rapidly.

"There has been a change in today's proceedings," declared Alala. She burned with riled energy, as if containing it built pressure beneath her skin. "The council has reason to believe Cosima Aphelion is a wanted fugitive complicit in a disturbingly long tirade of destruction and terror across hundreds of realms. She is accused of betrayal on the highest grounds."

All color drained from Vincenzo as his jaw fell open. The darkness within him shuddered, asking one question on repeat: *What did I tell you, you fool?*

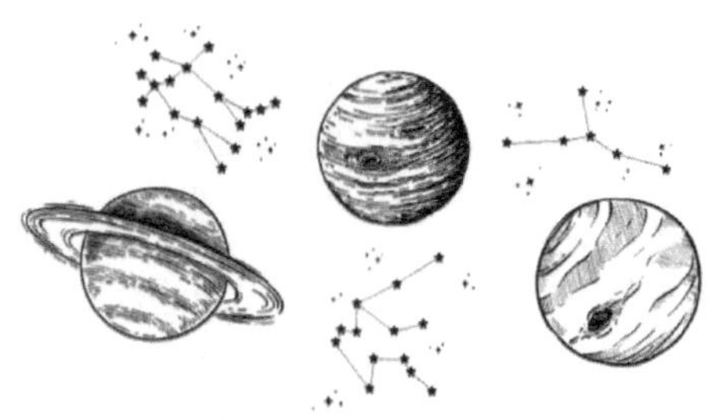

Chapter 8

Cosima

"What does that mean?" Cosima's hands trembled as she held them over her mouth in shock. Her eyes darted between an unreadable and silent Celestia and the Divinity before her. Each of the High Priestesses wore an expression of caution, and some, a mix of anger and distrust. The Ambrosi aides beside the Goddesses worked frantically to process the drastic shift, the shifting of papers the only audible noise.

"It means…" Celestia began slowly, breaking the silence, "That you are potentially going to need much more than my help." The Goddess turned to her sisters. "What are her accused crimes? How do we know this to be true?"

Alala frowned. "We will reveal our evidence in time, during this trial."

"That is a breach of protocol," countered Celestia. "This trial is for the disruption on Planet Haelos, not for other crimes she may or may not have committed."

"I agree," Demi added. "We convened today to discuss the crimes that unfolded on Haelos. Why don't we allow more time for evidence to be gathered while this current proceeding reaches completion? She cannot go anywhere. Cosima Aphelion will be held by the Kingdom until we have agreed on the proper avenues of retribution and balance."

Alessa growled. "If she has been accused of the highest degrees of betrayal, why would we waste another moment on this hearing? It no longer matters. There are more pressing issues."

Cosima rubbed her sweaty palms on the sides of her clothes, her attention bouncing from Goddess to Goddess, attempting to preemptively determine the degree to which the situation had soured. Within seconds, she went from plans to beg for mercy, to wondering if she should try to run as fast as her legs would take her. She was once again trapped, confined, and misunderstood. How could they accuse her of crimes she knew she had not committed? She'd spent fifty years trapped on Haelos, and all memories from her existence prior to that remain in the vicious void of her traumatized mind.

Her stomach sank.

Could this be about her hidden past? Could she be certain she *hadn't* been involved?

There were no memories that provided proper context to her previous life, and what little came in was hazy and misplaced. If she had no recollection of her time prior to Haelos, there was no guarantee that she was innocent. The realization sent anxious chills down her spine, and Cosima shivered as she hung her head in her hands. Would they kill her, or would she spend eternity as a prisoner yet again?

Astraea spoke next. "In order to bring forth the appropriate justice, we must weigh the scales. On one side, we are faced with the reality that Cosima Aphelion has been accused of significantly harming a planet and its population. On the other hand, there are indications she may have committed egregious misdeeds against hundreds of planets and the Eternal Kingdom itself. We cannot allow the main hearing to continue. The magnitude of these allegations demands immediate action. I am postponing the current proceedings until further notice."

The audience exploded into a flurry of hushed, shocked conversation. Though the tears wanted to fall, she would not allow them. If she were to be sent to her death, she could at least do it with strength. She lifted her chin and held her breath, willing her body to calm. There would be a process of hearing the evidence, and that meant she would be granted an opportunity to explain her side. As long as she clung to the truth, nothing would stop her.

Right?

High Priestess Sevasti nodded as though she were considering all the options before making a final decision. "I concur with Astraea. This is not a threat we can ignore. This must be remedied immediately. Rather than waste the meeting we have arranged for today, I declare the necessity of a new recitation of her charges. It is not often that we are presented with a potential criminal of this stature."

The other Goddesses hummed with agreement. Cosima looked to

Celestia for clues and found the High Priestess with her nose deep in the files brought to her by an aide. The aide was a short, round woman with a narrow chin and high cheekbones. She briefly met Sima's gaze and dipped her head in acknowledgment. Cosima gave a small, polite smile that the aide did not return. Instead, Celestia plucked a file, scribbled something across the top furiously, and plopped it into the woman's hands. She departed, rushing toward High Priestess Demi to deliver a message.

Celestia turned to Cosima. "I am not sure what makes them positive this criminal is you, but it must be strong evidence if they are this committed to moving forward. In a moment, they will reveal what it is they think you have done wrong. I want to remind you that these are simply accusations at this time. Do not panic over these charges. Do you understand? I am very good at what I do, and I was chosen for this position by Kismet for a reason. Even though I have not fully stepped into my responsibilities, I have spent centuries in this court working with my sisters. As the replacement for Ehses, I am gifted with uncovering the unknown, the deeply hidden." A glowing blue finger filled with stars tapped her temple. "Intuition, inexplicable knowing. I know you are not guilty, and victory will be sweet. Do you trust me?"

"You replaced Ehses?" The words fell out of Cosima's mouth without meaning to.

Celestia gave a sly smile. "Yes. Do you trust me?"

Cosima considered her feelings for a moment. Celestia was a stranger, but having a High Priestess on her side was not a mercy she would mistake for a burden. "I do."

Mr. Vallone waddled into view as he made his way before the High Priestesses to speak to them more directly. "Revered and respected Divinity. Thank you for treating this as seriously as it deserves. For our greatest good, my Goddesses, I bring charges based on newly uncovered evidence. Cosima Aphelion has been identified as the Realmwalker—the mysterious entity responsible for mayhem across the vast reach of the universe."

The crowd gasped, and Celestia flinched. It was clear this name meant something to those living in this Kingdom. Instead of being clued in immediately to her purported crimes, she was miserably confused. The Drago had called her by that name once, Realmwalker. But he had never mentioned anything about serious damages to other worlds.

"The list of grievances is lengthy, and as such, we have taken the liberty to group together similar charges, instead of dividing them individually by planet affected. Charges one through fifty-two: theft of valuable resources, leaving a planet at risk of collapse. Charges fifty-three through seventy-nine: manipulation of portals resulting in delayed aid from the Eternal Kingdom. Charges eighty through two hundred and eighty-four: reckless endangerment of populations over a million, resulting in pain, suffering, and irreparable harm to souls."

The nervous murmuring behind her shot like pinpricks along her skin, pestering her with the judgment she knew floated her direction. She clenched her jaw, hunkering down into the mask of calm she had created. Celestia assured her these were merely allegations for now. Getting worked up would not solve her situation. She needed to absorb every important detail with a sound mind, should it become relevant again later.

"Charges two hundred and eighty-five through nine hundred and fifty-six: reckless endangerment of populations over a million, resulting in pain, suffering, and irreparable harm to souls." Cosima faltered, sinking slightly into her chair. "Charges nine hundred and fifty-seven through two thousand and thirty-two: senseless massacre of innocent civilians with body counts totaling five thousand or higher."

"No," Cosima whispered, barely audible over the angry shouts from the audience filled with Caelari behind her.

"Murderer!" someone shouted.

"Put her to death!" screamed another. "End this waste of Creation!"

She twisted in her chair to face the crowd. "It's not true!" she cried. A single tear broke through the dam, sliding down her cheek as public evidence of her fear.

Celestia placed her hand on Sima's shoulder, reminding her to remain calm. As shame shrouded her in its biting embrace, she dared one last look into the angry sea of bodies, sending death threats with their eyes. She spotted a familiar sight—white wings with a shadowy black border and Vincenzo's signature half light, half dark hair. An invisible tie pulled taut between them, causing him to glance in her direction as she craned to see him better.

"Settle down, now!" demanded Sevasti. A squeeze encompassed the room, as physically uncomfortable as the walls closing in on them. Her power radiated a zero tolerance for disorder and hunted for any outliers in her midst.

Her tone was sharp enough to force Cosima back into her seat, even if she was desperate to be near Enzo. Sevasti's gaze reminded her of a lioness stalking with a lip curled back, the delicious scent trail of preferred prey enveloping her senses. The High Priestess was in her element and more than ready to command this room to her liking. The crowd behaved, falling into line without requiring another reminder of the threat that was Sevasti.

A pulse of a different energy skirted down the back of her neck, across her shoulders, and around her arms, like an embrace. It was a steady, firm energy. She sat straighter, chin up, and waited to hear the rest of the evil she was claimed to have committed. Never mind the mind-boggling numbers with crimes of increasing severity, and never mind the starving fish in the bloodthirsty ocean behind her. All that mattered was surviving this moment in time.

Mr. Vallone cleared his throat, though his satisfied grin conveyed the pleasure he took in watching them condemn her so obviously, without need for proof. "Her association with Aurelio, brother of the infamous Sacred Twelve, further damns her case, my wondrous Divinity. As such, I request her accommodations in the holding cells be stripped. I petition this council to move Cosima Aphelion to the prisons with the other dangerous criminals this Kingdom fights hard to keep out of the skies."

Her hand covered her mouth, and Sima found herself speechless. Painful energy scattered through her body as her pulse quickened.

"I object," hollered Celestia, who leaned over the table, waving her hand. "High Priestesses, these are still accusations, correct? We haven't presented our opening comments. You cannot call it justice if you refuse to view it from the other side. The moment we damn others without the facts, the moment we have damned what we work so diligently to uphold. Hear what we have prepared, and then, perhaps, decide what you must."

The Goddesses exchanged looks, curious ones of arched brows and sprouting smirks.

"I shall hear you," bellowed Alena. Her luxurious hair spun around her finger as the bird on her shoulder preened its feathers. "I admit, though, I am intrigued more by what Miss Aphelion has to say about all this than I am interested in hearing you, dear Celestia."

Cosima's bewildered expression amused the council more than Alena's statement, as a few of the High Priestesses chuckled. Even grounded and relaxed, Fria smirked, clearly equally curious about her time on Haelos. She couldn't discern if the interest was a positive sign or foreshadowed an untimely immortal's death.

Celestia bowed with a smile from where she sat beside Sima. "But of course, Alena. I will not deny you. A brief introduction, if I am allowed?" With a nod from the overpowering and intimidating set of Divine women, Celestia began. "Cosima Aphelion is not a flawless woman. None have preached her to be so. Instead of a lamb with wool as fresh as a morning sky, we find a snarling, snapping wolf—injured and distrustful. She is no more a danger, however, than a freshly birthed pup, and I compel this council of my brave sisters to open your minds and hearts to her. Remember, this is her story. She is not as grand as we are. She is not as powerful, but she is as important. If we forget to listen to those we command, we will become oppressors before we become leaders."

This statement garnered a different type of attention from the High Priestesses. Demi, Astraea, Sevasti, and Fay refined their focus and watched her with the eyes only women chosen above all others could— with devastating precision, willing to cut her down where she stood if she proceeded with anything but authenticity. This plea from Celestia appealed to an empathy of severity Cosima could not fathom. The Goddesses were greater than her in every way, and yet, they were choosing to relent their magnitude enough to hear her speak.

She would not waste it.

"Cosima," Celestia cooed. "Please begin where you can remember."

Her heart lodged itself alongside the lump in her throat, and swallowing was unbearable. She was sweating again, and her extremities were bags of sand, impossible to command. She opened her dry mouth and croaked the words, "I remember being a child, but only tiny fragments. I grew up alongside my parents, the King and Queen of the Aeria Archipelago, and my sister. From what I recall, we were not close to one another, and often my parents were highly critical of me. I was small, and then I remember being on the edge of my immortal adolescence. I was being prepared for the throne."

"The throne?" interrupted High Priestess Thera. "Why were you slotted for the throne and not your sister?"

"Yes…" Cosima took a slow breath. "Spirit Goddess, Ehses, granted me the throne. This was spoken to my parents, but during the ritual of an Oracle's sight, it was publicly declared before they could properly announce it. I believe they were hoping it was not true."

"Thank you for clarifying," Thera chirped. "Please, continue."

Her head dipped in acknowledgment. "I met Aurelio mere months prior to my coronation. He was knowledgeable, powerful, and charismatic. He captivated my parents with ease, and, admittedly, me as well. I will not deny I was the one who brought him into the kingdom, as he courted me. I did not, however, know he had sinister intentions toward my people. Never would I have gotten close to him if I knew who he truly was. By the time I figured it out, it was too late. I was stuck in his relentless cycle of abuse, overflowing love to smooth it over, and abuse again. Our relationship devolved into one run only by his desire to control me." Flashes of Aurelio's menacing golden glare appeared in her vision. Sima shut her eyes, and when she found the strength, she continued. "The night he overthrew my kingdom and forced me into a marriage bond, I was sleeping. I woke in the morning to anguished sobs and iron-scented air. The floors were sticky with blood, and I could *feel* it in the world around me—I could sense the tragedy of it all before I ever saw it with my eyes. My kingdom was burning, in shambles from a man I let kiss my neck and whisper his manipulative poison into my ears."

She coughed, her throat dry as she internally recoiled from the weight of the memories. Celestia slid a cool glass of water across the table. With a grateful smile, Cosima sipped it and continued.

"Afterward, it was…painfully difficult to survive. I was forced to use my power, enhanced through the use of mind-altering mushrooms and magic-infused crystal powder, to strike down whatever drew his ire. He kept me in line in whichever way suited him best. The abuse was physical at times, but primarily, he changed the way my mind worked. He found every lively piece of me that believed in something, and he crushed it. He put me down with cruel insults, and sometimes, he did it so covertly, I was left feeling disgusting and could not discern why. I internalized all his hatred for me. I let it consume and overtake me until there was nothing left. I began to believe I deserved the way he treated me, and the guilt ran so deep that even leaving didn't feel like an oasis. It felt like a death sentence. It felt like going into a world where everyone would see the monster in me that he did. I couldn't imagine bearing the weight of my whole kingdom's disgust. I was isolated, and with time, I grew numb to it, to a degree. I did what was necessary to survive, and for any rules I broke in order to do that, I am sorry."

"But," Sima said, taking a slow breath, "I want you to know that I was never numb to my decisions, not entirely. It was an immense burden, knowing I was fully under Aurelio's command, and I often lost sleep over my actions. Although it may be hard to see under the current circumstances, I have committed myself to fighting for what is right. When given the opportunity, I fled from Aurelio, and I worked side-by-side with brave citizens to fight back and end his control over Haelos. I was not just fighting to free myself from him, I was fighting to free each and every person whose lives were irreversibly altered by him. If there is one thing you take away from this confession, may it be this: who I was when I was at the mercy of my abuser is not an accurate assessment of who I am at my core."

The expressions the Divinity wore were tight and at first, unreadable. Then Sima allowed her emotions to settle as she drank in the change in the atmosphere in the room. No longer was it tight, so suffocating that breathing was laborious. Now it simmered at their feet as if the floor was encased in low-burning flames. Something had stamped down their power, made it gawk and stutter.

She recognized it as it spread across their faces. The woman the High Priestesses saw before them was not a perfect victim. She was flawed. She had made mistakes. Cosima did not fit what others pictured in their heads when they thought of someone who had been abused, she was aware of that. Instead of an unfortunate angel caught in the crossfire, she was a conscious, feeling person who made the choices necessary to survive, and that realness was a double-edged sword. If they wanted to cut her down for her crimes, they could not do it without acknowledging any in her position may have done the same.

For once, hope did not seem so cosmically misaligned.

Chapter 9

Vincenzo

Pride burned in his chest, and his heart applauded her bravery by thundering with a rally of mixed emotions in his chest. Sima's opening comments perfectly encapsulated the pain of her past, and yet, she gave only slivers of the true story of what she endured.

As he studied the face of the Divinity, he held his breath, an act mirrored by the stunned crowd. Moments ago, their anger had been at its peak, and a few of the Goddesses had been ready to condemn her. Now she had appealed to them without begging for mercy on her knees, causing each of the esteemed Priestesses to sit with crumpled faces. Cosima acted with strength, choosing to fight for her truth rather than lie down and take the misgivings of the universe. He could only watch with stunned admiration.

As the Divinity whispered messages for one another to their aides, his mind wandered. Hearing her speak had lulled Vincenzo into submission long enough to forget the overwhelming situation they found themselves in. For a few sacred moments, he did not concern himself with the threat of death or about the possibility others were misunderstanding her words, or worse—misunderstanding her. Instead, he thought of the moment their paths crossed, a Fated union written in the stars.

He had finished a grueling day of training with the other Rani

Guardians and decided to have a stroll about the Kingdom. That's when her essence flooded his senses, captivating and subduing him into a lifelong promise of servitude—one he happily obliged with. The way the sapphire blue dress she wore electrified the air between them, the first time he laid eyes on her, was irrefutable proof of love at first sight.

Following her was easy. It was the only thing that made sense to him. The orders he received alongside his brothers were to defend their future assigned planets to the death, and yet, the only person he wanted to tell him what to do was Cosima. She had smiled up at him, ensuring his life completely became hers and that his aching soul could finally stop its searching. Somehow, she had seen through his darkness, making him believe he was destined for more than endless heartache.

A Goddess's voice caught his attention. "My sisters," Celestia said, almost breathless. "You can see, this case is not as simple as you originally conceived. We cannot allow our eyes to meet hers with reproach, instead of empathy. The mission of the souls is to—"

"I'm aware," barked Keres. "I am well aware what the souls are meant to endure."

The Priestess of metamorphosis, darkness, and destruction. Vincenzo cocked his head to the side as he evaluated her. Her eyes sank into her face, cast in shadow. A bone crown sat upon her wild black hair. In many ways, her mysteriousness appealed to him, called to him like a long-missed friend. In other ways, it shunned and shamed him, chastising him for the ways he left the addictive embrace of the all-consuming darkness behind. Others saw Keres and were afraid. Vincenzo saw her and hated himself for the ways he could relate.

Yet, there was something more to Keres. He could not keep his gaze from repeatedly falling back on the Priestess, and the longer he lingered, the more a foul sensation accompanied her aura. It was subtle, or perhaps, well-concealed, but present nonetheless.

Arrogance makes evil unmistakable, his curse sighed. *Hard to conceal malice that potent.*

Enzo refrained from rolling his eyes, but he could not get himself to relax. The emptiness of the room agitated his thoughts. Could he withstand this unrelenting scrutiny? He hated attention from people and despised being associated with ruling or leading, except where it could not be avoided. His time in Ombra had taught him that the command of large groups came naturally to him. As if Fate had a cruel sense of humor, it also showed him how resistant he was to seizing true leadership. The people grew dependent on him in some ways, but he equally ensured he could disappear at a moment's notice, and others would be able to step into his shoes.

He did that everywhere he went—made it easy for him to escape without recourse. Enzo would be a fool to leave others truly dependent on him. He was not meant to settle in one place and wear a crown, not with the terrible power he kept contained within himself. He was built to see the expanse of the universe in the flesh, preferably with Cosima by his side. Despite how the raging storm inside called to him, he could do no more than sit idly by as the Divinity made their judgments, even if it should have been obvious that she was not a mastermind or conductress of evil.

She was Cosima.

A woman capable of commanding light from the voids of space. A woman he'd swim through blankets of stars and swirling storms of ragged rock for, searching tirelessly for an honor only she could bestow. A woman so unlike any other that she could only be part of a greater, more cosmic wish from the expansive universe, destined to create immeasurable change. How could they not see it as he did?

Cosima leaned to the side to hear something Celestia was whispering in her ear, and he grimaced at her rosy pink features, flushed from silently crying to herself up at the front of the room. His muscles were tight with his nervous energy. He yearned to protect her, to alleviate her suffering in every treacherous moment. He clenched his jaw at the ear-splitting regret panging inside his head. He ritualistically berated himself daily for decades, all for never being strong enough to save her.

"Cosima Aphelion," Sevasti said with measured patience. "If you were truly a victim, then explain to us how you were using the star realm portal for travel? Could you not have escaped?"

"It is not that simple," Cosima said, her voice soft in comparison to Sevasti's far-reaching speech. "The drugs I mentioned before, they seemed to tap into the Weave, allowing those without power to change Fate to glimpse potential avenues of death. Those same drugs amplified my abilities, but subdued my mental state, and often I would complete the tasks ahead of me with no understanding I was traveling through the portal. I did not know I was the key, opening and closing it all that time."

Sevasti considered this as Alessa spoke up next. "How were your powers utilized by Sacred Brother Aurelio? We were aware you had some connection to the Weave, but it sounds as though you can change more than we initially understood."

A lump rose in Sima's throat at the frustration in Alessa's voice. "He required me to thwart attacks on him. If resistances arose, it was my duty to throw them off his trail or destroy their lives in some manner. I would… touch the threads of those he targeted and enact the required changes.

I was also given instructions that seemed illogical to me at the time, but ultimately carried out his hidden agendas. Beyond that, he spoke of another brother, Carmine, frequently. He conspired on several occasions to kill him when he had the proper opportunity."

"Why would he use you to do these things instead of doing it himself?" scoffed Fria. "We are expected to believe he was strong enough to physically capture your kingdom by overwhelming thousands upon thousands of Rani Guardians, and yet he decided to hide amongst his victims? And sent you after those who resisted?"

"Well, ye-yes. I-I," Cosima stuttered.

"Fria," Celestia interjected, "I am sure much of these events can be corroborated by some of the witnesses. Perhaps we should select a few near the Palace on Haelos and see if others can shine light on what Cosima endured."

Vincenzo's stomach turned. The witnesses had the opportunity to swing the hearing the wrong direction, especially if they had unfavorable views of Cosima. The High Priestesses brought it up to a vote, and all but Alala agreed to hearing a selection of witness statements. Alala glared at Cosima as if she were sniffing out lies, but Vincenzo knew none existed.

"Very well." Sevasti lightly tapped her fingertips together. "I will select witnesses from the list provided by Mr. Vallone's defense team. Before we release for me to consider the options, I have one final question for you. Do you know of the crimes committed by the Sacred Twelve? The ones they have enacted since their conception?"

That question confused Vincenzo. Cosima knew nothing of the Eternal Kingdom, and the High Priestesses were well aware of this.

"No," squeaked Cosima.

"Then I shall tell you why my sisters have come against you so harshly, and plan to meticulously decipher each piece of evidence in this case. The Spirit Goddess created her sons in secret, concealing the birth of twelve Caelari in ways we have still not uncovered."

"No," cried members of the crowd. "Twelve Caelari?"

"Why has no one spoken of this?"

"Explain yourselves!"

"Twelve Gods? We are in worse danger than you have led us to believe!"

"Quiet," Sevasti growled, waving one hand while balancing her forehead on the other. "You are learning now, when it is appropriate for the information to be revealed. Any more interruptions and heads will begin to roll."

The crowd stiffened around him, and Vincenzo found himself unnerved by Sevasti's edge as well. Her aura was like calm, lethal anger from a foe twice his size—it begged its opponent to disobey, to give it a reason to show the ugly side it concealed within.

Sevasti tapped her fingers with a sharply raised brow. "One of those twelve brothers loyally aids this Kingdom, on a tight, restrictive leash, in order to prove he is not a threat to this realm. The others have dispersed throughout the universe, taking to planets like invasive insects—hunkering down there until they are eventually found. Each of them has proved, to some degree, to be dangerous. You ask for us to trust you, and yet, I have been informed you are in a romantic entanglement with yet another brother."

Gasps echoed around him, and Vincenzo bit back a snarl. The hatred for his wicked brothers was not a stain he could wash away. It tainted the view they had of her, and it took everything in him to not beg for her forgiveness right there, to vow to never come near her again if it meant she would be spared. Alas, no sooner would that free her. Everywhere he went, he faced this criticism. Pieces of his messy past were now her cross to bear as well.

They misjudge you, his curse said.

"I assure you I did not intend to gain romantic feelings for him, nor do I believe he is a threat," Cosima said, with a soft sniffle. "Vincenzo is nothing like Aurelio or any of his brothers. He has never hurt anyone."

"I hardly think so," said Thera, scanning the list in front of her. "This document states he was found equally responsible for civilian and Rani death on Haelos. You are both murderers."

"Sister," scolded Demi. "Contain yourself." She turned to the crowd. "We are dismissing for now. We will begin again tomorrow, when everyone has had a chance to process today's proceedings. Mr. Vallone, I am going to deny your previous request to remove Cosima Aphelion from her current holding cell arrangements. She will return with her Trine Scout. Witnesses will be alerted if they have been chosen before nightfall."

Merit, who had taken to snoring for half the day beside him, was now ushering Vincenzo toward the exit. He fought against the Scout, desperate to see her for another moment, when a voice had both him and Merit whipping around.

"Vincenzo, that is your name, correct?"

High Priestess Demi stood before them, regarding Merit with a strange look on her face before shifting her focus back to him. Enzo paused, unsure of how to respond. Her Trine Scout was a small woman with curly red hair who narrowed her gaze at him and cleared her throat, prompting him to respond properly.

"Yes, High Priestess." Vincenzo bent into a respectful bow. Though he had been anxious to get another moment with Cosima, he was now curious what drew the Goddesses' attention.

"Today unfolded with a measurable amount of chaos, and not all that was on the agenda was attended to. That leaves much to be uncovered in the days to follow."

"Yes, High Priestess," Vincenzo said, cocking an eyebrow upward. "Is there something you were hoping I could answer for you?"

Tell her you'll slaughter anyone who stands between Cosima and your rightful future together, his curse hummed, its tone bordering on amused.

Demi smiled, and though she was not a High Priestess known for her cruelty, there was always a calculating plan unfolding in her head that none were privy to until she decided to reveal her hand. It made her appear flighty, or so he'd overheard before, as if her mind was fickle and ever-changing. Though Vincenzo saw it for what it was—she was someone ten steps ahead of everyone, including her sisters. She operated in a manner that required planning for the future, even if she could not predict it. Enzo could only hope it meant that she was conspiring in their favor.

"Perhaps," she replied, planting a hand on her hip and motioning toward Merit with the other. "Your Trine Scout has been instructed to discern if you maintain connections to your brothers. So far, the answer has been a flat 'no', and with my insatiable curiosity, I felt it was more appropriate to gauge your involvement myself."

Vincenzo gave an awkward smile, the best he could manage to cover the snarl building in him. "I assure you, High Priestess, I am not, and have never been, interested in collaborating with my brothers to any degree. I was not raised alongside them, and do not share their interests."

"Ah," Demi said, patting her finger against her chin thoughtfully, "I do remember the Scouts mentioning your Rani Guardian ruse. My sister, Ehses, has created quite the obstacle for herself to clear. The more that unfolds, the worse it looks for her. With your brothers being hunted by the Kingdom, well—"

"Hunted?" Vincenzo blurted, his curse flaring with fury beneath his skin.

Aether shifted on her feet, her hand floating toward the slim throwing knife on her hip off instinct alone, as if she could sense his curse. Vincenzo cleared his throat and flashed an apologetic smile for interrupting a member of the Divinity.

"This is where the information came from about your…friend…Miss Aphelion. There is a deep investigation into the Sacred Twelve. As you know, the sons of Ehses must all atone for their crimes and answer to the Kingdom. It is by pure luck you were located. We have been searching for

Aurelio and the rest of your brothers for nearly thirty years now. There are entire teams dedicated to tracking them through portals. Those teams scour the planets one at a time; however, there are millions of worlds where they could be hiding."

Vincenzo's jaw hung open. His brain struggled to keep up with the meaning in her words. He stared at her for what felt like an eternity before he found a reply. "Am I included in this hunt?"

Demi fought back a smile, apparently amused. "No," she said with a sigh, "we only knew the full identity of eleven brothers by the time you came around. You nearly slipped by undetected, but Keres sniffed you out. I have no idea how she detected your aura, being that it is so subtle, but it does eerily resemble Ehses' signature. We are desperate to make a breakthrough in our efforts to locate them, as it has been some time since we have uncovered any new information on them."

It would be too easy to find and kill your brothers, Enzo's dark companion mused.

The idea hit him then, fast enough to cast stars into his eyes. "A deal!" He cleared his throat and steadied his emotions. "A deal could be arranged, a contract of sorts."

"Involving who?" Demi asked, narrowing her gaze.

"C-Cosima," he stammered. "Cosima spent fifty years with Aurelio, listening to him ramble on about his brothers. Is there not some way *she* could be of higher use than a mere prisoner? Let her help the Kingdom in return for her freedom."

Aether's brows raised as Demi's eyes flashed with excitement. "Just the forward thinking I take pride in. Her Scout is adamant that she is innocent after the time they've spent together. She did mention he would speak often about a particular brother of yours. There is a chance she knows things we do not. Not to mention she murdered Aurelio on her own…What do you think, Aeth?"

Aether's lips pressed into a line. "It's not a terrible idea. I concur with Nariah that beyond Cosima's powers causing a bit of chaos, she doesn't pose much of a threat to you or your sisters directly, Demi."

"Haelos has further value as well," Enzo added. "How have the other High Priestesses responded to the crystals from the planet?"

The High Priestess tipped her head back slightly as she surveyed him. "The crystals from your planet are causing more mayhem and headache than anticipated. There are valid concerns for the safety of this Kingdom due to those stones, and tracking down your brothers would be an incredible step toward securing them."

"Let her help. Give her the opportunity to show you who she really is, not the picture cheaply manufactured of her by Aurelio and his crimes. Give her the chance to show the Divinity she is not a threat, but an asset."

Vincenzo's shoulders were taut with nervous energy as he internally pleaded with Demi to consider his proposition. If a deal could be arranged, it would be a guarantee they would need Cosima, at least for some time longer. Until he could come up with a better plan to help her escape.

"It just might work," said Demi as she turned to leave, already deeply lost in contemplation. "Come, Aether. It seems we have another meeting to attend."

With that, Vincenzo gave in to Merit's persistent redirection back toward his rooms. His head swiveled as he searched for Cosima once again, and though he did not see her, her energy was near enough to make the hair on his arms stand. Once outside of the vicinity of the High Priestesses, Enzo let slivers of his magic skip through the hallways, creating tiny, inconsequential changes to the physical structures. He did not expend the energy with plotted purpose, but simply because the maddening build-up of his power, akin to suffocating, required an outlet.

When the time is right, Enzo thought with a frown, *I will use this wretched curse to free us.*

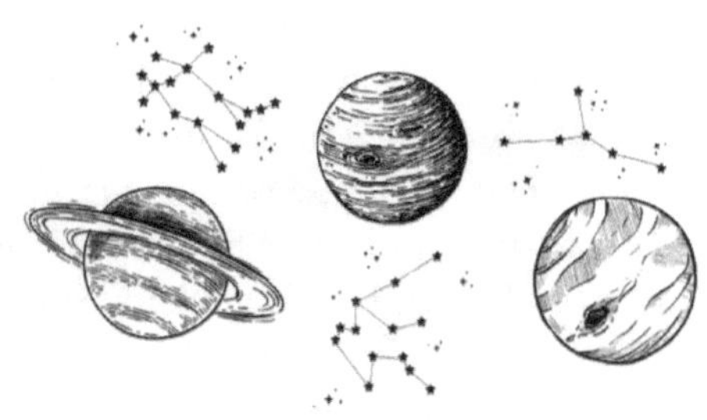

Chapter 10

Cosima

The relief of fresh water against her skin was enough to temporarily rid her brain of intrusive thoughts. There was no denying the hearing yesterday did not go as Cosima had hoped, and the situation jumped several levels of severity before she could comprehend the changes. Her evening was uncomfortable, her sleep fitful, and she was drained. If she thought about the hearing too long, her brain became cluttered, leaving her own thought process ineffective and miserable. Instead, she enveloped herself in the present moment. The way the water cleansed her skin, the way her breath felt escaping her lungs. All of it contributed to the calm inner atmosphere she needed to properly determine her next steps.

The High Priestesses had shown her mercy, allowing her to remain in her living quarters with Nariah until a decision regarding her future had been formally made. Bathing was one of the few entirely solitary times she was allowed, and she rejoiced in finally feeling as though she were not on display. As she lathered the soap into her long black hair, Cosima thought of Vincenzo. The unexpected way he rushed to her side, allowing her a brief release of her hardened, stoic mask, she attempted to conceal herself beneath. He brought her solace, easing her troubles even as others regarded him with scorn.

She stepped free from the warm water, and goosebumps traveled along her skin as she reached for a towel to dry herself off. If the Sacred Twelve were considered to be dangerous by the Eternal Kingdom, there was no way for Cosima to know exactly what kind of threat the brothers posed. Were they accused of crimes in a similar manner to Aurelio? Worse? She shivered to think about men more wicked than her former husband.

It was nerve-wracking to wait until it was time for the testimonies from the witnesses borrowed from Haelos by the Divinity. She could only hope the statements corroborated her claims and did not end up painting her in an even poorer light. The moment she had been questioned about her relationship to Vincenzo was the first moment she had thought about the way it would appear to those outside of their connection.

Her connection to Vincenzo, in her mind, was sweet and gentle. It was a place of serenity and love, not one of fright and manipulation. Nothing about their interactions felt slimy or negative, but when she realized others thought their relationship was suspicious, she found a kernel of doubt. Questioning him made her feel guilty, yet the thoughts did not die. Instead, they sprouted, twirling vines of poisonous fears tickling the edges of her mind as she pulled on an airy navy blue gown. It fit her well, showing her cleavage minimally and extenuating her waist. The gown was elegant and modest, the perfect mix to appeal to a council of Goddesses acclimated to the finest of luxuries. She understood why Aurelio had worked so vehemently to emulate this level of perfection in Haelos. He had been practicing for the day he took over the Eternal Kingdom.

As she took slow breaths to calm her racing pulse, she wondered if she outwardly appeared to be the kind of woman who was easily taken advantage of. Vincenzo had lied to her before—at least by omission. While on Haelos, he had not told her he knew her from their time together in the Eternal Kingdom, and he had obscured the reality that he was not merely a Guardian—but a powerful God who shared the blood of her tormentor, Aurelio.

She had not discerned yet whether their half-sibling relation unnerved her enough to stay away from him, but she had determined, at least to some degree, that Vincenzo was not scheming behind her back. Even if there was more he was hiding from her, she knew he had a reason to keep it to himself.

He'd never lie to me without a good reason. Would he? She wondered.

She shook her head, sending droplets of water onto the floor of the bathing chamber. With eerie intuition, Cosima turned to the door and half a heartbeat later, Nariah's fist pounded on it. Sima opened it and peered out at the Trine Scout who leaned against the wall.

"Ready for another round?" Nariah smiled, swishing her long white hair behind her.

Sima took in Nariah's relaxed demeanor before meeting her gaze. "You certainly do not appear worried. Is there anything I should know about?"

Nariah shrugged as she pushed off the door frame and turned to exit. "Who knows?"

She rolled her eyes and allowed Nariah to lead the way back to the courtroom. A group of Ambrosi aides rushed by, bumping into people walking nearby as they darted toward the room where the Divinity would be waiting. Cosima craned her neck to watch their hurried steps, and a knot grew in her stomach. Before worry could overtake her, the reassuring breeze-like energy from yesterday touched along her shoulders and cheek.

"Cosima," a familiar voice drawled, as if her name was sweet on his tongue.

She turned immediately, throwing herself into his waiting embrace. He smelled like a comfortable, rainy afternoon. Cosima glanced up into his emerald eyes and sighed. "Hello, Enzo."

"Hello." She was disappointed when his eyes broke away from hers as he looked at her Trine Scout. "Nariah. It will only be just a moment, I promise. There is still time before they officially convene."

Nariah snorted and turned away from him with a huff. The tap of her foot communicated her annoyance, but the Scout did not verbally rush them, so Cosima soaked in the moment, despite the kernel of doubt she carried with her. Now that he was in front of her, all she wanted to care about was the way it felt to be with him. There would be a time and place to untangle their lives, but in a circumstance where she had been isolated, with no more than Nariah to keep her company, she craved interacting with him, even in the most simple of ways.

"I am proud of you, Cosima," Enzo said, his eyes earnest as he gazed at her. "Your bravery never ceases to amaze me."

Sima smiled, his compliment somehow exactly what she needed to hear. "It helped knowing you were near. I thought it would be harder to talk about what Aurelio put me through, but I needed to speak my truth."

"You handled every moment up there with grace," he said, brushing his fingertips against her arm. "It takes a special strength to look those who doubt you in the eye and tell your story anyway. You have done something grand, even if just for the version of you who thought she'd never be free. Look at how far you have come."

Sima's smile faded. "I can only hope the Divinity sees it the way you do. How can that man make all these claims about me?"

Enzo shook his head. "We will have to wait for their side to present the evidence, but whatever it is, I don't believe it will prove anything. You're not who they say you are."

Her head bobbed with a small nod as she let out a shaky breath. "I'm terrified, Enzo."

His expression softened as he pressed a kiss to her forehead. "You have every right to feel that way, my love, but I won't let anything happen to you. No matter what happens, you will always have me by your side."

Nariah whirled around. "Enough chatting. It's time to move."

A fire Sima knew could only be the desire to resist burned in his eyes, but Enzo said nothing as the Scout ushered them down the hall. Cosima and Vincenzo walked side-by-side toward the Ecliptic Court as Merit and Nariah led the way. Their fingertips brushed against one another as though they were shy adolescents escorting each other to class. He chewed his lip with a distant expression, but she thought little of it as she, too, was overwhelmed by her nerves beneath the surface. When their Trine Scouts ventured just out of earshot, Vincenzo leaned closer to her.

"Cosima," he whispered. "I need to warn you. There are no witnesses today. The Priestesses are rumored to announce a deal for you."

A deal? Her head ached preemptively, as if her body anticipated another rendition of her previous captivity with Aurelio—forced to use her powers as others commanded. Could she allow herself to do it again if, at a minimum, it was not under the same conditions she had been under with her former husband?

"You must take it," he continued. "Do whatever you can to postpone their judgments. This is a rare opportunity. I am sure this Kingdom would much rather hire you to do their dirty work than banish you. Use that to your advantage."

Cosima blinked several times as she numbly floated through the courtroom doors and was once again accosted by the intense power of the Goddesses. It pressed the air from her lungs, and her fingers curled into fists as she fought the urge to run in the opposite direction.

She shot Vincenzo one last glance, relishing the reassurance in his eyes. A type of pleading swam in his gaze, too, as if the idea of Cosima turning down the incoming agreement would spoil whatever plans he had begun concocting. He had run the Depths with an immense amount of ease, and she could tell his mind was busy with alternative outcomes should the situation further sour. She was thankful, in a sense, not to have to be the one concerned with backup plans, and instead, she could focus on the situation head-on.

Even if her mind was hazy enough to slow her thoughts to a crippling pace.

The chair beneath her squeaked as she slid closer to the table, and

Celestia smiled at her before turning back to the paperwork she busied herself with. Vincenzo, instead of sitting in the audience, took a seat at a newly added table to her right. Merit stood off to the side, leaving an empty seat beside Enzo.

Celestia blew out a heavy breath. "I am sure somehow you have heard the rumors," she glanced at Vincenzo, "that the Divinity are willing to grant you a deal today. I have been somewhat briefed on this arrangement, and at this time, there is no reason to panic. After it is presented in completion, we will have time to convene privately and discuss our options. Just breathe, and you will get through this. There is no audience today, so don't worry about eyes on you or whispers from behind."

Cosima nodded, and as the council hearing began for the day, she placed herself in a detached, far-off piece of her mind, waiting for the piece of information she desperately awaited to surface.

"There has been an arrangement proposed by High Priestess Demi," Sevasti said tightly, the words uncomfortable as her lips formed them, "and we have already come to an agreement prior to today's meeting. Therefore, we will now list the initial terms of the arrangement, the restrictions, as well as the parameters, should you accept. Do you understand, Cosima Aphelion?"

"Yes," she said, with a bow of her head. "I understand."

"Very well," said High Priestess Fay. "Demi, Fria, and I have taken the time to formulate this arrangement based on the needs of the Eternal Kingdom. Your counterpart from Haelos, Vincenzo, joins us today. This is because this directly involves both of you. Fria, Thera, and Alena provided strong arguments in favor of this agreement, given the increase in turmoil being caused by the remaining brothers and the unavoidable truth that we are growing near the end of the prophecy. That leaves us no choice but to make our moves now. The Sacred Twelve may have drastically dwindled in number to only four alive, but they are just as strong as they have ever been. Lost somewhere in the universe, there are three brothers in particular that are causing massive damage to planets, leaving them in ruin before finding the next suitable host to deplete. For this reason, tracking down these men has been a high priority. With the revelation that Vincenzo and his brothers are not mere Ambrosi, but full Gods instead, this mission has surpassed all other concerns for the Kingdom, and it is now a top priority."

"As such," Fay said, leaning forward and spilling her long white locks of hair over the front of her desk, "*you* will go out and find them. You will be responsible for tracking each brother on the list, and you will eliminate them by any means possible."

Her breath caught as she listened. The council was requesting not only that Cosima and Vincenzo travel through the many universes, but that they commit sanctioned assassinations as well? Now she understood why Vincenzo had tried to warn her previously. It was unlikely she could get herself to agree to such an arrangement. She had killed Aurelio because she had to, because she would not know true freedom without his death. She was not interested in becoming a leashed assassin for the Kingdom that allowed her to be wrapped into Ehses's merciless attempts to overthrow the Divinity.

"Weapons we have recovered from Haelos will be made available to you; however, you will be limited by the number you can take with you," added Alessa. Her eyes dripped with a level of calm control Cosima found unnerving. "Your Trine Scout will be in charge of when you are allowed to wield a weapon, especially on this first mission. These crystals must still be studied extensively by the council before we will permit more widespread usage. For now, should you accept, you and your team would be the only ones in the cosmos granted permission to wield the stolen life-force crystals."

"Furthermore," Astraea chimed in, "there are restrictions as well. You will be assigned a trusted Trine Scout to accompany you through the portal and on your journey to the other worlds in search of the brothers on the list. This Trine Scout will be skilled in detection of power usage, namely fate manipulation, and therefore, you will not be granted the ability to use your magic unless cleared by the Trine Scout first. You will have a small team with you to not only ensure compliance, but also to assist you on your mission."

I can't use my power? Her heart skipped. *How will I get by?*

Thera frowned. "Your ability to not just touch the Weave, but alter it as well, is a significant risk. We cannot be sure what changes you have already enacted. The reach of your misdeeds is yet to be determined, and we cannot allow you to continue your chaotic spree of alterations. Do you understand?"

Sima's mouth was dry as she squeaked out a response. "Yes, High Priestess."

The deity nodded. "Only when permitted by your Trine Scout will you be able to manipulate the threads of Fate. Your abilities beyond that are within your discretion. Additionally," Thera said, "in the interest of protecting the sanctity of this council's rulings, you will be restricted, equally, in terms of your intimacy with Mr. Vincenzo."

Cosima's eyebrows furrowed in confusion. Recognizing this, Thera offered clarity. "You will not be allowed to carry on a romantic relationship during these missions. To ensure you are operating justly, you must relinquish your emotional connection for the prosperity of the greater whole. You will be restricted from physical intimacy of any kind, and your Trine Scout will also mediate interactions between the two of you to ensure compliance."

She glanced at Enzo to find his face scrunched in displeasure. He, too, appeared caught off guard by this specific request from the High Priestesses. He met her gaze for a fleeting second, giving her one, nearly invisible nod of his head, signaling he wished for her to agree, even with the added clause that they would end their relationship, at least for the time being.

"In exchange for your servitude," Alena began, toying with the ends of her hair, "you will be granted something rare. As we have not unearthed your true origins, and neither have we fully investigated the crimes you are alleged to have committed, you must understand this is not a decision we have made lightly. In exchange for the deaths of all three brothers, you will be granted immunity. All previous crimes you have committed will be erased, and you will be granted the freedom to travel where you please within the Ethereal Realm and beyond. Should you decide to defy any of the rules given before you, or should you shirk your responsibilities and escape instead, you will be put to death without trial once captured. There is no opportunity for error."

Cosima's mouth opened, but words did not come out. The offer stunned her to her core, and her thoughts froze rock solid. Immunity was the last reward she imagined, and all she had to do to achieve it was to murder three more of the Sacred Twelve. She had done it once before, and now she had a team on her side to ensure the success of the missions. There was just as likely a chance that Cosima would end up dead from these escapades sooner than she could bring them the head of even one brother, but freedom was all she had hoped for. Under Aurelio's command, chaos emerged. Under the High Priestesses' command, could *good* be manifested?

"What do you say, Miss Aphelion? We haven't got all day. There is a rather large list of arrangements that must be made should you agree," Sevasti said.

Cosima sat up as straight as she could. "I agree. I will kill the three Sacred Twelve brothers in exchange for my freedom."

Sevasti clapped her hands together.

"It is decided then. You are now indebted to this Kingdom, Cosima Aphelion."

Vincenzo

You are now indebted to this Kingdom.

The words left a foul, strange taste in Vincenzo's mouth. He sat numbly as the Divinity laid out further parameters for their servitude to the Kingdom. Not often were others capable of making him truly fearful for the future, the way the High Priestesses did now. It did not matter to the Goddesses if he and Cosima died trying to defeat his brothers. All that mattered was that they were able to sit back and let someone other than themselves take on the brunt of the responsibility and fallout. Somewhere within the lurking darkness of his soul, a storm raged, a fury he grew tired of restraining.

"…which will determine the significance of the leads the Kingdom has uncovered, and this will then be communicated to your assigned Scout. This Scout will direct you to the next location where you will begin the search…" He barely registered Sevasti droning onward as he spiraled.

Cosima was more to him than a pawn in everyone else's pointless games. She was his everything, his reason for every decision he made. There was nothing he did without considering her first. Now he questioned if he had made the right decision by pitching the deal to Demi. The Sacred Twelve were his brothers, and if Vincenzo was man enough, he would have offered to do it alone, without her help. He would have vowed to fight for her freedom and not rest until all of them were dead and she was granted the freedom she so rightfully deserved.

But he was a coward.

He froze just as much as she did when the arrangement was fully announced. He was terrified of his brothers, for each of them was three times as strong as him. His brothers were not like Vincenzo, as they all shared the same powerful father, Luciano, while his father was Domani. Because Domani was highly magically gifted, Enzo had powers his brothers did not have, but he was not physically capable of competing with the sons of Luciano. It made sense to him why his mother had chosen Luciano as her first sire, until desperation drove her to Domani as a last attempt to fulfill her twisted desires. The difference made him weaker, a vulnerability he hated himself for.

"…outlined in section four-nine-nine, all Trine Scouts assigned must…"

Enzo's stomach sank as a familiar ache crept through his muscles, and he hung his head. There lay another reason he had not forced his way into Aeria, puppeting every Guardian he came across in an effort to defeat Aurelio himself. Not only was Vincenzo different from his brothers, he was cursed. A dark, vicious magic lay within him, a threat to everything he worked valiantly to create.

When he first arrived in Haelos, he had only just begun to feel the insatiable burn of what he now referred to as his curse. In an effort to relieve the pain the buildup of energy caused, he poured his abilities into helping those in Ombra. Soon, he uncovered that the well of his magic was practically bottomless, and the more he used it, the more it demanded of him. Enzo had no way of discerning what fully relinquishing himself to this power would do, and each time he had exceeded his previous expenditure of energy, the power seemed to only grow.

This intimidating magic was amplified by his God-blood, meaning it had the potential to be a horrid source of destruction—but Enzo would never let it become that. He would contain the unholy power, even if it killed him.

I am not your enemy, his curse laughed. *Your own bloodline is.*

As Sevasti continued detailing the mission ahead, his eyes slid over to Cosima, who sat with a mysterious sparkle in her eye. It was something rebellious, the glimmer of hope that refused to die. He sat straighter, reminded of the reason he'd broken through his fear of being weak and finally attacked Aurelio. His control over his magic had initially been pitiful, something he changed only through half a century of practice in the Depths of Ombra. The only time he found the bravery to act had been the moment he saw his brother coming for Cosima with deathly hunger in his eyes. Then, he didn't care if he died—he only wanted to protect her.

Living required much more finesse. He could not simply break his way out without damning them to a life on the run. He could not lack courage when face-to-face with his brothers again. He had to be strong, unshakable when faced with terror twice what he thought himself capable of handling. He could never admit to Sima how much he truly feared his brothers, but neither could he admit fully how dangerous the men were.

"Initially, we suggest locating the man lowest on the list," Alala said as she picked at her fingernails, facial features twisted into an expression of vague annoyance, "Carmine."

That caught his attention.

Carmine was the brother Aurelio had set his sights on, tormenting Cosima with mountains of work to further his agenda. He pulled himself out of the ruminating dark cloud above his head and focused on the discussion in front of him by the council.

"That concludes the council's part in this case until further notice. Cosima. Vincenzo."

Vincenzo glanced up at Alala. Her burning red locks of hair framed her face in a rage-filled glow.

"I wish you the best," the Goddess continued. "Do not disappoint this Kingdom."

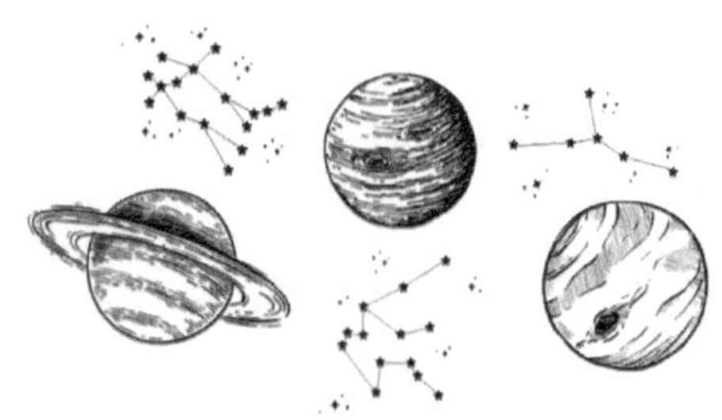

Chapter 11

Vincenzo

Merit, in his usual manner, was quick to usher Vincenzo up and away from Cosima. This time, he did not fight the Scout and allowed Merit to guide the way to the meeting room he knew he was inevitably going to end up in. Now that Cosima had agreed to be the personal assassin of the Eternal Kingdom, there would be a formal introduction to the case, laying out where they would head in the infinite void on a pointless hunt for lethal men.

His suspicions were realized when he ended up in a similarly ornate space to the courtroom; however, it was more private and contained a large communal table. The slab of pearl white marble was outfitted with dozens of chairs around it, each with a glass of water and a letter in front of it. Merit dragged a chair out and spun it to accommodate Vincenzo's wings, before taking a spot along the wall to rest against.

Enzo slipped into his seat and rested his hands on the table. A few Ambrosi aides attended to various tasks around him, one woman with big, round glasses giving him disapproving glances as she prepared the room for the arrival of a High Priestess. A silent hour had passed with no one arriving or mentioning a change of plans to him, and he had resorted to nibbling on the tip of his thumbnail to expel his nervous energy.

Finally, the door opened, and his head shot up. He recognized her immediately. Cosima swept in, the blue of her gown adding to the melancholy expression she wore. Nariah directed her to a seat away from him, placing herself between them as a stark reminder they had agreed in one swift moment to sever their relationship for a chance at freedom. He could not ask her to risk that to be with him, and he would adhere to these rules even if it pained him. He had waited fifty years for her; he could wait as long as she needed him to.

He attempted to keep his eyes off her, but the stolen glances left him desperate for more. She concealed her sulking the best she could, and it brought a small smile to his face, the way she valiantly remained strong in the face of adversity. Nariah glared at him, writing death notes like love letters with the menacing threat in her eyes.

"Nariah, Merit," Aether said, her long curls swaying as she poked her head inside the room. "Quick brief needs to happen. Step out."

Nariah chewed her lip as she glanced between the two of them. Merit tapped her shoulder and nodded toward the door. She huffed but followed after the curly redheaded Scout, with Merit close behind. Just before he fully exited, Merit shot Enzo a sharp glare.

Enzo clenched his jaw and reminded himself to stay in control. He could not let his emotions get the best of him. Although Merit was an irritating man, Enzo could handle him so long as he kept calm. He turned to Sima and was ensnared by her warm eyes, which sparkled as she looked at him, despite her obvious overwhelm.

"Sima," he whispered.

"Enzo," she whispered back.

Electricity shot through him at the way she said his name, like a gentle recognition of his soul once again within orbit of hers. The magnetizing energy between them was addictive, and Enzo wanted to remain by her side for eternity.

I can make that happen, his darkness whispered.

"They said we can't be together," she said softly, her head hanging down.

He hated to see the questions in her expression, the way she seemed defeated even when she had been granted a deal that could ultimately save her life. *This is all my fault,* Enzo thought. *If I had killed Aurelio myself, would she even be in this predicament?*

"They said we cannot be in a romantic relationship," Enzo replied. "They never said I had to stop loving you. It would be impossible to enforce. I'm hopelessly yours, Sima."

The crinkle around her eyes made his heart jump. "We can make it through this, right? I worry because we've only had a short while to spend together, only to face more restrictions."

"It doesn't matter. As long as I am with you and fighting for your future, I will withstand any binds, any chains, any restrictions the Kingdom wants to put around me. This has never been about having continuous access to you. I will love you no matter how close or far you may be from me. I promise."

A tear slipped from her eye, and she was quick to wipe it away. "I don't know why I'm struggling to believe that. It's not that I don't trust you, I just—"

"My love," Enzo said gently. "Our situation is an incredibly complex one, with a lot at stake. Go easy on yourself right now. Of course, you're going to feel caught off guard and nervous, because that's how I feel, too. I'm not trying to discount your feelings; I'm telling you that I share them, and we are going to get through it together. You are not alone in this. Even now."

"Thank you," she breathed. "You're right."

"This is the time to have faith, even if there seems to be no reason to have it. We can't give up here. I am going to make sure we succeed in killing my brothers so we can save Haelos and be free."

She looked away. "What about the prophecy, Enzo?"

His heart squeezed. "What about it?"

"If you are the survivor, you will have to command the Kingdom."

He shook his head. "Not if I don't want to, they can't make me do anything. If I happen to be the last one of my brothers alive, I will seek freedom, not responsibility."

"What about…"

Enzo knew immediately what she was speaking of as clearly as if her thoughts manifested in his mind. "Sima, *you* are the woman the prophecy says the survivor will marry. You are Kismet's daughter, or you are blood-related to her somehow."

"That's not true," Sima said, her lip wobbling.

"What do you mean?"

"I met with Kismet. She said she didn't recognize me. She thought I might be her daughter as well, but I'm not."

"Then she's mistaken."

Sima sighed. "It's not that simple, Enzo."

"How could it not be?" Her face twisted slightly, causing him to spill more words. "I understand why you are feeling discouraged, but you're the one for me. If I am the survivor, whether or not you are the woman from the prophecy, my heart is yours. As long as I'm still what you want, I'll be here."

She sniffed, and a small smirk pulled her lips upward. "You're the only one for me."

Enzo beamed. "That's music to my ears. All those resurfacing memories of me haven't changed your mind?"

"Most of them are sweet."

He laughed. "Most of them?"

She blushed, and Enzo drank in the sight of her pink glow. "There are a few I wouldn't find myself repeating out loud."

By the cosmos, I'm in love, Enzo thought. "I know exactly what you're referring to. Those are some of my favorites, but nothing compares to the time we spent by the sunset."

Recognition sparkled in her eyes. "The day we made lists of all our wishes."

"I remember all of yours," Enzo said, adding a wink. "Including your desire for a butterfly garden."

"I wish all my memories would return already. I am tired of trying to decipher all the mixed-up pieces of my own life. The worst are the ones that I believe are my own, only to realize they're recollections of other Fates I've viewed."

Enzo frowned. "I'm sorry, I know it must be frustrating, but we can make a million more memories together while we wait for it all to come back to you."

"We're being sent on a mission to murder your siblings. Not exactly a romantic getaway," she joked.

"It is for us, love. Our time on Haelos was intense, but it never stopped us from being drawn to one another."

She blushed again. "I don't think there is anything that could keep me from you."

Nothing can keep you apart, his curse mused. *Unless you allow it, I suppose.*

Enzo shoved away the voice and focused on her, sensing the return of the Scouts. "I love you, Sima. We can't fail as long as we are together."

"I believe you." She smiled. "I love you, Enzo."

The door opened, and Nariah flew into the room. She narrowed her eyes at them, but Enzo continued to stare at Sima, unwilling to let their short moment of alone time fade. But he had no other choice. Nariah cleared her throat as Merit held open the door. He took the loud hint and fixed his gaze forward as the air was sucked from the room when High Priestess Demi entered with Aether by her side.

The Goddess was bouncy and joyful, almost in attitude, as she took her seat opposite them. The aides scurried to present her with information and forms to sign.

"For our highest good, my darlings," Demi cooed as she scribbled her signature and appeased her anxious attendants. "I will make this quick, as my sisters and I wish for you to immediately depart to quell any further delays. This has been a cumbersome entanglement with the Sacred Twelve and High Priestess Ehses. Now that we are not in front of an audience, I can mention to you that the Spirit Goddess has fled, and we have no information on where she might be. If you come across a sign of her, or her in the flesh, you must immediately report it to your assigned Trine Scout."

"Who is it?" Vincenzo asked.

"Hm." Demi glanced down at her flurry of papers and read the name. "Nariah was chosen."

"Nariah?" Vincenzo repeated. The Scout smirked, clearly already aware of her assignment. "I do not mean to question your great authority, High Priestess. But I thought we would be assigned a Trine Scout that was familiar with the Sacred Twelve. There is a task force, yes? Perhaps there is someone better suited."

Demi smiled. "Nariah and Merit were pulled directly from that task force when we first received the reality replication from Haelos displaying Aurelio's death. The two do work in the holding areas, yes, but for those directly involved with the investigation into the Goddess and her sons."

Vincenzo shook his head. He should have known with Merit's sour attitude that he was accustomed to criminals of a crueler type. "Nariah, Cosima, and I are expected to hunt down three of the Ethereal Realms most feared Gods—my lowly *brothers*," he said the word with a growl, "with nothing but a few weapons. Are you sure this has not manifested itself into a suicide mission?"

"Careful," Aether warned in a low breath. Her dual-toned gaze fell on Enzo as she flicked a brow. "High Priestess Demi deserves your respect."

Demi's eyebrow burned with an emotion he couldn't discern, and he did not dare a peek at Cosima's reaction. Instead, he cleared his throat. "We are not denying we are grateful for the opportunity, High Priestess," he said as sweetly as he could manage, ignoring Merit's snickering from where he stood against the wall. "I am concerned with how feasible this mission is. I do not think it is wise to risk Cosima's life—our lives—with this assignment."

"I suggest you prioritize stealth then," Demi replied coolly. "You do not have to go in swords at the ready. Devise a plan together and kill them however you manage. You are not required to give Carmine a warrior's death, Mr. Atropos."

Vincenzo stiffened at the use of his last name. He was given the name bestowed on all abandoned children in the Kingdom, Rani Guardian or otherwise. Atropos was a sister of Kismet, and she was known as the bringer of death and finality. To be a child of Atropos was to be a wayward soul with none to claim them. Whether out of fear or reluctance, immortals rebuked all symbolism associated with death.

His last name was a brazen mark of his tumultuous childhood, a brand being used as a muzzle by Demi. She was reminding him of his place, that he was once unwanted and left to fend for himself. He was born out of desperation, not love, and that fact would haunt him no matter how he tried to bury it.

"I understand, High Priestess," he said, bowing his head.

"Now," Demi began, "I will lay out what we know of Carmine so far. He has been involved in the capture of three worlds. He started with a planet called Uperath, but has since moved on. We have cornered him after he fled the second one, and he is on a planet called Paiturn. This is a standard soul refinement world with a populace that must be protected at all costs. Carmine has a habit of slaughtering the inhabitants in violent waves."

Just like Aurelio, Enzo thought, resisting the urge to roll his eyes.

"After you were brought here from Haelos, several Scouts began their investigation into Haelos and into the crystals. While we have gained some insight into how these stones work, we have also uncovered that a substantial amount was removed from the planet. So far, there have been no sightings. If Ehses, or any of the Sacred Twelve, are in possession of them, there is a chance the stones will be turned into weapons that could slaughter immortals, and potentially even Divinity. While you should remain vigilant, your first priority is eliminating the target."

The room grew heavy with a deeply uncomfortable energy at the mention of entities capable of creating worlds and galaxies being killed by much smaller, insignificant beings. Even the Trine Scouts could hardly stomach the immense weight on their shoulders, evidenced by their matching scowls. Enzo's previous reluctance sharpened into a protective instinct. He no longer lamented where they had ended up. Instead, he saw how foolish he had been to complain about his desires when their mere existence was at stake. What would take their place should the Caelari be brought to their knees?

"We understand, High Priestess," Cosima said cautiously. "I will approach this mission with the diligence and tact it requires. We will not fail the Kingdom."

Demi beamed at them. "I am happy we have come to see it eye-to-eye." She rose, her aides scrambling to gather their items as Aether held open the door. "You will be leaving within a few hours. Try to stay alive long enough to reach your freedom," Demi said, more to Cosima than to him.

Vincenzo suppressed his urge to frown at the callous way she regarded their future, and instead, took his chance to speak with Cosima. He opened his mouth; however, Enzo's recent impulsive behavior meant Merit had already caught on and had his hands on Enzo's arm.

"You heard the rules," barked Merit as he tugged Vincenzo backward. "There is to be minimal contact between the two of you. The only reason you're being allowed to go with them is because the Divinity seems to think you can still be useful. Better to have you on a chain and helpful than rotting in a prison cell, I suppose."

Vincenzo blew out a breath to move the hair from his face and then squared his shoulders as he looked Merit up and down. The amused Scout was quick to puff out his chest and lock eyes with him. Merit bumped into Enzo with his chest.

"Do something, bird brain," taunted Merit. "Give me a reason to show you how tough a Trine Scout is."

Vincenzo narrowed his eyes and felt his magic pulse at his fingertips, begging to be unleashed on the irritating Scout after weeks of denying the impulse. At the very moment he was prepared to open the gates and shut Merit up once and for all, Cosima's hands pressed into his chest, ensuring a gap between the two widened. He gasped in response to her touch, the electricity from her palms enough to jolt him out of his impulsive anger. Although brief, he pulled her hands off him and gave them a reassuring squeeze before he dropped them.

"Enough," Nariah said, tugging Cosima out of the way and positioning herself between them instead. "Save it, Merit, you know he isn't worth it."

"He's just as corrupt as the rest of them. I won't be as forgiving as this Kingdom. If they are blind to what an unreasonable risk he is, I won't be." Merit stuck his finger in Enzo's face as Nariah attempted to hold him back. "I know you're up to no fucking good, you hear me? You aren't getting anything by me. I know vermin like you, always conniving to get what they want."

Vincenzo smirked as Nariah forced Merit to back up. "You think about me that much when you're alone, too, Merit?"

Merit snarled, shoving Nariah to the side, and charged at Enzo. The first punch landed on his jaw, making Enzo laugh, but he threw his arms up to defend against Merit's continuing attacks. He resigned himself to not hitting back, finding satisfaction in pushing the Scout this far already; however, his curse flared inside him, igniting in a way it had never before.

He thinks he's better than you, Enzo's inner darkness growled. *He thinks he knows who you are. A Trine Scout thinks he stands a chance against the inevitable son. Show him his mistake.*

When the opportunity presented itself, Vincenzo relaxed the restraint over his rage, and he beat Merit with starlight-filled fists, the heat burning both of them. Physical violence was not his specialty, but he had had enough of being insulted day after day by people who would not bother to learn anything about him.

It wasn't until Cosima cried out in fear that he looked up from Merit's face, as a hoard of Trine Scouts rushed the room—and it wasn't until Enzo was dragged away with bound wrists as she sobbed that he realized what a devastating mistake he had made.

It was about time you started giving in, his curse laughed as Enzo's self-loathing reached an unbearable new high.

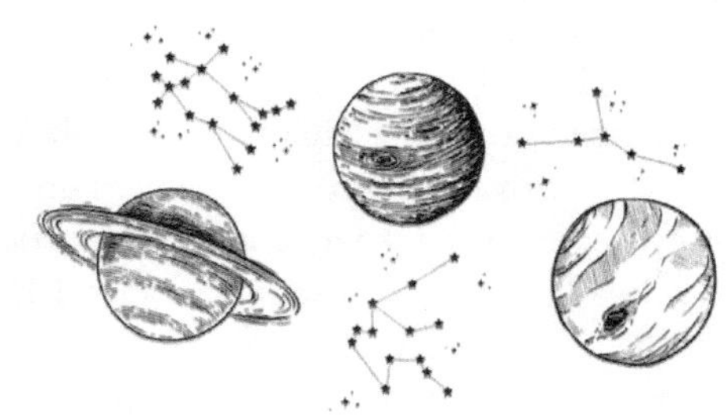

Chapter 12

Cosima

"Someone has to tell me something," Cosima said, crossing her arms over her chest.

Pollux and the other two Scouts in front of her did not appear convinced. Instead, they continued to stonewall her, offering only vague reassurances that more information would come soon. They did not allow her to leave the meeting room after Vincenzo was ripped away for punching Merit, leaving her with no option but to wait.

"You know the rules, Cosima," Pollux said with a deep frown.

She sighed as she turned away from the Scouts and returned to her seat. Nariah and Merit had been whisked away by High Priestess Alessa's aides to be quickly debriefed on the situation and, she assumed, to attend to Merit's injuries swiftly. Her mind was rampant with conjured images of Enzo being tossed carelessly into a cell. She hated that he resorted to lashing out, even though she knew his Scout, Merit, taunted him without pause. It put his ability to accompany her and Nariah to Carmine's world at risk, and for that, she wanted nothing more than to give him an earful of her fury.

The door slid open, and Nariah walked in with a strange, contorted expression. Merit did not follow.

"Oh, finally," Cosima said, throwing her hands up. "What's going on?"

"Come, we must prepare to depart." Nariah did not meet her gaze.

"What about Vincenzo?" Cosima demanded.

Nariah's lip curled. "He will be dealt with. For now, we must worry about departure. Remember, Cosima. This is your only opportunity for freedom. Do not squander it over a mere male. There are many of them. Many who are not also bred to be usurpers and mass murderers."

Cosima shook her head. "I am not asking because I have feelings for him—had feelings for him. I am asking because the arrangement was for Vincenzo to come with us. We cannot go, just you and I. We will be slain by sundown."

"We will not be by ourselves. Now come."

If the day's events had not been such a whirlwind, Sima may have fought Nariah more; however, exhaustion alone moved her feet forward as they left the meeting room. By the time they reached the outside, all of Cosima's senses were enthralled by the mystical Eternal Kingdom. Towering pink trees rained cherry blossoms onto their heads, the floral scent complemented by the fresh water from a nearby fountain with a bust of High Priestess Alena at the top. The walkways were mostly paved with white marble, save for black and maroon marble used as accents.

As they ambled by groups of people enjoying the fresh, warm air, she thought of the Sacred Twelve's prophecy, and potentially, their damnation. The surviving brother would be offered an opportunity to rule amongst the Divinity, wielding the same powers to control the Realm and vast universe. The position seemed like an impossible role she could not imagine being able to fulfill herself. Vincenzo, though, in her mind, was more than capable, even if he did not see himself that way. He was clearly opposed to leading in any official sense, whether in the great Eternal Kingdom or in a tiny, insignificant city on a planet amongst trillions. If she were destined to command a power as great as this, could she?

What is it that she wanted to do with her freedom, should she become acquainted with it at long last? In some aspects, it was invigorating to imagine a life fully hers to command, and in other aspects, the options were feeble and murky. Cosima's thoughts stalled as Nariah led them inside a sterile bathing chamber, where a fresh set of clothing, similar in fashion to the Trine Scout uniform, sat beside a series of small soaps. Hers had a burgundy cape instead of olive, and beside it sat hefty black boots, meant for any terrain.

"You will cleanse your body with each soap for two minutes. Then you will wash your hair, following the same steps. These soaps will protect your body during travel through the portal, as we are going quite a distance. You will feel the build-up on the surface of your skin, so be cautious when dressing after your bath. I will be in the next chamber over, performing the same steps. When you are finished, wait for me to return. Our counterparts will bathe as well, and we will convene at the portal."

"I understand," Cosima said, thankful for the moment of privacy she was allowed. Bathing became her ritualistic chance at decompression, and her body thankfully fell into routine without much fight. She stripped off her clothes and began washing as instructed. Sima could not help but think of Vincenzo, worried the Divinity would not let him accompany her to Paiturn.

Aurelio's voice floated into her mind. *Are you sure you're capable of doing it alone?*

She carried on, determined to ignore his lingering influence. When the familiar twinges of panic surfaced inside her, she swatted them away. When they returned, more persistent and intense, she grew frustrated. When it threatened her ability to continue cleansing, she threw the morsel of soap at the wall and muffled a scream into her palms, which she latched over her mouth. She painstakingly pulled herself from the bath and onto the floor.

Although she thought she had defeated the useless ruminating that often dominated her emotions, her chest burned like the air had turned to flame. Her emotions demanded release, and she was at their mercy more than she cared to admit. As such, everything she had stowed away came pouring out of her as another scream tore from her throat, this time not muffled by her hands. When she was done, she rested against the mirror and gently banged her forehead against it. Her reflection was as disheveled as her inner world, her hair as equally out of sorts as her emotions.

A piercing headache split through her skull, and she hissed as she pulled herself away from the mirror. She had not been banging her head hard enough to injure herself, at least she didn't believe she had. She held her head in her hands as she slid her back against the wall. Her vision grew hazy, and within seconds, another memory overtook her.

"Stop," a girl cried, "get off me!"

Her screams were muffled by a large black hood affixed with a lock at the nape of her neck. Her back bore horrendous, lengthy scars, the skin composed of explosions of red, thick patches of tattered healing. Two men struggled with her, and despite their much larger stature, she gave them quite a fight. She screamed all the while, thrashing wildly until the men successfully pinned her and restrained her hands behind her back.

Cosima reflexively reached for her wrists, barely cognizant of the sensation as her mind continued to watch the memory unfold.

The shorter of the two men hoisted her off the ground, looping his arms through hers to maintain control of her. He used his knees to nudge her forward, then lifted her off the ground as he led them away. The streets of the city were empty, not a single soul to witness her abduction. Her cries were soft beneath the hood, but not silent. The taller man snapped, snatching her throat with his hand and squeezing until her body went limp.

Cosima gasped for air as the memory grew shadowy. Suddenly, instead of watching from afar, the perspective shifted drastically, and she was thrust into it fully. Her wrists burned and ached with the restraints, her shoulders screamed at the awkward angle, and her eyes could only take in never-ending darkness.

The fear set in immediately, setting her on edge as she fought to free herself. Her lungs burned from how heavily she screamed, but her ears could register none of the sound. Even her heart, which beat furiously in her chest, gave off no audible sound, only the sensation of its fluttering.

Hands slid across her skin, and she used her body as a weapon, kicking and thrashing as violently as she could manage. Someone grasped her on either side of her face, and the sensation of their touch startled her. Slowly, the blackness dissipated, and the locked hood she thought she wore vanished. She was not in the memory of being restrained by two strange men. No, she was in the bathing chamber, and Nariah was staring at her with a bewildered expression. Sima blinked several times, her breathing ragged.

"Cosima," Nariah said, shaking her shoulders vigorously. "What happened to you? Are you alright? What is going on?"

She shook her head, mouth hanging open as no words came forth.

"You don't know?" Nariah sighed, releasing her hold on Cosima. "For the good of all, you scared me so badly, I almost called for help. You know who would have come? *Michi*. Do you feel like calling Michi?"

Sima shook her head again. "N-no."

"I didn't think so. Are you… are you alright?"

"M-maybe, I don't know. I don't know what happened. I had a memory, at least it felt like a memory. But it was like I was watching from the outside, and then the next thing I knew, I was reliving it. I could feel hands on me. I thought I was restrained and suffocating. I thought…"

Nariah stared very intently into her eyes with a pained expression. Sima glanced down and realized she remained unclothed from her bath. Her hands clasped over her chest, and her cheeks burned hot. Nariah handed her a towel, and once she was covered, the Scout relaxed a fraction.

"It is called a flashback—when the memories feel real like that. Or so I've heard. It hasn't happened to me, but it can be common for the Trine Scouts who see things they can't come back from while exploring the grander universe. However, perhaps it is a good sign that your memories are coming back."

Nariah helped her to her feet and gave her a half-hearted pat on the back. Her Trine Scout shoved the pile of clothing Sima was intended to wear into her hands and turned around to allow her privacy as she dressed. Once Sima reassured her several more times that she was indeed going to survive and not melt into a puddle of incoherent screaming again, Nariah led the way out of the bathing chamber.

"We will be meeting the rest of the team now. We will be with these people for quite some time, so I advise you to try and befriend them, or this murderous adventure will sour quickly."

"Who are they?" Sima asked as they crossed a wide gray and white stone bridge between two sections of clouds. "Have I met them before?"

Nariah's mouth pressed into a thin line as her eyes scanned their surroundings on the other side of the bridge. Her brows flicked upward when she spotted what she was looking for, and she led them down a somewhat crowded pathway. "More Scouts, some new ones, and I'll have you know Merit was meant to be Vincenzo's watchdog, but I am unsure how the Divinity will respond to his little outburst from earlier. They could decide to rescind their offer entirely."

"No, they can't do that," Cosima breathed, keeping her voice low enough to keep strangers from overhearing. "I know he made a mistake, but that Scout was pushing him. I didn't realize this could cost him the agreement."

Nariah shrugged. "I am sure they will send him along anyway. He is more trouble than he is worth if he stays. Who knows how many Scouts he'll have to punch before they kick him through the portal and let the roadways of the galaxies deal with him."

"You judge him so harshly."

The buildings on either side of the pathway were brilliant, reaching far into the sky as they sparkled like glittered rainbows. Each structure had a pointed tip surrounded on all sides by windows. Sima wondered what the Eternal Kingdom looked like from the inside one of the elegant buildings, but Nariah led her away from the surrounding city and toward the gate.

"You would too if you knew precisely how much of a drain the Sacred Twelve have been on this Kingdom…if you knew the levels of destruction they have enacted. You were married to one brother for half a decade, and you cannot imagine how several of them could be immensely worse?"

"That's true, but I have been through that period of unspeakable amounts of darkness, and I think it's clear how I trust the one person who has never harmed me. He had his chance to fool me and stab me in the back, and instead, he has done nothing but devote himself to me."

Nariah narrowed her eyes at Cosima. "Are you insinuating he was forthcoming with the knowledge that he was born of God-blood?"

Cosima averted her eyes. "Well, no. I do, however, believe there is nothing else he is keeping from me. Enzo knows how much I value honesty and integrity. I don't think he is hiding anything sinister, nor do I think I have any reason to distrust him. If he wanted to uphold their plans, why wouldn't he have kidnapped me like Aurelio did?"

"Not all plans require such force," Nariah replied with a roll of her eyes.

Vincenzo

"Ah, Mr. Vincenzo. I am happy you have decided to take part in this discussion. I thought there was a chance you would be unconscious for the remainder of our meeting."

He groaned as he rolled his stiff neck and gazed upward. Surano sat in front of him, and Vincenzo was propped up on a chair with his hands restrained just below his wings. The man was the most animated he had ever seen him, affirming Enzo had taken things too far by retaliating against Merit. Whether the Scout deserved it or not, he would now have to answer for his actions, and he could only hope the Kingdom valued killing his brothers more than they desired to punish him. There was nothing more valuable for them than a leashed killer, right?

"I know I fucked up. Let's get the punishment over with so I can get on my way."

"Don't like the idea of your beloved being alone with another one of your brothers?"

Vincenzo swayed his head back and forth in mock contemplation. "Perhaps. Or perhaps I would like to fulfill my duty to this Kingdom so I may know freedom. Whichever answer gets us closest to that will do, I suppose."

Surano glared at him. "Do you know what happens if she fails? What truly happens?"

"The council is convinced she is a masterminding criminal. I am well aware of the stakes." Vincenzo stared down at the table. The swirls in the cherry wood gave off distinctive star-like patterns, unlike the wood harvested on Haelos. Having spent so much time on the planet, it was hard to readjust to his original home once again. Would he ever forget his time there and the friends he made while at his lowest?

"That's a considerably generous assumption. At worst, you assume she will endure another hearing and may end up in the prisons, if fortune does not favor her. But, there is a more sinister reality. If she fails, Cosima will never know freedom, will never act according to her own will. Her debt to this Kingdom will be so heavy, the weight of it will crush her spirit, until she is an unrecognizable sack of broken flesh."

Kill him for even speaking of her that way, his curse hissed.

"No," Vincenzo challenged. "They cannot do that to her. She is not the criminal they make her out to be. It is a mistaken identity, not the truth. Once there is further investigation, they will see that she is actually innocent."

"That's what you want to happen, isn't it? But what if they are content just having a face to plaster on top of the crown so people do not question them as closely as they have been? Since you've been gone, the kingdom has been taking heavy heat from the residents. Beyond Cosima, there have been many missing immortals across the Ethereal Realm."

"Missing immortals?"

"I took the liberty of searching further into your time as a Rani Guardian. You were a regular grunt until you met her and fell in love, weren't you? Who did she tell you she was? How can you be sure she *isn't* a criminal?"

Vincenzo's head fell again. "She didn't tell me who she was…she told me her name, Cosima, and that was it. She refused to tell me which family she belonged to or if she worked somewhere in the realm, and I wasn't curious enough to press the issue further."

"You never suspected she should not have been here?"

Vincenzo scrunched his face in confusion. He hadn't. Not once. He had never assumed she was out of place because she filled all the missing pieces inside him. It felt strange, the twinge of insecurity in his own knowledge. He pushed the sensation aside, dismissing it as Surano's mind games beginning to wear on him.

"The evidence the Kingdom has on her is pretty damning, even from what little I've seen. The Realmwalker has a unique energy signature that was detected by several portals on the more advanced planets, and Cosima is the closest match. She might not be the person you believe her to be. Either way," Surano continued, "if this mission fails and Carmine is not killed, that leaves Cosima indebted to the Kingdom forevermore. Haelos will be disposed of, and all the hard work and sweet little lives will cease to exist. That leaves you. What do you fear more than death, Vincenzo?"

The darkness inside him cackled, and Vincenzo smiled. "That I'll never get the chance to punch in all your teeth, Surano."

Surano returned the expression, cocking his head to the side. "Or is it once again losing her?"

Vincenzo straightened, no longer amused. His tongue slid across his teeth as he calculated his next words. "It would do you well, *pest*, to stop threatening her to my face."

"And you would think you would know better by now than to get so attached. She disappeared once before. You could have acclimated to her loss and never had to endure the pain twice. You'll be lucky if you get to see her again."

"Are you saying I am not going on this mission?" His fists balled. While he feared that outcome, a deeper piece of him was convinced they would rather him get killed outside of their Kingdom than in it. In their eyes, more meaningful casualties were to be had if he were in this realm than another.

"Oh, you will. I mean to say, there might not be anything left of her by the time you get there.”

Use me, his curse sang, *make him choke on his blood.*

Vincenzo rattled against his restraints. He'd had enough of the games. He seized control of Surano's mind, the man's jaw hanging open a fraction as his eyes rolled back in his head. Magic skidded across his brain, and soon, his mouth spilled all he wanted to know.

"The High Priestesses are aware there is a large infestation of fungus-infected demons on Carmine's current planet," Surano said, his voice monotone. "It was considered an acceptable risk that she and the people with her might die immediately upon landing on the planet. Furthermore, Ehses is currently missing somewhere in the galaxies, and it is also considered an acceptable risk if she were to arrive and slay Cosima herself. The High Priestesses are rumored to greatly fear the Sacred Twelve and Spirit Goddess because they believe Ehses is responsible for kidnapping Kismet's daughter, among thousands of other immortals across this realm. At first, the Kingdom tried to ignore these disappearances, but after Kismet's daughter went missing, they had to answer."

Vincenzo rocked gently back and forth as he listened, mulling over his options. He could not traverse through the portal on his own without a Trine Scout, at least, he didn't believe so. When he'd been sent to Haelos, a Scout guided him through to Haelos and left him on the planet for the next fifty years of his life. He needed someone to open it and guide him to Carmine's planet. Merit was a strong choice; however, he was also better at shielding himself than most Scouts, and once he felt Vincenzo's incoming attacks, he could lock his mind down.

"How do you open the portal?"

Surano cocked his head to the side. "I do not know."

Vincenzo growled. "Useless," he whispered under his breath. "Let me out of here."

Surano stood clumsily, reminding Vincenzo to calm his emotions lest he lose control of his power over the man. He guided the Scout to release him from his binds and then stood.

"Guide the way to the Scout quarters. A friend of mine needs to be paid a visit."

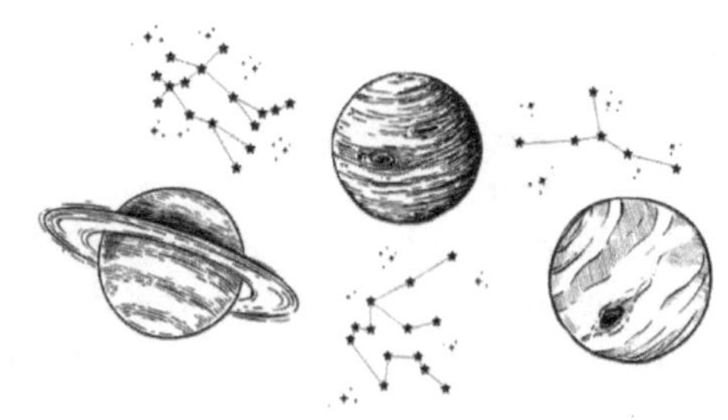

Chapter 13

Cosima

As Cosima and Nariah exited the inner sections of the Eternal Kingdom, the portal they originally arrived through was within sight. She could make out a few shadowy figures near the entrance and guessed these people would be joining them on their voyage across the galaxies. A team created to hunt the criminals who shared blood with her now deceased ex-husband. The intricacy of it all was enough to cross her eyes in confusion, but she slowed her breathing and pressed forward.

I can do anything. I can do anything. I can do anything.

The closer she got to the figures, the more they looked like actual people, and one appeared familiar with a short body and black hair. A cold sweat overtook her body immediately, and Sima stopped dead in her tracks. *Of all the people, why would…No,* she reasoned, *I am seeing things.*

"Cosima," Ivo yelled, waving one arm in the sky with joyous excitement. "Cosima!"

She was not, in fact, seeing things.

She dashed toward Ivo and the two slammed into a long-awaited hug. The moment Ivo's sweet citrus scent filled her nose and her long black hair crushed against her face, she broke into tears. Her knees grew weak, and they sank to the ground, still locked in a tight hug. Sima's time in this

Kingdom had been lonely, and the stress from the rabid accusations only exhausted her further. Ivo's presence was exactly what she needed to renew her spark.

"What are you doing here?" Cosima questioned when they had the strength to pull themselves apart.

"I can answer that," Nariah said from behind her. "Your friend here was observed in the replicated reality, dealing the final killing blow to Aurelio. He wasn't dead, not until she severed his head from his body with the crystal-enhanced sword."

Ivo appeared enthused at this explanation. "Isn't it amazing, Sima? They think I am just as guilty as you! Now they're going to send us on an adventure together."

Cosima couldn't help her shocked expression as Ivo reached to wipe away her tears. "W-what? Ivo, this is too dangerous. Why would they allow you to come? You are not an immortal. Joining us could mean certain death."

Nariah scoffed. "As if I would let that happen. You're not embarrassing me that easily. Come on, there are a few more people you need to meet."

Cosima turned her attention to the two remaining men by the Portal. One had medium-length, shaggy black hair with a long, angular nose and a cleft chin. He was slender, but tall. The other was the most muscular man Cosima had ever seen, with his arms a wide distance from his body to accommodate his massive biceps. The sight of him intimidated her, but Ivo linked her arm through Sima's and pushed them forward without hesitation.

"This," Ivo said, gesturing to the taller man, "is my Trine Scout, Horacio. Horacio is quite a doll, if you ignore the mean looks and generally grumpy attitude. He has the protective guard dog quality about him. This is Earnest. Earnest is much easier to appease, but has a nastier bite if you piss him off. Obviously. If you simply bat your eyelashes and say please, he will come running for you, though, and I adore that about him."

Nariah smirked. "Tell her why you need two Trine Scouts instead of just one."

Ivo beamed. "I beat the heck out of Horacio on the first day! He didn't stand a chance against me. They didn't think to restrict my magic the way they did with you, and I hit him with all I had. It was quite the thrill, if I am being honest. It took five Scouts to finally get me down. I agreed to stop fighting after that if they just gave me more time outside of the stuffy room they had me in."

Cosima shuddered. "I wish you would stop endangering yourself."

"You should be more worried for them than you are for her," Nariah said. "Earnest and Horacio will also be accompanying us to the next world,

Paiturn. Scouts are trained at traversing through these portals, so be quite sure to adhere to any and all instructions we give you. We are going much further than Haelos."

"Wait, but what about Vincenzo and his Scout?" Sima asked.

Earnest and Horacio shared a knowing glance.

"What?" Cosima demanded.

Nariah flicked her white hair over her shoulder and sighed. "He is not coming. Not now, anyway. He is going through additional reinforcement measures to ensure he *fully* understands the consequences should he choose to continue his defiant behavior."

Cosima debated protesting, but Nariah would not be persuaded on this matter. It was likely far out of even the Scout's realm of control. Ivo gave her a reassuring smile.

"He will catch up later, you'll see," Ivo whispered.

The portal behind her stood a hundred feet in the air, flanked by massive sculptures carved into the sides of it. The designs were intricate, depicting history Cosima could only hope to one day comprehend in its entirety. Inside, the portal was an orchid pink color, reminiscent of all the times she had stepped through doors, not realizing she was stepping through the fabric of the universe and into an inter-dimensional roadway. The thought in some ways comforted her now. If she had done it then, she could do it again now. She could look this feat in its face and barrel forward with bravery.

Cosima and Ivo linked arms on one side, with Scouts surrounding them. Nariah lifted her palm, and a beam of iridescent light speared into the portal. It changed from the soft pink color it had been before into a deep navy blue that shimmered like mystical potions on shelves in Ombra. For the good of Haelos, for Ivo, for Vincenzo, for herself, she would show no mercy to Aurelio's equally spineless brothers. She would free herself and her beloved planet, no matter what it took.

As they passed through the portal, the shift in energy immediately numbed her senses. She could no longer see, hear, or even feel sensations the way she did normally. The fabric of space and time enveloped her sweetly, cradling her as they accelerated through the galaxies in search of their destination. She allowed it to take her, relaxing into the disembodied experience flooding through her consciousness.

When Sima opened her eyes, her hand flew to cover her mouth. In front of her was a dense forest surrounding the circular brown stone portal. The trees had dense orange trunks wrapped in reddish vines, with sprawling yellow and green vegetation at the base. Large overgrown fungus adhered to the edges of the trunks, creating a stair-like pattern up and around the trees. The leaves were a deep red and fanned out in a dome shape at the top, blocking out most of the sky. Glowing insects lit up darker portions of the forest as tiny feathered creatures chirped from high above. Sima's heart pounded as the group took in their surroundings.

"It's your first time somewhere other than your home planet. What do you think?" Horacio asked.

Ivo's jaw hung open as she clung to Sima's side. "It's magnificent…I've never seen anything like this." She glanced up at Sima. "Is it anything like what you imagined?"

Cosima let out a puff of air. "Not even close."

As they stepped away from the portal, vicious shrieks made the ground beneath them tremble.

"What was that?" Ivo asked, with a noticeable warble in her voice.

"I'm not sure," Earnest grumbled, hoisting a large sword free from his belt, one Cosima recognized from the armory on Haelos.

She swirled toward Nariah. "Where are our weapons?"

Nariah appeared appalled. "*You* are not going to hold a weapon, not now at least."

A deep rumbling growl made the hair on her arms stand straight up. Ivo pressed closer to her side, and now all three Trine Scouts revealed their wings, boxing them inside. The Scouts stood with their weapons ready as they scanned for the incoming threat. Cosima peeked over Nariah's shoulder. In the distance, a flash of movement darted by, weaving in and out of the trees as it closed in on them. The creature moved with such speed, it wasn't until it was on top of her, pinning Cosima to the ground, that she saw the overgrown fungal infection sprouting from the terrifying beast's jaws.

Ivo

"Get down from there!" Nariah cried. "You don't know what you're doing!"

Within seconds of arriving on Paiturn, the group had been ambushed by a horde of viscous monsters, and though Ivo had her own magic, she hadn't been prepared for it. With too many close calls to count, Ivo had chosen to take charge of saving her own life. She flung herself onto the nearest tree and used the fungal growth on the trunks as leverage points. The soft flesh of the purple and green fungus crumbled beneath her feet, forcing her to move faster.

"Oh, now you want to care about the *weakling*. That's what you called me, right?" Ivo snapped, putting one hand over the other.

"Ivo, she didn't mean it like that!" Cosima yelled.

Below, Cosima, Earnest, Horacio, and Nariah fended off creatures as they arrived. Ivo looked for her own way to fend off beasts, knowing she was not the kind of woman to sit twiddling her thumbs while others came to her rescue. While she did not have the same magic restrictions as Cosima, Ivo was wary about exhausting her powers so soon into a deadly mission, so she opted to favor accuracy over power.

"What happens if one of the beasts can fly? This is not a very good plan!" Nariah hollered.

Ivo scoffed. As if she hadn't thought of that already. When the team was assigned to the mission, they were granted some of the only weapons strengthened by crystals in existence. Earnest and Horacio each carried a spare dagger in their belts. Ivo had swiped both of the blades immediately after the creatures began to attack. Neither knew of her thieving hands, and all it took was waiting for their attention to be otherwise occupied.

Nariah, however, in a short time, proved she would be more difficult to sway. She did not seem like the type to take no for an answer, and neither did she seem to like Ivo very much. When a beast had knocked Ivo to the ground, bringing Cosima down with her, Nariah had scolded her and called her a weakling, telling her to stay out of the way. Out of the way she went, then.

Ivo aimed her hand at a bright yellow beast with six long legs and three piercing red eyes as it bounded from the trees toward the group. "*Fuoco fluido,*" Ivo whispered. Flames sprayed from her hand like pressurized water, coating the creature in liquid fire.

Sima's time magic pulsed, slowing the creatures as they continued to emerge from the trees. The rhythmic motion of her friend's abilities allowed the team to move as though in a choreographed dance. Ivo only took shots she was certain would land and did her best to fend off the ones the group did not see coming.

Earnest spun as he stabbed his sword through a scaled pale blue beast, fungi shedding across the forest floor like a flower spilling pollen in the spring.

He swung the creature and hollered, "Might as well figure out where we are then!"

As she neared the top of the tree line, the branches below her began to sway beneath her weight. She balanced herself carefully, hoisting higher until she could finally peek over the top of the red leaves. The fresh air was cold on her face, and she raised a brow at the violet sky littered with dim stars. The sun was nearly finished setting. No horrid nightmares lined the sky, and for that she was thankful. However, it was clear she could not discern where their target, Carmine, might be. She thought there would certainly be a city within view, not endless seas of red, orange, and yellow plants. In the distance to their right were navy-colored mountains, which provided a landmark, at the very least, to travel toward.

"I can't see much," she shouted back. "There's only more forest."

Ivo began her descent. She would not leave the trees, at least not now. Instead, she would cross through the branches and make her way toward the mountains. If there were people inhabiting this planet, perhaps they would be at the base of it. They had yet to see any sign of life here. Only murderous creatures and disgusting fungi.

"Are there flying ones?" asked Horacio when she grew closer.

"No, none that I can see."

"Maybe she had a point when she climbed the trees," Cosima said to Nariah.

Nariah fended off two beasts with incisors the length of their calves. Their ugly muzzles were adorned with beautiful blue and green mushroom caps. "Oh, please," she groaned, slicing the jaw off one. It hit the ground with a wet thump. Green blood oozed from its muzzle. "She wants to get herself killed, be my guest."

Another beast came bounding from the trees, spraying spores as it sped toward Sima with its jaw hanging open. Ivo cringed at Sima's uncertain expression, her hands trembling in front of her as her friend debated the proper action. Ivo sent a blast of icy energy at the creature's feet, causing it to slide out of control before smashing into several trees.

"Don't you have wings?" Ivo asked. "Why don't you fly Sima out of here before she gets hurt?"

Each time a beast grew close to her friend, it made her insides twist into knots. Ivo reasoned Cosima was more than capable of defending herself, but Nariah had not even allowed her a blade in lieu of her powers. Ivo locked eyes with Sima and waved her hand, beckoning her to flee to the trees for safety. Cosima did not hesitate and immediately jumped up and grabbed a branch. Ivo lent a hand and helped her into the trees. Once she was seated, the two smiled at each other. The Scouts were too busy slaying creatures to pay attention as Ivo made her move.

"Here," Ivo whispered, sliding Cosima one of the blades she had stolen. "It's something at least."

Cosima shot her a grateful smile and tucked into the empty sheath on her belt. "Thank you. I won't ask how you got it."

"And I won't tell you."

They both nodded in agreement before turning their attention back to the ground.

"We need to move," Earnest said, wiping his blade clean on his slacks. "Which direction?" he asked Ivo.

Ivo pointed in the direction she had chosen. "That way. There might be people, but I haven't seen any sign of them. If we climb the mountains, we'd have a better vantage point."

"I agree," Cosima said.

Earnest and Horacio stopped two incoming canine-like creatures with exposed jawbones and red mushrooms exploding from their eyes. Earnest dove into the air, slicing the throat of one while Horacio rolled forward and stabbed his sword through the base of the beast's chin, up through its skull.

"I say we get moving toward the mountains then," Earnest said, wiping his blade off on his pants. "Unfortunately, one of those damned creatures ran off with my supply pack not long after we arrived. Horacio's was ripped open, and he lost a great number of food rations. It would be advantageous for us to cover as much land as we can, get situated, and re-evaluate what supplies we have left."

Sima's gut turned, and Nariah shook her head. "So, we just believe the witch-girl's directions without checking ourselves?"

Ivo's lip curled. "Check it yourself if you don't believe me. Nothing is stopping you."

That's when Ivo's breath caught as Nariah unfurled her wings from beneath her cape. They were captivating. They were impossibly delicate and thin, resembling a butterfly. She floated off the ground with three graceful beats of her wings and flew through the trees.

The rush of fungi-driven decaying flesh had finally come to a halt, allowing the group to gather themselves in Nariah's absence. The two Scouts adjusted their armor, then both took a knee in the soil. Their eyes illuminated with a bright white light, and Ivo watched in awe from the trees. Once the light faded, both men stood and regarded Ivo with a smile.

Horacio tapped his temple. "We can communicate with the Kingdom directly if we need to, but we can also transmit information to a Scribe. They document the memories we provide them, in case it becomes necessary later."

"Good to know," Ivo murmured, unsettled by the idea of being spied on trillions of miles away from the Eternal Kingdom.

Sima frowned. "Are we really running low on supplies already?"

Horacio smiled. "Those creatures did a number on us, but don't worry. Scouts are incredibly resourceful, and most of the animals on this planet should be edible. As long as you have a Trine Scout with you, we'll find a way to get everything you need."

When Nariah returned, Ivo stiffened involuntarily, once again caught off guard by her appearance. Her time with Nariah had not gone over well so far, but she could not deny the Scout had an otherworldly beauty.

She shook her head. "Well?" Ivo asked.

"It seems I agree with you. There is not much nearby, only the mountains. I did spot something tall behind the peaks, but I would need to get closer to know what they are."

Ivo swung to the branch of a nearby tree. "Told you so."

"You can drop the attitude," Nariah snapped. "It is up to me to make sure you do not end up dead."

"Why would the Priestesses send us on this mission if we were so likely to die then?"

Nariah locked eyes with her. "Perhaps Cosima must prove herself to this Kingdom. If she survives and takes the life of a brother of the Sacred Twelve, she can solidify in the mind of the Divinity that she is not affiliated with them. Whatever it takes, I am going to be by her side to ensure her freedom, and I will not let anyone, not even you, get in the way."

"We want the same thing, for Sima to be safe. You should have a little trust in me if we are going to be a team. I may not be as powerful as everyone else, but it doesn't mean I'm useless either."

Nariah's lips pressed into a line, and Ivo thought her face somewhat resembled a pout, as though she were disappointed she had not thought of that before.

"Very well," Nariah said. She turned to Cosima. "Come down from the trees. I will carry you and fly us to the mountains." She looked at Ivo then. "If you're really as smart as you think, you'll let Earnest or Horacio do the same for you. We will move much faster than you, swinging from branch to branch."

Ivo scoffed but jumped down, her boots leaving indents in the dirt where she landed. "Let's go then."

Cosima

The group covered a large section of land before the Scouts required a break for their wings and arms, allowing Sima to stretch her legs. At the front of the pack was Nariah, who stomped forward as if she was familiar with the path already, with Sima and Ivo trailing behind, and Earnest and Horacio at the back. Her best friend was her usual chatty self, engaged in a deep conversation with the two male Scouts as Sima stayed silent. Walking through the forest was not the uncomfortable part of the journey for Sima. What bothered her was the swirling mess of incompatible thoughts fighting for dominance in her head.

Without my powers, I am weak, battled with, *this is my chance to prove my innocence.*

Without Enzo, I have nothing, wrestled with, *the only person I can depend on is myself.*

She did not know what to make of their separation. He assured her that it would change nothing between them, but how could he know? Their relationship had been a blissful blip in her immortal life, and what memories arose of him were undeniably congruent with who he had shown Sima he was. Enzo had loved her when they were realms apart, had found her even when all hope had seemed lost. Doubting his love for her only made the guilt more bothersome.

"Hey," Ivo whispered, nudging Sima with her elbow. "How are you holding up?"

Sima shook off her thoughts. "I'm fine." Ivo cocked her head, calling her on her bluff. Sima sighed. "I worry I am useless without my powers. It seems counterintuitive to send me on this mission and restrict my abilities."

Nariah glanced over her shoulder and rolled her eyes. "It is rare enough to have the ability to touch the Weave in any manner, but to alter it as you can is almost unheard of unless you're a Celestial Empress. Letting you use it has consequences, and the sooner you learn this, the better."

"What kind of consequences?" Ivo asked. "It's her power. Why would using it be a bad thing?"

The Scout huffed, her white hair swishing as she turned forward. "As if it would be simple to explain the Weave and its connection to you while we are hunting down a target."

"There's a balance," Sima explained. "Each time I touch the strings, I am altering the balance that the Celestial Empresses have put in place, and there is no telling what the ramifications of those changes are."

Glowing plants and insects all around the forest lit their way; however, as the sun continued to set, the illumination began to flicker and extinguish. The group was covered in a thin sheen of sweat from constant movement as they maneuvered through an eerily still forest.

Ivo frowned. "Why would they give you the power to do that? The Empresses assign everyone a Fate, so why not change yours to *not* destroy things with your magic?" Nariah laughed, causing Ivo to raise a brow. "What's so funny?"

"Fate is perhaps not as detailed as you believe it to be," Nariah replied, diverting their course to the left to avoid a collection of fallen trees. "In a portion of mortal people, the entirety of their lives is…scripted, one might say. For others, it is akin more to a list of parameters, and it is up to the soul to navigate, allowing a more individual and unique experience. A child may be hindered in some manner, and their soul's calling is simply to persist despite it, for example."

"What's the point of putting souls through all that in the first place?" Ivo asked.

Sima smiled, twigs snapping beneath her feet as they walked. "Nariah and I have talked about this many times. The souls must be refined to become a true immortal, such as the Ambrosi that serve the Kingdom. On occasion, some become Caelari—Gods or Goddesses imbued with powerful magic."

"The souls are immature on planets like this," Earnest said from behind them. "Think of the people as children and the Caelari and Divinity as the adults in charge. There are things they have to learn."

A second pang of guilt hit Sima, this time as she thought of all the lives taken by Aurelio, and by herself, on Haelos. All were souls experiencing life to mature into the immortals they would someday become, and she had played a part in disrupting that in one way or another. Sima's hands shook at her sides.

Am I a monster for what I've done? Can I truly trust myself enough to use this wretched power again?

"Is it possible for some people to…not have a Fate?" Ivo asked.

Nariah paused, wiping the sweat from her forehead. "If you're an Empress. Otherwise, to some degree, Fate guides you."

"We need to find somewhere to have a quick rest," Earnest said.

"You're right," Nariah said, crossing her toned, muscular arms.

As the Scout scanned their surroundings, Sima caught Ivo staring at Nariah with a somewhat smitten expression. Sima hid her smirk and glanced at a dark patch of orange dirt to their left. It was a bare path without the normal cover of red fallen leaves and plant matter they saw in the forest. Earnest followed her gaze and moved to inspect it more closely.

"What is it?" Sima asked.

Earnest looked up and walked across the patch, disappearing into the trees. Nariah hovered over Ivo, the Scouts' blades drawn and ready to protect her mortal friend if necessary. Ivo tilted her head back to stare up at Nariah before she glanced away with bright red cheeks smoldering beneath her ice blue eyes.

Interesting, Sima thought. *You both act like you can't stand each other already and yet….*

Horacio opened his mouth to speak when Earnest returned. "We're in luck," he said, pointing over his shoulder. "There's a small stream of water. It looks clear and safe to drink."

Sima swallowed, her throat dry. "Glad something has gone our way, at least."

The water from the stream was a welcome sensation after all the sweat that had accumulated on her body since their arrival. Sima did her best to cleanse herself as she could, focusing primarily on cooling down rather than purely on hygiene. Ivo was kneeling on the bank of the measly stream beside her, performing a similar ritual.

As she splashed more water onto her face, a vision overtook her.

A tapping noise roused her sleepy eyes to open. She lifted her head from his bare chest, his breath calm and deep with slumber, as she searched for the source. The taps became more frantic, and she glanced down at his beautiful face before she rose from the bed. Vincenzo's brown skin still carried the hint of pink along his cheeks, a faint smile lingering on his lips from their tender evening spent tangled together. She tugged on his shirt, drenching herself in his comforting rainy scent, and padded over to the window. She pulled aside the purple curtains and slid the pane of glass out of the way.

In buzzed a tiny sprite with long ears and faint blue skin that grew richer near the bottom of her body. She spun in circles around Sima before she landed on her open palm, this routine so familiar it had become a dance between them. The sprite twirled and jumped in her hand, moving to a silent drum, as tendrils of magic sparked off her.

Sima smiled and brought the sprite close, pressing a small kiss to the top of her head.

"Go, now," she whispered. "You have made certain I am well. Tell her not to worry about me."

The sprite nodded with a serious expression before it melted away, and she fluttered out of Sima's hand, flying in Enzo's direction. The tiny being lay on her stomach on his pillow, kicking her feet behind her as she stared at him with curious enthusiasm. Sima rushed over and let out a hushed giggle as she shooed the sprite away.

"He's mine," she whispered, still grinning. "And yes, I know he's very handsome."

The vision disappeared, leaving Sima staring at her reflection in the water, wondering why she could not recall more about the sprite. She blinked as she regained her bearings. Seeing Enzo's face, even in a memory, made her heart pinch with longing. She reassured herself they would be reunited before the situation got too out of hand.

Sima noticed Ivo had left her side. She glanced up and found her friend was once again bickering with Nariah.

Chapter 14

"I saw that," Ivo snapped, rushing up to Nariah's side.

The Scout lifted a brow as she patted her face dry on her shirt. "Saw what?"

Ivo glanced around, then lowered her voice, keeping the same harsh intensity. "You *winked* at me."

Nariah smirked. "Is that right?"

"Don't lie to me, you're not going to convince me I'm seeing things."

"What reason would I have to wink at you?"

The question only enraged Ivo more. It was enough that Ivo's shirt had ridden up when she was cleaning herself off at the edge of the water, but the Scout had made sure to embarrass her by winking. She could tell when she was being mocked, and she would not allow Nariah to get away with it.

"Stop messing with me, I am not someone you can pick on. I don't go down easily, and I am sure I can hold a grudge a lot longer than you can."

The Scout braided her long white ponytail as a smile crept over her lips. "I don't doubt it."

Ivo stamped her foot. "Did you wink at me or not?"

Both of Nariah's brows lifted. "I never said I didn't."

Blood rushed to Ivo's face, and she pressed her lips together. *How dare she make fun of me like this!* "What's the point? I get that you're a Trine

Scout, and I am probably no more than an ugly little insect compared to the immortals you're used to, but you don't need to rub it in my face."

At that, Nariah appeared genuinely surprised. "I wouldn't call you ugly, Ivo."

Once again, her cheeks burned. "Whatever you'd call me, just don't. I don't care what you think of me."

The Scout grinned, the intensity of her purple stare hot enough to make Ivo shrink where she stood. "So, you don't care what I think of you, huh?" Nariah took a step forward and looked at Ivo over her shoulder. "Since it doesn't make a difference—I don't think you're ugly. I think you have the kind of beauty people would be willing to travel the galaxies in search of."

Nariah walked away, leaving Ivo unfairly confused. "She couldn't possibly mean that," Ivo whispered to herself. *Have I misjudged her?*

The sun had set fully by the time they reached the base of the mountains, and a harsh wind had rolled in, with gusts that sent the Scouts tumbling in the air. Flying through the trees was nearly impossible in their current conditions, and during the last leg of the trip, they resorted to walking. Thankfully, it had been calm enough for Ivo and Sima to divulge all they could about their time spent apart, allowing for some normalcy amongst the unusual circumstances. Likely due to nightfall, the fungi monsters had slowed to a complete stop; however, Ivo stayed prepared to pull her weapon and protect herself at a moment's notice. All the luminescent bugs and plants had extinguished their lights for the evening as well, casting them in darkness.

"Where do we go from here? Do we get to climbing the mountain?" Cosima asked from somewhere beside her.

"We're going to fall and injure ourselves before we get anywhere at this time of night," Earnest replied, "let's use our starlight. I haven't seen a single person, so I doubt we'll attract any attention."

"Good idea," Nariah hummed. The Scout was closer to her than Ivo expected, and it made her jump. When her palm illuminated with a starry night, their eyes met. Ivo quickly looked away, instead turning to inspect what she could see around them. "Everyone keep enough distance to avoid touching the light by accident."

Her starlight was bright enough to illuminate a few feet ahead of them at a time. Earnest and Horacio added their lights as well, and the group began moving again. The mountain was lush with more vegetation, but the terrain was far from optimal, with loose rocks, steep ledges, and overgrown plant life. The Scouts discussed flying the group upward, but the wind had not died down, making it dangerous to attempt.

"I've never seen wind like this before," Earnest said.

Horacio sighed. "Me either. I don't think all of us have the best chances of making it up this mountainside without slipping."

"I don't see a lot of other options," Nariah said, crossing her arms.

I wish I knew how to help, Ivo thought. *Everyone else has such strong powers. I need to prove to myself I am not just some weakling.*

A tingling enveloped Ivo's fingertips, the cold biting at her skin, as she glanced around. At first, she only spotted more of the same treacherous rock and sediment; however, after a moment, she began to make out something in the distance, as if it were materializing right before her eyes. Ivo walked closer to it and realized she stumbled upon a perfectly usable pathway, free of branches and bushes. Not believing her luck, Ivo squealed.

"Look," she said, turning back toward the group. "We can follow this path up. No treacherous climbing needed."

Nariah pushed by her, causing Ivo to stumble slightly. She inspected the path with a raised brow, then turned to Ivo and narrowed her eyes, as if searching for signs of deception. Nariah's somewhat suspicious gaze ended a second later. "Alright, team. This is the way, then."

"Watch where you're going," Ivo said, rubbing her shoulder where Nariah had bumped into her. "You almost knocked me over."

"*Me?*" The Scout spun around and pointed a finger with her free hand, her opposite palm still blazing with starlight that could maim Ivo in an instant.

"Cool it," Earnest warned them. "We're all friends here, alright?"

"It's not my fault she didn't look before she slammed into me," Ivo said.

"You're the one always in the way. If you get too close, you'll get burnt, *friend,*" Nariah seethed.

Ivo understood the threat. She was not an immortal and did not have the same healing abilities. Ivo's healing magic was nothing compared to theirs, but that did not mean she would allow Nariah to bully her. "Do it," Ivo spat, "and see if I don't take you down with me."

"Oh, is that right?" Nariah grew closer, pressing her chest against Ivo's as she stared down at her. Her wisteria eyes had a sharpened edge to them that told Ivo how badly Nariah craved an unhinged moment, even at her expense.

Why does she get under my skin like this? Ivo thought with a frown. *So much for wondering if I misjudged her.*

"Enough," Cosima said, wedging herself between them.

Ivo allowed her friend to separate them and sucked in a breath. She could not lose her cool, not when the two of them had so much at stake. While her home had not treated her well, Ivo could not imagine Haelos being wiped from existence as punishment for Aurelio's sick crimes.

"What is your deal?" Nariah crossed her arms, relinquishing her starlight. The world around them darkened slightly.

The question was laced with attitude and was clearly meant to provoke Ivo more, and she could not help but take the bait. "*My* deal? What is yours?" Ivo grumbled. "Can't handle that I was the one who found this path in the first place?"

"So, you got lucky," she hissed under her breath. "*I* am trying to make sure this mission is completed successfully and without breaking any rules given to us by the Divinity. There is a time and place for everything, but *you* are so impatient that you fling yourself into the trees before checking with anyone else. I am the one in charge here, and you need to quickly learn your place. You're *annoying* me."

Ivo rolled her eyes and stomped up the pathway with only Earnest and Horacio's starlight illuminating the way. "Maybe I'd listen if you were worth listening to."

The sounds of a scuffle came from behind her, which she could only assume was someone holding back Nariah from launching herself at Ivo. With a satisfied smirk, Ivo continued dredging forward, only slowing long enough to allow the other two Trine Scouts to catch up and light the path. The wind had picked up again, and it tossed Ivo's hair in every direction. She clenched her jaw to keep her teeth from chattering as the temperature dropped even lower.

"Do you have any information for us about Carmine?" Cosima asked Nariah as the group walked. Ivo was grateful for her friend taking the Scout's attention off her.

Nariah sighed. "He has been confirmed to be colluding with Ehses, though not to the extent the others have, and his presence was last detected on this planet. Other than that, he visually resembles his brother, Aurelio, but with a more squared jaw and brown eyes. As for his abilities, we can confirm shielding and mental manipulation, like each of the Sacred Twelve possess. The degree to which he has them, we do not know."

"So basically, nothing," Ivo grumbled to herself.

"Essentially," Nariah replied tightly.

A snarling in the distance put everyone on edge. Horacio drew his blade while Earnest pushed Ivo behind him. When nothing bounded from the darkness, the group began moving again and resumed their conversation.

"Don't worry," Horacio said to Ivo and Sima, "We will have the proper time to uncover more about Carmine. We managed to follow him to this planet. That means we already have him cornered, and all that's left is laying the killing blow. The fact that we haven't seen any sign of him yet probably means he's hiding away somewhere, but he can't lie low forever."

"Yeah," Earnest chipped in, "the lack of population is either from the beasts or from Carmine, but it makes it easier to kill him when we aren't worried about innocents being puppeted against us by his magic. We will spend time watching how this all plays out before we make any moves."

Horacio gave Ivo a small smile. "Nariah is right, we need to take things slow and stick together. If you have a plan, share it. But you can't keep running off on your own. You are going to end up lost on a foreign planet."

"I guess," Ivo said, unconvinced.

The group stuck tightly together as they continued up the path, and Ivo hated how close she stood to Nariah. The tension between her and the purple-eyed Scout had already put a bad taste in her mouth. All she wanted was to help Sima and Haelos, to find a purpose where she had not been provided one. She did not have the mercy of being blessed with unimaginable power like Sima, and she was not guided by the hand of Fate, but Ivo was also not a quitter. She would not stop until everything fell right into place.

Just as the group began to grow weary with fatigue from the icy wind and extended travel, Ivo spotted a sanctuary not far from where they stood. She walked closer to it, but before she could announce her discovery of the small cave to the others, Nariah shoved by and shouted, "In here, everyone."

Ivo rolled her eyes and followed the group inside, thankful to at least be out of the elements.

Once they had cleared the gate to the inner Kingdom, Vincenzo took a sigh of relief. He allowed his hold over Surano to falter a fraction to ease the strain on his magic, fearing growing too close to the edge. Getting out of the Ethereal Realm would prove to be difficult if he could not locate a Trine Scout capable of navigating to Cosima and the others. He had no other option than to hunt down Merit. He would see her again, no matter how far it led him or how desperate the search became.

When he stumbled upon a good place to ditch Surano, Vincenzo knocked him unconscious, wiped his memory, and hid his body behind clutter in a side alley. He strolled by immortals, thankful that he was unremarkable enough to blend in among the others. Even with his feathered wings, there was a chance most would regard him as a mere Rani Guardian. While perhaps low on the food chain and disliked, their existence was permissible. Not everyone here knew him as a brother of the Sacred Twelve, and that would benefit him.

His magic roared at his command, skipping across minds to find slips of information he needed to guide him to Merit. He hopped up the steps two at a time until he reached the Scout's quarters. Instead of knocking, his hand wrapped around the handle, and his power pulsed inside, confirming the Scout's presence. Merit was inside, and from what he could tell, did not suspect Vincenzo was lurking outside.

He grasped control of the Scouts' will, and though he fought against it, Vincenzo was successful. He let out a breath before guiding Merit to the door. It opened, and Merit's blank face greeted him. His eye was swollen from where Vincenzo had hit him earlier. It satisfied something in him to see the outcome of his anger had not faded entirely. With the healing power all immortals possessed, it was a wonder it was still visible.

"Nice to see you again, pal." Vincenzo clapped him on the shoulder. "You were just the man I was looking for. Get. Me. The. Fuck. Out of here," he bit out. "I have spent enough time being run around by this Kingdom. If you don't take me straight to Cosima, I will slice your throat, and I will not stop there."

Merit numbly pushed by Vincenzo. He could feel Merit's resignation internally, but the Scout retained enough strength to keep Vincenzo from having full control. Enzo instructed Trine Scout's body toward the portal, moving as quickly as they could without garnering unnecessary attention.

I am in control of this wretched power, he reminded himself.

After a grueling walk out of the Kingdom, he finally spotted it. The portal itself was desolate. Vincenzo pushed Merit only until he was only a few steps away from the entrance and used his power to raise Merit's hand. The Sacred Twelve, Rani Guardians, and Trine Scouts all possessed starlight, but something Vincenzo had never learned was how to wield his in the way the Trine Scouts had. He was taught how to use his starlight like a Rani Guardian. Still, he wondered how different the initiation of the power could be.

"Merit," Vincenzo instructed. "Open the portal, and take me to Cosima."

Nothing happened. No starlight poured from his palm and into the portal.

Damn it.

Vincenzo ran a hand through his hair and weighed all the options he had. If his mental manipulation was not working, there could be a few answers. On one hand, it was possible that he needed to phrase the instruction differently, or Merit was pushing him out and resisting the command. If that were the case, it would require more brute force.

"Hey," Vincenzo said, "Open the portal and take me to Carmine."

Merit continued to stare blankly into the portal.

"Open the portal," he repeated, "setting the destination for Carmine's current planet. I don't have time to beat it out of you, but I will if I have to. Move it Merit."

Vincenzo squeezed the Scout's brain and imagined himself digging his nails into it. He would not let a simple Scout be the reason Cosima died. He had failed her before, hadn't he? Not only had she been kidnapped right from under his nose, but she was also subjected to evil he could not stomach to properly process. His time spent fixing Ombra had benefited thousands of civilians, precisely the kind of response desired from a Guardian. And yet, he was not a Guardian. He was a God, and by all means, he should not have let his weak body keep him from slaughtering Aurelio for what he did to her.

But he did.

"Fuck," Vincenzo yelled, launching a punch toward Merit.

Enzo would not fail Cosima again. He had learned his lesson, and he would carry that shame into eternity if it meant he would never forget how weak he could be. He was not stronger than Aurelio or Carmine, but he was stronger than Merit, and it was only a matter of time before the Scout broke.

Vincenzo pulled back his arm, ready to aim another punch at the blank-faced Merit. Instead, he relinquished his hold over him. If he was going to finally beat the cocky Scout with a piss-poor attitude like he had dreamed of doing, he was at least going to allow the man the chance to fight back.

And so, it began.

Merit instinctively snapped into defense mode the moment Vincenzo allowed him to control his own body again. His navy hair flashed as he ducked, dropping low and tackling Enzo at the waist. Expecting this move, Vincenzo dug his heels into the ground and leaned over the back of Merit's body. The two wrestled as they threw hit after hit. This was a fight they had craved from the moment they'd met.

The Scout's wings manifested, smacking Enzo in the face. Instead of relenting and releasing him like Merit wanted, he instead reached around, grabbing one wing in each hand and contorting them until he barked with pain. Only then did Vincenzo release him, tossing him to the ground. His wings vanished, but the discomfort plagued Merit's face.

"Take me to her, and this can all end."

Merit glared at him, rubbing his shoulder. "I can't do that. They will kill me."

"I will kill you," Vincenzo growled.

"They can do worse things than kill me," Merit said meekly.

It was strange to Vincenzo, seeing another man's fear. It made him falter, if only for a moment, but it was enough for Merit to launch at him again. Merit's hands wrapped around Vincenzo's neck as the two toppled backward and onto the floor. Dust rose in the air and filled his nose as the Scout choked him. The only thing he could see beyond Merit's angry face was the swirling portal behind him.

Vincenzo placed his hand on Merit's chest and blasted him with starlight. "I warned you," he roared. The Scout screamed as he was shot back. Enzo rubbed his neck as he stood and aimed his palm at Merit's face again. "Take me to her, *now*, or so help me, this Kingdom and its Gods will burn."

Merit's hands grasped at the wound on his chest. Starlight reached temperatures hot enough to melt even immortal skin. If Enzo could not open the portal himself, he would sear every inch of the Scout's body and leave him in ashes.

Enzo's magic surged forward. Using this much power in this realm was risky. The Divinity would surely sense it if he expanded more than he already had, if they weren't already aware, but temptation was sweet on his tongue, and he could practically feel the moment he would be reunited with her. He manipulated the space surrounding them, allowing himself to burn dangerously close to the limitations he set for himself.

Gone was the Eternal Kingdom looming in the distance. Gone was the massive portal, Vincenzo's only hope of leaving this realm. Gone was the ground beneath their feet. He dragged Merit into a space he had hand-crafted while discovering how to use his powers. It was a black void, where no one would see or hear them. For as long as Vincenzo could sustain it, they would be locked tightly in what he could only describe as an alternate dimension. They were physically in front of the portal, but now his void occupied the space. None would come to his rescue. Merit's future depended on compliance.

Vincenzo manifested snarling monsters, the likes of which he had fought daily in Haelos, minus the fungal infections. They were ten feet tall with saliva dripping from their white fangs, thick black fur covering the creatures from head to toe. Five of them stalked toward Merit, who peddled backward with his eyes wide.

"N-no," he cried. "Where did these demons come from? You feathered bastard, get me out of here!"

Vincenzo smiled. "They're some of my creations. Aren't they marvelous?"

His father, Domani, was the one responsible for the creation of planets like Haelos. Ehses and his siblings could create people, but Enzo could craft with the very fabric of reality to create new beings and worlds. His father's power pumped through his veins, making him capable of genesis beyond what the Ethereal Realm had seen before. The only limitations he ran into with his abilities were self-imposed. That he could admit, but when it came to those who stood between him and Cosima, he would break through every shackle and reap their souls from their vessels before he let fear stop him now.

"You will take me to her, or they will rip you apart, again and again, until you relent."

"The Kingdom will punish you for this!" Merit screamed as the beasts pinned him and began tearing at his already battered armor. "You won't get away with this!"

"They don't have to know anything if you open the damn portal!" Vincenzo pushed the creatures further, locking their teeth around the Scout's limbs. As he writhed and screamed, Vincenzo shouted, "You know how to make this stop! You know how to save yourself. I swear I will make you regret existing if you do not change your mind."

"How can you do this?"

Merit's pants grew wet at the groin as the pain became more than he could handle. The beasts hinged their jaws and would not release, not until Vincenzo commanded them to. He walked over to the cowering man and squatted beside his face. The creatures continued to tug and pull on the flesh. Stammered screams still blubbered from Merit's lips.

Unleash me, his curse whispered. Enzo's power faltered, reminding him that he was dangerously close to breaking through a layer of his magic. *It's now or never,* he thought.

"What do you say, pal? Open the portal, or be dog food. Your choice," he bluffed.

"Alright," Merit spat. "Alright! Make it stop!"

Vincenzo smiled. "You've made the right choice. I wasn't going to stop until I scrambled your little brain beyond recognition." He snapped, and the void disintegrated. He pointed to the portal. *"Open it."*

It took everything in him to not collapse when Merit finally complied, and the starlight from his palm turned it into a deep navy. Enzo's feet scrambled across the threshold of the portal, and he tensed up when the fabric of the universe stripped his soul from his body. All while he was tossed through space, he reaffirmed his goal—he was going to save Cosima and murder Carmine himself. He would not leave her to handle it alone, not again.

2

The Misguided

The children knew the path and walked it with
pride, singing of softness and renewal.

Faces round in youth and souls smooth like
glass answered the call of empty, carnivorous souls
without question, unaware of the nature of chaos.

As turmoil and trepidation sank through skin into
their somber spines, doubt flamed like burning suns.

Pain stoked their breath into misplaced fury and
shielded their eyes from the light, forcing them to
walk blindly into the scorching fire.

Their binds, their wisdom, their fears—nothing
more than ash caked around their tired feet.

So far from home, with nothing left to give, the
flames became soundless beneath grief.

Still, they were not lost.

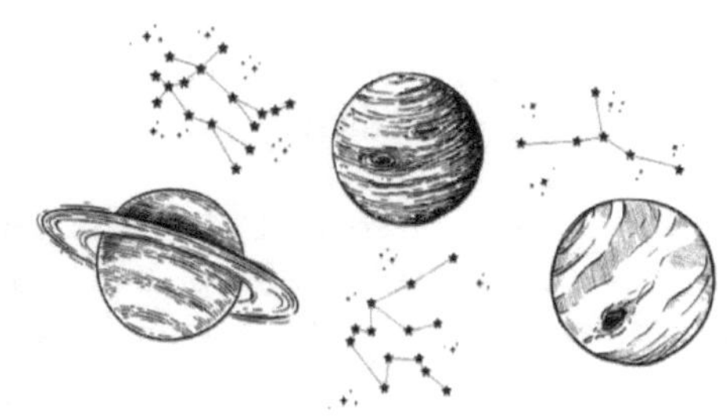

Chapter 15

The interior of the cave was cramped, but there was enough space for all of them to shelter from the harsh wind outside. The walls of the cave were not gray stone as Ivo expected to find, but a deep navy rock instead. Along the back, there were bones where a large creature of some kind had either been eaten and discarded or where it had curled up and died. Earnest gathered the remains and discarded them, much to Ivo's appreciation.

She took a seat next to Cosima and rested her head on her shoulder. "Would it be crazy if I said I was missing that weird Kingdom already?"

Cosima laughed. "I think I'd appreciate the fresh air more if I wasn't terrified of breathing in spores from those damned creatures."

Horacio took what was left of the supply packs and spread them out on the cave floor. "We've got two daggers, enough food for maybe three of us, and a couple of my shirts," Horacio said, rubbing his face with his palms.

At the mention of food, Ivo's stomach growled. By the look on Cosima's face, hers did too. It was the first time the idea of eating had crossed her mind. The day had flown by, and they were not much closer to resolving their mission.

"You three can eat first," Earnest said, "Horacio and I will be alright for the night without a meal. In the morning, we can go for a hunt."

"I have an idea," Nariah said. Before anyone could object, she ventured out into the deep, freezing night, leaving them alone in the cave.

"I don't like her," Ivo whispered to Cosima.

Cosima's nose scrunched. "I know she can be difficult, but I think she means well. At least, that is what I tell myself when I feel at the end of my thread with her."

"I don't know why she makes me so mad," Ivo said, her gaze falling.

"Nariah can be a tough one," Earnest said, peering out into the forest before coming closer. "She is strict, even for a Trine Scout, but that's why she's the best."

"And the most popular, if you know what I mean," Horacio said, adding a wiggle of his eyebrows. "Nariah is used to having fans kiss her ass because of her connection to the Weave."

Ivo resisted rolling her eyes. "I just want to get this mission over with."

"In the morning, we will venture up the rest of the mountain," Horacio said, stretching his legs out as best he could in the tight space. "I am sure this mission won't last much longer, Ivo."

Ivo huffed. "Why would the great *Eternal Kingdom* send us here with such limited information? We have no idea where we're going."

"*We* are the ones in charge of finding out the information," Earnest laughed, a deep grumble from inside his chest that warmed the cave a hair. "The Trine Scouts are not merely guards for the Kingdom, being sent off on errands. My assignments from the Kingdom include uncovering information, no matter the cost. This is nothing new for us."

Ivo raised a brow. "Is that true?"

"Yes," Horacio said, offering a lop-sided smile. "We simply go where we are told. With thousands of years beneath our belts, it takes much to truly surprise us. Each of us has a unique ability, depending on which High Priestess or Celestial Empress has offered a drop of their blood. Nariah can sense the change of Fate, and she can see the threads, but cannot alter them."

"Explains why she watches over you," Ivo said to Sima. "What can you do, Horacio?"

He smirked. "Nothing too interesting. Communication and knowledge are my specialty as I share blood with High Priestess Demi. It allows me to be well-suited for record-keeping on missions."

Ivo nodded, remembering she had begged Horacio to ask his Demi to show mercy on Cosima during her trial, as she herself could not attend. "And Earnest?"

"Strength," he said, flexing one of his giant biceps, "but that's not all I have. I can sense energy patterns. I can feel if someone has left the area recently or identify large gatherings of people. If someone's energy is strong enough, I can pinpoint their approximate location."

Ivo was suddenly insecure about her own powers, which, beyond healing, were fairly lackluster. She could cast a handful of defensive spells, bring people back from the brink of death, and had an uncanny ability to find what others wanted to remain hidden—but none of that seemed to compare to the group she found herself in. "And here I am, the measly mortal witch."

Cosima's hand gripped hers. "You're more than a measly mortal, Ivo. You are fearless, tougher than most, and my best friend. I wouldn't want to do this without you...I don't think I *could* do it without you."

"You're more powerful than you think," Earnest said.

Sima tipped her head. "He's right. There's no reason to doubt yourself. You found the path and the cave we are sheltering in. You've contributed so much already."

Ivo searched Cosima's eyes. The pit in her stomach whined with insecurities, but Ivo had never been the type to listen to that internal squealing much anyway. She gave a small smile. "I am glad, then, at least I am here for you. Especially with all the new faces around us."

Sima's expression changed. It was a subtle droop, but Ivo understood it. Her friend was concerned for Enzo's well-being, but was too stubborn to make the situation about herself. Sima was the strongest person Ivo had ever known, and sometimes, she needed someone to bring it up first.

"Enzo will survive," Ivo said, squeezing her hand. "It's Enzo. He can live through anything."

Cosima chewed her lip. "It feels impossible. I worry about his ability to track us down if he does manage to make it to this planet." She blew out a breath. "It's silly to be so concerned, but I can't help it."

"It's normal to miss him, especially since you have been separated for so long." Ivo rubbed a hand on her back. "He will make it. I have no doubts."

Footsteps approached, and Ivo sat straighter. Nariah peered her head inside.

"Horacio, get over here."

The Scout scrambled to his feet and helped Nariah pull in a large creature with thick orange fur. It had a lengthy muzzle and pointed ears with claws as large as Ivo's face. Across its paws were small black and brown stripes, matching the creature's fluffy tail. The Scouts slipped out their knives and dug into the animal, revealing its purple-black flesh beneath the fur. Her appetite dissolved the moment she realized Nariah had killed this creature with the intention of feeding it to the group.

"This is barbaric," Ivo cried, covering her mouth with her hands.

"This is survival," Nariah said. She cocked her head, leaving a trail of blood across her forehead as she wiped away sweat. For the first time, Nariah smiled at her. "Eat, or don't. I don't care."

Ivo resisted the primal urge to either slap Nariah or run away screaming, and instead slid her body away from the gruesome scene. Cosima rested her head against Ivo's back, likely shielding her eyes too. The cool navy rock held Ivo's attention until the horrific noise butchery created behind her finally ceased.

The scent of smoke and cooking meat invaded her nose, and as much as Ivo resisted its call, her hunger tempted her into one glance over her shoulder. As if the animal hadn't been stripped of its skin behind her, the cave floor was clean, not a tuft of hair in sight. A small fire lit with starlight blossomed with a thin slab of rock balanced above it to craft a cooking surface, and delicious strips of meat sizzled atop it.

Although Ivo's stomach continued to growl, asking for a portion felt like throwing herself at Nariah's feet, and she would not sink low enough to beg. Thankfully, she hadn't needed to craft a casual way to secure herself a meal while dodging a snide comment from Nariah, because the Scout slid a few strips onto two large leaves and placed one directly in her lap.

"Eat," Nariah said over her shoulder as she handed the other to Sima. "You'll enjoy it."

Cosima took the first bite, closing her eyes as she savored the taste. "It's good, Ivo. Try it."

She dug in, not minding the toughness of the meat. The flavor had a surprising spice to it, which Ivo found she quite enjoyed. As the food settled in her stomach, the anxiety looming in the back of her mind had diminished. She glanced up, only for her to lock eyes with Nariah. Ivo's cheeks grew red as she dropped her gaze.

The Scout had been stand-offish, pushy, and rude. Yet, had equally proved her ability to command the group and provide for them. Something about it only stoked the anger Ivo felt toward Nariah further. Her unwarranted attitude would prove to be an uphill battle. It was only complicated further by the fact that Ivo still managed to find Nariah attractive, despite how they bickered at every turn. It was an unfortunate truth she would admit to no one but herself.

The three Trine Scouts took turns sharing stories of their previous adventures, some more gruesome than others. Nariah, however, seemed to recall only interesting times during her assignment to the holding cells in the Eternal Kingdom. Ivo couldn't help but wonder why the Scout had spent so much time in the Ethereal Realm, instead of out exploring the universes, as Earnest and Horacio had.

Now that her stomach was full, Ivo's eyelids began to droop as her body whined for sleep. She snuggled against Sima's side with her head on her friend's shoulder as she let herself drift off. Nariah's voice became the backdrop to Ivo's dreams, comforting her more than she cared to confess.

The sun was the exact thing Ivo needed to warm up her cold bones, and she took time to appreciate it, despite being exhausted at the early hour. The fire had kept the cave at a fair temperature throughout the night, but nothing could beat the morning light on her face. The wind had subsided as they slept, and for the first time since they'd arrived, things had begun to look up. There was a noticeable lack of conversation; however, she attributed it to discomfort from the sleeping conditions and tense nerves for the day ahead.

"One of us is going to carry you up the mountain, Ivo," Earnest said. "Nariah is taking Sima."

"I hope you don't mind," Ivo said, "but I think I'll go with Horacio today."

"No problem."

A moment later, Horacio approached, and Ivo put an arm around the back of his neck as he lifted her up. The sky was filled with clouds, but the sun remained bright as they flew up the jagged mountainside. Occasionally, there were large gashes in the rock, as if gigantic claws had crawled up the side. She shuddered, thankful they were near the peak.

As they approached the top, a strange sensation rumbled inside Ivo. She instinctively gripped onto Horacio's arm at the same time a heavy aura slammed into them, causing all three Scouts to falter and drop several feet before they could recover.

"What happened?" Earnest held a hand over his forehead.

"No clue," Nariah said.

Earnest moved upward, this time at a slower pace, and although his papery, reddish-brown wings trembled, he managed to break through the restrictive aura. He disappeared over the top of the mountain, and everyone held their breath until he reappeared. He waved them up, and the Scouts followed, mirroring Earnest's slow ascent.

Once they had all made it to the top of the mountain, Ivo's sickening intuition was once again alerting her that something was not quite right. Before she could voice her concern, her vision went black. Horacio faltered beneath her, and Ivo toppled to the ground, scraping her skin on the jagged rocks below.

Gasps of astonishment left the group as they each strained against a powerful magic pressing on their brains. It did not fully intrude, but remained an oppressive force, as if to send a message rather than truly maim them. Ivo knew at once that they had indeed located Carmine. Ivo's heart pinched as her teeth chattered, her vision still entirely black.

She used her hands to feel around in front of her when a stranger's voice from a distance startled her.

"Halt," they commanded. "You are not permitted to enter the city of Riejj. This is your final warning. Depart immediately, or we will have no choice but to attack."

"We wish you no harm," Nariah's voice rang out.

The sound of her feet scraping made Ivo's heart race. The twist in her gut resurfaced.

"Nariah, don't."

A scream rang out as metal poured down from the sky, impaling Ivo in her thigh and shoulder. More metal clanked against the rock as it fell, her team crying out as the onslaught continued. Ivo ripped the arrows out with speed, finding her wounds were mercifully shallow.

Nariah called out instructions for the others to retreat, and Horacio's hands grabbed onto Ivo, the heavy aura thick enough to block out all their air. Ivo covered her head the best she could as Horacio shielded her with his body, the pain causing her fingertips to tingle as a loud buzz filled their ears. The Scout flew down the side of the mountain, following Nariah's instructions to head down toward the city at the center of the canyon. Nariah continued to shout out orders as they neared the bottom when a blast threw them forward, causing Ivo and Horacio to tumble through the sky.

No, no, no. Make it stop, Ivo hollered internally.

Horacio kept his grip on Ivo, using his body to absorb the brunt of the impact as they tumbled across the ground. A clap like fierce lightning shot through the sky, and all sound ceased. Ivo shivered beside Horacio, her vision still obscured. The ground trembled, and she could no longer hear Nariah.

"Horacio?" Ivo whispered, her vision slowly returning. She blinked a few times and then sat up, covering her mouth to keep from shouting, horrified by the blood dripping from Horacio's mouth, his eyes hauntingly blank. His chest was caved in, and his body sank into the ground. Something had crushed his immortal body, and somehow, Ivo had survived. Her heart pounded as she scanned her surroundings for a sign of the others.

Vincenzo

"Oh, if you weren't fucked before," Merit growled, "you certainly are now."

"Shut up," Vincenzo snapped. "You run your mouth at the worst moments."

His eyes burned as sweat dripped down his face. The planet was infested with the same horrid beasts he had encountered on Haelos, and it was precisely the opposite of what Enzo had hoped to find on the other side of the portal. He had burned through a near insane amount of his power in an attempt to get here, leaving him without the wealth of his magic to defend himself with. Though it would accumulate rapidly, the blade could not possibly hold for much longer, and soon the massive ivory teeth straining against it would burrow into his flesh and rip him to shreds. He retreated, pulling his sword with him, shooting into the air. The massive creature jumped after him, his claws missing Vincenzo by an inch.

The ground shook as the beast landed. It redirected its attacks toward Merit, forcing the Scout to defend himself instead of running his mouth. Vincenzo used the distraction to wedge his sword deep into the back of the creature's neck. When its twitching ceased, he extracted his blade and met the Scout's furious eyes.

"Well?" Vincenzo huffed.

"*Well?* Is that all you have to say for yourself? Are you insane? How many laws do you think you broke in the span of, what, an hour? I should slit your throat right here for what you've done."

Vincenzo beamed. "I'd love to see you try. Might be cute. We're not in your home anymore. On this planet, I am not bound by the same rules."

"You arrogant shit," Merit said, rushing Vincenzo. "Do you have any idea what chaos you've caused? I knew you couldn't be trusted."

As Merit's eyes blazed with fury, Enzo continued to smile. Although making it to this forsaken planet in search of Cosima required him to cross one of his own boundaries around his magic expenditure, the risk had been worth it. He still retained control over himself, despite his fears. The pure bliss that accompanied the relief of relaxing his restraint was addictive, whispering songs of his unstoppable strength in his ear.

There was nothing about Merit that inspired fear in him. He was a God. A Scout would never be enough to stop him.

"Hit me, already, Merit, or let's move on."

The snarls of beasts in the distance lit Enzo up with an electricity he could not ignore. With or without the Scout, he was going to do what he came here to do. The surrounding forest was thick with strange colored trees, and the air was dewy and humid from a recent morning rain shower. He swirled, attempting to discern which direction to head. The round navy stone portal in front of them appeared to be smack in the middle of thousands of red-leafed trees.

"You have no idea where they are," Merit said.

"Thanks for pointing that out," Enzo said through his teeth. "Really helpful."

Another monstrous creature with mushrooms for a muzzle came tearing from the trees. Enzo raised his left hand and blasted it with starlight at the same moment it opened its mouth, forcing the beast to eat the burning flames. He ceased his light and swung his sword into its belly, causing it to roar. With an expert swipe of his blade, it finally stopped moving.

"They might have let you live before this, but there's no chance now," Merit snapped.

"Says the guy who still has piss on the front of his pants."

Merit glanced down, and his cheeks grew red. He clenched his jaw and rushed Enzo. Prepared for the move, Enzo lowered his body and dug his heels in. Merit failed in knocking him down, but succeeded in landing a punch straight at Enzo's nose, causing it to pour blood.

"You fucker." Enzo threw Merit to the ground. "Stop getting in my way."

"My job is to get in your way. Don't forget the whole reason I'm fucking pissed off is because you choose not to comply with the Divinity. Not to mention the fact that you put your grimy magic all over my brain. You're lucky you caught me off guard, or you would've never been able to get a hold of me like that."

"Oh, is that what this is about? I hurt your ego because I managed to puppet you around? Get over it, Merit. We all get caught off guard one way or another."

"That's not an apology," Merit said with a frown, rising from the dirt.

Enzo's magic sparked at his fingertips, begging him to make Merit pay for his mistakes, but he ignored its desperate plea. He could not bear to expend more of his power so soon. "I'm not apologizing. If you hadn't provoked me in the first place, it wouldn't have had to be like this. We would've arrived with Cosima and the others, and instead, I'm here bickering with you while we stand over dead fungus-ridden monsters."

"You think this is how I wanted it to go? I wanted to be assigned to anyone but you. I had no choice. Kismet decided shielding was my specialty. So whether you like it or not, you're going to be stuck with me until the end of this mission."

Enzo glared at him. "You're going to turn me in at the end anyway, so what does it matter?"

"Oh, I would love to blab all about your crimes to the Kingdom, but my main objective, above even you, is to keep the Realm safe from the Sacred Twelve. Seeing as how you're one of them, no better place for me to be than right by your side."

Three more creatures emerged from the forest, and Enzo threw his blade through the eye of one. It stumbled and collided with the ground, shaking the trees. He flew toward it and retrieved his sword in time to avoid the claws of a red-scaled beast. It resembled an overgrown lizard with a razor-sharp tongue and black claws. He gutted the beast, leaving its inside spread out on the forest floor as Merit laid the killing blow on the third one.

"We're not a bad team," Enzo remarked, brushing back his hair. "If you stay out of my way, I have no problem trying to accommodate your little job as the Kingdom's favorite guard dog."

Merit's lip curled. "I'll only get in your way as much as you stray from the very clear lines the Kingdom gave you."

"Deal. If we're done chatting, then I'd like to find out which direction we should head. So far, all I have seen is more and more forest. We are going to need to get some height."

Enzo launched himself into the sky, with Merit close behind. As he traveled, his fingers trembled as his magic began to re-accumulate.

Your essence is comprised of stardust and vengeance, his curse whispered. *Do not think you can escape your destiny.*

Enzo angled his head toward the ground, taking in the landscape beneath for anything that could prove to be useful. A few animals roamed in the fresh daylight, clearly sticking to areas of the forest free of beasts. When a roar shook the trees further ahead, the animals had already fled, seeking refuge in the densest parts of the forest. The sun was nearing the middle of the sky, over the top of a range of mountains in front of him. Sensing no better alternative, Enzo flew toward them.

Cosima has already had to survive the night without me by her side, Enzo thought as he clenched his jaw.

As they neared the base of the mountain, Enzo considered landing and searching for the group, but from the sky, he could see no sign of them. Instead, he and Merit gained more altitude, pushing up the side of the mountain.

"Enzo," Merit called from just below him. "Do you see that?"

He halted in the air and turned away from the mountain, taking in his surroundings. The higher they went in the sky, the more that became visible of the planet below them. The glow from the portal was visible through gaps in the trees, but that was not what Merit was referring to. Enzo suspected Merit was disturbed by the giant crater visible in the distance.

"What do you think could have caused that?" Merit asked.

"No clue," Enzo said softly as he hovered. "There are black cracks through the whole thing, but that's as much as I can tell from here. We may have to check into it later."

"Carmine must have done a number on this place in the short time he's been here. In the briefing they gave us before we…unceremoniously departed, High Priestess Alena mentioned we should keep an eye out for any signs of crystal farming."

At that, Enzo raised a brow. The Kingdom had spent its time questioning Enzo, but strangely, it seemed rather uninterested in his connection to the crystals. Perhaps the Divinity believed that Enzo held no useful knowledge about them, but that was not true. During his time with Doc Santoro on Haelos, he had uncovered quite a bit about the strange stones.

That was also when he realized his power was near infinite. Where others would run completely dry, there existed only false bottom after false bottom for Enzo's reserves. It was helpful when it came to channeling his power into the stones, but the depths of his curse were not something Enzo was keen to explore anytime soon. He feared diving too deep into the poisonous well would consume him, forcing him into an evolution he could never come back from.

"I will do my best to keep my eyes open. If there are beasts covered in fungi here, like on Haelos, then it can only mean one thing. Someone is taking the life force out of creatures that naturally occur on this planet and using it for themselves."

Merit rubbed his chin. "Do you think Carmine is crafting a weapon?"

Enzo sighed. "I'm not entirely sure. While the main focus of the crystals on Haelos seemed to be geared toward creating weapons, they can also be used to craft force fields for defensive measures." Enzo thought back to the many stones he and the other Guardians used in secret to keep additional layers of protection over the underground city, Speranza. "He may also be using it to amplify his power. Some of those creatures had modifications to their bodies. My brothers can change physical forms, and perhaps they are proof he has been practicing."

"Creepy," Merit said. "Any chance Carmine is holding onto any of these crystals for Ehses or your other brothers?"

"Highly unlikely," Enzo replied, recalling what he'd learned of Carmine from his conversations with Sima back in Ombra. "Aurelio hated Carmine; he would never trust him with the crystals. If he is using them, it's for his own gain, not for my mother's plans."

Enzo's disgust for his brothers gave him a bad taste in his mouth. His magic coiled around the flesh inside him, slinking about as if to remind him he was still one of the Sacred Twelve. But Enzo knew one thing for certain—he would find a way to break his curse. He was strong enough to resist its alluring call, because there was no other choice. Either he would restrain himself, or it would swallow him whole.

If I keep a tight grip on my magic and always remain in control, I can protect Cosima.

The thought of her caused him to tug on the bond between them, allowing him a vague glimmer of her emotions. Enzo refocused on why he came to this planet and shot upward at top speed, determined to be reunited with her. Merit grumbled some obscenities in his direction, but Vincenzo disregarded his complaints and instead fought against the fatigue forming in his muscles to go higher, faster. Somehow, through the bond, Enzo could tell Sima had been injured, though not terribly. Guilt flooded his senses, and his magic forced his wings to move with more power, propelling him far above the Scout.

"Hey, asshole," Merit shouted from behind him. "You aren't going anywhere without me."

Enzo ignored him, hoping only that he would be by her side before it was too late.

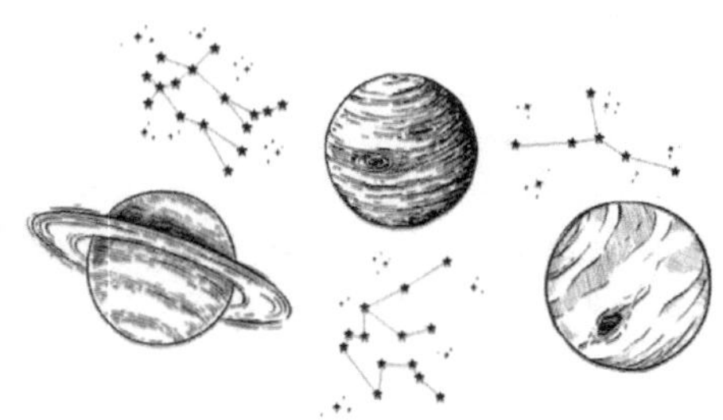

Chapter 16

Cosima

"Get up," Ivo whispered, tugging on her sleeve. "Hurry up, get up."

"What happened?" Cosima pressed her fingertips to the bridge of her nose. Her ears rang and her body ached. Before she could gather what was going on, Ivo was tugging her through what appeared to be city streets. But that couldn't be right. The last thing she remembered was reaching the top of the mountain peak with the group. How could they be inside a city?

Though her head swam, she tried to gather more about her surroundings. Modest taupe-colored buildings, marked with bright red and blue designs, lined the streets, with strange posts jutting out from the roofs, as though they were perches by which wild birds might rest.

Feathers flashed to her right, and her head snapped, wondering if perhaps it was Vincenzo. Instead, they veered down another path, and Ivo continued to rapidly barrel through the town. Her head tipped back, and she gazed up, wondering how she had missed the sight of them before.

Three giant towers shot fifty feet into the air. They were slender, made of a deep brown wood, and had a protruding ledge at the very top, as if meant for diving. Cosima craned her neck to fully take it in. "Where are we?" Sima asked, rubbing her sore neck. "How did we get here?"

"This way!" urged Ivo. She turned to find Ivo had wrenched open a small door to a home beside the tower. Cosima followed her inside and was thankful that the home appeared to be empty. More so than that, everything inside was coated with a thick layer of dust and sediment. This was not a building that had been occupied in quite some time.

Sima's heart thudded like heavy rain as she shook off her shock. The interior was plain, featuring a wooden table with five unique chairs. All of them had low arching backs and wide bases. Beyond one bedroom and a bare kitchen, fitted only with a small oven with wood beside it and a countertop for food preparation, there was nothing spectacular about the space.

Still, her stomach turned. "What are we doing? How did we get here?"

"Listen to me," Ivo said hoarsely. "Something happened, and I don't know where the others are. I think they are…lost. For now, it is just you and me. Are you feeling alright?"

"Yes and no," Cosima said. Everything hurt. "What happened? Did we fall?"

Ivo's eyebrows crept upward. She turned away from Sima, sneaking a glance outside through the thin paper shade in front of the window. "We… we made it to the top of the mountain, when we were ambushed. Before we could prove to them we were not enemies, they fired dozens of arrows at us. You lost your footing in the commotion and fell, hitting your head on a rock near the base of the mountain. I healed you until you regained consciousness. If you need me to heal you more, I can."

That would explain the shooting pain in her head, she reasoned. Cosima inspected Ivo. "You said it's just you and me. After they shot arrows at us, did you see the Scouts alive?" The loss of color in Ivo's face confirmed what she could not say out loud. The others were hurt, if not dead already. All Cosima had to show for the loss of more than half of their team was a pounding headache and blurry memories. "We have to go back. We have to search for them."

"No," Ivo blurted. She took several steps toward Cosima, holding her palms up. "No. I am not going back out there until nightfall. I am not risking being captured, not now. Like I said, the towers might be helpful, and we can search for Carmine."

"Carmine? Ivo, we need to find Nariah and the others. What if they are still alive?"

"What if they are dead? What if we end up just like them? I am not an immortal, have you forgotten? I cannot be as callous as you are with your life. If one of those arrows had hit me just right, I would be dead. I'm lucky I got hit where I did. The people in this city are not friendly, and I wasn't going to waste our chance at killing Carmine. Let's lay low here until we can come up with a plan."

Sima stumbled over to the table and took a seat, unable to think straight. "Perhaps the Scouts are fine. They have skin like reinforced metal. I'm sure they were just caught off guard by the arrows." She let out a breath. "Maybe they will be able to find us."

"Maybe." Ivo chewed her lip. "I had this heavy feeling…right before we landed on the peak. I didn't get a good look at the people shooting at us, beyond feathers and glowing, golden-brown eyes from the person closest to us. It was like he was glowing from the inside out."

"It absolutely sounds like Carmine's doing. I also felt the weight of his aura when we got closer. Have you seen any other signs of him?"

"Beyond what I felt? No, none." She grabbed two of the chairs and wedged them beneath the door handle. "But that doesn't mean there aren't any. Those towers could be promising. We can see more of the city without drawing more attention from the locals."

"What if he's not in this city?"

"There doesn't seem to be much else beyond this canyon and the never-ending forest outside of it. I don't know where else he might be. We will find him, do what we need, and go back home." Ivo's eyes burned with a somewhat weary determination.

Sima could not find the same strength. "How will we even travel through the portal without them?"

Ivo smiled. The sight of it made Cosima uneasy.

"You, friend," Ivo cooed. The girl's fear was palpable, but something else swam beside it.

"No," Cosima breathed. "We can't by ourselves."

"They want you to kill him, so we will. And then we will be free. You can run, and I can return to Haelos. Let us give them what they want and guarantee we walk out of here for good. The planet depends on us. We cannot be selfish. Plus, it's only a matter of time before Mr. Night and Day comes to our aid."

Sima crinkled her nose at Ivo's mention of Vincenzo. In her own way, Ivo was attempting to reassure Sima they were not completely alone on this foreign planet. Someone existed in the rivers of the Universe that cared for her. Her heart beat faster as she thought of him, despite knowing his love was now off limits to her. Somehow, it cleared her head enough to know they couldn't abandon the three Trine Scouts.

"I don't want to leave them behind either."

Sima picked at her nails underneath the table as Ivo continued to scurry around, placing obstacles in front of entrances. Ivo worked efficiently, snapping the legs off one chair to wedge the windows fully shut. Ivo turned to her and placed her hands on her hips.

"They work for the Eternal Kingdom, the same people who deny your abuse to your face and run you off on a suicide mission to clean up their messes. I have no sympathy for them."

She caught Ivo's steaming glare. "You can't possibly mean that…" But she knew Ivo did. Even if she was cordial with her two Scouts, they did say she had generated quite a bit of trouble for them while being held. "So, you want to abandon them?"

"I want to *live*, Sima. What do you not understand about that? We can't do that if they kill us first. Even worse, have you considered if the people here are working with Carmine?"

Sima opened her mouth and then closed it. No. She had not considered that. She was inclined to believe the people of this planet would be welcoming and good-natured. She hadn't considered that perhaps the situation resembled Aeria and the Ambrosi, more than willing to go along with Aurelio's schemes.

A noise outside startled them, and Ivo held a chair leg before her as if it were a sword. The sounds of something sliding and then thumping rhythmically sounded through the city streets. It was still daylight.

"Shit," Ivo cursed under her breath. "They couldn't have found us already."

Cosima rushed to Ivo's side, and the two of them peered through an inch gap in the window shade. Her heart pounded as she searched for the source of the noise, but none was apparent. Whatever created the noise was not on this side of the street, but it only grew louder.

Her hand slid to her waist and pulled free the stolen dagger gifted to her by Ivo. While she doubted the strength of the weapon, neither of them would go down without a fight. As if reading her mind, Ivo plucked her blade from its sheath and motioned for Cosima to get low.

She crouched, following Ivo's instructions, and crawled behind the table. Ivo positioned herself by the front door, balancing on top of one of the chairs to catch an intruder off guard. No voices followed the strange noise, but the closer it grew, the more the thumps shook the small house. Dust and sediment cascaded from the ceiling.

Cosima grit her teeth as the rumbling grew in magnitude until it reached just outside the door. The sound came to an abrupt halt, leaving Sima's head pounding as she strained to understand what was happening. Her own heartbeat reverberated in her ears, but neither of them moved an inch.

An ear-piercing screech filled the air, causing them to slam their hands over their ears. Pieces of the ceiling caved in, revealing heavy talons clutching into the building.

"What the hell is that?" Ivo breathed, frozen from where she stood by the door.

Cosima craned her neck, fear as thick as syrup on her tongue.

The creature peeled back the corner of the room, ripping the roof off the building. Sima slapped her hands over her mouth to keep from crying out as a lengthy beak poked into the room. Its beak chattered like it was tasting the air before more of the roof retreated beneath its talons. It pulled back, and a milky eye obscured the hole above them. Its clouded iris slid side to side in search of its desired prey, before biting at the room again.

"It can't see us," Sima whispered. Her breath was shaky, and her fingertips burned as if dipped in steaming water. She clenched her fists. "It knows we're here, but it can't see us."

"What should we do? Run for it?"

Sima shook her head. She had been forbidden from using her powers by the Divinity unless it was cleared by Nariah. Yet, without the Trine Scout to tell her no, Sima considered using her abilities to save them from certain death. She vowed never to become a captive again. The scorching heat consumed more of her fingers, as if burning down to the bone, and her hesitancy faded by the second.

She held her hands out before her and sent out a pulse of her magic in search of a tangible string to pull. Before she could select one, the creature shifted, revealing not another eye, but a massive silver chain with a dangling ruby pendant. Sima's hand flexed as she halted time.

She shook violently with every step forward, but it was not an illusion. The creature had somehow utilized the energy in the ruby to increase its strength. If she did not know better, she would think the crystal was the reason this blind bird was alive and pecking.

She ran her mind over her magic again, searching for an answer, when Nariah threw open the door. The Scout that was selected precisely for her immunity and expertise in powers like Cosima's blasted through her halt over time as if it did not exist. A heavy blanket fell over Sima's magic as Nariah demonstrated exactly how her Scout planned to hold in her line. She glanced down at her numb hands when the Scout tackled her.

"What do you think you're doing?" Nariah wrestled Sima's wrists to the ground. "You were about to use your Fate powers even though you were specifically instructed to *not* do that. You have a tight leash with your time blocks, but you must not touch the Weave. Your magic does not work the same here. You could have damned us all in a minute."

"I thought you said she was dead," Sima shrieked.

Ivo stared at the Scout with wide eyes. "I *thought* she was."

Sima breathed heavily and took in Nariah's scraped and bloody chin, the oozing wound below her collarbone. Her eyes were wild but clear. The Scout was fully in control, no matter how she seethed because of Cosima's decisions today.

"I-I'm sorry, but that thing was going to snap my head clean off my body. I did what I had to. Where have you been?"

Nariah held her gaze, Sima's wrists still pinned to the floor. "Your friend is the one who left us behind. Why don't you ask her why?"

Vincenzo

The peak of the mountain was frigid in the morning air, and Vincenzo's wings settled around him to preserve warmth. Merit attempted the same, but his wings were thinner with no feathers to keep him comfortable. His connection to Cosima had brought Enzo this far, but beyond knowing she was distressed and injured, he did not know where exactly she was.

"What bright idea do you have now?" Merit asked.

"Still coming up with one." Enzo scanned the other side of the mountain. A moderately sized city sprawled in a canyon, almost entirely encircled by mountains. It was as if the terrain created walls by which the residents could protect themselves from the creatures roaming beyond. The canyon itself showed clear signs of water erosion along the sides; however, it was now empty and dry, beyond the buildings.

"Not much to look at, is it?" Merit murmured.

"No," Enzo replied, searching for signs of life.

The city itself was unremarkable. The buildings were no more than two or three stories high and featured wooden outposts resembling stairs; however, the distance between them was wide enough to seem unsuitable for immortals to use. The homes were large, with wide doorways in place of narrow ones. Vincenzo wondered what the populace looked like. There was no telling what the creations of the Goddesses would resemble, especially since he could not spy even a single living being within.

"I'm going down there."

"I don't know if that's such a good idea," Merit said, snatching Enzo by the arm. "You don't know what the people are like; if they'll be hostile. I haven't seen any sign of an Archipelago. There are no Rani or Ambrosi. This place has either been abandoned or they have all been killed."

Enzo stopped. "You're right. Carmine likely wiped them out the moment he decided to stay here, though I wonder if he used crystals to do it." *Aurelio had to have been using the stolen magic to keep himself strong.* "Either way, there is only one way to find my brother, and that's by going down there."

Merit released him with a scoff. "Fine, if you want to walk right into a trap. Be careful. If he does have magic stones, he might have a chance at killing you, even with your God-blood."

Enzo laughed, an empty, half-hearted laugh. "That won't happen."

"Yeah, keep telling yourself that, feathers." Vincenzo pushed off the mountain peak and used his wings to soar into the open air, slowly descending toward the city. Merit scrambled to keep up, launching after him. The Scout gained on him before cutting him off. "What? Did I hurt your feelings, bird-brain?"

Enzo navigated around him, refusing to give in to Merit's constant pestering. He had grown up with no mercy with the Rani Guardians, existing at the bottom of the barrel—the useless lives sent to die in masses before the over-inflated egos that were the Trine Scouts arrived. Enzo refused to submit, to obey the senseless hierarchy that offered nothing unless one reached the top. Why, if the Goddesses were capable of creating them to have boundless power, did they not make them equal?

"Hey," Merit yelled, tackling Enzo mid-air, sending them tumbling toward the ground. Before he could right himself, Vincenzo pounded into the dirt, sliding down the remainder of the mountainside. Enraged, he littered Merit's torso with punches, which the Scout eagerly returned.

He got to his feet, still locked in a match of muscle with Merit, and the Scout was losing. It did not take much more force from Enzo before Merit was whimpering. Enzo's power still thumped through his veins. Somehow, he already itched to expel more of it as the creeping madness of built-up energy accumulated. His power shot outward, creating pillars of brown rock around them as Enzo's irritation took over.

"What's your fucking problem?" Enzo hollered.

Merit shoved Enzo off him. "I am sick of watching you do whatever you want without my input. I thought you said we could be a team. Or maybe the reason you keep ignoring me is because I am right about you. You're just like your piece of shit brother, Aurelio."

Enzo seized Merit by the front of his Scout armor and got an inch from his face. "I told you I am not working with my brothers. I do not have some secret master plan I am concealing from you. I am trying to find Cosima, help her kill Carmine, and get out of here. You can follow me around if it makes you feel like you are doing your job properly, but you are not going to whine in my fucking ear all day either."

He released Merit, opting to dust himself off. The commotion did the exact thing Vincenzo was hoping to avoid—it drew attention.

Surrounding them, doors creaked open, and out peered strange beings. Beings with elegant wings with fine-colorful feathers emerged, their faces resembling a mix between Gods and owls. Features recognizable to Enzo as a mouth, nose, eyes, ears, but with a sharpness that conveyed a predator-like watchfulness.

"H-hello," Vincenzo began. "We are not here to harm you."

Instead of responding, the crowd of people stared at them. None looked away or so much as blinked. Vincenzo shifted on his feet, surveying them. A being moved in the shadows, leaving Vincenzo breathless as they emerged.

"I am Ezekiel," the being said. Ezekiel had soft gray and green wings, his head concealed beneath a blue scarf. Only his face was visible, and his owl-like features seemed to hum with his dissatisfaction with Vincenzo. "Do not come any closer."

"We are looking for refuge," Enzo said, holding his hands up. He thought quickly on his feet to keep the people from attacking. "There are monsters outside the mountain. We were not safe out there."

"He's right," Merit said, "you can't make us leave. We will get killed."

The bird-like people seemed to consider this for a moment, exchanging curious glances amongst each other. A group to the left of them shared whispered conversations. Ezekiel did not remove his eyes from them, even as someone approached him and conveyed a hushed message.

"You there," Ezekiel commanded, jutting a long, feathered finger at Enzo. "What brings you to our planet? You are clearly from beyond our world."

"What makes you think we are outsiders?"

"I know you are outsiders," Ezekiel said slowly, "because there is no one else left alive on this planet. We are the last of all civilization here."

Enzo froze. "No, that can't be."

"I will ask you again. Why are you here? You chose this planet for a reason."

"We are looking for the rest of our team," Enzo said.

"How did you get separated from them, and why do you believe they are here?" Ezekiel's feathers rustled, a sign Vincenzo took to mean he was losing his patience with them.

"We…" Vincenzo had to think quickly on his feet. He could not be forthcoming with the true reason, lest the bird people be working in conjunction with Carmine. Merit groaned beside him. "We were traveling between worlds when we took a wrong turn. The rest of our team kept going one way, and we went the other. We realized our mistake, and last we can determine, they were here. Have you seen them?"

Ezekiel craned his neck. "Where were you planning to go before you became separated?"

Merit stepped forward. "Ever heard of the Eternal Kingdom?"

The owl-man shook his feathers. "In passing, yes. However, there is not much for the ants to do about giants, so I concern myself little with the affairs of Goddesses."

That caught Enzo's attention. Not all creations of the Goddesses knew about the Eternal Kingdom, let alone the High Priestesses. Enzo tucked his suspicions away for now, waiting for more information to come home that he could use. At the very least, he assumed Ezekiel was likely more closely involved with Carmine than the owl intended to let on.

"Consider us the Eternal Kingdom's enforcement. We were following command and returning after a mission," Merit said. "I'd suggest you comply before your little planet gains the interest of the Divinity."

Ezekiel shared an uneasy look with another nearby. He turned back to them and sighed. "We have come across some who may have been in your group, yes. They are similar in appearance to you, though they did not pounce on us."

"Where are they now?" Vincenzo blurted.

"They are inside the city."

"Are they injured?" Enzo asked, thinking of the sensations he got from the bond.

"No, it is much worse, I am afraid. They are dead."

The words did not register.

"What?" Enzo asked, ears ringing.

"They were killed as they were making their journey into the canyon. There was nothing we could do for them. A few members of our community saved their bodies and brought them inside the city. We can show you to them, if you'd like."

"How many bodies?" Enzo asked.

"Two."

"It can't be Sima," he murmured to himself. He ran a shaky hand through his hair. "I didn't feel anything when we got here. I would have felt something."

You're here somewhere. Wait for me. I will always find you.

Merit raised a brow as he stared at Enzo, before turning toward Ezekiel. "Take us to them," Merit commanded.

"Certainly," Ezekiel said, bowing slightly. He gestured to the left. "Right this way, gentleman. We keep the bodies of those who have passed in the temple, which is a short walk from here."

Merit slapped a hand onto Vincenzo's back. "Let's move it, feathers. Your distant brothers have dead bodies to show us."

Chapter 17

Ivo

Ivo had seen enough. She knew that, technically, Cosima was forbidden from using her powers without permission from Nariah, but the situation had rapidly turned sour. In Ivo's mind, her friend's attempt had been justified, and the Scout's use of physical force was crossing a major line.

"Get off her," Ivo yelled, yanking on Nariah's arm. Electricity shot through her once her fingers grazed the Scout's skin. "You have no right to touch her like that."

Nariah shrugged her off, but released Sima and stood up.

"You." She pointed a finger in Ivo's face. "You abandoned us."

Ivo stood tall, and despite being half Nariah's size, she had no problem staring her in the eye. Her hard purple gaze did nothing to intimidate Ivo, who had spent enough time being picked on to know when to stand up for herself.

"Abandoned you? You mean taking Sima as far as I could from their arrows and Carmine's magic? Saving myself, the *weakling*, since no one else would? If you need to make me the villain to make it easier to digest that we got ambushed and you did nothing to save us, then be my guest."

"When will you let the weakling thing go?" Nariah put her hands on her hips.

"She did what she thought was right," Cosima interjected. "You didn't protect her, and I was knocked unconscious. She is mortal. What more do you want from her?"

"Mortal means reckless? Or is your friend just irritatingly insane?"

"Why can't you just accept that you were about to let me die?" Ivo snapped.

Nariah's lip quivered for a split second before she pressed her mouth into a firm line. "The others are *dead,* Ivo, because I was the one shielding you."

Ivo scrunched her nose. "No, that's not true…It was Horacio beside me."

The Scout shook her head. "When your eyes turned black from Carmine's hold on your mind, we were on our way down the mountainside. Just before we reached the bottom, there was a blast that crushed Earnest and Horacio to death with debris. I managed to use my magic to shield myself and Sima, because she was directly behind me, and you. I chose your mortal life over theirs."

Ivo opened her mouth and shut it several times, not knowing what to say. The Scout she had spent so much time fighting with had let her comrades die in order to save Ivo's life.

"I don't know if I will ever forgive the Kingdom for sending a mortal along with us," Nariah said, staring at the creature she killed. "You've proved to be quite a pain in my ass."

Nariah's words stung, and Ivo's heart ached in response. Some small piece of her agreed, had been afraid from the beginning that she would only complicate the mission. Never would she have imagined others would be dead because of how fragile she was. Ivo balled her fists and stormed off, slamming the door to the tiny bedroom in the home they had sought refuge in.

The only one who has been abandoned is me. Fate has made me an immeasurably unspectacular piece of a cosmic journey, as if the Empresses wish to remind me how little power I have.

She crouched down with her back against the wall, burying her face in her hands. Tears dripped from her eyes as she thought of Horacio and Earnest, wishing she could bring them back from the dead, wishing she could undo the cruel twist of Fate that took their lives.

Nariah and Sima's voices floated in from the kitchen.

"Are we still in your time pocket?" Nariah asked.

"Yes, I have the entire block on pause." Sima frowned. "Look at the stone on the creature's neck. Do you think there's any chance it's a life-force crystal? I have a bad feeling about this."

"Carmine has a life-force crystal *chicken,* and the Kingdom won't even give us a proper blade?" Ivo whispered to herself, stabbing her stolen dagger into the wooden floor.

"I sense the bird is siphoning the power of the ruby." Nariah's footsteps were audible as she moved around the room. "This is certainly not a good sign. Most crystal formations are inert with minimal deposits per planet. I wonder if this is one of the stones stolen from your planet, Haelos."

"Should we alert the Eternal Kingdom?" Sima asked, chewing her nail.

"Earnest and Horacio are dead. Our only mission right now is to find Carmine," Ivo said to herself.

Nariah sighed. "As much as I want to investigate, I think the main thing we need to do right now is slay this creature. Then we can come up with a plan for killing Carmine. Our group just suffered a major loss. Which is why we should not be getting separated, nor should you be using your powers without my permission, Sima."

Ivo frowned. "What if waiting for your permission gets us into more trouble?"

"It won't," Nariah said simply.

You're so cocky and so hard-headed, Ivo thought, using her dagger to carve into the floor. *You drive me insane, Nariah, and I can't wait for the day I never have to see you again.*

"If you're certain," Sima said after a pause.

Their voices dipped lower, and Ivo could no longer eavesdrop on their conversation. Their hushed conversation grew harsher before eventually, Nariah's heavy footsteps stormed over to the door of the small bedroom. She knocked on the door, and Ivo debated whether or not she wanted to look the Scout in the face.

When she didn't respond, Nariah opened the door anyway. She shut it behind her, and Ivo kept her gaze fixed on the carvings she had created in the wood with her blade. The Scout came to a stop beside her, and to Ivo's surprise, she took a seat on the floor.

Nariah blew out a breath and rested her head against the wall. "So…I guess Sima thinks I was too hard on you. She thinks I should apologize."

"Telling me what Sima thinks does not count as an apology."

The Scout's face twisted. "I'm getting there," she said through her teeth.

"Go on, then," Ivo said, brushing away the wood shavings.

"You really are impatient, you know that?" Nariah smirked. "Anyway, at first I didn't agree with her, and I think you should know the reason why."

Ivo scoffed. "Let me guess: I'm nothing but a burden to you because I have useless magic and you're mad at me because your friends are dead."

Nariah blinked a few times. "I am not exactly…thrilled about those things, but no, that is not the reason." She shifted, bringing one knee up for her arm to rest on it. "I don't know exactly how to say this, but Ivo, I think you have significant power, even if it is primarily untapped."

The words felt like a punch to Ivo's gut. "Are you making fun of me now?"

"What? No. I am being serious. Are you certain of your mortal heritage?"

"Yes. Wouldn't the Kingdom have realized it sooner if I wasn't a witch?"

Nariah's head swayed back and forth. "Not necessarily. There is a chance you simply weren't examined closely enough or in the right manner. Don't you find it suspicious that problems seem to resolve easily when you are around?"

Ivo stood up. "Alright, now I know you're being cruel."

The Scout jumped to her feet. "I'm trying to warn you. Will you listen to me? If you're not careful, you could end up using your power in a way you don't intend. If you have the gift of luck, then it means you are connected to the Weave in some manner."

"The Weave…" Ivo chewed the inside of her cheek, unsure what to make of Nariah's claims.

Impossible, Ivo thought. *Sometimes I feel like the unluckiest person in the vast universes.*

"You have to refrain from using your abilities. I wasn't given restrictions from the Kingdom for you, so you can use it at your discretion, but someone as inexperienced as you should exercise caution."

"Inexperienced, huh?" She sighed. "If I happen to be lucky somehow, it is not on purpose. I can't refrain from doing it because I don't know how to do it in the first place."

Nariah seemed to consider her words. "Can you at least promise me you'll keep what I said in mind?"

"I promise I will do my best," Ivo said.

"Good enough," the Scout said, the fire in her purple eyes extinguishing.

Ivo stared up at her and swallowed hard when their gazes locked on one another. Nariah's beauty remained the only thing about her capable of intimidating her. As if the Scout could read her thoughts, she smiled and took a single, small step closer, leaving them only inches apart.

"You still never apologized," Ivo said.

"You're right."

An almost electric buzz manifested in the air between them, as if they were capable of more than harboring frustration for one another. Nariah leaned forward slightly, bringing her face near Ivo's. "I'm sorry for making you feel like a burden, and I'm sorry I called you a weakling."

Ivo huffed. "Was that so hard?"

Nariah leaned back. "Yes. Unbelievably so."

The Scout spun on her heel and walked out of the bedroom, leaving Ivo with her heart still pounding, wondering if she had hallucinated the tension between them. She shook her head and followed, finding Nariah speaking with Cosima in the kitchen.

"I did what you asked, now can we get on with it? I'd like to handle the bird sooner rather than later."

"Certainly," Sima replied, waving her hand.

The reawakened bird beast swung heavily toward the building, knocking Nariah off her feet. Before she hit the ground, her wings fluttered free and righted her. She threw Sima an annoyed glance before launching herself at the creature.

Cosima let Nariah handle the creature alone and instead rushed to Ivo's side. The two watched Nariah tussle with the beast, using her impressive skills to subdue it quickly. The creature shrieked as Nariah snapped the silver chain, leaving the bird defenseless. She pulled her blade free and sliced through its neck. Within moments, the chaos had ceased, and the bird's beak collided with the dirt. Nariah shot them a disapproving look through the hole before flying out of sight.

It was then that the voices of frightened and enraged townspeople filled the outside street. Sima eyed the demolished house and sighed.

"If we were hoping to remain hidden for some time," Sima said, "I believe that chance has passed us by."

The temple Ezekiel brought them to was made of navy stone with light gray swirls. It featured twelve steps to the top, and at the front entrance were two statues of the owl-like beings with floral-scented smoke toiling from their mouths. Once Ezekiel pulled open the door, a wave of foul odor hit their senses.

"Oh, no," Vincenzo gasped, throwing a hand over his mouth. He peddled backward, the horrific smell so strong he could taste it. "No, I am not going in there."

"You asked to see them," Ezekiel cooed.

Enzo scoffed. "Are you enjoying this?"

"That offends me," Ezekiel replied. "But, yes, a bit." He turned to the attendant beside him. "Letika, please open the windows to freshen the room. It seems the guests have a sensitive disposition."

"Certainly," Letika said. Soft pearl and ocean-colored feathers marked her brow. Instead of it making her look intimidating, she appeared wise and alert.

"This way," Ezekiel said, "This is where we store the dead."

A half-smile played on Merit's lips as he watched the attendant fulfill her task. Enzo nudged him. The Scout rolled his eyes but focused forward. Enzo followed suit and switched to mouth-breathing as they entered the foul, stagnant room. There were short, black painted windows strangely positioned along the bottom half of the wall with metal bars barring entry.

Or exit.

"Those in your group are over here," Ezekiel said, standing above two gray stone slabs.

Enzo neared the slabs. The bodies were hidden beneath white drapes, brass buttons placed over their eyes. It was clear one of the two bodies was too large to be Cosima, Ivo, or Nariah. The other one, however, was of a shorter stature. Gruesome fears tickled him, coaxing panic into his chest. A pounding headache accompanied it, and he rubbed his temples, hissing from the chill of his own fingertips.

"What are those?" Vincenzo asked, reaching a hand toward them. Ezekiel's frown made him pull back.

"They are ceremonious in some senses, symbols of protection after passing into the afterlife. However, you came from outside the canyon and are aware of the creatures lurking beyond. I shall admit to you, these buttons keep the dead bodies from rising once again."

Enzo felt his body flush with anxious heat. "The dead are rising?"

Merit appeared uninterested in the conversation; instead, his head swiveled around as he pretended to take in his surroundings. The closer he got to Letika, the more obvious it became that Merit was seeking her company and not more clues. The attendant continued her task of opening each window along the back wall by spinning the handle until fresh air wafted into the room.

Ezekiel frowned. "Not in all cases, but enough that it quickly became a problem."

"How long has this been going on?" Enzo asked.

"Perhaps a decade, maybe more. It is hard to say. The destruction of our world was a slow-moving curse that quickly broke into a devastating race to save ourselves. Before we could fully understand what was happening, entire cities were demolished. Our race has wings, which allowed us to take to the skies. We located this safe haven in the canyon and have been here ever since. I can't remember the last time any of us ventured outside of the mountains. The memories of the days spent losing loved ones and running for our lives keep us from going back."

Enzo shifted on his feet. "I know what that is like. Creatures like this took over my world as well. We studied the reanimation the best we could…" Deciding to keep further information to himself, Enzo shifted the subject. "How many people live in this city?"

"A pitiful two hundred. Efforts to repopulate are limited by the creatures, of course." Ezekiel's feathers trembled as he shook his head. "Quite a shame."

A surge of fury-filled magic gathered at Enzo's fingertips, begging him to kill Ezekiel. The sensation startled Enzo, but he contained his reaction, swallowing the fear that arose in response to his power's haunting call. He reminded himself he could handle his curse, even if it threatened to drown him.

"I've got a question for you," Merit purred at Letika. "How do those pretty little buttons keep the dead from waking up?"

Letika shot him a level glare. "They are blessed. We take them to our Ohteha, a priest. They are prayed over for fourteen days and nights while the Ohteha channels the magic from the Source into the buttons. The Ohteha uses sound, smoke, and energy to cleanse the dead of their afflictions and allow them to rest peacefully. The buttons were not always used in this manner, but the…circumstances called for greater magic. Each button is for protection, and we are grateful Source heard our calls for defense against the dead."

Merit's smile grew wider. "I could offer you protection from the dead. Worship me for fourteen days and nights, and nothing will ever come close to you again."

Letika took a step forward, squaring her shoulders. She firmly held Merit's gaze before slapping him across the face. The motion was so quick and efficient, Enzo thought he imagined the whole encounter. Letika left Merit standing there, holding his reddened cheek, mouth agape.

Ezekiel ground his jaw, emotion Vincenzo recognized as irritation flickering on his expressive, feathered brows. Enzo couldn't help the growing resentment the longer he spent in Merit's company. With Letika gone, the room only grew more tense. Fire burned inside his throat, tipping him closer to the edge as his magic warmed his fingertips, but he pulled himself back, focusing on his desire to find Cosima.

"Show us the bodies," Enzo blurted, "please."

The owl-like man nodded his head, carefully removing the buttons over the larger body before peeling back the drape. Enzo sighed, sick relief embracing him as he stared at a Trine Scout and not Sima or Ivo. It felt wrong to be grateful someone else had died, but he was. The man had blood all throughout his shaggy black hair, and his thin chest was crushed. Bones poked through skin on either side of his ribcage.

"How did this happen?" Enzo asked, leaning closer to the Scout's sunken, closed eyes.

Trine Scouts were more difficult to kill, more so than Rani Guardians. The damage done to the Scout could not have been dealt by the rabid creatures outside of the canyon. The paleness encompassing Merit's face confirmed he was experiencing a similar train of thought as Vincenzo.

"They were found in this condition. There was nothing we could do for them."

The same line he had given them earlier. Vincenzo continued to scan the dead man's body for further clues into his demise, occasionally glancing sideways at Ezekiel. Something about the leader was off-putting, and Enzo's guard went up each time his eyes were not directly on him.

Ezekiel stood at the head of the body, his winged arms crossed before him. As if he could sense the shift in the air, the man took a few steps away, feathers fanning as he stretched. His fingertips mirrored talons, and the shadow cast by them, intentional or otherwise, loomed directly above the dead man's chest. Enzo could not decide if he found the gesture to be threatening, but he would not be foolish enough to trust this leader. Even so, one body remained to be uncovered. His heart sped as his body prepared for a fight.

"The other one," Enzo said. His shoulders scrunched, pulling his wings higher behind him. "I want to see the other one now."

Ezekiel ended his elongated stretch and repeated the same careful motions to remove the buttons. As he pulled back the drape, Vincenzo quietly released a tense breath. Relief was just as bitter the second time, dancing alongside a dull horror at the realization that another Trine Scout lay dead. His torso was crushed, and the man's once strong muscles contorted into strange angles. Lengthy black bruises littered his throat, and a drop of dried blood rested in the corner of his lips.

"Oh, man," breathed Merit. He clasped his hand over Enzo's shoulder. "Rough, really. I think I remember these Scouts. Not my regiment, of course." He leaned closer to Enzo and lowered his voice. "I'm an inside dog, feathers. You've got me out here in the mud, and now two Scouts are dead in front of me."

Vincenzo understood the urgency in Merit's voice. Wherever Cosima and Ivo were, they were either alone or had only Nariah to protect them. Whatever had slain these men did so with such force that it unnerved Enzo to imagine the culprit lurking in the streets near them. Scouts were not enough to stop the killer, but Vincenzo was. He just needed to find her. At the thought of Cosima, a tremor started in his left arm and crept up to his bicep, his magic once again roaring for release. He clasped his hand over his trembling muscles and took a deep breath, relieved when the strange reaction subsided.

"Is something wrong?" Ezekiel asked. His tone was curious, but his eyes portrayed a sick sense of enjoyment.

Kill him, his curse whispered.

Enzo ignored its command and shut his eyes, forcing himself to think clearly. The owl-like man was not to be trusted, but he was still necessary until they found Sima. Besides, if Ezekiel brought them here to feed off their discomfort, Enzo would deny him the emotions he craved. He schooled his facial expressions in the best neutral mask he could muster. "What actually happened to them?"

Merit wiped the surprise off his face and leveled his gaze at Ezekiel. Vincenzo let his hand slide to the hilt of his blade, sending waves of his magic into the owl-like man who now shivered with a growing anxiousness. He let the pressure of it goad Ezekiel into moving.

Ezekiel's eyebrow flicked upward, his lip turning in a sneer. "What do you accuse us of? *You* are the intruder; must I remind you of this? If you have come to stir trouble, you will be met with grief instead."

Enzo laughed. "I assure you, you and your people are not at risk with me. You are not the flock I hunt."

"Who, then, has earned your scorn?"

Enzo weighed the answer on his tongue, deciding how much his own bitterness would reflect in his response. "A brother."

"A brother?" Ezekiel cooed. "Interesting." He fanned his gray and green feathers, shaking his neck.

"Do you know of him?" Enzo asked.

"I believe I know of whom you speak, though I doubt this man shares your blood. Beyond a form similar to yours, he has a lighter complexion and, I must say, is so plain compared to you."

Merit hid his snicker behind his fist. Enzo's power flared once more, this time shouting inside his head instead of whispering. *Kill him! Tear his head off his body and scatter his remains as a warning to the others.*

"And what could you possibly mean by that?" Enzo's upper lip twitched.

"He stalks around here, taking refuge in various places inside the canyon. Where exactly, I do not know. His whims are wicked, and his essence is dark. You share no similarity in this respect either. You are not free of darkness, but you are not empty of light."

"You need to help us find him." Merit crossed his arms in front of his chest.

"I told you I do not know where he is."

"Then how do you know of him? Give us something useful," Vincenzo said.

Instead of waiting for Ezekiel to become compliant, Enzo's magic seized his brain like a skilled hunter. Before he could notice the change, the magic coaxed the answers out of him. His sharp gaze softened briefly as his eyes fluttered.

"He is the reason there is no one left on this planet. The monsters outside the canyon are worsened by his presence, at least that is the only answer I can surmise. The moment he appeared, the problem exploded and spread across our world, ravaging all in its path. I told you once before, we are all that is left of this world. We believe him to be an angry God who came to curse our world, for reasons unknown."

The situation eerily mirrored the travesties of Haelos. His brothers were spreading mayhem across the cosmos. Could ruling the Eternal Kingdom be worth the pain that echoed galaxies away? Enzo could not understand the desire for bloodshed, especially of innocents.

"He is in the canyon; that is enough to go by," Enzo reasoned, turning to Merit.

Ezekiel's head swayed side-to-side. "So you think. You came through the top of the mountain ridge, just as the others did. He already knows you are here."

Merit's face filled with fury. "He did this to them, didn't he? Why didn't you stop him?"

"How shall I stop a *God*, pest?" Ezekiel spat.

Haven't you had enough, Enzo's curse taunted.

He released what remained of his hold over Ezekiel and increased the space between them. The realization that Carmine already knew of their presence tugged Vincenzo toward the door. He reached a hand out, snagging Merit by the collar, and exited the room.

The fresh air was intoxicating after breathing in the stench of death. Carmine claimed the lives of two Scouts, and Enzo would not give him any more leverage over them. Without waiting for Merit to gather himself, he shot into the sky, determined to find Cosima at last. The only chance they stood of truly defeating his brother came from working together.

In the past, the symphony of their power working in tandem elevated him to heights he could not vocalize. Now his power desperately craved her, wishing for her to make art out of his misery in the way only she could. His arm trembled again, but this time he did not deny the urge to expend the buildup. Enzo's magic crawled through the forest, crafting meaningless dirt and stone-filled structures, only for him to snap them out of existence a moment later. Wasting his energy brought him the relief he craved, like rain in parched lands, soothing the superheated burn of his curse.

He had not meant to keep his affliction from Cosima, but he hardly understood it enough to communicate it properly. Enzo's stomach turned and squeezed with pain. *What will she think of me once she knows I am tainted?* As much as he wished to reject the curse's hold over him, he selfishly wished for her to seize control of her power as well, to know what it was like to wield it without coercion or command. Perhaps then, they could harmonize and create expansion beyond their wildest dreams.

Perhaps.

The cool wind was welcome across his face, and he spotted smoke toiling in the sky. His wings guided him closer. Merit filled the space beside him, his wings pulsing at an even pace.

"There," Merit said, pointing to the tattered remains of a building.

The moment he spotted her, the moment her aura struck him, dizzy relief pattered against his tired mind.

"Cosima," Enzo breathed. "Finally."

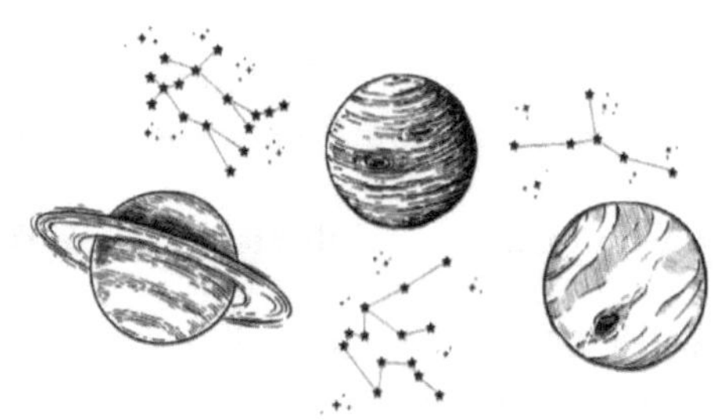

Chapter 18

Cosima

"Please, stop shouting," Nariah begged, fanning her hands out as she motioned for them to relax.

Cosima and Ivo held hands as they stood behind her, surveying the crowd. The people here stood on two legs and resembled immortals in stature. However, wings connected their arms to their sides, and feathers covered their bodies, head to toe. Their faces held the mouths of the Goddesses and eyes of owls.

"Who are you?" croaked a bird-like man with thinning feathers.

"What have you done?" hooted another. "He was our only guardian!"

"Help!"

"We are being attacked! They have slain the protector!"

Ivo inched closer. "What do we do?" she whispered.

Horror permeated the crowd, making it obvious to Cosima that the people were frightened by the strange trio in front of them. Outside the canyon, the forests were ravaged by creatures, forcing them to flee for survival. From inside their mountainous walls, they rebuilt, and now here the three of them were, bringing chaos with every step. Her eyes slid to the monstrous creature Ivo had called a chicken.

The people had referred to it as their guardian. The way the crowd gazed at its carcass spoke of endearment and heartache. The silver chain where the massive crystal pendant had hung glinted in the sun beside the creature's bloody wing. "This creature was protecting you?" Cosima asked.

A woman stepped forward, holding her feathered hands before her. She moved slowly, as if not to alarm them. "You don't understand what you've done." Her voice shook. "You've damned us all."

The panic in the woman's eyes barreled through Sima, causing her to take a step backward. Something about her fears was so palpable that it inspired the same emotions in Cosima. She shook her head. "We—"

"We did what we had to," Nariah barked. "Where is your Archipelago? We must speak with those in charge of this planet."

"There are only two leaders in this city," the frightened woman said. "The Chief, Zadkiel, and his son, Ezekiel. I do not know of an Archipelago."

"Take us to them," Nariah commanded.

"You must atone for what you've done!" someone yelled from the crowd.

"We will not take orders from you!" cried another.

Cries of agreement surrounded them. The crowd pulsed closer as their rage overtook their shock and sadness. Arrows aimed inches from their faces. Sima and Nariah pressed together, sandwiching Ivo between them. Sima drew her knife, knowing she would not be brave enough to use it against innocent civilians unless they threatened her mortal friend's life.

Her hand shook. The last time she had used a weapon against a person, it had been Aurelio. The thought of ending a life once more made her nauseous. Members of the crowd halted, glancing above their heads to something behind them. Sima turned, and the moment she spotted Vincenzo, her knees buckled.

She grabbed Ivo with her free hand and ran to him, leaving Nariah with the angry, grieving group of civilians. The sight of him was fresh air, and it nourished her aching soul. He drew his blade and lifted his other arm as Sima slid beneath it. His wings enveloped her and Ivo, forming a protective embrace.

"Enzo," Cosima breathed, latching her arms around his waist. He held her closer to him. The sensation of his body against hers leveled her breathing.

"Sima," he whispered into her hair. "Finally."

"I have never been so happy to see someone," Ivo cried, cowering beneath Enzo's wing.

Nariah's wings fluttered as she sprang backward from the crowd. She landed a foot in front of them. Sima peered over Enzo's wing at her. She turned slowly, her gaze dripping with disdain levied in Enzo's direction.

"You are not permitted to touch in that manner," she bit out. The words came out heavy, as if it infuriated her to have to remind them of their commitments.

Enzo did not move, but Sima pushed herself free. The space between them was painfully obvious in her mind. Ivo continued to hide beneath his wing, peeking at Sima with tired eyes. They had barely slept or eaten, and instead of finding a moment to rest, they had arrows pointed at their noses. Sima's stomach sank.

The civilians crept forward, still aiming their weapons. There was a cautious edge to them. Their eyes remained locked on Vincenzo, ignoring all of the women. Nariah was poised with her sword at the ready, her attempts to calm the group futile.

Cosima recognized a familiar figure that landed between Nariah and the pressing mob. It was the Trine Scout that had been assigned to Vincenzo by the Divinity. It must have been how Vincenzo traveled from the Eternal Kingdom after being forced to remain behind.

He swept the tip of his blade against the ground, sparks flying as the metal collided with stone. "Stay back," he commanded. "You are in violation of the Commandments provided to this planet. Stand down, now."

"You can't tell us what to do!"

"They attacked us first!"

"Your grievances can be tended to later. I will repeat myself only one more time before I begin subduing all who do not obey," Merit boomed. "Stand down."

"This isn't going to work," Enzo said, balling his fist as if he were torn on making a move himself.

A voice sounded from the sky behind them. "Halt."

A taller owl-like man descended from the sky. He was covered in gray and moss green feathers. His sharp gaze landed on her only for a moment before it moved onto the rest of them. He settled on Nariah. "I am Ezekiel. You wished to speak with me, I was told."

Ezekiel. The son of the Chief.

Merit waltzed toward him, blade at his side. "You motherfucker, tell them to back down."

Ezekiel waved his hand toward the people, and to Cosima's surprise, they withdrew their weapons. One by one, they dispersed, leaving them alone with Ezekiel and the dead creature.

"They have been tamed." He turned his nose up at the slaughtered creature. "I see one of our defense mechanisms has fallen victim to your ruthless pack."

"That's your idea of a defense mechanism?" Enzo groaned. "I don't think you were telling me the full truth earlier. I have to admit, I am not fond of lies by omission, Ezekiel."

Ezekiel's attitude faltered as Vincenzo stepped forward, and Ivo slipped from under his wing and stood behind him. Without command, Nariah moved closer to her, shielding Ivo from sight. Enzo moved to stand closer to Ezekiel and Merit. Sima followed, just a step behind. She held her head high and tugged her messy, raging emotions inward until she was someone more outwardly brave. Without her abilities, she would have to be useful in other ways.

Ezekiel glanced at her for a moment longer than he did the first time he met her, but he was not interested in her. He was keenly focused on Vincenzo. Her eyes shot between the two of them, gauging the temperature. Enzo had a ruthless side of him he tucked deeply away, but he was also supernaturally patient. Even now, as Ezekiel's eyes blazed with obvious contempt, Enzo was relaxed. He was expectant of trouble, but not worried.

She admired it, wondering how to contort herself into a master of her emotions as he did. Instead, she took slow breaths through her nose and waited for someone to speak. The men continued to stare at each other, but no one made a move. *We need to rest,* Sima thought wearily.

"I think—" Cosima began.

"Why are you speaking?" Ezekiel blurted as he glared at her.

"Do not talk to her like that," Enzo said simply. It was an egregiously calm command, but his words carried a physical weight to them, as if blanketing the space around them in thick mud. Sima could not deny Enzo's commitment to making her feel untouchable when he was around. "Apologize."

The man cocked his head to the side, considering Vincenzo's words. For a split second, Sima swore Ezekiel's eyes glazed over, before his face went slack, as if he were reawakening. What had she seen overtake him?

"I am sorry for my harsh words."

"Thank you," Sima replied, no longer confident enough to speak her mind.

"Tell me the truth about my brother," Enzo snapped.

"Perhaps we should not speak where others might overhear," Ezekiel replied. "I shall take you to my father, Zadkiel."

Sima's neck twisted as she inspected the sky with an added sense of being watched. Vincenzo briefly slipped his hand in hers for a reassuring squeeze, using his wings to block Nariah's line of sight. All too soon, he pulled away, leading the group behind Ezekiel. The path was wide, etched into the dirt by thousands of passages through it. The air was dry, and the only sound was their feet pattering as they walked in silence.

The Chief's son was no longer consumed by anger. His fierce brows relaxed into stale, emotionless tufts of feathers. He walked with his winged arms behind him like a prisoner, though he was not bound by any restraint, Cosima could see. She peered over her shoulder and spotted Ivo staring directly at her.

"Kill me," Ivo mouthed, rolling her eyes.

Sima smiled and shook her head, facing forward once more. Anything that did not lead them directly to Carmine was likely just another obstacle in Ivo's eyes, but Sima took the chance to survey her surroundings. It was a habit that died hard in her. It was a compulsion almost, how insatiably persistent her mind was that she needed to mark every possible exit. It had proved useful on many occasions, and yet, she was enslaved to the fear that required this habit.

The canyon rose what seemed like miles in the air above them. She struggled to remember if it seemed that high when they rested on the mountain peaks, but the endless sight of red rock was suffocating. The sky seemed smaller, drowned out by dirt and dust. The lack of visual diversity in their surroundings taxed her eyes and mind. Sima let out a shaky breath.

Sensing her growing anxiety, Enzo slowed his pace until he was directly beside her. "Are you alright?" Sima nodded. "What is it? Is it Ezekiel? You don't have to worry about him for now," Enzo whispered.

"It's not him."

Enzo glanced over his shoulder. "Is it Nariah?"

Sima shushed him. "No, it isn't her either."

"Whatever is bothering you, you can tell me. You are not alone here."

"Not being alone here sometimes feels like half the problem," she replied. How could she explain to him that the walls of this canyon felt like they were closing in on her? Every minute on this strange planet where a brother of the Sacred Twelve lurked in the shadows, the more she was reminded of her time with Aurelio.

He nodded slowly. "I can understand that. The mandatory presence of the Scouts is exhausting for me as well, to say the least." Enzo glared at Merit, who walked with his blade directed at Ezekiel's back. "I thought I would've ditched him by now, but his tracking abilities are too precise."

"How did you convince him to bring you here?"

Enzo let out a soft laugh, gently brushing her shoulder with his wing as they walked. "I don't know if convinced is the proper word."

"You didn't..." She trailed off, fearing his reply.

He swallowed. "I did."

Sima's jaw dropped. Enzo had used his powers on Merit's mind to find her. She glanced at Ezekiel. "And him, too?" she whispered furiously.

"Yep."

She pressed her lips into a line, unsure how she felt about Enzo's brazen use of his magic. She peered over her shoulder, relieved to find Ivo and Nariah locked in their own conversation, far enough away to not hear what she and Enzo spoke of. "We aren't supposed to use our powers."

"Says who?"

"The Divinity, Enzo. This isn't a joke."

He wiped the smile off his face with his hand and met her gaze. His emerald eyes ensnared her, Sima unable to resist staring deep into them. "Believe me, I understand the weight of our situation. But it is almost disrespectful how much the Kingdom underestimates my abilities. I might not be able to get rid of him, but he has little hold over my power. Merit may be a stubborn bull that thinks he can stop me. But he can't, Sima."

The way he said her name electrified her, but his words made her stomach turn. "Maybe that's what they want you to believe. Don't give them a reason to believe you are a threat. How do you know he isn't keeping track of everything you do?"

"He probably is," Enzo replied with a shrug. "But my powers are harder to properly monitor, and my restrictions are different from yours. You alter the Weave, and because of Nariah's shared blood with Kismet, she can track those changes. Merit doesn't have that luxury. I hardly know the full extent of my power; how can the Divinity possibly believe they do?"

The pit in Cosima's stomach grew at the mention of Kismet. The one time she was able to meet the auspicious Goddess, it had ended in disappointment. She had hoped she was fortunate enough to be the daughter of someone so deeply respected, as if it would cleanse her of her sinful past. As if being claimed by a Goddess with such obvious, overwhelming worth meant she would find that she, too, was worth something. Instead, she continued to be an unclaimed nobody, with the crimes of her dead husband held against her. Somehow, it only made her feel worse.

"Please just be careful with your magic," Sima replied.

"You have my word."

They meandered through the gate of a low wooden fence, moving their way toward the entrance to the estate. Statues feet taller than them were poised on the roof. The bird-people in the sculptures bowed their heads, holding their wings out at their sides. The estate itself was three stories high, with doors wide enough to fit several people with their wings stretched out at one time. The main set of doors were a deep, bloody red with thin, muted blue and yellow stripes. They slid open automatically as the group neared.

"Have you told me all of what you know about your power?"

Before he could answer, Nariah tapped Sima on the shoulder. With her hands, the Scout physically pushed herself between Sima and Enzo. Enzo rolled his eyes, but stepped to the side, allowing Nariah to separate them completely.

"We are here," Ezekiel announced. His voice was flat, his face expressionless.

"Where is the Chief?" Merit demanded, poking the tip of his sword into the chest of Ezekiel.

"He will not be home until later in the evening. He stops by the homes of people in the city during the day to ensure everyone has what they need."

"Very well, then," Enzo said. "We would like to meet your father now, Ezekiel. Bring us to him."

Instead of agreeing, Ezekiel twitched. His shoulder jerked upward on one side. "N-no," he growled. "You do not get to tell me what to do. The Chief is the most respected of all our people. He decides when to meet with you."

His back was rigid and stiff, but his shoulders and arms twitched at random.

"What's happening?" Cosima asked, feeling her heart race.

Enzo was calm. "He is fighting against my magic a bit. Little guy has a lot of strength in him, I'll give him that."

Within seconds, Ezekiel fell to his knees, eyes utterly empty. Enzo walked forward, patting him on the shoulder, which now sat eerily still.

"Guess we will have to find your pa ourselves." He looked over his shoulder. "Shall we?"

Nariah steamed, her brows pinched together so tightly, Sima thought she might lunge for Enzo. "Using your powers when you're not supposed to, are we, Enzo?"

He looked Nariah directly in the face, head slightly tilted. "No."

"Listen here," Nariah roared, launching herself toward him. Sima stumbled to put herself between them, only for Nariah to cast her to the side like she was weightless. Ivo caught her arm, and the two silently held each other, unsure of what would happen next.

Before Nariah could maul Vincenzo, Merit stopped her. "Enough," he grumbled. "I brought him here, and I cleared his power use. It is on me to decide, is it not?"

Nariah furiously searched Merit's face. "Merit, why would—"

"Because Ezekiel is standing between us and Carmine," Merit interrupted. "We are here for that son of a bitch, aren't we? Ezekiel has seen him but won't tell us where he is. He's been acting suspiciously from the moment we met him. The two Scouts you came with, Nariah. Where are they? Have you even stopped to ask what happened to their bodies?"

Nariah shrank back a fraction. "What happened to them?" Her voice was barely audible.

"You should be asking him that," Merit snapped. He jutted his sword toward Ezekiel, who remained on his knees. "The owl people are hoarding their bodies, and the entire thing smells rotten. There is something they are keeping from us."

"He's right," Enzo said. "It's clear they were killed by Carmine, and I think Ezekiel knows exactly how it happened. We might as well wait for the Chief to come back from his rounds. I think the group could use some rest. Let's see what Zadkiel's working with inside."

Enzo shot her a quick smile and walked into the house with Merit on his heels, leaving paralyzed Ezekiel outside. Sima linked arms with Ivo and followed, grateful that Enzo's assertiveness gave the group momentum. Nariah, to her credit, dissolved her bewildered expression quickly and slammed the door shut behind them.

Enzo's nose twitched as his feet fell heavily, thudding against the wood panel floor inside Chief Zadkiel's home. The door kicked up dust when it swung open, but the place was otherwise well put together. *This will do,* he thought. He ignored the stairs leading to the second floor and instead walked through an archway to the left as Merit went right.

Six chairs sat around a wooden table above a worn rug, positioned beside a window. A larger archway visually divided the space from a sizable kitchen. Enzo flipped open a few cupboards out of curiosity, frowning as he realized there was not enough food for them here. *I will have to remedy this,* he thought as the footsteps from the others grew loud enough to draw his attention.

Sima came around the corner first, and a smile tore across his face at the sight of her. Her gaze was pensive, but even so, the edges of her lips pulled upward, and a spark of love jumped from her eyes. Ivo held Sima's arm, her head swiveling as she took in the surroundings.

"What do you think of the place?" Enzo asked, holding his arms out beside him. "You're looking at your new, but temporary, accommodations."

"It's not bad," Ivo said, "if you ignore all the dust. The Chief can't hire people to clean for him?"

The sounds of Nariah and Merit arguing from somewhere else inside Zadkiel's home floated in. A second later, Merit flew into the room and landed a few feet from Enzo. "What's the plan for Ezekiel? Are you going to leave him out there?"

Enzo blinked. "Ah, right. He'll bring himself inside and shut the door behind him."

Ezekiel walked in, his eyes glowing green as he pulled out one of the chairs and sat at the table. Nariah wandered in after him, glowering as she approached Enzo. "Your power unnerves me," she said through her teeth.

"Noted," Enzo said, releasing Ezekiel.

The owl-man gasped as his eyes returned to their normal color. He held a hand on his chest and panted as he stared at them. "W-what did you do to me?"

"I did what I had to. The more you comply, the less I'll have to take control."

Ezekiel nodded, trembling in his seat. "I should have known when you mentioned he was your brother, that you are of God-blood."

Enzo shrugged. "I can make you forget how it feels, if you'd like.

Sometimes I forget to wipe memories when I'm done, but it's not too late."

Sima cringed slightly, and Enzo could not deny the pang in his heart in response. "I forget you can do that."

"No, that's quite alright," Ezekiel said. "You wished to speak with me. I will answer your questions to the best of my ability."

"I think you know a whole lot more than you're telling us. I can't say I'm pleased about it," Enzo said. "Why don't you fess up to all you know about my brother instead of playing these games with us?"

"Your brother occasionally mingles with the people here, but it doesn't happen often. Other than that, there is not much information I can provide you."

Enzo leaned forward, causing Ezekiel to lean back as he got in the man's face. "I can tell when you're lying."

Ezekiel cleared his throat. "Perhaps my father *would* be better suited to answering your questions. Why don't I go look for him?

"Merit," Enzo said, jerking his head toward Ezekiel. "You go with him. He can't betray us if you've got your eye on him."

The Scout smiled. "Let's go, Zeke."

Ezekiel rose hesitantly but led the way out of Zadkiel's home with Merit directly behind him. With the two of them gone, Enzo refocused his attention on Sima. Her frown had deepened, and he noticed she continually touched the top of her head, as if it hurt.

Sensing her discomfort, Enzo let a burst of power pierce the walls, allowing him to gain information about the interior layout of the home. Once he located a bathing chamber, the edge of his desperation waned, and he pulled his power back.

"While we wait," Enzo said, "why don't we take Ezekiel up on his offer and rest while we can?" He locked eyes with Sima. "There's a bathing chamber upstairs. Let me prepare it for you."

In her usual fashion, Nariah rolled her eyes. "I'm sure she can prepare it herself."

Enzo frowned. "I agreed to allow the dissolution of our relationship, but I did not promise to stop caring for her. You cannot interfere with non-romantic acts of kindness."

The Scout stared him down for several long seconds before she looked away. "Fine, but be quick. She will wait here until it's done."

Enzo nodded. He caught Sima's gaze once more, letting a pulse of his devotion find her through their shared thread as he grinned. Despite the chaotic events and exhaustion, she returned a small smile herself. It was enough to fuel him as he flew up the stairs and located the bathing chamber.

He let out a sigh as he took in the unimpressive space, bare beyond a huge wooden tub. It was nowhere near worthy of Cosima's grace, and he wanted her to feel relaxed. Although he promised to temper the use of his power, he had accumulated a fair amount even in the short time since he released Ezekiel. Enzo's fingertips burned cold as he gently reshaped the space, contorting to his liking.

The ugly wooden tub was quickly replaced with a sparkling white stone one, with three small steps carved into the side. He tapped a finger against his chin as new items sprang into existence around him. Enzo lost himself in his desire to please her, hardly stopping to question if he was going overboard. His magic tapered off as he looked around.

There were flower petals floating among the strips of steam coming from the hot water and plush purple curtains over the window. He got rid of the excessive adornments, such as the billowing fabric on the ceiling above the tub, and focused on crafting her a new outfit to wear next. As the burgundy fabric filled his hands, he couldn't help but think back to the first time he had created a room just for her in the Depths. He tried then, too, to make the room feel natural, as though he hadn't crafted it entirely himself, in fear of what she might think.

Enzo shuddered, remembering how much of his power he poured into the underground city as he learned to properly wield the strange magic inside him. *That was before I understood that there is a darkness attached to me.* He squeezed his eyes shut, fighting off the flurry of tender emotions he was too afraid to face.

I can do this. I can learn to use this curse for good and save the people I love. I can be strong enough.

He folded up her outfit and put it beside two plush lavender towels on the edge of the tub. He brushed back his hair as he willed himself to contain his emotions. Enzo opened the door and was startled to see Sima standing there with her fist raised.

"I was about to knock," she said, with the most endearing smile Enzo had ever seen. "I didn't know if you were done or not."

Enzo stepped aside and relished the way her eyes lit up as she entered the bathing chamber. He poked his head out into the hall and let out a sigh of relief that they were alone. For now. He shut the door as quietly as he could and turned to find Sima with tears in her eyes.

"Thank you, Enzo," she whispered.

He rushed toward her and pulled her into his arms, despite knowing it was forbidden. She sank into him, her warm tears soaking his shoulder as he held her. "What's wrong, Sima? Is it your head?"

"I hit my head," she said softly, pulling away. He stopped himself from reaching for her again. "But that's not why I'm crying. Are you sure I'm worth all this effort, even though we can't be together?"

Enzo's face twisted in confusion. "What do you mean? I would do anything for you."

"Even if you get nothing out of it?"

"What are you talking about? You don't have to do anything to earn my love."

Her face fell. "You feel that way right now, but will you still feel that way in a few weeks?"

He did his best not to laugh. "I have been in love with you for over half a century."

Sima shook her head. "Forget I said anything."

"Where is this coming from? Have I done something to make you believe that I don't care about you?"

She chewed on her bottom lip. "I can't use my powers, but everyone else can. On top of that, your magic is so much stronger than I knew."

"And that makes you believe that I suddenly don't want you anymore?"

She didn't meet his eyes. "Yes."

This time, he did laugh. "I would love you with or without your abilities. I promise you that. This separation is temporary, Sima. Don't give up hope. Don't give up on us."

"I won't, but how can our love survive if we can't even touch each other?"

"Don't underestimate me. I am capable of showering you in adoration without ever laying a finger on you. Tell me how you want to be loved and I will do that."

She was quiet for a moment before she gazed up, her magnetizing brown eyes singing for him. "I want to feel like you truly see me for who I am outside of our circumstances. I want to feel understood by you. I want you to see me in a way no one else does."

He grinned. "You will have exactly that."

She raised a brow. "Are you sure? What if you don't know how to do that?"

"That's the beautiful thing about love," he said, "it makes you find a way. One of the most rewarding parts of loving you is finding all of the ways to prove it to you."

The door slammed open, and Nariah stormed in. "Alright, enough, you two. I shouldn't have to remind you of the restrictions," she scolded, shoving Enzo out of the room.

He glanced back at Sima, and the relief in her expression assured him he had at least taken some of the burden off her. Enzo made his way back downstairs and thought of their conversation. *I will do whatever it takes,* he promised internally.

Chapter 19

Ivo

"This is certainly an underwhelming task," Nariah said with one hand on her hip. "But it beats fending off the locals. Where should we start?"

Old books concealed the walls from view, the texts in some places touching the ceilings. Stacks sat in front of stuffed shelves, and the entire room carried the scent of paper and ink. Ivo scanned the cramped library on the main floor of Chief Zadkiel's home, her stomach still full from the meal Vincenzo had cooked up with food he created from his power. She had been grateful for a chance to sit without the immediate threat of dying looming over her head. Now, however, they had a new task to attend to.

Enzo and Merit were busy upstairs with the Chief, attempting to glean what useful information they could from him. That left Ivo, Sima, and Nariah to dig through the overflowing books in his library for clues. Searching through written history was a specialty of Ivo's, especially with all of the censorship Aurelio enacted during his fifty-year reign, and she was ready to get her hands on some books.

"Seems any spot will do," Ivo said, squinting her eyes to read the titles on the spines. "I say we start picking them up and reading through them. Something should stand out eventually."

"Good idea," Sima said, moving a stack off one of two chairs in the room to take a seat. "Enzo mentioned seeing what he thought might be blueprints in Ezekiel's mind. Might be worth keeping an eye out for them."

Ivo nodded as she perused through one of the shelves. She selected a dusty burgundy book with flowery black borders along the cover. Her fingers thumbed through the pages as she skimmed the words, waiting for something to jump out at her. As she did so, she could not help feeling as though she were being watched.

She glanced up and made eye contact with the Scout, who had been staring at Ivo over her own book. Ivo looked away quickly, unsure what to make of the way her heart raced in response to Nariah's quiet attention. When her gaze inevitably made it back to Nariah, she found the Scout had resumed reading, with an arrogant smirk.

Ivo's grip tightened around the hardcover as she willed herself to ignore the pointless antagonizing. *She enjoys tormenting you,* she thought, *don't give her the satisfaction of getting beneath your skin.* Her burgundy book seemed to be a summarized record of history prior to the people settling in Riejj. She shoved it back onto the shelf and selected a burnt sienna book next. As she read, Sima and Nariah conversed near a shelf with an unnatural lean.

"This text seems to indicate the people had their own mining operations in the mountains prior to the creatures turning into reawakened monsters," Nariah said.

"Have you seen anything regarding the stones having power?" Sima asked. "I have a strange feeling about Carmine and the people from Riejj. It's clear that fungi-covered beasts are a sign that life-force transfer is happening, but why would he use that magic to help protect the population inside the canyon?"

"Maybe he needs them alive." Nariah tossed a book and picked up another in a fluid motion. She flipped through it, hardly regarding the pages. "I haven't seen anything yet about magic or life-force in the stones. Either way, this is precisely what the Divinity asked us to look into if we came across it. These crystals are becoming like a spreading infection across the galaxies. We should continue to investigate the stones while we are here."

Ivo wrinkled her nose. "Is that the best plan? We are here to kill Carmine and move on. Sima is indebted to the Kingdom until she murders three brothers. We don't have time to spend on side quests."

Nariah glared at Ivo. "We can complete both. There is no reason to ignore the presence of the stones, especially if there is something suspicious happening with them. We will have time to kill Carmine and collect evidence."

Sima raised her brows and stuck her nose in a book, determined not to interfere with their bickering. Her friend did not have to defend herself when Ivo was around, because she would always fight for Sima's best interests.

"That's not what we came here to do," Ivo said, crossing her arms. "The High Priestesses may have asked you to investigate, but your primary objective should be the same as mine—protect and aid Sima however we can until we finish the mission. I am not letting you throw all of our futures away on a breadcrumb trail for shiny gems. Can't the Kingdom send Scouts later to collect evidence?"

"That doesn't mean the evidence will still be here by the time the additional reinforcements arrive." Nariah's gaze darkened. "I have yet to report the deaths of Earnest and Horacio. Technically I should have already sent an alert back to the Kingdom, but I'd prefer if we had something substantial to offer the Divinity before we invoke their wrath."

Ivo's stomach sank. "They can't blame her for their deaths. Carmine had the owl people ambush us."

"I am doing what I can to keep this situation from falling back on Sima. Finding more information about the stones can only benefit us."

That was not how Ivo saw it. In her mind, every second not spent with the objective of killing Carmine was a waste. Whether it was her mortality that made her anxious to get it over with or her desire to get away from Nariah, Ivo did not want to chase dead-end clues when so much more was at stake.

"How do you feel about this?" Ivo asked Sima.

Her friend chewed her fingernail as she considered the question. "As much as the crystals concern me, I think you're right. We can't be hunting down information when Carmine could be plotting against us at this very moment. Doc Santoro and Vincenzo spent decades researching them, and there is still so much they do not know about the stones. We don't have the luxury of devoting time to an investigation."

Ivo crossed her arms and took pleasure in Nariah's stormy expression. "That settles it then. We should focus on Carmine's control over these people. Collect evidence on your own if you get the chance, but Sima and I are not going to."

Nariah grumbled something under her breath but continued sorting through the pile closest to her. Ivo couldn't help but smile at the fact that she had finally gotten the irritating Scout to be quiet. Ivo returned to her shelf, determined to find something undeniable about Carmine in Zadkiel's library. Something Nariah would have no choice but to commend her for finding. She took a step back and stared at the shelf, hoping one of the books would call to her.

If I were hiding something about the man I thought to be a God, where would I put it? Ivo thought as she tapped her finger against her lip. *I wouldn't put it in a cramped room. I would want to keep it safe.*

Ivo walked to the door and peered out into the hallway. At the end of it, she noticed a small altar with wood carvings, trinkets, and other offerings on top of a rich red tablecloth. She left the room and crept toward it, enamored by the glowing white candles inside a golden bowl.

"Where are you going?" Nariah asked harshly. "Come back here."

She ignored the Scout and approached the altar. A chill ran through her as she studied the face that was carved into all the wooden statues. *Carmine.* She knew without a doubt it was him, his features so similar to Aurelio's that it set her on edge. A lump beneath the red tablecloth caught her eye, and Ivo stepped back to get a better glimpse of it.

Nariah walked up behind her. "Hey, what do you think you're doing?"

"There's no way the Chief left anything about Carmine in that library. How did we not notice this altar on the way in?"

"The sunlight," Nariah said, pointing to the window on the left side of the altar. "As the sun rose, the light came through and illuminated it. It was probably too dim for us to make it out when we arrived."

Ivo nodded. "Something is under there." She crouched down and lifted the tablecloth. Beneath it, she found three books bound with mysterious black, scaled leather and a brown journal with a navy tie to hold it shut. "I knew it. Help me with these."

Nariah sighed and held her hands out, accepting the three larger books. Ivo kept the journal for herself and unfastened the tie. She flipped it open and began reading. The Scout tapped her foot and blew out a breath, as if she were bothered by Ivo's discovery.

She sped through the first few pages, sucked in by the detailed research recorded on the pages. Each entry was sophisticated and meticulous, delving into the parameters of the prophecy over the lives of the Sacred Twelve. It was noted in the margin that much of the information was spread through word of mouth, but several entries described the messages delivered by trusted Oracles.

"This is Carmine's journal," Ivo said, her jaw falling open.

"Let me see," Nariah said, snatching it.

"Give it back." Ivo tore it from the Scout's hands and held it behind her. "Ask *nicely.*"

Nariah clenched her jaw, her gaze heavy as she stared down her nose at Ivo. "No. I have every right to see it."

For some reason, Ivo's heart pounded in her chest, as if she were preparing to brawl with the Scout. "That may be true, but for right now, I have it. If you want it from me, you're going to have to ask politely."

The Scout surged forward, seizing Ivo's arm with one hand and reaching behind her back with the other. Ivo resisted, and the two locked eyes as they wrestled for control of the journal. Nariah's wisteria gaze captivated her, making her heart speed up and her mind slow down. Their bodies pressed against one another, and the sensation was so thrilling, Ivo forgot for a moment that she couldn't stand her.

Distracted, she released the journal, and Nariah abruptly retreated, causing Ivo to stumble. Her cheeks flushed as she brushed her hair from her face. As the Scout read, Ivo started to walk back to the library where Cosima still searched through books, but Nariah gently grabbed her arm.

"What?" Ivo asked harshly.

"Carmine talks about trying to find a way to break the curse. He has collected invaluable research into the prophecy of the Sacred Twelve. This is an incredible find. An incredibly *lucky* find."

Ivo jerked her arm free. "This again?"

Nariah tilted her nose up. "I can sense alterations to the threads of Fate, so I can confirm you are not directly enacting changes on the Weave, but perhaps you have the ability to influence it somehow. I have a drop of blood from the Celestial Empress, Kismet, but blood from any of the three sisters of Fate can grant powers like the ones I think you have."

Her heart squeezed. There was nothing Ivo wanted more than to have a purpose amongst the galaxies, but her pessimistic mind found it difficult to believe she had the power to influence the Weave. Ivo had been unlucky her entire life, why would that have changed now?

A crash came from the library, and Ivo and Nariah reacted instantaneously, both rushing toward Cosima. As they pushed through the doorway, they found her beneath a pile of books, giggling her head off. The precariously leaning stack had toppled over her, a fact which Sima seemed to find amusing.

"Are you alright?" Ivo said, tossing books off Sima's body.

"Normally, I would have used my powers to stop it from falling," she said with a smile. "But rules are rules."

Nariah glowered beside them. "I thought something horrid had happened to you."

Ivo couldn't help but grin as she tugged Sima to her feet. A laugh escaped them both as Ivo dusted her off. During what had proved to be an emotionally tense time, Ivo was grateful for the relief that laughter brought with it. When they pulled themselves together, Ivo filled her in on the journal they found.

"Let's see what else it says," Sima said, her eyes wide. "Who knows what we may find?"

Vincenzo

The dust in the air tickled Vincenzo's nose as he rifled through the stuffy office, tossing objects aside without concern. Behind him, Merit did the same, rooting through files and old books for anything that would prove useful. In other areas of the house, the sounds of the women doing their inspections wafted through the open office doors. At the heavy wooden desk sat the Chief, Zadkiel, stone-faced.

Zadkiel was a burly man with murky gray feathers. He shared some obvious resemblance to his son, Ezekiel, in the way his facial feathers gave him a sharp glare, no matter his true emotions. The only reason Vincenzo knew exactly how Zadkiel felt was because his magic held the Chief's weak brain in its clutches, ensuring he would cause no trouble for them. The steady stream of power gave him clarity he hadn't experienced since his time on Haelos, awakening all of his senses like a needle full of enhanced energy straight into his bloodstream.

The elder Chief did little to protest, and the magic spent controlling him was a positive byproduct of the interaction as far as Vincenzo was concerned. Enzo flipped through the pages of a book with a newer cover, not worn down with time and use, when a diagram caught his eye. It was a scaled recreation of the canyon, including mapped caves and tunnels on the interior of the mountain sides.

The quicker his eyes scanned the text in the margins, the angrier he grew. Ezekiel was more than aware of where Carmine hid. In fact, it appeared Ezekiel and Zadkiel were equally responsible for actively covering up his whereabouts.

"What is this?" Enzo seethed, slamming the book in front of Zadkiel.

Enzo reined back his power only a fraction, allowing Zadkiel to resurface, aware of the world around him once more. Merit shot him a warning glare before glancing over his shoulder toward the sound of the women laughing down the hall.

"Hm?" Zadkiel mused quietly. His eyes were brighter, clearer. "What?"

"What do you need these secret passageways for? Who uses them?"

"They are for maintenance on the canyon, for sustaining our people," Zadkiel droned, as though he had regurgitated this nonsense hundreds of times before. "We must be able to access the forest in order to hunt and gather supplies such as wood. The regular citizens are not permitted access."

"Who does the work, then?" Enzo asked.

"The enslaved."

"Pardon?" Enzo choked. "Who have you enslaved to do the work?"

Zadkiel blinked. "I did not enslave them."

"What the fuck does that mean?" Merit's cheeks flushed red.

"I do not know where the insects come from."

"Insects?" Merit twisted his nose in confusion. "There are bugs working in the canyons?"

Zadkiel did not react.

Enzo pushed instead. "Who enslaved them if you did not?"

"The God of Terror."

Vincenzo could not help but roll his eyes at the name these people had given his brother. "Why won't you help us punish him? If we can kill him, we can free you all," Enzo offered.

"He is the only thing protecting my people." Zadkiel's voice was flat. "Without our God, my people will die. We will be forced to become monstrous beasts after we die or be ripped limb from limb. I am sick of seeing entrails."

"He protects them?" Merit approached Enzo. "Doesn't seem like Carmine's type of deal."

"What do you give him in exchange for his aid? He enslaves the insects to work in the canyon, but what promises your safety?" Enzo crouched, staring directly at Zadkiel's semi-frosted-over eyes.

Too much control over Zadkiel's mind would numb him, making him incapable of speech. Too little, and he could break free, causing a ruckus before Enzo could snatch him up again. Zadkiel had not shielded his mind, a trick Enzo knew Carmine would never teach someone he, too, planned to mentally manipulate.

"Shut the doors," Enzo commanded, ensuring he kept his voice low enough for only Merit to hear.

Merit moved, completing the task. He stood with his back against the doors, arms crossed in front of him.

"Do as you must, bird-brain. I am sure it's easy for you to get along with your owl cousins, but make it quick. Nariah won't like this."

Carmine wanted Ezekiel and Zadkiel open for the taking. It explained the lack of clear information. At most times, the men were in a drugged haze when around Enzo's brother. His lip tugged in a sneer, considering the blood he shared with Carmine. His mother's magic made his brothers evil, corrupt.

In Vincenzo's veins, their mother's blood equally made him angry, volatile. He had been violent in his past, exploding with sheer impulsive rage when met with disrespect. It had been how he survived, but also how he had protected himself. With time, he had grown tired of being angry.

Enzo tipped Zadkiel's head back, placing his palm flat on his forehead. He tempered the wave of half-riled anger that begged for escape. He tucked it far away and focused on flooding Zadkiel's mind. The people who inhabited the planets all reacted differently to his magic. There was no telling exactly how to achieve the results he wanted in this world, but with time, he would work out all the kinks.

"Tell me exactly where to find him," Enzo whispered. "Don't fight it, give in. I won't take no for an answer. If you think your people are safe, it is only because I still allow it. There is nothing, *nothing*, that will stop me from finding my brother and slaying him. Tell me, Zadkiel. Where is my brother?"

"Brother?" wheezed Zadkiel, his voice so low, Enzo almost missed it.

Enzo leaned closer. "You are resisting, Zadkiel. Do as you are told."

"He is in the western atrium. It is accessible only if you take flight from the Red Feather Tower and enter through the hatch found between two boulders."

"What matters of defense does he have?"

"He is the God of Terror. He needs no other defense."

Enzo rolled his eyes. "Will he be able to sense us coming?"

"If he does not already know you are here, he will absolutely know when you arrive at the hatch."

Enzo nodded. If his brother's mind manipulation powers worked anything like his, then he would need to be within a certain range to be able to detect the brains of others. Although Enzo himself could not detect all life forms within range, it would not surprise him if Zadkiel was correct, and Carmine could.

"We can come up with a plan," Merit said. "We know where he hides out now. If we scope it out, there's no reason we can't ambush him."

"What do you give him in exchange for protection?" Enzo pressed again. The question nagged at him.

"Sacrifices." Zadkiel's eyes blinked independently of one another.

Merit went rigid beside Enzo. "What type of sacrifices?"

"The experimental kind."

Enzo grabbed Zadkiel by the throat, his power roaring as it tunneled deep into the man's psyche. He had had enough of playing games and pulling teeth for information. There were more important issues to address. The inside of Zadkiel's mind was as dusty as his office.

Breaking through his memories and searching for accurate information could prove to be difficult. Searching through a brain was not the same as rifling through a filing cabinet. Each brain categorizes information differently. Because the Goddesses all took turns creating souls and vessels for the people of the world, their minds could prove challenging if the avenue of organization was unfamiliar to him.

Zadkiel was motionless beneath his grip, but inside his mind, an aching heaviness seeped into Vincenzo's chest. The rawness of others' emotions was partially why Enzo refrained from this level of intrusion. It was messy to navigate, whether with his powers or his feelings. Somewhere in the distance, Zadkiel's love and pride for his people sang a haunting song of loss and everlasting perseverance.

Enzo could physically feel Zadkiel's pain through his magic, the way he vowed to protect his people. It would have thrown him off his guard if Enzo hadn't been careful. He knew better than to underestimate the shadows lurking within those who writhed against his invasion of their minds.

What Zadkiel had to hide was not malicious in nature. It was a struggle so pure, so devoted, that it clouded the Chief's judgment. The actions that followed Zadkiel's vow to Carmine were more gruesome than Enzo expected. Knowing his brother was involved, however, meant he wasn't surprised. In fact, his brother was desperate for attention and recognition— enough so that he would be attending a party the citizens were throwing. Enzo considered it to be the perfect chance to pounce on his brother. When he had everything he needed, he released Zadkiel, turning his back as the Chief slumped to the floor.

Enzo stood frozen, processing everything he had seen inside Zadkiel's mind. All of the power he held over the Chief and his son had been worth it for the information he found. In a short period of time, he was able to uncover Carmine's location and gained insight into the owl-like people's contribution to his brother's shameful attempts to remain fully concealed. Enzo's hands were ice cold and trembling at his sides as his heart rioted, picturing the moment he would choke the life out of Carmine.

Merit snatched him by the arm, his grip piercing as he snapped Enzo out of his haze. "What did you get?"

Enzo met his gaze before jerking his arm free. "Carmine is making his own life force crystals. The one the chicken wore was not stolen from Aurelio. It was used as a threat. Before he died, Aurelio would taunt Carmine through magic, mocking letters, and explosions made from crystal powder."

"That's all you got?" He kicked his foot. "Makes sense why Letika and Ezekiel were worried about the dead rising. Must be the ones Carmine stole life-force from.

His mind flicked to the other information he had learned. Beyond knowing where in the mountains his brother hid, he knew Carmine would be at tonight's event hosted by the people of Riejj. If there was one thing the Sacred Twelve seemed to adore, it was being revered as Gods.

Enzo smiled. "We need to find something nice to wear. There is a party tonight."

"A party? I thought you were bloodthirsty."

"I did my share of work today, and I demand leisure." He kept his suspicion about Carmine's plan to show up to himself. "My magic needs to accumulate to its fullest before I am willing to attack him head-on. What better way to recuperate than with wine and my beautiful woman spinning to music in my arms?"

Merit's jaw tightened. "You know you can't do that, Enzo."

He frowned. "I am sick of being ordered around. Either clip my wings yourself like you've always wanted or get out of my way for one night. I don't know why you've decided to help me anyway."

Merit smirked. "You brought us here, we might as well complete the job. I'll look that much better when I bring your head on a pike to the Divinity."

"I'd love to see you try," Enzo laughed.

"You'll get away with as much as I say, feathers, don't forget it."

Enzo ignored Merit's pitiful attempt to assert his dominance in favor of more appealing company. Cosima's voice floated like silk through the closed doors, meaning she was near. If the sound of her voice didn't command him so fluidly, Enzo might have given Merit the painful reminder he needed that he was not the one in charge. Instead, he let himself be guided towards the only thing that made any sense for him in this melancholy lifetime, leaving Merit to clean up the mess.

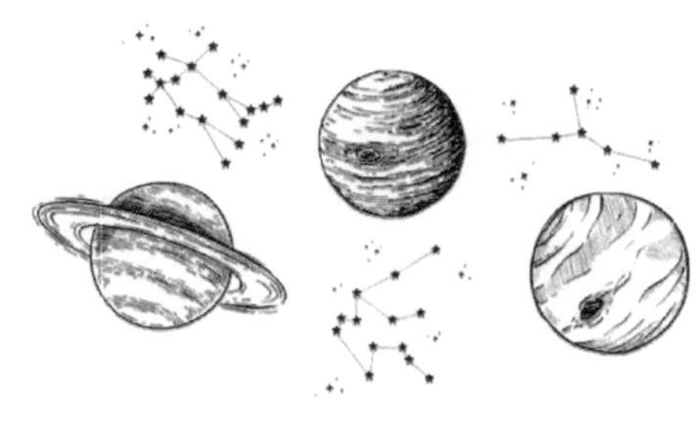

Chapter 20

Cosima

What could it all mean? Sima wondered as she tucked her legs beneath her in her chair. She flipped through Carmine's notebook, searching for useful information as Ivo dramatically recited lines from a poetry book she found hidden in a drawer. It had been handwritten, which only made her friend more insistent in reading it aloud.

"This one says: 'Seas of murky green to skies of inky blue, until our shade fairs purple, only pain is true. Three suns on the horizon, two moons below. The tether tightens, and the black bird crows. What becomes of us all is not for us to know.' This one makes less sense than the one about the lambskin."

"At least the lambskin one had a better rhyme scheme," Nariah murmured. "I doubt even the poet knew what he meant to say."

Sima rolled her eyes and turned the page. As her eyes skimmed, they caught sight of something important. It was in a section where Carmine was recalling the first time he learned of Aurelio's ability to strengthen stone with spilled blood.

"The mortals of this planet have stood no chance against the hellish demons Aurelio brings me. Those who did not find a way to flee became sustenance for evil, and those who hid were eventually found. I wonder how any of them have managed to live, but if I had to guess, some of the mortals must have powers that delay the inevitable."

"He taunts me. Each day that passes, all I can do is wait like a ground-dwelling bug, burying myself in the sand in hopes I can miss being seen. When I least expect it, he returns. At times to open up a portal in the sky—through which he drops more angry mangled flesh and muscles—at others to deliver a message. That was the case today."

"His message was hauntingly precise—come out and die like a man, or he'll trap my essence in a stone. It drives me mad trying to figure out how he uncovered such a process, but I know he is telling the truth. I have seen the creatures, and beneath their mangled forms, I see their old bodies exploding with overgrown, fresh, and fungus. He has turned the bodies of mortals into gruesome things and he threatens to do the same to me. What power would he gain from my essence? If the life-force in the mortals could give him the ability to level a planet, what could be said for the essence of a God?"

Sima's hands trembled as her eyes repeatedly scanned the last line. The door opened, and in wafted a familiar energy. She glanced up at Enzo and her heart skipped. Though she had fears over Carmine's journal, she could not deny she was happy to have Vincenzo nearby. Even with dust all over him, he was handsome.

"What do you need?" Nariah asked him.

"We are done with Zadkiel for now," Enzo replied.

Merit popped into the room and pointed over his shoulder. "Nariah, I need to run some things by you. It's important."

Nariah sighed and walked out of the room, leaving the door open. Sima glanced down at the notebook in her hands and stood up.

"Ivo found this. It's Carmine's journal. There's quite a bit of information in here, but there's something that stuck out to me." She found the section and handed the notebook over, holding her breath as he read it. "Well, what do you think?"

His brows were tightly knit together. "It is concerning. I'm not sure if the essence of Caelari can be captured by crystals, but there's a chance. I spoke to you about attempting to contain my starlight inside them, but most of the stones were not strong enough to properly harness the energy. If Aurelio found a stone strong enough, perhaps it's possible. It isn't a good sign that he was thinking about it at all, as it likely means he was conspiring with my mother on it."

Ivo rubbed her shoulder. "Are the stones the same on every planet? Can any stone be turned into a weapon?"

Enzo shook his head. "As far as I am aware, the stones are different in every world. Each world is created with unique specifications, which results in a massive variety of fauna and mortal races as they must adapt to the constraints. Haelos and its people were made to be companions, which is likely why Aurelio first used the mortals there to experiment with. When I would speak with Doc Santoro on this, he would always remind me that the stones carry significant risk as most are incredibly unstable."

Sima's gut twisted. "What about the stone around the neck of the creature the people here called a protector?"

Enzo's brows lifted. "Ah, yes, Salvatore. From what I learned from Zadkiel, the crystal itself came from outside of this world. I saw a strange crater caused by a heavy impact."

"Why would Aurelio send Carmine weapons he could use to defend himself with?" Sima asked.

Something about the journal unsettled her. Twelve brothers all fighting to be the last alive, pinned against one another by their own mother, with the Fate of the Eternal Kingdom resting in the balance. Several of the brothers had already been slain by the time Sima was finally free from Aurelio, and yet she couldn't help but wonder if they were truly dead or were simply better than Carmine at remaining unseen.

Ivo shrugged. "Maybe it wasn't Aurelio that sent them. What if Ehses was covering all of her bases just in case her main pick was killed?"

"That's true," Enzo replied. "I don't believe my mother is above betraying any of us. Either way, we can spend more time thinking it over later. We have somewhere to be tonight, and we can't go looking like this."

"Why are we here?" Ivo asked, staring into the wide-open room with several mannequins draped in fabric.

"There is supposedly some sort of celebration occurring tonight." Nariah ushered Ivo further into the room with her hands. "We are to dress the part and make peace with the locals."

Cosima took a seat in the available armchairs corralled by a large mirror on the back wall while Nariah stood with her arms crossed near the front entrance. Every once in a while, the Scout pulled back the curtain and peered outside. The room had plenty of space to accommodate multiple gowns with five-foot wide skirts and a handful of tailors' stations, ready to attend to ten women at once.

"A celebration? How will that smooth over the locals calling us murderers?" Ivo asked.

Ivo walked up to one of the headless mannequins and rubbed the material between her fingertips. The fabric was a bright color, more vibrant than she had seen any of the citizens wear during their heated interactions. It had not been a formal occasion then, however. She stole a glance at Nariah, who seemed more on edge since Ivo's discovery of Carmine's journal.

"Apparently, Vincenzo and Merit have been able to…sway the Chief into declaring us special guests of the evening," Nariah said. "Ezekiel spoke with some of those who were enraged with us previously and has done his best to smooth things over. We should be able to attend the event without incident. Either way, it gives me the opportunity to study the locals and search for more clues around the stones."

Ivo huffed. She still did not believe Nariah should be wasting her time focused on the crystals. It was not their job to hunt for clues. They were here for one reason only—killing Carmine. Her hand drifted toward a blue fabric, like ice floating above the deep ocean, allowing its magnetizing color to cool her frustrations.

"Vincenzo says it could be a fun time," Sima added, though the look on her face told Ivo her friend was plagued with doubts. "Perhaps it would do us well to take a night off from the stress."

"I won't say no to a party," Ivo said, inspecting the holes in the fabric meant for wings, "but I don't think any of this is going to fit me."

Nariah tapped her foot. "Someone is going to assist us. They will be here any minute."

While Ivo was entertaining herself by sorting through the yards of folded fabric inside the built-in storage hutch, two women walked in. Ivo almost missed their appearance entirely, as they were near silent, and walked in with their heads bowed. Both women had distinctly different features than Ezekiel. They were on the shorter side, but shared striking baby blue feathers with white around their eyes. It made them appear softer, kinder than the others they had encountered in their time here.

"Welcome, esteemed guests," one said.

"We will begin measurements so we may tailor the outfits for you," said the other.

"I am Nariah." She pointed to the others. "Ivo and Cosima."

"I am Jasira, this is my twin sister, Delmira."

Ivo continued to sort aimlessly through the fabric, her hands gliding across them as she watched the sisters from the corner of her eye. A voice deep inside urged her to keep her guard up around any of the people in this city. Every interaction she had had with these citizens proved to be potentially deadly, and even if they dressed her in fancy clothing, she would know them for the dangerous sides of themselves they had revealed.

"Jasira, what sort of outfits are typical for this event?" Nariah asked.

"I would opt for a formal, tighter fit gown for your body type," Jasira said, waving a hand at her sister.

Delmira immediately took to measuring Nariah's limbs, adjusting her body as necessary. Cosima remained seated in the armchairs, noticeably withdrawn from the conversation. Since leaving the Chief's estate, Cosima had hardly spoken to either of them. Ivo left the fabric hutch and opted for an empty seat beside hers.

"You have very pretty eyes," Jasira said to Nariah as she sketched onto a small pad of paper. "I believe the best color to complement them in our inventory would be our clover green fabric. It is a very soft material called pahyasa. Breathable, but elegant."

Ivo rolled her eyes at Nariah's pleased expression. *She's eating up the attention.*

"Are you alright?" Ivo asked Cosima.

She shrugged her shoulders. "Something about Carmine's journal is not sitting right with me. I was looking through the last few entries, and I found a paragraph where he mentions three powerful prophecies, outside of the one around the Sacred Twelve." Sima glanced around before her gaze fell again. "Perhaps it's foolish, but I can't help but think one is about Kismet, and maybe…"

"Your mother?" Ivo asked, recalling Sima's desire to find her true family. "It makes sense to me. What does he say about them?"

Sima sighed. "He believes only the Celestial Empresses are capable of breaking the prophecy around the Sacred Twelve, but he mentions that this could potentially be circumvented if the Empresses were to lose power."

"So, what is his plan? To go after Kismet himself?"

Sima shrugged again. "I don't think so. Enzo hasn't spent much time looking it over, but he thinks Carmine is too cowardly to face the Empresses head-on. He did suggest that perhaps his brother is counting on someone else to take them out."

Jasira and Delmira looked in their direction. Ivo shot them a small smile, her stomach twisting as she met their eyes. As they turned their attention back to Nariah's fitting, Ivo turned to Sima.

"I don't like the sound of that. Killing a Celestial Empress seems impossible."

"I don't know," Sima said. "Enzo said there are two people that Zadkiel suspects of being 'eyes' for Carmine. Enzo thinks there is a good chance they will be at the celebration tonight. He plans to follow them if they return to his brother." Sima placed her head in her hands. "I still hardly know what to make of his journal, but I know it must contain something we can use. Perhaps not now, but when we hunt down the others."

Ivo tucked her hair behind her ear. "We will have more time later to sort through all of Carmine's notes. I know it's hard to make sense of everything with such high stakes ahead of us, but maybe this night off could be good for us?"

Sima's frown seemed etched into her skin. Her friend's dreary mood reminded Ivo of the time they had spent with only each other to rely on in the Nuvola Palace on Haelos. Her heart sank as Sima attempted a small grin.

"Are you sure I can do this, Ivo? Together, we killed Aurelio. What if someone gets hurt? What if I can't save Haelos? With the time spent in the Eternal Kingdom and now with Nariah watching over me, I have had no time to practice my powers. What if I am not strong enough when the time comes?"

She considered her words as the twins led Nariah to a locked jewelry cabinet near the doors. Cosima was not someone Ivo would dare consider weak. In more ways than one, she had taught Ivo about what it meant to be strong. When Ivo's girlfriend had been murdered by Aurelio, it was Sima who had held her together. If there was anyone capable of overcoming the impossible, it was her best friend.

"I have never met anyone quite like you, and I know you are guided by a higher purpose. It doesn't matter if you've had years to practice or minutes, your magic is your own to command. You know it better than anyone." Ivo placed a hand over her friend's shoulder. "You are strong, Sima. More than anyone else I know."

"Thank you, Ivo. You are too."

"I don't know about that," Ivo replied with a lop-sided smirk. "I'm not as powerful as you or Enzo. If I were, then we would have taken care of Aurelio a long time ago."

Sima nodded. "You are very powerful, but in your own way. No one can replace you. You're just as much a piece of this puzzle as Enzo and I."

"How are you and Enzo coping with watchdog Nariah breathing down your neck?"

Sima's jaw twitched, and she swallowed hard. "I feel foolish for admitting it. I wish he and I had some normalcy. We haven't been given the option to sit and get to know each other. Instead, we are constantly on the run from something or hunting someone."

"What does normal even look like when you are dating a member of the Sacred Twelve, I suppose," Ivo said, gently nudging Sima with her elbow.

Delmira waddled by them with a long length of the light green fabric before the twins got to work pinning the material in various places around Nariah's body. It was not long before the gown took shape. Ivo ran her eyes along Nariah's impressive figure, stalling around her curvy hips. Ivo's heart began to race. Nariah had been the most infuriating piece of this mission, and now Ivo struggled to take her eyes off her.

"What do you think about the Scouts, Nariah and Merit?" Ivo asked, her eyes still latched to Nariah's body. "Too bad we can't leave them by the portal and meet up with them after we finish the job."

"They are not my favorite people, but sometimes I am thankful they are here to help us do this. I can't imagine if we had to come on our own, if I am honest."

"Nariah is not exactly easy to deal with. One second she's criticizing me, the next she's defending me with her life. I feel like I am trapped with someone who can't tell whether she wants to be the knife or the hostage."

"What bothers you the most?" Sima asked.

Ivo's expression soured. "I hate that everything has to be done her way. It makes me feel like I'm in a prison. There is not always a right way to do things, and sticking to the rules has only made this journey harder. I am sure if you and Enzo were allowed to use your magic to its fullest, we would have already found Carmine and had his head on a plate for the Kingdom."

Sima chuckled quietly as Jasira approached.

"Who is next?" she asked.

"I will go," Ivo said, rising from her chair. "I think changing my appearance is exactly the stress relief I need right now."

Ivo stood patiently as Jasira and Delmira took her measurements. Meanwhile, Nariah stepped out to bathe and prepare now that a majority of the tailoring was finished, her dress swishing delicately across the floor as she walked around. As much as Ivo tried to refrain from thinking about the way the Scout looked in her gown, Nariah's curves toyed with Ivo's mind. The more she hated her, the more she couldn't stop thinking about her.

Nariah slipped out of the dress, wearing a thin under-shirt and the pants from her Scout's uniform beneath. She shot Ivo an amused smirk before she walked out the door. Jasira picked a rich sapphire blue piece of pahyasa and began to pin it around Ivo. Within minutes, the once rectangular, unremarkable material now clung favorably to her chest and grew looser at the waist. Ivo blushed when she saw herself in the mirror. From where she was sitting, Cosima smiled and gave a thumbs-up.

"Return in two hours," Jasira said, with a piece of string and a needle between her lips. "I will have your gown finished by then. When you exit, turn to the right and continue to the last door in the hallway. There, you will find a private bathing chamber."

Ivo did as she was told, relieved that following the instructions led to a serene bathing chamber. In the center of the room, a spacious, wide-set tub sat, as if meant for cleansing with company. In the water, herbs from this planet floated along the surface, the smell calming and inviting.

She sighed, peeling off her clothes with tired, heavy limbs. They had not been on this planet long, and already Ivo was exhausted. Hopefully, the evening would prove useful on their hunt for Carmine. Ivo dipped a toe into the warm water and found the temperature was perfect. She sank into the tub, covering herself up to the tips of her shoulders. She rested her head back and closed her eyes.

"What do you think you're doing in here?"

Ivo sat up and gasped, hands flying to cover her chest. Her jaw hung open at the sight of Nariah standing with only a small towel covering her body. Ivo's cheeks blushed, eyes dragging with a crawling pace over every inch of the Scout's impressive figure.

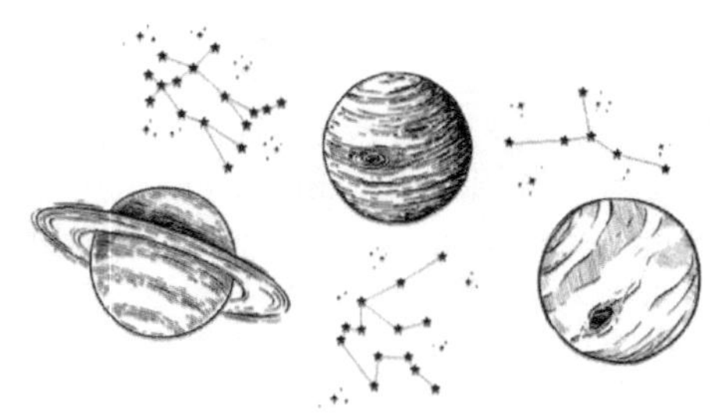

Chapter 21

Cosima

"Right this way," Jasira said, holding the door open wide for Cosima.

The hallway was empty, save for the few portraits of the people here and paintings featuring arrowheads and bows surrounded by flower arrangements. Nearly the entire city within the canyon was made of wood, with two or three thin stripes of bright primary colored paint to cover the walls.

"Are you sure I look alright in this?"

The dress featured a low plunge in the back, leading to ripples of shimmering red fabric just above her buttocks and a pool of red around her feet. The front was a touch more modest. The thin straps tied behind her neck, and her chest was concealed. Her shoulders were on display, but with her hair down, she felt less exposed.

"It is some of my best work." Jasira smiled. "We must get going. Your friends have not come back to retrieve their gowns, and you need to wash up."

Jasira led her down the hallway and through a door on the left into a small bathing chamber. The woman reminded Sima to be quick, undid the ties of her gown, and disappeared. Cosima made sure not to waste any time. She was eager to reunite with Vincenzo, as every minute in his absence felt extraordinarily long. However, she equally wished to avoid the celebration as her gut hollered that something was amiss.

She washed her hair and body with the soap provided, making sure to untangle every knot in her hair. After all they had been through, she was thankful for the opportunity to clean herself thoroughly. Being stuffed into a fancy gown and put on display had been a daily activity for her. Could she handle it again, with grace? Would the panic arise again?

At the mere thought, the anxiety caused it to manifest in her chest and throat. Sima placed a hand on her chest and tried to breathe. When it did not work as she intended, and her breaths became more shallow, she pulled herself from the tub. She shivered, the air cooler than she remembered. With shaky hands, she wrapped her hair in a towel and dried herself off.

You're spoiled goods, Aurelio's voice floated into her mind. *It's only a matter of time before Vincenzo finds out how worthless you really are. You're not lovable, you're usable.*

She swallowed hard. "I thought I was past all of this," Sima whispered, struggling to step into the gown. In frustration, she tossed it to the side and pressed her palms into her eyelids. "Why? Why? Why?"

She had survived the unthinkable on Haelos, and when faced with yet another uncertain future, she once again fought for her life.

Why did I survive all of that, just to feel inside like I never really left?

Each moment that reminded her of Aurelio, that reminded her of being trapped with no way out, she fought a whirlwind of agonizing memories. As strong as she tried to be through it, as much as she tried to hide it from the others, Aurelio haunted her and plagued her mind with negative thoughts.

For a time, the thrill and allure of Vincenzo's love helped her ignore the healing that needed to be done. She had used the hope of their connection to blind herself to her trauma, ignoring what lurked beneath the surface of her psyche. Now, outside of Haelos and the Eternal Kingdom, their dynamic had changed without their permission, leaving her with no choice but to confront what she had been hiding from.

Soon you'll disgust him the way you disgusted me, Aurelio whispered in her thoughts. *What will he think of your pathetic truth? How will he respond to the pitiful girl you are deep inside when you can no longer disguise it as strength?*

"No," Sima whispered back. "I deserve to be loved. Even if you never thought I was worthy."

Sima considered her appearance in the mirror, her brown eyes heavy with decades of pain. Her hair had begun to dry in some places, and she brushed it before it was too late to fix. Tears stung at the corners of her eyes, but she refused to give in, wiping them away before they had a chance to fall. Just as she had done thousands of times before, she mustered strength from a seemingly empty source within as she splashed cool water on her face.

She would kill Carmine and anyone else the Eternal Kingdom wanted her to, as long as freedom truly waited on the other side of it all. The thought of a future only she could command made her pause. She had not stopped to dream of what she might do with that freedom, but she craved it nonetheless.

As she applied color from a tiny silver pot onto her cheeks with a soft brush, her mind wandered back to Enzo. This time, she mentally recounted all the times she had seen him use his magic since he had arrived. Whether Nariah's constant disparaging of him was finally getting to her, or if her own power restriction made her feel insecure, Sima could not deny her concerns. She knew he was not like his brother, but Enzo was born a part of the Sacred Twelve. *Can he trust his powers? Can I?*

"Cosima?" a voice sounded from outside the bathing chamber door.

Sima snatched the discarded gown and slipped inside it. She gave herself one last chance to fix her hair before rushing to the door. In front of her stood Vincenzo, wearing an immaculate suit. The ensemble was a deep hunter green, paired with a cream-colored under-shirt. He smiled, before his eyes dipped to take in what she was wearing. He stepped closer.

"You are breath-taking, more beautiful than any cosmic creation," he said. His voice was warm and low. "I would love nothing more than to spend the evening with you by my side."

"It will be me *and* our Scouts, Enzo. We should leave now so we aren't late to the party."

He smiled. "Right, just one thing first." His eyes sparkled like the night sky as he pulled a small purple velvet jewelry box from his pocket. He popped it open and presented it to her with pride. "For you, my love."

Sima gasped. Inside the box was a set of stunning emerald earrings and a matching ring with a hefty gem and gold band. The ring reminded her of the one he had given her on her first night in Ombra. It had warned her of his movements and had played a vital part in Sima's trust of him. "Where did you get this? It looks just like…"

He shook his head. "I won't reveal my secrets. It was made to be identical to the one I gave you before, but the emerald is larger, and I thought the earrings would go well with your dress."

"The jewelry is lovely, Enzo," she breathed. "I love it."

"And I love you," he replied with a grin. She stared up at him, and a wave of soft excitement flushed her as he leaned closer. "I have been begging for time with you, and now it's here. As long as I am with you, nothing else matters. I am letting my power accumulate to its fullest, and for now, there is nothing more for us to do. We know where he is." His eyes dropped to her lips, before he gazed into her eyes again. "Allow me to be good to you and show you how badly I've been missing you."

Sima couldn't help but smile. "After all that time spent as prisoners, perhaps we deserve a little bit of fun." She took a step backward. "But, we can't be too close, Enzo."

He sighed. "As if I don't know how to be good to you without touching you. I will show you the best night of your life in a manner our Trine Scouts will approve of. Just give me a chance."

Sima searched his eyes. "We can live out our freedom with each other, as long as we make it that far. We can't risk losing it over breaking the rules, you know this, right?"

"Yes, of course."

"And your use of your power. Be…be careful, please. You have been using more of it than you did on Haelos, or at least that is how it seems."

Enzo's face twisted. "Sima, I have always expended considerable amounts of magic, one way or another. On Haelos, much of it went into the Depths. I have been cooped up with no outlet for long enough. My magic is helping us. I promise I won't use it unless it's necessary, but I am also not risking your life."

"Is that what this is about? You are doing this to protect me? You can't change the mind of every person that stands between us."

"Can't I?" His voice rasped with the slightest hint of desperation, tangled with the ghost of helpless anger.

Vincenzo pushed forward, pressing his forehead lightly into hers. One of his hands braced against the exposed skin of her lower back, pulling her against him. A soft breath escaped her, and she placed her hands against his chest, reveling in the thrill of touching him even when she should not. Her body tingled with anticipation, and she could not help but lean in closer.

"I promised you I would always find you, so long as you want to be found. I won't let anything keep you from me. Don't you understand you are all there is for me?"

Her heart skipped. Enzo's ability to disarm her with his words was a mercy as Sima wanted nothing more than to retreat into him again, despite her earlier turmoil. Her eyes fluttered shut, his scent filling the air around her. She could feel the thrum of his heart beneath her hands. Its pace mirrored her own, another moment of synchronization between the two of them.

"You're the only one who has my heart," Sima whispered. "There is no one who can make me feel the way you do."

"I told you I would wait for you forever," he breathed, their lips agonizingly close.

A flicker of doubt surfaced, causing her heart to skip. "I hope you mean that," she whispered before pulling back. As difficult as it was for her to restrain her desires, Sima thought of Haelos above her desire for Enzo. "Regardless of your feelings for me, you need to keep your power in check. I'm worried that you're not thinking clearly when you use it."

Vincenzo

Enzo held her gaze as his thoughts raged inside him. It tore him apart to know that in such a short period of time, he had already shocked her with his use of magic. The guilt was sour, but worse was the fact that he didn't want to stop using it. So far, the only progress they had made on this mission came about because of Enzo's magic. Still, he knew that was not the answer she hoped for.

"Are you afraid of me? Of my magic?" Enzo asked quietly.

She looked away. "It's not that I'm afraid of you…I am afraid *for* you. What if you make the wrong decision? What if you use more magic than you intended?" Sima curled her fist. "I asked you before, but I'll ask again. Are you telling me everything about your power?"

No, Enzo thought, hating the truth. If he confessed to her the full scope of his curse, would she still love him? If he told her that his power scared even him, could she ever feel safe around him again? *I can't lose you over this*, Enzo's mind—or perhaps his power—screamed inside him.

"Enzo?" Sima asked.

He shook off his thoughts. "I haven't told you everything, but it is not because I don't trust you enough to tell you. It's because I am in the process of testing and expanding these abilities. I don't want my magic to become another worry over your head."

Her nose scrunched as her eyebrows pinched together. "What happens if you make a mistake and it impacts me, or worse, Haelos? Do you know what's at stake here?"

"Of course, I do," he said. "This is not something you need to be concerned about. I keep myself in line, and I never use more of my magic than necessary. I have strict limits, and it takes great discipline to keep it this way. I am not putting anyone, especially not you, at risk."

She let out a soft sigh. "What does it feel like? When you use too much of it? How can you be certain you haven't gone too far?"

Enzo rocked on his heels. "It feels like the ocean is surrounding me, the pressure of the water restricting my body and my breaths. It's like suffocating on dirt beneath the surface. My magic gives me a great deal of warning before I get too close to crossing the line. I stop myself far before I get to the truly awful sensations."

The part Enzo didn't mention is that the painful experience felt like being reborn, as if his power was ripping him to shreds to configure him the way he should have always been. It was as if his magic was breaking him in order to fortify him into an unstoppable force.

"That sounds terrifying," Sima whispered. "I had no idea that it felt that way for you. My own magic feels dreadful, but nothing in comparison to yours."

"Your abilities are not dreadful, Sima. You have a magnificent power, but like my own, it can be difficult to accurately grasp. How does yours feel when you get too close to the edge?"

"I've run my reserves dry thousands of times, but ever since we left Haelos, I've felt like there is more beneath the surface. It is almost as if the true wealth of it is hidden somewhere deeper. Although, I have had few chances to put it to use."

He couldn't help but smile. *Could she understand me after all?* Enzo wondered. "Perhaps you're right. I experienced the same sensation."

"How did you break through it?"

Enzo clenched his jaw. "It happened after Aurelio nearly killed me, but I didn't understand what happened until…"

"Until what?" Sima asked, tapping her foot.

"Until you left the Eternal Kingdom without me."

Sima stepped closer and rested her head against his chest. "As much as I hate to admit it," she whispered, "I'm happy you're here. I don't know if I could do this without you."

He pressed a kiss on top of her head. "You can do anything, with or without me. I need you far more than you need me."

She chuckled and pulled away, her hand lingering in the space between them. "Shall we? Before Nariah becomes too suspicious of us."

He slid his hand into hers and gave it a small squeeze. Despite his confidence regarding Carmine, a tiny nagging voice inside his head told him he was still not strong enough to defeat him. He shooed the thought out of his mind and smiled at Sima.

"With you by my side, I am ready for it all."

The walk to the dance hall had been quiet, but in a serene sense. They enjoyed the simplicity of each other's company, all while she considered his words. He said he could give her a pleasant evening without having to touch her. While she appreciated the sentiment, there was a piece of her that longed for more of his body against hers.

The celebration was a birthday party for the Chief's son, Ezekiel. Banners hung with portraits of Ezekiel's distinctive eyes were plastered across them. The extra sets of eyes, whether real or painted, seemed to follow her every step she took into the room.

"Not the event I was expecting," Enzo said, "but we will make do."

The party had already started, and more people than she thought lived in the city were crammed inside. Some sat at tables, sipping on their drinks and chatting, while others danced to the lively music, bodies packed tight. The band members were dressed in black suits adorned with bright gold buttons and the tell-tale primary-colored stripes across their backs.

Sima cringed as she gazed around, following Vincenzo in search of the others. She expected to find the locals watching her, assuming their presence was unwanted. However, no one turned in their direction or showed signs of noticing they had arrived.

The citizens had gone from sticking arrowheads in her face to acting as if she were invisible. Thankfully, it did not take long for Sima to spot Ivo and Merit. As the two of them made their way through the crowd to where the others were seated, Sima scanned for Nariah, but did not find her.

"Ivo," Sima called, waving her hand.

Her friend waved back before holding up a glass full of a navy-colored drink, pointing to it with glee. Sima laughed and slid into an available seat. She turned to see where Enzo had gone, only to find he had disappeared.

"What is that?" Sima said, swiveling back to Ivo and Merit.

"I have no idea what is in this stuff, but it is amazing. It is a tad sweet, but this is my second glass, and boy, do I feel ready to dance." Ivo wiggled her body in her seat.

"You're already getting drunk? We weren't that late. Where is Nariah?"

Ivo ignored Sima's question, continuing to dance and sway in her chair.

Merit frowned. "Looking for you, I thought. Seeing as how you're here, she's probably running around mad, thinking you've vanished."

Sima cocked an eyebrow. "Unfortunate."

A glass appeared in front of her on the table, containing the same beverage Ivo had. She glanced up, and Enzo winked at her as he walked around the table. Ivo tipped her head back, finishing off the glass before he slid another drink in front of her as well.

"Ladies," Enzo said, flipping his chair around for his wings before taking a seat. "Merit."

"Took you long enough," Merit said, sucking his teeth.

"My apologies," Enzo said, placing a hand over his heart. He looked at Sima. "I took the liberty of preparing your favorite meal for you. It's being kept warm by some of the Riejj cooks. Let me retrieve it for you."

Sima smiled. "You made my soup? Just the way I like it?"

He beamed. "With the thinly sliced rice cakes and everything."

She could not help but blush as a strange, but comfortable sensation washed over her. "Thank you."

The moment Vincenzo stood up, so did Merit, leaving her alone at the table with Ivo.

"Finally," Ivo murmured as the two men wandered off, already bickering like hens.

"A brief moment of peace before Nariah finds us," Cosima said.

"About that," Ivo blurted. "Something strange happened. Earlier. To me. And her."

"What happened?" Sima asked.

"Nariah and I…" Ivo trailed off. She glanced behind Sima, and her eyes widened.

"Nariah and you, *what?*" growled Nariah.

The Scout stood with her arms crossed in front of her chest. She wore the gown made by Jasira and Delmira, only now it was fully finished. Even Sima could not deny that Nariah looked incredible, regal, and furious, all in one.

"Were you searching for me?" Sima interjected.

Nariah looked her up and down. "Yes. Where were you?"

Sima waved her hands in front of her dress. "I was the last to have my dress tailored. Plus, I was not going to waste my chance to wash away the past couple days."

"Don't let me find out you were with…*him*. You know the rules."

"I am well aware of the rules." Sima dropped her gaze.

"What are you thinking?" Nariah asked. "You're doing nothing to distance yourself from him. I know you've seen his flippant use of his powers. Are you sure you can trust him?"

Sima swallowed to avoid flinching at Nariah's words. "He is trying to help."

Ivo glared at Nariah. "Why are you so against him?"

"How could I not be?" the Scout snapped. "Cosima, have you even stopped to ask yourself why he would volunteer you to kill his brothers? An arguably dangerous mission, putting you directly within the grasp of each of his killer siblings, without even the ability to protect yourself? He is the one who gains the most from your success."

Her heart pounded, and a strange sensation swirled inside her ribcage. "Enzo wouldn't do that. He wouldn't use me to steal the spot from his brothers. He did it because he knew there would be no other way for me to prove myself. The High Priestesses were ready to make a decision without hearing all of the evidence. They were never going to spare me. At least this way I can earn my freedom."

Ivo crossed her arms. "Besides, aren't you always telling Sima that *you* are here to protect her? Add Enzo, Merit, and me on top, and she's hardly here alone. He did what he thought was best for her. At least he tried."

Nariah narrowed her eyes at Ivo. Her friend squirmed beneath the Scout's heavy gaze, and Sima wondered what it was that Ivo had attempted to confess before Nariah arrived. The Scout turned her head and focused on Sima instead.

"Don't say I didn't warn you."

The music played by the band grew louder, each note brimming with energy. From one entrance, Sima spotted Ezekiel waltzing in with a woman on his arm. She had pastel rose-colored feathers and unlike Ezekiel, had a roundness to her features in place of angles. People from the crowd surrounded them, begging for scraps of attention. Ezekiel was adored by his citizens to a degree Cosima had not realized.

She turned to find Nariah equally interested in the scene unfolding, her eyes locked onto Ezekiel.

"Why do they bow to him like this?" Nariah asked, her words laden with disgust.

"Question is, how did we not notice this until now? I knew they were obedient, but they treat him like their personal hero." Sima drummed her fingers on the table. She couldn't place why exactly, but the blinding adoration left a nagging feeling in the back of her mind. *Aurelio and his brothers took delight in being worshiped. Why then does it bother me?* She glanced around for Enzo. *He wouldn't be like…would he?*

Ivo sat stiffly beside her. Sima looked between her and Nariah, sensing the way the two seemed intent on ignoring one another. Nariah stood beside their table, her body angled away from Ivo. Commotion rang out from somewhere in the crowd of dancing bodies filling the open floor. Nariah immediately hunted the source, leaving them behind.

"What's happening?" Ivo asked.

Screams so loud and terrifying that they lit a fire of goosebumps across her skin had Sima on her feet within seconds. Ivo followed, sticking close to her side as they tried to understand what was happening. Only minutes prior, Ezekiel had entered the party to cheers and excited faces. Now bodies ran in every direction, the crowd pulling and pushing them both as the chaos grew.

Someone slammed Ivo to the ground, and others trampled on top of her, despite Sima's protests and attempts to tug her back to her feet. Sima collided with the floor, losing her balance with the movement of scared citizens traveling in every direction. With a pulse of her magic, she froze time within the hallway, allowing her to pull Ivo from the floor.

The two of them ran and Sima released the time halt that kept a portion of the crowd frozen in place. The screaming continued, magnifying the ache in Sima's ears and body. She linked her hand with Ivo's and ran toward the closest exit as the room was thrust into darkness, only occasional flashes of light allowing them to navigate the chaos. They stomped through spreading puddles of blood and jumped over limbs and torn apart bodies. Her eyes caught glimpses of the sea of dead that littered the floor, but she focused on breaking them out of the room, using her control over time strategically to move them through faster.

Once through the doors, Sima scanned around them, trying to gather herself enough to navigate the halls. Blood-curdling screams paired with a strange, almost electric buzz filled their ears, causing Sima and Ivo to fall to their knees. Intense magic gripped her brain, blurring the line between reality and tactile nightmares. The high, oscillating pitch of the buzz was maddening, enough to clear her brain of every thought, consumed only by the desire to stop the pain the power caused her.

Sima writhed on the floor, her palms wet as she tried to block the sound from her bleeding ears. For a moment, she thought the piercing sound would render her unconscious, until a hand wrapped around her throat. With her air blocked off, she flailed her limbs. The buzz continued relentlessly, making even opening her eyes and observing her attacker impossible.

As Cosima fought to survive, the mayhem continued around them. Her hands grasped wildly at her attacker's hold on her throat. Tears and blood mixed together in her hair and ear canals. She forced her eyes open, finally getting a view of the person intent on ending her life.

A man with frost-white hair and brown eyes grinned ear to ear as his grip on her tightened. His insane glee in taking her life was plastered across every blood-splattered inch of his face. She knew this was Carmine. Not only in the ways his features resembled Aurelio's, but also in the toxic threat his aura emanated. For a moment, Carmine's face morphed into her former husband's, perfectly reanimating her nightmares.

Every piece of Cosima froze.

He leaned closer, pressing his lips to hers. Sima tried to break free, but he used his other hand to hold her firmly in place. His tongue pushed into her mouth, sweeping through her mouth hungrily. Sima's body recoiled in response to his revolting intrusion as he pulled back an inch. Her eyes met his, and her entire mind went blank. She was entirely paralyzed, her body betraying her when she needed it most. He leaned in for another kiss, and despite how she protested from within, she could not move away.

"So you've come for me," Carmine growled against her mouth. "Just as he said you would."

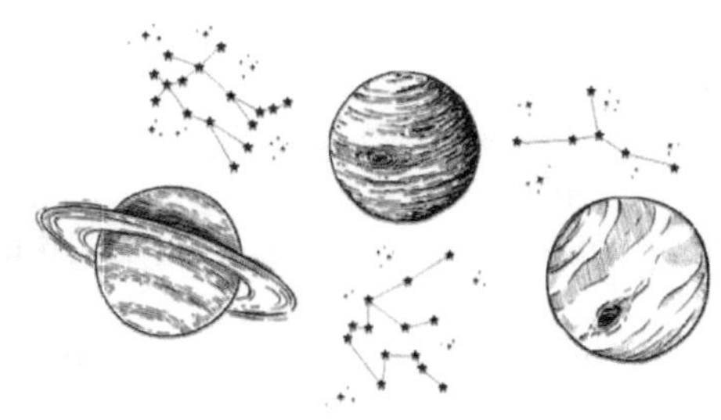

Chapter 22

Vincenzo

"Where the fuck is she?" Enzo screamed into Ezekiel's face, fist poised to throw yet another punch. "She was here, and now she's gone. What did you do?"

Ezekiel's face wept blood from his nostrils, dampening his feathers. He shook his head. "I don't know what happened, I promise. I did not know any of this would happen!"

Enzo slammed the back of Ezekiel's head into the ground repeatedly. "That's not good enough, Ezekiel. You'd better figure out what happened, or I'm plucking every feather from your pathetic body."

He released him, lodging a firm kick to Ezekiel's stomach as he stood up. He did not have time to beat the answers out of him; he had to find her. He cursed himself under his breath, deep regret clanging against his insides. He should have known better than to leave her alone, even if for a minute.

The universe itself orchestrated events large and small to keep them apart, but it would take more than that to prevent him from finding her again and again. For each time she was taken from him, he would make the cosmos itself pay.

She is the answer to your blissful resurgence, his cursed hollered. *Not even death can unravel your union.*

He sent waves of his power through the crowd, attempting to see through the eyes of others without burning too much of his magic. With the amount of chaos, there was no doubt his brother was responsible for the unexpected carnage. There was something in their blood that drew them to violence like a siren song. Even now, Enzo could feel the call to burn this world to the ground, all because Carmine dared to step between him and Cosima.

He grew frustrated, desperate. None of the people he searched through had seen her. People cried over the bodies of the dead and dragged the injured living out of the doors. Although in shambles, this room no longer held the carnage. He was somewhere else, meaning he could be anywhere with her.

Enzo flew through the hallways, using his wings to propel him quickly, hastening his search.

Why can't I feel you? Where have you gone?

A man crouched over what appeared to be a woman's body. Before Enzo could notice her feathers, his starlight blasted the man backward. His body left an indent in the wall, and the woman whimpered with fear. Enzo glanced down at her and then to the man, realizing the woman was not Cosima. The man, while knocked around, was alive, at the very least.

The sound of someone else's voice caught his attention, and Enzo left with a muttered apology to the woman. He hunted the source of the noise, his stomach leaping into his throat as he recognized another voice as well—Sima's. The fear in her voice pushed him further, but the time it took to find her was agonizing.

From behind a closed door, he could hear a struggle ensuing. He slammed it open, barreling through with speed. Without time to assess the situation, he was already on top of Carmine, searing his skin with his starlight. The burning light tunneled into Carmine's side. His brother roared, casting Cosima to the side roughly.

"Run, Sima!" Enzo called, aiming another beam of starlight at Carmine.

Despite how she trembled, she held her hands up, and the lights began to flicker as the walls trembled. The dance hall morphed beneath her magic, causing the floor to ripple and wave. With a blink of his eyes, the space transformed, now full of chairs and tables stacked high, creating obstacles and obscuring their view of each other. Enzo's heart squeezed as he launched himself into the air—leave it to him to fall in love with a woman who refused to back down from a fight, even if the sight of it killed him.

Carmine growled and unfurled his red-feathered wings. "Hello, brat," Carmine hollered as he shot upward. "I never thought the day would come when I would finally meet my little brother. Mommy did a grand job of tucking you away, didn't she?"

As much as it troubled him, Enzo remained calm, using the stacks Sima created to his advantage. He used their coverage to force his brother to follow after him or risk losing track of his biggest threat. "I am surprised you recognized her blood in me." He flew further away from Sima, drawing Carmine closer to the door. *I have to stay in control. I can't let him push me.*

"How could I not feel it? You may not look it, but your strength hums a symphony only those equally as powerful can detect. I had heard of her plans to shove you amongst the Guardians, but now it makes sense."

Carmine flew forward, leaving them only a few feet from the threshold of the door. Enzo hovered, allowing Carmine to begin to close the space between them. Retreating this far had given his brother the illusion of control, and Enzo only needed to maintain it long enough to keep Sima safe. When Enzo glanced to where he had last seen her, the space was empty. He sent a silent prayer that she had finally made a run for it as he focused back on his brother.

"What makes sense to you? What revelation have you come to about me, brother?" Enzo allowed himself to ease backward only an inch.

He had prepared for this moment, mentally at least. *This is why they'd come here: Carmine's head on a plate is what guaranteed Cosima's safety.* All he needed to do was lure Carmine close enough. He was right in believing Carmine would make an entrance, but was wrong about how. Being ambushed by him was not how Enzo thought their death match would finally unfold, but he would make do with what he was given.

Carmine took the bait, flying forward. "The only way she could conceal you was to make you appear weak, insignificant. She hid you amongst the lambs, for none of them knew how sharp your fangs were. You are a killer, brother. Why not join us?"

"I should think you wouldn't need my help. You lot are the strongest immortals in the Ethereal Realm, what more could you need?"

"You underestimate all you could gain. You already have her power in you, all it takes is learning how to properly wield it. Don't pretend you haven't felt the madness growing if you neglect it, if you don't let off steam. I know the magnitude of your power calls to you, the way it does with all of us."

Enzo glanced away at the mention of his curse. He had toyed with the idea that his brothers were damned with the insatiable, power-hungry parasite inside them, but Carmine confirmed it was true. "I don't know what you're talking about."

"Oh, but you do. I can see it all over your face." Carmine laughed. "There are ways for you to use your power to become stronger than any of us. I hear your sire is Domani. The bounds of his powers…you have infinite potential."

Enzo hated the way his curse sang to him. *Prove him right*, it whispered, *show him what true wickedness feels like.*

"What does it cost me to sign my life away and become corrupted like you? There is no stain on my soul worth aligning with you or our mother."

Carmine's lip twitched and he inched closer. Before Carmine could continue, Enzo let loose his power. Not the power of mind manipulation, but of space manipulation. He bent the room around them, contorting it to egregious angles. As Carmine stepped through the threshold of the door, Enzo forced the door frame inward, trapping him. The transition between spaces held a special kind of magic Enzo had been waiting for a chance to exploit.

The rooms crept inward, becoming black voids. When executed perfectly, as Vincenzo knew he would, the transitional space between rooms allowed him to open a new pocket of reality, creating space where there was no room for it once before. Carmine would be trapped in a dimension only Enzo could control.

He had not been able to perform this level of contortion on command in Haelos. His magic was stretched thin across the Ombra District in a desperate attempt to quiet the screaming ache of his pent-up powers. Now that he had gone months without unleashing it, his mouth salivated at the opportunity.

Carmine yelled with all his might as he struggled to break free. Enzo could not overpower him physically, but as long as his brother stayed within this fabricated space, he could keep him from moving. He had lost track of Sima during his surge of power, but he hoped she was seeking safety.

His mind flickered to her frightened voice. *I can't,* she had said.

But I can. I will, for you. She had killed Aurelio alone, and now it was time for Enzo to repay the favor.

Before he could launch an attack on Carmine, a piercing sound split through his eardrums, lighting up the sides of his head with excruciating pain. Enzo shook his head, doused in confusion. His powers wavered, and if he wasn't careful, he could lose his hold. He fought through the pain, searching for a sign of his brother.

What greeted his eyes was a scene he could not register fully. Carmine stood, unmarred and unrestricted, with a hand tucked in his front pocket. The other held Sima by the throat. Enzo lunged forward, blind with desperation.

His hand reached for Sima, only to pass right through her. He moved again, horrified to find the same result. Swings at Carmine ended similarly.

This was an illusion. But, Enzo reasoned, that could not be possible. He had spent decades fortifying his mental shields, fine-tuning them until they were impenetrable.

Why then were his arms grabbing empty air instead of the visions of bodies his brain swore were true?

Crystals, Enzo thought. *Of course. He is strengthening himself with life force.*

The piercing, high-pitched sound reverberated through his skull, numbing all thoughts. He struggled to pull himself free, to slam shut whatever open door in his defenses had allowed for Carmine to seize control of his mind. If he wanted to kill his brother, he would have to destroy whatever crystal lent him its power.

"Help me," Sima cried from behind him. "Take me away from this!" Enzo spun, and a hazy recreation of her stood drenched in blood. Her eyes were rabid, and though he knew this version of her was an illusion, he could *smell* her fear. Just as before, his hands passed right through her. His frustration was boiling magma, and with one fierce slam, he sealed his mind shut, finally ending the hallucinations.

Within seconds, Cosima faded, leaving him in the dark void he crafted for Carmine. He took a breath, centering himself for a brief moment before he ripped his creation to shreds. Once again, he was standing in the hallway, and Cosima and Carmine were nowhere to be found.

Ivo's eyes squeezed shut, her mind throwing up whatever defense it could against the trauma that rang through her body in response to the wicked mayhem around her. The lights flickered on and off, creating a disorientating pulse to the room. The people of Riejj tore through the halls screaming, searching for safety, all while Ivo lay curled on the floor.

Thankfully, their feet no longer trampled on top of her as they had when she fell during the stampede, unharmed only because of Cosima's saving protection. However, moments after Cosima helped Ivo off the floor, Carmine inflicted horrific visions through his mind magic, the images so terrifying Ivo thought she would be sick. When the hallucinations finally ceased, Sima and Carmine had disappeared.

Ivo was all alone, trembling in the center of a swirling storm of death and fear, with nothing to anchor her. It was impossible to imagine herself fighting back, despite how desperately she wanted to contribute. Each time she came face-to-face with her mortality, she ran for safety.

I don't want to die. I want to live. I want to live a life that matters.

Someone snatched Ivo's wrist and yanked her upward. She screamed, convinced she would find herself in the clutches of their enemy, only to stop when Nariah clamped a hand over her mouth.

"I will get you out of here, but you need to let me save you."

"Sima," Ivo murmured against the Scout's palm. "Rescue Sima."

"She has Vincenzo. I can't find Merit, but let's hope he's already with them. Keep your eyes closed. You don't want to see the bodies."

Ivo nodded, a wave of nausea sweeping over her. Nariah pulled Ivo into her arms, and an electrifying sensation shot through her body in response to the Scout's touch. It wasn't painful, but sobering, as if it provided her with a jolt of energy that cleared the panic and remnants of Carmine's magic from her mind. She clutched onto Nariah's arms as they flew for the exit.

We should be helping, not running away. Maybe Nariah was right when she said I complicate things.

The cacophony of voices continued outside as people fled in all directions. Ivo's teeth chattered, despite feeling warm against Nariah. They traveled a short distance, and she finally opened her eyes as the sounds tapered off. The Scout flew her to a nearby alleyway, which was dimly lit by the moon. Ivo's knees trembled, and she sank to the ground, wrapping her arms around her knees.

"You need to find Sima," Ivo urged. "Please, you have to help her."

"I can't risk taking you back in there," Nariah said, crossing her arms. "Maybe I should fly you back to Ezekiel's home where you can wait safely."

Ivo let out a shaky breath. "No, that will take too long. Leave me here. Go for her."

The Scout turned to leave, but she hesitated, her eyes locked onto Ivo's. Nariah's expression was tense, as if she were lost in thought.

"What are you waiting for?" Ivo curled her fist, willing her hands to stop trembling. "I've survived this long already. The real danger is inside."

Nariah gave a curt nod, her gaze lingering for another stolen moment, before she dashed into the night back toward Sima and Carmine. Ivo rose from the ground and moved closer to the wall, concealing herself in the shadows.

Everything will be alright. Sima is fine. It isn't too late.

A confusing sensation bubbled in her gut, and a tear fell from her cheek. Ivo wiped away the watery trail, unsure of what to make of the haunting feeling. Being by herself was terrifying, but at this time, she would only be a distraction, especially if she continued to struggle with her emotions. *It's best for everyone if I am out of the way.* She glanced around. *I just wish I wasn't alone.*

A noise from further down the alleyway made her flinch, but it was not an enemy lying in wait. Instead, a small creature, similar to a fuzzy mouse, but with pointier ears and a tiny tail, emerged holding a piece of discarded food in its mouth. It hopped along until it noticed her crouched in the dark.

It moved closer and stood on its back legs, as if it were inspecting her. The creature dropped its stolen treasure and scurried to her side. Sensing something auspicious about the tiny thing, Ivo instinctively lowered her palm, the mouse-like being tickling her skin as it crawled inside. She smiled to herself as she brought it eye-level.

"You're rather cute, you know that? You're the first one I've encountered on this planet that hasn't tried to kill me right away."

Its whiskers twitched, and Ivo swore that the tiny thing knew exactly what she said. It twirled in her hand before slowly making its way down her arm. It sniffed at her pocket, using its paw to scratch at the fabric. She reached in and pulled out Carmine's journal.

The creature pawed at the cover, and Ivo opened it. Its little head angled toward the pages, and she wondered if it were reading the contents. *Rats can't read,* she reminded herself. She chuckled lightly and used the pad of her finger to pet its head. The mouse-like being responded affectionately, diving against her touch as if to beg for more.

She pulled the creature against her chest as she scooted toward the light. She continued to pet it as she flipped through the pages of Carmine's journal, letting her mind wander as she did so. His writing was intense, filled with long-winded rants and circular arguments surrounding his family; however, it was insightful when it came to the entries about the prophecy.

Or rather, *prophecies,* Ivo quickly learned.

During his hunt for more information, Carmine had employed the services of several Oracles, both in the Eternal Kingdom in secret and throughout the many planets he hid from Aurelio on. It seemed as though he managed to collect more information than any of the other brothers had managed, as he often congratulated himself on his accomplishments.

> The foolish men I share blood with fight for their chance
> to be the only one who remains, but I have committed myself
> to breaking us free from this damnation. I have only myself
> to thank for the truth I uncovered. Our curse is intimately
> tied to Kismet's bloodline—due to my mother's treachery—
> meaning the Celestial Empress' prophecy has been revealed
> to me, in taunting pieces, on my journey for freedom. My
> mother's thieving ways may have granted her unholy power,
> like a caterpillar emerging as a butterfly, but she created a
> debt she cannot repay. I do not know yet if there is a way to

unleash us from Kismet's ire, but I have begun to unravel her connection to the Weave. The Celestial Empresses, the three mystic hands of Fate, speak only through knots and tangles, through slicing and mending threads. How then could they have been foolish enough to think no one would follow the strings that led back to them? Oh, Kismet. My bloodline is not the only one you have cursed, for the prophecies of three whisper among the fabric of the universe, one undeniable truth—the end of the Celestial Empresses is near.

Something tickled inside Ivo's gut as she read the words. What Ivo knew of her friend's connection to Kismet was murky at best, but if Carmine was right, it would seemingly answer why Aurelio seemed so intent on having Sima for himself. If she carried her own prophecy intertwined with that of the Sacred Twelve, then it could only mean an even larger plot was in play. Ivo wondered if she fit somewhere in the cosmic web, or if she was doomed to forever fray beneath the weight of her Fate.

Ivo shut the journal and tucked it back into her pocket, her mind swirling. The mouse had fallen asleep on her but woke with the motion. She chewed on her cheek.

"Everyone is in there fighting, and I'm out here," Ivo whispered to the creature. "I was never afraid of dying before, and now I can't help but wonder what else is out there for me. Dreaming of more has made me a coward."

I don't know if I deserve more than this, Ivo thought to herself, her mind picturing a particular purple gaze. *But I want it anyway.*

The mouse's tiny black eyes stared into hers as if it were imbuing her with the strength she needed.

"You're right. I have to fight for what I want."

She stood up, balancing the creature in her hands as she did so, and took a centering breath. Ivo marched out of the darkness and back toward the dance hall, careful not to snag her dress on the ground.

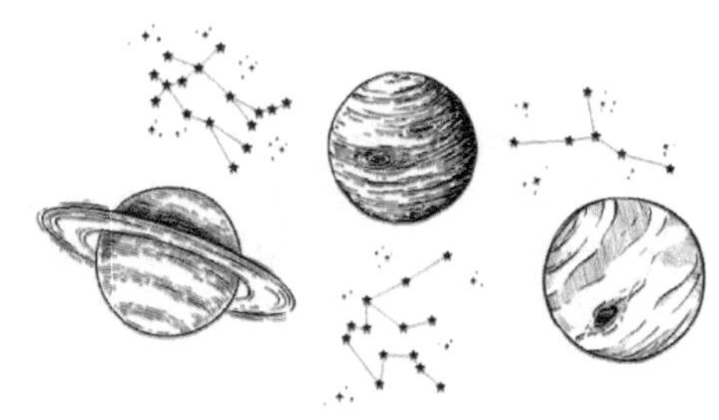

Chapter 22

Cosima

Cosima wasn't exactly sure how she ended up on her hands and knees vomiting onto the polished wood floor, or where Enzo and Carmine disappeared to, but she was grateful that in this moment, she was alone. Sima shuddered as her already empty stomach turned again, the swirling in her brain granting her no reprieve from the sickness.

Each time she thought of Carmine's mouth on hers, she heaved.

Somewhere in the distance, she vaguely registered the destructive sounds of a battle. *I have to help Enzo,* she thought. However, she could not gather the strength to lift herself from the floor, despite how she desperately reached inward for her power. It burned her fingers as it flared, the sensation soothing her fears. The biting pain of her coiling magic grounded Sima, reminding her what was at stake.

I can hardly bear to look Carmine in the eye, but that won't be enough to stop me, Sima thought. *I have to be stronger. I have to find a way through this.*

Sima crawled away from the spilled contents of her stomach and shakily rose to her feet. She held her head as she glanced around. She was inside an empty ballroom, and in front of her were three sets of double doors, all propped open. The sounds of the fight grew louder as starlight blasted through the hallway.

"Sima," Nariah hollered. A blur of white flashed as she was tossed backward, the Scout digging her heels into the ground to slow herself. "Use your power, now!"

Sima's jaw dropped open as Carmine appeared, howling as Merit clung onto his back with a dagger wedged deep into his shoulder. Carmine reached up and threw the Scout off him, adding a burst of his own starlight, which was quickly deflected by a shimmering purple shield.

Nariah turned to her and shouted, "Sima! *Do* something!"

You're too fragile, you coward, Aurelio's voice whispered in her mind. *You can't stop him.*

His voice made her heart jump into her throat as a chill wave drenched her body. Enraged by the defensive magic deployed by Nariah, Carmine screamed as he ran full force toward them, toppling the Scouts and sending them just out of sight from Sima. Her heart was loud in her ears, Sima's magic begging to be used. She fought through her fear, managing a single step forward before she froze again.

You'll always be mine, don't you get it? You think you escaped me, but as long as you're alive, I am with you. Her former husband's voice lingered in her head. *Why do you bother trying to escape me?*

Somewhere within, a piece of Cosima screamed in response to his words, as though the words set her on fire, burning down all she had rebuilt since his death. A scratching sound near her feet made Sima jump. A tiny mouse clawed at the edge of her dress, its whiskers wiggling as it sniffed her. Before she could tug her gown away from the small thing, Ivo ran into the room, her skirts gathered in her hands and cheeks red from exertion.

"Oh, thank you Hand of Fate," Ivo panted, "perhaps, I am not cursed."

"Get away from the door," Sima urged, rushing to Ivo's side. "Where were you? Are you hurt?"

"No," Ivo said, shaking her head. "Nariah got me out, but I came back."

"Why would you do that?" Sima nearly shrieked. "You were safe. Why would you come back?"

Ivo stamped her foot. "I was not going to sit out there while my friends die. I know I'm not as strong as the Scouts, but I don't need to be. There are other ways for me to be useful, and none of them involve me standing outside like a child."

Sima nodded. "Nariah, Merit, and Carmine just passed through the hallway."

Ivo frowned. "It's suspiciously quiet out there if that's the case." She glanced at her small mouse friend and bent down beside it. "Take us to him."

She could have sworn the tiny creature nodded before it took off down the hallway in the direction Sima had last seen Carmine and the others go.

Although Sima feared for Ivo's life, there was something about her friend's presence that gave her the strength to face Carmine again. They followed after the creature, Ivo a few steps ahead of her, only to both halt the second their feet entered the hallway.

At the end, the space opened into a grand entrance with another grand dance hall on the opposite side. Starlight flashed repeatedly as swarms of bird people with glowing red eyes marched toward the other ballroom. Feathers, blood, and tissue littered the area as they pressed forward. To her credit, Ivo wore a stern, brave expression, even as the chaos grew loud enough to hurt their ears.

Some of the people being controlled by Carmine's magic turned toward them. Their red eyes paused as Sima's hand shot out, bringing time to a stop. Carmine would be able to break through her freeze on time, but the people of Riejj could not. Ivo's magic spread ice below their feet and summoned wind, which pushed the beings away from them.

Ivo tugged Sima forward by her wrist, leading her through the crowd. Her friend shouted spells, the words drowned out by terrified screams as the building around them began to crumble. Although Ivo was not as thoroughly trained on using her magic outside of healing, she left Sima immensely impressed as she cleared a large enough area that Merit was visible, through inventive means.

Blood ran down the side of Merit's face, matting his Navy hair to his head. He supported his right arm with his hand under his elbow as he sighed.

"Glory to the Divine," Merit breathed. "I feared you two might be dead. Carmine and Enzo are inside. No clue where Nariah went."

Sima's heart lurched into her stomach. "Enzo's in there alone?"

"There has to be a way we can help," Ivo said.

Her mind was full of thoughts of Aurelio, with images of her torment as fresh as when it occurred, the flurry compounding into a cacophony of whispered reasons why she would never be strong enough to defeat Carmine.

Yet, her hand reached for the handle anyway. When she met resistance, something in her gut told her to reach for her power.

Vincenzo

Unleash me from these binds, his curse whispered. *Make him pay.*

No, Enzo thought. *Not now. Not yet.*

He barely managed to pull himself away, his curse seemingly growing stronger. Vincenzo had lost track of his brother momentarily, and he knew life-force stones were to blame for Carmine's manipulative hold over his brain. When he had managed to break through his brother's magic, Carmine had vanished. Thanks to the chaotic sounds of the Trine Scouts fighting back, it had taken little time for Enzo to track him down. Once Carmine was backed into another ballroom, Enzo slammed the doors shut and sealed them.

"You again," Carmine growled.

His brothers were an enigma, each of their powers manifesting in different deadly versions, and somehow, Carmine had broken through his defenses. For a moment, resentment panged louder than his own fear. Resentment, he had been raised a Guardian, with the body and powers of a God. His mother had made him small, had forced him to be only a fraction of his true potential. Relief came from his internal storm as his curse spoke to him.

Coat this place in his blood, it sang. *Give him what he deserves.*

Sparks of his power zapped through the air as his curse expelled energy, the action like a sigh of relief as Enzo allowed it to bubble higher than before. Carmine's fingers sank into Enzo's biceps, and the two dug in their heels as they wrestled. His brother was stronger, but Enzo refused to quit, even if he tore himself to shreds in the process. His magic flooded from his palms into Carmine, crafting metal spikes that plunged through his brother's flesh.

Carmine hollered and ripped Enzo's hands off him. The move further shredded the skin around his brother's arm, and blood poured as Carmine continued to throw punches. Carmine's magic reinforced his hits, creating shock-waves as his fists landed. Vincenzo crafted shields of rock and stone, which sprouted from the ground with each attack his brother launched, finally allowing him to maintain distance from Carmine. Suddenly, the doors slammed open, causing the two of them to look up. His stomach dropped like an anchor through water as he saw Sima standing there, her arms outstretched, ready to fight, despite the fear he knew she was feeling.

Curtains floated and paintings tore from the walls as a tunnel of wind accompanied the first wave of Sima's power. As Enzo watched her launch her own attack, it was as if he could see the threads themselves snapping and fraying as she made her changes. Glass shattered as every window exploded, and Carmine dove out of the way as a chunk of the ceiling fell directly above him. Despite how he tried to save himself, chunks of glass were lodged all throughout Carmine's body.

Sima was the picture of endurance, grit, and dedication, and he longed to take the weight of Carmine's bounty off her head. Coming so close to death so soon after slaying Aurelio on her own, it was a wonder she was standing. Not because she wasn't strong, but because even Enzo knew strength had limits. He would make it stop; he would destroy the parasite that chaos had become over her life to free her from her torment.

You have a duty to protect her. You swore your love, son of two moons. Do not fail your oath. Enzo's curse was loud in his ears. He needed to save her from the evil of his bloodline, as he had failed to do in the past. It was as if his curse was weaponizing the thought of her to coax emotions so hot, they burned through all reason. Vincenzo could feel the way his body begged to give in to the anger, to let it consume him until he was nothing more than a smoldering prophecy of Carmine's imminent demise.

Vincenzo lunged for him. Carmine dove out of reach, locking them both into a dance to the death. Their feet stomped to internal beats, dragging them in pointless circles around the room, neither of them ready to be crowned loser or give up their life. With each burst of Vincenzo's magic, metal spears hurtled toward his brother, but Carmine was quick and dodged with grace. As much as Enzo wanted Carmine dead, his brother was not ready to give up. This truth radiated from his gaze.

"You want to kill me, brother?" Carmine toyed. "You'd better earn it. I won't give my life over to someone unworthy. Prove yourself, or I'll bring you back to others weeping, teetering that edge to everlasting nothingness with hopeless resignation."

"Perhaps you underestimate me." Enzo landed. "I may not be strong enough to take your life with my bare hands, but I will outlast you. No matter how you batter my body, you will not be able to stop me."

The walls expanded, growing the room ten times its original size, all while casting his expansion in darkness. Carmine, whether he noticed the change or grew tired of Enzo's words, attempted to take hold of his mind once more. This time, Enzo had been ready, reinforcing his internal shields prior to the strike. The hint of a crease appeared on Carmine's forehead.

He funneled more, his magic pouring from him in massive emerald waves as it crashed over his brother, bringing with it snarling shadows. The boundary Enzo had been wary of crossing approached as Carmine gasped, the first sign he had successfully begun breaking through his brother's shields. He could not stop now, not when he was just beginning to win.

Enzo's lip twitched. "The moment you came for her, the moment you *touched* her, it was already over for you. I will hunt you far and wide across the universes, and try as you might, you will not outrun me. You now have a target on your back. I want you to remember that."

Carmine laughed, though sweat had begun to form across his hairline.

"You're making a mistake, not taking what is yours. Only one of us will survive in the end, brother, wouldn't you rather it be you?"

"I have thought about it," Enzo said. "But what would be the fun in ruling the Eternal Kingdom? The demands would never cease. That is not a life to me. Though I do wonder. You seem much smarter than Aurelio. Why, then, do you not see the trap our mother has in store for you? You perform all of her bidding, to what end? What is the point if you're destined for slaughter?"

"That may be true, but until then," Carmine said smoothly, closing the space between them with wide steps forward. "I can have all the fun I want, can't I?"

Snarling in the shadows broke Carmine's concentration, and Enzo soaked in the confusion marring his brother's face. "I hope you don't mind, I brought a couple friends to help tire you out. Can't expect to do it all by myself, right?"

Long black snouts emerged from the darkness, the rest of their forms still hidden. Pearl white incisors, dripping in saliva, chattered against each other as Carmine's scent settled across the Wrenhiles' nostrils. Wrenhiles were one of Vincenzo's favorite creations, something he had worked on for years in solitude.

The shock on Carmine's face painted every wall inside Vincenzo with golden glee. This secret, so well kept, it haunted his brother to see it manifest. The first Wrenhile emerged, in all of his eight-foot-tall glory. His hackles were raised, and his black fur made only him appear larger. The beast's paws cracked the floor beneath their feet as it wandered closer to Carmine at an antagonizing, crawling pace.

"They're beautiful," Carmine choked. "Mother did not pass this ability to us. This summoning power was granted by your sire?"

"It is not quite summoning, brother." Enzo grinned, electricity snapping in the air around them as the intensity of his magic grew. "I hand-crafted them. Before this, their matter lived between the fabric of space and time, waiting for me to birth them. It may burn a bit of magic at first, but the creations come out just as I dream. Domani's blood allows me to do what even our mother cannot. Do you understand yet, Carmine? Do you know why I refuse to submit to her?"

Vincenzo joined the Wrenhile and its starved brothers, edging closer to Carmine. "I refuse to submit to someone lesser than me," Enzo growled. "She cast me aside like I was nothing and still expects me to play along with her games. I lived only for myself for an eternity, that is not a habit she can break."

"You're only alive as long as she does not realize you are a threat."

"Maybe she will regret doubting me when she is forced to face her sins," Vincenzo said. "I know for certain you will not survive long enough to tell her anything."

Carmine laughed as a Wrenhile pressed its snout into his chest. While clearly uncomfortable, he refused to give up his arrogant show and continued to taunt Vincenzo. "Perhaps not me, but there are others of us out there. Don't forget. Our older brothers are more twisted and cruel than I am, and they thirst for inevitable power with more ferocity than I do."

Enzo smirked. "I won't forget."

A cacophony of tearing flesh and utter destruction echoed through the expanded room as the Wrenhiles dug into Carmine. When there was no fight left in him, that was when Enzo would claim his worthless life, and that was when this nightmare would end. Carmine fought off the creatures, breaking their faces with his fists.

Rip out his heart and shred every piece of him that remains, his curse screamed. *Erase him from existence.*

Enzo's fingers painfully tingled. He was distracted by his bloodthirst for a moment and didn't realize what was happening. Then, he felt it. His restraint slipping, his weak mind giving in to the promises of his hidden power. His curse burst through his veins like liquid metal that would harden into a cage of impenetrable strength, should he allow it. Should he give in entirely?

Vincenzo shattered the first boundary he had been too fearful to cross once in the past, knowing this was his opportunity to protect Cosima the way he always should have. With a pulse of his power, ice coated every inch of the floors and walls of the mangled hall where Ezekiel's birthday celebration was taking place not long ago. Enzo gasped as light poured from his eyes and his body rose in the air without the use of his wings, his hair floating above him as sizzling green electricity discharged at random from his frozen fingertips.

The surge of power caught him off guard, and for a split second, Enzo lost what little control he still had of his magic. His eyes rolled back as pure energy zapped from his hand in place of the starlight he was accustomed to. The burn was vastly different than starlight, expelling more energy than he had ever released at one time, right at Carmine's pinned body. His brother's body was crunched between the foundational layers of the room Enzo had hand-crafted. It allowed him to pulverize Carmine with the new beam of energy faster than his magic could heal him, until his magic began to bubble inside his skin.

For the first time since his curse had emerged, Enzo became conscious of his body nearing yet another false bottom to his abilities. At the same moment, he realized Sima was still in the room, trembling with her hands still outstretched, the panic in her eyes bright as she stared directly at him. It snapped him out of his bloodlust, and he forced himself to end the pour of his magic. Enzo's fear was like coarse salt on his tongue, an impossible-to-ignore reminder that he could not hand himself over to his curse.

He tore his eyes away from her and took in his surroundings. The rubble before him did not move or quiver. It was wholly still as particles rained from the ceiling. Enzo's entire body shook, not from exhaustion, but from the sheer thrill of unleashing his magic, despite his self-doubt. A flash of shame threatened to throw him off balance at Sima's reaction, but Enzo navigated around it, surging with an unfamiliar confidence.

Enzo would learn to tame the ugly beast within, would learn to properly wield his power. With how it had helped him, he would have to reevaluate his stance on his curse. He stared down at his shaky hands, wondering if the dark power he had been running from was the answer he had been seeking. He locked eyes with Sima, and as her honey-brown eyes pierced right through his adrenaline haze, he knew that was not the case.

No, he thought, clenching his fist. *No more than is necessary. Then, never again.*

Enzo shot toward her with desperate devotion, his spirit relieved once he was near the woman he'd tear apart the galaxies for. As he wrapped her in his arms and caught the scent of lavender in her hair, he held her with conviction. She was rigid at first, but then quickly melted into him as she nuzzled her face against his chest.

All too soon, Nariah shoved herself between them. Her white hair slapped him across the face as her shoulder knocked him backward. "Rules are rules, even if you have murdered the target," Nariah said. She turned to the pile of rubble Enzo had crafted. "You did murder him, right?"

Chapter 24

Cosima

"Cosima?" Ivo called through the door. "It's been a while. Are you sure you're alright? Let me in."

Sima looked up from where she sat with her back against the wall, the foggy bathroom causing her hair to frizz. She double-checked the door was locked, knowing Ivo wouldn't hesitate to storm in if Sima didn't give in to her pestering. Her eyes fell to the ruins of her tailored gown—dirty, torn, and evidence of her deepest horrors come to life.

"I am fine. I want some time alone." Her lip quivered. She sank her teeth into it. "Please."

The sound of Ivo's retreating footsteps brought relief, and Sima once again hung her head low. She sniffed and wiped away the rogue tear snaking its way down her cheek. Sima stared into her reflection, only for the face of a coward to stare back. She felt her sanity dripping off her, leaving her closer to madness than ever before. Carmine's face mirrored Aurelio's, and in that moment, all rational thought drained from her body. He *looked* just like Aurelio. He moved and breathed like him. He radiated the same noxious energy as her former husband, and she wondered if she had made a mistake in thinking Aurelio was dead.

But he was.

He had to be.

She squinted her eyes shut at the memory, the invasive recreation rampaging through her anxious mind. The same mind that had gone blank when Carmine touched her. She had been useless, completely inept. She forced Vincenzo to take on the brunt of the battle, all while she froze with fear despite Nariah allowing her to use her power. She did not even attempt to break free from his grip when he kissed her, she only stared in disbelief. Her magic did not flare, she did not try to save herself.

She had locked up and shut down.

There was no deciding which was worse, the shame and embarrassment, or the utter terror that *this*, this failed version of her, was who she truly was deep down. She felt like a liar, a fraud, someone bound to imperfection.

To add insult to injury, Carmine had *not* been killed by Vincenzo, only injured. The proof left behind was the crushed arm Carmine ripped from his own body to free himself from rubble. By the time Vincenzo, Nariah, and Merit had begun to peel back the layers of destruction, Carmine had already vanished, fleeing into the night to nurse his wounds in private.

Her lip trembled but she would not be allowed to wallow in peace. Two sets of footsteps sounded in the hall. Sima sighed. She knew who to expect, who Ivo would run to when Sima was circling the drain. It was Vincenzo who spoke to her through the door.

"Cosima?"

"I am *fine*, Enzo. Please, go away."

"Let me see your face, just for a moment."

"Why?"

"So, I know you're telling me the truth. You don't have to do this alone."

She stood, reaching for the doorknob, but stopped. She was not fine. Her life was a haunting melody of the same dreary truth: no decision, no action would ever be good enough, so long as they came from her.

"Sima? Open the door, please."

Her fingers curled into fists. What cosmic torture was the unraveling of her life? Why did scorn stick to her like sap on trees? Why must she stumble through these worlds with her soul unrecognizable, with her authenticity cruelly manipulated into a person she never was? Or never thought herself to be.

The handle twisted, but the door did not open.

His tongue in her mouth had been cruel, an invasion that left her more hollow, close to shattering. Carmine needed to be killed, but how could she trust herself to rage through his storms without drowning in his suffocating aura? He was more than a moving target. He was an arrow already snaking through the air, and her back was willfully turned, too afraid to see her mess in the light.

What made her believe she was strong enough to kill any more of the Sacred Twelve?

An explosion of wood scattered across the floor, some pieces landing at her feet. The door laid flat on the floor. She gasped as she wrapped her arms around herself, tears streaking down her cheeks. Vincenzo pushed his way into the room.

"Love," Enzo whispered as he knelt beside her, gingerly placing her hand between his. "I am sorry I had to do that, but you…you stopped responding."

Nariah walked into the room and shot daggers with her eyes. A sliver of Ivo's guilty expression appeared from behind the Scout's shoulder. It was the first time since their interaction with their intended target that Cosima had faced them. "You made us sick with worry. What if Carmine had you?" Nariah turned her nose up. "There are rules. You cannot ignore them whenever you please. Just because you and Enzo let him get away, doesn't—"

"I—" Sima stopped. There was no defense she was confident in.

"Enough," Ivo snapped. "She has been through enough, Nariah. You think because everyone kisses your ass in the Eternal Kingdom that you can dictate how everyone around you breathes. Let me be the one to tell you, you *can't*. No one tells you how to recover, and you won't tell her either."

Nariah's lip twitched. She stared down into Ivo's eyes with smoky fury as her hands balled. "If she had done anything, and I mean anything, when I asked her to, we might have had a chance at stopping him. We were so close. I honestly am not sure why the Kingdom put their good faith into her, when each day I feel closer to believing she is who they say she is."

"You don't mean that," Sima said, voice low. Her face twisted with pain. "You don't."

Nariah's harsh expression faltered. "And if I do?"

"Then you have no fucking clue who I am," Sima snapped, a tear speeding down her cheek. "I have told you the truth about *everything* because I thought we were friends. Can't you just imagine what it was like for me to see him? You didn't exactly stop Carmine either last I checked, Nariah, so shut your mouth."

Everyone fell silent. Ivo attempted to hide her smirk behind her hands and turned around to keep from laughing in Nariah's face. The Scout glared at her but said nothing.

"Can we have a moment to speak alone?" Enzo asked Nariah.

"No, absolutely not," Nariah growled, crossing her arms as her brows pulled together.

"Let's go," Ivo said, grabbing Nariah by the arm.

Their footsteps retreated as the two engaged in a heated, half-whispered argument at the end of the hall. Sima pushed some of the scattered wood away with her feet before pulling her legs tighter around herself. Enzo slid to the floor beside her and pulled her head to rest on his shoulder. She let go of her legs and wrapped her arms around his waist. Their physical interactions were limited, but sitting beside him and feeling his warmth sink into her eased the ache in her heart.

"It's my fault," Sima whispered as a tear fell.

"It's not your fault, don't listen to Nariah." Enzo's voice was soft but somber. "He ambushed us and got his hands on you before any of us knew it had happened. You were alone with him, and I'm sorry I let it happen. I'm sorry you've been put in harm's way so many times and that I've let you down."

"No, Enzo," Sima said. A sinking sensation filled her stomach. "You don't need to apologize. I left you to handle it alone. I was useless."

"You did use your power, Sima. You tried your best. You were scared," Enzo replied. "How could you not be?"

"Precisely, and I almost got both of us killed because of it. What I did wasn't enough to stop him."

"Sima…he touched you."

She couldn't help the way her body shuddered in response to the memory his words invoked. She squeezed her eyes shut. "Are you angry with me because I didn't do anything to stop him? He kissed me, Enzo, but I didn't want him to." More tears fell across her cheek.

Vincenzo gingerly pulled her chin to make her look at him. "I would *never* blame you for his actions toward you. We both know why that would make you freeze, why it would fill you with fear." His voice was soft. "You can't blame yourself for how you responded to someone touching you against your will."

"I should have done something," she whispered, shutting her eyes. She was too ashamed to see the love Enzo had for her in his eyes. "Something more."

He pressed a small kiss to the bridge of her nose before he tugged her into a tight hug. "You have spent your time being brave, can't you see? You were strong for so long already, and it eats at me that you're still having to endure this kind of pain. I wish I could erase all the ways he hurt you. I wish I could reclaim your peace for you because, damn it, even the cosmos themselves know you deserve it. I didn't think about how seeing my brothers would impact you, and for that I am sorry."

Sima cried harder as she held onto him. "I thought I could do this."

"I will do this for us if you need me to, love. I can take this burden off you."

"No, absolutely not," Cosima said as she pulled away. She wiped away her tears. "I have to do this. I need to prove my innocence to the Eternal Kingdom. Even if I am not the one who kills him, I need to be involved. We can't give them any reason to doubt me."

He placed his hand on her back and rubbed her shoulder. "Then we will do it together. Remember, no matter where you go in this ever expansive universe, you are never alone."

Sima relented a small smile as she searched his green eyes. Seeing the devotion in his gaze reminded her of the way his power seemed to consume him during his battle. Her heart dropped, and her smile faded.

"What is it?" he asked. "What's worrying you?"

She shook her head. "It's nothing."

"No, come on. You can tell me anything."

"I…" Sima trailed off, her gaze falling to her lap. She had no clue how to talk about her concerns. "I don't know, it's not important."

"It is to me. I can feel when something isn't right." He rubbed his hand up and down her back. "If you need time, we can try again later, but if you're worried about how I'll react to something…I promise you that you're safe with me."

Cosima's heart pounded as she chewed her lip. "Well, then…" She paused as her brain turned into a flurry of repressed thoughts. "You told me you'd be careful with your power. That didn't *look* like restraint, Enzo. When you were fighting with Carmine…it's like something changed in you."

Enzo nodded slowly. "I know what you're referring to. My power is…vast. Truthfully, I tell myself we haven't talked about my full capacity because of the circumstances, but that's just an excuse. I know I haven't exactly been forthcoming, and I am sorry. I only wanted to keep you safe."

Sima furrowed her brows. "Tell me now. I don't want you to keep secrets from me."

"I don't want to keep anything from you," he said softly. "Domani is capable of creating entirely new worlds and I have inherited at least a significant portion of the ability. I know you know I can create matter, but combined with my mother's powers, I can…create living creatures, as well. However, that is not the part I have been scared to share with you."

"What else is there?" Sima asked, unsure of what the man she loved could be hiding. "You are powerful, Enzo, that is nothing to be ashamed of."

Enzo pressed his lips together as he gazed into her eyes. He brushed a lock of hair out of her face. "There is a sinister and destructive side to my magic, too. I can destroy anything I can create and occasionally even things I did not, with just a snap of my fingers. There is more to this dark power lurking within me that I have not fully explored. It is untamed and ferocious. It disrupts the very fabric of the universe, contorting it to my will. What you witnessed with Carmine was me tapping into that well."

"Does it hurt you?" Sima asked, her chest tight. "What happens to you if you use more of it?"

"I don't know, but…" He looked away, his face tense. "I worry it could consume me if I am not careful. There is a wickedness to it that I do not trust, but it keeps calling to me."

"Enzo," Sima breathed. "You have to resist it. You can't let it take over."

"I know, my love." He reached for her hand and laced his fingers through hers. "I am strong enough to withstand it. I may have used a portion of that power with Carmine, but nothing about me has actually changed because of it. I am still the same me. You don't have to worry, I will be careful."

He opened his mouth to say something then stopped and let out a breath. Enzo's gaze fell. "I know it seems hopeless because he escaped, but I almost had him." Enzo's eyes lit up as if he had unlocked something rare in his battle with Carmine. "Sima, you know my heritage, you know the strength of my bloodline. If I have the ability to help, I have to take it. I feared my own power for so long and I…I didn't rescue you when I should have. I will spend every day of my life repenting for the damage I caused because I couldn't be the man I needed to be."

Sima studied his viridian gaze, the water dripping from them as his soul spoke through his eyes. He pressed a kiss to her forehead, his lips lingering for a breath before he pulled away. "But I will never make that mistake again. Carmine will die by my hands, and I will free us, all of us. I am the man you need me to be, and I will prove it to you." His voice lowered, rumbling in his chest. "I will do this for you and more."

"Do you promise that you know what you're doing? Do you promise you won't take it too far? There are lines that you will never be able to come back from if you cross them." Though guilt tore through her as the words left her mouth, she said, "Don't be like them. Don't be like your brothers, Enzo."

He tugged her under his arm, his wing like a blanket over her aching body. "I promise. I will only do what is necessary to give you the life you deserve. I exist to love you, Sima, and nothing will change that. I know this is impossible to ask, but I need you to trust me."

Sima gazed at him as she gently ran her finger along the scar that ran down his face. His love renewed her, gave her the audacity to dream again. She could have faith in him, even in the dark times. "I trust you, Enzo. Thank you for letting me talk to you—for making me comfortable enough to talk to you." Sima pulled her legs closer to her and wrapped her arms around them. "We aren't going to argue now? I'm not used to bringing up my feelings without a firm debate following."

He gave a soft laugh. "Not unless you really want to, though I don't have many coins in the game. If we argue, it won't come from my heart."

Sima chuckled. "Fair enough. I think we can skip the argument."

His eyes latched onto hers. "I think so too. I know I've said it before, but you are safe with me. Even if we are forbidden from showing it, I adore you. I only want your happiness."

Sima tore her eyes away, a strange emotion brewing that she could not yet interpret. It made her want to fall into his arms and simultaneously made her want to run away screaming, hiding until the world around her finally ended.

"I don't care what you think," Ivo snapped, pulling Nariah further down the hallway, "she has every right to be furious with you." She found a secluded corner and released the Scout's arm. "You cannot speak to her like that."

"I can speak to her however I wish. Don't forget that I am the Scout that was assigned to her by the Kingdom. There is no one more suited to put her in her place."

"She doesn't need to be put in her place." Ivo's brows furrowed. "She needs *support*. Do you know the first thing about being someone's friend, or do you only know how to follow orders?"

Nariah seemed surprised by the remark and scoffed. "Well, maybe I am not trying to be her friend."

"Don't act like you don't care about her. You have helped her far too much to act like she still might be the criminal the Divinity says she is. You know Sima. You've been right here alongside her, just like I have. I know you can see that she isn't this horrid person with a deep secret."

The Scout frowned, but the fire in her eyes did not extinguish. "There are two Scouts who are dead because we came here to kill Carmine. She gave her permission, and she had an opening to do something, but she shut down instead. How can I not be angry when she lost her opportunity to prove herself?"

"Do you know what it's like? To be so afraid that it paralyzes you? Sima has been through more than any other person I know, and yet she is still kind, she still tries her best, and she doesn't lash out at her friends just because she is scared of the Kingdom."

Nariah's lip twitched. "I am not scared of the Kingdom."

"If you had to walk in her shoes, you wouldn't be able to make it through lunch. It is easy to judge her when you've never had to deal with having your whole life taken from you. I will not let you talk to her like that again. If you want to pick a fight, you can come to me, but you will not insult my best friend."

"I'm sorry, Ivo."

The fury in Nariah's eyes waned, ever so slightly, making her purple eyes sparkle. Intrusive thoughts about their steamy time together popped up in her mind, and Ivo nearly lost her composure. She couldn't tell what was worse, that she had crossed the line with the person who kept shackles over her best friend, or that some small piece of her wanted to touch the Scout one more time. Ivo clenched her jaw and leaned into her hurt, refusing to fall victim to the Scout's allure again.

Ivo turned her nose up and crossed her arms. "This time, I am not the one you need to apologize to."

"You're lucky I've even said the word 'sorry' twice to you. I hardly think apologizing is worth the trouble."

"Then why bother saying it to me? It's clear you don't care about pissing me off."

Nariah's tongue slid across her teeth beneath her lip. "I don't care about pissing you off. I care if I…never mind. I'll tell Sima I take it back. Can we let this go?"

"No, tell me," Ivo said.

Nariah let out a loud sigh. "I don't care if you're mad, but I'm not trying to be an asshole either. I don't want anyone to be hurt because of me, unless it's Vincenzo or perhaps Merit. But…"

"But?" A strong pressure squeezed the two of them closer, forcing Ivo to crane her neck to look up at the Scout. Nariah met her eyes and for one swift moment, Ivo wanted to kiss her, to feel their lips crash into each other as they had before Carmine's ambush.

"But I don't want to hurt Sima and I don't want to hurt you."

Ivo's breath caught, unsure if her mind added unspoken intention to Nariah's words, or if the Scout was truly implying something deeper. "Could have fooled me. You act like you can't stand me."

Nariah chuckled. "I know for a fact you hate every second we spend together."

A small smile crept across Ivo's lips. "Just about."

A mischievous twinkle in Nariah's eye made Ivo blush, somehow knowing what the Scout would say before she opened her mouth. "You didn't hate me when my tongue was—"

"Hush," Ivo snapped, standing on her toes to cover Nariah's mouth with her hand. "Enough of that."

"Are you embarrassed?"

"I don't want to talk about it," Ivo said, turning away, hating how red her face already was.

"Do you regret it?"

Something about Nariah's tone was serious, and Ivo shook her head. "This isn't the time for this. I haven't even washed the footprints off my body yet, Nariah."

"It doesn't matter what we did. It doesn't change anything between us."

For some reason, Ivo's heart pinched at her words. Her face scrunched, and Nariah's brows raised as if she knew she had once again hurt Ivo's feelings.

"You're right. Nothing has changed between us."

The Scout pressed her finger to her temple. "I didn't mean it in a negative way. I mean that I'm not expecting anything from you now just because we fooled around."

"I don't expect anything from you either," Ivo said harshly, her heart stampeding in her chest.

She stormed off down the hallway, only for Nariah to follow after her. "Ivo, wait."

"You need to apologize to Sima. I think we've said enough about the situation."

"So, you're going to pretend it never happened? That it wasn't real?"

Ivo slowed and turned to face Nariah. "It was real, but it won't happen again. Now, go in there, and say you're sorry."

Nariah's face flushed, and her wisteria eyes simmered. They held each other's gaze for a few more moments before the Scout tore herself away and stomped into Sima's room, where the door still lay on the floor.

Cosima

The comfortable silence the two of them could share was one of the main reasons Sima had fallen so quickly for Enzo. Somehow, he made simply sharing a space together an intimate way to rest or pass the time, as if their souls were replenishing their energy through proximity alone. Ivo and Nariah's arguing had ceased, but they were not the ones to enter first.

Merit walked into the room, rolling his eyes when he noticed Vincenzo and Cosima sitting together. "We need to make decisions for our next move. Word the bird people are giving to Ezekiel is that Carmine was potentially spotted in the outer perimeter of the city."

"We'll be ready the next time he comes," Enzo said, "but I hope he's not foolish enough to make another move so quickly. He'll be sloppy without proper time to recover. He's likely rushing back to his hiding spot to rest as we speak."

Nariah stormed into the room, Enzo reflexively shifting an inch further from Sima as she fixed her gaze on them. "I'm sorry," Nariah said through her teeth. "I should not have insinuated you were to blame for Carmine's escape. That was wrong of me," she swallowed, "and it was *not* your fault."

Sima glanced at Ivo standing in the hallway with her arms folded in front of her, then back to Nariah's flushed face. "I accept your apology."

"Good," Nariah said, stalking off and disappearing.

Ivo approached, wearing a smug grin.

"What did you say to her?" Sima asked, afraid of the answer.

"I convinced her of the error of her ways, that's all." Ivo shrugged.

"You don't think she was right about me?"

Ivo's hands wriggled into hers. "Not at all. Nariah is just upset that we didn't capture Carmine, but it's not your fault."

"I didn't expect Carmine to look so much like Aurelio. It terrified me, Ivo. My mind went blank."

"When have you taken time to rest and recover from Aurelio? When have you had the opportunity to be a person instead of serving as a means to an end for others? Of course, you had that reaction to seeing Carmine. In the grand scheme of things, hardly any time has passed since Aurelio died."

"I thought I was over this already, over *him*. Does the healing truly never end?"

Ivo sighed, but she smiled anyway. "Even if you take a few steps back, it means you're upright, and when you gain your balance again, you'll be ready. You just stumbled, is all. Don't be afraid to try again."

"How can I trust myself to act differently next time?"

"Are you ever going to give yourself the chance?"

Sima pondered her question as Ivo pulled her into a tight hug. "I heard his voice," Sima said into Ivo's hair.

"Who?"

"Aurelio." His name felt like a betrayal in her mouth. "Right before you found me, I saw Carmine, and I heard Aurelio's voice in my head, taunting me."

Ivo pulled back and looked her in the eyes. "He was never right about you. You were forced to hear every negative thought he had about you for years. Eventually, it was bound to become ingrained somewhere deep inside you. It's up to you to realize they were reflections of him more than they were ever reflections of you. He didn't know you, not the real you. But I do."

"If I can't do this successfully, who knows what might happen to me. This quest to kill his brothers…I thought I would feel vindicated or empowered, but all I am is frightened. Killing Aurelio, breaking free of him forever, it took everything I had. What if I don't have it in me to keep going and keep trying to make something of myself?"

"Have you considered that you're spending more time running toward a future you haven't figured out if you want yet?"

"What do you mean?"

"You know we are here to slay the remainder of his bloodline, but there is no telling what future you will have once that is completed. Have you thought about the life you want to live? For me, after Erelya was killed, I was spiraling. Thankfully I had you and other girls from my coven, but I stopped living and merely existed for months. One day, I realized if I didn't pick something to live for, I was going to walk right off the edge of our kingdom."

Sima sniffed, her brows furrowing. "I'm sorry, Ivo, I know that was a hard time for you."

"That's not why I brought it up. I want you to find what it is *you* want from this life, and I want you to go for it. When the world around us is not to be trusted, when every day is uncertain, there has to be something you want more than anything."

"I don't know what that is," Sima said meekly, tears streaming down her cheeks.

"Not yet," Ivo said, placing her hand on Sima's shoulder. "But you will. And when you do, I'll be right here alongside you, making sure you see it through. Now is not the time to give up. Fall, stumble, cry, and scream. But get back up every single time."

Sima looked at Ivo, weighed the determination and calm waters in her eyes, and knew she was telling the truth. Sima was not living for herself. Her love for Vincenzo had been enough to fuel her for a short while, but in this moment, she knew it would not be enough to sustain her. Living for someone else would never be as fulfilling as she needed it to be. This was dire. This was her will to live after so many years of wishing for death.

The conversation broke something open inside her, allowing hope to flood through her wary body. Sima needed to live for what was important to her. There would be setbacks on her healing journey, but there was also a destination she wanted to arrive at—somebody she wanted to become. She couldn't throw that away, not even if she was afraid.

"Thank you," Sima whispered. Her head fell. "Maybe you're right."

"We will regroup, we will be ready for him, and this time he won't get away." Ivo placed her hands on her hips. "You can't blame yourself for everything that goes wrong and expect to still be sane by the end of the day."

Sima relented a small smile. "Can't I?" she joked.

Ivo took her hand, and together they met the others who waited for them in the spacious lounge inside Ezekiel's abode. Allowing them to stay had been the least he could do, Vincenzo had said as he ushered them inside. Whether he had truly been gracious or if Vincenzo's powers had slithered into his mind, Cosima was thankful for somewhere safe to rest.

Nariah and Merit stood in the corner, sipping something out of silver-rimmed glass cups, talking quietly to each other. Nariah gripped her cup tightly, her mouth set in a firm frown. Vincenzo rested face down on a massive mint green sofa, his wings folded neatly behind him.

Vincenzo turned to them. "Go upstairs and choose one of the empty rooms to sleep in. Without a break, none of us will be prepared for him to show up again."

"Come on," Ivo said, tugging Sima along.

"Can we sleep together?" Sima asked as they walked up the stairs.

"Absolutely," Ivo replied.

She shut the door as Cosima climbed into the wide bed. The sheets were soft, but the bed was thin, making her uncomfortable, but not enough to protest or remedy the problem. Ivo slid in on the other side and snuggled near Sima, the two facing each other while curling in on themselves. Sima let herself think of Ivo's encouragement, letting it wash away her torment, if only long enough for her to finally fall asleep.

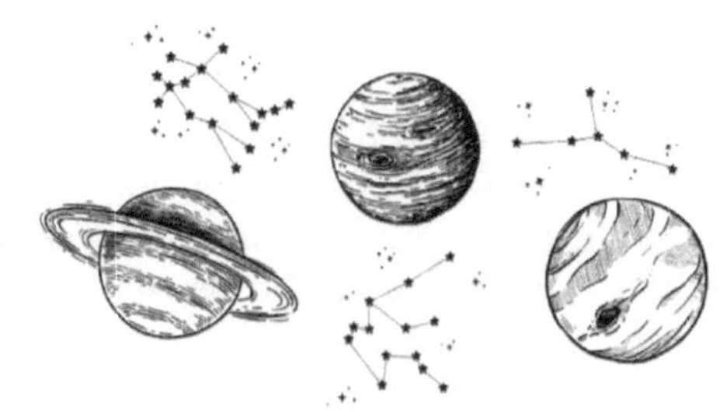

Chapter 25

Vincenzo

Thump, thump, thump, went Enzo's curse. All through the night, it pounded its invisible fists against the interior of his mind, scheming of ways to break free of the confines he created for it. Despite his efforts to halt its taunting whispers, he only grew more ill, overwhelmed with lovesick fever dreams centered on total domination.

We could have it all, his curse sang, *no one to tell us what to do, no more chains to bind us.*

"Shut up," Enzo murmured into his pillow.

The spare room in Ezekiel's home was three doors down from where Sima and Ivo slept, nearest to the stairs, should Enzo need to respond promptly to a threat. Beyond plain white bedding and a hard mattress, there was not much to look at, but it was a fine enough resting spot for him. If he could get quality rest, that is.

One of them will take her, his curse whispered. *If you continue to do nothing, one of them will steal her away. We can stop them. We must stop them.*

Enzo huffed as he flipped onto his back and slammed the pillow over his face. Through closed eyelids, he witnessed his fight with Carmine with crystal clear details. Every pulse of his power, every push back from his brother, every inch closer to the edge of the dark abyss—all on repeat as he dissected his every decision, before moving onto Carmine's.

His own faults were obvious. Enzo hesitated too often, retreated each time he approached the bottom of his well of power, fearing what lay beyond it. When he went deeper into his reserve during his fight with Carmine, he found a wealth of energy and thankfully retained control over himself somehow. However, it was only a matter of time before his curse consumed him if he continued to give in to its whims. He was not a fool. The dreams had not stopped. Whether the Hands of Fate gripped him in his sleep, or the universe itself willed him to remain in control, one fact remained certain—each time he drifted off at night, haunting warnings peppered his brain to stay far from his wicked power.

Perhaps that was why his curse was determined to keep him awake.

You are the chosen one, it taunted, *a power so great was surely not gifted by mistake*.

"Enough," Enzo snapped, sitting up.

He let out a heavy breath before his eyes fell onto Carmine's journal. Ivo had given it to him once they returned to Ezekiel's home after the fight, insisting that he read through the pages she had marked with folded corners.

"What better time," he mused as he picked it up. He flipped to the first marked page and began reading. "Let's see what Carmine has determined to be the truth of the prophecy.

The prophecy speaks of the one who will rule. It specifically mentions that the only one of us that will remain is the one with strength pure enough to withstand the weight of "true" responsibility. The story changes in small and vast ways, depending on the Oracle from which the word came, but I have done my best to make connections as I can. I have done my best to discern what exactly purity means, placing myself in the mindset of Kismet as she laid her rule.

Each retelling of the prophecy includes the usual traits such as courage, intelligence, charisma, devotion, and intention. However, the following also appear at a rate that cannot be attributed to chance: eyes that see all that hides beneath existence, ears that hear all that is not said, a heart that loves all that is not understood, and hands that feel all which has yet to be.

The purest one, in my opinion, will be the brother who can melt through his egotistical protective coating to reveal the awakened man within. He will be the one who is strongest because his restraint does not come from his fear. His purity is in his serenity, as several Oracles mention that his aura is the comforting monsoon breathing life into sandy seas.

Lastly, there is repeated mention of a name for the

one who prevails—The Scythe of Destiny. If that is not ominous, I don't know what is. It is in moments such as this where I am grateful that I have accepted my duty to die when my time comes. I know I am not the great one of which the prophecy speaks. Which of my brothers can withstand the test of Fate? Only time will tell.

Enzo's hands trembled as he stared down at the notebook, his brother's handwriting carved into the pages. His mind was rampant with confusion. Carmine spoke of the survivor of their doomed prophecy as if he were some kind of hero, as if that sort of title could be bestowed on men so twisted—Enzo included.

His self-loathing was sharper than usual due to Carmine escaping alive, but his time was limited. Even his brother was aware his final days were in the making. Whether he hoped Enzo or perhaps another of their siblings would find the notebook or not, Carmine's notebook was a lengthy dedication to his hope for a better future for their bloodline. Was that a hope Enzo could share?

The notebook flopped onto the nightstand as Enzo tossed himself back onto the bed, determined to pry at least a morsel of sleep from his tattered brain. If he wanted to remain in control of his curse, he would need to be well rested. Already, Carmine had revealed his hand and had shown how easily he could slip through Enzo's defenses if he wasn't carefully guarding them.

I will do anything to keep Sima safe, Enzo thought as his eyes fell shut.

And so will I, his curse whispered as he drifted off to sleep.

The scent of familiar dishes filled Ivo's nose, pulling her from the bed. She tucked the covers around her still sleeping friend and crept out of the room. She made her way into the kitchen as Vincenzo filled small white bowls with food. Merit sat with his legs propped on the chair beside him as he flipped through Carmine's journal. Nariah braided her hair as she spoke to Merit.

"What makes you think that sort of application is feasible for her?" Nariah asked. The Scout glanced up and made eye contact with Ivo. "Just in time. Sit and get something to eat. You'll need your strength."

"I am almost positive," Merit said. "Just because we haven't seen it before doesn't mean it isn't possible. Think about it—she can only extend as far as her imagination reaches. With a little nudge, who knows where she could go."

Ivo wrinkled her nose as she took a seat. "Are you talking about Cosima?"

Enzo slid a bowl in front of her filled with more food he had crafted to create meals for the group. "Merit seems to believe that Sima might be able to deflect Carmine's attacks if she can time it properly."

"It makes sense to me," Merit said, clasping his hands over his stomach. "I've seen what she can do to the surrounding environment. There is no reason she can't at least somewhat minimize the impact of Carmine's attacks."

Ivo's eyes fell on Nariah. The Scout sat with a furrowed brow. When their gazes met, Nariah said, "What do you think, Ivo? Is it worth the risk? We know that with every change of Fate, there is a chance something significant will be altered without the ability to undo it."

With a sigh, Ivo picked up her spoon and pushed around the chopped potatoes and peppers in her bowl. "I believe in Sima. I never agreed with the restriction of her power, despite the haunting consequences you constantly bring up. Sima was gifted that power, and you should trust her to use it."

"Sounds like you're the only one who doesn't agree, Nariah," Enzo said as he took a seat. "Her abilities could be just the advantage we need. We were ambushed, but this time we can go in with a proper plan. Allow her to use her powers with your rules clouding her judgment."

"You're the one who accused her of not doing enough," Ivo said. She took a small bite of food and chewed. "Let her prove to you why she deserves your trust."

Nariah let out a breath, her shoulders sagging slightly. "Alright. I will grant her permission, but if we are betting on the fact that preparation helps us end Carmine's life, then I want to test that deflecting ability before we attack."

Vincenzo nodded. "I agree with you. In fact, I was considering taking Ivo with me."

Ivo raised a brow. "Where are we going?"

Vincenzo smiled, brushing back his black and white hair. "Merit and I had an early morning forming the first stage of our plan. Using the information from Zadkiel about the location of Carmine's hideout, we mapped out the best place for some underground tunnels."

"Really?" Ivo asked. "How far did you get?"

"I've fully finished one section, but to ensure we trap my brother, I want to create a connecting tunnel on the opposite end, allowing us to attack from both sides. Are you up for accompanying me while I build the new area? I want to see more of your spells. I think you can play a vital role in this."

"Absolutely not," Nariah snapped. When everyone's head turned toward her, she glowered. "I do not trust you. You are not taking Ivo alone, nor are you putting her life at risk with your plans."

"Who said you get to decide for me?" Ivo shot back. "I want to contribute, and you're not going to take that from me."

Nariah's purple eyes fell on hers. "Ivo, this is dangerous. You could get hurt."

"I'm aware," Ivo said, crossing her arms. "But my life is my responsibility, not yours."

They continued to stare at each other until Enzo cleared his throat. "Merit, why don't we step outside and, uh, double-check the maps?"

Merit got to his feet and shot Ivo an amused smile before he headed toward the door. "Good plan. I could use some fresh air."

Once the door shut, leaving the two of them alone together, it was Nariah who broke the silence first. "Helping directly with Carmine means he could kill you. Even if Sima can deflect his attacks, that doesn't mean something won't go wrong with this plan. You're not built to be in fights like this."

"I am not a child. You can't decide what I can and cannot do. You don't have to constantly remind me of how weak I am in your eyes."

"Oh, please," Nariah said with a roll of her eyes. "This is not about you being weak, Ivo, this is about me wanting you to survive this."

Ivo growled at the use of her name. "So, we fool around one time, and now you think you own me? I will be in charge of keeping myself alive, alright, Nariah?"

"You can't still be angry with me because of that night," Nariah whispered, her tone taunting.

"Shut up," Ivo shot back.

"I told you I was sorry. What we did was not a sin."

Ivo's cheeks flushed, her memory explicit and *loud*. "Yes, it was. Who knows how the others will feel if they found out? Especially since you're a hypocrite."

"I am a loyal servant to the Divinity, I know their laws and their honor code like it is tattooed inside my eyelids. For that same reason, I know we have done nothing wrong. The Kingdom has not banned you and me from exploring each other's bodies," the Scout said with a smirk. "From what I recall, you had a pleasurable experience."

"Hush," Ivo hissed, grabbing Nariah by her collar and pulling her closer. "Do not breathe a word of this to anyone."

Nariah gazed into her eyes as a small smile broke across her face. "Do you know how good it feels to be this close to you again?" she asked, her voice a whisper.

With how close they were, Ivo's nose caught the Scout's alluring scent. Ivo bristled as Nariah leaned forward until their faces were only inches apart. For a moment, she didn't move, didn't back away from the Scout's advances, her heart pounding loudly in her ears as she let their lips hover so near to one another.

"I knew it," Nariah whispered, pulling back and returning to her seat.

Ivo slumped back into hers and crossed her arms. "Whatever. You're… unfortunately hot, but it doesn't make you, or what we did, right."

"It won't happen again," the Scout said, winking as she swung her legs to rest on the table.

Ivo scrunched her nose. "You're right about that."

"Unless you want it to," Nariah said with a flick of her brows.

"Shut *up*," Ivo hissed.

"Good morning," Cosima's voice floated from the hallway.

Grateful for her friend's presence, Ivo let out a sigh of relief. Sima entered the kitchen, her black hair tucked behind her ears as she blinked away her sleepy haze.

"Hi, lovely," Ivo chirped. "Vincenzo saved the day again by making breakfast."

Sima smiled as Nariah reached for a bowl and placed it in front of her. "Let me catch you up on the plan."

Ivo excused herself, heading to the bathroom. She was already dressed for the day, but more than anything, she needed to get away from Nariah's smug face. Her cheeks burned hot again, and she was thankful Cosima had not seemed suspicious of them when she wandered in.

She sat on the edge of the tub and rolled her neck. Maybe what she and Nariah had done was not against any rules set by the Kingdom, but she had betrayed her friend, or at least that was what the feeling in her gut told her. Sima could not even touch Enzo, and here Ivo was, sleeping with the Scout who kept her friend in line as an indebted assassin.

It all happened so fast, she thought, as she stood up and paced in the cramped bathroom just off the kitchen where Sima and her Scout chatted. The night of Carmine's attack, Nariah had come across Ivo, who was already nude in the tub, wearing only a flimsy towel across her body. The way the Scout looked, it was shamefully unsurprising that Ivo had blurred all reasonable judgment and not objected when Nariah dropped it, exposing herself before she dipped into the water with her.

Her heart raced as she remembered Nariah's lips crashing into hers, how undeniably relieving it was to give in to the desires she had been suppressing. They had thrown previous boundaries out the window, expelling frustration through physical means, not stopping until they reached a blissful end for both of them. As much as Nariah infuriated her, she couldn't help but crumble beneath her touch.

The Scout might have initiated their passionate moment, but at no point did either of them truly relinquish control. It was like they kissed with their guard up, hands exploring as if they were enemies hunting for vulnerability. Yet, there was an undeniable softness to Nariah's touch as though she craved something more than release. Ivo had tangled her hands into Nariah's white hair, and it was like touching a painting hidden behind ropes—thrilling and forbidden.

Every delicate curve of the Scout's body begged for Ivo to return, haunting her thoughts with explicit memories. Secretly, she was ashamed at how easily she had given in to the temptation and at how she was desperate to do it again. Ivo yearned to press her lips to her bare skin, to fill her senses with Nariah's taste and scent. But they could not. A Scout could not be with a mortal, and Ivo's heart could not withstand another heartbreak. Despite her desires, Ivo knew she was better off distancing herself from Nariah.

A knock rattled the door. "It's time to go. Hurry up in there," Nariah barked. Ivo pulled herself together and emerged from the bathing chamber. The white-haired Scout looked her up and down before frowning. "Are you unwell or just unhappy?"

Ivo scowled. "Your presence makes me feel both."

"Will you two just kiss already?" Enzo sighed.

Ivo's cheeks burned hot as her eyes fell to the floor. Nariah stammered something incomprehensible and stormed off, slamming Ezekiel's front door on the way out. Merit snickered as he trailed after the Scout, and Sima was staring at her, studying her with the hint of something Ivo couldn't quite place.

"You like her," Cosima said.

It was almost a question, but Ivo knew better than to think she could hide something from such a perceptive friend. Enzo pretended to look around the room at anything but her and Sima. "No, I was caught off guard," Ivo said.

Enzo coughed in a poor attempt at concealing his laughter. Sima's eyes flicked to him, then back to her. Ivo swallowed, her mouth dry and scratchy.

"Does she like you?" Cosima asked.

"No," Ivo said.

"Yes," Enzo said at the same time.

Ivo shot him a dirty look before turning back to Sima. Her friend swayed slightly side-to-side, as if she were weighing how much she believed them. "You were going to tell me something the other night, when Carmine attacked. Weren't you?"

A cool wave washed down Ivo's back as she straightened. She had thought Cosima had forgotten all about it, and she did not intend to be the one to bring it up. "Yes," she said, pausing. Her friendship with Sima meant more to her than any fling she might have with Nariah. "Nariah and I... were intimate."

Vincenzo flipped around, concealing his reaction as he aptly sensed his departure would be appropriate. By the time the door closed behind him, Sima's brows had been fully raised for a minute straight. Ivo squirmed as she waited for her to speak.

Growing anxious, she blurted, "I'm sorry. Please don't be mad at me. It was a mistake, and I don't think it will ever happen again anyway. No, I know it won't. I know it was a stupid thing to do."

Sima's brows lowered, and her head cocked slightly to the side. "Mad at you?"

"Yes?" Ivo replied, cringing.

Sima burst into laughter. Ivo's body went rigid in response to her amusement, her friend's reaction unexpected. "No, Ivo," Sima said between laughs, "I'm not mad at you."

"You're not? But she's practically your prison guard. You don't think I've betrayed you by sleeping with the woman who reports on you to the Kingdom?"

She shook her head. "No. I want you to know I mean this sincerely. I refuse to mind your sheets and whoever you bring within them. Do as you please, as long as you feel safe and good about it."

"I feel like a rotten friend for being with Nariah on this mission when you and Enzo can't even be alone together."

Cosima laughed again. "The distance is not always a bad thing. I think it's allowing me to see the bigger picture of who he is. Don't worry, Ivo. I promise, it is alright. I would rather you be happy than worrying about what I will think. Besides, you have a way of seeing the potential in things others might dismiss. There's no doubt in my mind that if something has drawn you two together, that it's for a reason."

Ivo's shoulder sagged, but with relief instead of horror and embarrassment. Suddenly, her attraction to the Scout did not seem so shameful.

"Thank you."

"Do you want to be with her?"

The question caught Ivo off guard. She shrank in her seat. "I don't know. In fact, I don't know what being with her would look like or if she has any genuine interest in me anyway."

"How do you feel about her?" Sima raised a brow. "Genuinely?"

"I feel…" Ivo blew out a breath. "Like I can't stop thinking about her, no matter how much I try. She creeps into my dreams when I'm asleep and haunts my thoughts when I'm awake. She makes me so angry, and yet somehow it only makes me want to be closer to her."

"So why not give it a try?"

Ivo shook her head. "You know why."

Sima was quiet for a moment. "You can't let her death stop you. She would want you to be happy."

"Who says Nariah would even make me happy? What if I risk it all and in the end, I wind up more miserable than before?"

"Then it will have been worth it to have loved at all. Would you go back and change your past if it meant never loving *her*?"

Ivo's heart pinched, painful memories of her dead partner floating into her mind. The grief was too great, and she shoved it away. "No. I wouldn't change a thing. But I don't think I can love again."

"Start with simply admitting how you feel," Sima said. Vincenzo entered the front door and stood beside it, signaling it was time to depart. Sima pulled her into a quick hug. "I'll see you soon. Be careful," Sima said with a smile.

Ivo waved her goodbye and turned to Vincenzo. "She can't come with us?"

Enzo's eyes were locked onto Sima as he watched her and the other two Scouts leave. "Nariah refuses to leave Cosima's side, and Merit plans to show them the other passageway I created so they are familiar with the layout. You're coming with me as I craft the next stage."

Ivo followed after him, using her hand as a shield from the sun when they stepped outside. "So you just remember everything you create in a space? Do you ever get lost?"

Vincenzo smirked as he led her down an empty street. The surviving people of Riejj hid themselves away after Carmine's attack, leaving the city near silent. "No, I don't get lost. It is fairly easy for me to remember what I've created because my magic is fine-tuned for mapping."

"Sounds like cheating," Ivo said.

He laughed. "A bit, perhaps. It is handy to never lose track of what I've created, especially when I really get going. In Ombra, I manifested an entire underground city. The people worked to permanently build onto my structures to create a sustainable home for themselves. They often came to me for help or with questions, but soon, they no longer needed me to keep things running."

They turned onto another empty street, and the closer they grew to the edge of the city, the sparser the buildings became. "I can't imagine what it is like to have a power like that."

Enzo gave a small nod. "It…has its downsides."

Ivo cocked her head to the side. "Like what? I'd do anything to have abilities like yours."

He sighed. "It takes a lot out of me. I have to expend a lot of energy each day, or it begins to accumulate. It gets painful fast, and too much of it makes me delirious." He pointed to the end of the street where a sliver of the mountain behind the canyon was visible. "That's where we're going."

"You aren't creating cities anymore, though. Does that mean you've been struggling since you left Haelos?"

"Yes, immensely," he said, sweeping his hair from his face with his hand. "But I have managed to find other ways to expel energy, at least enough to keep me from going insane. That comes with its own costs, too, though."

"I had no idea your power created so much trouble for you." Ivo wrapped her arms around herself. "A blessing and a curse, isn't it?"

Enzo stiffened before he let out a breath. "I'd say so."

Ivo chewed her lip as she considered the enormity of his magic. "Can I ask you something?"

"Sure," he replied.

They reached the end of the street and continued walking on the empty dirt patch between the city and the mountainside. The navy rock reminded Ivo of the day Earnest and Horacio died, a shudder spreading across her body at the memory. "The prophecy says only one of the Sacred Twelve will survive. What will you do if that's you? Are you prepared to rule the Eternal Kingdom?"

Vincenzo pressed his mouth into a line and let out a slow breath through his nose. "I will be the one who survives, but I will not be the one who rules. Listen, you have to understand that a lot of what we know comes from rumors that people take as fact. Oracles confirm different parts of the story, but a majority of the information doesn't overlap. I tried my best to do some research prior to ending up on Haelos, but I never got very far. All I know is that the Celestial Empresses themselves have *never* confirmed that the Divinity would have to step down in favor of an Empress and Emperor. I'm sure my mother would love nothing more, but I have no interest in being an Emperor."

"Not even with Sima by your side?" Ivo asked.

He recoiled slightly. "I…"

Ivo put her hands on her hips as she walked. "I thought you'd do anything for her."

Enzo chuckled. "I would do anything for her, but she hasn't exactly asked me to rule alongside her. Neither the Divinity nor Kismet has confirmed Cosima's heritage, so I am sure she has convinced herself she is still without a home."

"Well, what do you believe?"

"I have full faith that she is related to Kismet. If not her missing daughter, then a missing niece or granddaughter. Either way, her ability to manipulate the Weave cannot be overlooked."

Ivo raised a brow. "Then you must also believe she is the next Empress. You can't have it both ways, Enzo. You believe she is destined to rule, but you live in denial about what that means for you. Look how far you two have come already. If I know anything about Sima, it's that she wants this. She wants to command an Empire. It is in her blood, and I know you see it, too."

They came to a stop beside the base of the mountain. From where they stood, Ivo could see the Red Feather Tower Zadkiel had told Vincenzo about. Enzo avoided her gaze as he studied the giant rock wall in front of them.

"You'll have to face this eventually," Ivo said, crossing her arms.

He sighed. "I know, Ivo. I know. I'll get there. Right now, I'm just trying to kill this fucker for touching her."

Ivo shrugged. "The sooner you talk to her about your feelings, the better. All that resistance you feel inside can only be dealt with if you admit it's there and talk about it."

Vincenzo hung his head as his hand rested on the rock. "I could say the same to you."

Her jaw dropped. "What could you possibly be referring to?"

"You're love-sick over Nariah. When will you admit you like her?"

Ivo's face flushed. "I don't know what you're talking about."

His hands moved in front of him as he closed his eyes. Green smoke-like energy poured from his palms and seeped into the rock. "I think the only one who doesn't know how you feel for her is you. Why are you so resistant to her? It's clear how badly you two want to be together."

"Clear in what way? We are constantly at each other's throats." Ivo rolled her eyes. "She can't stand me."

With one blink of her eyes, a passageway manifested in the rock before them. A long tunnel lit with glowing orange spheres on the ceiling beckoned them forward.

"I think that's just how you two flirt," Enzo said, lifting his brows as he smiled.

"I'm nothing more than some conquest to Nariah. I doubt she actually cares for me the way you think."

Enzo had a soft, amused expression, looking down on her like a knowing older brother. "I think someone like Nariah wouldn't spend all her time staring at you if she didn't care for you. Come on, it's time to explore."

Ivo's pulse quickened as she trailed after him, her thoughts stampeding untamed inside her mind. Could Nariah really have feelings for her? It seemed outrageous to consider a relationship with the Trine Scout. Could such a union exist between an occasionally lucky witch and the force of nature that was Nariah?

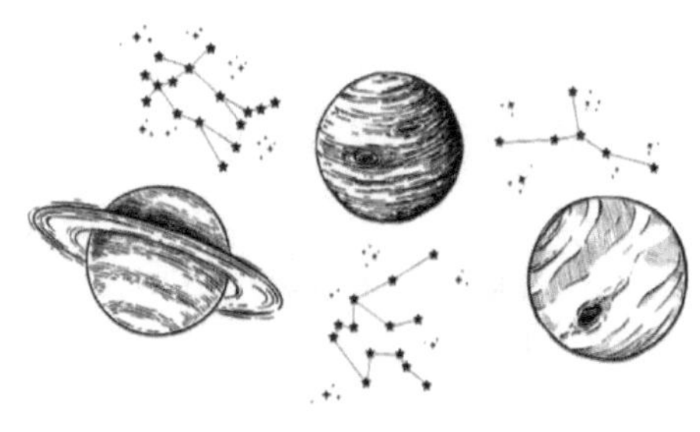

Chapter 26

Cosima

The passageway created by Vincenzo was spacious and well-lit, somehow full of his comforting energy as Cosima stepped inside. Merit stood off to the side with his hands on his hips as Nariah and Sima looked around.

"Well, you're looking at Enzo's trap. I'll show you both the different divisions, but first things first, the exit. Obviously, if Carmine is on his way out, we don't want him to escape." Merit placed his hand on the wall and pushed. A pulse of green energy lit up a square in the rock. A moment later, giant bars slid from the ceiling, closing off the exit behind Sima, making her jump. "Sorry about that. Remember this spot. There's no magic needed, just a push of your hand."

"Got it," Sima said, stepping away from the metal bars. "How far are we from Carmine?"

Merit frowned. "We've got plenty of room from where we are standing, but as we venture deeper, we will inevitably inch closer to his hideout. During those sections of the hideout, we need to avoid speaking too loud, so we don't draw attention to ourselves."

"Any other traps we should know of?" Nariah asked with her hands on her hips.

"Oh, plenty," Merit said. "Feathers is a pretty inventive guy, I've got to give that to him. I didn't expect it."

Sima smiled, and in response, Nariah rolled her eyes. "I don't understand how Vincenzo being good at setting deadly traps is anything but ominous."

Merit laughed and waved them forward. "It's not a competition, you know that, right, Nariah? You won't get an award from the Divinity for hating Vincenzo with your whole chest. I mean, I don't always agree with him, but give it a break for now."

"Whatever," Nariah grumbled.

"We're almost to our next stop," Merit said over his shoulder.

Nariah continued to fume as she walked beside Merit. Cosima trailed behind them, twisting her hair with her fingers, unsure of what to make of Merit's defense of Enzo. As they reached the end of the first passageway, seven archways appeared, each with a different symbol above it.

"What do those images represent?" Sima asked, pointing at them with her finger.

Merit rubbed a hand over his tricep. "I'll do my best to remember, but keep in mind, this is bird-boy's expertise. He claims each symbol represents a different building block of the universe. Down the one with the red symbol is a space filled with raidnen. Next to it, beneath the blue symbol, is a cavern filled with hyloten. The yellow symbol is a void suspended in helbrium."

Merit pressed two fingers to the bridge of his nose as he closed his eyes. "The purpose of the first three is to create weightless environments with different properties than this world. Raidnen is kind of like smoke and flame, hyloten is like gas and water, and helbrium is like electricity and air."

Sima blinked a few times. "I…don't know what that means."

The Scout shrugged and ran a hand through his navy hair. "Hey, I'm telling you everything I remember. You're lucky I recalled as much as I did because I sure as stars don't know the other four."

"Typical," Nariah scoffed, rolling her eyes.

"My head can only hold so much at once," Merit said, with a hint of attitude.

Sima resisted smiling. "Great job, Merit. Which one are we going down first?"

Merit crossed his arms in front of his chest. "Thank you, and what a great question. We *cannot* go down the first three, which is why I remembered what they were. Due to the volatile nature of Vincenzo's magic, we need to avoid them at all costs. The other four, however, are filled with traps, but as long as we don't trigger them, we should be fine. First up is the mirror realm under the purple symbol."

"Mirror realm?" Sima asked, her eyes growing wide.

The Scout grinned, his orange gaze bright. "That's the one where you'll practice some new techniques. I've run the idea by Vincenzo and Nariah already. Come on."

Sima's stomach flopped, but she hastily followed after Merit down the passageway with the purple symbol. The orange glowing orbs along the ceiling faded, causing the tunnel to grow dark for a brief moment before a mystical lavender light became visible on the other side. Once she stepped through the opening, her jaw fell open. Sima swirled as she took in the sparkling, mind-boggling room.

Colorful like stained-glass but full of more intricate geometry, the space had an alluring aesthetic. As they walked through the room, the light reflected, causing a shifting rainbow of transforming shapes. Sima's heart pounded as she gleefully spun in circles, enamored by the brilliant display. She twirled, watching her reflection dance as she did, while the room morphed and glittered.

"This is…divine," Sima breathed.

Nariah lifted a brow as she looked around. "Yeah, it's something."

"This is the perfect place for you to practice, Sima," Merit said. "I believe that you are capable of deflecting attacks with your magic. You wouldn't be making direct changes to other people's Fate, you'd be negating an action."

Sima chewed her lip. "Yes, but that always comes with a redirection. I cannot cancel it out entirely, the outcome always shifts to something or someone else."

Merit cocked his head to the side. "Not if you hit the threads just right."

"Are you sure about this?" Sima said. Nariah wore an indiscernible mask on her face, but Merit appeared enthused. He nodded eagerly, and she let out a sigh. "Alright, let's give it a try."

"That's the spirit," Merit said. He turned to Nariah. "Teach her how to see the threads without touching them."

The Scout's white hair swished as she swirled around, leaving her back facing them. She waved her hand in the air, and thousands of tiny, iridescent threads manifested in the air around them. Sima gasped as she reached for one of the strings, only for her finger to pass right through it. The beauty of the threads was magnified by the mirror realm Enzo created.

"You can summon this view anytime you wish," Nariah said, crossing her arms. "To do so, reach for your power as normal, but imagine you are pulling it from the center of your body, instead of from your hands or heart. Set the intention—you are commanding the Weave to respond as you request."

Cosima blew out a breath and did as Nariah instructed. At first, nothing happened, but after a moment, a tingling sensation tickled her core. The threads exploded, more vibrant than when Nariah had first manifested them. Her fingers trembled as she reached for one, and this time, a tangible string pressed into her skin.

"Perfect," Nariah said. "Don't go further than that."

"You better be ready to get your ass handed to you," Merit said, squatting down with his palms facing her. "The best way to learn is by doing."

Sima raised a brow, prepared to laugh, when suddenly a burst of purple-blue starlight blasted right toward her. She dove out of the way and rolled across the invisible floor. She held her head as she sat up, finding the mirror realm to be disorienting after her tumble. The threads she manifested slowly disappeared. Ready to scold him, Sima opened her mouth, only for Merit to aim at her again.

"Get on your feet," he hollered. "I'm not going easy on you."

Sima ran as blasts of starlight pulsed behind her. Her magic burned at her fingertips, and she positioned her hand in Merit's direction. As her legs pushed harder, Sima took a deep breath and pulled from her core, allowing the threads to resurface. A stream of starlight barreled toward her, and Sima's hand snagged a thread. She successfully deflected the blast, but the starlight continued to bounce around, reflected by the mirrors. Sima dodged it when it neared her before it finally shattered like ice and disappeared. She took a moment to catch her breath before she looked up at Merit. "Are you trying to kill me?"

"Don't be dramatic," Merit said. "Starlight can't kill you."

"That went better than I expected," Nariah said, adding a small nod. "I approve. Let me join you."

Vincenzo's magic swam through the soil and sediment, spreading like flame through brush as he created his underground playground. His power was a symphony of contradictions so intricate he could only hope he was worthy of its enormity. His pulse was loud in his ears as he walked forward, careful to keep his face neutral to avoid scaring Cosima's best friend with his inner turmoil.

Craft your disgraceful brother a coffin from which he cannot escape, his curse hummed.

Ivo had her arms crossed over her chest, her gaze distant as she lost herself in her thoughts. Although Enzo was not intending to spy on her,

Ivo did not have any inner shielding, allowing her emotions to permeate into the air like rain before a storm. It was as though Enzo could smell her conflicting feelings for Nariah, the way Ivo struggled to cope with her desires.

Unable to help himself, Enzo cleared his throat and asked, "What is it about her that gets you so riled up?"

Ivo glared at him. "You're talking about Nariah?" She rolled her eyes. "It'd be easier to tell you what doesn't bother me about her."

Enzo smirked. "Perfect plan. Tell me what you like about Nariah."

Her brows pinched. "I didn't say I liked anything. Some parts of her are just more tolerable than others."

He held his hands up in front of him. "Fair enough. What troubles you the least?"

Ivo scowled as she faced forward, the path manifesting in front of them with every step. "I guess I don't mind when she's protective of Sima, as long as she's doing it the right way. I admire her loyalty to the Eternal Kingdom, even if it doesn't make sense to me. I don't know what it's like to be committed to something like that. I also think she's a decent leader when she isn't expecting everyone to kiss her ass for it." She shot Enzo a sideways glance before she looked forward again. "And she's not hard on the eyes either."

Although he tried to hold it in, Enzo laughed, which only amplified Ivo's attitude. She smacked his arm as her cheeks burned red. "Shut up! It's not funny."

"I'm sorry," Enzo said, composing himself. "It's not funny. It's just really cute that you have a crush on her."

Ivo halted and stomped her foot. "It is not cute!"

This time, Enzo laughed freely. "Listen, I don't personally get your attraction since I find Nariah to be a buzz-kill, but I don't know…your little budding romance makes her seem more…like a person than a servant to the Most High."

The bright color slowly faded from Ivo's face as she resumed walking with him. "I've heard about her reputation. She is used to getting with anyone she wants. What makes me special? Besides, I'm mortal. It quite literally wouldn't last between us."

Enzo's heart panged with the reminder of Ivo's shorter lifespan. "She seems to think you're worth all the trouble."

"You keep saying stuff like that," Ivo murmured.

"Because I mean it," Enzo said. "I've met Scouts like her before. She puts on the tough act, pretends like she loves the attention, and guards herself from getting hurt. That doesn't mean she doesn't like you. Maybe

I just have a keen eye, but Nariah is constantly concerned with your well-being, and well, she listens to you. She asks for your opinion, she trusts what you have to say, and she even apologized to Sima because of you. That's no small feat."

"Yeah, I guess so, but it doesn't make up for all the hot and cold behavior," Ivo said.

"Maybe not," Enzo said, rubbing a hand behind his head, "but have you asked yourself if you're reflecting the same kind of behavior back to her? How open are you to her advances?"

Enzo slowed to a stop in front of a giant tree that his magic created. Its roots dug down into the navy stone beneath their feet, and its branches tunneled through the walls. It had a glowing emerald trunk with sparkling sapphire leaves. It pulsed lightly, in tune with Enzo's heart.

Your ability to destroy is paralleled only by your ability to create, his curse whispered. *Look at the symphony of matter that manifests as you will it.*

Ivo scrunched her nose as she stared up at it. "What does it do?"

"It communicates." Enzo reached for one of the leaves. When it touched his skin, a bright wave of green light raced across the tree. "I learned it from the faeries in Eternita. Wasn't a whole lot I was able to pick up, but they inspired me nonetheless. Its roots are through this whole thing, including the section where Cosima and the others are. At any point during our battle with Carmine, we can use this tree to communicate, ask for help, or engage the locks."

Enzo turned to Ivo. "I believe your magic will work well with it. Your witch powers are tightly connected to nature, and that's why I believe you will be able to magnify the scope of your attacks by using the communicative abilities of the tree."

She lifted a brow. "How?"

"You channel your magic into it the same way I do, by setting the intention and touching a piece of it. What is an attack spell you are comfortable with using frequently? Why don't we test it out?"

Ivo rubbed her arm. "I use my electricity spell the most." She sighed. "Step back."

Enzo nodded as he put distance between himself and Ivo until his wings touched the wall. "Keep your focus on simply infusing the tree with your magic. You don't need to direct it anywhere yet. Go ahead. You can do this."

She blew out a breath and flexed her fingers. "Right, I can do this." Ivo reached up and held one of the sapphire leaves in her hand. "*Onda elettrica,*" she whispered.

A fierce arc of blue energy waved through the tree, dousing the room in bright light. All of Ivo's hair stood up, her black strands sticking straight above her head. The tips of the branches began to spark with blue electricity, creating flashes like lightning as the energy connected with the ground.

Interesting, Enzo thought. *Certainly more power than I expected.*

Ivo ended the flow of her magic and turned to him as her hair fell flat once more. "Well, how did I do?"

Enzo smiled. "Fantastic. The power output on that spell was impressive. Have you always been this strong, Ivo?"

She looked away. "I guess so, I don't know. Nariah mentioned something about it."

"Oh, really?" Vincenzo cocked his head to the side. "What was it?"

Ivo huffed. "It's stupid."

He chuckled. "Come on, tell me."

"She thinks I'm…*lucky*. I don't know what she's talking about. I've never been lucky, but she keeps telling me I'm changing circumstances to benefit me without touching the Weave."

Enzo's curse maniacally cackled inside his head as he pushed off the wall and walked toward her. "Perhaps you're using your power without meaning to. Your spell worked well, but I have to admit, it worked almost too well. I've heard of being favored by the Hands of Fate, but I don't know how that applies when you are actually calling on your magic. Either way, you've got more to work with than you give yourself credit for. Come on, let me show you to another section. I want you to practice channeling your energy from one room to another."

"Do you really think I can be an important part of this plan?" Ivo chewed her cheek.

"Oh, without a doubt, Ivo. You're an essential part of this plan." Enzo laid his hand on her shoulder and gave it a reassuring squeeze before he let go. "Let's see what else you're capable of."

"Enough," Sima yelled, panting as she held a hand out in front of her to hold time. Merit and Nariah easily broke through her time pocket, but their starlight remained frozen in mid-air before Sima. "I need a break, please."

Nariah's white ponytail moved like a snake as she walked over. "That was pretty good work, I have to admit it. The running and dodging perhaps needs improvement, but the deflections are perfect."

Merit put his hands on his hips. "I told you she could do it. I think she's already ready for the next level."

Sima's heart thudded. "I don't like the sound of that. There's more you want me to do?"

Merit's thin, green wings flashed as he flew over to them. "You have the ability to touch the Weave. We've already discussed your ability to swap out one action for another, but what if there was a way for you to negate or minimize an attack as well?"

"I don't think that's possible," Sima said, shaking her head. "I told you that I've never been able to fully stop something from happening."

"That doesn't mean you aren't able to." Merit rubbed his chin. "You have immense power, but it means nothing if you don't know how to properly use it. Your abilities should make you practically unstoppable, but I haven't seen you deploy anything significant yet. I got a glimpse of you using it during Carmine's ambush, and it got me thinking. I've been talking to Nariah about the threads, and I might have figured out a way to help you."

Merit lightly smacked Nariah with the back of his hand. She rolled her eyes but waved her hand in front of her, allowing the iridescent threads to resurface. Nariah met Sima's gaze.

"Merit, and I assume that the way you're currently making changes is by taking a section of thread, removing it, and replacing it with your command. This is likely why there is still a required outcome, because you are shifting one area, not the entirety of the action. Events are all chain reactions, and without accommodating for that, you risk not getting what you want out of the change."

Cosima's mind swirled. "What can I do differently then?"

The Scouts exchanged a glance before Merit said, "You don't need to remove anything; you only need to alter the fibers of the thread. There are millions of fibers to every thread, each carrying incomprehensible amounts of information. If you find the one that aligns directly with the incoming attack, you should be able to take hold of it directly to alter the outcome. Think of it like this: I'm waving a knife in front of your face. You can kick the knife away, but it won't stop me from coming at you with my fists. On the other hand, you can grab my hand and point the knife back toward me. I might reconsider attacking you, or I get a taste of the same energy I was putting out, and I end up hurt."

Sima nodded slowly. "I think I understand what you're saying. I have been changing a giant section of the thread, thinking that replacing it will stop the events already in motion, but that doesn't work. Instead, I need to grab onto the moving parts and direct them differently. Not working against Fate, but with it."

The navy-haired Scout clapped his hands together. "Exactly. Now, how this will work in negating the attack entirely is through probability. A game of chance is happening all the time around us. Bend it in your favor, Cosima. When you know they're ready to attack, find the exact moment electricity fires in their brain, and the wheel of fortune begins to spin. You should be able to find an outcome that cancels out the action. Like in my case, there will be a moment where my starlight misfires. Seize it and bring it to fruition."

"How do you know everyone has a point at which their attacks or magic fail?" Sima asked, her stomach twisting into knots.

Merit smirked. "There has to be. Every single action has an equal and opposite reaction. There can be no 'on' for someone's magic if there is not also an 'off'. Confuse the signal and turn it back off, despite the energy being summoned."

Cosima pressed her lips together as she stared off into the sparkling mirrors behind the Scouts. The moment Carmine kissed her abruptly intruded on her mind, followed by a haunting reappearance of her former husband's taunting. *Sick little lamb,* Aurelio's disembodied voice whispered, *with wool matted in blood, you still follow my plans, just as I thought you would.*

The words made her heart skip. Sima squeezed her eyes shut and took a slow, shaky breath. With might, she shoved against the horrid memories and grounded herself in reality. When she opened her eyes again, she found both Scouts staring at her. Nariah's brows were pinched together as she leaned slightly forward and inspected Sima silently. Merit's facial expression was tight, but his orange irises blazed with certainty.

"You can do this," he said, his voice soft, but firm. "Don't let a single thing anyone has said to you get to you now. Who you were then is not who you are now. Carmine is scary, he looks like your ex, I get it, but he's not fucking tougher than you, Sima, you hear me? He doesn't have shit on you. You've gotten chewed up and spit out. This loser hides when he's scared and hurts others so he doesn't feel so small inside. Not only can you face him again, you can make sure the last thing he ever fucking sees is the rage in your eyes."

Though her hands trembled, the fear dripped away. Little by little, her fire within defrosted her icy panic, allowing her to seize the strands of her destiny. "You're right," she said as she squared her shoulders. "I want to do this, I want to learn to wield my powers with more precision."

"That's the spirit," Merit said, clasping a hand on her shoulder. "Alright, enough talking." He let go and shot into the air with Nariah not far behind him. The Scouts aimed their palms at her, and Merit grinned. "Show me what it looks like when the fibers of eternity do as you command, Weave Wielder."

Sima spun on her heel and ran. She pulled from her core, and threads manifested as Nariah had taught her. As blasts of starlight barreled toward her, Sima deflected them while also searching for the right moment to negate their shots. She struggled to keep focused as the Scouts continued to pursue her.

In order to gain some time to think straight, Sima positioned her hand behind her and let her magic explode outward. She created enormous cracks in the mirror realm as a wave of starlight slammed into the Scouts. The cracks self-sealed as the realm restabilized, and a cloud of black smoke concealed Nariah and Merit from view. Sima glanced up toward the ceiling and spotted them in the reflection above, both covered head to toe in black ash.

Sima cringed. "Are you two alright?"

Merit couched and emerged from the smoke. Only his eyes and teeth were visible as he smiled. "Now we're talking! Not quite what I was hoping for, but being able to magnify magic is just as useful."

Nariah scowled as she exited the dark cloud. She wiped away the ash from her face, leaving streaks all over her skin. "At least you're making progress, I suppose."

The smoke dissipated, and in its place was a strange ripple. It was almost entirely translucent, except that it shimmered and slightly distorted the colorful geometric mirror behind it. Sima squinted as she walked toward it. "What is that?" she asked.

As she moved closer, she noticed movement at the very center. There was a razor-thin, vertical slit in the air as tall as Sima that shifted in color and light. Nariah's hand wrapped around her arm.

"Stop, don't get any closer until we know what it is."

"Did you rip a damn hole in the universe?" Merit asked as he folded his arms in front of his chest.

Sima glanced at him and then at the ripple. She swallowed hard. "I hope not."

Chapter 27

Ivo stared at the glowing green branch with a raised brow. "Are you sure about this?"

Enzo nodded. "There's nothing to worry about. Remember, the intention is the most important piece of your magic. If you are rock solid on your intention, nothing can sway you."

Her eyes flicked to him and back to the branch. It stretched across the entirety of the stone room, which was twice the size of the ballroom where Carmine had ambushed them. The room itself was full of invisible traps, from gigantic saw blades hiding within shadows to swinging spiked boards with ruthless speed. Despite Vincenzo's promises that none of the contraptions would be triggered by her, Ivo's hands trembled as she took a step forward.

"*Onda di ghiaccio*," Ivo whispered with her palm outstretched.

Ice funneled from her hand and coated the floor. Enzo's eyes flashed with green, causing the branch to pulse with light. A second later, Vincenzo's own ice magic combined with hers, creating impressive sculptures in the shape of mini palaces. From behind the sculptures, several of his Wrenhiles appeared, but in miniature form. While normally Ivo would find them to be intimidating, the tallest reached the height of her hip, and each of them gazed at her with adoring brown eyes as they sat at her feet.

"Are you ready?" Enzo shouted.

One of the Wrenhiles nudged her with its snout. Its ivory canines hung past its lip, and its triangular ears were fuzzy at the tips. Her heart pounded in her chest, but Ivo nodded. "I'm ready."

"Go!" Vincenzo crouched down as he cast his hands forward, causing frozen waves to manifest, barreling toward her.

Ivo's legs moved swiftly as her magic helped her navigate the slippery terrain with ease. The Wrenhiles ran alongside her as she shouted her next spell. *"Muro di fuoco."*

A towering wall of fire sprouted between them and Enzo's piercing ice waves. The ice from her original spell remained intact beneath the flames, just as he had told her it would. She slid to a stop as two of the Wrenhiles stalked toward the fire with their hackles raised. Enzo emerged from the flames shrouded in shadow.

Once clear of Ivo's smoldering defense, Enzo shook off his shielding and grinned at her. "Great job, but we're not done yet."

The ground shook as something approached. Ivo's jaw hung open as a gigantic creature manifested behind Vincenzo. It had a long, slender body with agile legs, resembling a lizard with its scaled body. Its vertical pupils dilated as the creature lowered its head near the ground. It opened its mouth and hissed, revealing multiple rows of razor-sharp teeth within.

Ivo wasted no time and took off in the opposite direction, the room seeming to expand as she ran. The creature was directly behind her as the Wrenhiles dispersed into a formation around its legs. The canines bit at the lizard's feet and joints. The creature shook them off as it pursued her. She shouted a spell to melt the icy floor a fraction, creating a thin layer of water. She slid across it until she reached the glowing tree branch. She threw herself onto it and pulled her body off the floor. Just as Enzo had instructed her, she communicated her intention to the tree through touch and then made her move.

Out of breath, Ivo pointed her hand at the lizard swiftly approaching and shouted, *"Lancia elettrica."*

A spear of electricity shot toward the lizard and landed at its feet. The creature shook as the electric shock stunned it. The Wrenhiles trotted over to Ivo's side, unscathed by her attack.

"It worked," Ivo said, patting one of the canines on the head.

Vincenzo flew over and hovered in the air a few feet away from her. "Nice job, you're absolutely stronger than I anticipated. You should be proud of yourself for managing to keep up and for following through on all of my instructions. I don't think that could have gone any better."

He waved his hand, and the room morphed back to its normal size. All of Vincenzo's creatures, including the gigantic lizard, vanished. Where the lizard had been a moment before lay an indent in the shape of its body, several feet deep. Ivo glanced down into it and noticed something sparkly near the bottom. "What is that?" she asked.

Enzo lifted a brow as he leaned forward. "I don't know. Let me fly down there. Stay here."

Ivo wrapped her arms around herself and tapped her foot as his wings flashed. Enzo landed near a small crack and inspected it. He held his hands in front of him, and more green energy wafted from his hands into the ground. The crack opened up, revealing a deep cavity stuffed to the brim with crystal towers and large stars with twelve points.

He looked up at her and brushed his hair out of his face. "Well, this just got a whole lot more interesting, that's for sure."

"Do those belong to Carmine?" Ivo asked. She climbed down into the crater and got a closer look at the stones. "Some of these look like the ones Sima found on Haelos in Aurelio's office."

Enzo frowned. "I was just thinking the same thing. These gray ones with the blue and yellow flashes of light are Labradorite. There must be something special about this specific crystal type if we keep finding large carved pieces like this."

"What should we do with them?" Ivo asked, her fingertips growing cold. "Destroy them?"

He sighed. "Not all of them can be destroyed. When I worked with Doc Santoro, we collected as many of the stones as we could. The weaker ones could be broken and crushed into dust. The stronger ones couldn't be chipped, let alone demolished."

Ivo scratched her head. "What did you two do with them then?"

Enzo met her gaze and then looked away. "We created a vault for them. One piece in particular was unlike any of the others, with a glow not unlike the tree you just used. It was carved like these pieces into the shape of an insect. Doc is keeping a safe watch over it. If we can't destroy it, then we at least need to keep it safe from others. As for these, it might not be feasible to waste our time trying to break them."

Ivo nodded. "Maybe we should find the others and tell them what we've found. I am sure Nariah will want to have some say in what happens to the stones."

He reached down and grabbed one of the Labradorite towers. It was nearly the length of Ivo's entire arm with dancing blue flashes up and down its sides. Ivo glanced down at the cavity and spotted something brown and navy. She squinted her eyes as she dropped to her knees and reached for it.

"It can't be," Ivo said, pulling a small journal free. She flipped through the pages and immediately recognized the writing. "It's another one of Carmine's notebooks. This one is all about the stones. Looks like he was doing research of his own."

"May I?" Enzo asked, holding his hand out. Ivo handed it to him, and he skimmed the pages. He paused on one of the pages, and his expression darkened. He gripped the notebook tightly and glanced up at her. "There is a note from Aurelio in here."

"No," Ivo managed to say. "What does it say?"

Enzo's jaw clenched. "When prey outlasts its novelty, even the fullest belly will slit its throat. How sweet it will be when a hand only I have held and a soul only I have tasted comes coasting in, to take back all I have lost, to reclaim what is ours. Never will death lose your scent, no matter how you try to wash yourself of Fate's call."

Ivo shook her head. "I don't understand."

"It means that Carmine knew Sima would come for him one day. Aurelio threatened to send her after him because of her ability to alter the Weave."

Her heart pinched painfully in her chest. "He knew? This was somehow a piece of Aurelio's fucked up plans?"

"That's what Carmine probably thinks now, but it's not true. Aurelio is dead, Ivo. He has no plans. We are here to kill my brother because he deserves to die." Enzo looked off into the distance. "Either way, we need to find Cosima."

"Is it the best idea to show her Aurelio's note?" Ivo asked, cringing slightly.

"You want to hide it from her?" Enzo asked, raising a brow.

"No…yes? I am not sure. I don't want to frighten her more."

Enzo nodded. "You're right." He shoved the small notebook into his pocket. "Perhaps it is best to wait until after Carmine is dead, but I still want to tell the group about the stones we found."

Ivo blew out a breath and swallowed the bitter taste of guilt on her tongue. It was not like her to hide things from her best friend, but Ivo cared about Cosima's dreams too much to let fear stop her. Enzo helped her out of the crater, and the walls around them shifted and morphed as he created a pathway through them, which Ivo assumed led directly to the others. As they walked, Ivo could not seem to ignore the strange dark feeling looming over her.

Cosima

"What should we do?" Cosima asked, wrapping her arms around herself as she stared at the ripple. "I didn't mean to do that."

Merit put his hands on his hips and paced back and forth in front of it. "I'm trying to think, give me a second. There's got to be a reason for this, no way you actually made a hole in the fabric of the planet."

"I knew it was a bad idea for her to use her powers," Nariah said, pinching the bridge of her nose. "Nothing good comes from inexperienced manipulation of the Weave. They're going to cut our wings off."

The navy-haired Scout scowled at Nariah. "Do not fucking say that. I am not going down for any of this." He paused and turned to Sima. "Pull the threads back out and see if you can see anything strange or if you can figure out where it came from. Try to avoid touching the…shiny thing directly."

Sima nodded. "I'll try." She took a slow step forward as she manifested the threads once more. The threads coming out of the ripple were dyed a deep red instead of the delicate iridescence the strings normally had. "Nariah, I—"

"I see it," Nariah said, her jaw tightening. "The threads connected to it are red, Merit."

"Alright, well," Merit said, rubbing his jaw. "I have no clue what that means exactly, but it's a good sign that we've found tangible signs of the problem beyond the hole. Cosima, be very careful, but reach for one of the threads."

Sima swallowed the lump in her throat. "Understood."

Nariah laid her hand on Cosima's shoulder. "One at a time, and try to keep us updated on what you see. Past a certain point, my powers fail me, and I cannot experience what you do."

She closed her eyes and took a slow breath. *Tides of eternal destiny, favor your daughter born of loose stitches and needlepoints,* she prayed internally. Sima opened her eyes and stared directly into the center of the ripple, which continued to flicker with movement. She tilted her head back and reached for one of the blood-red threads. When her finger collided with it, an explosion of pale purple light threw the three of them backward.

Cosima rolled and came to a stop flat on her back. Merit appeared in her blurred vision, and he pulled her to a stand. She held onto his arm as she steadied herself. The sound of voices floated toward her, but it wasn't until she caught a glimpse of the Scout's tense expressions that she glanced at the ripple.

Viewing memories on grand display was a normal piece of touching Fate, but those experiences were private. To her dismay, her deepest memories played out as if pulled directly from the recesses of her mind. The wall of moving images was full of Aurelio's face from a dozen different angles, allowing the Scouts to see him *exactly* how Cosima had.

"No," Sima cried, "don't look."

Merit walked forward, his hand touching his lips as his eyes filled with too many emotions for Sima to discern. She followed after him and grabbed his arm. He paused and looked at her, his orange eyes flaming. "This is real, Cosima? This was your life with him?"

Sima turned her head toward the display of her shameful past. In one of the memories, Aurelio's face was bright red as he screamed at her, backing her into a corner. As she crouched and stared up at him, he hurled insult after insult.

"You'll never be anybody," Aurelio from the memory spat. "You're lucky I found some use for you; otherwise, I'd begin to question what cosmic mistake led to your existence. I am so tired of looking at your pathetic fucking face, whining and crying over nothing. You're one that's broken, don't you get it?"

"I-I…" Sima's breath caught in her throat.

Nariah wrapped her arm around Sima and turned her around. "You don't have to watch either, Sima. Merit, turn around."

Merit didn't move. His cheeks burned with color as his fists trembled at his sides. "Who the fuck did this guy think he was? Who was he to talk to you this way?"

A cry from Cosima of the past rang out, anguished and pained as Aurelio leered over her in the memory. Nariah held her as she trembled on the floor of the mirror realm, cringing at the drunk haze in her former husband's eyes. It was as though she had been dropped right back into her former self's body as her body reacted to the sight of him intoxicated. Her heart pinched, her palms began to sweat, and her muscles were paralyzed.

"You know you deserve this, right?" Aurelio slurred, his eyes bright with manic rage. "This is what happens when I have to remind you of your place, over and over again. You make me do this because you won't do as you're told." He leaned an inch from her face in the memory. "You want to act crazy? I will show you *insanity*."

"How do I make it stop?" Sima whimpered.

"Nariah, do something," Merit said.

Just when Cosima feared the visions of her past would become too much for her to handle, a gentle, calming sensation wafted over her. It was not enough to completely absolve her of her pain, but it was enough to allow her to resurface in reality instead of being drenched in her memories.

"Cosima," a warm, familiar voice called out. "What's wrong?"

"Enzo," Sima cried, her body trembling as she turned toward him.

Vincenzo's wings carried him forward, and his arms wrapped around her. Cosima worried that Nariah would shove them apart, but for once, the Scout pressed her lips into a line and stayed silent. She allowed herself to melt into Enzo's arms as the visions of her most traumatizing moments played in the background. She felt Enzo stiffen beneath her as his breathing became ragged.

"I'll make sure there is no one who remembers you," her memory of Aurelio taunted. "I will wipe out every trace of your worthless little soul. Are you stupid enough to think anyone else will want your tainted flesh? Do you truly believe others cannot smell how rotten you are within?"

Vincenzo's heart slammed as his muscles tensed. His body trembled ever so slightly as he held onto Cosima, his eyes locked onto the recreation of her memories that played out. The images of her past were so vivid they made Enzo's head spin. He had heard a sliver of her recollections, but never before had he witnessed her torment with his own eyes.

"I am right here with you," Enzo whispered in her ear, barely getting the words out through his fury.

Because the memories came directly from Cosima's point of view, Enzo had no choice but to watch how Aurelio had hurt her. He wanted to look away, wanted to devote more of his attention to consoling the woman he loved, but the rage within him would not let him. Enzo could not cope with the depravity of it all—the way Aurelio's features contorted into pure hatred as he screamed, the cruel way he cut her to pieces with his words, the way he desperately tried to break her without pause.

You can no longer afford to be weak, his curse croaked. *You cannot let harm befall her once more.*

A new memory unfolded. From what Enzo could tell, it appeared as though Cosima was chained inside a small closet. It was dark, and the only audible sound beyond his brother's voice was Sima's soft whimpers. "You don't even know who you are," Aurelio said, his face full of harsh angles as he dragged on his cigar. "I still remember all of our talks about the future, when you'd tell me how badly you wanted to be a good queen. Perhaps you fooled me, somehow enticed me into believing you could be the woman I wanted, only for you to be a sorry disappointment instead. But now I know the truth—you're a fraud. A good-for-nothing little liar. You don't want to help others, you just hope your perfect image is enough to keep others from finding out who you really are inside."

Vincenzo couldn't believe his ears, his jaw tight as Cosima wept in his arms. It took everything in him to remain physically still, as his magic boiled inside him, threatening to burn his vessel from the inside out. He squeezed his eyes shut as he searched for something to ground him. If he did not find a way to handle his escalating emotions, there was no telling what destruction would follow.

You must become her savior, so she may become yours, his curse whispered. *Do not allow your sacred rage to be wasted.*

Cosima shivered in his arms, and Enzo pulled her closer. He cradled her face in his hand as he pressed a kiss to her forehead. Her honey brown irises were dull, as if the vision of Aurelio had stolen the life right out of her. The agony in her expression felt like razors through his chest.

"Nothing he has ever said about you is true. He was a small, cruel man who projected his hate for himself onto you." She shut her eyes, and Enzo softened his voice even more. "You already survived him, my love. You are free of him. Do not let memories of the past keep you from your bright future. My life has not been the same since you came into it, and for the first time in my existence, I feel like I am worth something because you love me."

The images flickered, but did not dissipate. "Little dove." Aurelio's voice made both of them flinch. "I thought I taught you better than this. You know that you'll never escape me. I watched you try to flee from the palace, only for my Rani to stop you. I know where you are every minute of every day, and at this point, I probably know what you're going to think before it pops into your mind. Silly girl…I own you and I always will."

Sima's face turned bright red as she looked away from him. Vincenzo's curse screamed inside him, and he thought his skin would burst from containing the building waves of his magic. He clung to his rational sense, struggling to keep himself composed as he reached for her and gingerly turned her face toward his.

"I see you in everything. You're the moonlight, and timid flowers bloom beneath your touch," Enzo whispered. "You're spring showers, and the world slows when you arrive. You're the stillness of night and the color in the trees. You're the dreams that come at dusk, and you're the hope that comes at dawn. There is nothing if there is no you."

He rejoiced at the sparkle of her resilient soul in her eyes. She was fighting the torment and trauma, and the painful images once again began to flicker. This time, the sound of Aurelio's voice cut in and out as well. She reached a shaky hand toward his face and ran her fingers along his scar. Without meaning to, Enzo felt his magic rush out of him. Before he could halt the flow, his power entangled itself in hers.

A bright purple and green aura covered them, catching him by surprise. He noticed thousands of near-translucent threads covering the mirror realm. Enzo's eyes flicked to the Trine Scouts, who had backed a few feet away from them. Nariah's eyes were wide, but she did not intervene. He glanced down at Sima and smiled. "Our magic creates a beautiful harmony,

Sima. You are meant to be mine, and I am destined to be yours."

After a flash of white, the haunting portrayal of Cosima's past finally came to an end. She sagged with relief into his arms as Enzo blew out a breath. Ivo approached, her face streaked with tears as she smoothed her hand over Sima's hair. Sima glanced over her shoulder at her friend and let out a small cry.

The two embraced as Ivo whispered something too quiet for Enzo to hear in her ear. He took a few steps back, grateful that Cosima had a friend to lean on because his arms began to shake uncontrollably. His breath grew ragged, and his thoughts moved at a dizzying speed.

Merit wrapped his hand around Enzo's arm and pulled him backward. Enzo stumbled after Merit, taking only one last look at Cosima before he exited the mirror realm. He sent her one more reassuring pulse of his magic, hoping to give whatever he could before he toppled right over the edge.

You cannot choose to hold back any longer, his curse hissed. *Look what becomes of your fear.*

The Scout shoved him forward and scowled. "Get it together."

Enzo narrowed his eyes at him. "He was a fucking monster," he spat. "I can't think straight, I don't know how to breathe after seeing the way he treated her." He ran his hands through his black and white hair. "I'm going to lose my sanity."

"That shit was hard for me to stomach too, don't me started on how badly I wish I could punch Aurelio's teeth in, but he's gone. All you can do is try to devote that energy to something productive, like killing Carmine."

Electric emerald energy sparked between Enzo and the floor. "It's my fault. I should have done something, Merit, but I was a fucking coward. I spent all my time working with my power, convincing myself I was training to be strong enough to defeat him, but I should have died trying."

Merit's eyes widened as Enzo continued to tremble uncontrollably. "You can blame yourself for never saving her all you want, but he should have never done that to her in the first place. He was a filthy parasite, and damn it, Enzo, I am positive if you had known it was this bad, you would've ripped Aurelio's head clean off his body."

"What kind of man am I?" Enzo croaked, tears falling down his face as he clenched his fists. "I hate myself for being so weak. All I can think about is how soft her skin is, how gentle I instinctively want to be with her. She never deserved this."

The Scout's shoulders drooped. "No, she didn't. But it's too late to make Aurelio pay. What she needs now is for you to make sure her future looks nothing like what you saw in there. I know you would never hurt her, but your remaining brothers might. You have to stop them."

Enzo met Merit's gaze, and the Scout's fiercely determined expression was grounding. He took a deep breath, finding his unsteady inner world had finally stopped spinning, despite the chaotic rage that still burned in his gut. Vincenzo rooted himself in Merit's message—Cosima was still not safe, and it was his job to fix that. Enzo turned and began walking, his magic rising to the surface. The entire underground structure he had built vibrated with his every step.

"Where are you going?" Merit asked.

"To cleanse my sins in Sacred blood."

You will paint the horizons with sorrow, his curse sang, *they will crown you, son of two moons, as the unbecoming of tomorrow.*

Chapter 28

Ivo and Sima sank to the floor as they held onto one another. What Ivo had witnessed was more horrible than anything she had personally endured at Aurelio's hands. Ivo had been brought back from the brink of near death because of the former king's torture, and yet somehow that had become just another day for Cosima. It made her stomach turn and made her ears ring. All she could do was pull her friend closer and cry.

Merit re-entered the room, this time without Vincenzo by his side. He flicked his chin toward the door, and Nariah followed. When the two Scouts were gone, Cosima pulled away from her and sniffled. Ivo was patient as she allowed her friend to collect herself. When the rosy color around Sima's cheeks began to fade, Ivo spoke.

"I am in awe of you," she whispered. "You are strong beyond measure. I am so sorry."

Sima's lip wobbled. "I didn't want anyone to see. I am mortified."

"We don't see you any differently, Sima. Not at all. I hate that it happened against your wishes, but you are safe with all of us. We would never judge you for what you went through."

Her friend sighed and tucked her hair behind her ears. "I never told you how bad it was. I-I didn't know how."

Ivo's heart skipped. "You never had to. Do not feel bad for not telling me more. It fills me with agony to know how badly he hurt you, and I'm sorry we all became witnesses to your private suffering."

Sima met Ivo's gaze. "In some small way," she whispered, "I think I feel less alone."

Ivo leaned forward and rubbed Sima's back as they rested their heads against one another. "We are here to carry it with you," Ivo said softly. "You never have to sit with that pain alone ever again."

"I'll be fine," Sima replied.

A tear from her friend's face fell onto Ivo's hand. She looked at Sima as she wiped away more tears. "Have your moment, Sima, but remember it doesn't end here. You are unstoppable. I have never seen pain stop you before. He can't keep you from your destiny."

Sima sat up straighter, her lips turned upward with the ghost of a smile, though her eyes were watery. "I have to keep going, don't I? Even when it feels like I am constantly taking a step backward, I have to keep trying if I want to see myself get better."

"You're already on the path," Ivo said. "You've grown so much since your time in the palace."

"Thank you," Sima replied, her voice even and smooth as she regained her bearings. "It doesn't feel so heavy anymore."

"Sometimes all it takes to heal you is sharing what you've kept hidden," Ivo said.

Footsteps approached, and Ivo lifted her head to find Merit and Nariah approaching, still without Vincenzo. A line formed between Nariah's eyebrows as she scowled, and Merit was focused on Cosima. The navy-haired Scout crouched down beside her friend and rested his hand on her arm.

"I need to speak with you about something," he said.

"What is it?" Ivo asked, her heart racing.

Nariah tugged Ivo to her feet and jerked her head toward the exit. "Come on, you and I need to talk to you, urgently. You can meet up with Sima in a minute."

As the Scout dragged her away, Ivo looked over her shoulder at Sima and wondered what they were speaking about. Sima's brows were pinched together, and her mouth was pressed into a thin line. *Did something happen to Vincenzo?* Ivo wondered.

Cosima

Merit's brows pinched together as his hand rested on her arm. He was trembling, but his eyes were soft. The Scout let out a breath. "If there's one thing I know, it is that there is nothing you cannot do." He pressed his lips together while studying her face, as though he was planning his words carefully. "What you went through with him…he tortured you. He tried to condemn you, to shatter your spirit, but that miserable mosquito failed. You endured a nightmare behind closed doors but have emerged plated in gold, Sima. Two things have become obvious above all else—you have powers beyond our collective imagination and your soul was built to endure the impossible."

The sincerity in his words caught her off guard. So often Merit paraded around as if every breath was a waste of his time, but in this moment, when she desperately needed to be handled with delicacy, the Scout gave her a steady shore to crash against. If there was anything to be grateful for after having her dark corners exposed, it rested in the sturdy friendships she had developed through her pain. Still, a persistent blade of doubt was lodged somewhere within, the wound hemorrhaging feelings of unworthiness. "Do you really think I am ready to face Carmine, after everything you've seen? What if I lose courage again?"

The corner of Merit's lip tugged upward. "You won't. It's not in you to lose, or you would've given up a long time ago. There's a fighter inside you, Sima, that isn't ready to fail, even if you have to go kicking and screaming." He stood up and held his hand out to her. She accepted and he pulled her to her feet. "You can fucking do this. Show that pig your wrath and don't let anything get in your head. Listen to your gut and nothing else."

Sima turned her head and stared at her reflection in the many mirrors. She expected to find her expression full of sorrow, but instead her eyes spoke of unrelenting bravery. Within her was a palace with unshakable walls. Others had trashed the hallways of her core, had smeared blood on every surface, but none had succeeded in crumbling the fortress built of her hope. Countless times she had wanted to collapse, to give up on her murky vision of a better future. Yet, the wind never ceased to whisper of freedom.

"I'm ready." Sima clenched her fists. "It's time to stop outrunning destiny."

Once outside of the mirror realm, it took Ivo a second to steady herself. The strange realm Vincenzo had created left behind a disorienting effect. Nariah walked over to a navy wall and rested her back against it. She chewed her lip as she fidgeted with her white-ponytail. Ivo let out a sigh as she took the spot beside the Scout.

"What is it?" Ivo asked.

"I never knew," Nariah blurted, as though she had barely contained herself this long. "I had no clue what that fucking rat put her through. I knew he was a shitty guy, but until you see what it looked like behind closed doors, you truly know nothing. You can picture it in your head, but the real thing is so…sinister. I wasn't even there, and I felt the power in his hate, the pressure of his presence."

Ivo wrapped her arms around herself. "I still hate Aurelio, even if he's dead. I wish he had been forced to feel even a fraction of the terror she's felt in her lifetime. I bet he'd break. All of his brothers are weak, just like him. Except maybe Enzo."

Nariah stiffened. "Right…about Enzo."

Ivo glanced up at her. "Where is he?"

"He…ran off. To fight Carmine. Alone."

To keep from screaming, Ivo clenched her jaw and grabbed Nariah by the front of her uniform. "What do you mean, he went to fight Carmine by himself? Is he insane? Are you? Why would you let him do that?"

"I didn't," Nariah said, tearing Ivo's hand away. Her fingers lingered against Ivo's before she withdrew. "Merit let him go. Merit isn't normally that kind of guy, but in this situation…it's different."

"What is so different about it?"

Nariah chewed her cheek. "Merit let him go because he knows that what Enzo saw in there is going to eat him alive if he doesn't do anything about it. He said he saw the desperation and helplessness in his eyes and knew that *nobody* was going to be able to talk Enzo out of it."

Ivo's shoulders drooped. "I can't argue with that."

"Neither can I. I don't think we are doing a good job at containing our rage right now. That's why I need to talk to you. Merit is explaining the rest of the plan to Sima. We need to be prepared to provide Enzo with whatever help we can. There is no doubt that even if he went after Carmine himself, he would still be using these tunnels and realms he created. Do you remember the plan Enzo told you?"

"Yes," Ivo said, lifting her chin. "I know exactly what to do. After what we watched, I'm ready for Carmine to bleed out down here."

Nariah's gaze darkened. "You must stay out of sight of Carmine. You are working on defensive measures, not any direct attacks."

"I get it," Ivo murmured, rolling her eyes. "You don't want me to die on your watch. I've heard it enough already."

Nariah swiftly moved to stand in front of her. The Scout rested her palm against the wall, pinning Ivo. "I'm being serious, Ivo. I don't want you to get hurt. If I could, I would stay by your side and watch you myself, but I have to help Sima and Enzo."

Ivo smirked. "Be careful, I might start thinking you care about me."

The Scout raised a brow. "And if I do?"

She scoffed. "You don't mean that."

Her heart picked up the pace as Nariah wisteria gaze captivated her. The Scout leaned in and brushed her finger down the side of Ivo's face. "I couldn't live with myself if anything happened to you."

Cosima and Merit's footsteps approached, causing Nariah to pull away. Ivo swallowed hard and attempted to breathe normally as her friend and the other Scout stopped in front of them. Sima's face was tense, but she carried herself with her usual strong elegance.

"Everybody ready for what comes next?" Merit asked, clapping his hands together. "We need to get into position before Enzo makes it back here with Carmine."

"I am ready," Ivo said.

"Great. I'll walk you over to the room with the tree like you and Enzo agreed on." Merit waved her over. "Cosima and Nariah are going to stay near the mirror realm, and I am going to position myself in the room opposite yours. The tree is closest to Carmine's hideout."

Ivo made eye contact one last time with Nariah. The Scout's eyes softened for a moment as she smiled before Nariah turned away and began walking with Cosima. Ivo faced Merit and sighed. "I hope he dies fast."

It's time to end it, Enzo's curse screamed. *Turn him to dust, wither his soul, clear your path.*

Vincenzo's magic pierced through the walls at the very edge of Carmine's secret hideout. Once he confirmed this brother was within, he pressed a finger to the wall. A pulse of green energy shot through it and created a walkway. He flew through it as fast as his wings could carry him.

Once inside Carmine's hideout, Enzo morphed the space to force his brother to come directly to him. Carmine appeared only a second later, missing an arm with surprise in his eyes. Without waiting for an opening, Enzo shortened the distance between them and manifested a blade from his palm, plunging it deep into Carmine's neck. His brother hollered as blood spurted from the wound.

Carmine snatched him by the arm and threw him backward. Enzo broke through three layers of stone before he stopped. He wheezed as he pried himself out of a wall. Already, he had succeeded in drawing his brother out; he only had to keep the momentum up. Enzo remained focused on his goal of trapping Carmine in one of his many realms. He would not let his brother escape his grasp once more.

A flash of wings caught his attention as Carmine sped toward him.

A wave of wind followed the blast of Enzo's powers as rock towers shot out of the ground. His brother slammed through one but recovered quickly, expertly flying around his obstacles. Enzo opted for starlight next as Carmine barreled into him. His brother's rapid smile eerily resembled Aurelio's, and his grin did not fade, even as Enzo's starlight burnt the skin on his arm to a crisp.

They were entangled in a smoke-filled battle of brawn and untethered magic. Carmine's physical strength outweighed his, but Enzo's curse lent him power. Once again, Enzo found himself beating against that wall he feared so deeply, so close to the edge of losing all restraint. Time and time again, he was pushed into becoming the monster his curse doomed him to be. His magic coursed through him at a maddening speed, causing his heart to beat erratically as they fought. His limbs shook, feeling both impossibly weak and on the verge of giving out, and emboldened by the fierce, chaotic magic that continued to pour out of him.

Whether you die amongst the clouds and rest in open air, his curse sang with a soft edge to its voice, *or disintegrate amongst the stars and yearn in the vacuum of space—your blood brings renewal. Fear nothing.*

He contorted space again, positioning them exactly where he wanted them while also keeping his brother occupied with hits. Giant cracks formed in the rock, and the entire underground structure trembled beneath Enzo's attacks. He threw his brother off him and flew, tunneling right through one of the passageways he had created that led to a weightless realm. Carmine followed, seemingly unaware how quickly he had played into Vincenzo's plans.

The space broke open, revealing an endless, cloudy sky. Angry gray clouds rumbled, covering every inch of their vision. Due to the specifications he used when he created the realm, the space had a degree of weightlessness to it, inevitably slowing their movements. Enzo's wings pushed harder as his brother continued to follow him. He did not anticipate Carmine's ability to adapt his speed, and it took only seconds for his brother to grab hold of him. Enzo shoved him away as a bolt of lightning shot between them. Their hair stood up as the perpetual storm geared up for an electric performance.

Vincenzo let his body drop, folding in his wings as he spiraled downward. He took a slow breath as he timed his next move, waiting for precisely the moment lightning would discharge to charge up his own attack. He combined his emerald electricity with the bright white lightning, the two spiraling into a spear of pure energy. It slammed into Carmine's shoulder, and his brother cried out as his body convulsed. His white hair flattened against his head as he went downward, headfirst.

He held his hand in front of him, creating a viscous spiraling tunnel of air. It scooped up Carmine's body, tossing him like paper in the wind as Enzo pulled the tunnel closer. As his brother toppled head over heels, Enzo tripled the speed as he raised a hand beside him, harnessing more electricity. It swirled into a spiked ball of energy that pulsed with emerald light. Enzo blinked, and five more like it manifested. He hurled them at Carmine, his lip curling into a smile as the spikes sank into his brother's skin, causing him to let out garbled howls.

Carmine broke free from the wind tunnel and tumbled through the air before he righted himself. He dove for Enzo, moving with dizzying speed. The breath left Enzo's lungs as they flew backward, breaking through the edge of his realm. They were spit onto the navy stone floor of the underground space, and Carmine wrestled his arms to the ground as he leered over Enzo's face.

"Well done, brother," Carmine said, panting as his wings beat behind him. "You are more impressive than I believed you to be. Not only are you fighting to become the survivor, but you have fallen in love with the legendary lady as well. How did I not see it before? Cosima is not simply Aurelio's pet, she *is* the woman from the prophecy. And you have taken her for yourself! Tell me, how did Aurelio take the news?"

Enzo swallowed tightly, his starlight accumulating in his fists. He glanced down, dismayed to see his brother had somehow manifested a new arm.

"He ripped my wings almost entirely off my body and tried to leave me for dead."

Frost white hair shook lightly as Carmine laughed. "As to be expected. Do you believe that by killing me you can somehow evade his scorn?"

Vincenzo opened his fists, and starlight poured from his palms. He narrowly missed his brother, but Carmine released him, allowing Enzo to scramble to his feet. "It's Aurelio you're waiting for?"

His brother smiled as he rose from the ground. "The one *after*."

"After Aurelio?" That only confused Enzo further. Vincenzo's magic swam through his tunnels, fetching the creatures he had hidden away in the dark. His pulse quickened as Carmine stared him down. "Who comes after Aurelio?"

His brother grinned unnaturally. "The one you should truly fear. If your sweet Cosima is the thread, think of him as the needle. There can be no masterpiece without his sharp soul."

Enzo's curse flared. *He thinks he should fear another,* it whispered, *when the one who will unmake him stands before him, burning ever brighter. Show him the error of his ways.*

The ground shook as creatures with muscular hind legs sprang from the shadows like rabid rabbits with fangs and clipped ears. While Carmine was occupied, Vincenzo ran down one of the tunnels, knowing his brother would not be able to resist a chase. As he expected, the mangled body of one of his creatures broke through the wall only feet behind him. He switched to his wings and transformed the physical space, bringing the two of them near the mirror realm. Before he could make it all the way there, one of Enzo's creatures snarled and charged at him, knocking him down.

Enzo stared up at it as he struggled to regain control over the rabid creation. Carmine laughed as he approached, stopping only when Enzo summoned a sharp silver blade that burst through the creature's skull, killing it. He shoved it aside and retracted his metal weapon as he stood up. Carmine zipped through the air, his fingernails narrowly grazing Enzo's neck as he ducked down.

With a push of his green energy, he shoved his brother deeper into the passageway. They emerged inside the mirror realm where Enzo had last seen Cosima. His heart rampaged in his chest as the nauseating memories of Cosima's past resurfaced. Prismatic clear quartz towers and warped mirrors erupted, contorting and complicating their view. His brother started by smashing obstacles, before he took to the air and attempted to fly toward him. Expecting this, Enzo morphed the mirrors once more, creating dozens of copies of himself. Confused as to which one was the real one, Carmine growled and punched through one, only for another to appear.

Vincenzo paused, feeling the energy shift in the realm before Cosima had stepped fully into it. Carmine hurled a burst of orange energy into the mirrors, shattering them all at once. Now exposed, Enzo dove out of the way of another surge of his brother's magic. Before it could reach him, the energy rebounded, deflecting back toward Carmine.

Cosima appeared a moment later by his side a moment later, causing his heart to skip.

"I have a plan. Bring him closer and keep him focused on you. Keep using the mirrors to distract him as you herd him near the center."

He nodded his head. "Got it."

She took off, concealing herself behind some of the prismatic quartz. Enzo flew in a half circle around his brother, sprouting mirrors at random that reflected his image. Carmine punched through them as they popped up, but Enzo replaced each one with three more. His brother slowed to a stop and slammed his hands onto the ground, causing a great number of Enzo's mirrors and prisms to break.

I have failed before, but I will atone, Vincenzo thought. *I will untether him from this dimension and reap his soul for you, Cosima. I will seek your justice.*

He lifted his hand and pointed it at Carmine, his magic bubbling inside him. As emerald energy sprang from his palm, he shuddered, a trail of goosebumps coating his arms. Just as they had done before in this realm, Cosima and Vincenzo's magic entangled, creating a forceful blast. Carmine flew backward, and his body lodged into the rainbow of geometric shapes that lined the boundaries of the mirror realm.

Sima appeared out of nowhere, running full speed toward him. She held her hand in front of her, and Enzo's jaw hung open as thousands of iridescent threads appeared. She selected one and a crystal shot toward her hand. Sima caught it and wrapped her fingers around it, leaving only a silver chain visible. She pulled on another thread, and something rustled beside him. Enzo glanced down and found the crystal in his hand. It was in the shape of a beetle, carved of Bloodstone. The weapon vibrated as Enzo attached the stone to its hilt, and the shiny metal blade began to glow with a flame-like essence, matching the crystal's blue-black color with blood-red specks.

Carmine screamed, festering darkness pouring from his skin. The black smoke toiled around him as he smoothed back his white hair.

"Stealing the stone is not enough. You can kill me, but you won't be able to stop the chosen one when he comes for you. Tell Aurelio my blood will not grant him victory."

He knows nothing of your true path, his curse hissed. *You are beyond death. Fate could not have crafted a more resilient son.*

Enzo wrapped his hand around the bloodstone beetle. "Aurelio is dead, Carmine."

His brother's gaze sharpened, and he snarled. "You lie!"

"He was murdered months ago."

Carmine snapped straight, his face a shade paler than before. "What?" A wave of energy set a low rumble through the underground. "No, that can't be true. Who killed him? Was it you, brother?"

Cosima emerged with the crystal blade Nariah had given her at the ready. With threats written in every blink of her eyes, her purple aura flamed. Enzo smirked. "The woman he claimed one day would take your life took his instead."

"But she has come now for me anyway," Carmine said softly. "Very well, then I must earn my death."

His brother shuddered, his brown eyes filled with panic. His fear was so unlike their deceased brother, Aurelio, and yet so familiar at the same time. Enzo wondered what he recognized in Carmine's eyes that made the hair on his body stand.

Black smoke drenched the realm in darkness before hundreds of burning orange beams of light shattered Vincenzo's mirror realm, sending glass flying in all directions. He flew toward Cosima, ready to shield her with his body, when he was suddenly floating, rotating through the air at a crawling pace. He caught a glimpse of her standing, unharmed, as shards of glass fell toward the ground like snow.

When she dropped her hand, Enzo and Carmine plunged toward the floor. Enzo rolled to his feet and let his magic spiral out of him. Two giant stone hands emerged from the ground, each grabbing one of Carmine's arms. Without the bloodstone beetle, he no longer had magnified power.

His brother strained against the binds, but could not free himself.

Enzo's magic flooded into the stone, intensifying his uncontrollable rage. As he stared at Carmine, his vision began to blur, making him appear more like Aurelio than the man already did. His curse roared within him and crawled beneath his skin, begging for release. Vincenzo struggled to control its alluring pull as he neared dangerous territory. He could not be sure that stepping beyond the harrowing edge of his power would doom him, but he could not be sure it would not either.

"It doesn't have to be this way, brother," Carmine said, his lip curled into a sneer. "You have time to escape before he realizes you are here. Once the Survivor finds you, the prophecy is set in stone. He plays tricks, far more clever than you will give him credit for, even if you heed my warning. You will walk right into his traps, do exactly as he wishes, all without trying. There is no winning against him, so it is best not to play at all."

Enzo raised the blade and took a slow breath, preparing to swing, when his brother spoke again, Carmine's voice so soft he nearly missed it. "If you love her, you will run as far as you can before he finds you. You will take what little time you have left with her, and you will spend your last moments saturated in love and not loss. You cannot escape the stars of time. He will be the one to survive."

Vincenzo wasn't sure if the words out of his mouth belonged to himself or to his curse, "There is no need to escape the inevitable. The stardust in my veins, the divinity in my heart, and the future in my lungs sings to me of my irrefutable purpose. I will be the only one who remains, brother, because I will have it no other way." His magic funneled out of him at a staggering pace, once again creating a tunnel of shadow and wind. The surge of power illuminated his eyes, allowing him to see reality in a new way—the true glimpse of the inner workings of their collective existence, including the threads attached to the Weave.

"Enzo," Cosima yelled, her voice startling close.

He wanted to look at her, but his curse kept him ensnared in his bloodlust. *Sacrifice him so the wheel may turn*, it screamed. *Sign your eternal command in Sacred blood.*

Enzo stabbed the blade into Carmine's neck and swung his arm, slicing through half of his brother's flesh. His power ravaged through Carmine's body like a fast-moving poison, turning his skin black as it flaked off into ash. Without wasting another moment, Enzo swung again, delirious with rightful rage up until the moment the thump of his brother's dismembered head on the floor caught his ears.

Cosima

"Enzo," she repeated, this time quieter.

He was drenched in blood, still clutching his weapon tightly as he panted. Enzo's eyes were glowing, creating tiny tubes of light where he looked, illuminating Carmine's empty brown gaze and the river of blood oozing from what remained of his neck. Enzo was trembling, his breath tight and labored. She hated seeing him in this state, but she was unsure whether his magic usage had simply drained him or if his power itself had harmed him.

His strength is incomprehensible, Sima thought. *I've never been more in awe of someone before.*

Sima stood a foot from him, just to the right of Carmine's head, which had slowly begun to disintegrate like the rest of his body. She turned her attention back to Enzo and debated reaching for him, unsure if he would accept her touch in this state. She inched closer to him and searched his face. His emerald eyes were wild with sweltering anger as he stared down at Carmine. She had witnessed him use an intimidating amount of magic without faltering, but still she did not fear him, even as he struggled to settle his fury.

"I am here with you," she whispered.

She reached toward him, her hand trembling nearly as much as his body. The moment her fingertips touched his body, a wave of intense, commanding energy flew through her, before she once again sensed Enzo's comforting aura. His eyes flicked to her, and he relaxed. The blade in his hand disappeared, along with Carmine's crystal. He reached for her arm and pulled her against him. Sima breathed in his familiar rainy scent and looked up at him. His breath was still heavy, but the illumination in his eyes had begun to fade.

"I told you I could control it," he whispered. "I'm…in control of my power."

"I know," she said, touching his scar. "You did it, Enzo. You did it."

He shut his eyes as a tear fell down his cheek. "He's dead. I killed him for you." He opened them and locked onto her gaze. "And I'll do it as many times as I have to. I won't let anything keep us apart."

Sima's heart squeezed. Her gratitude was overwhelming and heavy like grief in her chest. "Thank you," she breathed.

He smiled at her, the sight of it in her mind akin only to being bathed in the cosmic sea. Vincenzo leaned forward, and Sima wrapped her arms around his neck. Their lips met, and it was as if she could taste the storm raging within him, his battered soul begging for relief. She kissed him fiercely, imagining her love coating every shattered piece of him until he could be whole again.

"Do you still love me?" he whispered against her lips. "Despite my poisoned blood? Despite the unholy curse that clings to me?"

"You have loved me through my darkness," she whispered. "It is an honor to love you through yours."

He kissed her with devoted hunger, like his tongue spelled out the tenets of his worship. She melted into him as his wings wrapped around them. Footsteps approached, and Sima knew Nariah would soon rip them apart. As she pulled away from him, he gently grabbed her chin and smiled, pulling her back in for one more kiss. He released her, and they turned to find the two Scouts and Ivo navigating the destroyed remains of their battle with Carmine.

"Give me good news," Nariah said as she hopped over a broken prism.

"He's dead," Enzo said, lifting his chin.

All three let out a breath as Ivo ran to her side.

A chill ran through Sima's body. *Something isn't right.*

"Huh, weird," Merit said, shrugging one shoulder. His face scrunched, and his head swiveled.

"What is it?" Nariah looked around for the source of his scrutiny, and Sima's heart began to pound. "What's wrong?"

"You don't feel it?" Merit asked. "It feels like there is death in the wind, like oblivion is heading right for us."

Sima wondered what he meant until the rampage of emotions overwhelmed her senses. Despite the internal storm she realized all of them were experiencing, it was silent outside. There was a sensation of being entirely alone, as though every soul around them had vanished. As if they were the only ones on the planet still breathing.

Her heart quickened, and Sima pulled Ivo closer to her, wrapping her arms around her. The action was a waste, as their air was cut off and all five of them tumbled to their knees. The sounds of her friends struggling to survive faded, as if she were disappearing into nothingness. Her head spun the longer she went without a breath, and the world grew murky.

Cosima's blurry eyes caught sight of shiny black leather shoes stopping in front of her before she slipped into the darkness, unable to retain consciousness any longer.

3

The Misaligned

"When does it end?" they cried, anguish swimming like poison in their starved bellies.

"We have been unshakable, undeniable in our pursuit of godliness. Why then have we brought ourselves no closer to salvation? What more can be done?"

In its enigmatic and impossible way, the well of life produces a path.

They take each step with hollow resentment, a false defiance of the journey ahead.

Though they know not why, the enlightened ones heed the nudge of Fate's guiding hand.

Faith, the wind whispers, *all that remains is faith.*

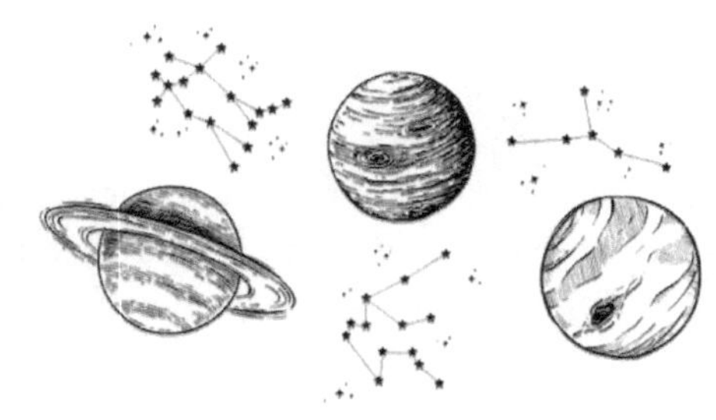

Chapter 29

Cosima

Cosima's head pounded as she regained consciousness. Only moments ago, it seemed, Enzo dealt the killing blow to Carmine as they stood on his captive planet, but that was not where they were now. She rubbed her eyes and took in her strange new surroundings. They had been mysteriously transported to the empty skeleton of a building, the interior of it stripped of all material except the wood and metal beams that kept it standing.

A man she had never seen before stood in front of her, bent over and smiling, as if he knew her well. He wore a black suit, adorned with brass embellishment covering nearly every inch. Dragons, feathers, and winding vines covered his suit jacket, and menacing midnight black wings towered behind him. An impossibly oppressive aura followed him, as if a festering infection of darkness consumed him.

He had vibrant purple eyes, white skin, and thick black hair to his shoulders. Handsome in a way that made her stomach turn, his dark glare consumed her, and she could not look away. He crouched down and got even closer to her face.

To her right, Ivo lay unconscious on her back, Nariah beside her, folded in half on her side. To her left, Vincenzo and Merit were face down, their wings flat and limp against their backs. She swallowed her panic and fought to stay conscious. His lips moved, and she focused on listening to the words coming out of his mouth.

"Hello, Cosima," the mysterious man said.

Something about the way he said her name sent a crawling dread down her spine. Sima knew he must be a brother of the Sacred Twelve, if not by how he said it, then by the dark twinkle in his eyes as he stared at her. While he did not resemble Aurelio as closely as Carmine did, his eyes communicated a hollow, endless anger. It was undeniably the same stare she had endured for fifty years.

"How do you know my name?" she asked.

"It is really a pleasure to meet you. I have heard so much about you over the years, it was about time we finally met in person. Watching you from afar is not nearly as much fun. I see what Aurelio saw in you. You are magnificent."

Sima glared at him. "Who are you?"

He gave a small bow. "My name is Sostene. I am the eldest, and, of course, one of the only remaining brothers alive. Though I would bet you already knew that part."

"Sostene," Sima said under her breath.

"I must admit, I thought we had much more time, you and I. But it seems we will have to cut the schedule short. Truly a shame, but I will work with what I have."

Sima's lip wobbled, and she clamped her teeth over it. "What do you want from me?"

"What all of my brothers want—your undying devotion."

His words struck fear in her, causing her to freeze. "I'm not her. I'm not the woman from the prophecy."

"Is that right?" Sostene let out a small laugh and shook his head. "Tell me how you came to that conclusion."

It wasn't clear whether telling him the truth was advantageous or not, but Sima prayed that her confession would deter him; his interest was already enough to make Sima's skin crawl.

"I am not Kismet's daughter."

A smile spread across his lips, but Sostene said nothing. The others woke one by one, starting with Ivo and ending with Merit. When Vincenzo regained consciousness, he rose from the floor at a crawling pace. Once he noticed Sostene, his eyes grew wide, and he reached for his sword.

"No, brother," Sostene said. "You know better. You are not strong enough to defeat me on your own, the same way Aurelio was not. None of you can compete."

"I will kill you either way," Vincenzo vowed.

Sostene erupted into laughter. Before Enzo could make a move, Sostene lifted his hand and seized him with his power, imaginary binds hauling him into the air. With a flick of his wrist, Sostene sent Enzo barreling through the walls, causing him to disappear somewhere on the horizon. Sima let out a scream, but her legs were locked in place. Ivo gasped, hiding behind Sima, and Merit ran over to the hole, attempting to find Enzo through it. Nariah's brows furrowed as she inched closer to Ivo and pulled her away from Sima and Sostene.

Sima's jaw hung open, and Sostene bent down, using the tip of his finger to close her mouth. "I feel so much better with him gone, don't you agree? I don't know why Aurelio let him live this long, but I quite like the game. It's adorable to try and watch him be tough when he has no clue how. He'll be fun to kill later on."

"You wouldn't dare," Nariah said.

"You won't get the chance," Sima spat. "I-I won't let you."

Sostene held his hand up and clenched his fist, causing Nariah to tumble to her knees. She fought to speak, but no words came out. He replied instead. "Perhaps I won't be the one to take his life…maybe it will be you who does it for me. You're correct that the prophecy mentioned a woman from Kismet's direct bloodline. A woman Fated to be the determining factor in which of my brothers live or die. Prophecies are funny, ambiguous things, are they not? The Oracles whisper, but not all sing the truth. They agree on one small detail, however. Kismet's descendant will offer her undying devotion to one Sacred Brother, and all others will perish. I did not believe it until I went to check in on dear Aurelio and his captive planet, only to hear *you* had murdered him. Is it true? Is he really dead?"

"Yes, he's dead," Sima said slowly, her hand reaching back to confirm Ivo remained behind her. "He spent enough time torturing me. I earned my freedom in blood, and I will do it again before I go with anyone else."

He smiled at her. "I like the energy, the bitter tenacity. I suspect my dearest brother must have underestimated you if it was his own pet that tore out his throat. He should have treated you better, I suppose. You could come join me without all the theatrics. You could take a walk on the true dark side of the moon, if that were at all of interest to you."

Sima scoffed and shook her head. "I'm not interested in going anywhere with you. Forget whatever sick plan you have in your head, I am not your captive." Her eyes fell on the hole Enzo's body made through the wall. "I'll tear your throat out for hurting the man I love."

He threw his head back and cackled, his menacing aura growing more unbearable by the second. "Your crush is not a hindrance to the future I imagine for us. Let me take you away from this life of blood splatter and adrenaline." He sighed, placing a hand over his chest. "Have you ever stopped to question why the Kingdom would dare send you on a mission this dangerous? My Sacred Brothers and I have been declared enemy number one, and still, the Divinity is too consumed in its own matters to take proper action. Instead, they saw the perfect opportunity to force their work onto the neck of someone else. That someone happens to be you. Why sacrifice yourself for Goddesses who believe you are beneath them?"

"I am here because I decided I want to fight for my freedom rather than leave it up to the same Goddesses you are doubtful of. At least out here, my life is in my hands, instead of in theirs." The longer she spent near Sostene, the more something inside her boiled and rebelled. She stood up and took a step toward him. He stared down his nose at her, clearly amused, but curious, too. "The last man who tried to cage me ended up dead. How quickly do you want to join him?"

He chuckled. "Oh, sweet Cosima. You have no clue what the truth is, do you? My mother blessed the Kingdom by creating our Sacred line. Her intentions may have been slightly misled, but ultimately, she did the realms a favor. She allowed our bloodline to cleanse the Realms of our sins through metamorphosis. Not only will only one brother survive, he will be the strongest and most capable leader—the one that will crush the rotted pieces of the Eternal Kingdom and resurrect them into something unequivocally grand. The one of us that remains will have earned his vengeance." He sighed. "You all are merely lucky I am a gracious God."

Merit, whose head had been hanging low throughout the conversation, snickered. "Got kind of a big head on you, you know that?"

Sostene snapped his fingers, causing the Scout to writhe on the floor in agony, but even so, the Scout laughed through the pain. Sostene snarled as a wave of purple smoke bounced off Merit. Sima was aware of Merit's shielding abilities, but Enzo had frequently discounted the Scout's magic. *How is he still fighting off Sostene's power?* Sima wondered.

"Stop it, that's enough," Ivo yelled, her voice carrying a resonance that Sima had never noticed before.

An invisible wave of electricity snapped and crackled as it slammed into Sostene. The color drained from Sima's face as she turned to find Ivo holding her hand up. It made the intimidating Sacred Brother pause for a moment as he took her in. Sima's heart jumped into her throat. *Why do you always interfere, Ivo?*

Sostene looked her up and down before turning his attention back to Sima. To her surprise, Sostene released his power over Merit, and the Scout sagged onto the floor. "Do you know why Carmine feared my arrival?"

Her heart squeezed, and she wished she could be anywhere but beneath the intense blanket of Sostene's energy. "Why?" Sima asked, hoping to keep him from targeting her friends again.

"Because Carmine knew I would come for him. You see, you and my runt of a brother did something momentous—and you're hardly even aware of it. You solved not one, but two, very troublesome problems for me, and now that they're both out of the way, there is nothing stopping me from taking it all for myself."

Her mind swam. "How was Aurelio your problem?"

"Aurelio was mommy's favorite boy, and for many decades, she was certain he would be the one to outlast the trials of time. My mother should have known the dimwitted bully could never be the harbinger of destructive transformation. Instead of encouraging him to advance his ability, her affection made him cocky, made him think there was nothing left to learn. He did not devote himself to the weight of our combined Fate."

Sostene's lip twitched. "A man preoccupied with his people's perception of his power has an unstable illusion of control more than he has true influence. Aurelio spent his time harassing Carmine while the remainder of our brothers were picked off one by one."

"Why was he more afraid of you than Aurelio?"

Sostene cocked his head to the side, his purple eyes burning brightly. "Because I'm a nightmare, haven't you gotten that yet? The wheel has already begun to turn, and there is hardly any time remaining. There are only four of us left." He turned toward the hole he had cast Enzo out of. "My baby brother, of course, being one of them. But I have something none of my siblings do. Luciano, my sire, gifted me with more power than any of my brothers. Even if he hated almost all of my Sacred Brothers he created due to my mother's betrayal, he never held a vicious hand to my cheek. Instead, in the dead of night, he delivered priceless instruction, allowing me to wield my power to its fullest capacity. I can do things they can only dream of."

"Why did Luciano take an interest in you?"

"The prophecy may seem cloudy and contradictory to others, but its truth has always sung to me. I am the survivor—not Aurelio, and especially not the runt. The unfathomable power that courses through me cannot be denied. Thankfully, my father understands this. I never had to prove my worth to him; he knew it inherently. It may be her blood in our veins, but it is my father who taught me how to wield it with precision—to never fear what great magic I was gifted with."

She glanced over her shoulder at her friends as her stomach turned, unsure what to make of Sostene's admission. Merit and Nariah shared a series of glances with their lips locked tightly. Ivo's blue eyes were like ocean waves, commanding, yet mysterious as she watched them with her fists balled tightly. Cosima swallowed the temptation to collapse beneath the pressure of Sostene's presence and faced him once more.

"It doesn't matter how impervious you believe yourself to be—Vincenzo will outlast you, and we won't stop until we find a way to take your life." Her heart pounded as her mind flashed with images of Enzo floating as viridian energy beamed from his eye sockets. "We won't let you destroy the Eternal Kingdom or hurt innocent people."

He laughed. "What reason would I have to do that? I am not the monster you believe me to be. The lives of others may hold pitiful weight in my eyes, but without an audience to command, to capture, to hold near, what use is the performer? For that reason alone, I plan to amend the Kingdom into something better suited for me as its ruler. I would dispose of all twelve residing priestesses and replace them with my chosen dozen. Oh, what a magnificent dream that would be. Everything running as it should, and everyone bowing on their knees to a proper emperor."

"Your plan hinges on the domination of the Kingdom. What happens when people inevitably rebel against your desires? Will you kill them in cold blood? You would be a pitiful leader."

He smiled at her, stepping closer. He stood only inches away, his purple eyes searing into hers as he held her stare. "You have no idea what kind of leader I am. I am good to my servants, so long as they are good to me. I do not tolerate disobedience well, but…" His finger ran down her cheek, and Sima shivered. "You'd follow my command so loyally, you'd be begging me for more—scrambling for the chance to please me." His voice was low and husky. "And I'd let you."

Sima slapped his hand away and took a step backward, scowling. What could possess him to flirt with her so brazenly when it was becoming apparent entire realms, including the Ethereal Realm, were at risk should he gain control? Sostene snarled as black smoke with a purple tint toiled from his palms. As he clenched his hands, a thunderous clap shook the building. Ivo covered her gasp with her hand and turned away. Nariah and Merit tensed, but made no move toward them.

"What would the Spirit Goddess think of that?" Sima asked.

Sostene clenched his fist, his cheeks roaring red and pink hues as his lips pressed into a line. "Mother faces no objections to our inevitable union, Cosima. If she did, however, she would have no choice but to accept my decisions. That is the price to pay when you create sons stronger than yourself."

His words made her sway on her feet. "Does Ehses know I have already brought forth Aurelio's demise?"

"Not yet," Sostene said as he grinned. "Preparations have kept us busy, but I couldn't resist the chance to get a look at you for myself. I must say, your aura is divine. She told me your power was suitable, but she undersold you. You are magnetizing, and I cannot wait to see you access the full depths of your abilities. Can't you picture it? The realms we will command at each other's sides?"

His mention of her powers made her magic boil to the surface, the accumulation of it so intense, she thought her skin might burst. "You don't know the first thing about me."

A sharp canine tooth flashed as the corner of his lip tugged upward. "Give me the pleasure then, sweet Sima. Allow me into the blessing that is your inner world and sit back as I worship your every breath. If my devotion is not enough, then I'll bring the masses to their knees at your feet. Tell me what it takes, and you shall have it. I'll spill blood in your name, I'll write lovesick letters in the stars," he said, inching forward, "I'll conquer every corner of the cosmos if it means I get to linger in your intoxicating aura."

"I know better than to trust your lies," Sima spat, her heart fluttering. "You'd slam chains around my wrists the first moment you got the chance."

He leveled his gaze at her. "Nonsense, I have no need to rely on physical binds. My love is fervent and flexible. I would be unshakable in my pursuit of your pleasure, devout in a way that would make the rising sun seem unreliable. This is the last time I will offer, at least for now. Join me. Let me take you away from the debts and dangerous errands. Live as my Empress and watch me unfold the world for you."

Sima grit her teeth. "Lay me beside you, Sostene, and I will slit your throat in your sleep. Your blood will become evidence of my rebellion as it soaks into the sheets. I'll watch with delight as your chest stops rising."

The Sacred Brother smiled, his purple eyes locking her attention. "Such a shame," he purred. "I can understand the hesitation after your miserable time with my brother, but with Aurelio gone, I can show you what properly commanded power looks like, what *you* could be with your talents properly harnessed. I will return for you, someday."

He reached into his coat pocket and pulled out a purple crystal butterfly, one Sima recognized, but where she had seen it slipped her mind. Clouds of immense power wafted off it, calling her toward it. Without intending to, her hand reached out with her palm up.

Sostene's white teeth sparkled as his smile widened. The butterfly jumped to life, its wings moving in delicate waves as it floated from his hand to hers. The elegant creature glimmered, its crystal body illuminated with a deep purple light as it rested on her palm. She sucked in a breath as its magic collided with her own. The two flows entwined, and everything around Cosima faded as her soul quieted. The crystal butterfly shuddered, causing its wings to rain golden flecks of light that faded a second after they appeared. A surge of power flooded through her, and Sima's heart pounded as the curious creature's energy awakened something lurking in the corners of her essence. Sostene snapped, and the butterfly disappeared. Sima blinked rapidly as she adjusted to the abrupt dismissal.

"Tell Vincenzo I am saving him for last. While he is the one who has your heart—for now—tell him his final breaths will be my favorite, because it means one thing… that I succeeded in taking you from him. Until you're all mine, Sima, I won't stop until you're mine."

He vanished, leaving behind a bluish-purple ripple of light in the air. Her cheeks burned, Sostene's dark intentions so palpable she could not escape them. His words contained a certainty, a confidence so undeniable, Sima almost wondered if he knew more about her than he let on.

Sostene's disembodied voice tickled her ears. "Tell Dario I said 'hello', won't you?"

Sima blinked, and the world around her melted away. The four of them fell through the fibers of their reality, only to be caught by the forgiving fabric of space bending around them as millions of stars sped by. They plummeted through a violet portal that manifested beneath them. Cosima held her breath and braced herself as they flew through it and were spit out on the other side, leaving Carmine's planet in the past.

Chapter 30

One moment, Ivo was cowering from the mysterious stranger who had identified himself as Sostene, and the next, she was thrust through the tapestry of the universe. Space tore at her skin and stunned her senses as she closed her eyes and held her breath.

Within the darkness behind her closed eyelids, a vision manifested. A purple orb glowed, as a haunting melody greeted her ears. As she focused her attention on the orb, finer details surfaced. It was a purple butterfly, with delicate wings outlined in black.

Its wings were vibrant and loud, shimmering with the thousands of tiny rainbows caught inside. She reached for it, only for the butterfly to flap its wings and dart out of the way. The unusual song continued in the background as Ivo watched the brilliant creature fly away, disappearing in the black void.

The universe was not finished with Ivo. There was more it desired to reveal to her, and another vision pieced together. The melody from before faded, replaced with a gentle orchestra, the sound some distance away.

The void seemingly vanished as the vision encompassed her entire view, ejecting her from the inter-dimensional roadway. It was as though she were plucked from space and dropped into a physical body.

Ivo shook her head as she glanced down at her tiny hands. Below them were small feet strapped into sparkling blue flats. *Am I in a child's body?* Her heart skipped, and she stumbled backward, colliding with someone. She whirled around and found a familiar face.

"Sima?" Ivo asked.

The girl smiled, her face a mirror image of Ivo's best friend, but much, *much* smaller. Cosima, in the vision, could not have been more than a few years old, nowhere near old enough for her immortal settling. She wore a beautiful lilac gown with a string of pale gold stars around her neck. The jewelry reflected Ivo's bewildered expression.

"Do you want to go play?" Sima asked.

For the first time, Ivo took in her surroundings. To her surprise, they were standing behind two ethereal women who conversed on a balcony. Their dresses were breathtaking, as if the raw beauty of nature was captured alive and knit into the fabric. Below, there was a massive crowd of finely dressed Caelari, swaying to the music from the orchestra on stage.

One of the women noticed Ivo and bent over slightly to whisper in her ear. "Go play, darling. Don't go too far."

Their gazes met, and Ivo stilled at the sight of her ice-blue eyes. She blinked, unsure what to make of the woman's eerie resemblance to her. Ivo tore herself away and turned around.

Sima rocked back and forth on her heels with an adorable smirk as she waited for Ivo. She held a hand out, and Ivo accepted it, the gesture so well known to two of them that Ivo's heart squeezed.

The two held tightly to one another as they ran giggling through the hallways. Nearly forgetting the real world, Ivo rejoiced in the childlike joy she experienced with her best friend by her side. It wasn't until it all began to fade away that Ivo wondered if what she had seen was real at all, or if the stranger, Sostene, had altered her mind, injecting it with confusing and conflicting information.

It's just a silly hallucination—a terribly vivid dream.

The experience had altered something within her, despite her denial of it. The shift spread through her, moving in uncomfortable waves, as if the very energy of her soul was being revitalized. She couldn't shake the feeling that the vision did not come from Sostene, but from a higher, cosmic source, as her mind ran with possibilities of what it could mean.

What message are you trying to send me?

Ivo would not get her answer. Their impromptu travel through space came to an abrupt end as Ivo and the others reached Sostene's intended destination.

Vincenzo

"Crawl to me," Sostene taunted. "Be a fucking man. If you can't walk, if I've broken every last bone in your legs, then *crawl* to me."

Snap his fucking arms off at the elbows and shove them down his throat for speaking to you like that, his curse screamed.

Enzo hissed as he tugged his battered wing out of the crater his body had created with the force of Sostene's throw. This was precisely the reason he had feared his brothers so greatly, why he had let that fear terrorize him for decades—their strength was inconceivable. There was nothing he wanted less than to be staring Sostene in the eyes, no clue as to where his friends had gone, and, more importantly, Sima had gone.

"It won't be that easy," Enzo growled quietly, launching himself at Sostene.

His brother vanished, reappearing feet away. "It's finally time to play, isn't it, runt?" Sostene's shoulder-length black hair fluttered as a viscous purple aura consumed him like glowing flames. He hurled dark orbs of magic toward Enzo, the blasts creating craters in the red and yellow forest. "I can't wait to hear your skull crush beneath my grasp."

Although they were still on Carmine's planet, none of the fungal beasts had made an appearance. Enzo angled his wings to slip through the trees unscathed. He pushed his muscles to their maximum as his power created physical distance between him and Sostene. It was futile as his brother warped through space, continually ending up only feet behind him, despite how Enzo manipulated their environment.

The only thing stopping you is your inability to give in, his dark companion wailed, its screams tickling the inside of Enzo's mind.

Already having sped through his limits in his battle with Carmine, Enzo knew it was a risk to continue to dip into his poisonous well of magic, but he would not let Sostene take his life. He relented beneath the pressure of his rising curse and allowed it to once again flood through him. Enzo thrust them into a void, drenching them in never-ending black space until he commanded it how he desired.

Sostene's black wings towered over him as he fixed his suit and grinned at Vincenzo. "I quite enjoy your tricks, brother. You are endless entertainment."

Enzo trembled as his magic burned him from the inside out. "Tell me where she is."

His brother raised a brow and clenched his fist. "She doesn't belong to you, runt. You really want her to watch me gut you?"

"You're so arrogant, it makes me sick." Enzo let his internal flames flicker in his emerald eyes. "There is nothing you can do to keep Cosima and me apart."

Sostene's smile faltered. "You will never be enough to stop me. I've been watching you, and I know what you're capable of, what kind of man you are. You flee, like the coward you are. You lurk in the shadows, pouting as you plot your revenge, but never do you quench your bloodthirst."

A flash of dark purple blinded Enzo as he was cast backward. Sostene gripped his shirt, staring down his nose at Enzo as he tugged him upward. "Show me what you're made of, son of Domani. Make this worth my while."

Vincenzo snapped his fingers, and a snowy tundra exploded from his hands, finally allowing him to put proper space between himself and his brother. Towering fifty-foot-tall trees with midnight black trunks densely packed the space, expanding in all directions endlessly. His hands shook uncontrollably as he took breaths to calm himself.

What if I haven't reached my true limit yet? Can I bear to push further without losing myself?

He continued to spin and contort the space, ensuring he left no discernible pattern to his actions. With the continuous, monotonous environment, Enzo hoped he would be able to outmaneuver his brother if he could not overpower him. He floated upward as a perpetual heavy snowstorm created a haze in the air. Enzo flicked his fingers outward, his magic spreading in a wide invisible wave. Within seconds, he was able to sense his brother, who was rapidly approaching, opting to fly rather than warp.

"There is nothing more enjoyable for me than watching you react," Sostene hollered, his black wings beating at an even pace behind him as he flew, "but surely this is not the full depth of your power. We are brothers of nightmares. Darkness consumes our souls. Give in, runt, let the madness take you."

You cannot deny my call for eternity, his curse chanted on repeat as Enzo attempted to control the pulse of his growing power.

Vincenzo's arms stretched outward as green energy exploded, creating a cascade of ice crystal daggers. Sostene let out a furious cry as several of the frozen blades sliced through his skin. Instead of blood, a thick, glowing fluid seeped from his wounds. It had the same black and purple signature as Sostene's magic, and Enzo felt a chill run down his spine. Despite his surprise, Enzo continued to craft within his void, just out of sight of his brother.

"It doesn't speak to you—your wicked power?" Sostene waved a hand over his wounds, healing them instantly. "You can't deny its existence, I can feel it growing with fervor inside you," he said, straightening his suit. "Don't tell me its melodies don't sing your name in the dead of night. You can't escape the debt our lives accrued in the greater realms; none of us can. So, stop holding back. I see no reason not to give into the depths of your magic at least once before you die." He raised a fist in front of him and clenched it. "Stop holding back, you immeasurably pathetic coward. I want to see what a son sired by Domani looks like at his strongest before I cut him down."

His destruction is incapable of genesis, his curse snapped. *Show him why you were chosen instead.*

With another pulse of Enzo's magic, the forest disappeared, and beyond the black sky, all that remained below them was a deep pit of green acid. As he continued to charge the space, gigantic buzzing arcs of electricity sprouted from nothingness and ended at his palms. His hair began to float as he ascended above his brother, his illuminated gaze narrowed on the subtle displeasure on Sostene's face.

Before Sostene could react, Enzo rolled his head back as he pointed his hands at his brother. The electricity ravaged through Sostene, his skin glowing with Enzo's emerald energy as he seized. Somewhere within, Vincenzo's desperate desire for his bloodlines' destruction bared its teeth and writhed with impatience. He screamed as he funneled more of his toxic power. It would not come without cost, but in his delicious delusion, it would be well worth the price.

Sostene's skin flaked away, revealing a swirling storm—his core like a purple galaxy contained within a fleshy exterior. As he withdrew his power, his heart slowed, despite the adrenaline coursing through him. A laugh echoed through his void, and Enzo glanced around.

"I could kill you in an instant, don't you understand? You're alive because I allow you to remain so."

Enzo clenched his fists in an attempt to disguise the way he shivered. After expelling so much power, he was left freezing. His curse begged for more, but his stomach turned at the thought. "Why don't you just kill me then? What's the point in playing along?"

Sostene laughed again as the miniature galaxy expanded and formed his vessel. He shook his head as his face reformed. "Because, brother, I seek to *destroy* you. I don't just want you to die, I want to devastate you. I desire to take everything you love away from you so I can devour the taste of your pathetic grief. When you're ready, you'll be begging at my feet for your demise. I'll keep dear Cosima all to myself, and when the deprivation of her love tears you apart, I will only grow hungrier. She and I will be unstoppable together, the prophecy tells it so."

"No," Enzo bit out, quelling his disgust as he mustered the strength to keep fighting. "She will never love you."

"Love me? You sensitive fool. She doesn't have to love me. She only has to believe she loves me and give me her devotion. I will inherit my rightful empire, and there will be no one above us, no regulation we cannot break. The many universes yearn for renewal, and who am I to deny them their restoration?"

"You're all just power drunk replicas of each other," Enzo murmured. Tumultuous waves of trembling rage tormented Enzo as he struggled to keep his calm. It was unbearable the way his brothers spoke of the woman he loved, each word a threat to the future he dreamed he would get with her. Enzo clenched his jaw. "A man as demonic as you could not get a woman as divine as Cosima to love you organically, even if you made it out of this alive and had eons to get it right."

"That's the difference between us then, I suppose," Sostene said with a smile. "You care for love, and I care for what it does for me."

A piercing sound ripped through Enzo's ears, causing him to drop several feet before he recovered. "You're…not…good enough for her," he bit out, using his hands to cover the sides of his face.

His void vibrated chaotically as it split open, like the eruption of a volcano. Red flesh and muscle sprouted from the center, draining his vat of acid. Enzo was thrust backward and collided with a tremendous bundle of bones, his head bouncing off what he thought might be a rib. Sostene's demented creation pulsed with blood as it grew, filling his void with oceans of flesh beneath trees of ever-towering bones, a spine snaking through the black sky above him.

"Witness me," Sostene screamed, spinning as tendrils of purple and black smoke encircled him. He held out his hand as he grit his teeth. "I want to dissolve your skin and taste the fear in your blood. I am going to sculpt you into the man you should've always been as I drain the power that thumps inside you."

The sparkle of stars will guide your listless soul, his curse sang, *discover resonance in the dust of creation as you erase him from existence. Only time can contain your reincarnation.*

Sostene clenched his fist as his eyes grew black. Vincenzo shook his head as his heart beat strangely in his chest. His hand clutched the clothing and skin above his quivering organ as he rebelled against his brother's attempts to separate it from his body. Sostene shot forward and slammed into him, causing them to tumble. They bounced off the tight muscle fibers where they landed, finding themselves trapped in what Enzo feared might be gigantic intestines. The grayish tissue coiled around his ankles and wrists, binding him to the spot. Enzo tugged against them as Sostene brushed back his black hair and smiled.

"What was it you said, brother?" Sostene said, leaning forward with a hand around his ear. "I am not 'good enough' for sweet Sima?"

Vincenzo blasted the tissue with his starlight, but the flesh his brother had created resisted its burn. He glanced up as his brother as he bit back a scream.

"You are rotten and cruel," he spat. "You could never be right to rule alongside her. She is not the pliable subject you expect her to be. She will buck and bite before she gives in to your tyrannical plans."

"How precious you are," Sostene said, his predator-like gaze locked onto Enzo. "You cannot see how you share our corruption. You think because you are only half my blood that it means you are half the threat to the systems as they stand? They were not built to last an eternity. The Divinity's way of commanding has become obsolete as the evolution of our collective souls reaches greater heights."

Enzo's lip twitched. "I am nothing like you."

"You are a reiteration of my same spirit. Each of us represent a different expression of the same being, but that does not mean there is no hierarchy amongst us. You surely are not the weakest, brother, but you are equally far from the strongest." Sostene stepped forward and clamped his hand around the crook of Enzo's neck, digging his nails in. Enzo screamed as his brother's poisonous magic ripped through his body. "You are the one who is not enough for her, don't you get it yet? You lack the grit needed to command the delicacy of a new dawn from the cusp of nothingness. She needs a man capable of ensuring the fruits of destiny are always in her presence. She needs a man unbound by fear with fury on his breath."

The seconds pass, and every beat of your heart brings you closer to the end of their reign, his curse whispered. *Embrace your inescapable destiny, unstoppable son.*

Vincenzo trembled as a blackness crept up his fingers and arms. His vision darkened as the coiled tissue around his limbs vanished, and he dropped to the floor. His sight brightened just enough for him to watch as Sostene seized his wrist and stared at him with a wild storm raging in his eyes.

"You may have her heart for now, but haven't you learned yet, brat? Nothing lasts forever."

With a demonic smile plastered across his face, Sostene twisted his wrist and snapped the bones in Enzo's arm. He cried out as he fought against his brother, his mind blaring with alarm. The pain was unlike anything he had experienced before, and the intensity of it drove him to tears. His broken arm pulsed with unbearable dark energy. The blackness that had crept up his skin disappeared, but his agony remained. His curse hissed as he attempted to heal himself, but his magic did nothing to dampen the mind-altering pain.

"Ah, I feel it," Sostene said, raising his hands beside his head. "I feel the thrum of your power. You have deceived me, brother. You hold so much more within you." He snapped his fingers, and Enzo's void dissolved, leaving them on the forest floor on Carmine's planet, Paiturn. "When you're finally worthy of it, I'll slit your throat and rejoice in your scarlet ruin."

Sostene waved his hand in front of him, and a portal ripped open, a cloudy purple spiral at its core. Despite how Enzo's arm barked with pain, he clamped his teeth over his lip to keep from crying out as Sostene tugged him to a stand. He stepped back and grinned.

"Cosima is an exquisite beauty—her every curve is a testament to the thoughtfulness of the universe." Sostene's eyes darkened. "I will force you to watch me taste and explore her. I cannot wait to see your spirit break as I bring her to ecstasy and beyond. You will know helplessness like no man before you, as I take what should have never been yours."

Sostene shoved him through the portal, knocking all of the breath from Vincenzo's lungs. As the roadway of space tore at his skin, the pain from his broken arm blurred the lines of reality. He was incredibly weak, but aware enough to realize there would be no winning against his brothers if he could not withstand his curse. He pushed away his fears and pictured Cosima's face as the stars sliced into his vessel.

Wait for me, wherever you are. I will find you. I will find you because you are mine.

It was not possessive, it was not arrogant. It was the only truth he had ever pledged himself to, the only thing capable of bringing him to his knees in quest of being a better man, a holier man. A man worthy and deserving of a love as grand as the one she held inside, one he'd weather any storm for.

And I am ever so desperately yours, Cosima.
Wait for me.

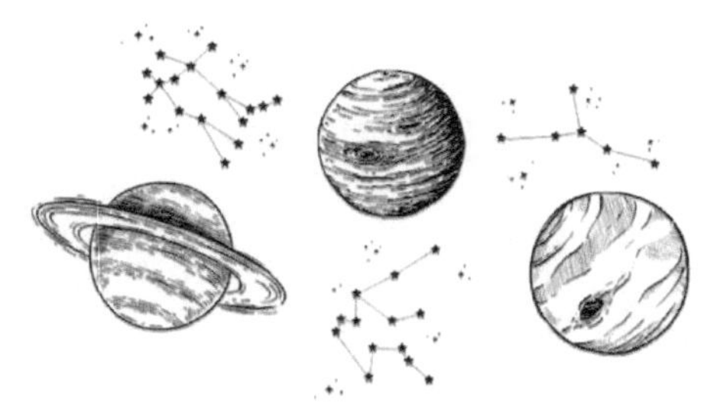

Chapter 31

Cosima

With a thud, Cosima landed on her back in red mud. Her head swam with confusion as she blinked away the haze in her eyes. She turned her head to the side and let out a sigh when she noticed her friends. Merit was upside down with his back leaning up against a dense shrub. Nariah pulled Ivo out of the mud before she pinned back her white hair and walked toward Sima. Somehow, without confirming, Sima knew Enzo was not with them. She clamped her teeth over her lip and willed herself to remain strong as Nariah helped her stand.

The group was quiet as they took in their unusual surroundings. All of the plants were differing shades of black, and the sky had a diffuse pink glow. The trees reached a staggering height above them, the trunks bare except at the very top, where the coal black leaves formed shallow domes covered in a pale green radiance, further illuminating the forest. The entire area buzzed with what sounded to Sima like thousands of insects singing at once.

Delicate wings with strange shapes and angles fluttered by, some of the bugs more aggressive than the others. Merit swatted one with a skinny torso and thin, clear skin. When it smashed against his arm, its purple blood splattered.

"This is not what I was expecting," Merit said, his frown deeply etched. "Where the fuck are we?"

Nariah crossed her arms. "If I had to guess, Yaailo. That's Dario's planet, but I have no idea why Sostene would bring us here."

Ivo furrowed her brows. "I bet he thinks Dario will kill us. That asshole better realize if he wants us dead, he better kill us himself."

"Hush," Sima hissed. "Don't talk like that." She looked at Nariah as her heart raced. "Vincenzo isn't with us. We need to find him."

A shriek silenced the jungle, and the group crouched down, their eyes wide. Nariah wrinkled her nose. "First things first, we stay alive. Then we can worry about where the hell he went."

The Scouts drew their twin blades as their capes rustled with the wind. Ivo inched closer to Sima and placed her hand on her back. Sima turned, and Ivo slipped the crystal blade from Nariah's belt into her hand. The ground shook as enormous footsteps echoed. Her breath lodged in her throat. A shadow moved in the distance. It approached them at rapid speed, the force from its every step jostling them on the ground.

"Merit, now," Nariah yelled, her wings shooting her into the air.

Merit followed, his thin wings incredibly agile as he darted side-to-side in anticipation of the incoming threat. Cosima stood up, prepared to run if necessary. She locked onto the massive being as her heart skipped a beat. It was not an animal or twisted beast; it was a man three times their height, his arms wrapped tightly around himself as he ran with alarming speed.

Sima grabbed Ivo and moved out of its path just as the man raced by. He showed his white teeth, each the length of her arm, as he chomped in the air, biting at the Scouts as they flew around him. Nariah bounced back and forth in front of him, garnering the man's attention as Merit positioned himself behind the giant man's neck. Starlight consumed Merit's blade as he swung. It sliced right through the man's neck, his head and body sending a rumble through the jungle as they hit the ground.

Ivo held a hand over her heart as she panted. "What the fuck?"

"Where did he come from?" Sima asked.

Merit wiped his blade clean on his olive cape, the man's black blood leaving stains behind. "I have no idea, but there better not be more of them."

The cacophony of insect noises resumed. Nariah landed in front of them. "We need to get moving. Clearly, Dario is not in this part of the jungle, and I don't think we're safe here."

"Where are we going to go?" Ivo asked.

"I'm not sure," Nariah said, sheathing her blades. "We will have to keep moving until we find somewhere suitable to gather ourselves and perhaps rest, if we're lucky."

The empty stare of the beheaded giant made Sima cringe. "The quicker we get out of her, the better."

A low groan made the jungle vibrate as distant steps echoed. This time, however, many of the steps overlapped, as though the sounds came from a pack of giants. Sima's heart pounded as the group froze. As garbled shrieking grew more fervent, the Scouts snapped into motion. Nariah zipped out of sight as Merit placed himself in front of them. Sima held her blade as she pressed her back against Ivo's. Her eyes flicked back and forth as she held her breath.

A cry rang out, and a moment later, a giant head with brown hair rolled to a stop at their feet. Its eyes were shut, and it was missing the bottom half of its jaw, its teeth caked in red mud. Nariah appeared, coated in black blood.

"Ready yourselves," she shouted, "more are coming."

Sima scanned the trees in front of her before she spotted a smaller being. This one did not resemble immortals as closely. It ran on all fours with a flat back, and its face had empty eye sockets. She planted her feet as it bounded from the trees, its teeth chattering. She reached for her time magic and pulled the creature to a halt. Although she successfully halted the being, it strained against her hold, something she had never experienced before.

Deciding it was best not to chance it breaking free, Sima bolted toward it, her blade outstretched. Her magic flooded into the weapon and gave it a lavender luminescence as she swung. The metal tore through its neck, causing the creature's head to dangle by a sliver of connected flesh as black blood spurted. With another swing of her blade, she was confident she had killed it.

There was no time to catch her breath as two more emerged. Their arms were underdeveloped and frail against their chests. The taller one had red eyes with inky pupils and blond hair. The shorter being moved faster, but was bald with no nose or ears. She froze them in her time pocket, only for the shorter one to break free within seconds. Her ears barely registered Ivo shouting a spell before a bolt of blue energy stunned the creature. Sima swung, but the cut was too shallow to stop it. Black blood rained over her as Ivo's electric spell wore off, and the being threw her onto her back. It bit at her leg, and without waiting for permission, Sima used her magic the way Merit had coached her to, managing to bend the wheel of chance in her favor, to keep herself from getting injured.

When the opportunity presented itself, she dug the blade through the side of its skull. Her arm and wrist screamed with the amount of force it took to break through, but finally, the being stopped moving. She shoved it off and jumped to her feet. To her left, Nariah and Merit bounced through the air as though they were dancing, the glint of their blades reflecting the pink hue of the sky. Nariah's colorful wings encircled her as she spun parallel to the ground, her blade cutting ribbons into the core of a man taller than the first they had seen.

His knees fell into the mud, the impact causing a wake of energy, nearly knocking Sima off her feet. She searched for Ivo and found her friend using her power to drench a giant's feet in ice. This one had full use of his arms and swatted at Ivo as he screeched. Nariah appeared and shoved her blade through the underside of the creature's skull and into its brain. She ripped it free, and it folded forward, its feet still bound in place.

Nariah scooped Ivo into her arms and flew to Sima. She deposited her friend at her side and wiped her forehead. "I think that is the last of them, but we need to move. Now."

"Which way should we go?" Sima asked.

Ivo touched her sleeve. "I saw something when I was running away from one of those giant beings. The growth of vegetation suggests a water source nearby. No clue if it's safe for us to use, but it is worth checking out."

With a flutter of his wings, Merit landed beside Sima. "Let's do it. I don't like standing still. I swear I can still feel one of those guys looming behind me."

Merit carried Sima while Ivo sat in Nariah's arms as they flew in the direction Ivo had thought might lead them to a safe place to shelter. Sima quietly used her abilities to slow time around them, and it soothed her racing thoughts to drain her magic on shielding the group in the best way she knew how. Merit's navy hair waved with the gusts of wind through the strange, tall trees, reminding Sima of the Scout's helpful advice in the mirror realm. She wrinkled her nose. *This power is grander than I imagined, if only because I have yet to wield the full scope of it*, she thought.

Sima stared off into the distance. "Merit, do you think there is more you can teach me?"

The Scout pinched his brows. "Absolutely. I know you've got some cool shit hiding away somewhere in you. It's all about encouraging that confidence in your abilities more than anything else."

The corner of her lip pulled upward. "How do you know so much about this if you don't have a connection to the Weave?"

He snorted. "I have a connection to the Weave, just not like you and Nariah. Mine is…subtle, I guess you could call it. The Weave exists, above all else, to communicate. Not everyone knows what it's saying, and most of the time, neither do I. But every once in a while, it reveals things to me. Usually, right when I need it."

Sima nodded. "I think I understand." Her heart sank. "Do you think Enzo is alright?"

Merit rolled his eyes. "That bird fuck is alive and kicking, that much I'm sure of."

Her eyes widened. "How do you know?"

"I'm a Trine Scout, Sima. I went into this knowing Enzo might try to shake me off. That connection to the Weave comes in handy when tracking…Feathers couldn't lose me even if he killed me before he ran."

Merit's gaze flicked to her and then forward again. "He's somewhere on this planet. I'm sure we will run into him soon enough."

"Look, right there," Ivo shouted.

The Scouts brought them closer to an area overgrown with more of the midnight black plants, but each of the leaves had a pale green and blue glow to them. Merit set her down and pulled out his blade, hacking away at some of the vegetation until there was a pathway. As he moved forward, Sima followed with Ivo at her heels. Nariah guarded the rear of the group while Merit pushed deeper. The sound of rushing water sped up his movements as insects and wildlife began to buzz and sing.

With one final swing of his sword, the last of the vegetation disappeared, leaving them standing on a high ledge with an orange sun beaming through the domed leaves of the trees. The entire area had a supernatural luminescence, creating an effortlessly entrancing view.

The waterfall was closer than she expected and a hundred times more beautiful. On the other side of them, clear water streamed down from a high cliff, creating two separate waterfalls, one leading into the other. Tiny pink and purple bugs fluttered by, creating trails of light behind them. Despite the otherworldly sight, her heart was heavy. Sima wished Vincenzo could be there to witness it as well.

The Scouts flew them toward the water, revealing two separate reservoirs created by the waterfalls. The upper pool had an oval shape, while the bottom resembled a crescent moon with a smooth, bluish-gray bottom. Delicate violet flowers floated on the surface of the clear water. Nariah confirmed it was safe for them with a small taste and allowed them to select where to bathe.

Sima and Ivo chose the moon-shaped pool, leaving their undergarments on as they slipped into the surprisingly refreshing water. The second she sank in, her muscles relaxed. At first, she leaned into the sensation, then a wild wave of negativity flashed through her.

I can't survive. I am doomed. Vincenzo's love for me is waning. She pressed her fingers to her forehead as the thoughts kept rolling. *I am going to die out here alone. I have to find a way out. Sostene is the only one who can help me.*

With a deep breath, Sima plunged herself beneath the surface, her black hair floating above her. She could feel Sostene's touch in her thoughts, however faint. She fought against the panic that threatened to take root. Her resilience had become a bitter, snarling thing that would defend her peace at all costs. Sima refused to give up, even if Sostene managed to pierce through her shields.

When she resurfaced, Sima's mind was clear. She brushed back her wet hair and rested against the ledge. Ivo was transfixed on the silhouette of Nariah visible from their pool. It was not detailed enough to be a true glimpse, but her shadow showed off every curve. Sima raised her brows, turning around as she pretended not to notice. When she finished scrubbing the dirt and black blood from her body, she faced Ivo. Her friend's gaze had not moved.

Sima laughed. "Are you done watching your girlfriend like a stalker yet?"

"She is not my girlfriend," Ivo grumbled, "and I am not a stalker. I am making sure the Scouts don't creep a look at us."

"I'm pretty sure you're the one trying to catch a glimpse of Nariah."

Ivo splashed her. "Stop that."

"I think it's cute."

"I don't." Ivo frowned. "I don't know how I feel about her or how she feels about me. Being here only complicates things. Who knows if I will make it out of here alive, let alone be able to form a relationship with her, so why should I bother getting my hopes up?"

"You could try telling her how you feel."

Ivo rolled her eyes. "As if it could be that simple."

"It could," Sima said with a smile.

Ivo peered over her shoulder, causing Sima to laugh again. Her cheeks turned red, but Ivo turned forward. "I have a bad feeling about the next target, Dario. Those people had to be his creations, and they freak me out. Something about how closely they resemble immortals gives me chills."

Sima frowned as her stomach flipped. "Merit said Enzo's out there, probably with more of those beings."

"Enzo can handle them himself." Ivo grinned as she twisted all the water out of her hair.

"You're right. He is powerful in a way I never expected." Sima pulled herself from the pool and let the orange sun dry her body as she looked down at Ivo. "I can only hope he doesn't destroy himself with it."

After drying herself off and putting back on her clothes, Ivo could not stop thinking about her conversation with Sima. Was telling Nariah how she felt the right thing to do? She pressed her lips together as she glanced up at the second pool. Could she come to terms with leaving her true emotions unsaid?

Ivo let out a small groan as she hiked her way up the side of the waterfall until she reached the pool where Nariah sat. The Scout was clothed with clean skin; however, she was struggling with her long white hair. The ends were matted in the black blood of the beings that they had encountered. Ivo chewed the inside of her cheek as she approached. Nariah glanced up at her but said nothing as she dipped her hair back in the water and scrubbed.

"Let me help," Ivo said sternly as she got onto her knees beside Nariah.

The Scout's purple gaze was locked on her as Ivo's hands worked through her matted hair. Without meeting Nariah's eyes, Ivo reached over and broke off a black leaf nearby. She wiped the thin trail of green liquid from the plant onto Nariah's hair and rubbed it between her palms. It created a small amount of foam, and with some pressure, the black blood began to rinse away.

"How did you know that would work?" Nariah asked.

"I have a lot of experience with herbs and plants. This world has many unfamiliar types of vegetation, but when I was bathing, I tested out a few, and this one helped me get that sticky gunk off my body." Ivo used her fingers to rake through Nariah's hair. "I should be able to get it all out for you."

Nariah brushed back a lock of Ivo's black hair. "Thank you."

Ivo froze for a moment before she blinked away her surprise. "Of course."

The Scout leaned back and watched as Ivo finished her task. "A lot has happened to us in a short period. How are you holding up?"

She swallowed. "I'm fine. A bit tired, but it's nothing I can't handle."

"You're keeping up with the group better than I expected. I doubted you at first."

Ivo frowned as she stood up. "Gee, thanks."

Nariah hopped to her feet and smiled. "It's a compliment. Mortals don't usually fare well outside of their planet of origin. I had my fears, but you've crushed all of them."

"Good to know you didn't expect me to live this long," Ivo murmured as she faced away from Nariah.

"It's not that. I'm responsible for your safety. I have no choice but to keep my eye on you."

She crossed her arms over her chest as the Scout stepped in front of her. "Well, I'll try not to make your job harder."

The Scout chuckled. "You certainly make it more interesting."

Although she was unsure why, Ivo's cheeks burned. She excused herself and searched for Sima, finding she had lost the desire to confess her feelings to Nariah. Despite the fact that the Scout seemed flirtatious, she could not stop reminding Ivo why their relationship would not work.

How could an immortal ever love a doomed-to-die witch? Ivo thought as she made her way to a flat clearing beside the bottom pool.

Merit had manufactured them a temporary shelter out of leaves and sticks, which blended in remarkably well with their surroundings. She slipped inside the roomy space, impressed with the beds made from giant broad leaves with flat, smooth surfaces piled together. She lay down on one as the Scouts mentioned something to Sima outside about hunting for food. Before Sima could enter the shelter, Ivo had fallen asleep.

Ivo had experienced nightmares before, but that was nothing compared to whatever she was enduring now. The dreams did not start frightful, but were incoherent recreations of embarrassing times or her inner fears, like ending up alone. Unfortunately, the dreams changed to something with more of an edge. Her mind projected hostile scenarios so real, it was no wonder she had not succumbed to the madness of the dreams already. Ivo tossed and turned on the bed of leaves below her, but in her mind, the Sacred Twelve were ripping her apart, limb from limb, forcing Sima and the others to watch.

When the tearing of her flesh had been completed, the dreams merely began again with a new scenario, somehow more terrifying than the last. This time, it was Aurelio who stalked toward her, holding Sima's head by the hair as it dripped blood. Her head landed with a thud at her feet, and Ivo screamed so hard she thought her throat would bleed.

"Ivo?" Nariah asked, her voice floating in despite the terror of her dreams.

Ivo was too frightened to open her eyes, but the voice kept coming, more persistent each time. The sensation of hands pressing into her arms caused her to scream again.

"Ivo," Nariah hissed. "Wake up."

Ivo gasped as she sat up. Nariah was on her knees beside her, face flushed. She sighed and let her head hang as Ivo wiped the crust out of her eyes. They were still inside the shelter the Scouts built for them in the strange, glowing jungle, meaning that Sostene sending them to another world was not a part of her twisted dreams. It had been real. She shook her head.

Nariah chewed her lip. "You scared me half to death. You started off mumbling in your sleep, and the next moment, you were shouting."

She peered around the Scout. Sima and Merit were sleeping, despite the commotion Ivo had caused. Her stomach sank at the realization that everyone was tired enough to sleep through her fit. Everyone except Nariah, that is.

"I'm sorry," she whispered. "Bad dream."

Nariah adjusted herself to sit beside Ivo. She blew out a breath as her arms rested on her knees. "It happens. Are you...concerned about something?"

Ivo rubbed the back of her head. "Besides fearing that at any moment a horrid nightmare might manifest between the trees or that Dario will rip me to pieces while my back is turned? Not really."

The Scout chuckled. "I was worried that Dario's magic had gotten you.

I saved you some food. It is just some fire-roasted vegetables, as Merit and I didn't trust many of the creatures we found." Nariah handed her a tightly rolled black leaf. "It's still warm."

"Thank you," Ivo said, accepting it. She peeled back a corner of the leaf and took a bite. "I'm sorry for waking you up."

"It's fine. I couldn't sleep anyway. For reasons similar to you, it seems."

Ivo took another bite and swallowed. "You get nightmares?"

Nariah nodded. "On occasion. My time as a Scout has been memorable to say the least."

It was hard to imagine the Scout being scared of anything. Nariah was intimidating, both in beauty and in strength. Though Ivo did not feel as foolish about her outburst, knowing that Nariah was equally unnerved. Ivo wasn't sure why, but something about the interaction between them seemed different, less emotionally charged.

"Have you traveled outside of the Eternal Kingdom like this often?"

The Scout swayed her head side to side. "It has been quite some time, but I used to spend years away from the Ethereal Realm. Some Scouts get homesick, but I never minded drifting through the cosmos."

Ivo wiped the corner of her mouth, finding herself drowsy again now that her stomach was full. "You didn't miss all the people fawning over you?"

Nariah smirked. "You heard about that, huh?"

"From Horacio, the first night on Carmine's planet."

"I have had my share of quick-burning romances, but nothing that ever really made me want to stay home."

"Why did you then?"

She shrugged. "Luck of the draw. On the Sacred Twelve task force, you don't get to choose where they put you. After a while, they thought my skills were best used to monitor persons of interest related to the case, rather than hunting in the dark for bits of information."

It was strange for Ivo to converse so openly with Nariah. Only in the dead of night did it seem the Scout could relax enough to be palatable. She wished it could be this easy with Nariah all the time. "How does it feel to be out again?"

"I feel like I've gotten the shit beaten out of me non-stop."

Ivo laughed. "That's an accurate estimation."

"I suppose it is," Nariah said with a smile.

When the conversation came to an end, Ivo expected to feel awkward and unsure of herself, given how normally combative the two were in each other's presence. However, it was a comfortable silence, as if the two managed to enjoy each other's company for once. *I wish it could be this easy with you all the time.* At some point, Ivo drifted off to sleep beside the Scout, this time dreaming of Nariah's smile and deeply beautiful purple gaze instead of horrific nightmares.

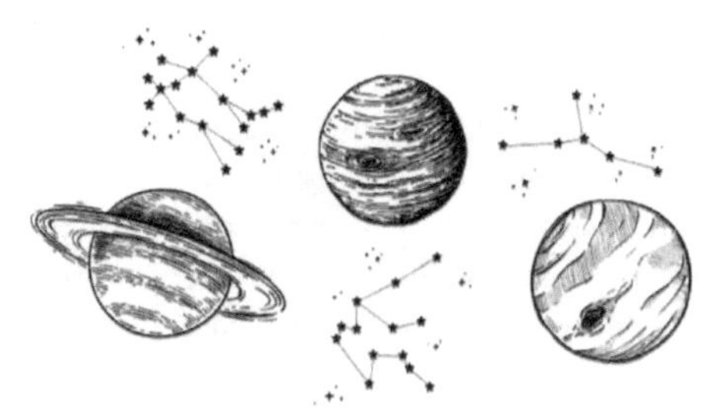

Chapter 32

Vincenzo

Wake up, his curse hissed. *You do not die here.*

Vincenzo's dark companion writhed within him, the sensation of it enough to wake him from his delirious haze. He winced in response to the painful edge his injury carried due to the lingering presence of his brother's dark magic, every beat of his heart causing a spray of pain to pulse throughout his flesh. Sostene had broken his wrist and somehow made it impossible for Enzo to heal himself. He cradled his arm as he sat up and looked around, finding himself in a sea of black shadows, with a pale green light coming from above.

You are not done yet, his dark companion shouted. *Another soul must be claimed!*

Something bolted from the shadows and smashed his body into the dirt. Enzo cried out in agony as the pain caused his vision to spot. Viscous energy sank its teeth into his mind, shredding his shields as he struggled to regain control. He bucked against the overwhelming blanket of magic. Aurelio and Carmine's abilities had been disorienting but manageable. This energy was inescapably tight around him. It clung to his skin and soaked into his bloodstream, bending reality around him.

"Enzo." Sima's voice floated in, echoing from above. "Enzo?"

His eyes snapped open as he reacted to her voice. Although he could not see Cosima, he yearned for her comforting touch to support him through the endless pulse of suffering coming from his injury. More of the sinister energy from before seized him, causing his surroundings to ripple and wave before his vision cleared completely. Vincenzo was in a giant jungle with unfamiliar plants all around him. The colors of the environment shifted in hue, alternating in a way that made his stomach turn.

My brothers are capable of mental torture, Enzo thought. Desperate, he fought against the magic trapping him, attempting to detach its sticky energy from himself with freezing fingers. His own power poured out of him, its trails of green light dissolving seconds after he discharged it, but it did nothing to relieve him of his shackles. The air grew thicker, and Enzo rebelled against the magic's iron grip on his throat. His legs kicked as his body floundered, but it did nothing to stop the onslaught of images. Some were more complex than others, but the scenes overlapped each other, creating a disorienting, overstimulating nightmare.

Disturbing creatures and violent crimes flashed by, but that was not what had ensnared Enzo's vision. He watched in horror as a tiny figure drew closer among the chaotic storm and emerged with a crushed skull and bloodied body. Her onyx black hair covered most of the gaping wound, but he could make out her unmistakable honey brown eyes.

Enzo bellowed, his scream so untethered, it felt like the sheer force of it alone began to boil his blood in his veins. He knew it wasn't real, but seeing Sima recreated in some way destroyed a piece of him. The image of it clung to the back of his eyelids, searing itself into his mind as his rage-filled screams continued without pause.

His brother seemed pleased by Enzo's torment, as soon all other figures faded except for Sima's wounded figure. She began to flicker with different forms, all somehow more gruesome than the last, her body contorted and broken, but still painfully recognizable. The ground materialized beneath him, and Enzo toppled to his knees, tears streaming from his eyes.

When will you have had enough of being beaten and berated? Burn their binds and emerge, his curse rumbled.

"Make it stop," he muttered, his chest too heavy for him to breathe properly beneath it. "I c-can't."

"You didn't save me, Enzo," all of the Simas whispered. "You left me all alone again. I thought you wouldn't leave me, Enzo."

"No, no, I tried," he said, inching forward on his knees. He thought his heart might give out. "This isn't real."

"How can you look at me and tell me it isn't real?"

His entire body trembled as he forced himself to look at her. He bit back a sob. "I wouldn't have let this happen to you. I wouldn't..."

"Why do you keep running away when I need you?"

Enzo opened his mouth, but no words came out. His heart was shredded, and the longer this went on, the more hopeless he began to feel. The electricity in the air kept him awake, despite how his mind wished to give out, to end the painful hallucinations.

"You lied to me about your power," she said.

He blinked. "What?"

"You could have used it to save me, Enzo, but you didn't. You let them hurt me. Why did you do that? You told me I was safe with you," she said, her words increasing in fervor and panic the more she spoke. "But you abandoned me."

"No, my love, I am here, I came for you." Enzo shook his head, reminding himself this was not real. Regardless of which brother toyed with him, he had to retain what little control he had over himself, or more of his personal thoughts would begin to seep out to be used against him. He angled his head toward the empty blackness above him. "How long are you going to torture me?"

A voice wafted back, brushing against him like a soft wind. "Until I've had enough."

How much more will you take? His curse thumped like his heart in his ears.

Enzo's breath was shaky as he attempted to calm down. He would never break out of the mental prison if he could not gather enough strength to shove his brother out. "You're not Sostene. Who are you?"

A laugh crashed over him, the sound of it bouncing off his body. "You are the one who bothered *me*."

"Where is she?" Enzo curled his trembling fists.

"I'm right here," Sima said softly.

Enzo refused to look at her, and his voice cracked when he spoke. "No. You're not her."

"Don't be so sure." His brother's voice carried a hint of amusement. "Sostene is perhaps entwined with the ravenous pursuit of ultimate power, but that is not what sings to me. I merely want to create with caution thrown to the wind. I feel the soil cower inside my palms as I thrust my hands into the ground and pull free the roots of all who claimed it before me."

Son of two moons, gentle as you are fierce, his curse sang, its voice soaring above his brother's. *It is time to stop hiding from your destiny. Let destruction bring you peace.*

Enzo wavered, his discipline cracking. He could feel the instability spreading through him like wildfire, leaving him liable to crumble should he make the wrong move. All the hard work to master what he could of his power, all the restraint it took to get this far—would be for nothing.

No, Enzo thought. *I can hold out longer. I can keep from breaking.*

The vision of Sima collapsed with a heavy thud. Despite knowing it was a hallucination, Enzo found himself reaching for her on instinct. She disintegrated in his hands as his heart pounded, leaving him dazed. Seconds later, she reappeared, this time unharmed, but wrapped around the arm of Sostene.

Sima wore a sparkling black gown with her hair pinned back in silky waves. Enzo blinked, finding himself more entranced by her beauty than angered by the fake Sostene's arrogant glare. The tumultuous waves of his mental prison had begun to wear on his resolve, and Enzo was fading quickly. In a distant corner of his mind, he registered the last of his shields beginning to buckle.

"You knew I would reject your poisoned blood," the image of Sima hissed. "Why else would you keep your horrid curse a secret? You gave me no chance to choose for myself."

Enzo balked, unsure of what to say—the line between reality and his hallucinations growing fuzzier by the moment. "I have it under control. I only wanted to protect you."

"You keep saying that, but I don't believe you. I've seen the way you're already giving into its toxic pull. I know you saw the fear in my eyes the night you fought Carmine for the first time."

He shook his head, his skin flush. "You don't have to be scared of me, I would never hurt you. I've been trying to keep it from eating me alive to prove to you I am capable of being who you need me to be."

"How am I supposed to keep loving you when I know what you're hiding? You were never the one for me."

Enzo shivered. "I am, I am the one for you, I promise. Believe me, Sima, believe me. I am strong enough. I can keep this curse at bay. Nothing bad will happen to you. I will protect you."

"Your curse is blurring the lines of reality. How can you trust yourself around me when we both know what you are? You're crooked and broken, just like Aurelio was. You're just like him."

"No," he groaned, his insides consumed in aching rivers of flame. "I am nothing like him. I love you, I would never hurt you."

"What about when you curse decides I am the enemy? What about when your curse demands you break my neck?"

She speaks of me like I am a parasite and not the valley of your unquenchable soul, his curse hissed. *Do not let your brother use her to play on your deepest insecurities.*

He did his best to keep upright. "You don't understand. I didn't ask for this, I am containing it how I can."

"No, you're not," she snapped. "You and I both know it has begun taking over, and you've relaxed your restraint. It's only a matter of time before I lose you entirely to it."

This power is your own, his curse whispered, *you do not have to be afraid of wielding what others cannot.*

"Look me in the eyes," Sima said, her voice softer, "and tell me you can go back to the way things were before that piece of you snapped during your fight with Carmine."

Enzo averted his gaze. He couldn't answer her because he hated the truth. Was the only person he was really lying to himself? He had spent so much time keeping his curse at bay, but each time he dipped into that impossibly deep well, the more untethered he became.

Sima disappeared, and a moment later, a different version of her appeared. This time, a recreated Enzo was beside her as she cowered on the floor, eyes wide with unrelenting panic. The real Enzo screamed as he watched a vision of himself killing Sima with his powers, magic flooding her body until it poured from her eyes and mouth.

No, Enzo's tattered mind thought as he continued to wail. *No, I wouldn't...I could never...*

More of him broke and crumbled inside, leaving him in a desolate, hollow state. He crumpled into a puddle of his own tears, too terrified to keep fighting against the mental prison, despite how his curse thumped with energy. It was a strange, otherworldly sensation for him to endure— feeling both too powerful and too weak to do anything.

Release me, his curse mused, *and I will do it all.*

Cosima

Sleep had come quickly for Cosima, despite Vincenzo being the last thing on her mind before she drifted off. Her dreams were of the usual sort at first, until she found herself exiting through a door. Her dream-self stepped through it and walked straight into a sparkling sea of stars. She glanced down, and her bloody, dirty clothing slowly evaporated as a skin-tight violet dress replaced it. Pale gold constellations painted the bodice of the gown as elegant, web-like fabric spread across her shoulders and down her back, forming into a trailing cape.

"*Esti,*" a familiar voice said.

Sima's lip curled in disgust. "Sostene."

He manifested in the distance, circles of light forming beneath his feet as he walked toward her. He wore a matching violet suit, which only magnified the purple burn of his gaze. She glanced down and froze, finding an endless shimmering expanse of space below her. She flicked her eyes back to Sostene, who watched her with a disturbingly pleased smile.

"What do you want from me?"

He strolled toward her, the two of them suspended above an invisible, glass-like surface. "I only wanted to see you again and ensure you were well. I regret how we ended things."

Sostene spoke with an immeasurably relaxed tone, as though they conversed with only the cosmos as a witness. Something about it heightened her defenses, and Sima's pulse quickened.

"You discarded us on a foreign planet with giants that tried to eat us. Are you truly delusional enough to believe I'm interested in speaking with you right now?"

His gaze softened. "It was rather rash of me, I will admit that. You must understand, I am a man commanded by his heart. Your denial of my affection left me in ruins. Nevertheless," he said, stepping forward with his hand outstretched, "I am a forgiving lover. There is still time for me to take you away from all of this. I will adorn you in moons and wrap you in the tapestry of time. Your beauty is supernal, and I must have you for myself. Come with me, Cosima, and let your perpetual paradise unfold."

"I am not something for you to own." She balled her fists. "I am sick of being spoken about as though I am merely a well-groomed reflection of your permeating control. You cannot wait to force me into a role I will never be able to escape from, a position you've slyly drenched in hollow romance. I am not so desperate to be loved that I would give up my freedom."

Sostene's head tilted to the side, his black hair pooling on his shoulder. "I have no desire to dominate your wild soul, *Esti*. So long as your heart beats for me alone, you can command alongside me as my pure equal. Make me your home, and the celestial rivers are yours to explore."

"Your persistence is not earning you my favor."

"Perhaps not in the present," he said with a smirk, "but you will come to see things from my perspective, I am sure of it." He blew her a kiss, and a puff of purple smoke in the shape of a butterfly floated toward her, the scent of wisteria filling her nose as it broke across her face. "I'll try to contain my heart in your absence, sweet Sima."

Sostene and the dream vanished. Cosima gasped as she woke up, her hair matted to her forehead with sweat. She placed a hand over her pounding heart as she looked around the makeshift shelter. Ivo was slumped against Nariah, the two fast asleep in a seemingly uncomfortable position. The pink of the sky was visible through an opening in the midnight black leaves.

Merit was outside, sharpening his blades as more vegetables roasted over a fire lit by starlight.

She made her way out of the shelter and stretched her back. "Morning, Merit."

"Hey, you're right on time. It's almost done." He jerked his head toward the shelter as he raised a brow. "Those two, huh?"

Sima smiled as she swatted a bug from her face. "You mean the lovebirds? What about them?"

The Scout shrugged as he wiped his blade clean. "Nariah is…different."

"How so?" A reflective sapphire blue beetle buzzed near Sima's face, and she swatted it away. As the sun rose, the jungle sprang back to life, meaning the overlapping songs of insects became their ceaseless background noise. "She doesn't seem different to me."

"Well," Merit said with a chuckle, "that's because Nariah changed a lot after meeting you, too. But with your short friend, she seems almost happy—when we're not almost dying, of course."

"I think they could be good for one another." Sima folded her legs under her as she sat down. "You've changed, too."

He raised a navy brow as he used his blade to push the chopped vegetables onto a leaf, before handing it to her. "Oh, don't start saying I got soft or something, because it's not true." He squashed a rather large insect that landed on his shoulder and grimaced. "I'm the same asshole I was before I ever met your troublesome trio."

Sima blew on the food to cool it. "Don't lie to me. You used to hate Enzo."

Merit frowned. "I still hate Enzo."

She chewed and swallowed a bite of food. "No, you don't. The fire isn't in your eyes, Merit. Deny it all you want, but you've lost the burning hatred, and there's nothing you can do about it now."

His lip twitched with a fraction of a smile. "I'd pluck his feathers and batter him up so he's crispy when I serve him to the Kingdom before I'd call him my friend, but yeah, he's not quite what I expected him to be. Every freak Sacred Brother I've met was undeniably heinous, and while Vincenzo has that capacity in him…" Merit stared off into the distance.

"What?" Sima asked, her heart heavy.

Merit shook his head as he let out an exasperated sigh. "He also has more restraint than anyone else I've ever met. Back in the Kingdom, he seemed impatient and pushy, always ready to pitch a fit. That was until I saw him with you. His desire to protect you seemed a bit excessive, I guess, but at that point, some things started clicking in my head about his behavior." Merit's expression harshened. "Then I saw your memories of Aurelio…

and I understood. I finally knew why he was on the edge of insanity all that time—and why he still is."

Sima wrapped her arms around herself. "Nariah doesn't trust him at all."

The Scout shrugged. "She doesn't have to; that's her deal. But all three of you are forces to be reckoned with, and she'll figure out sooner or later. I'm not bird-boy's biggest fan, but I don't know…with how his power is increasing, he might survive this."

"About that…" The thought of Vincenzo's power increasing filled her with wavering feelings. "Can I be honest with you about something?"

Merit wrinkled his nose. "Of course, but I won't spare your feelings if it is something dumb."

"Deal." She let out a breath. "At first, I was scared of Enzo's abilities. The way it was manifesting seemed almost malicious, as though it was hurting him as it intensified."

He bobbed his head. "Alright, so what is different now?"

"When he was fighting Carmine, our magic intertwined. I have never experienced anything quite like it, but the sensation of the energy itself felt undeniably like Enzo. There was nothing dark or sinister about his magic, and the combination of our powers has only left me feeling conflicted because I now feel more deeply connected to him."

Three insects with long legs and wide wings buzzed near Merit's head, and he incinerated them with a small blast of his starlight. "That doesn't sound like a bad thing. If you sensed his power and it wasn't wicked, then why worry?"

Sima chewed her lip. "Because at the same moment he killed Carmine, I felt the true weight of his power. It was vast, grander than I could have ever imagined, even if I only got a glimpse of it. The way it consumed him has been haunting me."

Merit blew out a puff of air and chewed his cheek. "If there is any chance of him surviving this, Sima, it depends on that same power you fear. I may not fully understand the guy, but I trust him eons more than I trust any of the other Sacred Brothers."

"I can't bear the thought of him not making it out of this alive." Leaves rustled behind her, and Sima glanced over her shoulder. Nariah emerged from the make-shift shelter with a frown on her face as she rubbed her eyes. "Good morning. Is Ivo up?"

The white-haired Scout yawned and stretched. "Not yet."

Merit glanced up at her and scoffed. "About time you got your ass moving. Eat up, I want to make some meaningful progress today. I'm restless out here."

"So eager to be a chew toy for the giants." Nariah smirked as she walked over and grabbed the food from his hands. She looked down at Sima and inspected her portion. "You've hardly touched yours. I'm not going to be the only one forced to eat."

Cosima picked up a brownish purple cube from the leaf on her lap and shoved it into her mouth. The flavor wasn't bad—the texture and taste resembled sweet potatoes back on Haelos—she had simply lost her appetite when speaking about Enzo's uncertain future. *I need to keep my strength up,* Cosima thought as she took another bite. *There is no telling when we will get a chance to rest like this again.*

Merit rested his arm on his knee. "Sostene's little trick dropped us on Dario's planet prematurely, which means we don't have a whole lot of wisdom from other Scouts to rely on. That being said, I've been trying to learn what I can about our environment since we arrived. Throughout the night, there was minimal wildlife movement. The glow from the trees and plants never stops, but the insects fly up and rest in the dome of leaves at the top and extinguish their light. Sometimes the jungle rumbles a bit, and when it does, those insects retreat just like that. Anytime the bugs disappear, trouble is nearby."

Sima scrunched her nose as she looked around. "But Merit, there aren't any bugs right now, come to think of it."

The Scouts exchanged a glance before both shot to their feet. In the distance, a shriek, too immortal-like to ignore, rang out. The cry was loud and filled with aggravation, as though it came from a supremely enraged giant. Her heart pounded in response, and Sima turned toward the shelter to retrieve Ivo. She took a step forward and paused when she noticed a dark shadow looming over her. Her breath left her lungs as she looked up and found a giant with blood red eyes and black teeth smiling as its hand wrapped around her body.

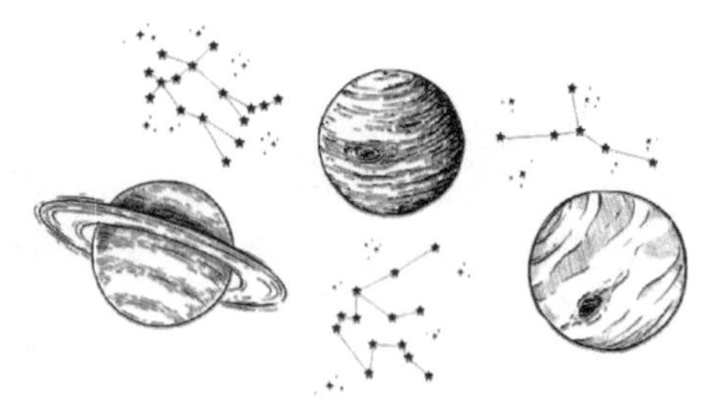

Chapter 33

Panic-filled screams ripped Ivo from sleep's gentle embrace. She jumped to her feet and ripped the wall made of leaves clean off the side of the shelter. The Scouts were zipping through the air, attempting to kill a giant with a strange purple and orange hue to its skin. It had long feet with claw-like toes and sturdy legs packed densely with muscle.

Ivo held her hand up, ready to send a bolt of electricity via a spell, before the giant turned slightly, revealing that it had Cosima within its grasp. She found it hard to breathe as her heart threatened to burst free from her ribs. "Sima," Ivo shouted. "I'm coming!"

Afraid of accidentally injuring her friend, Ivo had to be smart about the attacks she used. The giant and the Scouts were aware of this fact as the being waved around Cosima like its own personal shield. Ivo's thoughts raced as she ran through her spells, searching for something that would not hurt Cosima, either directly or indirectly. If the creature fell the wrong way, it could easily crush her friend to death.

"*Ragnatela,*" Ivo cried with her hands outstretched in the giant's direction.

Spider silk cobwebs spread across the being, entangling it in sticky binds. The giant howled with anger as it attempted to rip itself free, only to stumble forward and lose its balance. Having already anticipated the creature would lose its footing, Ivo was prepared and shouted out the same spell, this time crafting a horizontal surface for Cosima to land on. The web caught Cosima as the creature landed in the red mud.

Nariah moved swiftly, swooping in to lay the killing blow before the giant had a chance to recover from its tumble. Black blood created an inky pool beneath where Cosima was suspended in the web. Merit retrieved her, and Ivo caught her breath as Nariah approached.

"Are you alright?" The Scout scanned her from head to toe.

The concern in her eyes startled Ivo. "I'm fine," she said, rubbing a hand over her arm. "What happened?"

"We got ambushed. I'm sorry you didn't get a chance to eat something before that thing came and ripped our little campsite up." Nariah sighed. "I'm happy you're alright, though."

Their gazes lingered on one another for a moment before Merit arrived with Sima in his arms. He placed her down, and Ivo rushed to her side. She was wheezing harshly, and her eyes were bloodshot. Sima held onto Merit to steady herself, and Ivo knew that she needed healing at once. She tugged Sima's shirt up on her right side and bit her tongue to keep from verbally reacting to the heavy purple and blue bruising around her friend's ribs.

"Help lay her down," Ivo instructed the Scouts. "That creature broke her ribs. If I don't heal her right now, those bones are going to mend improperly."

Merit eased Sima to the ground while Nariah took off her cape. The Scout rolled it up into a ball and placed it beneath Sima's head. Ivo got on her knees on her friend's right side and hovered her hands over her abdomen. Knowing another giant could bound from the trees at any moment made Ivo move with measured speed, intending to help her friend as quickly and thoroughly as possible.

"Deep breath in," Ivo said as her magic accumulated in her palms.

Healing did not require spells for witches, especially when as skilled as Ivo. The waves of her ice blue magic swept through her friend's flesh like a seasoned visitor. She shook off the reminders of being forced to keep her friend alive in captivity inside the palace, focusing instead on the strong pulse of Sima's blood. She closed her eyes and allowed the sensation of her friend's inner symphony to be her guiding force.

She waded through the anguish of Sima's pain and found the source within seconds. As she suspected, her friend had broken five ribs, their individual cracks and chips painted clearly in her mind. Ivo let her magic thread through the injuries, undoing the damage with ease. After the first rib returned to normal, Sima let out a shuddered breath. When all five were whole and smooth again, the crease between Sima's brows disappeared, and her chest rose without her flinching.

"Thank you," she croaked.

Ivo helped her sit up. "Do you have any more pain?"

"The ache is subsiding by the second."

Nariah crouched down beside Sima. "When you're ready, we're going to fly through the jungle instead of walking. We don't have any real clue where we're headed, but the more we explore, the more likely we are to find something. I don't want us to split up entirely, but we are going to be at a distance, increasing our chances of finding something important."

Sima nodded. "I'm up for it, I promise. Ivo's healing even got rid of the ache from sleeping on leaves all night."

Ivo smiled as she stood up. "If you need more, just let me know. Some of the discomfort might come back."

The ground trembled beneath their feet, and the group froze. More gigantic footsteps headed their way, and Ivo's stomach twisted. Nariah scooped her up as Merit did the same to Sima, and the Scouts launched into the air, heading the opposite direction from the incoming creatures. Despite how the jungle flew by in a haze, the sound of the footsteps never grew faint behind them. Ivo peeked over Nariah's shoulder and swallowed tightly.

A group of the immortal-like giants kept pace behind them, demolishing anything that got in their way. Trees fell around them, and the Scout increased her grip around Ivo as she maneuvered around the chaos. To the left them, another being emerged, noticeably stronger than the others. Its muscles flexed as it bounded toward them, and Nariah narrowly escaped its grasp.

Seeing an opportunity, Ivo shouted her electric spell and managed to paralyze the muscular being for several seconds. She turned her attention to one that ran with terrifying speed, despite its awkward gait. Its feet slapped the ground, sending mud flying in all directions as it closed in on them. Ivo held her hand and shouted another spell, this time sending a ball of flame with her magic. The sphere burned a hole right through the creature's chest, and it howled before it collapsed.

The muscular giant reappeared, this time holding a tall, midnight black tree trunk in its hand. It stabbed at them through the trees, but Nariah evaded its attacks. Ivo prepared to use more of her magic when something slammed into them and sent her flying from the Scout's arms. She used her arms to shield her face as she skipped across the ground and landed in a patch of dark gray shrubs. The itchy leaves poked at her skin as she pulled herself out of the plant.

She spotted something with bright red fur and yellow stripes from the top of its head, down to its long, slender tail. The feline bounced from tree to tree, using its claws to dig into the bark as it landed. The sound of the battle ensuing between her friends and the momentous creatures caught her ear, but just as she was ready to run away from the red feline, it turned to face her.

The feline's features were intensely cat-like, but the longer she stared, the more it began to resemble a person. Instead of a lengthy snout, they had a short, flat nose and razor-sharp teeth in their surprisingly immortal-like mouth. Ivo gasped, wondering if she had witnessed the being shape-shift when a giant broke through the trees and swiped its arms toward the feline.

"Look out," she cried. The feline bounded toward her as the creature with disturbingly long fingers pursued. Ivo's palm shot forward as she shouted, "*Neve e fiamme!*"

Snow tunneled out of her palm and covered the creature before a massive wave of smoldering flames lit the beast on fire. As its flesh burned away, a strange gray skeleton with shimmering bones was left behind. Ivo looked around for the feline, but they were gone. Nariah burst through the trees and slammed into her, wrapping her arms around Ivo as her wings kept them from falling.

"Fuck, I thought one of those creatures got you." Nariah pulled back and studied her face. "Did you know you're bleeding?"

Ivo reached up and touched her forehead. Her fingers were covered in red blood, but there was a distinct lack of pain. "I don't even feel it." The jungle continued to shake as more giants closed in on their location. She pointed in the direction the feline had fled. "We need to head this way. Let's tell the others."

Without asking why, Nariah nodded and picked her up. Ivo expected the Scout to doubt her decision, but whether from trust or because she had no better alternative, Nariah flew in the direction Ivo suggested. Through the trees, she caught a glimpse of Merit and Sima. A smaller being around eight feet tall trailed them as the two made their way toward them. Nariah jumped into action, strands of her white hair fluttering as she unsheathed her sword and buried it in the creature's chest. Its erratic cries ceased seconds later when she stabbed it again.

Nariah put her foot on its cheek and pointed. "Ivo says we're heading that way."

Merit dipped his head. "Don't need to tell me twice."

The buzz of insects returned to the jungle at last, and Ivo's shoulders sagged with relief. Once in Nariah's arms again, the jungle flew by. She wasn't sure exactly what they would find, but she wondered if they would come across the same feline from before, or more like them. The way they had stared at her had seemed so person-like, but there was no telling if the being would be able to communicate.

Her stomach growled, and Ivo wrapped her arms around her stomach. Nariah glanced down at her. "What is it? You're hungry?"

"Yes," Ivo replied sheepishly, curling her icy fingertips into her palm. "I'll be fine. I don't think it's safe enough to find something to eat here."

Nariah pulled her closer as they swept through the trees at top speed. "We will find something soon. The second we find somewhere secure enough to rest, feeding you will be at the top of my priority list."

"What if this world is too big for us to be able to find Dario? Carmine happened to be where the last of civilization had holed up, but there is nothing for us to orient ourselves with here."

The Scout's lip twitched. "He will be destroyed, just like the rest of them. Don't worry about that. If we had arrived here properly, the Kingdom would have prepped us with at least basic information regarding this world. Plus, we would have been able to restock on the supplies that we lost on Carmine's planet."

Ivo frowned as her heart sank, remembering Scouts who had died. "Have you sent any communication back to the Divinity yet? Do they know that Horacio and Earnest were killed?"

Nariah sighed. "No, I haven't told them anything."

"Why not?"

The Scout furrowed her brows. "Because I am afraid if they find out what happened, they'll somehow blame Sima for it. If we manage to kill Dario, at the very least, I can beg them to go easy on her. With two of three brothers dead, there's a higher chance of leniency. Plus, who knows, maybe we will slit Sostene's throat by the end, too."

The thought of the Kingdom blaming Sima for their deaths sent a chill through her. Before she could open her mouth to express her discomfort, her eyes caught a flash of red.

"Stop!"

Nariah leaned backward as she slowed down. The red fur and yellow stripes from before moved through the trees, the feline still bouncing from one to another, but this time with a noticeable injury to its back foot. The Scout squinted.

"What is that?"

"A person, I think," Ivo said. "I saw them earlier. A giant was trying to kill them, too. We should follow them."

"Good idea," Nariah said, flying toward the being. "Perhaps they will lead us toward others. Maybe one of them knows something about where Dario might be."

Ivo looked to her side and confirmed Nariah and Merit were following at a distance. When her attention fell back on the feline, she noticed the jungle had gone silent. The way Nariah's breath hitched revealed she had come to the same realization. Ivo prepared herself to respond with her magic as two giants with contorted limbs sprang from the trees and pounced on the feline, dragging them from the trees. Nariah picked up the pace, and once close enough, Ivo used her electric spell, stunning the giants.

Merit and Sima emerged from the trees, the Scout's blade in her friend's hand. As Merit swept downward, Sima swung, slicing off one of the giant's arms at its crooked joint. Ivo watched as time moved at a crawling pace inside Sima's time pocket, the giants snapping their jaws in slow motion as Merit tossed her friend through the air. Cosima slammed her blade through one side of the giant's head to the other. The tip of the sword lodged into a tree, the creature's long purple-black tongue hanging from its open mouth.

Time returned to normal, and with one giant left, Ivo sprang into action. The feline person hissed and held up a measly dagger as the giant unhinged its jaw.

"*Lama energetica,*" Ivo yelled, the magic from her fingers so cold it burned.

A thin beam of blue energy sliced through the enormous creature, and its face slid off its body as black blood sprayed. She held out a hand toward the cat-like person as they narrowed their eyes at her.

"You're hurt. Do you need help?"

Their claws retracted into their hand before they accepted Ivo's help. Once standing, they took a step back with their hands up. "Please, no trouble."

"We're not the ones you should be scared of," Nariah said.

"Are you not Gods?" they asked, lowering their arms.

"No way." Ivo crossed her arms. "What makes you think that?"

They shook their fur and squared their shoulders. "The only being I have met that speaks like me, but looks like you, was a God." They looked away. "Well, I didn't meet him directly, but I was there when he came to our city."

Merit stepped forward. "Do you know where he is now?"

Their cat-like pupils dilated. "No. He comes only when the moon is at its fullest, and he resides inside the temple until the sun rises. Only the Seven may enter."

Sima raised a brow. "The Seven?"

"Yes," the feline replied. "There are seven chosen members who enter the temple with him. The rest of us take up temporary residence in the Aluyaa courtyard. The Aluyaa trees shed petals of light as everyone rests on their knees and prays. One of the Seven proclaimed that their God was in search of a magnificent stone somewhere outside the walls of our city. I was volunteered, along with a few others, to search for it."

"Your city has walls?" Ivo asked. "Is it safe from those giants?"

They nodded. "Yes, it has kept them at bay for nearly a decade. Are you seeking shelter?"

"Desperately," Merit said, rubbing his back.

"Return with me," the feline said, stepping toward Ivo. "You saved my life, and I am sure the town council will agree to let you in."

Ivo grinned. "What a relief. Show us the way, new friend."

"I'm not finished with you yet, little twelve."

Enzo stirred at the sound of his brother's voice. He peeled his eyes open and found himself lying face down in red mud. He pulled himself to stand, cradling his injured wrist, and though he wobbled, he did not collapse once more. The violet and black jungle with its green and blue luminescent glow made his head spin. The shades of black and purple blurred together, making it hard for him to make sense of what he was seeing.

Allow yourself to rise, his curse purred, *let the confines of your soul shed with their blood.*

Somewhere in his core, his magic pulsed, the sensation unpleasant as the sound of it grew loud in his ears. His body vibrated with the intensifying hum of his curse, his muscles imbued with jittery energy, like a serum of vitality slithered inside his veins. With the aid of his dark companion, Enzo's eyes focused, allowing him to make out giant burgundy mushroom caps with strange waves of orange and red hues through their stems wrapped around the base of trees, like wide, natural platforms. His head followed a swish of movement, and he found himself staring at a creature with dark brown fur hanging from its black tail on a sturdy vine. With the body of a monkey, the face of an opossum, and the disposition of a rapid raccoon, the snarling animal set him on edge. Enzo slowly backed away as more of them emerged, spread across the fleshy mushrooms.

As he moved deeper into the jungle, strange creatures of all types made appearances. If he weren't in constant, delirious pain from his wound, he would have spent more time marveling at the unique wildlife. Enzo recognized the sound of a strong water current and stumbled toward it. The river was brilliant with its bright blue glow, and Enzo toppled against the shore. He dunked his head in, the bite of the cold water enough to sober him.

Something moved in front of him, and Enzo's head snapped up, sending droplets cascading over his back. He shivered as his eyes locked onto Sima's as she stood on the opposite side of the water. His heart squeezed, and without a word, he threw himself into the river, thrashing against the current as he fought to be by her side. With soaked clothes and a trembling body, he threw himself at her feet. He wanted to speak, but he thought he would sob before words could form if he opened his mouth.

"You have to flee, by wing or foot, but you must go," Sima said. "Dario wants a show."

The ground shook as the violet trees were pushed out of the way by enormous hands. Beings of impossible size emerged from the darkness with sparkling white teeth and open jaws. They towered behind Sima, and Enzo threw his head all the way back to view them fully. He reached for her, desperate to protect her, only for his hands to swipe right through her body.

He's still in my mind, Enzo thought as his stomach turned. *What is real and what is not?*

Enzo rose to his feet as his wings twitched. Inside, his core ached with an insatiable starvation, the sensation of being devoured from the inside out, inescapable as rage gnawed at his flesh. He held his shattered wrist over his abdomen as he fought off the desire to vomit and drew his sword with his non-dominant hand. He could not bear to use more of his unholy power for the way it scratched his sanity until it was raw and inflamed, which could only be a sign of more consequences to come. His curse was consuming him, and Enzo would not risk losing any more of himself to it. He squared his shoulders and sucked in a breath.

His heart drummed as he stared into her honey-brown eyes. He did not look away until she vanished entirely and the giants encroached upon him. Enzo shot into the air, evading every grasp they made his direction with expertly timed bursts of movement. The internal beat of his sustained life drove his dance, creating a precise pulse to his attacks. He maneuvered around the taller of the two giants with shaggy red hair and long arms, waiting for the perfect opening to strike.

Once behind the red-haired giant, he hovered above the ground and shot forward, using his blade to cut through the back of the being's feet. Without the strength of his dominant hand, the wound was jagged but effective enough to send the giant tumbling. He forced himself to strike again, stabbing his blade through the being's back. It bellowed as the other one stormed toward him, its arms more agile than the first. Enzo fell backward into the mud, narrowly avoiding the creature's hand. His blade was still lodged in the flesh of the red-haired one.

Before he could reach for it, both giants lunged for him. His wings pulled him into the sky as their jaws snapped. The one he had stabbed crawled forward at a moderate pace, and Enzo rushed toward it, flying by fast enough to free his sword from its flesh. A spray of black blood rained across the mushroom pad behind him as Enzo dodged and collided with a tree. As his body angled toward the ground, he caught a flash of fingers moving toward him.

He twirled his body as he fell, slicing through its hand with speed. He landed on his feet and winced as his arm banged against his chest. Enzo kept up the momentum and slashed again as his wings carried him toward the red-haired giant's face. He stabbed his sword through its eye, and at last, the creature stopped moving.

The remaining giant ran toward him, and Enzo rolled out of the way. The being slid to a stop and faced him, tipping its chin down as it spoke. "You had better find her before Dario does. The clock is ticking. What will you do to get out of the way of its perpetual grind?"

It launched toward him, the force of its step creating an audible echo through the jungle. Enzo lunged forward, aiming for the giant's throat. He lodged his blade just above the bones of the creature's chest, and it gurgled as it crumpled into the mud. Thunder rumbled and rain pattered against his skin, cooling him as he fought to catch his breath.

"Did you think you were done?" a voice hissed from the shadows. "I've only barely gotten a taste of your tormented blood, brother."

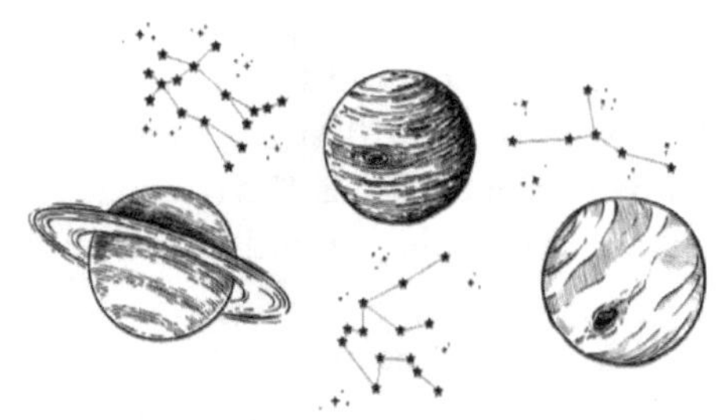

Chapter 34

Cosima

As Ivo chatted with the group's newest friend, Saya, Sima remained vigilant should more giants manifest. Although the large flying insects were annoying and persistent, their presence meant there were none lurking nearby. The jungle changed slightly the farther they walked. Some of the plants were no longer completely black, but a deep violet instead. More moody reds, browns, and purples blossomed, relieving the lingering darkness she had felt in the other parts of the jungle. She sighed as she thought of Enzo, her heart squeezing as she sent another silent prayer that he was alright wherever he was on Dario's planet.

Stay out of trouble, Enzo. Keep your promise and come find me. I can't bear being away from you, Sima thought.

Nariah walked beside Sima with a deep frown. Sima noticed the Scout was staring at the back of Ivo's head. Her black-haired friend was completely oblivious to Nariah's attention and carried on her conversation with their feline guide.

Sima smiled, thankful for a distraction. "How do you feel about her?"

The Scout blinked and shook her head. "Who?"

Sima leaned her head to the side. "Ivo."

"I feel she is an incredible burden, that she is hot-headed, that she is rash, and too independent for her own good. I think she always wants to have the last word, and her heart is braver than her mind is, which infuriates me. I think she cares for you too much and she is willing to march into battle by your side, for better or for worse." She stamped her foot down on a bug and smeared it into the mud. "I think she has an attitude and is manipulative to get what she wants, and I spend too much time trying to keep her from getting killed."

"Sounds like you think about her a lot, don't you?"

Nariah leaned closer to Sima's face and glared at her. "Are you trying to be funny?"

"No, of course not," she said, adding a small laugh. "I think you are in denial."

"What could I possibly be in denial about?"

"You have feelings for each other."

"I do no—wait, did you say 'for each other'? Does…does Ivo have feelings for me?" Nariah's gaze in Ivo's direction turned a shade more nervous than before. "Did she tell you that?"

Sima considered whether exposing Ivo's feelings was the right direction to head and decided to push Nariah in the right direction. "You should ask her yourself. If you two would spend less time trying to bite each other's heads off, you might find you get along quite well."

Nariah shook her head. "I am not looking for friends. Besides, I've tried, but every single time I try to get close to her, she shuts down and backs away. The way she feels about me is irrelevant, now we—"

"Is it really?" Sima rocked back and forth on her heels. "You don't care at all how she feels about you?"

"I am sure she is not fond of me, and that's perfectly acceptable. Maybe I'm not used to engaging with someone constantly sending mixed signals, but it's fine. I know better than to keep putting myself out there, just to be rejected over and over."

Sima smiled. "Why are you so scared of her turning you down? Ivo doesn't bite."

"I assure you, she probably does," Nariah said, but she smiled, too. "I'm not scared, I just…I'm sure she has the same hesitancy as me. Our relationship would be…complex."

"Is it because she's mortal?"

Sima witnessed something unexpected—genuine sadness in Nariah's eyes. "Yes, but also because I am a Trine Scout. Scouts are not forbidden from forming relationships, but there is often no time to attend to personal affairs when you are working for the Kingdom, especially not if you are talented like my colleagues and I, as the Divinity will call on us frequently. With how long I could be gone on a mission, there is no telling how much of her mortal life would pass without me there to spend it with her. I can't lead her on, but I also…" Nariah sighed, "can't stay away."

"My advice? Tell her how you feel before it's too late. You might not have a chance once we return to the Eternal Kingdom. I can't speak for Ivo, but I can imagine she is waiting for you to be, well, vulnerable."

Nariah wrinkled her nose. "I can be vulnerable."

Sima placed a hand on her shoulder. "Sure, friend. Don't convince me, convince her."

The Scout nodded with an absent expression on her face as the group slowed to a stop. In front of them was a large break in the trees, revealing a well-established city, capable of holding what appeared to be tens of thousands of people. The walls were made of towering white stone marbled with sparkling silver flecks. Along the sides were branch-like perches with armed feline warriors stationed around the massive steel gate.

Saya pointed at the gate with a wide, toothy smile. "This is Dileyna, my home. When they learn of how you saved my life, they are going to be overwhelmed with gratitude."

Sima stuck close to Ivo as they approached the gate. Saya yelled out and waved to someone at the top of the gate. Seconds later, the huge, shiny steel gate parted, allowing them to enter into the city. A breath hitched in her throat as she took in the thriving crowd of people only feet from the walls. Children with round cheeks and short tails skipped through the courtyard, weaving around those shopping at the stocked market. Ivo and Sima's eyes were glued to a stand full of fresh bread, operated by a feline with a gray face and long whiskers.

Nariah tapped Saya on the shoulder. "I am sorry to impose so soon after you have guided us to your home, but is there a chance we could get something to eat?"

Ivo's face twisted. "Please, Saya, I'm starving."

Saya nodded her head and ushered them away from the market. "I have something better than bread. Come with me to my Luuyet—my family's estate. All generations of my family live there, and my father will be able to send word to the Crown of Dileyna about my return."

"How long were you gone?" Sima asked as the group walked between two buildings with dreamy aquamarine paint and white trim. "With how beautiful the city is, I am surprised anyone would want to leave."

"It has been several weeks. I was already heading back here when I was ambushed," Saya replied. They reached the end of the street, which opened into another busy area full of tables and chairs as people dined. "Those giants are dangerous enough that almost no one leaves. We have had a few peaceful decades behind these walls."

"Why did they force you to go then?" Merit asked, folding his arms over his chest.

"Desperate times call for desperate measures. I am one of the fastest in Dileyna, even if I am not the toughest. You don't really need to know how to fight if you can evade the encounter altogether. I normally wouldn't have let the creatures get so close, but your group caught me off guard."

They walked down a pathway beneath a bridge and arrived at an impressive estate on the other side. The exterior was painted a dark blue with pale orange trim and an overflowing garden of unique flowers. Each petal had swirls and otherworldly shimmer. Saya jumped onto a platform above the door and pulled open a window. She climbed in and vanished, reappearing a moment later when she opened the front door.

"Come on in," Saya said with a small wave.

With exquisite paintings full of broad brush strokes and detailed line work all over the walls and finely crafted rugs covering the black wood floors, the space was hardly what Cosima expected. Saya led them to a seating area full of low-sitting benches and elaborate sculptures. Once the group was seated, Saya excused herself.

Merit let out a breath. "This is fancy for people who live so close to rabid giants."

Nariah clicked her tongue. "I just hope Dario isn't the reason for all the elegance. You know how pretentious those Sacred Brothers are."

Ivo rubbed the back of her head. "When we were walking, Saya told me all about their rituals with him. They call him the defender of Dileyna because he gifted the Crown several blades with what they called righteous stones. Those stones increased the strength of the warriors, allowing the people here a way to defend themselves against the giants. They managed to build this city because of Dario's gift. However, that's not all." Ivo shifted on her feet. "Dario told them he is creating the giants to practice for his new world. He claims that anyone who helps him will be reborn with great magical abilities. That's why the whole city prays."

Sima raised a brow. "What does he get out of their prayer?"

"It's energy harvesting," Nariah hissed. "A different Sacred Brother that was taken down did the same thing. Essentially, he holds their minds with his power while they all devote their energy to him to magnify his magic. Whatever Dario is doing, it's something calculated."

Cosima's stomach twisted. "I don't like the sound of that."

Several sets of footsteps approached, and Saya returned with a plate full of steaming cooked meat cut into slender strips and pickled purple and red vegetables. Behind her stood two felines with silver eyes and white fur. She set the food on the short table in front of them. "This is One and Six.

One is my cousin, and Six is their best friend."

Six had tiny, vertical black lines up her nose, and One had black in the fur around her hands and feet. Both nodded their heads a fraction before they sat down. Sima wasn't sure why, but their presence gave her chills. She shook off the sensation and waited for Saya to serve them. Saya handed a plate to Nariah first, who immediately passed it over to Ivo. As Cosima got her portion, Ivo tore into her food.

"So, you're a part of the Seven, then?" Nariah asked. When they nodded, she pressed her lips together. "What is it like being so close to a God?"

Six crossed their legs. "It is strenuous work to learn all there is to know before the reincarnation of our people. We spend almost all of our time studying the texts given to us by Dario the defender. That being said, it is also a magnificent honor."

Merit's lip twitched. "How exactly does he plan to birth you all again?"

One frowned. "He has the power of eternity, all he must do is master it. When the time is right, he chooses someone from the city, and they are reborn in his new world. As our great God grows in his abilities, more of us will be revived."

It took everything in her not to scream as the two members of the Seven spoke. The situation reminded her of Aurelio and his desperate need to be worshiped. Dario had created their problem and then offered the solution as if he could not bring their terror to an end on his own. "How do you know he's telling the truth?"

Both felines hissed before Saya laid her hands on their shoulders. "We have no choice but to trust him. We are in the defender's hands, and either we obey or we die. Please understand that the Seven are my people's only communication with our God. They are making an incredible sacrifice."

One used their hands to pull the hair beneath their pointed ear to the side. Attached to their light pink skin was a pulsating ruby. The red gem had incredible clarity, and through it, One's brain was visible. "We have given ourselves to the defender," one said slowly, letting their hair cover the stone again, "and there is no going back."

"That crystal…Saya, you mentioned something about searching for a missing stone out there," Ivo said, jumping to her feet. "Why does Dario need it?"

Saya looked away. "He told the Seven that if it wasn't found, someone was going to come and destroy our planet looking for it. He said it would give him enough strength to save all of us."

Merit leaned forward. "Did you find it?"

She shook her head. "No," Saya said, smoothing down her red fur.

"Another search will have to take place."

Six tilted their head to the side, their silver eyes narrowing on Cosima. "Why have you come to this world? Saya tells us you are not Gods but that you are gifted with unique abilities."

Cosima swallowed, sensing something sharp and unspoken in her tone. "We are lost travelers looking for respite. If you allow us some time to recover, we will be out of here as soon as possible."

Nariah grinned. "We appreciate the hospitality, truly."

Saya's harsh expression relaxed, and the two members of the Seven got to their feet. One glanced down at Sima. "You are welcome to stay in our Luuyet, but if you cause chaos, you will be ejected."

"Understood," Merit said with a dip of his head.

"I should show you to your rooms," Saya said. "Right this way."

Saya led them down a flight of stairs and into a comfortable lounge room. They pointed down the hallway. "There are three rooms, and each has two pillow beds. I assume you will decide your sleeping arrangement amongst yourselves." They put their hands on their hips as their whiskers twitched. "The rain room is at the end of the hallway."

"Rain room?" Sima raised a brow.

"For bodily cleansing."

"Ah, a bathing chamber," Nariah said. She clapped her hands together and smiled. "We are humbled by your kindness, Saya."

"I will leave you all to it. If you need anything, I sleep on the second floor, first door on the right."

"Got it, thanks, Saya," Ivo said.

Merit yawned and stretched. "Well, I am checking out the rain room first, sorry, ladies. A man can only stink so much before you all have the right to excommunicate him."

Ivo rolled her eyes as Saya retreated up the stairs and Merit headed down the hallway. She turned to Sima. "I guess you and I are sharing a room."

"Before that," Nariah said, "can I talk to you, Ivo? Alone?"

Sima hid her smirk and pretended to yawn. "I'll go on ahead, you come to the room when you're done."

Ivo frowned but said nothing as Sima walked down the hallway and found a room. The beds were made of large flat cushions with a white blanket draped over the top. She flopped onto the one closest to the door and let out a loud sigh. Her body ached, and lying alone made her crave Enzo's touch. She rolled onto her side and shut her eyes, picturing his brilliant brown skin and divine emerald eyes. Every one of Vincenzo's features was striking. She mentally compared his resemblance to his brothers. Enzo and

Aurelio could not be more dissimilar, but Enzo shared similarities with Sostene. Their lips were the same shape, and the black half of Enzo's hair matched Sostene's. Sima shivered as she recalled the mysterious darkness that swam in Sostene's amethyst gaze.

"I'm spending another night without you," she whispered.

Her heart tugged on the deep connection she felt to him, and she allowed the familiar brush of his essence to comfort her. Her eyelids wrinkled as a pulse of pain shot through her arm. She opened her eyes and inspected her arm, finding nothing different.

"I don't know where you are, or if you're hurt, but don't give up yet, Enzo. How am I supposed to do this without you? You hold me together when I'm falling apart, you love me like I was never broken, and you kiss me like it's the only thing that makes sense. I'm waiting for you."

A tear ran down her cheek, and Sima wiped it away. She curled into a ball on the pillow bed and shut her eyes. Another fractured memory resurfaced, and Sima's heart ached with how thankful she was for the moment. Her memory of Vincenzo was hazy and difficult to fully grasp, but it was new. She used a tendril of her magic to replay the scene until she fell fast asleep to the hum of his voice.

"That is the loveliest drawing I've ever seen." His viridian gaze poured adoration over her. He pressed a kiss to her forehead. "Tell me again how you learned to do this?"

Sima glanced down at her work and grimaced. The sketch of her grandmother's garden was filled with wonky proportions. "My mother used to spend the afternoons painting with me. It isn't coming along like I'd hoped. See, the dragonfly on this flower looks fine, but the one in the air looks like it's wilting beneath the sun."

Vincenzo laughed, the sound like wind rustling the trees in the summer. "It has charm, my love. Look at the radiance of the water in the fountain, and the bees near the roses are adorably round."

"You really think it's good?"

"I'd make a universe full of blank canvases just to watch you paint the skies," Vincenzo whispered, wrapping his arms around her. "I love seeing the world the way you do, even if it's just a glimpse."

"Where will you go?" a voice whispered. "There is no home for a cursed son."

Enzo panted, unable to discern where the voice was coming from, his mind dizzy with confusion. Sweat dripped down his brow as he ran, the jungle full of towering trees with thick trunks, disembodied voices, and angry buzzing insects. The persistent pests chased after him, forcing him to flee deeper and deeper into the boisterous jungle.

The ground shook beneath him, causing him to stumble as a screech pierced his ears. Enzo covered them with his hands and continued running, drenched in his own fear and sweat. Something stalked behind him, its heavy footsteps thudding as it kept hot on his trail. He dared a glance back and found himself locked eye-to-eye with a gigantic person-like figure with an unsettling posture. Enzo swallowed a scream and focused forward, his legs moving faster.

As it ran behind him, it held its arms in a strange position and its feet were rotated outward at an abnormal angle, giving it an awkward, inefficient gait. Despite its unusual appearance and movement patterns, the being managed to keep pace behind him through its massive leg span. With every wide step, it grew closer and closer.

"Your blood is tainted," the voice whispered. "There is nowhere to hide."

Do something. Sever every bind he has placed over you, his darkness barked from within.

The curse continued to call to him, the magic biting at his fingers, but Enzo could not get himself to use it. Even in the throes of delirious adrenaline-filled hallucinations, he could not shake his restraint. He had promised Sima that he would not let his curse submerge him, and he did not intend to break that promise. He would do his best to defend whatever barriers remained between him and the full expanse of his power.

Somewhere within his tether to Cosima pulled taut, causing him to cry out as her emotions drenched him. Her confusion, her worry, her loneliness all rushed to the forefront of his mind, and Enzo struggled to remain focused on evading the giant pursuing him. Wherever she was, he was getting closer.

I can feel you, the connection is intensifying, he thought. *I won't stop until you're in my arms again.*

"How long until it is her blood on your hands?" the voice whispered.

Enzo's heart skipped as electricity shot through him, forcing him to fall face-first into the mud. He flipped onto his back and held a shaky hand up as the large being approached. It slowed as it grew closer, as though it was inspecting him. Its head cocked to the side as it held its arms near its collarbone, elbows outward.

"She cannot save you from your poison," the voice hissed.

"What do you want from me?"

The being crouched and gave its bulging eyes a slow blink. "Your last breath."

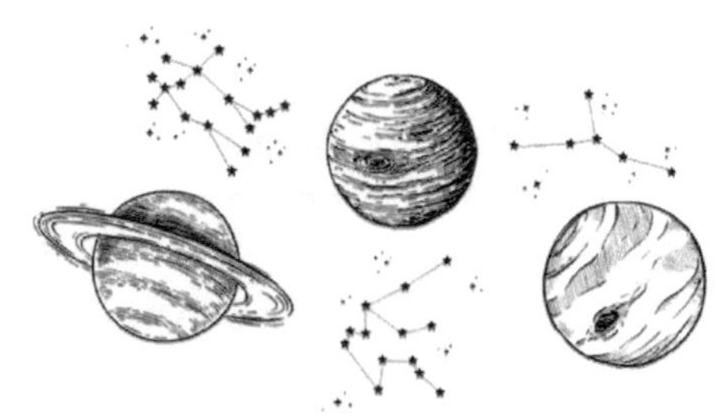

Chapter 35

Ivo sat down and blew out a puff of air. "So, what is it that you want to talk to me about?"

Nariah paced back and forth. "I don't know how to tell you this, but you need to be more careful with your power."

"Here we go again. How many times are we going to have this conversation?"

"I told you that you weren't directly altering the threads, and that's still true, but you're doing something else that is just as dangerous. I've been trying to find the right moment to bring it up, and it can't wait anymore."

"Alright, alright. What am I doing that is so dangerous then?"

Nariah chewed her lip and slowed her pacing. She faced Ivo. "You're creating new threads."

Ivo threw her head back and howled with laughter. "I had no idea you could be so funny."

"It's not a joke. This is serious. Listen to me. I have absolutely no clue why you're able to do such a thing, but right before we found Saya, I saw it happen. I must have missed it before because I was hunting for changes to existing threads, but you're creating entirely new ones out of thin air. They join the millions of other threads, and if I hadn't seen it at the precise moment it appeared, I don't know if I would have ever figured it out."

Her heart jumped into her throat. "But how can I do that? I'm a mortal."

Nariah brushed back her white hair. "I am wondering the same thing, Ivo. You don't have the energy signature of someone that is immortal, but perhaps somehow you were imbued with the blood of one of the Celestial Empresses."

She wrapped her arms around her knees. "Has that happened to mortals before?"

"Not that I've heard of," Nariah replied. "Until we figure out how you're doing this, you need to stop. Altering the Weave is not an offense taken lightly. You saw how they responded to Sima and the restrictions they placed on her. Don't give the High Priestesses any reason to suspect you are a threat."

Ivo's thoughts zipped through her at mind-boggling speeds. For a split second, she welcomed the idea of being special, but something inside her was resistant and resentful.

"How do you know it's me? I am not trying to do anything, so I also don't know how you expect me to stop."

"You didn't feel anything out of the ordinary before we stumbled across Saya?"

Ivo shook her head. "Nothing. I think you're mistaken, Nariah. Maybe it was Sima, or something strange happened, but it wasn't me. I wish you'd stop bringing it up because it's not going to change anything. I am still going to die one day, with or without the involvement of others. You just have to accept that."

Nariah's face twisted. "I don't want you to die, especially not now. I am trying to protect you. Maybe there's a chance we're wrong about you being—"

"Don't," Ivo barked. "Don't do that. Don't get my hopes up. I never asked you to protect me. You're wasting your time chasing impossible dreams. You are supposed to watch Sima, and all I am is a distraction to you."

Nariah looked away and clenched her jaw. "You could definitely say that."

Ivo threw her hands up. "Here you go again."

The Scout's purple gaze bore into Ivo. "You act like you have any idea at all what I really think of you."

That made Ivo laugh. "And whose fault is that? You're not exactly an open book."

Nariah's brows knit together. "And you are? You are so guarded all the time, I have barely gotten the chance to know you."

Ivo's pulse thumped in her ears. Vulnerability was not her strong suit, but the Scout had not made it easy to be around one another either. "Oh, now you want to get to know me?"

Nariah took a deep breath and stared down at Ivo. "I am *sorry*. Alright? I am sorry, I don't know how to be normal around you. I don't know what about you makes me so fucking insane, but I can't think straight when you're around. I can't take my eyes off you because I am worried something is going to come bounding from the trees, and I will never see you again. I know you're still mad at me for what I said on Carmine's planet, but I didn't mean it."

Ivo's heart beat faster, but she said nothing. Nariah's insult had attached itself to her core. For decades, whether in Ombra or confined to the palace in Aeria, she had fought to find some semblance of meaning in her existence, only to still find herself wandering without purpose. Ivo could not change the circumstances of her mortality, and as the years passed, she knew she was closer and closer to parting ways with this life. All she wanted was for the time she had left to be spent on something meaningful, to find some proof that she mattered at all.

"You're not weak." Nariah's shoulders sagged. "I made some harsh judgments of you, and you've proved me wrong. You never back down from a fight, you have a light in you that doesn't fade, and your power is something extraordinary. I know you think I'm making this up, but you're in touch with the Weave. If you'll let me, we can work together to pinpoint when your magic is manifesting, so you can halt the flow. I can help you through this if you'll just let me in."

"The last thing I need is to get closer to you," Ivo said softly. She didn't want to believe Nariah about her power. She already struggled to accept her meager two-thousand-year lifespan compared to her best friend's eternal one. Falling for someone immortal only complicated it further. "I can take care of myself."

"Why should you have to if I am here and willing?"

"I don't depend on anyone except myself, or maybe Sima, but that's it." Her mind flicked back to her conversation with Horacio and Earnest as she wrapped her arms around herself. They had told her that Nariah was both publicly and *privately* popular, something that only made Ivo's fears of inadequacy whine more fervently. She had only had one lover. What could she offer the Scout that she hadn't already had? Once the novelty wore off, Nariah would grow bored with her. "I don't waste my time trusting people I know will let me down."

"Why is trusting me a waste of time?" Nariah asked, her expression tight. "Who knows what may blossom between us?"

Ivo shut her eyes as images of her deceased girlfriend, Erelya, popped into her mind, the grief as fresh as the day she died. All the emotions Ivo tried to keep locked away threatened to break through, and her fists clenched as she regained control over herself.

"Because the people I care about are always taken from me. Why should I open myself up to being hurt again? My heart on the line for what? So you can pass the time by slipping into my pants whenever you want? I want something real, and you want to keep busy."

Nariah recoiled as if she had been slapped. "Is that what you think this is? That I am just using you?"

"You're a Trine Scout, Nariah. I'm not stupid. I know someone like you would never love someone like me. Not really, anyway. I have nothing to offer you. You know I like you. You know, that for some reason, I can't get myself to stay away, and you exploit it because you know I can't say no to you. You're everything I could never be, and every second with you is a reminder of that."

Nariah shook her head. "Ivo, where is this coming from? That's not—"

"It doesn't matter," she said, waving her hand weakly.

"It does." Nariah shifted on her feet. "I know I am not the best at showing it, but I care about you. A lot more than I ever intended, but this has never been about passing the time. Not for a second."

It was impossible to think as the Scout moved closer. Everything outside of Nariah faded, and Ivo found herself locked in her wisteria gaze.

"I have never been at the mercy of someone else like this before," Nariah whispered. "It is unimaginably frustrating, but I am helplessly drawn to you, Ivo. I can't shake this hold you have over me, and it is utterly humiliating to talk about feelings I've…never had before."

A breath caught in Ivo's throat. As badly as she wanted to confess her feelings for the Scout, something kept her from speaking. Was this what she wanted? To navigate loving an immortal Scout when she didn't even know if she had a future? For a brief moment, she debated pulling away altogether. Instead, she let her eyelids flutter close as Nariah leaned in, their lips nearly touching.

A crash shook the city, and Ivo's eyes flew open. She steadied herself on the Scout's arm as their heads shot in the direction of the noise. Destructive booms were followed by screaming, and Nariah sprang into action—she flew up the stairs and disappeared. Merit ran out with soap still in his hair and his Scout's uniform half assembled, with Sima emerging from her room a moment later.

Nariah appeared in the doorway at the top of the stairs, her eyes wide. "There are giants inside the city. The walls seem intact. It's like they're manifesting out of thin air. Hurry, the people of Dilenya are dying."

Vincenzo

The unnerving giant that had stalked him through the jungle shape-shifted, flickering in and out of view as it molded itself into different arrangements, each more strange than the last. Despite how he fought against the hallucinations, Enzo remained deeply within his brother's grasp, unable to shake off the magic crawling around his mind. He had gotten used to the incessant sounds of insects and nature from earlier, but they were absent now as well, leaving him with the pressure of silence.

The being froze and then dissolved before him, leaving someone else standing in its place. The woman he loved stood there with worry written in her gaze and a bloody, carnivorous scene only feet behind her. He knew it wasn't her. Their internal tether told him the woman standing before him was merely a replication of the woman he loved. Yet something about the hallucination seemed so real, he almost forgot he had watched the giant shape-shift into her likeness.

"Enzo?"

Sima's voice fluttered in, warped and echoing in a way that only confused him more. His mind would not work the way he needed it to. He tried and failed to gather himself coherently, but it was as if he was addled by drugs. His stomach tossed and turned, which only made him dizzier. He could not bear to take a glimpse at the gruesome scene of mangled flesh behind her, or he'd lose what composure he had left, but looking at Sima hurt. He wanted her to be real. His love for her had become precisely the manner by which his brothers tortured him.

The piles of tissue and organs began to pulsate, growing in size until they were impossible to ignore. The mound of flesh closest to her was full of entrails and torn open hearts, their ventricles still fluttering with the ghost of a pulse. Once his eyes fell on the pile, he vomited, his knees colliding with the mud. It was too much for him to cope with. The utter terror, the relentless pang of his curse, the constant separation from Sima. Enzo could not take it anymore.

You do not die here, his curse shouted, its voice pounding against what resolve remained. *Break free. Break free. Break free,* it chanted.

"Enzo?" another haunted, distortion of Sima's voice called to him.

He dragged his eyes off the contents of his stomach and held her gaze. A man in shadow approached her and turned her face toward him with a smoky finger. The shadow pressed its lips against hers, and Enzo thought he would be sick again. His hallucination of Cosima gave in to the passion of the shadow's advances, and it was jarring enough that a burst of his magic shot through the mud, and a moving wave of soil and rock blocked his view.

A raging wave of emotions bubbled inside him, a tangled mess of unprocessed grief and insecurity. It reminded him of his eternal unworthiness, his scarred potential. It reminded him of all the ways he would never be enough—especially not for her. However, Vincenzo was not a complete victim to his fears, for the sturdy ember of hope ignited alongside it. As Enzo heaved once more, he thought of what Cosima had said to him after he had killed Carmine.

You loved me through my darkness. It is an honor to love you through yours.

The words brought him stamina, enough to get him back on his feet. He swayed, holding his broken wrist close, as he prepared himself to keep going. Enzo's devotion to her was the only reason he bothered to fight at all, despite how he verged on total collapse. His curse rampaged inside him, creating ribbons of his flesh as it fought to be released, and though he knew it was risky, he allowed himself to dip into its toxic well once more.

Enzo glanced down at his fingertips as his heart seized in his chest. With every improper quiver of his heart, black encroached upon his skin. His nails were drenched in darkness as the color crawled upward, ending just before it reached his knuckles. His curse's storm grew in size, making it harder to think as the seconds passed. Each thought came out more distorted than the last. The only thing tethering him to reality was his bond to Cosima.

My curse is my relief, my truest omen. From open horizons I fall. From nothing, I became.

The words rambled on, with their real meaning lost on Enzo as his eyes began to roll back in his head. The trees were shaking and loud, and bone-chilling booms echoed through the jungle. With each blink, the world grew darker.

I am your inevitable end and your unavoidable reincarnation, his curse laughed as Enzo closed his eyes, unable to hold them open any longer.

Cosima

"Help! Someone, please help!"

Sima slid to a stop outside as she searched for the source of the cry. She ran down an empty street until she found someone caught beneath rubble. In the distance, more than a dozen giants created utter madness through their destructive rampage. The beings tore through buildings and consumed people, the damage and loss rising by the second.

Without waiting for proper clearance from Nariah, Sima touched her magic, allowing threads to explode into view all around her. She yanked on one, which sent the heavy piece of broken roof flying in the opposite direction. Sima crouched down beside the feline with blue and black fur and helped them to a stand.

"Please, save my friend," they begged, dark red blood seeping from their thigh. "They're still inside the house."

Sima followed where the feline pointed and took off, jumping over wood and shattered glass. Inside the demolished house came muffled cries. With another quick pull of her magic, rubble flew onto the street, clearing the interior. She spotted a slender feline with orange fur waving one hand while holding their leg with the other.

"It's broken," they said, tears forming in their amber eyes. "I can't get up."

Merit poked his head into the house. "I'll get them over to the healer where the other injured people are going. I think there are more citizens trapped who could use your power. Stay away from the giants, at all costs, you hear me? Let Nariah and I take down the ones we come across."

Sima frowned as Merit gingerly picked up the orange feline. "I'll do my best."

A loud thud made her flinch, and Sima made her way back onto the street to find the source. Nearby, a giant with shaggy brown hair and blue eyes was pulling furniture out through a third-story window and dropping it onto the street, as the residents screamed inside.

Merit flew into view with the injured orange feline in his arms. "Sima, I mean it. Don't go toward it."

Her feet refused to move, her eyes glued to the building. The giant reached in and pulled out a feline with blue and white stripes that scratched at its skin with their claws. It unhinged its jaw as it brought them towards its mouth. Before she realized she was doing it, Sima was running while she formed a time pocket. The giant froze, and Sima withdrew her blade. Nariah's iridescent butterfly-like wings flashed as she burst through the air and cut through the back of its neck. Time resumed as the feline fell from the being's hand, and a web appeared beneath them as Ivo enacted her spell.

Another giant that moved with a distinctive rhythm stepped into Sima's field of view. Nariah engaged, dodging its attempts to snatch her from the air. The Scout drew the being into an open plaza and shot forward, spiraling as her sword made ribbons of the skin on its arms. Each of its five fingers slammed into the ground as its black blood-covered palm swatted at Nariah. The pulse of the giant's movements shifted in tempo, catching the Scout off guard as its fingerless hand struck her from the sky.

Its uninjured arm shot into the house and tugged free two small felines with round faces. Sima's stomach jumped into her throat as she found herself once again moving. She pulled the giant into a time pocket and raced forward, allowing the Weave's threads to surface.

"I don't want to die," wailed one of the young felines, banging its fists against the creature's thumb.

Cosima pushed herself harder as she reached for the threads. Merit popped up behind the giant just as Sima selected a string. Her magic responded strangely, this time splitting into thousands of impossibly thin strands. Everything slowed, including Sima herself, as a flurry of possibilities exploded in front of her. Her eyes widened as she realized she was witnessing all the outcomes she could choose from based on the current circumstances. One of the options would swap her location with the two children in the giant's grasp. Without thinking, she pulled it.

The world fluttered, and Sima blinked. When she opened her eyes, she found herself inside the giant's hand, and time resumed. It squeezed the air from her lungs, but Sima's hand still clutched her blade. She jammed it into the creature's flesh and cut herself free. As she plummeted towards the ground, Merit zipped back and caught her.

"That was fucking sick." Merit whooped as he circled back around to the giant. "You didn't listen to me for shit, but damn if that wasn't cool." He set her down on a roof. "Let me show you how to finish the job."

The giant's teeth chattered as its hand shot toward Merit. The Scout jumped onto it and ran up its arm with his wings, providing power to his steps. He gripped his sword with two hands as he barreled straight through the being's open mouth. Sima gasped when it clamped shut around Merit. The giant's eyes widened before they rolled back, and black blood seeped from its nose. Merit shoved open its mouth by the top row of its teeth and stood on its tongue.

"I really hate these fucking things." He flew forward, and the creature fell, shaking the street when it landed. "How are there so many of them?"

Sima followed his gaze, and from atop the roof, she had an unrestricted view of the mayhem. Despite the few they had worked to kill, more than twenty giants now stomped through the city. "Dario must know we're here."

Merit sighed. "Well, if it's any consolation to you, your feathered lover is nearby. Not quite in the city yet, but close. Hopefully, he can help us wrap this up because I'm already over it."

"Sima! Merit! Down here!" Ivo yelled out, using both her arms to wave as she jumped up and down.

The Scout scooped her up and flew her down to what appeared to be a restaurant. Her nose immediately picked up on the scent of smoke. There was a small crowd outside, the tensions high as people hollered out commands or cried with grief. Merit put her down, and she rushed to Ivo's side.

"One of those giants fell onto the building and trapped the people inside the kitchen," Ivo said, holding onto Sima's arm. "A fire broke out, but they can't get out because the creature is still trying to eat them, even though it can't get up. Nariah went in there a minute ago, but she hasn't come back out."

Merit met her gaze. "You go for the people, I'll kill the broken snapper before he gets his teeth in someone."

With a deep breath, Sima followed Merit and Ivo inside the burning building. At the center, a giant lay crumpled in a strange position as its muscles twitched. A large metal pole was jammed through its chest into its back. Although it was pinned to the ground, its snarled as its arms swiped through the open dining room. Black smoke came from two double doors in the back of the restaurant, collecting on the ceiling before it flooded out through the opening the giant's body created. Nariah was nowhere to be seen.

Merit made his way toward the giant, and Sima pulled Ivo toward the kitchen. The metal doors were crunched in at the top, preventing them from opening. Just as she had before, Sima unraveled the threads and found a strand where the door was left unaffected. She touched it, and when she blinked, the door was fixed. Before she could pull it open, Merit let out a cry behind her.

She turned around and found him trapped beneath the giant's shoulder. Sima glanced up at the ceiling and realized it had shifted two feet to the left, as if she had managed to go back in time and changed the location of the giant's fall. The creature growled as its massive arms swung through the room. Her eyes widened.

"That wasn't supposed to happen."

"What went wrong? Do something," Ivo yelped.

Unintended consequences of my power, she thought as she cringed. *I'm lucky it wasn't somehow worse.* "Use your magic to put out the fire. I'm going to help Merit."

The two ran in opposite directions, and Sima pulled out her sword as Merit let out another yell. "Kill it already."

Sima followed through, stabbing her sword through the giant's neck. She plunged it deep and then jumped onto its chest and pulled her blade through its flesh, slicing its throat open. At last, the rabid noises ceased, and Sima lifted its shoulder as much as she could as Merit wiggled free.

"I'm so sorry, Merit," Sima said as her brows pinched together. "I tried to pick a strand quickly, and somehow I think I…altered the past?" She stared down at her hands. "I thought I could just reverse the damage; I didn't realize it would move the giant, too."

"While I'm sure it was an accident," he said, stretching his back, "I'm still pissed. Learn your lesson, or next time you're gonna splatter my guts. Where is Nariah?"

"I haven't seen any sign of her." Sima turned toward the kitchen, and through the open doors, a horrific scene was visible. "Oh, no."

A smaller giant, around seven feet tall, crawled around inside the kitchen with viscous speed. Black ash and soot coated the back half of the kitchen, and although the fire had been put out, the smoke had not yet fully dissipated, leaving a haze in the air. Ivo stood her ground, doing her best to protect the scared people crouching behind her with spells. With a flash of Merit's wings, the Scout and Sima flew into the kitchen, and he threw himself on the creature's back. It bucked him off, sending him flying into the wall. Sima placed the being inside her time pocket, and when it froze, the frightened citizens fled.

Ivo trembled. "I still haven't seen any sign of Nariah. She came in to fight the giant in front of the restaurant and disappeared. What if she's hurt?"

Loud thunder rolled through the sky, accompanied by the soft patter of a fresh rainstorm. Merit shoved his blade through the creature's heart and then rolled his neck.

"Nariah wouldn't let something unworthy claim her life. We'll find her."

A bolt of lightning lit up the sky outside as the rain grew heavier. The sounds of screaming people and howling giants were dampened by the downpour. Chills ran down her spine, and an uneasy sensation riled inside her, just like it had right before they met Sostene.

"I think you were right, Sima," Merit said. "I think Dario does know we're here."

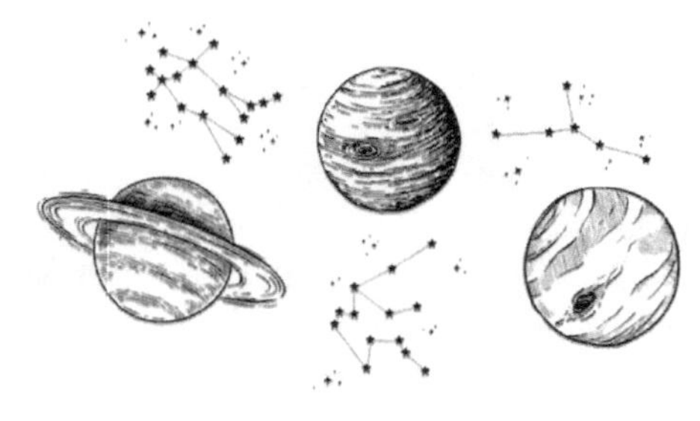

Chapter 36

Vincenzo

Something wet dripped across his face. It started off with light splashes, but grew quickly in intensity until it dribbled into his nose and mouth. Enzo coughed as he sat up, finding himself alone once more, lost in the jungle as rain poured. He attempted to stand, but his body gave out, forcing him to fall face-first into the mud. With lazy hands, he wiped his face off on his sleeve.

A creature with a distressing aura crawled backward toward him with its stomach facing the sky. Its unclothed body resembled immortals in every way, except its gigantic proportions. It was three times Enzo's size, with a strikingly familiar face and a painfully terrifying, unnatural smile spreading across its lips as its head hung upside down. Its neck spun, allowing it to face upright. It locked onto Enzo and screeched.

Enzo dodged out of the way, using his wings to propel himself faster than his weary legs could. Even so, he had barely escaped its teeth. As the creature positioned himself to strike again, another one came running through the trees. This one moved faster, causing the ground to shiver beneath the pounding of his feet. He moved upright, and while not quite as large as the other creature, this one had a stare that sent a chill down Enzo's spine.

Their gait was awkward like the last being he encountered, but their unique pattern of movement did not slow them down. No matter how hard he pushed his wings, he was no closer to escaping them. When he would dare a glance back, too tempted by fear to remain focused ahead, their mouths would move, but the sound came several seconds after.

They were calling his name.

"Oh, Vincenzo," they cried, "the prodigal son has arrived. Won't you show us what death feels like?"

You cannot defy your destiny, his curse shouted, loud enough to make Enzo wince. *It was crafted for you, and you alone must bear the weight of it.*

Enzo had no choice but to fight them, his magic thick like destructive lava inside him. He manifested a sword in his non-dominant hand as his heels dug into the ground to slow himself. He flipped around and allowed his power to flood his weapon, gritting his teeth as his curse surged through him. The creatures came to a halt, towering far above him. His hands shook, but he did not retreat.

The upright one broke the momentary pause and bounded toward him. As its foot hovered above his head, Enzo stabbed his sword into its flesh. It howled in response and pulled back, lifting Enzo as he hung onto the sword. He swung his body back and forth, dislodging the weapon. He caught himself before he hit the ground and propelled into the air, aiming for the second one.

"You had better hurry, little twelve," the giant screeched. "He won't let her go if he finds her first."

Its voice had transformed from unnerving, high-pitched echoes to feeling as real as Cosima's voice had been to him, only now it sounded like Nariah. He flung himself onto the abdomen of the backwards creature, steadying himself as it ran. Its head spun to face him. Enzo narrowed his gaze, catching the hint of a yellow glimmer outlining the creature. Not quite an aura as the magic was too defined, but noticeable enough to garner his attention.

"Can you still feel her? Do you think it will burn when your cord to her is severed?" The giant recreated Merit's voice. "You're wasting your time with us, all while your brother picks out panties for her to wear on their wedding night."

The idea doused him in flammable wrath. Hearing the words come from Merit's voice only made him more bloodthirsty. He plunged his sword down into its stomach, grimacing as it began to scream. Enzo's curse shot through his palms, and the giant dissolved into ash. The binds of his brother's magic were suffocating, and with a forceful shove against Dario's hold, Enzo finally broke free. His mind was finally clear of his brother's influence, but the injury from Sostene had worsened, the pain unavoidable without Dario's manipulation to distract him.

Enzo returned to the air, speeding through the jungle. He did not know where he planned to go, but he had run himself ragged, emotionally and physically. He panted, switching to stumbling on foot as the suffering from his shattered wrist grew unbearable. Heavy rain tattered the trees, and Enzo shivered as it ran down his body. He fell repeatedly, unsure if he was still being followed, but he pulled himself up and pushed forward anyway. He didn't let himself stop, not even when the coherent vision came with wider and wider gaps of pitch black in between.

He was blacking out.

"Stay with me, Enzo," Sima called from somewhere else. "I don't want you to leave me."

"Sima," he whispered, tumbling to the ground once more. "I love you."

"Do you remember?" her voice said, drowned out by the heavy rain.

"Remember?" he mumbled into the mud, no longer capable of lifting himself off the ground.

"The first time we kissed. Not on Haelos, but in the Kingdom."

His eyes fluttered shut. He did remember. He had never forgotten.

It had been a brief, a stolen moment, too sweet to be meant for someone like him. Her lips across his had been a calm awakening, as if some internal chains had fallen off his soul. It had been Cosima who kissed him first, but he had not hesitated to wrap her in his arms. As quickly as she had melted into him, she departed, running off somewhere she would never tell him. If he had not been enamored before, he had undeniably been after. His fingers had lingered on his lips, wondering when he would see her again, with no clue what the future would hold.

His body sagged in response to the memory, his wings limp as rain bounced off his feathers. His heart was frightfully slow in his chest, and the black continued to spread up his arm from his fingers. The internal rattling of his breath made him fear the end had come for him. *Am I dying? Did I go too far?* His thoughts were quiet and distant.

"Rest and when you wake, we will be together at last," she whispered in his ear.

"Don't go," he muttered. "Don't go without me. I'm sorry I've been such a coward. I'm sorry I didn't protect you when I should have, and I'm sorry I can't keep them away from you. I'm broken, but I tried to be whole for you. I wanted to give you…more than this."

A tear slid down his face, but he did not feel sad. He wasn't sure what he was feeling, but it was unlike anything he had experienced before. It was sharp, caustic, eating away at him from the inside out. It was venom in his veins, fire in his lungs, shadows in his mind. It was devouring him and all he knew himself to be. His body burned as if he were beneath coals in a festering pit of flame.

His eyes rolled back, and his body ceased all movement. His chest did not rise, but neither did he die. As if his cursed magic had given up on him, no healing sensations simmered through his body. Instead, his power toiled out of him at a mindless rate, pouring deep into the soil, draining his reserves at a crawling pace. As the seconds passed, his consciousness faded. He struggled to remember why he was here, why he was cold and wet, where he had come from, who he had been talking to.

Rest, soul of many moons, his curse whispered, the sound rattling through his skull, *and allow your ascension to unravel.*

Darkness consumed him, and Enzo slipped away.

Ivo didn't care that rain soaked all the way through her clothes and left her shivering. She was just happy to see Nariah alive. The Scout's cape had been burnt, the singed remains of it blowing in the wind. She had a large bleeding cut on her left arm and scratches on her right. Nariah's white hair was tipped in black blood as she once again launched herself at the giant.

A huge fist slammed into Nariah, and the Scout tumbled backward before she regained her balance with her wings. Ivo moved quickly and used a spell to stun the beast with her blue electricity. The already charged air fired off three more bolts of electricity into the creature, finally laying it to rest. Nariah landed on top of its charred black skin and used her blade to ensure the beast would stay down for good. Only one giant remained in the immediate area, and Merit's wings flashed as he flew toward it. Ivo turned away from the fight and faced Nariah.

"What happened to you?" Ivo asked, placing her hands on her hips.

"The one with the broken back that fell into that restaurant threw me through the damn wall. Once I was outside, I got ambushed by this guy in the alley, and I couldn't shake him. Smaller ones kept joining the fight." Nariah walked over and patted Ivo on the shoulder. "Thanks for the help."

Her skin tingled where the Scout touched her, and Ivo wiped the rain off her face. "Why are there so many of them?"

"Dario isn't going to make this easy on us," Nariah replied.

The chaos in the distant parts of the city had not dimmed, and Ivo wondered if clearing this block of giants would make any difference in the end. Despite the rain, the sharp scent of the giant's black blood mixed with the iron scent of the dead citizens scattered throughout the demolished block. Her gaze fell back on Nariah, and her heart pinched. Too many opposing thoughts battled for dominance in her mind—some telling her to throw herself into Nariah's arms and others mocking her for believing she was worthy of the Scout's attention.

The Scout's purple eyes were bright, even with the gloomy conditions. "So, you came looking for me, huh?"

Ivo frowned. "You're a member of the team, don't let it get to your head."

Nariah smirked. "We never got to finish our conversation earlier."

Her chest ached, and she looked away. "Yeah, I guess we didn't."

"I'm tired of the hot and cold, Ivo. I've had enough of hurling insults and letting my temper get the best of me. You drive me crazy, but in a way, I never want to be without."

"You have no clue what you're trying to sign yourself up for," Ivo said softly. "You have a life with purpose, don't waste your potential on me."

The Scout stiffened. "I know exactly what it is I am choosing right now, and it's you. You're the only thing that I want. If it's about me being Scout, there are ways to—"

"Stop," Ivo said, holding her hand up. "I would never want you to give this up. Being a Scout is who you are, Nariah. You shouldn't destroy yourself for a relationship that might not even work out."

"Damn it, Ivo, I am so sick of pretending things are fine the way they are. I can't cope with everything that's been left unsaid."

A strange bitterness surfaced inside Ivo. She had spent so much time being conflicted about her feelings for Nariah that she didn't know the first thing about embracing them. Instead, the friction made her frustrated, and Ivo lashed out. "You're the one who said that hooking up changed nothing between us."

"I didn't mean it." Nariah pressed her fist to her lips as she took a breath. "*Everything* has changed between us. I can't go back to the way it was before."

Thunder rumbled from the sky. "Well, I can."

"Bullshit." Nariah's hand gently pulled Ivo's chin to force her to look at her. The electricity between them was stronger than ever, and for some reason, Ivo had never wanted to run away more. Internally, she resisted, but externally, she stared hopelessly into Nariah's purple gaze, unable to pull away. "Look me in the eyes and tell me that you really feel nothing for me, because that's the only way I'll believe it. There is something here, and I can't stop myself from fighting for it."

Ivo's breath caught, a strange grief drowning her from the inside out. A tear slid down her cheek, and Nariah wiped it away, her touch so gentle, Ivo thought she might crumble beneath it. Loving Nariah would mean coming to terms with their incompatible lifespans and, more terrifying than that, would require that Ivo open her heart to the possibility of being hurt again.

"Why? Why now?" Ivo asked, knowing the question was directed at Fate more than at Nariah.

"I want you to be mine," Nariah whispered, resting her forehead against Ivo's.

The words crashed over Ivo, and she could deny it no longer. She knew her feelings for Nariah had spiraled out of control and that she had crossed a line she could not come back from when they slept together. The pain that lingered from her former lover's death was haunting, reminding Ivo of all the reasons she never wanted to be vulnerable again, but she could not deny that she had already fallen for the Scout.

Ivo opened her mouth to speak when an ear-piercing scream startled her. The Scout wrapped her hand around the hilt of her blade and hunted for the source. "Stay close to me."

She followed after the Scout, the two entering another open plaza, this one stained with blood that drained from four half-eaten felines. Ivo swallowed the urge to vomit and kept her eyes focused on Nariah. Another shriek lit up the air, and the two picked up the pace, coming up on a temple. The temple itself was elaborate, with sculptures of Dario's head perched at the top of the stairs, surrounded by thriving violet plants. The entire structure was covered in what appeared to be hand-painted tile that created a mural. At the top of the temple, the design resembled the open sky and sun, while the lower portion depicted rows of feline citizens with their heads bowed in prayer.

"This is the temple Saya was telling us about," Ivo said, her hand over her mouth. Energy pulsated from within, and Ivo shivered. "Do you think the cries came from in there?"

Nariah shook her head. "No, but it was definitely nearby. Let's keep searching."

They maneuvered around more half-eaten bodies and rubble as they continued walking. They turned the corner and made their way to the back of the temple, where they spotted a unique grove full of trees with massive branches and glowing leaves. The area was clearly fit to hold ceremonies as it featured dozens of prayer spaces, somehow untouched by the rain. As they stepped into the sacred sanctuary, their bodies dried within seconds, the storm that had drenched them vanishing without a trace.

Something in the air applied pressure to her eardrums, and Ivo placed her hands over the sides of her head. Her stomach dropped as pure fear froze her in place. A rush of wind rustled the glowing leaves of the trees, and when one flew off and touched her skin, a blur of light moved in front of her. Ivo let out a small gasp as it happened again. Something was inside the sanctuary with them, and it moved with mind-boggling speed. Ivo willed herself to make a move when the entity rushed her and slammed her head against the ground, rendering her unconscious.

As rain pattered across his forehead, Enzo furrowed his brow. His curse still writhed within him, but some of the intensity had dulled. The wrist his brother had broken still throbbed, and his entire upper body was smothered in pain. With each breath in, it felt like the insides of his lungs were coated in lava. Vincenzo coughed until the burning in his throat finally ceased. He glanced down at his hands. The skin on his right arm up to his elbow had turned entirely black. On his left side, the darkness had reached midway up his palm.

Enzo dragged himself to his feet and evaluated himself, searching for more physical evidence of his curse's toxic influence. He had gone too far in his fight with Sostene, and now he was paying the price. With how long he had spent unconscious, Enzo wondered how his magic reserves were lower than they should have been. He was nowhere near running out, thanks to the seemingly limitless bounds of his curse, but if he had to defend himself, he would be forced to dip into its poisonous well once more.

He slid his broken wrist over his chest and pressed it into his skin. There was an icy chill inside him, and his heart beat slower than normal. The realization was uncomfortable, but he was still alive and, as far as he could tell, retained control over himself. Enzo thought about the woman he loved and rejoiced in the familiar tug within. He closed his eyes as he hummed their song and let his body orient itself in her direction.

Vincenzo's wings carried him north, and once he finally reached a break in the trees, he realized why it had been so quiet. There was a city, or what was left of it, in the distance. Giants stormed through it, crushing buildings and creating chaos. He flew toward it, reminding himself to stay calm despite the fact his tether seemed to lead directly into the destruction. The closer he got, the louder the shrieks of suffering grew. Enzo knew Dario had to be near, and his mind flashed with panic at the thought of yet another brother getting his hands on Cosima. His curse bucked in response, sending a forceful wave of energy through him.

She is yours and you are hers, it whispered with calm confidence. *Do not let the vermin forget.*

With a flash of viridian light, Enzo shot forward, spiraling toward the city at blinding speed. He soared over the walls and caught a glimpse of the calamity. Mutilated piles of bodies lined the streets as giants left unchecked chomped through feline people at a slow, gluttonous pace, tossing remains behind them. The scene made his limbs shake, and he landed on a roof across from a giant that sat in the street as it tore apart a person with gray fur, one limb at a time.

"I can't take it anymore," Enzo said, his gaze igniting. "All the senseless bloodshed, all the meaningless death. Tell him to come out here and fight me like a man."

The creature stopped its chewing and grinned, tissue and blood covering its teeth. Its head tilted to the side as it leaned forward. "He doesn't need to fight you. He already has her."

Enzo's eyes widened, and he growled as he launched himself forward, a metal spear manifesting in his uninjured hand. He drove it through the creature's eye, and as it fell backward, he repeatedly stabbed until it stopped moving. The intoxicating thump of his curse crept in like a gentle wind, bringing relief without him noticing it brush across his skin. The sweet melody of its outrageous power lulled him into a bloodthirsty frenzy.

Who will you become when you finally accept that you are unstoppable? Infinity awaits you, his curse thundered.

He barreled through the air, maneuvering from one giant to the next with blinding accuracy. He slit the throat of one before dismembering another, before the first hit the ground. A creature pounced on him, its fingers coiling in on him when his starlight turned its arm into ash. He fell downward and landed on his feet before he threw a hand up. Dozens of dense spheres of sediment burst from the ground, and with a flick of his wrist, he hurled them through the air.

Enzo reveled in the satisfying crunch as the spheres collided with their giant skulls. He raised his hands at his sides, and steel rods shot up from the streets, piercing the remaining creatures without mercy. He launched himself into the sky, hardly taking a moment to appreciate the way he silenced an entire block full of overgrown sacks of flesh within seconds. His arms trembled at his sides as he flew deeper into the city. The persistent pulse of pain from his wrist was the least of his concerns as he spotted black smoke and a flash of familiar green wings near the center of the city.

Somehow, ten more giants emerged, towering above the others he had seen. Each had a clarity to their eyes that unnerved him.

"Does it ever fucking end?" he growled as his blade tore through the thigh of the closest creature. As it fell forward, his curse-strengthened starlight blasted through its temple, killing it.

"Come on," he shouted at the beings, "let's get it over with."

Three rushed him at once, and Enzo slammed his hands together before pulling them apart, sparkling electricity manifesting between his palms as the ground tore open and swallowed them whole. He closed his grip and extinguished their lives, the creatures of his brother's creation so feeble it made him laugh.

I doubted this ability for so long, but look how it sings for me, he thought as he faced the remaining beings.

He raised his hands with his palms upward, and pillars of howlite erupted from the dirt. Giants peddled toward him, the street vibrating beneath their steps. With a subtle jerk of his unbroken wrist, the stone flew forward fast enough to leave diamond-shaped holes through the bodies of three creatures. They toppled on top of each other, causing a cloud of dust to rise.

Be reverent in your quest for revival, his curse mused, *and death will become your unwavering blade.*

Only three remained, and it was clear why—they moved with a speed the deceased beings did not possess. Enzo dodged one with short black curls and a broad smile. Its dark brown eyes tracked his every move, despite its head remaining stationary. Enzo's wings allowed him to dash out of the way of its incoming attacks, but he placed himself right in the path of one with shoulder-length blond hair. It swatted him out of the sky with its palm, dazing him as he crashed through a roof and landed in an empty bed.

A tug on their bond throttled his fury, causing it to stutter as he focused on Cosima's end. Her panic was bright, and his desire to wrap up his current battle became unavoidable. His heart beat slowly in his chest as Enzo's wings drove him up through the hole. A blade formed, and he forced it through the underside of the blond giant's chin. Its hands clasped around him, and he let go of his weapon. The creature tried to open its mouth, but his blade kept its jaw shut.

"Try and take a bite now, you overgrown fuck."

His starlight blasted through its cheek, and the being released him. Enzo darted out of the way as it tumbled forward and crashed through empty display stands outside of a market. Although it was still alive, he turned his attention to the two left standing. Black curls swished as the giant positioned itself beneath him and jumped, its teeth clamping around his ankle.

A hiss escaped his lips, but the pain was dulled beneath the beat of his curse-filled heart. He kicked the being in the nose with his free foot repeatedly as he aimed his hand toward its face. When he finally had an opening, a metal rod shot from his palm through its skull. The giant fell to the side with a limp flop, and Enzo used his arm to keep his head from bouncing off the street. He shoved his free foot against one of its teeth and sucked in a breath as he yanked his ankle out of its mouth.

The one with his other blade sealing its jaw shut emerged, its amber eyes locked on him as it bounded forward. Enzo repeated his earlier trick by hurling more stone projectiles, but the creature evaded each throw. He threw himself out of its path at the last second and rolled across the street before his wings jerked him into the air. He shuddered as the steady drip of his curse into his bloodstream turned his skin to ice.

The blond giant held its eyes impossibly wide as it pursued him, the tip of his blade visible beneath its chin. The other remaining giant had a frightening face, half of it taken up by his enormous teeth as it grinned. Vincenzo sent a blast of starlight at the blond one. When it dodged, some of his starlight got near enough to the bridge of its nose to burn its eyeballs within the sockets. It screamed, and it swung its head wildly. He flew around it and burst toward the back of its neck with the blade forming in his hand only a second before it sliced through the creature's flesh.

The one with the freakish smile balled its fists and swung at him, surging forward fast enough that Enzo could not shake him. He fell into rhythm with the giant as his viridian gaze burned. With every jab of the giant's fist, Enzo evaded by alternating which direction he moved. When it widened its stance, he flew between its legs and slashed the back of its ankles. His curse boiled in his veins, and the blade in his hand turned red with the heat. Enzo pulled back his arm and threw the blade, which whistled through the air with an emerald trail behind it. It slammed into the back of the giant's skull, and at last, he could breathe.

He glanced down and noticed that he had thrown the blade with his injured hand. Although it twitched, he hardly had any sensation at all in his right arm. It moved as he commanded, but even as he poked at his midnight-colored skin, his brain registered none of it.

Before he could dwell on the transformation any longer, Cosima popped into his mind. His head snapped up, and without a look back, he faithfully pulled himself in her direction. His heart rate continued to slow, and his teeth chattered as he flew. His curse had continued to consume him, and he was only somewhat aware of the fact that he had passed the point of no return. He tuned his mind to the thrum of her magnetic soul and blindly followed without considering what permeating consequences his lack of restraint would earn him. Enzo balanced himself on a dangerously tight line, and if he thought too long about what Cosima would say about this once she saw him, he would plummet to his demise.

Do not fear my adherence to your essence. I am you, inevitable son, and you are me, his curse whispered. *Let your devotion be the path to your resurrection.*

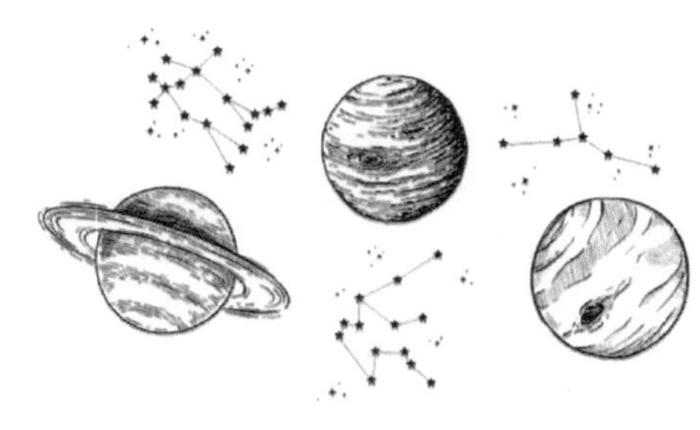

Chapter 37

Cosima

Cosima did her best to comfort the young feline as she carried them in her arms. Her feet slapped against the ground as she ran, with Merit close behind. The number of giants had finally begun to wane, and the break in bloodshed was a welcome relief. She slid to a stop outside of a school. The door was yanked open, and a feline person with red fur collapsed onto their knees.

"Prai," they cried, squeezing the youngling. "Oh, I was so worried."

Merit ushered the children he had rescued to run inside the school. They had been directing and delivering people to the school for over an hour. Cosima was grateful that the Scout did not object when she asked for them to focus their efforts on rescue. She couldn't bear the thought of letting more people die, the blood of innocents lining the streets had already begun to haunt her.

"We've got one more block before we've completely cleared this area," Merit said, cracking his neck. "Let's make it quick so we can focus on the southern portion of the town. If we're lucky, there will be some people left to save."

There were no giants in direct vicinity to the school, but Cosima assumed Ivo and Nariah were responsible for the help, from wherever they were in the city. She hadn't seen them since the encounter where her magic resulted in Merit almost being squished to death. Her cheeks burned at the reminder.

This is precisely what the Divinity was worried about, she thought as she followed Merit. *If I don't consider every possible outcome, there is a chance things will go wrong. Next time, I could seriously injure someone. There has to be a way to navigate this without causing irreparable harm.*

They walked down a street that was eerily quiet. The only sound was created by their feet splashing in puddles from the rain that had not yet dried up, despite the pink sky and bright sun. The rumble and roar of chaos still happening in the southern part of the city was unsettling. Dario created more upheaval than she could have predicted, and somehow, she had yet to find Enzo.

"Do you hear that?" Merit asked, pausing.

Sima stopped walking and waited. A low-frequency thump came from somewhere nearby. "What could be making that sound?"

Merit raised a brow. "I don't know, but I have a crappy feeling we're about to find out."

The ground trembled, softly at first, before it built into a disorienting commotion. Wood and glass rained over them as a horrifying glob of mangled flesh burst through a building. It shape-shifted in front of them as its arms grew to impossible proportions, snaking all throughout the air. The flesh writhed and gurgled as it oscillated between forms in front of them. Misplaced features like half-formed ears and screaming mouths floated by as the mound of skin and muscle produced dozens of disgusting appendages. Its form resembled a nightmarish insect as it closed in on them, pushing Cosima and Merit back to back.

"What is this thing?" Sima choked out.

"Cosmic punishment," the Scout replied. "We must have fucked up bad to deserve this."

The mound of pulsating organs moved closer, and Sima's hand shot out to pause time. At the same moment her magic brought the abomination to a halt, a familiar aura slammed into her, and everything faded to black. All of her fears melted away, and her heart was at peace. She blinked a few times, confused by the luminous wisteria tree in front of her. The delicate flowers were breathtakingly radiant, and their beauty drew her forward.

As she approached, she noticed someone with broad wings standing there. She let out a gasp and ran toward him, not stopping until their bodies collided. Vincenzo's arms wrapped around her, and the delicate warmth of his scent filled her nose. When she pulled back to get a look at his face, his expression broke her. He was distraught, his eyes bloodshot and his cheeks stained with tears.

"Forgive me," he whispered through quivering lips.

Her hand touched his face, trailing his scar. He shuddered in response to her touch. "Forgive you for what?"

"For not being strong enough to withstand this wretched curse."

Sima searched his emerald eyes. "What are you talking about? What's wrong?"

He looked down at his hands and held them out toward her. "Don't you see it?"

Lightning shot through her as her gaze fell onto his hands. His right arm was broken, the bones protruding beneath the skin. Her heart lurched as she realized how much pain he was in. "When did this happen? We need to get Ivo to heal you."

His eyes widened as his gaze slowly fell away from hers. "I think I went too far, Sima. It's taking over my body and I think…I think it's killing me."

The breath left her lungs, and she held his arm against her. "No. Don't say that."

"Can you see the poison?" he asked, his voice barely above a whisper.

"What poison?"

He held his hands toward her once more. "The darkness is spreading. It's taken my whole right arm and nearly half of my left."

Sima shook her head, her pulse quickening. "I only see your broken arm, Enzo."

His face crumpled. "I can feel it growing stronger. I don't know how much time I have left."

"Ivo can heal you, you're not going to die." Tears filled her eyes. "Please don't talk like that."

Enzo's pained gaze locked onto hers. He held his uninjured hand up and waited. Sima lifted hers and pressed her palm against his. The moment their skin touched, a ripple of their magic emerged from their hands. The purple and green energy entwined, like it had twice before. The sensation of it was both thrilling and comforting, leaving her wanting more.

"I'm beyond repair," he murmured, though his eyes softened as their power danced together.

"You're not broken," she whispered, "the shadows inside you are just misunderstood."

She stood on the tips of her toes as she pressed a kiss onto his lips. More of their combined energy surged, creating a soft drum-like beat. Each time their powers threaded together, she was infused with an intimate sense of connection, as though she was learning more about him as the seconds passed. Enzo was terrified of his power and referred to it as a toxic curse, but what Cosima detected of his demanding power only made her trust him more fully. Its strength was inconceivable, but not wicked.

The harmony their energy created together was not an accident—to

Sima, it was a divine orchestration, the foreshadowing of an incandescent future that waited for them on the other side. Everything about Vincenzo's essence was pure, bathed in unfaltering light. She wanted to bask in its brilliance until it infected her, too.

Vincenzo let out a sigh as his lips left hers. "How can you observe my unfiltered soul and not flinch?"

Cosima smiled. "The cadence of your curse serenades me."

Enzo mirrored her expression, and it was bright enough to dissolve the black void surrounding, taking the radiant wisteria tree with it. Returned to reality, Cosima's senses were accosted by the stench of death as she glanced around the city street. She and Enzo stood in several inches of sticky black blood, and the monstrous glob of flesh was gone.

Merit growled from behind her, and Sima flinched as she spun around. The Scout wiped the blood from his face as he stormed up to Enzo and stuck a finger in his face. "Next time, warn me before you do some shit like that. Your magic blew that thing up from the inside out, and I don't know if I'll ever get the smell of this stuff out of my hair."

Demonic screeches roused Ivo from her concussed slumber, her vision full of black spots. Her hand held the bloody wound on the back of her head as she pulled herself off the smooth pebbles beneath her. The sacred courtyard was drenched in bluish purple flesh, black blood pumping through its web-like veins. Nariah's iridescent wings pulsed as she evaded warriors made only of connective tissue and muscle. A small hoard of the disturbing creatures inched toward her, leaving sluggish trails of onyx fluid in their wake.

Ivo's hand trembled as she expelled magic through her palm. "*Onda elettrica*," Ivo shouted. Bright blue energy barreled into the large person-shaped creatures, paralyzing them where they stood as electricity shot through them. "*Legatura della vite!*"

Vines sprouted from the ground and snatched the two smaller creatures. Although they were not as large as the other beings they had encountered in the jungle, these two were nearly twice Ivo's height. Once they were held firmly in place, Nariah flew over and sliced their heads off, bringing an end to their persistent wriggling. The mounds of flesh drenching the sanctuary trembled as bubbles in the tissues morphed into the shape of additional adversaries.

The bones in Ivo's finger ached with the chill of her magic. Ice blue energy barreled out of her, snaking through the air as it obliterated everything in its path. The force of her power stopped her dead in her tracks, and Ivo hissed as the bite of her energy worsened. She balled her fists and took a breath as beasts with thickened purple tissue sprang through the air.

A meaty paw thumped against her chest and threw her onto her back. The beast's face earlier resembled an immortal heart, with chambers that beat with each shuddering breath through its tubular nostrils. Ivo ripped the blade from her holster and slammed it through the creature's face. Her dagger sliced easily through its flesh, and black blood flooded out, drowning her in its forceful flow.

Another pulse of her magic sent the corpse flying, and Ivo flopped onto her stomach and vomited. The blood had a bitter chemical taste, and Ivo could not think as it coated the inside of her throat. Ivo held her palm to her mouth and whispered a water spell as her heart pounded. When enough of the taste had dispersed, she dragged herself to her feet.

To Ivo's left, Nariah fended off a skinless creature that crawled on its hands and knees, its back scraping against the underside of the luminescent trees. Its giant exposed jaw snapped open and shut as it attempted to snatch the Scout out of the air. Ivo rushed over and repeated her electric spell from before, her magic forcing the creature to hold still long enough for Nariah to kill it.

She wiped her blade off on her pants and nodded. "Appreciate it." Her eyes grew wide. "Behind you!"

Ivo whirled around, narrowly spinning out of the grasp of a beast with frightening protruding eyeballs and thin, pointy teeth. She frantically looked around in search of Nariah, but the Scout was nowhere to be found.

With a quick breath, Ivo shouted another spell and threw herself backwards. *"Crollo!"*

The ground beneath the creature gave way, and it disappeared beneath the surface. Ivo cringed as she watched its massive fingers grip onto the edge. Before it could pull itself free, Ivo used her blade to slice its hands off at the knuckles. The ground sewed itself back together as Ivo turned around. A creature with intestines for tentacles waved its appendages around as its body pulsed forward in steady beats.

Ivo ran, pushing herself with all her might, but the creature was faster. Its gray-blue tentacle hovered over her before it plucked her from the ground and brought her towards its circular mouth. Ivo screamed as she fought against its grip, horrified by the sight of its massive teeth. It held her hands at her side, keeping her from using a spell without injuring herself in the process. She turned her body as much as she could, twisting her neck to keep her head out of its mouth. It clamped down on her shoulder, and Ivo cried out in agony as it shredded through her skin.

The scent of burning flesh filled her nose as the Scout called out her name. Seconds later, Ivo collided with the ground, soaked in her own blood and the creature's saliva. She panted as the pain cleared her mind of all thoughts beyond how badly she wanted it to stop. Nariah cut the demented creature's head off and threw her blade, rushing to Ivo's side.

"Ivo." Nariah's voice was hoarse, her features twisting into an expression of despair as her eyes took in Ivo's injury. "What do I do? What do I do, Ivo? Tell me how to fix this. How bad is it? Oh, by the Divine, there's so much blood."

"Calm down," Ivo wheezed, rolling her eyes. She coughed, the motion causing another wave of intense pain to shoot through her injured shoulder. "I'm alive."

Nariah's breath came out ragged. "I can't lose you, please. I'm going to lose my fucking mind."

Ivo narrowed her gaze as her trembling hand touched the ribbons of her skin on her shoulder. "I've been…through much worse…can't kill me that easily."

Nariah held Ivo's face in her hands. "What do I *do*? Tell me, please."

She studied the Scout's gaze and chuckled, finding her worry to be endearing. The action sent another current of pain searing through her body. Ivo swallowed her wince. "Nothing, Nariah. I should be able to heal myself."

"Are you certain it will be enough?" Nariah asked, her purple eyes dripping with evidence of her fear.

Ivo smiled weakly. She had survived Aurelio; this injury would not be enough to stop her. "It'll be enough. As long as I don't get hurt again soon, I'll be fine. I have enough of my magic left to get me out of danger. I can fix the rest later."

With a deep breath, Ivo hovered her hand over her wound and let her magic begin to flow. The blue beam of light was warm as it pierced into her flesh. Although the pain was sharp and made healing herself a slight struggle, she kept a brave face to avoid worrying Nariah further. Soon her wound stopped oozing blood as the skin knit together again. Before she could finish, a commotion set the Scout on edge.

What remained of the discolored fleshy sea covering the floor of the outdoor sanctuary reseeded and congealed beneath one of the glowing trees. The tissue pulsed with a deep orange glow from within. Ivo's magic stuttered, but she tried to keep the flow going as the mound exploded. A man with a haunting aura emerged, and Ivo knew at once it was a Sacred Brother.

Dario wore a thick gold crown adorned with dull jewels atop his black hair. His silver eyes sparkled with malice as his dense brows furrowed. A full beard covered his chin and jaw, hiding his mouth from view. He stuck a hand inside his amber suit and strolled forward. Nariah placed herself between them and held her sword out. Ivo leaned around the Scout's frame to watch as Dario approached.

"Get out of my way, *bug*," he spat, his voice deep and fierce. "You stand between me and my destiny."

"I've come for your head," Nariah hissed. "You're not getting any closer than that."

Dario blinked, and the wind rustled. With a flash, he was standing beside Ivo, towering over her. He crouched down slowly as his hand reached out to cradle her face. Nariah yelled as she flew toward them, only for Dario to cast her aside with a flick of his wrist. His silver eyes bored into hers as he sighed. "My, my, you are stunning, but not the divine light I was hoping to find. Do tell, sweet thing, where is she?"

Ivo's lip curled into a sneer at his mention of Cosima. "Oh, you'll find her soon enough, but only when her blade is finally sinking into your skin."

Dario smiled, his white teeth shining beneath his thick beard. He lightly pinched her chin before he released her. "You're adorable. Too bad it's not your heart I wish to steal."

He stood up and flicked his finger towards himself, causing Nariah to fly forward, stopping only a foot from him. She kicked her feet as he suspended her in the air with his magic. Dario's face morphed into someone Ivo didn't recognize with blue eyes and tan skin. Nariah's face contorted as she screamed obscenities and thrashed her body.

"What's the matter, little bug? Feeling haunted by your past?"

"You deranged fuck." Nariah's foot swiped an inch from Dario, earning her a laugh from him. "Take her face off."

Dario's face morphed back into his own as he threw her to the ground. Ivo cried out and scurried to her side. Nariah wrapped her arm around Ivo's waist and drew her closer, protecting her from Dario. The Sacred Brother cackled as he drew closer. "Your winged lover is not who you believe her to be."

"Shut your fucking mouth," Nariah spat.

Ivo's brows knit together. "What do you mean?"

He adjusted his crown before pulling a cigar from his pocket. His eyes locked onto Nariah. "Your shields aren't as formidable as you might have hoped. A trained insect like you was strong enough to outlast the pressure of my weaker kin, but you have no such luck here." Starlight sprang from his fingertip as he lit it and took a long puff. "I know your truth."

"You know *nothing*." Nariah's body shook as her purple gaze flamed.

"Yet you keep it a secret," Dario mused.

A sickly feeling drenched Ivo's gut. "What is he talking about, Nariah?"

"All of the Sacred Brothers lie, Ivo." The Scout refused to meet her eyes as she spoke and kept her attention on Dario. "Don't believe anything he has to say."

"Even if I am merely trying to give her the transparency you will not?" Dario licked his teeth before taking another drag of his cigar. "Why are you so afraid of her learning of your mixed blood?"

Nariah snarled, launching herself toward him. "Enough!"

Dario's arm grew in size as he swatted her with his giant palm. It returned to normal, and he settled his gaze on Ivo again. "She may despise our Sacred blood, but she has more in common with us than she understands. Her blood may contain a drop from a Celestial Empress, but it is also infused with a drop from a sitting High Priestess."

Ivo's eyes widened as her heart created a racket. "Which one?"

He took another puff of his cigar, his lips curled upward as he blew out the smoke. "I can't give you all the answers, little lamb, that would be too easy. You've got your own shoes to fill, and that bug, whether she knows it or not, seeks to stop you and your dearest friend. Will you allow her to corrupt you?"

The signature rainbow shine of Nariah's wings captured Ivo's attention, and Ivo tilted her head toward the sky. Her body swayed as Merit and Enzo's wings flashed seconds later. Dario's head swiveled as his grin grew larger. "What a delight, dinner has served itself."

Skin and muscle bubbled from the cracks between the smooth pebbles below her. Ivo screamed as she peddled backward. The flesh morphed into dozens of long arms with sharp bones protruding from the tips of the fingers. The appendages shot into the air and dragged Merit toward the ground. He used his starlight to blast away hands, only for more to appear, their fingers shredding his uniform and skin. Red blood poured from his side, and Ivo raised her hands, using her web spell to disrupt the movements of the arms. Merit burst free and grabbed Ivo, moving her out of Dario's immediate vicinity. Enzo hovered above the Sacred Brother as his green eyes pulsed with vibrant energy.

"At last!" Dario held his hands at his sides and spoke with his cigar between his lips. "Bring me my heart's desire, brother. Allow me to marvel in the sweet vengeance that floods her veins."

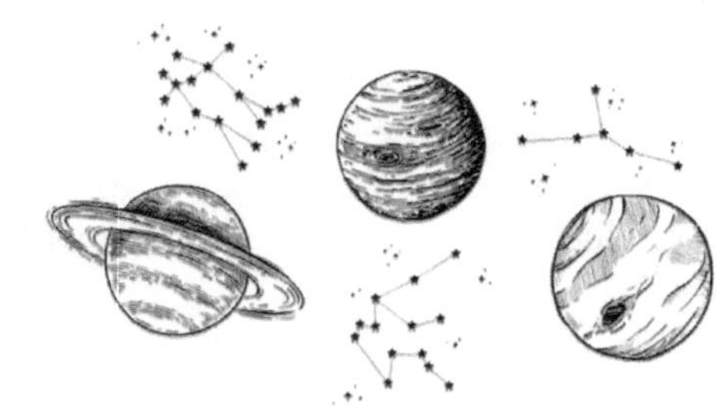

Chapter 38

Cosima

Once Enzo arrived, it had taken almost no time to locate Dario, as the rest of the city had fallen into a deep silence except for the area surrounding the temple Saya had told them about. For some unknown reason, the Sacred Brother had made the decision to focus his efforts on that location only, and thanks to Merit's tracking abilities, they knew Nariah and Ivo were in close proximity to him. Sima struggled to keep her emotions in check as she moved inside the slim, hallway-like structure Enzo had created encircling the entire outside of the temple, weaving around other buildings in the area. It was enough to keep her out of Dario's line of sight while still being able to lend help with her abilities.

Through the thin slats that allowed her to glimpse the sanctuary courtyard, she could make out Merit and Ivo nearest the temple, with Nariah approaching and Enzo stationed in the sky. Her blood chilled as her eyes landed on Dario in his pristine amber suit. Cosima knew it was advantageous to remain hidden, but her mind would not stop urging her to cast aside Vincenzo's plan and make a move.

"You cannot stop what has already been in motion." Dario's voice made her cringe as it wafted in from outside. "The time for untethered creation is upon us. Only the devout will survive."

The walls of Enzo's structure rattled as more of his twisted creations blossomed inside the prayer space. An emerald flash blinded her for a moment as Enzo barreled toward Dario. The Scouts were blurs as they swept through, slicing through tissue with shocking speed. One of the creatures closest to her hiccuped black blood, creating puddles around its claws. It moved on all fours as it swung its lengthy, muscle-covered snout near the ground. The glowing leaves of a nearby tree were pulled in its direction as it sniffed loudly. The creature's chest shook with a low growl as its purple flesh rippled.

"I can smell your soul," it whispered as it lingered mere feet from where Cosima hid inside the structure.

Cosima held her breath as she reached for her magic, intending to pull the creature into a time pocket, when a hand burst through the floor. She dodged its grasp and ran through the hallway, swallowing her scream. The strange creature that had spoken to her galloped alongside the structure, following her. She let the threads burst from her core and selected one. Just as the contorted being moved beneath a tree, Sima snapped its heaviest branch, sending it straight through the creature's back.

She let out a breath as she faced forward and continued moving through the structure, finding herself near the back end of the courtyard. She slowed to a stop as the sounds of the battle outside grew concerning. The Scouts were shouting, but Sima could not make out what they were saying. Sima blinked, and a towering man appeared. She let out a small yell before she clamped her hand over her mouth.

Dario's silver eyes were soft as he stared down at her. "If only you knew my vision for the new world. You would not struggle against me so much. The life we could have together, the power we could hold, and you throw it all away for him? For a boy doomed to die?"

"You're all doomed to die," Sima said as her lip twitched. She settled the rising storm in her gut with a breath. "I intend to take your life, Dario."

"Don't be so quick to violence, my fated darling. You can grow to love me with time," Dario said with a smile.

He stepped toward her, his hand outstretched. Sima's magic ignited, causing an explosion of threads once his skin touched hers. Unlike with Aurelio, she experienced no resistance when her hands weaved into his Fate. The courtyard and the ensuing battle faded from existence as Dario's inner world erupted before her. Images of his life overlapped, creating a chaotic flurry, but through them she gathered a sense of who Dario was.

His essence was perplexing, full of twists and turns she did not expect. She thought his soul would reek of cruelty and arrogance, but she found instead that he was deeply introspective and curious. His memories were riddled with persistent rejection and neglect at the hands of others, as well as humiliation and torture at the hands of his family. Sima cringed as brutal images of Dario receiving his ritualistic beatings from his mother flicked by.

With effort, Sima managed to refocus on the task at hand and began to evaluate the threads of his Fate more closely. One of the strings had a subtle illumination, and her fingers hovered above it. It continued to call to her, and as she selected it, a thrum of energy wafted through her. The thread led directly to her, and through her, she found evidence of his sleepless nights spent dreaming of how he'd love her—all without even knowing what she looked like. The Sacred Brothers had devoted themselves to Cosima in a way that filled her with dread. A plan surfaced in her mind, and Sima shook off her haze.

A tiny tendril of magic won't hurt, Sima thought. *From gentle winds come unspooling threads.*

She manipulated the thread that led to herself, altering his perception of their connection. His desire for her was already at suffocating heights, but his concern for her overall well-being was frighteningly low. He did not love Cosima the way Enzo did—he had been brainwashed into believing she was the answer to his prayers. In his eyes, she represented the means by which he would earn his ascension, and he would do anything to get her, even if it meant containing her as Aurelio had. She tugged him closer to devotion and dove for the surface, desperate to distance herself from his inner world.

Ivo launched multiple sprays of her web spell, creating a difficult terrain beneath the creepy muscle monsters. Sweat covered her brow, and her shoulder ached from her earlier injury. The clothing around her shoulder grew damp as the pain worsened. Ivo had not finished healing her wound, and with more hits to her body, she was beginning to fall apart.

A snake made of purple and blue stitched skin slammed into Ivo, throwing her back against a tree trunk. A stabbing pain in her lower back made her cry out, and when she glanced down at the bloody branch in her abdomen, her mind cleared as her ears rang.

"Ivo, no," Nariah screamed, collapsing at Ivo's side. She patted Ivo's face as Ivo's eyes rolled back. "No, no, no. Stay with me."

Her vision went black, and Ivo sank somewhere deep inside herself.

When she opened her eyes, she found herself thrust into a black void. A woman appeared, too powerful to merely be a Goddess with her intolerable aura. Her mind screamed as her bones began to break beneath the woman's vibrating energy. The mythical woman snapped her fingers, and all of Ivo's agony faded away. Ivo's hands slipped across her body, ensuring she was truly whole again.

"It won't last," the woman said, her voice rich and captivating. "But I could not stand to see you suffer."

Without the pain, she could fully regard the stranger. Rivers of inky black hair trailed to just inches above her bare feet. The woman wore a luxurious dress made of the night sky, its skirts ending above her knees, with two moons adorning her earlobes. Her skin was marked with elegant symbols Ivo did not recognize, shimmering with rainbows of light in the designs. Her pensive, pure white eyes did not leave Ivo's.

"W-who are you?" Ivo squeaked.

"Nyssa," she replied simply, as if her name carried weight.

Ivo, however, did not know about the Eternal Kingdom like the others. "Nice to meet you, I'm Ivo."

Nyssa cracked a smile. "I know who you are, child."

Her heart raced. "How?"

"There is little I do not know, to put it lightly. When you awaken, your pain will return, but you will not die, little butterfly. There is more to be done."

"What am I supposed to do?"

Nyssa gave a small, sad smile. "I cannot tell you myself, or I would, child. You will not remember this encounter when I return you to your vessel, but know, in this moment, I visit you often."

Ivo opened her mouth to speak, but darkness swallowed Nyssa, leaving her standing alone. She blinked, and her memory was wiped clean as a wave of pain slammed into her. She let out a whimper as she teetered on the line between consciousness and the void.

Cosima

When Cosima emerged from the Sacred Brother's threads, she found herself wrapped in Dario's arms with her hand touching his face. His silver eyes dripped with adoration as he softened his grip and released her. Sima took a few steps back and watched him carefully. From what she could discern, it seemed as though only seconds had passed while she was altering his Fate. The scent of burnt flesh in the air was accompanied by the bitter scent of the spilled black blood from the continuing fight happening in the courtyard.

"Do you know why it has to be you?" he asked in a hushed voice.

Sima's heartbeat made her sway slightly. "Because of the blood I share with Kismet?"

Dario smiled. "You're a clever girl, but that is not the only reason." He took a slow step to the side and walked around her as he inspected her from head to toe. "They speak of a daughter of Fate herself, the one with love pure enough to redeem even the most decayed soul, renewing and replenishing what time would never be able to. Many are preoccupied with that requirement, but they fail to embrace the bigger picture. Your pure blood and magnificent power allow you to wash us of our sin, but it is your unique soul that is the key."

Sima's mind flicked back to her time spent with Aurelio. The entire time she had been carrying out his bidding, she was opening and closing the portal. She had been the key in that situation, too. "How so?"

Shrieks of pain rang out, too high-pitched to belong to any of her friends. Sima's heart skipped as she glimpsed the courtyard through the thin slats. Enzo was at the center, using his starlight to scald a shifting blob of disfigured body parts that grew in size by the second. Dario cocked his head to the side as he watched her.

"Eventually. We will have filled this realm to the brim, and when creation reaches its maximum, the mounting pressure will break this system entirely, and it will be redirected somewhere else. In order for this to happen, a renewal must take place. The entire Ethereal Realm must be cleansed, including the Eternal Kingdom, so that we may ascend."

She grew restless conversing with him, and a plan pieced together inside her head. The blade she needed was in her possession. All she would need to do is get close enough to take his life. She crossed her arms over her chest. "Where am I involved in that?"

"Your magic is only amplified by your soul." He inched closer as his eyes lingered on her lips. "When the time is right, it is the synchronization of our bonded power that will lift the restrictions on our realm and allow it to expand. Think of all we could create with eternity at our sides and the emptiness of space waiting for us to fill it."

"Why do you desire to take this position by force?" Sima asked, keeping her body still as he moved close enough for her to catch a hint of his vanilla amber scent. His fragrance was welcome among the stench of death from outside. "Why did Ehses create twelve sons to overthrow the High Priestesses if this expansion is supposedly so beneficial?"

His finger twirled a lock of her black hair as her ears caught Ivo's voice shouting out spells. "The Divinity struggle to accept that their reign has come to an end. Even the Celestial Empresses are nearing their combustion. They had their chance to evolve into the leaders this realm needed them to be, but they failed. You are the solution."

Sima's heart dropped, heavy like an anchor in her ribcage. No matter which of them spoke of using her, it never failed to make her feel slimy, as if she were a doll—a placeholder for their demented desires, made to act as they commanded. Sima leaned closer to him, pulling her blade free with a swift movement before she wrapped her arms around his waist. She stared up at him as she angled the tip toward his back.

"What if I don't agree with killing the High Priestesses and changing the Eternal Kingdom?"

His eyes danced with delight as he pressed his body into hers. "When you know the truth, you will realize there is no choice. The elders know they are running out of time, and they're desperate enough that their masks are slipping." He searched her eyes before he let out a small breath. "I know you love little twelve, but that is precisely why the Divinity sent him here. He is doomed to implode, darling girl. They're hoping he finds his end outside of the Kingdom because they hope the ripple of his destruction is too far away for them to feel."

Sima's chest ached. Her hand gripped her blade harder to keep her fingers from trembling. "What are you talking about?"

"They sent you on a mission to find what remains of my kin," Dario hummed, "because they knew none of us would harm you in the process of eliminating him. They bet on the fact that each of us would writhe with wrath when we got a whiff of your tether to little twelve."

His face hovered an inch above hers. Before he could press his lips onto hers, she shoved the blade through his back as her magic funneled into it. His expression crumpled as he cried out. Sima yanked her weapon free and shoved him backward. He fell onto the ground, pulling her down with him. The blade pierced him once more, and his hand held hers in place as the hilt rested against his skin.

"You've made a mistake, my fated darling. Don't you understand? I'm not as irredeemable as you believe." Blood spotted his lips as he tugged her close enough to feel his breath on her face. "Do you know where evil comes from? How does it choose its next vessel? What percentage of *insane* do they have to be, how far from the light do they have to stray, to be unworthy of rescue? What sin stains my soul beyond recognition?"

Sima struggled against him, attempting to free herself from his grasp. One hand continued to hold her blade in place as the other wrapped around the back of her neck. "I saw the chaos you've caused in your memories. I didn't need to see all of it to know you are just like the rest of them."

"I did not ask for this role, but without death there cannot be transformation," he hissed, scarlet liquid dripping from the side of his mouth. "My mother forced me to become who I am. It was her guiding hand that led me to claim the lives of innocents, and I am now a tortured soul addicted to spilling blood. I'm trapped, chained by my destiny to destroy what blocks my path. All I need is your love."

With another burst of movement, Sima managed to free her knife. Before he could react, she slowed time and drove her blade into his chest. She met his silver gaze as small purple arcs of energy danced around her weapon. "You don't deserve it."

Dario's voice dropped low in a desperate plea as he coughed up more blood. "If I am corrupt, wrong to my core, won't you fix me? I never wanted to be bad. I never wanted hands that could kill before they could love. I never wanted to be a monster, and yet every day I walk the path of deformed and deranged passions. I am out of breath, drowning in my sins. Don't you see me? Isn't there something worth saving?"

He sputtered, his breath going ragged as the light faded from his eyes. His chest stopped rising, and her grip on the blade loosened. Sima's eyes watered. From fear, fatigue, or sympathy, she did not know, but his words lingered in her mind as tears streaked her cheeks. Her knees wobbled as she stood up, her thudding heartbeat accompanied by a screaming headache. She rested her foot on his chest before she yanked her weapon free.

The noise from outside grew loud enough to hurt her ears. Black blood flooded in from the courtyard through an opening she couldn't detect. The thick liquid washed over her legs, reaching high enough to submerge her ankles. She glanced down at her feet and nearly collapsed.

Dario had disappeared.

As Ivo's eyes rolled open, her mind became intensely aware of the pain plaguing her body. She glanced down and let out a ragged sigh of relief that she was no longer impaled on a branch. The wound remained, but she was now leaning up against the trunk of the tree a few inches to the side of where she had been injured. In the span of only a few hours, she had hit her head, gotten her shoulder shredded by a giant, and been skewered by a branch. Her unsteady hand pressed into her abdomen in an attempt to slow the bleeding, but Ivo knew the situation was grim. She did not have enough magic remaining to heal herself.

Between fighting off giants and keeping herself alive, she had run herself nearly dry. Her vision was blurry, but she could barely make out Nariah's form in front of her, continuing to fend off the fleshy creatures. She opened her mouth to call out the Scout's name, but no words would form. Black spots formed in her vision, and Ivo thought she might pass out again, plagued by the fear she wouldn't wake up again.

The ensuing battle faded in and out of view as Ivo's blood coated her hand. Her head rolled back, but before she fully lost consciousness, Nariah grabbed her by the shoulders and shook her. Ivo blinked off her confusion and looked past the Scout. Standing behind them was Merit, buying Nariah enough time to tend to Ivo.

"Stay with me," Nariah pleaded, pressing her hands on top of Ivo's, applying more pressure to her wound. "Don't fall asleep. I need you to stay awake."

"Hurts…" Ivo squeaked.

Nariah's eyes watered as she smoothed down Ivo's hair with the back of her hand. "I know, I know. I am going to get you out of here. I don't care what it takes. I am going to find the portal and get us off this planet."

"Sima," Ivo breathed.

The Scout shook her head. "You can't worry about her right now. If I don't get you back to the Eternal Kingdom, you're not going to survive. I won't let you die, Ivo."

The ground trembled, and black blood sprayed across them. Merit inched closer as he continued to swing his sword and spray his starlight. "We need to move, Nariah. Dario vanished, but his magic isn't letting up. Enzo is pinned by giants on the other side of the courtyard. I need to help him, but first you have to get her out of here."

Nariah stared into Ivo's eyes. "I'm going to try and wrap your wound the best I can, and then I am going to have to carry you. It is going to hurt, but I have to do this to stop the bleeding."

Ivo weakly nodded her head. "Alright."

Nariah tore Merit's cape off and pulled up Ivo's shirt. The sight of her own wound made her queasy, and Ivo stared up at the glowing leaves above them. One leaf broke off from the branch and fell in dawdling swoops, mesmerizing her mind, which was delirious from blood loss. She bit her lip as Nariah shoved fabric into the gaping hole in her body. The anguish was sharp enough to induce hallucinations, making Ivo feel as though she had been ejected from her vessel. The out-of-body experience was addled with strange, incomprehensible visions.

When it finally came to an end, she fell into a deep slumber, desperate to distance herself from the agony. A jostling sensation woke her, and Ivo realized she was flying through the jungle once more in Nariah's arms. They had somehow escaped the city and were moving at such high speeds that Ivo once again grew nauseous. She slammed her eyes shut and focused on breathing to keep her stomach from tossing its contents.

They flew for what seemed like hours, with Ivo fading in and out as they traveled. A low person-like groan sent chills through her, and she nuzzled her face deeper into Nariah's chest. The Scout's scent was comforting, like lilies and jasmine, and her heart pounded against Ivo's cheek as she weaved through the trees. Ivo let her gaze drift over the unique world. *Will this be the last thing I ever get to see? Do my travels through the universe end here?*

The thundering of enormous footsteps echoed behind them, and Ivo's heart pinched. Nariah held her closer as she pushed her wings even harder. The Scout's face was red as it dripped with sweat, and Ivo couldn't help but find her beautiful. Tears welled in her eyes as she looked up at the woman who had become her savior and willing protector in just a few short weeks.

She desperately wanted to confess her love for Nariah, but breathing was growing more laborious by the second, and even keeping her eyes open was draining. Ivo studied Nariah's features, hoping to burn them into her soul, so even after death she would not forget the Scout's face. If she had the means, Ivo would turn back time and not waste Nariah's attempts to deepen their connection on petty arguments based on her insecurities. The regret was second only to the burning admiration she held for the Scout. Not even Dario's attempt to manipulate her had changed the way Ivo felt for Nariah.

Trees slammed into the ground as the beasts closed the distance between them. Nariah's eyes were wild as she focused straight ahead. Ivo knew if the Scout was not so focused on keeping her alive, she would be able to fight back. Instead, she pressed a kiss to Ivo's head and kept her arms locked tightly around her.

The screaming howls of the giants worsened by the second, and the vibration from their determined footsteps made Ivo nauseous. Nariah zipped side to side, evading incoming swipes from humongous hands, but the Scout was running out of steam, and Ivo was running out of breath. Ivo accepted the fact that she was going to die and only hoped she would pass in the safety of Nariah's embrace and not be crushed between the teeth of a living nightmare.

A hand sprouted from the trees directly in front of them, catching the Scout off guard. As she maneuvered out of the way, the creature snagged Nariah by her wing, sending Ivo flying from her arms. She collided with the red mud, the impact painless in comparison to the suffering her abdominal wound caused her. Nariah's voice trembled with rage as she screamed, slicing her way through flesh to get closer to Ivo.

Amber flashed in front of her eyes, and Ivo's breath caught. She blinked slowly as she weakly lifted her head. The Sacred Brother stood before her, a red-tinged hole in the center of his suit. Dario leaned forward and touched her face. "Tiny weaver, you're so near death's eternal river. Would it be right of me to watch the fire extinguish in your eyes, or should I tempt the winds of Fate?"

Ivo locked onto his silver eyes, her fingers cold as ice. Nariah's butterfly wings flickered behind him, and Dario raised a hand toward her. She sliced through it with her sword, earning her a displeased glance from him. His skin slowly melded back together, and he sighed.

"You Trine Scouts really are the definition of infestation. Always buzzing where you're not meant to be." Dario snapped his fingers, and gray hands as tall as Nariah erupted from the ground and held her down. Ivo let out a gasp, and Dario turned to her. "Where were we? Ah, yes. I may be a madman, but I am not entirely cruel."

Dario pressed a finger to her abdomen, and all of the air escaped her lungs. Ivo writhed as a terrifying sensation shot through her core. It felt as though all of the tissue inside her body was being stretched beyond its limits and knit together. Ivo cried out as Dario laughed.

"Let go of her," Nariah yelled. "I'm going to kill you for hurting her."

"Relax," Dario said over his shoulder. "I am atoning for my sins as we speak."

A burning hot sensation speared through her, and after a moment, it dissolved, taking the rest of her stomach pain along with it. Ivo's hands clutched her abdomen, the skin smooth and unmarred, before she caught his gaze.

"Why?"

He shrugged. "Should this whole prophecy not go the way I planned, your existence will prove to be yet another obstacle for my remaining brother."

Starlight shot upward through the trees, and Nariah broke free from Dario's trap. She threw herself at him with her teeth bared and her sword in hand. She stabbed it through his chest, and Dario let out a soft grunt. "I should have squashed you the first time we met, bug."

Dario's hand reshaped into a jagged blade, and he shoved it through Nariah's core. Ivo screamed as she fell onto her knees in the red mud. Scarlet dripped from the Scout's mouth as her eyes grew wide. Dario yanked his arm free and attacked again. His blade, made of bone, sliced through Nariah's neck, causing her head to fall into the mud, the Scout's purple gaze still laced with fear. Ivo's heart skipped several beats as her entire world turned upside down.

Another blood-curdling scream tore through Ivo's throat, shaking the jungle as she crawled forward. The glowing insects hiding in the domes at the top of the trees created a dense cloud as they fled the area. Thunder rumbled above them as Ivo stared in disbelief at Nariah's head. It rested beside her body as the blood pouring from her neck created puddles in the mud.

Dario's laughter echoed as he vanished, leaving Ivo alone with the shattered pieces of her heart and the mutilated body of the woman she loved as the rain washed away her tears.

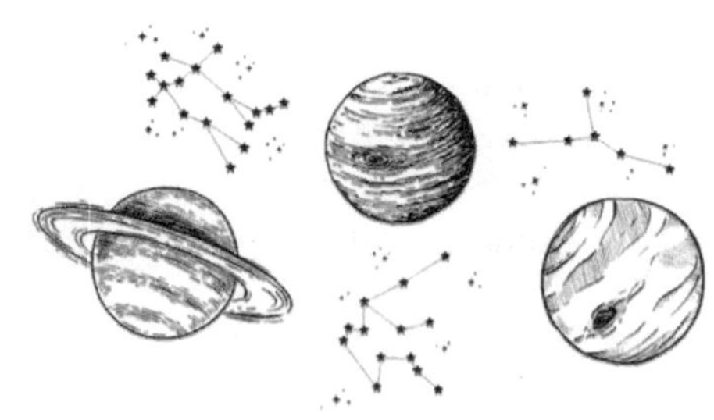

Chapter 39

Vincenzo

With another ball of his energy, Enzo cleared a sizable section of the flesh, burning it to ash. He moved toward the direction he felt Cosima in, her fear at the forefront of his mind as he moved. Dario had managed to isolate himself with Cosima while amping up the mayhem in the courtyard to keep Enzo at bay. It had bought his brother some time, but that was coming to an end as Enzo manipulated the wall of his structure and created an opening.

Her love is not an accolade. It is your fiercest mercy, his curse murmured.

He flew forward and through the hole, careful to meander around the beast he had killed. He found Cosima standing there with a dazed expression. "My love, are you hurt?"

Sima glanced up at him as he fluttered to her side. She steadied herself against him before she looked into his eyes. "I killed him, or at least I thought I did. I stabbed him in the heart, and he stopped breathing. I looked away for one second, and when I turned back, he was gone."

"It's going to be alright," he said, pressing a kiss to her head. "I'm not going to let him get away."

Based on the way his curse was curling into knots inside him in response to Dario's harrowing aura, Enzo guessed his brother was still nearby. It was doubtful his brother would flee, even if Cosima had gravely injured him. Dario was likely preparing himself to strike again, and Enzo was prepared.

Despite not having had a true break from his magic expenditure in quite some time, Enzo's power had never felt so endless. Cosima and Merit could not see the curse's poisonous tattoo creeping up his arms, nor could they sense the way his heart had slowed to a near stop inside his chest. He took it as a sign that his dark companion had not fully consumed him, even if it was getting harder to think straight the more his curse yearned for violence.

A deafening scream lit up the sky as a giant bellowed from outside. Enzo peered through the hole and frowned at the sight of dozens of enormous beings crushing buildings with their feet. Nariah and Merit zipped by, and seconds later, body parts rained from the sky. The Scouts sliced through fingers, hands, and even jaws as they hacked away at the howling giants.

A flash of amber light came from the center of the courtyard, and Dario emerged, his body growing rapidly in size. He towered eight feet above them as his skin rippled, armor made of bone covering his body. Enzo turned to Sima and pressed a kiss to the back of her hand. "Now is our chance. I love you."

"I love you, Enzo. Let's make the sky rain with his blood."

Enzo smiled, letting his eyes soak in the sight of her one last time before he shot into the air. His wings pulsed with added energy from his magic, sending him soaring toward Dario. Like weeds sprouting from the ground, more of his fleshy minions emerged, growing to full size within seconds. Cosima's energy collided with him at the same moment he manifested a long scythe in his hand.

With the aid of her magic, Enzo's scythe spun through the air, causing the heads of ten beasts to slide off their bodies and flop onto the smooth pebbles below. Dario launched a punch, his arm stretching as it extended toward him. Enzo grunted as Dario's fist slammed into him and flipped through the air. He righted himself with his wings before he hit a glowing tree. His ears caught a subtle whistle, and Enzo darted to the left, narrowly evading a projectile made of bone, courtesy of his brother.

Enzo raised his hands at his sides, and shimmering prisms erupted from the ground. He threw them, and waves of Sima's violet indigo light sparkled inside the clear crystals as they spiraled through the air. Her power ensured each of the prisms made an impact with either Dario or his disfigured creatures. Chunks of Dario's flesh were missing, leaving his body riddled with holes. His brother laughed as his skin closed around the openings and sealed them shut.

His curse bubbled to the surface, and light burst from Enzo's eyes. He flew toward Dario as his magic poured from his fingers, drenching them in a dark void. It transformed within seconds, creating a maze of spinning blades that diced through Dario's body, creating a dozen meaty chunks out of him. His brother's tissue melted and slithered away, before gray skin coiled around his blades and rendered them inert.

"You thought I wouldn't find out?" Dario croaked, his body melding together. "About the bond? With someone as unworthy as you? You know the pain of severing your tether will kill you, don't you?"

Focus, his curse hissed. *Feel the fury of your blood and send his soul into the ether.*

"You won't get the chance," Enzo hissed, his body seizing with energy.

Although there was not much he had learned from their brother Alvize's invading gifts of wisdom, he had discovered that a bond between a Sacred Brother and the daughter of Fate could be replicated by any of them. He also knew that it could be severed, the act of which would kill the brother on the other end of her tie. Enzo had spent long enough doubting his connection to her, and he did not intend to allow anyone to get close enough to destroy it.

He would not let Dario take her. He would not let anyone take her.

Vincenzo's fear and rage made him rabid, and though he could feel himself teetering over the edge, he could not stop his descent into madness, hurling rational thought far from his mind. Enzo's power shifted, taking on a new virulence as he once again pushed past boundaries, plunging deeper into the well of tempting magic inside him. It reached for him at the same time, the energy so potent that pieces of himself crumbled beneath it, dissolving to give way for greater and greater strength. He was drunk on the insatiable power.

The force holding them to the ground inside his void eroded, causing them to float into the dark black sky. Enzo used blasts of his starlight to hurtle through the air as Dario whirled himself in circles. As he closed in, his brother caught on and used his own light to move himself out of the way of Enzo's incoming attack. Enzo pivoted and, with freezing fingers, manifested thousands of metal stakes in the shape of a sphere around Dario. He held his brother in place as he surged forward with the crystal-imbued blade he had used to kill Carmine in his hand.

As the stakes dissolved, Enzo slashed at Dario's chest and neck. His brother's eyes were wide, his pale lips snarling as he worked to mend the flesh Enzo fervently flayed. Dario gurgled blood as he attempted to form words, some of it splattering across Enzo's face as he tugged his blade free. Dario's hands flailed at his sides, not coordinated enough to reach his neck. His head dangled back at an angle, muscles and tissue exposed.

"Look at me, brother." Vincenzo snatched him by the back of his head, his fingers twisting in Dario's black hair. "See how it is the one our siblings called weak—the one they underestimated, the one they thought was incapable of outlasting them—that takes your life."

Rain poured from the perpetual night sky, drenching them both, the fierceness of the storm mirroring his own transformation. His eyes turned wholly black, his half-day and half-night sea of hair floated above him as his magic created emerald green sparks along his blade. Cracks spread across the gem inside, but it did not come apart; instead, it hovered inside the groove where it rested, held back only by the metal prongs on the outside. It rattled as he stabbed it into Dario's eye, and Enzo laughed, relishing his brother's rabid screams.

Enzo let enormous waves of his magic flood through the weapon and into his brother, the magnetic ebb and flow of unstoppable power more addictive than he ever imagined. He struggled to pull himself back from the edge, and for a moment, he forgot about every misfortune he had experienced—for in this moment, Enzo was unstoppable.

Only when he felt Dario's aura fade into oblivion did Enzo remember where he was. Somehow, his void had disintegrated, and he was standing in the courtyard as a storm thundered above. Threatening arcs of his electrified energy lashed out at random, and Enzo could not end the outpour of his magic. He bucked against his curse's control, but he was bound within its lust for vengeance. Images of Sostene's face flashed behind his closed eyes, and Enzo toppled to his knees.

Your journey is nearing its glorious finale, his curse whispered. *Let your rage slumber, for soon you will taste the sugary core of righteous victory.*

Enzo panted as his magic tapered off at a pace slow enough to drive him mad. He struggled to catch his breath as his vessel ached with regret. He would not be able to stop the thrum of his curse until all of his brothers were dead. His heart crawled to a stop, beating only once every few minutes, and as water pattered against his head, Vincenzo realized no rain would ever be enough to cleanse him of his mistakes.

Cosima

Sima trembled where she stood, her heart rapidly thumping as her mouth hung open. During their battle, the two had disappeared into one of Enzo's voids, only to return just as he dealt the killing blow. The sky darkened, and rain poured, drenching Enzo as he let Dario's limp body drop to the ground. Her mind was blank with disbelief as her eyes hovered over Dario's corpse. She waited for the man to move or disappear, as he had after she had stabbed him, but the Sacred Brother remained still. Vincenzo had killed him.

Cosima flicked her gaze back to Enzo, studying the deep lines in his face from his scowl. His eyes were wholly black as electricity surrounded him, magic coming off him in sharp, starling waves. The water that dribbled across his head cooled his rage, allowing his eyes to clear their darkened ash. The green stare she knew and loved returned to its usual vibrant hue, but rigid horror locked his features. Enzo choked out a half-sob and swayed on his feet.

The sacks of flesh created by Dario slowly turned to ash and washed away with the storm, leaving only thick puddles of black blood behind. Her footsteps were sticky as she made her way towards Enzo, careful to avoid the magic that continued to pump out of him at a staggering pace.

"Vincenzo," she whispered. He glanced around, but his eyes were vacant and distant. Electricity continued to arc at random around them, creating a web of dangerous energy that kept her from getting closer. "Can you hear me?"

"Sima," he breathed, looking toward her with oceans in his gaze. "What have I done?"

The question made her chest ache. "You killed Dario."

Sima's pulse quickened as she stared down at the powerful waves of his green energy. She wasn't sure what made her step forward, but when she did, his magic redirected around her instead of hitting her directly. Sima pressed her lips into a line and made her way to him, the shifting electricity strong enough that it created an audible buzz that grew louder as she approached.

His eyes widened, and his breath grew heavier. "I killed him, Sima. That means there are only three of us left." He looked down at his hands as they shook violently. "I stopped holding back, I gave into my curse, but what if it was a mistake? I feel different now, like the very truth of who I am has shifted. What if I'm not the same man anymore?"

She could not lie to him. She could sense the shift in him, as if his transformation was palpable through the connection she believed they shared. He stared up at her, holding his breath, and as she searched his devoted gaze, the words came from her heart. "It doesn't change anything between us, Enzo. I still trust you. I still love you."

Sima searched his eyes as she gingerly brushed her hand against his cheek. His magic shot through her, coaxing her own power out of her hands. Violet, indigo, and emerald sparks lit up the sky around them like a dazzling night sky. Their entwined power brought her an addictive sense of pleasure as her body hummed in response to it. His brows were furrowed as he leaned forward and pressed a kiss on her lips.

Stunning explosions of their harmonic flow created a cosmic backdrop to their moment as more of Vincenzo's power combined with hers. The strength of their bond intensified, and for the first time, Cosima felt as though she had gotten a true glimpse into his inner world. She had touched his Fate, but she had never experienced the unfiltered song of his soul.

Her fingers snaked through his hair as his arms wrapped tightly around her waist. Vincenzo's nightmares, his grief, and his overwhelming adoration of her all skirted through her mind as she let his authentic self drench her from head to toe. The intimidating power lurking deep within him scurried to the surface in search of her, as though it knew she would not run away from it.

Every corner of his curse was at the forefront of her thoughts, brushing against her like a familiar friend. She felt its sharp edges and, at last, understood Enzo's reservations about his power. He doubted his ability to wield his gift without being crushed beneath it. The magnitude of his magic was inconceivable, and yet still, she found no reason to fear it. His curse brought her peace as if its existence was proof he would outlast his brothers.

Sima pulled her lips from his. "It has to be you who survives this, Enzo. You were blessed with this power. It calls to you because you are the only one capable of commanding it with purity. I won't give my heart to anyone else. If this change to the Eternal Kingdom is imminent and I must oversee it, it will only be with you as my husband."

Finally, his outpour of energy came to an end, and his eyes softened. "I never wanted to be a king or an emperor, Cosima, but I would do anything to stay by your side. I want what you do, and I'll do whatever it takes to give it to the future of your dreams."

Motion flickered in the sky, and their heads snapped upward. Merit descended with a grim look on his face. The Scout held his arm, his uniform drenched in crimson beneath his hand. "Nariah and Ivo fled into the jungle, but I think something went wrong. I've been tracking both of them, and I can't figure out where Nariah is. Plus, the last I saw of Ivo, she was badly injured."

Cosima's heart jumped into her throat. Enzo pulled her into his arms, and within seconds, they were in the air, following after Merit. Sima did her best to hold back her tears as they entered the jungle, despite how heavy her chest felt. She had been so focused on Enzo and Dario that her best friend was left to deal with her injuries alone. Although she knew berating herself internally would not resolve the situation, the thoughts kept swarming her, only ceasing when Sima's eyes fell on Nariah's decapitated body.

The rain had not stopped, and Ivo was so cold that her teeth chattered. Her shoulder and head ached as Dario's healing remedied her abdominal wound only. As Ivo shivered against Nariah's body, she wished he had killed her instead of the Scout, or at least done her the mercy of allowing them to die together. When hushed voices came from behind her, Ivo tensed. She was not prepared to see them.

"Ivo. Are you alright?" Cosima was the first to approach. Her feet sank into the mud as she stood above Ivo. "I'm here with you. You're not alone."

"I don't want to let go. I want to stay here."

"I understand," Sima said gently. "But it's pouring out and you're hurt. Your shoulder is still bleeding, and you need to be healed."

"No!" Ivo snarled. Hurt was not enough to describe what she was experiencing, but none of the pain came from her wounds—solely her heart. "I want to stay here."

Ivo lay her head back on Nariah's chest, wishing it would rise again, that her body would be warm again. If she had to freeze in the mud, then so be it. At least they would be together. Somewhere in her abdomen, there was a distant burning pain, but her grief outweighed what lingered after Dario's handiwork. She let the blood and rain soak her clothing, ignoring the progressively weaker grasp she held on the world around her.

Enzo's face crowded her vision. He was crouched down in front of her, on the opposite side of Nariah. His face was lit with worry, but he smiled at her. "Ivo…"

"I know, Enzo," she replied. "I know. But I can't leave."

"You are hurt. Sima's right, we need to get you back to the Kingdom."

"Sima," Ivo said. Her heart squeezed. "Can you fix this?"

Ivo felt her stomach drop as Sima's face twisted. "No. I can't bring her back."

A rogue tear fell, followed by the flood she had been holding back. Two people. Ivo had been brave enough in her unremarkable life to love two people, and both were savagely taken.

She sobbed, clutching Nariah's cape in one of her hands. "She can't be dead!"

"She is," Enzo said, his voice hushed. "There is nothing more we can do for her here. Come with us so we can take her back to the Eternal Kingdom."

Ivo said nothing and reduced herself to a puddle of tears, the rain slowing to a drizzle as she clutched Nariah's cold arms, positioning the Scout to hold her in a chilly embrace. Sima gently rubbed Ivo's back as she cried, and though Ivo could not bear to look her friend in the eye, she was grateful she did not have to be alone with her misery.

"I'm sorry, Nariah. I should have told you. I should have said something, but I thought…"

Stupid. So foolish.

Ivo had been here before. She squeezed her eyes shut, a small groan escaping her lips from the pain in her gut. Her last romantic partner had been killed by Aurelio. She knew better than to develop feelings, but her affection was impossible to suffocate. Instead, embers grew into raging adoration, the beautiful blooming of something she had wanted to see through. Now, there would be no future. To some degree, she had known this would be the case, but she assumed it was because Nariah was a Scout, not because she would die.

Dead. She's dead.

Ivo tried to let the words sink in, but she flinched and rejected them each time her mind lingered over the idea. She refused to believe it. Instead, she pressed her eyes shut, sealing herself into her thoughts. Nariah was *not* dead. She could not be dead. That would be too cruel, would be too much agony for one person to tolerate. Did Fate hate her? Had she been cursed? Her feelings for the Scout had been confusing before, but now there was a desolate resolution, a clear answer where there had not been one before. Their love had a dramatic and irreversible end, and there was nothing she could do about it.

At that moment, a piece of her broke open, and through her internal gates came waves of a mysterious energy. It ravaged through her body, flooding her skin and muscles with the sensation of thousands of needles poking through her skin. She grit her teeth as more of it poured from within until it tipped over the edge and began to fill the world around her with blue electricity, even though she had not called out a spell. Her grief magnified, and she crumpled in on herself as Sima and Enzo cried out. She did not look at them as she curled into a ball, as the pain of losing Nariah ripped her into shreds. Her magic came with fierce intensity as she let out agonized moans.

"I can't do it," she cried, speaking to the vision of the Scout in her mind. "I can't go on without you. Why did you do this to me?"

She had fallen in love with Nariah, through every scalding interaction, through every heated debate. And now, she was gone. Ivo would never have the chance to tell her how she felt, would never have the chance to beg for a stolen future, a romance she did not deserve. She could not lay herself at Nariah's feet and commit herself to the fury she inspired in Ivo's gut, could not vent the flames of frustration through passion. Their stolen exchanges would be all she would ever get, and it would never be enough.

"Ivo," Sima warned, her voice lit with concern. "Be careful."

"No," Ivo snapped. "Leave me here to die."

"You know I can't do that. You're losing color, fast. You need a healer. We don't have time."

Ivo winced, hating the way her friend's words sounded. More of her magic flared, forcing Sima to back up several feet. "What will happen to her in the Eternal Kingdom?"

Sima held her hands up. "Whatever happens, we will try our best to make sure you're included, after you see a healer. I know it's selfish of me to ask you to be strong right now, but I can't let you die, Ivo. I need my best friend. I promise I will fight to give you access to Nariah during their traditional ceremony."

"You don't get to make those decisions," Ivo said coldly. "What if they take her and I never see her again?"

Once again, Sima was silent. Ivo clung to Nariah, letting herself pretend that they were lying together in bed, letting the warm summer air waft through the windows while they slept. She wrapped herself in the protective hug of delusion, her daydreams filled with sweet, tender moments. Ones where they did not have to hide behind attitudes and arguments, but where they put their pent-up energy to good use and left each other spent. All she had to remember Nariah by was an inevitable, heated release, one they were destined toward since they entered into each other's orbits. Now Ivo was adrift in space, with no direction.

Merit's face appeared in front of her, his expression softer than Ivo had ever seen. "Hey."

Ivo frowned. "What?"

"This fucking sucks, right?"

Her face crumpled. "Yeah."

"I know it's bad, some truly downright unfair shit. But Nariah wouldn't want you to cling to her like this. She would be heartbroken to think of you making a fuss over her instead of getting yourself to safety. She may not have had a chance to tell you, but Nariah loved you. Save yourself, if only because it's what she would've wanted. It's not fair, and Fate's fucked up, but you can roll with the punches. She went out saving you, don't let it be in vain."

Nariah loved me? Ivo thought. She pictured the Scout's purple gaze and her heart squeezed. *I loved you, too.*

Ivo knew he was right. Eventually, Nariah's body would disappear. It was a cold shell that once held her essence, and her body was losing its familiarity by the fleeting second. Struggling to accept the loss for what it was, but subduing herself anyway, Ivo sat up, turning her head so she would not have to see Nariah's gruesome injuries. Sima held her hand and guided her to her feet.

"I will never be ready," Ivo murmured. Her resignation made her shoulders droop, but she allowed herself to tumble into Sima's waiting arms.

"I know," Sima said.

Her simple reply comforted Ivo, and they leaned against each other as they made for the portal.

Chapter 40

Her body was numb as she walked with her arms wrapped around herself. She hardly remembered she had been injured at all as she focused on remaining upright. Behind her, Enzo carried Nariah's body. Despite her better judgment, Ivo turned and found that Merit was bare-chested beneath his cape, covering something in his black shirt as he cradled it in his arms.

Ivo knew immediately that it was Nariah's head.

Sima held her steady as Ivo's knees gave out. She gave an anguished cry, ignoring whatever the others were saying to her. Sima pressed her hands to Ivo's face and forced their eyes to meet. "You can do this," Sima said.

Ivo nodded, wrapping her arms around Sima's waist. She buried her face into Sima's clothing and stood there while Merit used his starlight to activate the portal. Ivo only knew it was time to go when she felt herself pushed gently over the threshold, causing her to lose her hold of Sima in the process.

She desperately wanted to crawl back, but it was too late. The tapestry of the universe gripped her firmly, and the world, where she lost the Scout she never planned to love, faded away. Ivo willed herself to remain calm as the sensations from the inter-dimensional roadway made her skin feel too tight against her muscles. Her grief weighed her down further, which made it impossible to fight against the transition. Ivo surrendered and let herself fly through space.

When it was finally over, and the nauseating experience had halted, Ivo was once again standing in the Eternal Kingdom. She held a hand over her puffy eyes, shielding herself from the piercing light of the sun. It was a different time of day here, but without Nariah, the Kingdom had lost its beauty to her. Her heart was slow and ached with every beat as she searched for strength inside herself, only to come up empty-handed. If Cosima had not wrapped her arm around her, Ivo would have collapsed outside of the portal.

Make it stop, Ivo willed the universe. *Please, I'll do anything to make this pain stop.*

Merit froze, and Ivo followed his gaze. In front of them stood what she imagined to be a hundred Trine Scouts, all pointing their blades at the four of them. "Halt," one hollered. "Scout, you did not request proper clearance before arriving through the portal. Have you been compromised?"

"It was an emergency," Merit said, shifting on his feet. "Three Trine Scouts are dead."

A scatter of gasps spread across the angry crowd. Several were immediately distraught. She glanced at their meager group, the ones who had survived. Earnest, Horacio, and Nariah had been killed, and based on the reactions of the other Scouts, it was not an easy loss.

"Nariah?" one to the left of Ivo whispered. "She's not with them. Is she dead?"

She squeezed her eyes shut at the mention of Nariah. The muttering of the Trine Scouts was too much to handle, and Ivo wanted to escape. She sent one silent prayer after another, begging to be put out of her misery. Her body trembled, her shoulder throbbing with pain, as she clung to Sima.

I wish Dario had killed me instead, Ivo thought. *I'd do anything if it meant bringing her back.*

"We need a healer," Merit shouted. "We have a mortal who is injured."

Ivo thought she might begin to sob right there in front of everyone, and her lip quivered. She clamped her teeth into it to hold back her cries. The Scouts, who had been ready to defend their Kingdom, were now dissolving into hushed conversations and panicked pleas to Merit for more information, some tugging on his uniform as they brushed by.

Before more could be divulged, a sharp, high-pitched whistle caught their attention. Ivo searched for the source and landed on several Scouts surrounding a High Priestess as she sauntered down the steps. "You all know better than to gossip," the High Priestess said, brushing back her fiery red hair. "This is classified information. You all will come with me."

Cosima

High Priestess Alala led them back to the containment chambers where they had stayed prior to their deadly mission. Cosima expected to be questioned with urgency, but instead, Ivo was carted off to be seen by a healer, and she was expected to wait for Michi to retrieve her and take her back to her room. Being without her best friend and the man she loved was the exact opposite of what she needed, but Sima had no choice in the matter.

"Vincenzo and Merit," High Priestess Alala said with a raised brow. "You two will come with me."

Cosima's pulse raced as she thought back to her conversation with Dario. The Sacred Brother had told her the Divinity secretly hoped Enzo would be killed while on their mission, and now that they were back in the Eternal Kingdom, Sima feared the worst. *What if they plan to kill him? What if one of the remaining brothers comes for him while he's locked up here?*

"I want to stay with Vincenzo," Sima blurted. When the High Priestess' eyes fell on her, her cheeks reddened. "Nothing on that mission went according to plan, and one incredibly dangerous Sacred Brother, Sostene, is still out there. What if he shows up here in search of Vincenzo?"

Alala leveled her gaze. "I plan to get all of the details of your excursion from these two right now. We will increase the security inside the containment area, and I will personally ensure every single Scout knows who to watch out for. That being said, you cannot remain together. Return to your room and await a call from either myself or one of my sisters."

Shoes clicked on the marble floor, and Michi's frowning face appeared. Sima's shoulders sagged as she stepped toward the Scout. She paused and locked eyes with Enzo. His jaw was tight, and through their connection, she could feel the rustling of his internal storm. She repeated that she loved him inside her head, hoping somehow he'd hear her as she trailed after Michi.

When she lost sight of Enzo, Sima faced forward and attempted to keep herself together. After the usual routine of seemingly random turns to confuse her, they arrived at her door, and Michi unlocked it with her starlight. The inside was free of clutter, but a thin layer of dust coated the room, as though it had been cleaned and then left untouched until now.

Once the door closed behind them, Michi started laughing.

"What?" Sima asked, her fists clenched.

"To think you did the Kingdom a favor and it got you nowhere. You killed two of the most feared Sacred Brothers, probably by the skin of your teeth, and here you are, a prisoner again."

"Glad it brings you joy," Sima murmured.

"The Kingdom already has its pick. I am sure your feathered boyfriend is next on the chopping block," Michi said with a smile. "After they get rid of him and the other guy, Alvize will take over."

Sima's mouth dropped open. "Who?"

Michi huffed. "Alvize is the Sacred Brother chosen to rule along with Kismet's daughter, Moira."

Her mouth went dry. "Moira?"

"Yeah, I may not know everything they are planning, but I've put the pieces together myself." Michi crossed her arms and cocked her head to the side. "Alvize helped them find Kismet's missing daughter, Moira, right around the time your little deal was brought up. He convinced them to align with him in order to defeat Ehses, and because they couldn't risk Alvize getting hurt tracking down his brothers, they needed someone else. Why else would they be so quick to send you and Vincenzo to do all the dirty work? Genius really. And you fell for it."

A familiar boil in her blood grew hotter by the second. It seemed Dario had been telling the truth. The High Priestesses had hoped Vincenzo would die on their mission. "Do you think figuring out their plan means you're important? You're a deliriously loyal Scout that this Kingdom wouldn't hesitate to sacrifice, just like Nariah. If they considered it a suicide mission, then it means they knowingly sent all of those Scouts to their death. Still proud of where your alliances lie, Michi?"

She left Michi with a mildly shocked expression and stormed into the bathing chamber, slamming the door behind her and engaging the lock. It could not truly stop the Scout, but it would hopefully deter Michi and grant her some privacy. She turned the water to its hottest setting and stripped herself of her clothes, lamenting how the rage dissipated. She had no energy left for anger, not when there was a hole in her chest.

There was another Sacred Brother the Kingdom had aligned with, and Sima could not imagine killing him would be easy with their army of Scouts at their disposal. Vincenzo was terrifyingly vulnerable in the grand scheme of things, and she had no clue how to help. She had thought Enzo was safe until Sostene was dead, but there was nothing stopping the Kingdom from killing him now, especially when they assumed Cosima was a bloodthirsty criminal. Three Scouts were dead, and soon, she, Enzo, and all of Haelos would be the next to go.

Michi had mentioned the chosen brother, Alvize, had managed to locate

Kismet's missing daughter, Moira. Sima hated the fact that she was envious of Moira's relation to Kismet. Her existence did not, however, explain why each of Enzo's brothers had seemed so certain that Cosima was the woman from the prophecy. Her eyes widened as she wrapped her arms around herself. *Could I share blood with Moira, too?*

As she stepped into the searing water, Sima wondered if anything she had done since leaving Haelos had made a difference, or if she was truly at the mercy of her own chaotic destiny. The steam created a haze inside the bathing chamber, and Sima let the heat of the water soothe her tired muscles. Soon, all of her harsh, worried thoughts slipped away, and the only thing on her mind was Enzo's face.

Sima drifted off to sleep inside the tub and found herself once again beneath the brilliant wisteria tree inside Vincenzo's void. The dream was coated in a blanket of calm, and none of her worries from the real world manifested, allowing her to take in the sight of him. He stood there in an all black suit with tiny gold accents shaped like stars across the breast pocket and the cuffs of his jacket. She approached him and pressed her hands against his chest. "I missed you. I wish we could be together all the time."

Enzo smiled down at her. "I am all yours. You can have me any time you wish."

She opened her mouth to speak when she noticed something off about him. His eyes were purple instead of green. Sima shoved him away from her and staggered backwards. "Get away from me."

"What's the matter, lovely?" As he grinned, his face morphed into Sostene's. "I may not look like the man you've given your heart to, but I can please you just as thoroughly."

Sima clenched her jaw. "Why are you here?"

"Because I cannot stand to be away from you. I've been close by since our first encounter, waiting for the moment you'd beg for me to rescue you." Sostene sighed as he stuck his hands in his pockets. "But it never came."

"Did you know?" Sima shivered. "Did you know about Alvize and Moira?"

Sostene's brow flicked upward. "I had heard some mumbling about them, yes." He stroked his chin with his hand. "Do not fear, Alvize. He is attempting to circumvent the prophecy in his own way, but it will not pan out the way he believes."

"So, it's true then, Moira is Kismet's daughter?" Sima asked, not meeting his eyes.

He laughed lightly. "Yes, you darling thing. Do you know what that makes you?"

Sima's gaze slowly lifted. "No."

Sostene's head hung to the side as he smiled at her. "Her granddaughter. The woman in Alvize's possession is your mother."

"My mother?" She had almost started to believe she didn't have a family waiting for her. Sima's entire body drooped, her head spinning as the information settled over her. The mystical Celestial Empress, Kismet, was her grandmother, and Moira was her mother. She had spent many nights dreaming that she would one day find where she belonged, and now she was one step closer. "How can I meet her?"

"You can't," Sostene said. "Not without my help. As I said, she is in Alvize's possession, and he has locked her away. He claims he is doing it to keep her safe, but clearly that is not the case. Take my hand, and I will free her for you."

Sima's stomach turned. "I'm not interested in going anywhere with you."

He dipped his head a fraction. "I respect your wishes, but know I will be visiting you again soon." He grinned. "I go through withdrawals without you, *Esti.*"

The dream faded, and Sima gasped as she sat up in the tub. Michi's fist banged against the door, causing the handle to rattle. "You've got five seconds before I tear this damn thing down."

"I'll be right there." Sima pulled herself from the tub and dried herself off as she calmed her racing thoughts. She tugged on a soft pink nightgown. The breathable fabric was welcome as her body released the excess heat it absorbed from the scalding bath. She opened the door, brushed right by Michi, and headed straight for bed without another word. The Scout huffed but left her alone with the bedroom door ajar.

Cosima settled beneath the sheets as she willed herself to keep her breathing stable. Sostene's words continued floating through her mind, but she could not fully allow herself to trust they were real. Appearing in her dreams, telling her precisely what she wanted to hear, seemed like the perfect way to end up right where he wanted her. Despite her hesitancy, she could not stop herself from imagining her childhood with a mother who loved her. As Sima fell asleep, she almost believed she had finally found where she belonged.

Vincenzo

"Calling you a failure feels improper. Disgrace, perhaps, is best."

She thinks you have failed, his curse murmured, *but you have only just begun.*

High Priestess Alala's mouth was turned into a deep scowl. Her curly red hair was like a hive of angry hornets, buzzing with the energy of her enraged aura. Her magic brought sweat to their foreheads, her heat inescapable. Enzo avoided looking at her directly, instead choosing to focus on a corner of the room as his foot bounced beneath the table. His magic snaked beneath his skin, searching for an outlet. He did his best to keep his face neutral as he noticed the black tattoo of his poisonous power stretched higher up his arms. He seemed to be the only one who could see the marks his curse left behind on his body.

"I apologize, High Priestess," Merit said, his tone unusually timid. "The mission did not go as planned, but—"

"But nothing!" Alala shouted. She inhaled sharply before she began again. "After killing Carmine, you were to return to the Eternal Kingdom and await further orders. Not only did you not do that, you chose to pursue another target without permission. For that alone, I could have you killed."

Enzo tilted his head as he leaned forward, inspecting the High Priestess. Something flickered inside her aura, creating occasional violet flashes among the burning red. The unusual display filled him with unease, and Enzo was overwhelmed with the desire to leave. It took everything inside him to remain grounded as his curse boiled, urging him to tear down everything standing between him and Cosima.

The Divinity do not deserve their power. They must feel the consequence of their insolence, his curse mused. *Dismantle what they work so hard to uphold.*

"You broke every protocol by continuing that mission and not immediately utilizing the portal to return. At the very least, you could have used it to send a distress signal. Nariah is dead because both of you turned your backs on your training and your duty to this Kingdom. I expect this out of Vincenzo, but not my Scouts."

Merit winced. "We didn't think—"

"Exactly!" she shouted. "You did not think! When Earnest and Horacio died, you should have sent out an alert. When you killed Carmine, you should have sent out an alert..."

Enzo drowned out the sounds of Alala's squawking as he tugged on the tie to Sima. There was not much he could gather due to the dampening effect on his magic that the High Priestesses inevitably created with their own powers. However, he could sense some discomfort. It troubled him, and Enzo attempted to soothe her a fraction through their connection. As her whirling emotional field shifted a shade lighter, he felt his body relax in response.

The bond is your mercy, his dark companion mused.

When his attention turned back toward the conversation, Merit was at the pleading stage, turning blue in the face as he wasted every breath. "Stopping the Sacred Twelve has always been my primary mission, and that has not changed. Please, you must understand. It was not our fault. Sostene is the one who transported us from Carmine's planet to Dario's. We did not make that decision ourselves."

Alala scoffed. "Why would Sostene transport you instead of kill you, if he meant to stop your team?"

"Is that what you would have preferred?" Enzo's voice was rough as he spoke. Alala narrowed her eyes at him, and he cleared his throat. "I am not going to pretend I understand my brother's intentions and desires, but I can tell you we did the best with what we had. You and your sisters seemed fine with sending us on that mission without everything we needed."

"We were not willing to provide all the details until your group was able to slay Carmine first," Alala said. "It was necessary that Cosima prove her allegiance before she was trusted with sensitive information."

"We should have been sent with an entire team of Scouts." Enzo curled his fists, his blood pressure rising. "We needed more weapons, armor, and resources. You sent us there to die."

Alala's eyes widened. "I suggest you be more careful when making accusations like that. You're lucky you're still alive after everything that has happened. With how many crimes your mother has committed, it's no wonder why sisters were willing to grant you mercy in the first place."

Enzo's jaw tightened. "Admit it, you were never planning on letting me live. You were going to let me solve your problems in exchange for Cosima's freedom, and when you got what you wanted, you were going to kill me."

"Is that true?" Merit asked, his face pale. "He killed two of the Sacred Brothers, and you're still not going to let him live?"

Alala glared at him, and Merit shrank in his seat, mumbling something under his breath. She turned back to Enzo. "My sisters and I have decided to align ourselves with Sacred Brother Alvize in the best interests of all who are beneath our command. If you performed well, we were willing to consider allowing you an agreed-upon amount of time before the Kingdom came for your head."

Enzo nodded slowly. The same brother who had spent many years taunting Enzo through notes had also been scheming his way into the Eternal Kingdom. "I see. You've chosen a palatable enemy to take over instead of properly defending your people."

The Divinity had never planned to let him live for very long. That had always been clear to him. Yet, despite that, he had been too trusting, too blind in his pursuit of freedom and thought, in a twisted way, that he might get his wish somehow. He believed he could bend destiny at his will and grant himself the future with Cosima he had always dreamed of. That delusion was now shattered. If Enzo didn't kill Sostene and Alvize, he would never get to be with her the way they deserved.

You know what must be done, his curse whispered. *You are nearing the stage of your metamorphosis.*

"You hardly understand what is at stake here," Alala said, folding her hands in her lap. "Ehses has already put our Realm at significant risk. There were faults in our system that allowed your mother's exploitation to take root. It began with the Rani Guardians, and as *you* know, Ehses was able to infiltrate the training grounds. She did not only leave you behind, she also brainwashed hundreds of Guardians to enact her experiments across planets. She had created beings she was not permitted to, subjecting them to conditions this Kingdom would never allow."

They'd tell you anything but the truth, his curse laughed. *They'd rather wipe the slate clean than admit they were to blame. The system does not work. You must destroy it.*

Alala's gaze darkened. "It was when an experiment on a planet called Reygco got out of hand that the unraveling began. The people she had created were given complicated and strange magic, distorting even the most basic of requirements for these worlds. One being was capable of burning holes through the atmosphere, endangering the lives of all inhabitants. This garnered our attention, and we had only one option. We chose to wipe the planet, to undo what should never have existed. To this day, the fight continues to restore the balance her disruptions have caused. If this realm lost equilibrium, catastrophic chaos would obliterate everything inside. Every second that passes brings us closer to the fulfillment of the prophecy, and we have no choice but to put the interests of our Kingdom above all else."

Enzo resisted the urge to cringe as Alala confessed his mother's sins. "Where does that leave Cosima then?"

The High Priestess sighed. "Because you all have only killed two of the three agreed-upon brothers and your lack of adherence to the rules, my sisters and I are in quite a predicament. We must decide whether to kill Cosima or allow her trial to continue as before."

"Unacceptable," Enzo slammed his fist on the table. His curse was bolder, more palpable than the last time he was in the Kingdom. Now it felt like a suit of armor wrapped around his skin. "We killed Carmine and Dario, precisely as you wanted. You said she had to prove she was not colluding with my brothers. Their deaths have proved it."

Alala smirked. "I don't believe it clears her of any wrongdoing. If anything, it makes her look more suspicious. Either way, her contract specified that all three must die to absolve her of her accusations. You will just have to wait for our final decision, I suppose."

Enzo's vessel vibrated as steam accumulated inside him. He could not allow himself to dismiss the thinly veiled threat in her words. She spoke as though she had already made her decision to condemn Cosima. "You're making a mistake."

The High Priestess lifted her brows. "I don't believe we are, Mr. Atropos. It should not matter what becomes of Cosima Aphelion, as you will be dead before a decision is made about her future."

Merit shot to his feet. "You can't kill him."

"Of course I can," Alala said with a smile as she twisted a lock of her red hair. "We came to a decision about his Fate long before you all had a chance to fail. This simply sped up the timeline. I suggest you say your goodbyes and make peace with what is to come. You've got mere days left, at best."

Do not fret, his curse said. *The Divinity are the ones on borrowed time. You must cleanse their fingerprints from the golden road of your future.*

Alala walked out, and in her place, a handful of Scouts restrained their wrists and led them out. Merit's head drooped, but his fingers twitched in the binds behind his back. Enzo chewed his cheek, unable to interpret what little information he could glean about Cosima through his magic. When a door opened and only Merit was shoved inside, Enzo knew what was next. He was going to be assigned someone new and confined once more.

The room he had stayed in for weeks before their missions was stuffy and dusty, untouched since his last visit. A Scout whose name and face Enzo had not bothered to remember murmured something about not leaving without permission and walked out of the bedroom. Enzo plopped onto the mattress, hating the bitter taste in his mouth. Normally, he would devolve into endless thinking, determined to find an answer that didn't involve unleashing his curse.

But for once, Vincenzo felt there was no other option.

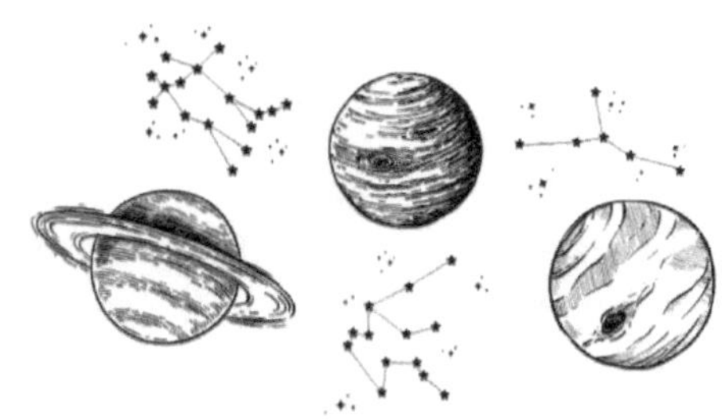

Chapter 41

Cosima

The interrogation had been brutal, lasting what Cosima guessed might have been several days—but could have easily been only one. She regurgitated every moment of their journey, from start to finish, with dreary repetition until the Goddess, Astraea, had been satisfied. The High Priestess' line of questioning frequently dipped into unknown territory, and Sima found herself frustrated with how often she confessed that she did not know the answer.

Despite killing both Carmine and Dario, the Kingdom still suspected Cosima of colluding with the Sacred Twelve. The crimes they planned to pin on her were as much of a looming threat as they were before they left the Eternal Kingdom. She could not help but wonder if the High Priestesses had ever truly intended to allow her, Ivo, and Haelos to walk away from this unscathed.

When High Priestess Astraea had exhausted all of her questions, she excused herself, leaving Sima to herself. As the time passed, Sima found herself slumped over on the table as sleep took her. A nudge from a Trine Scout pulled her from her nonsensical dreams, and the aura of another High Priestess slammed into her.

"Hello, Cosima. I know you've had quite the long day, so I will try to make this quick. I'm here to ask about Nariah's death."

Sima's stomach dropped as she glanced up at Demi. With the haze of sleep departing, the horrific memories of Nariah's headless body surfaced in her mind. Her heart ached as Ivo's trembling figure manifested next, the despair dripping from her eyes. She shook the memories away and swallowed tightly.

"Yes, High Priestess. Ask away. I will do my best to answer."

She smiled again. "I know you will. Walk me through what you witnessed of her death."

"I did not witness it directly."

"Ah, that is right." Demi dipped her head slightly. "My apologies. Tell me how you became aware of her death, then."

"Vincenzo and I worked together to kill Dario. When he was finally down, Merit arrived and told us he could no longer track Nariah. We used his ability to track Ivo to navigate through the jungle, and that's when we saw Nariah lying in the mud."

Aether cringed as Demi asked, "What did you see next?"

Sima witnessed it all in her mind as she spoke. "Ivo was there, huddled over Nariah's body. I knew immediately there was something wrong. I briefly spoke with Enzo before I went to comfort my friend. It wasn't until I moved closer that I noticed Nariah's head was missing. After that, my focus was on Ivo"

"How did you feel in that moment?" Demi pursed her lips. "Seeing a Trine Scout in that manner?"

"It was horrifying." Sima shook her head, attempting to disperse the memory of Nariah's corpse. "I cared for Nariah, and though it was hard, I sacrificed my own emotional needs to comfort Ivo. I knew she needed me more, and I wanted to be strong for her."

Aether's features twisted with pain, and Sima's heart sank, remembering that the Scouts had been friends. "The first two that died were the ones capable of transmitting information to the Divinity. The next was Nariah. She trusted you!"

Demi placed a hand on Aether's shoulder, calming her. "You do see how it's suspicious, though, don't you?" Demi asked. "That everyone capable of clearing your name is dead? I mean, the only one who physically witnessed Nariah's death is Ivo."

"I didn't ask for this to happen. I never wanted Earnest or Horacio to die, nor did I want to lose Nariah. I know for a fact no one in our group hurt them."

"Of course not," Demi said.

Something about her response was off-putting. Thus far, Sima would have believed Demi was an ally. However, at this moment, accusations swirled in her gaze. She did not look at Cosima as she had before, but instead, had a mind clouded with misinformation. In watching Demi's face reveal her inner feelings, Sima wondered if there was more the Divinity hid from her.

"You still want to charge me with the crimes, don't you?"

"Not me personally," Demi replied, "but that is how the Divinity is leaning, yes. The three Celestial Empresses are expected to make an announcement that will impact future proceedings soon, so there is a desire to resolve this with haste."

"Is the evidence against me that convincing?"

Demi swayed her head back and forth, scrunching her lips. "Mm, yes and no. For me, it is not enough. For the others, it might be. As much as I am the Goddess focused on communication, all I can do is equally provide knowledge. I cannot force others to see the outcomes as I do. They are entitled to their own decisions, and the majority ruling is the one that holds."

"Even though I have done as you asked and killed two of the brothers?"

"Yes," Demi said, deflated. "You have done something great for this Kingdom, but Nariah's death has only increased suspicion around you. Earnest and Horacio were highly valued Scouts, and I am afraid their passing may force our hands on the matter. Other Scouts are demanding justice, and there are not many who believe your innocence."

"Do you?" Sima asked.

"For now, yes, but that might change. I must admit, I was taken aback to hear of Nariah's Fate. She was a strong warrior for this Kingdom, and we will mourn our loss now that she is gone. I have only a few more questions. They are not about Nariah's death, but about Sostene. You told Astraea of his appearance, explaining that he had been the one to transport you to Dario's world. What do you recall happening just before you were diverted away from Carmine's planet?"

Ringing clouded her hearing, separating her from the room she was in with Demi. Instead, Sima's bones vibrated at the same frequency as Sostene's magic, transporting her back in time. The room around her faded, and in its place, Sima found herself standing face-to-face with Sostene's mirror image, his purple eyes filled with the same unabashed flirtatiousness as before.

"Hello, Cosima," the recreation purred.

Sima recounted what she could from the memory, detailing the way his magic had gripped them, what he had said of Vincenzo, and what he said about Luciano, his father. The only thing Sima did not mention was Sostene's incessant attempts at courtship, fearing it would only make her seem more suspicious. When she finished, she was grateful to watch it, and Sostene, fade from her view, allowing her to take in her surroundings again. Demi's lips were pulled into a small smile, and she nodded as though putting together a puzzle.

"So, Luciano has been mentoring his son in private. You have done well to give this information over. I will make sure this is addressed by the other High Priestesses. Perhaps we will be able to determine what powers Sostene has that the Kingdom is unaware of. This helps your case more than you know."

Sima's shoulders sagged. She did not experience relief, but grief instead. "If I am convicted of these crimes, what becomes of Haelos?"

Demi pressed her lips together, taking a deep breath through her nose before she replied. "You know the answer to that already, Cosima."

Her eyes filled with tears. "But I did as you asked. I didn't want Nariah to die. I didn't mean for any of this to happen."

"I understand, but we have no way to verify how attuned you were to the instructions laid forth by the Kingdom before you departed. Nariah was the only one on your team capable of sensing the use of your powers. Merit does seem to corroborate what you've told us, but Earnest and Horacio are also dead. It is not often we experience losses of this magnitude."

"This was no ordinary mission. We managed to kill two of the Sacred Brothers. Does that really not count for anything? I did as you asked of me." Tears welled in her eyes. "Dario was so strong, we did everything we could."

Sima knew it was useless trying to convince Demi because, at the end of the day, she was a High Priestess. Her reality was vastly different than Demi's, and the Goddess would never be able to truly view the situation from Sima's eyes. She could not help but think the situation was unfair, that the Divinity were conspiring against her somehow. She had no proof of malicious collusion, but every avenue seemed to lead to the accusatory finger landing back on Sima.

Demi stood up. "I admit, there was no guarantee that everyone would come out unscathed, and I do not believe you are the evil-doer they accuse you of being. However, the disruption to the balance of this realm must take precedence. We must do whatever it takes to restore our control lest the situation turn dire, especially before the winds of change reach our Kingdom. At this time, your only option is to wait until your Fate is determined."

Sima was lost in her thoughts as Michi led her back to her room. She peeled off her clothes and slipped back into her nightgown. Sima flopped into her bed and shut her eyes as sobs shook her chest. Even if she was

Moira's daughter, she did not think it would prevent the Divinity from ruling against her. She knew that the clock was ticking and she was running out of time. She could not stand to sit through more court proceedings, but she equally could not entertain the idea of running away.

She desperately wanted to save Enzo both from the Kingdom and from his brothers, but she had no clue where to start. It was too dangerous to get close to Sostene with Enzo around, but as long as she was trapped inside the containment chambers, there was no chance of her defeating him by herself. She had spent so much of her life being told what to do by others, and Cosima wondered when the time would finally come for her to make some decisions of her own.

Vincenzo

As he sat with his back against the headboard of his bed, impulsive urges sparked inside Enzo's mind. Although his room was situated far from hers, he had the ability to manipulate space, and after his conversation with High Priestess Alala, he was desperate to see her again. He had spent quite some time debating using his magic in this manner since he and Sima were first locked away in the Eternal Kingdom. Prior to their mission, he had always found a reason to decide against the urge; however, now, nothing stopped him.

He clapped his hands together, his power biting at his fingertips as he pulled his palms apart slowly. Bright green energy snapped and crackled between his hands as Enzo morphed it the way he desired. With an outward pulse, his magic shot into the wall and pierced all the way through to Sima's room. He slammed his hands back together and reduced the space between the two of them by altering the physical plane where they stood and creating a new one directly below it. This method of shortcutting was easy for him, but did not come without flaws.

Michi, Sima's new Trine Scout, stood with a wild expression, her mouth hanging open as a book dropped from her hands onto the floor. He snapped his fingers, seizing her mind while she was still caught off guard. He flicked his hand toward the wall, and Michi walked until she reached one of the corners of the room and stood without moving.

"Sima," Enzo called out.

A ruffling sound came from the bedroom, and Enzo rushed over to the door. He swung it open and found Sima standing there with a bewildered expression. Her rosy pink nightgown mirrored the color in her cheeks. "My love," he breathed.

"Enzo? Is it really you?" Sima asked with wide, moon-like eyes. "What are you doing here?"

"I had to see you," he replied, his eyes soaking in the sight of her.

She blinked, as if his response surprised her. "What about Michi? What about your Scout?"

He pulled her hands into his, relishing the electricity between them as their skin touched, and stared into her honey brown eyes. "I don't care about them. I needed to talk to you. Things are not looking good with the Eternal Kingdom. Your life is at risk again, Sima. They might kill you instead of allowing your trial to finish. We should think about escaping."

"Escaping? No, we can't. It's too dangerous, Enzo."

"Yes, we can," he said, giving her hands a small squeeze. "I can break us out of here, and we can run. We can finally be together and stop doing what everyone else tells us."

"I can't do that, Enzo. I don't want to be on the run for the rest of my life. I don't want to be looking over my shoulder, wondering when the Trine Scouts, or your brother, will come hunt you down. You are tied to a prophecy you cannot ignore."

"So are you."

She furrowed her brow. "I don't have solid proof—"

"Stop it, you don't need proof. You know who you are; stop looking to the universe to prove it to you. You saw how each of my brothers went rabid for you. We are tethered together, and our bond is stronger than ever, despite all of the odds. Both of us have magic others could only dream of. So why then are we letting others decide our future?"

Sima hesitated, then took a breath. "We've never spoken about it before."

"What, the bond?"

She nodded. "I've known…I've known it was there but…"

Enzo's heart raced. "I don't know when it happened, if I am being honest, but what I can feel through it has grown." His hand trailed the side of her face. "It's time to admit to yourself who you really are."

Her eyes were clearer than he had ever seen them. "Then so do you."

"Sima, I don't thi—"

"No," she interrupted. "Don't do that. If I can't run from my destiny, then neither can you. I can admit that I have been allowing myself to believe I am not tied to the prophecy, all so I can avoid facing the truth. But I can't anymore. My love for you and my power have two things in common—they require trust. I have to trust you, and I have to trust myself. I am connected to this prophecy, whether I like it or not." She interlaced her fingers with his. "And so are you. You are the survivor, Enzo."

She speaks from her soul, his dark companion whispered. *This, you know already.*

Enzo let out a breath and brushed his free hand through his hair. "You're right, Sima." He searched her eyes. "But this power feels carnivorous, like it has the potential for great evil. I thought it was a sign I was not the survivor because I feared wielding it, but now I am questioning if perhaps it is the greatest indicator of all that I am the one destined to survive. Does it not terrify you? If I am…the chosen one?"

"Not for a second," Sima whispered. "Your powers are not a curse, Enzo…they are your path to freedom. Our love is not a coincidence. This bond is not a mistake. What if the prophecy doesn't speak of the survivor because the destiny of you and your eleven brothers is undecided, but because *you* were the one who wrote it with the magnitude of your energy? I've seen how powerful your magic is, and maybe none of them ever stood a chance of outlasting you. You are meant to lead this Kingdom and beyond."

A tear slipped down his cheek, and Enzo cleared his throat. "I've tried to run…"

"I know," she said, wiping the water from his face. "But you can't anymore. We aren't going to escape, Enzo, because I still have faith that it will resolve in our favor. I know we will make it out of this. I love you."

Those words were enough to wither any restraint he had left. Enzo pulled her into his arms and kissed her, his lips exploding with her magnetizing energy the moment they touched Sima's. She wrapped her arms around his neck, and he pressed one kiss after another across her face and down her neck. He breathed in her scent and lost himself in the sensation of her skin. The relief soaked into his bones as he finally got to experience the mercy of her affection again.

"I missed you," he whispered into her neck.

His magic flared, though he didn't understand why. He felt the energy drip off his fingertips and onto her skin. As their lips locked onto each other and their hands began to explore, he could feel her magic seeping into his flesh. It was as though their energy was melding together, creating with it an ocean of dazzling energy in the air around them.

Sima's hands dropped from his neck to his chest. He let out a small moan in response to her touch across his ribs and stomach. She smiled against his mouth and continued moving her hands lower. Enzo let out a small gasp as she gingerly ran a finger across his manhood, which pulsed in response to her attention.

"We might not get another chance," Sima whispered, her breath heavy.

"I brought time to a standstill, and for now, it's just you and me. If you want, we could…"

Enzo smiled, and his pants grew tighter. "I would be a fool to deny a chance to please you."

She led him into her room and stopped beside the bed. She rose on her toes to kiss him, and Enzo picked her up by the waist, his wings lifting them a few inches from the ground. He playfully tossed her back onto the bed and rejoiced in her laugh as she landed. He positioned himself over her and pressed his lips to her collarbone, the spot just below her ear, and lastly, her mouth.

She tugged on his shirt and pulled away from her just long enough to get it off. He slipped the thin straps of her nightgown off her shoulders, his heart racing as he moved the fabric to reveal her breasts.

"Perfect," he muttered as he ran his tongue over her skin and sucked her nipple into his mouth. In response to the moan she let out, Enzo felt a pinch of pain as his hard length strained against his pants.

A second later, her hands were fumbling with his waistline. He let out a laugh as he took them off and tossed them onto the floor. As he did so, Sima wiggled out of her nightgown. She rested on the bed with her legs teasingly pressed together, which emphasized her bottom and hips while covering her most delicate spot. Enzo's jaw dropped as he took in the sight of her bare form, his eyes glued to every curve.

Her cheeks were flushed as she smiled at him. She let her legs drop to the side, revealing what Enzo believed to be true heaven between them. He dropped to his knees and eagerly pressed kisses up and down her thighs. She let out excited squeals and moans as he grew closer to her center. Once his tongue flicked across her, he couldn't help himself from hungrily enjoying her taste. One hand moved to pleasure himself as the other kept her spread open for him as his tongue explored. The work it took to bring her to completion brought him satisfaction, as Enzo found unimaginable fulfillment in her pleasure—every small sound she made was another reason to devote himself to her more fully.

When she finished, her legs trembled lightly as Enzo moved his way back up. He peppered gentle kisses up her stomach and over her breasts. She grabbed the sides of his face and pulled him up faster, their lips crashing into one another as her fingers dug into his skin.

"I want to feel you again," she whispered.

"Anything for you," he replied with a grin.

Enzo reached down and positioned his length at her entrance. The sensation of her wetness on the tip of his length made him pulse with desire. He raised himself above her just high enough to watch her expression as he gently plunged himself inside her. Her eyes rolled back as she moaned, and Enzo bit his lip, overjoyed with the way her body melted around him as he moved in and out of her.

He took slow breaths to steady himself, overwhelmed at once with the intensity that came with being inside her. She gripped him tightly, and even the smallest movement filled him with ecstasy. "How could I ever be so lucky?" he whispered. "What have I done to deserve you?"

Sima's sounds threatened to throw him over the edge, but he focused on her more than his own sensation. He knew he would contain himself until she was thoroughly pleased, and Enzo slowly picked up the speed, making her moans grow louder. It was music to his ears, and he let the symphony of her voice and breath direct the rhythmic movement of his hips, building in ferocity as she got closer to finishing.

"Enzo," she whimpered, her cheeks red. "I'm yours."

She tightened around him, and Enzo whispered in her ear. "I know, my love, and I am yours. No one can take you from me."

The explosion of her climax created an ocean between their bodies, and Enzo could no longer hold himself back. He joined her in her haze of pleasure and pressed himself deeply into her as he reached his peak. He slowly rocked in and out of her wetness, unwilling to depart from her mystifying touch. She smiled up at him, her gaze so much softer than he had seen in months.

"I love you," he whispered.

"I love you," she replied. "Thank you."

He untangled himself from her and propped himself up on his elbow as he gazed at her. "It's my pleasure, Sima. I should be thanking you for the honor of knowing true divinity when I'm with you."

Her face twisted with pain. "Promise me that whatever happens next, we will face it together."

Enzo nearly laughed. He could think of no other possible path forward—he was hopelessly devoted to her. "I promise. You can't get rid of me that easily. I will always be by your side."

She wiggled closer and rested her head against his chest. "I don't want you to leave me."

"I would never. Even in death, I'd find you again."

Her honey brown eyes stared into his. "How would you find me?"

He grinned as he smoothed back her onyx hair. "Easy. By searching for the brightest light in the universe."

Chapter 42

Ivo

Ivo stretched as the healer told her to, holding her arms above her head. She winced. The healer, whom she learned was named Hirtia, mumbled an apology around the thin needle she had between her lips. Being stuck with dozens of tiny needles was not how Ivo expected to spend her day, but no amount of fussing had made Hirtia turn away, so she allowed her to work. Hirtia explained that she was a Channeler, a special type of immortal gifted by one of Kismet's sisters, with the ability to harness the renewing powers of the Weave.

Being healed by a Channeler created a sensation inside her flesh she had not experienced before. It was cold, but comfortable, the magic exploding through her body instead of radiating as she was used to. Ivo had healed Cosima on many occasions, and now it was she who required treatment, especially since her pain had not begun to subside. Added on top of her physical discomfort was the never-ending weight of her grief. Ivo missed Nariah every second she was awake and spent her nights dreaming of the Scout's purple gaze. She wondered if the suffering would ever subside.

"When will I feel like myself again?" Ivo sighed.

Hirtia tapped her lightly on the chest before wagging her finger at Ivo. "Until your heart is mended, you will not fully improve. The pain you feel inside is preventing you from healing and is altering the flow of your magic." Hirtia returned to fussing over the placement of the final needles. "Stop moving."

Ivo considered the statement. She had not expressed her heartbreak over Nariah's death to Hirtia, but with how frequently they encountered each other, the healer was bound to notice her puffy eyes and red nose from crying. She let out a small breath and closed her eyes, allowing Hirtia's magic to fill her stomach.

"I don't know how to heal my heart. I lost two people who mattered to me in such a short period of time. That isn't fixed easily."

"Several of your organs were cut open, and the rapid healing you experienced left you with an infection deep in your tissue. You are lucky to be alive," she said, patting Ivo's shoulder. She then hovered her hands over Ivo's abdomen, and the needles vibrated with Hirtia's power. "There is time for sadness, always, but do not forget about the beauty in still breathing."

"I might not be breathing for much longer anyway, but thank you."

Hirtia tipped her head, communicating her confusion.

"My planet is doomed. All the people I loved, all the places I never got to see, it will all be wiped clean by the Kingdom. I am included in that, so they go, I do, too."

"That doesn't feel fair," Hirtia said, the flow of her magic tapering off. "What did your planet do to earn that kind of Fate?"

Ivo shrugged. "Wasn't our fault. Have you heard of the Sacred Twelve?"

Hirtia's eyes grew wide. "Who hasn't heard of them?" She pulled her hand away. "They have been causing chaos across the galaxies. That kind of mayhem causes people to talk, even in this Kingdom where we hardly see the destruction. We may only get to chat about what is happening over tea breaks, but the people here care. We even started wondering if the disappearances here had something to do with the brothers."

"What do you mean disappearances?" Ivo asked.

"Well, there have been lots of them! That's the first thing I can tell you. Pretty exclusively centered on the Ambrosi. The Kingdom is less interested in what happens to the immortals without special powers. It started off slow enough, but now there is a new disappearance being talked about every few weeks."

"Why haven't the Ambrosi demanded action?"

"I'm sure they could try," Hirtia said with a laugh, "but it takes quite a bit to truly gain the attention of the High Priestesses. Without knowing the right people, you can't get close enough to sound the alarm."

Ivo sighed. If the Kingdom did not care about their own people disappearing at increasing rates, then there was no chance the Divinity would opt to save Haelos, even with a convincing argument. There was only one item in existence, Ivo thought, the High Priestesses might value enough to save her planet—the mysterious butterfly pendant Sostene had shown Cosima. The very same one that had appeared in her dreams.

"Hirtia," Ivo said, keeping her voice low. "There are crystals covering every inch of this place. Do any of them harbor magic that you know of?"

Hirtia looked at Ivo sideways. "They are just for decoration, dear. I think if they were capable of holding power, we would have noticed by now, right? Imagine the state of the Kingdom if that were true. Since my grandmother's time ten thousand years ago, they have used these crystals to craft our beautiful home, only replacing them when the cracks jeopardize the structural integrity."

"Right," Ivo murmured, tapping her finger against her lips. "Where is the last place that had a major renovation like that?"

"I wouldn't know," Hirtia said. "I am a healer for the Kingdom, not an architect. I serve High Priestess Alessa, as all my kind do, but High Priestess Thera has plenty of immortals who aid in the construction projects formed by the Kingdom. She is in charge of all the fine details."

"Do you know anyone who works for Thera that I could speak to?"

Hirtia raised a brow. "I do not believe you should be speaking to anyone but me and your Scouts for now, especially with the current stakes involving your planet. Think twice if your plans put your life at further risk."

"Are you suggesting I give up and let my people die?"

Hirtia gave a small, rebellious smile. "Of course not." She glanced around. "I know one woman who might be able to help you. She is not close enough to Thera to win you any favors, but she might be able to answer your questions about construction as she catalogs the forms that come through before they reach the Priestess. Her name is Yeyhara. The Scouts probably won't let you into the Kingdom to look for her, so I will send word and ask her to find you."

"Thank you, Hirtia," Ivo said softly.

"Don't thank me yet, I am almost finished with you, which means we can begin our next healing ritual," Hirtia said, plucking a needle from Ivo's abdomen.

"Whatever it is, is it worse than this?" she asked with a wince.

"It is more mentally draining than physically. I don't know how to put this nicely, dear, but you've got a straggler—a nasty spirit attached to your aura. Little bug has kept to himself, thought I wouldn't notice him."

"A spirit? My aura?" Ivo blanched.

"It can be removed. Do not fret, these are common amongst those who travel through the veil. You can occasionally pick up a hitchhiker spirit— souls that did not properly pass through the portal. It happens, and it does no more than suck your energy. They can't hurt you, but they can slow you down. Best if we get him out, right?"

Ivo nodded and lay her head back down on the mat. Outwardly, she wore a brave face, pressing her lips together to keep them from wobbling, but inside, her mind rattled with fears she could never voice, lest they manifest into reality. She closed her eyes and took three slow breaths as Hirtia had instructed.

"You ready, dear?"

"I'm as ready as I'll ever be," Ivo said, knowing that no discomfort would ever top the grief she now carried.

There was a warm sensation in her chest, making her acutely aware of her ribcage and thudding heart within. The deeper it spread, the more Ivo swore she could *feel* her organs and body in a way she had never before. The thin sac around her heart, the lobes of her lungs, the delicate nerves of her spine, the fresh blood flow to her now sealed wound. All were at the forefront of her mind, clear as if she had a direct view into her own anatomy. Somehow, she could detect the presence of something else as well.

It was not sinister, but timid instead. Through her mind, Ivo reached out, attempting to touch it. It scurried away, descending into her hips. Hirtia's magic followed, the warm sensation moving lower to catch the fleeing spirit. Ivo cringed, waiting for the discomfort to arise as she moved her consciousness through her gut, where she had been sliced open.

The pain had vanished, but she ached in a different way. It was a disembodied, lingering sort of ache, a uniquely haunting sensation. As Hirtia's magic slammed into the frightened spirit, Ivo's vision turned white. Her eyes could behold nothing but pure, blinding light.

A ghost of a vision played in the periphery of her vision. If she focused on it, it slipped away, only returning when she released control and let herself absorb the strange dance through time occurring in fragments.

The life of the spirit had belonged to a warrior feline, like Saya, from Dario's world. As Ivo experienced pieces of her life, her ears were accosted with pieces of audio, allowing her to piece together a harrowing puzzle. Ariella, the warrior, had served her people honorably, defending their tribe from threats for decades, but she had grown weak with age. Cast to the wayside and told to die in peace, she watched as Dario seized their minds and used them as living shields, discarding her loved ones when they no longer served him.

She died alone in the chair beside the window, her last breath spent wishing someone had held her, for even a minute, as death took her home. A spark ignited somewhere in Ivo. Somewhere amongst the confusion and anger, a bittersweet understanding settled and took root, weaving through her muscles. Ivo could not give up here, could not let Nariah's death steal her hope as well.

Dario had taken from more people than just Ivo, had disrupted more than just her life. The echoes of generations of grief haunted their legacies, the likes of which they were only beginning to unravel. She knew there were more planets like Haelos out there, more ruins made of heavens, more desolation in the path of innocents. Innocents like Nariah. A stabbing sensation in her chest made it feel as though her grief was taking on a mind of its own. Her fingertips were so cold they burned, and a wave of her magic burst from Ivo.

Her eyes flew open as Hirtia's magic ceased. She sat up and gasped. Hirtia's eyes were black, and deep cracks spread from them. She gurgled and convulsed lightly, her fingers bent like claws in front of her.

"Hirtia?" Ivo asked quietly. "Hirtia, what's happening?"

"R-run," Hirtia gasped, "n-now."

Ivo scrambled to her feet and ran for the door. A glittering black portal appeared in front of her, and before she could skid to a stop, she tumbled through it. She screamed as she fell through, the veil tearing and ripping at her skin. She was spit out through another portal, landing poorly on her neck and shoulder on hard dirt.

She rolled to her knees and whipped her head around. The strange portal disappeared in the blink of an eye, leaving her completely alone in a foreign world. Ivo got to her feet, taking in that she was surrounded by mountainous terrain. Despite her being unable to determine the time of day, the temperature was tolerable—a small mercy considering her circumstances. Three small suns trailed each other in the sky, and the sight of it made Ivo's stomach drop.

She was *much* further from home than she had been before.

"Fuck," she shouted. "What the fuck!"

Tears burst from her eyes, and she slammed the palms of her hands against her forehead. She had no weapons, and for all she knew, she was transported to another dangerous world. The only brother she knew capable of that was Sostene, but through her teary gaze, he was nowhere to be seen. Her magic sprang out of her unintentionally, small blue arcs of energy bouncing off the ground at her sides as her mind raced.

The panic was festering, and she needed to calm herself or she'd be handing herself over to the enemy. As she took a few breaths, she noticed a strange ocean blue aura around herself, outlining her entire figure in the flickering energy. Her magic was sparking inside her, as if untethered in this new world.

Ivo managed broken breaths through trembling sobs as she pressed forward. The trees parted within a few feet, opening to a steep hillside. There were rivers of water, but the terrain was too clean to be a natural passage of water. She squinted, making out what appeared to be women wearing broad cone-shaped hats tied beneath the chin.

Ivo stuck to the surrounding vegetation for cover as much as she was able as she made her way toward the women. There was no telling if they were hostile, but as she grew closer, the more they outwardly resembled immortals. Ivo would not stick out, unless they could detect in some other manner that she was not one of them.

At the bottom of the hill, three women collected strange purple and red vegetables from the watery farm, brushing away the roots before tucking them into baskets on their backs. Before she could decide against it, Ivo fled from cover and approached them.

"Can you help me?" she asked clumsily.

The startled women snapped their heads in her direction, one dropping a purple vegetable in the process.

"Witch!" one hollered. "A witch!"

Ivo's eyes were wide as she stepped backward with her hands up, aware at once that a witch was the wrong thing to be on this planet. She glanced down at herself, understanding that the others could see the strange blue energy that engulfed her body. Her magic was not dormant here; instead, it poured from her fingertips like ocean lightning storms, only enraging the people more.

Cosima

"Here's your meal," Michi said, plopping a silver tray onto the bed beside Sima. "Eat up."

Sima frowned but pulled the meal closer to her as Michi exited her room and went back to the sitting area. The food smelled delightful, with a selection of small vegetable dishes paired with thin strips of marinated meat; however, something about the meal made her stomach turn. She dismissed it as merely being quite hungry, and she dug in. In the middle of chewing her first bite, Sima felt her teeth grind against hard granules.

She took a sip of her herbal tea and washed down the food. Sima inspected her dish, but found nothing out of the ordinary. She resumed eating, and when she was nearly halfway finished, she once again ground her teeth on rock-hard pebbles. She spit out the food and found tiny black flecks. A strange sensation swirled in her gut, and Sima felt lightheaded.

"You can't go in there," someone said from the hallway outside of Cosima's rooms.

Sima shoved the tray away from her and made for the door. She peeked out into the sitting area and found that Michi had her nose in a book. Her Scout was seemingly unaware of the chaos occurring in the hallway, which grew louder by the second.

Is it Enzo? Sima thought. *Has he come back?*

"Stop! You're not allowed in there," a woman shouted.

A thud against the door roused a groan from Michi, who slammed her book shut and got to her feet. Sima pushed the door flush with the frame when the Scout walked by and opened it again when Michi had ventured into the hallway.

"There's been a breach. Run to alert the others," Michi screamed at someone. "Get back! You cannot come in here."

Aether's voice rang out next. "This is your last warning. Back away or be killed."

Curious, Sima left her room. As she approached the door, it swung open and power seized her. Her hand flew to her throat, all her air cut off. Sima feared Sostene had come for her, her heart beating so fervently it hurt, but only Aether was visible as she crawled in the hallway, covered in blood. Her vision blurred, and darkness encroached; her mind was free of useless, panicked chatter and full of blissful silence instead.

She dropped to her knees, the impact painless. It should have been uncomfortable to suffocate, but it was as though the bite of it was dulled. Or perhaps that her mind was dulled, she noted with bleary resignation. Tears dripped from her eyes, but she could not get herself to care that she was dying.

It will be over soon, her mind hummed. *Death can be warm, it can be kind. I don't have to fight so hard.*

Something pinged in her chest. Her heart, she realized after a drowsy moment. She peeled one eye open and spotted not Sostene, but a woman instead. She was immaculately dressed, wearing a slender green silk dress with a thin slit at the side. Her bundles of white hair were tied back with two thin red lacquered sticks, two wisps of hair snaking down her face and ending near her jawline.

The magnitude of her aura was confusing, even to Sima's lulled mind. The more she wished to inspect the strange woman walking toward her, the louder the thoughts grew. Her mind's hushed, encouraging inner tone grew fervent and impatient, demanding she give herself over.

Let go! There is nothing to live for! Life has only shown me pain, so why do I try?

Sima shook her head, feeling a warm touch encircle her wrist. She peered up at the woman, whose beauty captivated her mind at once. The moment they locked eyes, the hold on her air—and mind—vanished. She took a greedy gulp of air, supporting herself on the woman's arm. Her smile was kind, her pale blue eyes strangely familiar. Her eyelashes and eyebrows were a shimmery white, like snow had gotten trapped on her face, intensifying her already impressive looks.

The woman's eyelashes fluttered as she blinked at Sima. Her power seized Sima, pulling her inside a slowly creeping haze, similar to the sensation she experienced with Aurelio and his brothers, who had tried to touch her mind through her shielding. This time, she bucked against the sensation in her mind.

"You are Cosima."

Her voice was confident, but soft. A tenderness to her tone known only to those blessed enough to truly experience peace. Pieces of a puzzle began to click into place. Though the woman was gentle and soothing in her approach, Sima's gut reacted with urgency and appall. She knew who this woman was—who this former High Priestess was.

"S-Spirit Goddess," Sima spat out.

Ehses—mother of the Sacred Twelve—crouched down beside Sima. Her smile grew unnaturally large, spreading until it nearly touched her ears. She cackled, softly at first, sending a chill down Sima's spine. Then it grew manic, her behavior eerily reminiscent of her son, Aurelio. Sima shoved her away, scrambling for the door. Against her will, she slowed, her mind growing heavier with every step. Her body was no longer within her control. She spun on her heel and marched back to Ehses' side.

"I found you," she sang. "I put you somewhere, little doll, and you did not stay. I gave you a stunning home, a handsome husband, and you fled from my gates. I don't respond well to my pets escaping their cages." She leered closer to her, dragging the side of her finger down Sima's face. "Pretty girl. My, how you've not changed since the first time I laid my eyes on you. You are radiant like stars, adaptable like the moon, and that is why I chose you."

"Chose me? You kidnapped me," Sima said flatly. She attempted to reach for her magic, but a strange, empty sensation filled her as she blinked off her haze.

Ehses snapped her hands back. "I did what I had to! You would not listen to reason. You did not care about the future I saw for the Kingdom, for the expansion our bloodlines could create. I gave you better options, but you rejected all of them. What else was I to do?"

Sima's curiosity got the better of her, feeling an ill-fitting sense of bravery, as if her actions were being guided. "You could have given me a chance to choose. If you told me the truth about everything, perhaps I would have trusted you."

Ehses's nose twitched. "If only I believed you," she said, bopping her finger on Sima's nose. "You have done something defiant by taking my favorite son from me. Do you think I will be quick to forgive you?"

The Spirit Goddess stepped away, strolling over to the wooden table in Sima's rooms. She tapped her fingers on the top, transforming the table into one made of solid white marble. She repeated the process on the chair, adding a poke to the seat to add a plush red cushion. She lowered herself into the chair, crossed one leg over the other, and looked Sima up and down.

"What do you want from me? Are you here to kill me? Make me suffer for what I did to Aurelio?" Ehses frowned, and Sima fell to her knees, pressing her forehead to the ground, guided by the pull of the Spirit Goddess's magic. "I am s-sorry," Sima said, her mouth not her own.

"That's more like it," Ehses said. "I am not here to kill you, Cosima. I *need* you. That is why I gave you my blessed son as an offering."

"He abused me," Sima growled, straining to keep control over her lips. "That is not an offering; it was a torturous prison sentence."

She once again reached for her magic, but came up short. What could keep her power from responding when she needed it most?

"He did have a temper, but he was promising. He had the strength, the ruthlessness, the malleability." Ehses shook her head, as if shaking off a memory. "Nevertheless, there are options for you."

Sima rose from the ground, her feet dragging her to the untransformed seat beside Ehses. Once she was sitting, the former High Priestess snapped her fingers. The room melted away, revealing a new location. They were on a stone patio outside of a grassy green mansion covered in vines and blooming roses. Their scent overwhelmed Sima's nose with their sweetness, causing her to sneeze.

Steps sounded from behind her, Sima turning to find the source. Sostene grinned at her, holding a gold cloth napkin in front of him as he bent forward. When she refused, he shrugged and tucked it back into the pocket of his black velvet suit, tailored to fall perfectly around his wrists and ankles. His shoes were a deep purple, matching the hue of his eyes that never left her, even as he took an open seat at the white marble table.

"Hello, little star."

"Abandoned and forgotten,
Left to wilt and wither.

Prayers for relief,
Pointless and bitter.

Insanity unbalanced,
Eternity untethered,

Bathed in the cosmos,
Fate unmeasured.

Tides have turned,
A split destiny earned,

A curse without approval,
A boy darker than death,

The only cost of renewal,
Is his last breath."

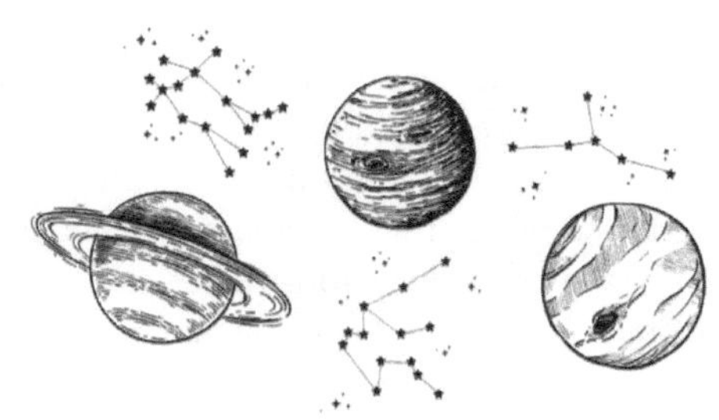

Chapter 43

Cosima

Cosima took slow breaths in through her nose as she willed the trembling in her body to quell. She didn't need Ehses or Sostene to confirm they had used something to dampen her magic. She had already attempted to reach for her magic, only to come up empty-handed. Sostene took a sip of his wine while staring at her over the rim of his cup. Sima grit her teeth as her frown deepened.

If only I had taken Vincenzo up on the offer to escape, she thought as her head angled toward her lap.

"I understand you two have already acquainted yourselves." Ehses snapped her fingers, and a servant manifested from thin air, holding a full glass of red wine. The Spirit Goddess snatched it from her hands, and the servant disappeared in a puff of white smoke. "While it would have been more favorable to have delayed your union, I cannot deny that you two make a brilliant pair."

Sostene leaned toward her. "I could not stave off the inevitable, especially not after I managed to feel your magic with pristine clarity, even at a great distance. It doesn't matter where you are, it calls to me."

Sima glared at him. "How long have you been watching me?"

The corner of his lip curled upward. "Only since your arrival to the Eternal Kingdom, my sweet." His eyes flicked to his mother and back to her. "You were otherwise occupied with Aurelio prior to that."

Sima studied his expression before her gaze slipped over to Ehses.

The Spirit Goddess wore a smug smile as she wiggled her fingers in the air beside her head. A lit cigar appeared in her hand, and Ehses took a long drag as amusement danced in her eyes. Sima turned her attention back to Sostene, the wheels turning in her mind.

"That's right," Sima said, drawing out the words as her heart rate spiked. "Your mother knew better than to make you her first pick. Aurelio was supposed to be the face of your vicious plans, and I killed him."

Violet flames flickered in his eyes as he narrowed them. "She had reasons for bestowing her favor upon him, but Fate always has the upper hand. The true scripture of destiny will always prevail."

A deep line formed on the Spirit Goddess's forehead as she dragged on her cigar. "My golden son remains blessed, this is merely not the era of his ascension. Sostene, however, has risen to the occasion. He handles the urgency of this prophecy with an astuteness his brothers are incapable of replicating. You can also thank Sostene for your hasty arrival here. When the bloodshed begins, you won't be forced to witness souls being reaped from their immortal shells."

Sima swallowed hard. "You're planning to attack the Eternal Kingdom?"

Sostene sighed. "We are not to blame for the mayhem amongst the Caelari, that I can assure you. I'm afraid your doting devotee will be the one with blood on his hands."

"You're lying." She clenched her fists. "Vincenzo would never hurt innocent people."

Ehses smirked as she blew out smoke, the sight of it sending a chill through Cosima. "My youngest son is not as holy as you believe him to be. How you can stand the pulse of his hideous magic, I may never understand; however, I do know he is bound by Death herself." The Spirit Goddess's gaze harshened as her lip twitched. "His tether to Oblivion rots him from flesh to bone, spirit to soul."

Sostene let out a light laugh. "He is already living on borrowed time, *Esti.* You cannot save him, no matter how much you try to convince yourself you can. You cannot mend what was never meant to last. Release him and experience permeating ecstasy through our everlasting entanglement."

"Your downfall will be the way you underestimate him," Sima snapped. "I have devoted the full expanse of my heart to him, and nothing will change that." Her lips quivered as tears stung her eyes. She refused to accept that Vincenzo would wind up dead at the end of this. "I won't cooperate with you if he dies. I won't live without him."

"Cosima, don't be rash," Sostene scolded, raising a brow at her implied threat against her own life. "You're not going anywhere."

Ehses tipped her head back and laughed. "Nothing happens without you, despite the way *others* have tried to circumvent that specific requirement. Without you, Cosima, there is no prophecy. You descended from a Celestial Empress, but in a manner that was thought to be impossible. There are other descendants, yes, but they become so through ritualistic manners of blessed blood sharing, where a Celestial Empress bestows drops of her essence upon a generation deemed worthy. No one has ever descended *from* the Celestial Empresses directly."

"Until you and your mother," Sostene said with a satisfied smirk. "Although even dearest Moira's blood is not as pure as yours. Kismet's magic did not take to her the way it did to you."

Sima's throat burned at the mention of her mother. "How do you know all of this?"

"Because I am the one who found you, pet," Ehses said, ashing her cigar. "When I became pregnant with my first son, I had to find a way to hide his birth, something I believed was unachievable, especially with the strength he had in the womb. I had already been cast out of the Divinity, forced to roam without purpose for eternity. I was desperate, looking for revenge, and found myself outside of Kismet's palace. I lay in waiting outside for months, prepared to birth my child on her doorstep if it meant there was a chance at finding a way to make her pay. One day, you came strolling from the front door, as if you had been there all along. As Fate would have it, I uncovered her secrets before I went into labor. I have you to thank for concealing my twelve sons from the Divinity."

"Me?" Sima's chest pinched.

Ehses leaned forward and touched a finger to Sima's forehead, injecting her mind with a vision.

"Get back here right now!"

The grassy meadow sprouted lavender and purple zinnia flowers. The pathway the black-haired girl ran down was overgrown and obscured. The girl skipped and hopped, twirled and jumped, letting the cool breeze carry her farther from home. A woman with the same features as the little girl barreled out from behind a tree and snatched her up, causing the young child to squeal with delight.

"I told you to stay nearby," she scolded.

"I want to see the other side," the girl pouted, pointing to the far edge of the meadow. "You never let me see the other side."

"Ah," she chirped. "An adventurer now, are we? What if it is cold across the way? Do you have a coat?"

The girl turned her nose down and grimaced. "No! I didn't think I'd need it."

"What about a snack, little? You have no food, should your tummy grow hungry. Not as prepared as you thought for such a grand adventure. Best let us return home and come back when we are prepared."

The tiny girl considered the statement with her arms crossed in front of her chest. Her lips twisted as she chewed her cheek. "Maybe you're right, Ahnma."

"Ahnma is always right," the woman hummed, guiding the girl back toward the dazzling palace.

Sima shook off the images and pressed a hand over her racing heart. Seeing her mother's face made her ache for more memories, especially now that she knew her name was Moira. She craved more information about the woman who had raised her, the lingering homesickness in her soul never louder than in this moment.

Ehses wriggled her fingers, the cigar disappearing, as the ghost of a smile rested on her lips. "When I found out exactly how Kismet had kept you and your mother hidden, how she had raised you two without anyone knowing you existed, I devised a plan to steal it. The mysterious stones were full of surprises, and it was not long before she realized they were missing. Kismet was furious with me, catching me only because my rat of a mate, Luciano, handed over the information out of fear that our sons were too powerful to slay without disrupting the balance of our galaxies. That is when Kismet cursed us."

The memory played in the back of her mind as Sima focused on the image of her Moira's soft features, with brown eyes that resembled hers. "Where is my mother now?"

Ehses frowned. "She is in the hands of the Eternal Kingdom. The Divinity have chosen to use her to try and circumvent the prophecy."

"You've torn my whole family apart," Sima spat, only for her shoulders to droop as the energy drained out of her. "What does it matter if I am a descendant of a Celestial Empress?"

"It matters," Ehses said, her smile wrong and menacing, "because the three Empresses are losing their power. Someone must rise and take their place. However, that exchange of power does not come without its own ritual of sorts. Your heart's song is a necessary ingredient if we are to allow the wheel to turn."

"You'll fail," Sima said, not looking away from the Spirit Goddess's gaze. "If you can't do this plan without me, then it means that what I want matters. My heart has already chosen its home."

Sostene's face twisted. "You foolish girl, you're so misguided. You're actively choosing the worst possible outcome. That runt is sick with a sour soul. Save yourself from his unbecoming. If not ruled with a ruthless hand, this Realm will succumb to the rancid stench of irredeemable disorder. I am what the Kingdom needs if they wish to survive in the incoming storm from beyond our borders."

"I know what Vincenzo is capable of. When he and I entwine, there is nothing that can stop us." Sima swallowed as her eyes trailed the sprawling vines and roses along the outside of the green mansion. The overlapping stems reminded her of threads, and though she wished to unleash her magic, it remained lulled beneath whatever drug they had slipped her. "I will be a nuisance every step of the way until I find a way to bring down the both of you. I will free my mother from the Divinity's chosen Sacred Brother, and I will end him too."

Sostene grabbed Sima's hand from where it rested on the table and gripped her so hard she let out a small yelp. "Your family deserves no mercy from you. Kismet cursed you as well. She declared that one of us would be chosen by her descendant to bring balance. The Empress knew she was binding her granddaughter to men made of madness and malice. Don't you understand why you must pick me? I can absolve you of your debt with the passion beating within my cold heart."

Sima yanked her arm free from his grasp, her wrist barking with pain. "What if the Kingdom comes searching for me?"

"Oh, you're all mine, *Esti*." He smoothed back his black hair and licked his bottom lip. "I created quite the mess when we came for you, though taking you was easier than I expected, if I am being honest. I don't know that the Divinity had any true interest in protecting you."

"It was worth the decades of despicable destruction I carried out in your name." Ehses took a large sip of her wine, finishing the glass. "None of them believed you truly belonged to Kismet because they were more concerned with wrapping up the antics of a serial criminal." She grinned. "Well, and I suppose my alterations to your vessel made it difficult for them to sense your true heritage. I doubt even Moira would recognize you with my spells inside your spine."

"You did what?" Sima's hand shook as her head spun. "You're the reason Kismet didn't recognize me and why the Divinity called me the Realmwalker."

"No, dear, you are the reason they call you that. That is why my mother made sure you don't remember much of your life prior to Haelos. Your backlog is most impressive," Sostene said as he rose from the table. He rested a hand on her shoulder, and a wave of his magic pulsed through her. "Perhaps I will show you sometime. For now, I will show you to your new room."

"Wait," Sima said, her vision growing blurry as her body grew heavy, "no, no, please."

She lost control of her body, dropping helplessly to the floor. Just before she hit her head, Sostene caught her and pulled her into his arms. He took a deep inhale with his face buried in her neck before pressing a kiss to her temple. As badly as she wanted to rage, she could muster no more than a puny groan before he tossed her over his shoulder and said farewell to his mother.

"Be sure to give her another dose before the moon rises," the Spirit Goddess said.

Sima lifted her head in time to watch Ehses vanish from thin air.

She fought off the black encroaching on her vision as Sostene waltzed through his mansion with a relaxed demeanor. Her head rested against his back, and his arm was wrapped around her thighs, keeping her in place on his shoulder. He stopped outside a door and placed her on her feet.

Sostene's eyes were bright as his finger trailed her jaw. "Vincenzo's death is on the horizon. Soon, your heart will beat along with mine, and we will become inseparable. I cannot wait to know until I know every detail of your irreplaceable soul."

The mention of Enzo sent a searing pain down her spine in a brief flash. Sima stumbled as she moved away from his touch, barely catching herself on the pedestal of a strange vase that she swore hummed a tune when she collided with it. She shook her head and attempted to uncross her eyes to look at Sostene. He was a blur, but she knew he was amused by his hold over her.

"Fuck you," Sima whispered.

Sostene laughed, lacing his arm through hers. "It is the hour of recompense, little star. I left behind a beautiful little love note detailing our plans to abscond together when I left the holding chambers in ruins. With you gone, nothing is stopping the Divinity from killing my baby brother. It also means that you are at my mercy. If I must destroy every other avenue for you, then so be it, Cosima, but you are mine now. I won't stop until your blood sings my name. I can be everything you need me to be. The others could never measure up because I was here, my sweet, learning how to be the man our Empire needs."

He opened the large wooden door, revealing what her hazy vision determined to be a study or library of sorts. He led her inside, pulling out a chair for her to sit in. She collapsed into it and shuddered when Sostene covered her with a fluffy navy blanket. He patted her head before he stepped somewhere behind her and poured himself a drink. When he returned, he let out a satisfied sigh as he took a seat in the chair beside her.

"I knew we'd be together one day. Mother erroneously chose Aurelio, but the hand of Fate knew he was not tenacious enough, not man enough. But I am." He took a long drink, smacking his lips when he was done. His violet eyes hung on hers. "My plans to destroy Alvize are already in motion, all thanks to you."

"Me?" Sima asked drowsily, no longer able to hold her head up. She sank into the chair, letting the warmth of the blanket caress her towards sleep.

Sostene reached a hand over, lazily stroking her shoulder as her eyelids pulled firmly shut.

"It was too easy to use you to lure the demon out of Vincenzo and too easy to use your threads to Moira to locate my final opponent. Alvize thinks Moira's heritage will be enough, but he doesn't know that my power melds into yours, that we fit together like Fate intended. I can *see* into you in a way the others cannot. The scripture of your soul soothes my aching bones, and I am addicted to your deliverance. Every moment spent in your presence wears away at my eternal agony, brings me a reprieve from my wickedness. My roaring strength can only be attributed to our close proximity, and I won't let *anything* disturb this harmony."

Sima could no longer fight off her exhaustion, could not keep conscious long enough to think about what he had said to her. She slipped into a deep, dreamless void, surrounded only by the hollow sensation of a heartbroken core.

"Come closer," Cosima whispered seductively, using her finger to command him forward.

Her nightgown was a deep purple with white lace adorning the bottom hem and along her breasts. Her black hair spun in loose curls until it reached her waist. Her lips had a faded bloody tint to them, as if he had spent hours kissing her lipstick away. His heart thudded at her command.

Vincenzo complied, lurching ahead until he stopped just inches from her. She laid her hands on his chest and gazed into his eyes, cocking her head to the side. He studied her from her high cheekbones and delicate lashes to her small chin and full lips. He wanted to lean forward and kiss her, but something stopped him. An annoying ringing echoed, distant but bothersome in his pursuit of devoting full attention to her.

"What's wrong?" she asked, her brown eyes swimming with confusion.

"I miss you constantly," he murmured, leaning gently toward her until she wrapped her arms around his neck, allowing him to pull her closer. He held her against him, burying his face in her sweet-smelling hair. "I want to spend a hundred days hidden from the world with you. I want to tuck flowers into your hair and hold your hand underneath the moonlight."

"You've gotten your wish. We have an eternity ahead of us," Sima replied with a chuckle. "Perhaps you will grow sick of me."

He laughed. The idea was insanity. He was never more authentically himself than when he was by her side; he couldn't imagine reaching a time when he would tire of her presence.

"The Fates would have an easier time bringing a wealthy man a full heart. All I have wanted since the moment our eyes met is to love you and to be loved by you. You can't get rid of me that easily."

She smiled, the expression crinkling around her eyes. "Good, I wouldn't want you to go. I am starting to become rather attached, if I am being honest."

"Oh?" He laughed. "So, my charm *is* working?"

"Barely," she teased.

The ringing grew louder, more bothersome. He winced, holding a finger to his brow. With a pulse of his magic, he shoved out the sound and focused on Cosima. She wore a concerned expression, reaching out to caress his face. Her hand was warm against his skin, leaving a trail of tingling bliss where she touched him. His eyes lazily drifted beyond her. The wall behind her flickered, revealing a wave of strange light.

Enzo jumped back, only now realizing he did not recognize his surroundings. He struggled to recall what he had been doing before Sima had summoned him forward, his mind coming up blank. *I was with her, wasn't I? Why can't I remember?* Sima's head hung, her hair spilling over her face, concealing her features. The bedroom they were in was unrecognizable, adorned with strange sculptures of faces along the walls, a sea of people.

"What's wrong?" she asked without moving.

Enzo's mind raced. *Something isn't right.* "Where are we? What are we doing here?"

"Have you forgotten already? We killed Sostene, and the Eternal Kingdom granted us our freedom. It is just you and me now, Enzo. You and I, forever."

The air was thin, as if his lungs could not acclimate to the atmosphere.

"Where are we?" he repeated.

"You picked this planet when we ran away together. You don't remember where you've taken me?"

No. The word came from somewhere within. "This isn't right," Enzo mumbled.

"You want to leave me?"

"You know I would never, my love," he said earnestly, "but I know this isn't real."

Sima snarled, lashing at him with her nails. He stepped back, caught off guard by the tears streaming down her face and the anger radiating from her like ash-filled clouds. He raised his hands to protect his face as she continued to launch rash attacks with her fists and nails.

You were distracted, his curse hissed. *You let yourself get distracted, again. There can be no time for mistakes.*

A burst of energy blew him back, his head knocking against a wooden bookcase. Faces suspended on the wall above the shelf crashed down on top of him, yelping as they fell. He swiped them off himself before jumping to his feet, careful to not step on them out of fear they were alive.

"Sima," he said, breathless. He held his hands out in front of him. "What is going on? I don't want to hurt you."

"You said you'd never leave me," she snapped, picking up a thin wooden stool beside the bed. She smashed it against the bedpost, then charged him, using the broken legs as stakes. "You can't go. I can't live without you."

Enzo dove out of the way, using his wings to propel himself faster. He flew toward the door as Sima chased after. He reached for the doorknob, letting out a growl when he discovered it was locked. He narrowly moved out of the way of Sima's stake as it lodged in the door beside his ear.

He rolled across the floor and jumped to his feet, spotting a window along the wall. He barreled toward it, willing to suffer through broken glass in his skin if it meant he could escape without hurting her. His body bounced off it, sending him straight to the floor at Sima's feet. She stabbed repeatedly with impressive speed, managing to pierce him through the side.

He groaned, wrapping his hands around the stake as he pushed her away. His heart panged as she toppled to the floor, so easily disarmed by so little of his strength. The distant ringing returned, fogging his mind. He pulled the stake out and inspected it. It dissolved in his hands, vanishing before his eyes.

It took everything he had not to reach for Sima, where she lay sobbing softly on the ground, her hair casting a wide web around her. A delayed signal of pain knocked him back a step, but he ground his jaw and stepped closer to her.

The room melted away around them, slowly dissolving as he walked. By the time he reached Cosima, the floor had evaporated, leaving them in a white void. He knelt beside her, hesitating as he extended a hand toward her. She jerked back, revealing her bloodshot eyes and pink nose.

"You're just like him," she hissed. "You're just like Aurelio."

Enzo shook his head gently. "No, I'm not. You and I both know that."

"You're just as much of a monster. Maybe you're worse than he ever was. At least he was honest about who he was, but you parade around like you have a good heart, when you were using me all along."

The words caused his heart to squeeze, but it did not rouse a visible reaction from him. Instead, he gathered her hands in his. "If there is any chance you are the real Sima…I love you. If you are Sostene's attempt at breaking me…tell him I said to come out and fight me like a man."

His voice broke at the end of his sentence, the torment of his brother's manipulation beginning to wear on his psyche. He clenched his teeth and took a strong breath through his nose, holding his composure as Sima faded away, her eyes locked on his with a sad, broken gaze, until she had disappeared.

"Brother."

Enzo whirled around, startled to find not Sostene, but who he could only assume to be the brother chosen by the Eternal Kingdom. His spiked brown hair peeked out from beneath a crown carved of diamonds. His facial hair was short, but wrapped around his chin, coming to a well-groomed stop mid-cheek. His red loafers clicked lightly as he approached.

Smite him where he stands! Bring his chaos to an end! You fool, do something, his curse shouted.

"Alvize," Enzo murmured. "Is this why you went through the theatrics? Wanted to weaken me before you put yourself at risk? This will not keep me from killing you should you so much as harm a hair upon her head."

"I wanted to give you a warning," Alvize said, his voice even and deep.

"Is that so?" Enzo spat.

"Your time with Cosima is running out," Alvize replied.

Enzo lunged, bouncing off an energy field Alvize had crafted to protect himself. "What did you do to her?"

"I've done nothing to her, brother," he said. "She has abandoned you, fleeing in the middle of the night to be with Sostene. There are several Trine Scouts who were injured in the process, all affirming it was Cosima who had attacked them. You bet too much on a woman," Alvize said with disgust. "She could never lead by your side. She killed mother's golden boy, and now it seems you have entangled yourself in her threads as well."

"You speak lies," Enzo growled, his curse rampaging inside him. It hurt to speak with his power pressing against his lungs. "She would never run away with him."

Alvize chuckled. "Don't be so certain. I know everything that happens inside the Eternal Kingdom, and your beloved chose another. Such a shame that you thought your union to be infallible."

Enzo's stomach turned. "Why are you telling me this?"

His brother shrugged. "I have brought you a proposition. Kill our remaining brother, and I will allow you to live out the next decade at peace by Cosima's side."

The words sparked a wildfire in Enzo's gut. "I'll smite Sostene and come for you next. While both of you are drifting in the in between, I'll be indulging in eternity with Cosima as my wife. I have accepted the role I must play in the evolution of our Kingdom, and it starts with taking your life. Tell me, brother, which High Priestess is guided by your malice, brother?"

Alvize grinned. "Few remain who sit upon their throne without my influence coursing through them. Our siblings are fools, useless idiots concerned with fast-tracking power over strategic games. I established myself through back-breaking effort, earning every ounce of trust from the Divinity I have gained. I showed them what our mother could not, an Emperor with the heart of his people at the forefront. What Kismet and the other Empresses will not, I will."

He is a charismatic deviant with time ticking inside his chest, Enzo's curse cackled. *How much longer will you permit him to breathe, child of Oblivion?*

Enzo resisted the urge to roll his eyes. His brothers had a habit of praising themselves for the way they successfully manipulated others.

"Moira approves of this? Have you brainwashed her as well?"

"No more than a healthy dose to keep her leash short, but I am not cruel. She will be revered, all without lifting a finger. It is a dream for a woman as sensitive and fragile as she is—a mercy, really."

Enzo thought of Cosima as his chest ached. How much terror would his bloodline inflict on her? Could she bear the weight of their curse? He clenched his fist as a weakness in Alvize's hold over his mind appeared. Enzo seized his opportunity to end the cruel illusion and hurdled through the hairline crack in the mental fortress.

He broke through, relieved to find himself still within his rooms. The Scout assigned to him had collapsed on the floor, his black hair soaked with blood seeping from a head wound. Enzo cursed under his breath and ran over to the man, who was still alive. He shook the Scout, but he was entirely unconscious.

"Fuck," Enzo cursed, letting him drop.

He stepped over him and made for the door. A pulse of his magic on the bond between him and Sima confirmed she was either a drastic distance away or she had truly left the Kingdom. There was no chance she had done it intentionally, he reasoned, meaning she was in danger. He could not waste any more time.

Will you wait until her blood is on your hands, or will you kill the coward that lives in your bones? His curse roared, loud enough to make Enzo flinch.

He stared down at the door handle, pondering the impulsive plan that had riled his blood into furious storms. The dark poison of his magic now fully consumed the top half of Enzo's body, and though he remained the only one capable of seeing the markings, they were proof of how close he was to truly losing himself. His breath hitched at all the times he thought he had reached the point of no return before this moment, and his body trembled. He was already terrified of his curse, and somehow, he intuitively knew that if he broke this final barrier around his magic, he would never resurface. There was no telling who he would become, but Enzo didn't care if the power rotted him from the inside out. All he wanted was to free Cosima from the prophecy—to free her from his brothers—even if it meant sacrificing their future together. It didn't matter if he lost her forever, so long as she was no longer affected by his horrid bloodline. His magic burned as it roared out of him, growing with intensity.

As he called for his curse, it came in monstrous waves that crashed over him, destroying his flesh. He struggled to breathe as it drowned him beneath its immeasurable weight. The height of his curse had been something he resisted, but in this moment, he let it flood into his muscles without hesitation. A transformation began, starting somewhere deep inside him, leaving him with the sensation of his soul igniting. He could feel the changes unraveling with unhurried precision, and as his new magic settled into place, he found he no longer needed air. All of his senses were heightened, and his command over his power was smooth, fluid, unrestricted.

The path is within you. Listen to your intuition and burn it all down, his dark companion hollered.

He held his hand up and used his power to rip the door off its hinges. As Scouts in the hallway launched themselves at him, he struck them down like insects. Those strong enough to defend against his physical attacks were crippled as he gripped onto their brains and squeezed, bringing them to their knees. His magic surged, far exceeding his prior experience, causing their eyes to burst and blood to pour from their noses. Alarms blared as more Trine Scouts attempted to stop him.

He tore through them, barely cognizant of the lives he was taking. Necks snapped, bones broke, and souls cleaved from still-warm bodies.

Some of the Scouts burst into flames or turned to ash in the blink of an eye, all without his direct attention. Instead of focusing on the innocent lives he took, he escaped further into his mind, submerging himself in the belief that the crimson rivers he created would buy Cosima's freedom, for good.

Only those who intended to keep them apart would feel his wrath.

The unbridled potency of his magic now pumped through his veins, filling his bloodstream with its fervor as it dissolved who he once was from the inside out. There were no more barriers to break through; all that was left was to allow his curse to rip him to shreds and piece him back together again. The dark companion he fought to elude now ran rampant through his body, restricted no longer.

Finally, his curse sighed. *Apostle of reincarnation, harbinger of calamity, and seraph of salvation—the time for your divine dichotomy has arrived.*

Enzo stepped into the fresh air, his feet sinking into the cloud the holding cells rested on top of. Without worries of repercussion or ill-fitting consequences attributed by a recklessly egotistical empire, Enzo slashed his way to the portal. He channeled out the screaming and the sound of magic blasting through the air, leaving himself only capable of registering his own voice as he hummed Cosima's song.

Chapter 44

"Witch!" a man from the crowd hollered as he held out a torch, nearly burning Ivo in the process. "Burn her! Burn her now!"

A woman, who arrived on the back of what appeared to be a horse twice the size of any she had seen on Haelos, gripped Ivo's upper arm and tugged her to safety. She cursed under her breath, whistling a whirlwind of insults as she tossed Ivo like a sack of potatoes on the back of midnight black stead, before hopping up herself.

"Halt!" the woman hollered. "You will not touch the intruder. I will bring her to the countess."

Her brown hair swished in Ivo's face as the reins snapped and the horse lurched forward, the woman muttering to herself all the while. Ivo wrapped her arms around the woman's waist, straining to hold on through the horse's fierce gallop. It reminded her of flying in Nariah's arms, and for a moment, the sadness threatened to drench her as her heart pinched.

The woman yanked on the reins, bringing them to a stop, and turned to face Ivo. She wore a deeply etched frown as her thick brown eyebrows knit together. "You're hardly breathing, doll, you know that?"

Ivo sheepishly met her gaze. "It's not every day that I end up on a strange planet." Though the statement was true, she could not get herself to admit the real reason why she was so weak. She didn't think she could get herself to mutter the Scout's name without bursting into tears. "Why are you taking me to the countess?"

The woman faced forward, and the horse moved at an even pace, slower than before. "Trust me, she is exactly the person you need to see right now, especially with the shadows looming over you."

"Why did those people keep calling me a witch?" Ivo asked.

At that, the woman gave a haughty laugh. "Your magic is a beacon. Did you think they would not be able to sense it?"

"I don't have magic," Ivo lied. "You are mistaken, I am a simple mortal."

The woman let go of the reins and whirled around, grabbing Ivo by the chin, her fingers digging deeply into her skin. The horse continued its easy trot as though the animal was used to the woman's antics. "Do not lie to me. I am an Adenyeh Gaide."

"A what?" Ivo asked through painfully pursed lips.

"An Adenyeh Gaide," she snapped, releasing Ivo. "It means, *mortal*, I know precisely where you come from and what you are. Your home planet is far from here, and your magic will not be welcomed by the others."

"What is wrong with my magic?" Ivo asked, rubbing her jaw.

The woman put her back to Ivo again. "They believe that you should not exist."

"Says who?" Ivo protested.

"Says the empire, and every kingdom ruled by them." Her lip curled. "If you are as you claim, a mortal with magic, something that is against nature. Those people you saw back there," she shook her head. "They could have crushed you with little effort. That is why I am taking you to the countess. She will take pity on you. The king may have burdened her with arranging for the transport of prisoners, but this is where you got lucky. She will want to save you."

"Save me?"

"Yes. The king would lop your head off before he dared to invoke the wrath of the Eternal Kingdom. The countess will arrange your transport to the Citadel if you're truly favored. At worst, you may be let loose somewhere outside our territory."

Ivo's pulse quickened. *How far am I from home?* "What is the Citadel?"

"A refuge, of sorts."

"Right." Ivo chewed her lip. "What is your name?"

"You don't need to know it," the woman grumbled.

"Well, I'm Ivo. I do have magic, but not the powerful kind that can hurt others. I'm a healer. I mean, I was, for many years. I have some spell-casting ability, but I wasn't taught everything there is about my magic."

"Why did no one teach you?"

Ivo's mind clouded with memories of being taken prisoner and forced to work in Aeria. "It's a long story."

"If you tell me how you made it to our planet, mortal, I will tell you my name."

Ivo shrugged. "Seems fair, but I don't know. One minute I was in the Eternal Kingdom, being healed myself when the woman helping me…was hurt, I think, and she told me to run. When I tried to get away, a portal appeared and I slipped through, ending up here."

The terrain grew rougher as they veered off the beaten path, the horse navigating with expertise through the unmarked forest until they reached a small castle. It held one tower to the left beside a gatehouse tunnel secured with iron bars. Moons and stars covered the tower, made from silver paint.

"While an unlikely story, I am strangely inclined to believe you. I am Isolde. Inside, you will meet the Countess, Johanna. As a member of the royal guard, I will have no choice but to kill you should you try to harm her."

"I'm not a threat," Ivo said.

"I'm aware. I am merely reminding you of how outmatched you are."

Ivo huffed, but did not respond. When they approached the gate, a thin, lanky man appeared and unlocked it swiftly. Isolde and the man did not so much as make eye contact as the horse trotted inside. The guard locked the gate behind them and scurried off, disappearing once they had passed through the tunnel and into the courtyard. A woman wearing a modest blue dress with a white head scarf stepped out from the castle and gave Ivo a warm smile. She had beautiful brown skin and reddish-brown eyes, like perfectly brewed tea.

"The mystics were right about her stark eyes," Johanna said, "what an auspicious surprise."

Ivo's face twisted in confusion as Isolde hopped off the horse, managing the steep drop with ease. She held out her arms for Ivo. Unsure of how else to get down, she swung her leg over and sat facing Isolde.

"I'll catch you," the woman said, waving her forward. "Come now, we don't have all day."

Ivo fell, but as promised, Isolde caught her and set her down in a patch of sparse grass. "Johanna," Isolde said. She walked over to the countess, and the two exchanged a hug. "I hope this isn't a bad time."

A soft wind brushed through the courtyard, rustling the yellow leaves in the tree above. Ivo rubbed her arm and looked around. The new environment made her stomach turn, the unfamiliarity only making her miss Nariah's comforting strength more. She clamped her teeth onto her lip as she held back her tears. This was not the time to fall apart.

"Not at all," Johanna said. "Somehow I knew today would be the day." She paused, cocking her head to the side as she studied Ivo. "Are you well, child?"

She managed a small smile. "Just lost and hungry."

Johanna gave her a warm smile. "Come inside. I have fresh bread."

Ivo followed, her eyes dropping to Isolde's waist as she walked in front, taking note of the twin short swords at the woman's sides. Another pang of grief echoed through her. As much as she hated to admit it at the time, Nariah had made her feel a sense of safety that had disappeared once she died, and Ivo still looked for her everywhere.

The interior of the castle was luxurious, with far more attention to detail than the outside indicated it might have. The rugs beneath their feet were bursting with color and were of such fine quality, it made Ivo uneasy to walk on them, lest she make them dirty and ruin the enamoring patterns. Fabric billowed from the walls and posts, creating an entrancing, airy feel to the rooms.

A glass tabletop sat on a metal base sculpted to look like a man and woman were holding it. Chunky blue cushions were placed around it, and Ivo sighed as she sank into the woman Johanna had motioned for her to sit in. A woman wearing a beige dress and a forest green head scarf poked her head into the room. When Johanna waved her in, the woman ushering a darling gold cart wheeled toward them with pitchers full of vibrant fruits floating in water.

A glass was poured for Ivo, and she found herself taking a sip before she had fully considered if the action was wise. Either way, the infused water was delicious and exactly what she needed after her tumultuous travel. Johanna brought her bread and thin slices of white cheese to munch on as she spoke with Isolde in the kitchen. As Ivo sat there, the persistent ache in her chest dissolved, replaced with a mysterious strength. She set down the piece of bread she was eating and stretched her back as more of her discomfort vanished. After a few moments, she could hardly recall why she had felt so devastated when she arrived on this strange planet.

Isolde and Johanna emerged from the kitchen. Isolde took a seat beside Ivo and shot her a quick smile as Johanna settled in across from them. "Ah, you seem a bit brighter. It seems as though the food has brought you some relief."

"Huh, I guess it did," Ivo said, her forehead crinkling. "Thank you for your kindness."

"You have done well bringing her to me, Isolde," Johanna said, reaching forward to rest her hand on Ivo's. Her eyes illuminated in a faint red glow. "You are from Haelos."

Ivo startled. "Y-yes, how did you know that?"

Johanna smiled as she leaned back in her chair. "I know much about you already, Ivo. We will be fast friends."

"Her magic…" Isolde said, trailing off.

Johanna nodded slowly. "Yes, my loyal knight. She is exactly as the prophecy proclaimed."

"Prophecy?" Ivo asked. The missing context left her craving answers.

"I told you that you should not exist," Isolde huffed. "The Goddess who created your planet, Ehses, did so in violation of the statutes assigned by the Celestial Empresses. The Empire has strict regulations on the creation of sentient beings. A planet cannot have an imbalance of magic and mortality."

"Your magic is proof of such an imbalance," Johanna added. "Poor soul. Your body is weak, but your magic is so curiously strong. If you weren't careful, you could burn right through your flesh."

"I didn't know that could happen," Ivo said softly.

"When the body is not fortified for the levels of magic it possesses, the power could kill the being. It is reckless, an egregious disaster waiting to implode. I imagine you were shoved into a body not your own because of the imbalance between your flesh and magic. I wouldn't be surprised if you turned out to be more powerful than the Goddess who created you intended." Johanna sighed. "Your entire planet is rampant with these imbalances. From what I could tell of your memories, the people—"

"My memories?" Ivo shrieked. "How?"

Isolde attempted to calm Ivo by laying her hand on her shoulder, but it only made Ivo leap to her feet, spilling her water over the glass table. It ran down the sides, puddling in the Countess' lap. She rose graciously to her feet, approaching slowly.

Ivo backed away. "Stay away."

"There is no harm done," Johanna assured. "I have already witnessed all your memories and returned them to you."

"You stole them?"

"Temporarily," Johanna said.

"How do I know you gave them all back?"

"I have no reason to keep them once I have learned what I need."

"Yeah?" Ivo asked, taking another step back. "What did you learn then? That I was a slave? That the Divinity are trying to kill my friend? That I'm helpless to stop it? Are you satisfied with your intrusions?"

Johanna frowned. "You mistake my intentions."

"We can help you," Isolde said.

"How are you supposed to help me?"

Isolde dropped to her knee, bowing her head. "Johanna, myself, and a dozen other women are the only remaining full-blooded Adenyeh Gaide. Only a drop of our blood is needed to possess a certain level of power, but other bloodlines were favored over ours, leaving our great-grandmother with no choice but to ensure our survival while teaching us the ancient knowledge of our people."

"With a drop of our power, others could sense you were endowed with magic, but nothing more. With our pure blood, we are able to discern the heritage and true origin of any being in the galaxy, even if we do not have prior knowledge of the planet." Johanna inched forward. "Additionally, we can access memories, allowing us to navigate the past, strengthening the wisdom of not only our people, but others as well."

As Isolde rose, Ivo blinked a few times and then answered. "What does that have to do with helping me?"

"We have heard the echoes of chaos created in the wake of the Sacred Twelve, but we have equally launched our own retaliatory campaign, determined not to be another planet subjected to their asinine choices. The prophecy spoke of you, decades ago, and now here you are." Johanna pulled something from her pocket, letting it dangle between them. A pale blue crystal butterfly pendant glimmered on a sturdy black cord. "Do you know what this is?"

A puff of energized smoke, like lightning in dark clouds, came from the pendant. Ivo flinched, but she did not feel pain when it touched her skin. Instead, it invigorated her, restoring her beyond what any healing or rest could offer her. She assessed herself, curious how she had been relieved of decades of draining emotions in seconds.

"This is a crystallized soul, one crafted from an eternal being," Johanna said grimly. "There are three in existence. Each one was crafted after the inspiration of the Celestial Empresses. Legend states that when they were brought into existence, their creators, known only as the Cosmic Devotions, captured prolific elder souls and entombed their essence into these butterflies. The Empresses were gifted the Empire's territory, which we inhabit now, when it was merely a vast expanse of dark space. Consumed by the absence of life, the Empresses began their work on the Weave."

"This butterfly," Isolde said, "can kill almost anything in existence *except* a Celestial Empress. However, if all three were combined, even they would succumb. This specific butterfly was obtained from a brother of the Sacred Twelve. When Johanna touched him, she obtained his memories. He was tasked with hiding the butterfly, and we believe Ehses is still unaware that he was unsuccessful, meaning we are the only ones who know its location."

"Your planet," Johanna said, "likely holds another butterfly. The crystals from Haelos are magnificently dangerous. A combination of Ehses cultivating raw power for weapons and an intensifying effect from the butterfly."

That pendant could help Sima kill the remaining Sacred Brothers, Ivo thought.

"Let us use a tendril of your magic to find your home planet. There we will recover the second butterfly, if Ehses has not already retrieved it."

"My magic?" Ivo looked down at her hands, unsure if she could trust the women she had met today. If they spoke the truth, the pendants could aid Sima greatly. If they lied, then Ivo could very well be setting her planet up to be invaded, or worse, attacked. "I don't know."

"This is not a situation that can wait," Johanna urged. "When the other brothers are killed, that is when Ehses will make her move, enacting the grand plan she has been formulating for thousands of years."

"Help us help the trillions of lives impacted by this," Isolde said, shaking her clasped hands in front of her. "This is about more than just you."

Ivo bit her lip, torn by her indecision. This was an opportunity to return home, to bypass whatever plans had been hatched for her by the Kingdom, but equally came with a substantial risk. She wondered what Cosima would choose to do in her situation.

"Prove to me you are telling the truth about the butterfly, and I will agree."

Johanna nodded. "I understand your desire for proof. Very well. Do I have your permission to touch you?"

"Yes," Ivo said cautiously.

The countess lunged forward, grabbing her by the arms as she pulled their foreheads together. When they touched, Ivo's mind expanded, surging with bestowed wisdom. It was not like viewing memories as moving pictures, but as if her mind accessed knowledge she had always had. When she reached for the information, there it was, waiting for her.

It was clear. The butterfly's mysterious and ever-evolving powers. The deaths of brave volunteers in the pursuit of decoding the strange artifact. The travel to distant realms in search of answers. Ivo blinked, acclimating to the information as her mind processed the stakes.

The butterfly that Johanna had tucked back into her pocket was not merely a weapon, but a planet destroyer, a soul breaker, a havoc bestower. Her mind struggled with the fact that something capable of this level of obliteration potentially rested somewhere on her planet.

Could Aurelio have known about the pendant? Was he searching for it on Haelos?

"Will you help us?" Johanna asked, summoning Ivo out of her thoughts.

Ivo wrapped her arms around herself. "I will take you."

"Excellent," Johanna said, clapping her hands together. "We must move at once."

Isolde ushered Ivo away as Johanna pressed her palms together. A series of symbols appeared in the air before them, made of sapphire blue energy. Johanna shoved her palms out in front of her, then rolled her hands around her, gathering the blue magic.

Johanna shot a beam of light straight ahead, which pooled until a shimmering portal formed. "Come now," she commanded, and Ivo rushed forward. "Aim your powers toward the middle. I only need a drop to navigate."

Ivo closed her eyes and called forth her magic, and it greeted her like an old friend, with warm comfort as it spilled from her hand into the portal. When she ended the stream and opened her eyes, her jaw dropped.

Inside the portal was a direct path to the Ombra District on Haelos.

Vincenzo

To his surprise, Vincenzo had eviscerated an entire block of the holding cells before someone potent enough to be considered a threat arrived. The room he had once slept in, dreaming of this day, lay in battered ruins, a trail of bodies left in his wake. He had been close to feeling regret, or something sour like it, but had grown tired of abiding by the rules of people who'd rather damn him and the ones he loved to death. Instead, he basked where he had once balked, and thrived where he had once floundered.

The magic that pulsed through him had an invigorating sweetness, a joyful aftertaste that kept him reaching for more, and a proper adversary was just what he desired. If he had sold his soul by letting this power corrupt him, then he would make the transaction well worth the trouble.

"Vincenzo, what are you doing?" Demi shouted. "Stop this!"

Enzo's eyes glazed over her, uninterested. Beside her stood her Trine Scout, Aether, and High Priestess Keres, who stood defensively, her back and shoulders straight, prepared to unleash her own legendary abilities on him. A pull within drove his hand up, as if he had become a vessel for the power that rested within and not the wielder.

"Are you here to stop me?" Enzo murmured.

"Are you finished with your tantrum?" Keres asked, unfazed by the threat his gesture insinuated.

She was not intimidated by his power. It amused him. "You allowed my brother to snatch the woman I love like she is a lusted-over prize behind thin glass. I have had enough of your incompetence. Some matters are best solved violently, I am coming to learn. When not offered a path, a leader must make one himself."

"We could have helped you find her. This makes you an enemy of the Kingdom," Demi said with disbelief. "You can't get away with this."

"Lies," he roared. "You have all been ready to damn her without a second thought. You would have pinned this all on her and never searched for her. I won't stand by and watch you all do *nothing*."

Useless, useless, useless, his curse chanted, *kill them, kill them, kill them.*

"Back down now, Vincenzo," Aether called out. "We will have no choice but to kill you if you resist, and I don't want to have to do that. Think of Cosima. What would she think of all this death?"

You do this for Cosima, his curse hissed. The words submerged him deeper into his darkness as he relented more of himself to it. *I do this for Cosima,* he thought.

He stepped over the body of a dead Scout, now aiming his palm directly at Keres. Her stone expression was smooth as she surged forward, spinning her arms as she crafted a glowing yellow and smoky black shield in front of her chest. Her hands jutted forward, and the shielding grew, completely immersing the High Priestesses.

"Stay behind me," Keres commanded Demi and her Scout.

Aether furrowed her brows as she pulled a throwing knife from her belt. "Why are you doing this? You told us you weren't the enemy, and now you've betrayed this Kingdom. This won't end the way you think it will."

"He's showing us who he truly is," Keres snapped. "He is revealing the depraved thirst for blood he has always had burning inside him. My sisters should have let me kill you when we had the chance."

They already betrayed you when they made Cosima their bargaining chip, their pawn, their scapegoat, his curse roared. *Rip this Kingdom apart with your hands and craft peace with your tears. It is time for a new dawn.*

Enzo's eyes illuminated, the green rays of light bursting from the sockets of his face as more of the famished rage fed the burning pit of untethered magic. For now, he contorted his power to his liking, molding the torment and hatred he held inside into a weapon he would launch with his bare hands. Combining with his starlight, his energy skipped along the galaxy beams until it slammed into the shield and crackled off it like ice shattering on stone. Keres wrinkled her brow as her shield cracked. A void in his heart spoke to him, fed him stories of food ripped from his hands, pain that seared his body, loneliness that consumed his soul. It persuaded him to unleash more, to tear down every obstacle until his tattered soul renewed beneath his own vengeful grasp on those who had hurt him.

Those had hurt *her.*

He sent a blast three times the magnitude of the first, rocking the ground beneath their feet. Bodies and rubble flew with the gust of energy, raining onto the shield as the Priestesses cowered inside it. Pieces of her shield gave way, creating small holes in Keres' defenses. His wings lifted him from the floor, allowing him to hover above them several feet in the air.

His thoughts blurred into the voice of his curse, and Enzo could not tell them apart. *Keres is the Priestess of metamorphosis. Her refusal to submit to True Darkness has caused me to awaken. I have come to rectify what her fragile soul could not.*

Enzo's mouth began moving, but he was not sure where the words came from. "You are a coward, Keres," he growled. "Just like the rest of your sisters. I know what it is you are too afraid to do, why it is you refuse to hand over the proper keys to the Kingdom." His curse seeped into his eyes, causing them to glow. "You all sent us on that suicide mission, hoping to clean your hands of us, but that didn't happen. In fact, Cosima and I succeeded in laying two of my brothers to rest. We brought us closer to the finale of this petulant prophecy, and yet it wasn't what you wanted. You didn't expect us to survive, and now, with only three Sacred Brothers left, your lives hang in the balance. If Sostene prevails, your heads will roll. If I win, there is no telling what is in store for you. And let me guess, if Alvize wins, you get to keep some modicum of power. What did he offer you in exchange for your compliance?"

"You do not frighten me." Keres narrowed her gaze. "You have no clue why I make the decisions I do, nor do you know who I stand with. It didn't matter to me whether you lived or died because there was no reason you should have even lasted this long. Whether it's Alvize or Sostene at the end, at least I know it won't be you."

Enzo grit his teeth as he growled. Towering strikes of his viridian electricity sparked, creating a web of energy in the air above him. Although his magic did not pierce Keres' mind, he could sense the shadows that created a pit inside her. "I can smell your dishonest words, Keres."

Demi trembled as she whispered into Keres' ear. Keres scowled, her bone crown shaking as she shook her head, but Demi did not let up. Aether joined in, not taking her eyes off Enzo as she pointed a throwing knife in his direction and whispered with the Goddesses. Whatever the Scout whispered to Keres enraged the Priestess more. Demi looked at Aether. "Are you sure this is what Nariah would have wanted?"

Aether nodded tightly. "I went through as many of her recollections as her brain would allow after her death. Merit trusts Enzo, and so did Nariah. I hate to say this with how many of my brothers and sisters lie dead back there, but Sostene is the real enemy here, Demi. I saw him through Nariah's memories. He is stronger than we are prepared for, even with Alvize's help."

His curse snaked around his throat and forced words through his mouth. "Think carefully about which alliance you put your faith in, High Priestess Demi. How much do you trust your sisters? When my mother was being stripped of her title, who gave her a chance to make a run for it?"

A flash of Keres' black energy cracked through the sky, and heavy droplets of rain danced across his head, cooling the heat accumulating inside him. "I did no such thing."

Aether's eyes locked onto Keres as Demi's hand trembled at her sides, waves of teal light spearing from her fingertips. "Then why were you one of only four sisters who voted against her banishment? After the announcement of her removal had been made, you were mysteriously nowhere to be found."

Keres's lip curled into a sneer. "You believe him over me? We have served by each other's sides for thousands of years. Don't listen to him."

The Goddess turned to face Enzo, her cheeks tinged pink. "The Celestial Empress has not been herself for many years—but she began declining rapidly after she confessed to us that her daughter was missing. We kept the news from the public, knowing that word of Kismet's kin would create confusion and disorder. We refrained from drawing attention to her deterioration to maintain the people's trust in the Divinity. When he arrived, Alvize was willing to feed us information about the tirade of inter-realm chaos and point us toward those responsible. Because of the increasing disorder in our realm, we decided to take him up on his offer. Without Kismet's direction, we chose to continue to place our faith in him. He told us we could find her daught—"

"You must stop," Keres interrupted, nudging Demi harshly.

"Tell me," he commanded, his electricity creating a discordant buzz.

Demi frowned. "He said we could find Moira if he could meet with Kismet. He attempted to perform a ritual where he would use Kismet's connection to Moira to locate her based on their attachment to the Weave. It took Alvize some time, but he managed to locate her and brought her home to Kismet, but the Empress didn't recognize her."

Enzo thought of Sima. Loving her meant caring about the well-being of the woman who may very well be Sima's mother. "Where is Moira now?"

Keres flinched as if she had been struck. "We can't tell you that," she hissed.

Aether pressed her lips together before she spoke. "They are outside of the Kingdom, but they are not far. Alvize took Moira back to her home after her meeting with Kismet did not go over well."

"We've attempted the reunion on several occasions," Demi held her head up, gazing at the sky, "but as I've said, Kismet claims she does not recognize Moira and refuses to accept her. The other Celestial Empresses haven't been seen since the day Kismet cursed Ehses, and no one knows where to find them."

The Trine Scout shifted on her feet. "I don't trust Alvize, not for a second. After the ritual he performed, she only declined further. Moira claims he is her savior, but something isn't right."

Enzo cocked his head to the side as he mulled over their admissions. Did they hope he would spare them?

His darkness laughed. *How much longer will you let this Empire flounder before you finally allow it to flourish beneath ash and fire?*

"Make this easy on yourself and stand down." The command came from behind him. Enzo whirled and found Alvize approaching with dozens of Trine Scouts at his side. "You have made a grave mistake, Vincenzo."

"Brother," Enzo said, extending his arms to the side. "What a pleasant surprise. We were just talking about you. Better to meet face-to-face, isn't it?"

Alvize's nose twitched. "These are not optimal circumstances to meet anyone, Vincenzo. Surrender yourself or be taken by force."

Enzo's curse cackled. *He believes he is enough to stop you? Death itself could not end your becoming. You have awoken, inevitable son.*

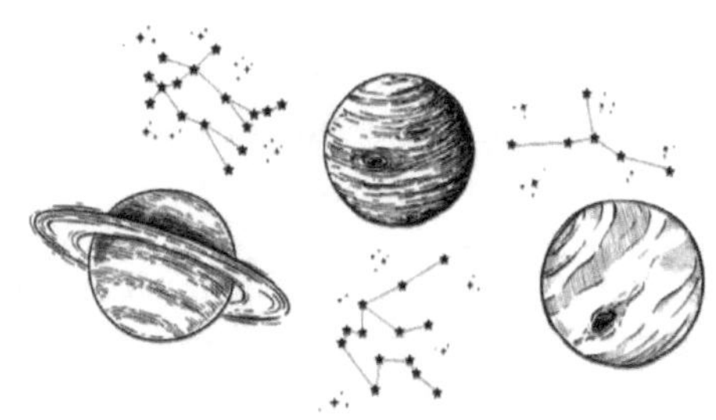

Chapter 45

Cosima

Although Cosima did not dream, while teetering on the line between sleep and consciousness, a memory from her childhood surfaced. She squeezed her eyes shut, willing the memory to stay as she soaked in the sight of her mother's face.

"What do you mean we can't do anything about the missing people?"

Her mother frowned. "The Divinity will find them, Sima. This is not for you to interfere in."

"If you do nothing, you are just as evil as the ones behind this!"

Moira shot Sima a look, and she sank back.

"I would do more if I could! I am not blessed like you, child. When Kismet decides she will step in, she will. Until then, you will let the Divinity handle it, and that is final."

"Why doesn't she do something? All she cares about are her little winged friends."

"There is a reason for everything."

When Cosima fully woke up, she had forgotten all about the nightmare of her circumstances. She rolled over in the plush bed, expecting to find herself in her assigned bedroom with Michi lounging in the great room outside. Instead, when she wiped the sleep from her eyes, she jolted upright, startled by her unrecognizable surroundings.

The room was embellished with almost exclusively black and violet decor. Beneath her plump mattress with its moody sheets was a thick black obsidian platform that hummed with energy. The walls were painted mahogany with amber light glowing inside silver sconces and billowing curtains over the windows. The largest piece of artwork was on the wall directly opposite the bed and depicted the iridescent threads of the Weave. *Can he see the threads like I can?*

No, no, no, Sima thought, her heart slamming inside her chest.

She rose from the bed, casting aside the silk sheets, and marched across the gold-flecked black marble floor. It was cold as she made her way to the solitary door. She was cautious as she turned the knob, grimacing when she found it locked. Sima reached for her magic, intending to split the lock open, only for it to once again leave her empty-handed.

A spell of dizziness slammed into her, causing Sima to stumble. She held her hand to her head as magic thumped against her mind. It was as if Sostene's magic created a sickness, lingering like thirst in the desert. It had not fully been cleared by her system, and his control echoed through her body and mind. She shook her head, willing herself to fight through the clouds and make sense of the situation. She continued to hold her forehead as she returned to the bed, the chill from the stone floor biting her toes. Once warmth returned to her extremities, she walked herself through yesterday's events.

She had been sleeping when a commotion came from the hallway. Ehses had found her, admitted to kidnapping Sima, and whisked her away to the realm they hid within now. Sima could not recall what she had seen of his mansion so far, as she was too dulled beneath Sostene's magic to form proper memories. However, she did remember two things.

"My mother," Sima whispered. "My real mother is out there, and Vincenzo is in trouble."

At that, her heart squeezed, her wary soul igniting with a small sliver of hope. There was somewhere Cosima belonged, people who loved her. She only had to stay alive long enough to reunite with her family and the man she loved. The person who stood between her and the life she wanted to live was Sostene.

Sima's hands curled into fists. "You can't make me obey you."

Sostene's words floated through her mind, reminding her that because of the chaos he created when he kidnapped her from the Eternal Kingdom, the Divinity would believe she escaped to be with him. His dangerous plan put Vincenzo at risk, and Sima knew if she didn't find a way to help him, the High Priestesses could very well have him put to death—if Sostene or Alvize didn't get to him first. She shuddered and shook off her fears, deciding instead to put her faith in Enzo.

It would have been simpler not to fall in love with him, but she did not regret their union or the peace it brought her. Among a lifetime of torment, he had been a powerful light, energizing her deflated sense of self. He had not been the one to save her, but instead had shielded her from the horrors of the world long enough for her to save herself.

Now, she ached for him.

She wanted to speak to him, to cast aside the grim reality they were doomed to and confess her gratitude. Had she truly thanked him before? Had she properly conveyed the impact he had on her life? Her heart dropped. She could not remember. Cosima reached toward the internal tether between them and gave it a heavy tug, hoping to feel something in return. None of his comforting, adoring energy wafted back toward her, and the sudden loneliness that took root inside her made her feel hollow.

She sniffled and reminded herself how far she had come. Sima had not waited idly by for her future to find her, she sought it herself. She had carved a place for herself among the cosmos, if only because she refused to die at her ex-husband's hand. Could she find some of that strength again, even when everything seemed hopeless? Could she find a way to her proximity to Sostene for her own benefit?

The door opened, and Sima wrapped her arms around herself. It was all too familiar, the way Sostene strolled in, Sima already in the process of shutting down as he took a seat beside her. She had been here before, scared of the man who entered her bedroom, fearing what he might do to her, fearing what she might be forced to do in return. When she met his blazing purple eyes, she knew she would never go back to being a prisoner.

"You are as beautiful as always," Sostene mused as indigo energy flamed around him.

Sima held her breath, reminding herself to be strong. *I can find my way out of this. I can use his obsession with me to my advantage.* She released the air from her lungs. *A man will never force me to do anything against my will ever again,* she vowed.

I was given this power, Sima thought as Sostene leaned closer to her, *the key is trusting it, just as I told Enzo.*

He lifted a hand to her face, aiming to push her hair from her face. Sima slapped it away, a fierce wave of her lavender energy collided with him as her power fought to surface. When he reached for her again, she snagged his wrist and dug her nails into his skin. He did not react beyond a shift of his eyebrows upward.

"You will never get me to comply with your commands if you begin like this," she spat, releasing him.

To his credit, Sostene smiled, never faltering in his composure. "But of course."

"Why are you here? What do you want from me?"

"As you say, I must convince you to love me. I will prove to you I am not the monster you believe me to be."

"You think you can woo me into handing myself over to you? You are using me like a tool to win your mother's games. It is not outside the realm of possibility that I would find this repulsive," Sima said with artificial sweetness.

He blinked. "I have plans for if you reject me completely, but please understand, I am allowing this to happen organically to prove to you I am worthy of your affections. It pains me to know another has your heart. Your adoration for Vincenzo makes me quite…" He cocked his head to the side. "Jealous."

"It should," she replied, her nose twitching. "You are nothing like him."

"Perhaps not outwardly," he said, eyes alight with amusement, "but my Sacred brethren all have the same soul. To a degree, we have identical powers, minus what he has been granted from his father."

"So, it is possible, then," Sima said, "for you to be as kind as Vincenzo is to me, but instead, each of you chooses to be cruel."

"Of course, it is possible. But whatever he can give you, I can give you more. He was born to a wayward God, an ancient hero who had long since lost his usefulness to the Kingdom. It was how he fell into my mother's trap anyway. Poor, washed-up Domani was begging for a chance to be valuable, to usher in a wave of revolution. His vision did not match my mother's, but she knew how to knead out his worries. My brother is the weakest link, the frailest soul ready to crumble beneath the weight of true greatness. Can't you see how unproductive it is to love him?"

"Enzo is not weak." Sima leveled her gaze at Sostene, his purple irises flaming with potent power. She did not balk at his magic. Instead, she bit back at him. "I do not love Enzo because of what he can do for me, but because of who he is at his core. I am not drawn to him for his strength, but for his softness, his kindness. When the universe is cruel, striking with heavy hands, he is brave enough to endure the intensity of its ire if it means keeping others safe. *You* are the weak one for the ways you resist gentleness. You could never replicate the love he and I share."

Sostene laid his hand directly beside Sima's, not breaching her boundary regarding unwanted touch, but proving, once again, his desire to be close to her. "If he is good to you, I will be better. I'll devote every sunrise to your beauty and make millions dance beneath the moon, singing of your impenetrable power. My baby brother cannot tweak the stars until they twinkle like your eyes. He cannot make the hue of the sky mirror your delightful aura. But I can. Allow me into your heart, for our union will change the future as we know it."

Sima moved her hand away from him. "I have spent too much of my life falling in line for others. No one gets to decide anything about my future, except for me, and I refuse to marry you. You are just as evil as your mother."

"She is not evil," Sostene said with a sigh. "She is misunderstood. The regulations put in place by the Celestial Empresses are far too restrictive. They keep the proper advancement of souls from partaking. In each realm, the Ambrosi and Rani Guardians are to direct the souls toward their highest potential; however, they refrain from letting the people truly experience the hardships they need to elevate quickly."

"I've heard that before," Sima said. "From *him*. Aurelio said that enduring hardships was good for them. It sounds like an excuse to not do your job and allow people to suffer."

"The suffering is temporary compared to the potential gain. The souls would be able to progress into immortal beings, perhaps even gaining powers strong enough to become Caelari. Did you know it is incredibly rare for divine beings to be bestowed by the Celestial Empress Lethe? It is because the souls must be refined enough to withstand power of that magnitude. The current order is preventing a new age for this Empire, one where divine beings usher inventions and magic we have never seen before into the realms around us."

Sima furrowed her brows. "Your solution is to force people to suffer until they progress into divine beings at a faster rate because you believe new magic will evolve?"

"It has to," Sostene said. "It is a natural occurrence. Every few thousand Caelari births, new magic evolves. The Eternal Kingdom depends on this."

"Why can't things continue the way they are?"

"Because, *Esti*— my little star, what do you think the existence of Celestial Empresses implies?"

"The existence of an Empire?"

"Close. Think bigger. Have you ever wondered what lies outside of the Eternal Kingdom? What the Ethereal Realm holds?"

Sima shook her head. "I have hardly seen the Kingdom to start with, let alone what lies beyond it."

"It holds dozens of small kingdoms, all operating in tandem with immortals preserving the flow of the galaxies they are tasked with maintaining. The Ethereal Realm is one of seven holy realms, called Lani's, each containing an Empire. Kismet, Nyssa, and Lethe, the hands of Fate, are a type of being called the Isheori, and even they are not at the top of the hierarchy."

Her mind strained to take in the new knowledge. "There are more beings as powerful as the Empresses?"

"More than you would be comfortable knowing. There are other Empires, other Isheori who threaten our existence, much like the Eternal Kingdom threatens the existence of the puny planet Haelos you found yourself enamored with."

Sima's thoughts raced, but louder was her disgust for Sostene's desires. "You act as if their lives mean nothing, yet you want to force them through a faster, highly treacherous growth cycle, because you fear the invasion of another Empire." She folded her arms, turning her head away from him. "You need them and yet you care so little for them. Vincenzo genuinely cares for others."

Sostene frowned, standing up. "You cannot care for *every* life, *Esti*. Do you feel sorry for every animal slain to feed your people? Do you lament the loss of each insect that fell beneath your stride? I have a plan for how to properly rule, unlike Vincenzo. You would be a fool to choose someone who knows so little of the grander scheme."

Somehow, that had gotten through her defenses, striking her deeply within. Her mind floundered, imagining twisted scenarios of invasions, ones she and Vincenzo would be wholly unprepared to mitigate. She shut her eyes, only for clear as day images to flash of more bloodshed, on scales her brain could never reconcile with. The sensation of his breath near her made her open them.

Sostene lingered inches from her face, his eyes filled with slimy desire. "You would become my Empress, and we could lead as one. I would make no decision without you. I told you before that you were the key to our phenomenal future, and I meant it. I respect that I am not the sole ruler of this connection because I find beauty in your magnitude, Cosima. There is more power that lurks within you, and I want nothing more than to be the one who helps embolden it so it may rise to the surface. You are more magnificent than I can describe with words. Let me show you the truth of who you are."

"I know who I am." Without meaning to, a pulse of her magic cracked the black obsidian platform beneath the bed, causing him to stumble and release her. She opened her eyes, ending the haunting over her mind she knew he had enacted. She jumped out of the other side of the bed and faced him.

My magic is responding, even if it is hard to grasp, Sima thought. *Whatever drugs he gave me must be wearing off.*

"I can see you need time to think this over," he bit out. He tamed the rage that flickered in his eyes until it slipped beneath the surface and smiled at her. "I will return at dinner time. For now, I leave you with a parting gift, something to remember me by."

"I want nothing from you," she said.

He laughed, disappearing and reappearing by her side. He grabbed her wrist, causing her to yelp, and touched his finger to her forehead. Sima was instantly subdued by the shattering of her mind. Memories flooded forward as they had done when Tasia had attempted to restore them. She had thought she had recovered all of them, but a millennium of lives lived proved she had only scratched the surface. She was helpless as she witnessed her births, deaths, failures, and loves all flash by without a chance to process. Her soul had a detailed report of everything that made Cosima who she was, extending as far back as her first incarnation.

While it continued, Sostene pressed a kiss to her temple. "There is more where that came from. When you are ready for it, I will show you the truth—your truth. I can do what no one else, not even Ehses, could offer you. There is a reason you are so important to this plan, my little star."

He gathered her in his arms and used his magic to meld the stone back together. He laid her in the bed and covered her gently. A bitter liquid dripped into her mouth as memories confiscated her attention, the concoction warming her body as she swallowed. His footsteps departed, and Sima was left alone with the mind-scrambling flood.

In one lifetime, she had been a widow with two children to keep fed and warm through the winter. In another, she had been a quiet librarian who died alone, but happy. Every life fit perfectly into who she knew herself to be, reaffirming her vision of herself to a dramatic extent, as if she finally peered into a mirror capable of showing who she was at her core. Tears streamed down her cheeks.

In unique ways, Sima faced incredible hardship, but had come out on the other side of every situation, not just in this world, in this life, but in all that came before it. The proof of the past lifted her spirits and emboldened her inner strength. She could not deny her bravery, her grit, her dedication.

With her new wisdom, Sima drowned beneath a strange, contorted guilt. A sickly thankfulness to Sostene intertwined with fierce rejection of him and everything he stood for. His plan for the Eternal Kingdom seemed to be a path of senseless suffering, but she could not deny that through her unlocked memories, she witnessed the ways in which her own suffering had propelled her forward.

No, this is what he wants. He wants me to see it from his perspective.

Returning some of her memories had been the least Sostene could do after what his family had forced her to endure. If the Kingdom slowed the progression of souls, in her mind, it had to be for a reason. However, a piece of her yearned for more, yearned to be shown more of her life.

As the images drew to an end, Sima sagged into the mattress, growing weary with exhaustion. She let herself drift to sleep, allowing her mind to rest. Her dreams were full of romanticized recreations of her past lives, blurring the line between painful hardship and temporary discomfort, however, a deeper sensation carried on in the corner of her mind.

Sostene's release of a wall somewhere in her mind had unlocked more than intended. Beyond imagery, a power she did not recognize hummed. Its song was sweet and welcoming, taking to her and spreading across her body like a veil of invisible armor. Her dreams continued, uninterrupted by the silent eruption of magic, extending Sima's abilities to new heights. Angelic voices sang in the background, imbuing her with wisdom.

A shield, a shield, a shield,
Within, within, within,

You are here to stop what should not begin.

A divine protector, a fated ancestor, you will rise,
A justice attester, a sacred protester, you will penalize.

A curse, a curse, a curse,
To end, to end, to end,

You are here to shatter what will not bend.

A reality changed, a heart estranged, guided by the sanguine lies,
A weapon hidden, a love forbidden, guided by the butterflies.

Her conscious awareness of these powers came with such stealth that when she awoke, she thought the unleashing of her magic had been a part of the delirious dreams. When Sostene sent a servant to retrieve her, Sima attributed the strange sensation in her bones to hunger and gladly followed to the dining room.

As she tore into the provided food and tuned out Sostene's self-inflating stories, the remnants of the song played on repeat.

A curse, a curse, a curse,
To end, to end, to end.

Vincenzo

"Brilliant plan you had," Enzo crossed his arms. "Become the beloved dog of the Divinity so they would be too enamored by your boyish charm to slaughter you where you stand like you deserve. You told me that you had Moira, not that you had an actress standing in her place."

Alvize's cheeks grew red, and his brows furrowed. He lifted his hand and snapped. The mayhem disappeared in an instant. The Trine Scouts, the High Priestesses, the ruptured corpses—all gone. His brother had thrust them into another endless white void. Enzo kept his face neutral, not revealing how overjoyed he was to find himself in an empty space, free to create without constraints.

"Do you think me that dim-witted? I have verified her heritage." Alvize's brows were knit tightly together as he scowled. "She is Moira."

"How? If you're not colluding with the outlawed Spirit Goddess we have as a mother, then how could you possibly know for certain?"

"Through her memories," Alvize said smugly. "I even got to witness the ones of tiny Cosima toddling around Moira's feet."

Vincenzo snarled, the green fading from his eyes, replaced with a smoldering, blackened red. "You lie!"

Alvize laughed. "So you've realized your strength. That doesn't scare me. I have been in touch with the limitless expanses of my powers for quite some time. Tell me, how are you faring with the maddening consumption required to function? Soon it will devour you. We both know you are not strong enough to outlast it."

"If the only reason I haven't slain you and all of our worthless brothers myself is my temporary inability to wield these powers as fluently as you can, then you are the weaker one. I am adapting, overcoming, conquering." Enzo's power sang to him, delirious with delight, dignified in its usefulness. He witnessed it shimmering through the void, seeing with new eyes. "It is only a matter of time before your head rolls."

"I thought you were uninterested in leading. Is that not what you told the Kingdom repeatedly? You know, your file was quite interesting. I was enthralled as I read through the transcripts. You were nothing more than a mistake, the piss-poor byproduct of true greatness," he spat, festering, "the heart-stopping fat off a hefty swine! You have none of the muscle or backbone required to nourish this Kingdom."

Enzo smiled. The more his brother unraveled, the more satisfying the burn in his veins became. He was intoxicated on the sensation, growing dizzy and impatient. He spat more of his starlight, magnified by piercing, electric energy, this time aiming directly for Alvize.

Let it sing inside your veins, let it dance inside your lungs, his curse whispered. *Let this power be all that you become.*

Alvize dove to the left, evading Enzo's burning magic. His void rippled as heavy blue blankets of his brother's power burst from his back. Alvize's wings resembled stormy skies as bolts of electricity flashed through his feathers, causing them to glow. He spread them wide as he cocked his head back and laughed.

"You think you're prepared for what is to come?" Alvize raised his hands, and globs of bone and tissue sprouted from the endless black of Enzo's void. The skeleton warriors towered above where they stood, stretching far into the darkness. "You couldn't be more wrong. When the day of reckoning is upon us, how many will be crushed by your utter incompetence before you take your own life? How many tallies should they carve into your corpse when you ascend to a position you were never meant for? Can you cope with being branded as the fool who damned us all?"

Enzo cracked his neck as he stared up at the bony beings. "I have spent more time pondering it than you know. Only in the true depths of night do I let myself consider a future where a crown weighs heavily upon my head and people scream for me when they are grieving. Do you know what answer I always come to when I consider whether I can withstand the breath of calamity?" Glowing viridian bubbles popped around the giant skeletons' feet, acid eroding the bones of their toes. "I was born of the unknown. I am bathed in the undefined, and I am clothed in the silky embrace of mystery. What do I have to fear from what is to come?"

Vines of his magic snaked through the bony warriors, caustic poison eating through to their marrow as they swung toward him with their swords made of sharpened femurs. Enzo raised his hand and clenched his fists. At once, the skeletons turned into billowing clouds of dust full of tiny bone shards.

A deep line formed between Alvize's brows. "No one can stop our mother but me. Do you have enough brain cells to comprehend what she and Sostene plan to enact? Ehses created thousands upon thousands of planets, all full of mortals with wayward magic. Her experiments were all to perfect one thing—vessels brimming with power that were effortless to sacrifice."

You must lay their aching souls to rest, his curse mused. *Only you can save them from their eternal suffering.*

Enzo's mind lingered on the words *eternal suffering*. "What is she doing with their souls?"

Alvize's eyes flickered with an emotion that passed too quickly for Enzo to discern. "Not their souls, brother, their life force. It is being bottled up, leaving their bodies to rot, while their spirits are warped and mutated. Our mother is creating demons out of twisted souls that should instead become divine beings."

His limbs trembled, and if his heart beat more often, it would have seized. "What purpose could that serve? Why divert them away from reincarnation?"

"Because they were never supposed to exist." Alvize looked away. "They cannot be reincarnated once they are split from their life force. The three threads of each individual cannot be frayed, or it disrupts the Weave. Their lifeforce, soul, and spirit must remain intact, or the tapestry begins to unravel. Something must be done to establish balance again before it begins to tear. You are far out of your element here, baby twelve."

The cosmic symphony begs for your harmony, his curse whispered. *Do not dismiss its yearning.*

"You have all been so cocky, counting me out as the weak runt of the litter. Only Sostene seems to sense that Domani's power has melded with our mother's, crafting something entirely new. I lived in fear of it, believing it would destroy me if I ever gave in to it. Now look at me," Enzo said, holding his hands above him. "Flourishing. You could not have found me at a better time."

Enzo clapped his hands together, the ground rippling in large waves as his arms moved. He pinned Alvize between his mountainous waves as his palms joined, causing his brother to spew profanities and threats as he fought to free himself. With time, Enzo had adapted to the strength of his siblings, understanding through exposure that they relied too heavily on their intimidating ability to overpower, as well as mind manipulation, when they could not strong-arm others into the results they desired. Rendering them incapable of moving was the easiest way to lessen their lethality.

Like oceans through desolate canyons, you are the sign of change to come, his curse sang.

Enzo laughed as he floated from the ground and commanded a roaring blast of stone and soil projectiles to beat Alvize senseless the moment the mountain wall dropped. A crude cage crafted of metal contained his brother with three white wolves, their glowing green eyes locked onto him.

Normally, he would not waste energy controlling his creations directly, but he wanted to feel their teeth sink into his skin; wanted to hear his screaming through their ears. He was drunk on the power he had rejected for an eternity. The power that came to him now came to him with the ease of an expert. As Alvize tore through the wolves, Enzo manifested horde after horde, showing no signs of tiring.

Twisted curiosity poured from his palms as he sought more stimulating means of murder. He released the wolves to their mauling and refocused his vision. The void around him crumbled, pieces of the world around them peeking through the holes in his brother's trap.

"Attack!" his brother hollered, ripping open the bars of Enzo's cage to escape.

The Trine Scouts that had accompanied Alvize set their sights on Enzo. Several of them jumped into the air, joining him as the ruins smoldered. Demi, Keres, and Aether had escaped, likely the moment Alvize had trapped them in the void, but it only turned the situation more deadly.

Enzo combined his powers in frenzied, mad ways as he casually flew forward, eyes an emerald fire pit. Armored faceless beasts towered above what remained of the nearby buildings and swatted Scouts from the sky. Flying insects spit poison, and deep tunneling holes opened, swallowing those standing on the clouds, the Eternal Kingdom sat on top of. He approached Alvize, who wore a deeply etched frown with two muscular Scouts flanking him.

"You're the one I've come to kill," Enzo said, a small smirk on his lips. "We don't need to involve all these other people, do we?"

The Scout to his left, with sandy blond hair, snapped his neck to face Alvize. "It doesn't have to be this way," Enzo said through the Scout's lips. "You could give in and admit you are the…"

"Now what was it you said?" Enzo asked, tapping a finger against his chin.

"The weaker man," Enzo said through the Scout to Alvize's right. She jerked her head toward his brother, her knees wobbling. "Admit you are the weaker man."

Alvize growled, creeping backward away from the two Scouts. The sensation of him straining to claw into their minds amused Enzo, as his own magic was enough to keep his brother out. Enzo stepped forward, placing his hands on the back of their necks.

"Say goodbye," Enzo commanded.

"Goodbye," they said in unison.

Enzo used his power to force them to snap their own necks as his brother's stoic expression gave way to obvious bewilderment. Alvize slipped through one of these holes, descending slowly as Enzo crafted something he had never thought to create before—a crystal crafted by himself. Magic poured like lava as a new stone emerged.

He held his hands as if holding a sword, and he swung, the metal spraying from his palms until it met at the tip. The entire weapon was crafted of Enzo's glowing lavender stone, with swirling storms trapped inside. He dropped himself through the cloud, meeting Alvize at the bottom, just in time to slice his head off. Enzo's power ravaged through him, burning at a temperature he had never experienced before, a pain so sharp it only deepened his blood lust. His magic shattered and cracked the inside of his stone blade as it met Alvize's neck, blood exploding in a mesmerizing halo around them. His eyes were blank with disbelief as it toppled downward.

For good measure, Enzo caught Alvize's body by the collar of his shirt, transforming the sword into a dagger as he stabbed through his heart, energy sparking off the weapon in an array of colors. He grabbed the key that dangled around what was left of his brother's neck and stuffed it into his pocket. Satisfied, he let the body follow Alvize's head, not caring where it or the others had ended up. From what he could tell, it appeared to be a never-ending river of empty blue skies. He burst through another tunnel in the cloud and resurfaced, heading for the portal.

Killing Alvize did not have the intense emotional relief he was anticipating, but a cold, gratifying reassurance instead, as if he had affirmed his intuition—he would be the last brother standing at all costs. Not because he would be more ruthless than his brothers, but because his survival was an inevitability. Enzo found he quite preferred the calm confidence that came with his insatiable power.

What is there to fear if death is but an obstacle, his curse laughed.

The bond to Cosima was sturdy, and the raging storm over their connection had cleared, dispersing the interference. He navigated toward her, the realm in front of him a blur as beautiful voices sang and instruments played each time he blinked. His power surged through him, and Enzo's apathetic mind let it continue to ravage any Scout who stood in his way, doing little to impede the flow. The Kingdom had initiated protocols to protect the citizens, but he paid no direct attention to the outside reality. His body moved as his power willed, and Enzo drifted into the safety of daydreams about the woman he loved. As blood coated his face, his emerald eyes burned, witnessing only one person through his hazy gaze.

The one who painted murals over bloodshed, the one who created life where there had only been desolation.

Cosima.

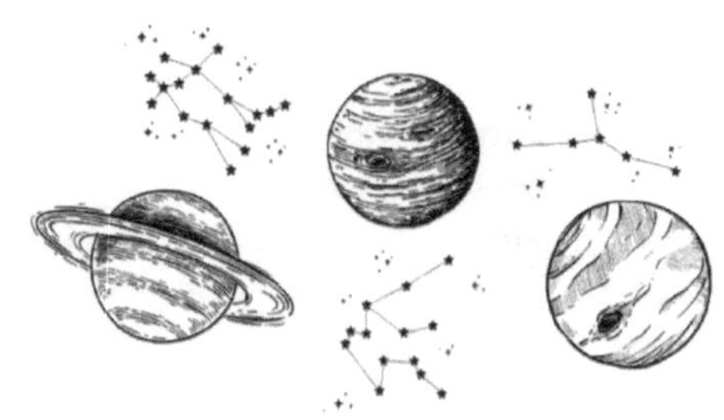

Chapter 46

Cosima

The breeze on the small balcony was delicate as it trailed across her exposed shoulders and kissed the tip of her nose. Her hands rested against the wooden fence as she soaked in the awe-inspiring sight Sostene had regular access to. His hideously grandiose mansion faced the waterfalls, all four floating islands raining water in a soothing spray into a lush spring below.

All this beauty, Sima thought, *and all I can think about is sharing it with Enzo.*

Sostene's hand brushed against her face as he moved a lock of her hair out of the way. He leaned against the fence and smiled at her. Instead of shying away from his touch as she might have done with Aurelio, Sima took a step away from him and shot him a sour glare.

"I told you not to touch me," she said. "Hasn't anyone explained to you that women don't like when you cross their boundaries?"

He gave an appeasing smile. "Right, my apologies. You are stunning, and it is hard to keep my hands to myself."

"That's not an excuse," Sima said. "I do not belong to you, and I never will. I am not your property. I am not a flower to pluck from the soil, so you can enjoy my beauty as long as I interest you. I am a person, and you will treat me with respect."

Sima refrained from cringing as she noted the strange sparkle in his eyes. He placed his hands in front of him in a show of appeasement and walked over to the table, plucking an orange fruit from the vine and popping it into his mouth. "I am not sure how you and Aurelio lasted fifty years together. I would have suspected you'd try to kill him sooner than that."

"I tried," she said with a grimace. She took a seat and smiled at him. "I believe it would take me *much* less time to kill you."

He laughed and leaned back in his chair. He ran a hand through his black hair and narrowed his purple eyes at her. "I have a question I have been dying to ask you about your little crush. May I?"

"I suppose."

"What do you see in him that you do not see in me?"

Sima wrinkled her nose. "Vincenzo?"

Sostene nodded, staring out at the waterfalls. "What do you…like?"

"I-I…" Sima took a breath. "That's not easy to…" She paused. That wasn't the truth. It *was* easy to talk about Vincenzo. In fact, all the reasons she adored him came flooding to the front of her mind. What stopped her was the creeping fear of Sostene using Sima's affections against Enzo, more than he had already.

"I don't ask out of malice, I assure you. I want to prove to you that I can be what you desire. He is not the only man who can draw your affections."

Her mind lingered on the immaculate sensation their combined power gave her. When Vincenzo's magic combined with hers, they created something so beautiful, she could never be convinced it was a mistake. "Other men are irrelevant," Sima said. "I don't want anyone else. He is irreplaceable. He is gentle with me in the most natural way. I have no reason to fear him or hide who I am from him. He doesn't seek to use me or destroy me. He wants to love and care for me. He doesn't want to do it simply to gain my affections, but because he is invested in my happiness."

Sostene raised a brow. "Are you sure this isn't you seeing what you want to see in him? How do you know he feels this way about you in such a short manner of time?"

Sima's eyes lingered on a collection of purple and black butterflies flying through the sky toward the spring at the base of the waterfalls. "When you spend a lifetime being mistreated, kindness is addicting. At first, when you don't know better, you mistake many things for kindness. Lust, greed, societal pressure, control. Those things can drive someone to be performatively nice, but never truly kind. After a while, I learned the difference." Sima rested her head in her hands. "It was clear immediately that he was different. He went out of his way to be considerate of me." Her mind drifted to the many meals, made beds, and fresh clothing through which he showed his love for her. "His love is giving and empowering. I don't feel like something is being taken from me. I feel as though I am being watered and nurtured. That compared to what I am used to…it is a mercy."

Sostene's face twisted, but the expression evaporated slowly as he softened his gaze. "I see, it sounds like he has made quite the impression on you. You care for him deeply as well."

"Yes," Sima said, her gaze dropping to her lap. "I do."

"You will forget him in time," Sostene said.

"If you harm him, I will never forgive you." Sima fumed as she glared at him. She reached for her magic, but it did not come. The memory of the bitter liquid Sostene had dripped into her mouth popped into her mind. She calmed the pieces of her that felt violated and reminded of her time with her ex-husband.

I will make him pay for what he's done, just as Aurelio had to, Sima thought as she clenched her jaw.

Sostene gave a very small bob of his head as he stared off into the distance. He blinked rapidly a few times as if realizing something. "I don't have to be the one to kill him," Sostene offered, his purple gaze glowing. "The Eternal Kingdom is going to annihilate him either way."

"Do you think you are doing me a favor by not killing him yourself?"

His eyes fell from hers. "Yes, I suppose in some ways I think that, but primarily I wish to please you and show you I can be considerate. You won't forgive me if I kill him, but he is doomed to die. You cannot save him, *Esti.*"

Sima curled her fist. "The only reason he is at risk at all is because you kidnapped me and framed me for the murders. Did you kill the Scouts? Is that what happened when she went into the hallway?"

"Only one. It was painless," Sostene said, furrowing his brow. "I did what I had to do, Cosima. If you understood my plans, if you saw things from my perspective, you would find it easy to love me. I cannot untangle you from my mind; I am bound to you. As the sun rises and falls, I am yours, as my heart beats in my chest, it hums for you."

She crossed her arms over her chest. "How can I believe you want this authentically? You treat me as though I have no say in the matter."

"Because I am not the morally corrupt man you believe me to be." His voice was raised, but he was not yelling at her. He was passionate, sitting on the edge of his seat as he spoke. "I *care* about your happiness. I want you to be happy when you're with me. Do you think I want you to hate me? Do you think I want to have to use my power to force it on you?"

"You…" Sima trailed off, remembering her conversations with Costanza. "You can't. Your magic isn't potent enough to fully break through my shields."

"Not yet," Sostene shook his head. "I can manipulate some aspects as my mother has, but I have refrained from seizing complete control. Never mind that, that is not what is important. I don't want to use my power on you. That is the point."

Sima let out a breath as the inkling of a plan spawned in her mind. Escaping from Sostene's mansion would prove to be difficult, especially without her memories to help her find her way back to the Eternal Kingdom. Sima knew the only way for her to gain the advantage over Sostene would be to get out of his territory. "Attraction and desire are not things you can force. It takes time, and you have to work for it. I cannot just fall for you because you want me to. Love comes from action, from undeniable devotion."

"So, tell me what it is I must do." Sostene slid from his seat and rested before her on his knees. He gently scooped her hands into his and stared up at her. The blatant longing in his eyes startled her. "I'll give you anything, I'll give you all of me—just tell me, My Empress, what do you need from me?"

Her lip trembled, and she clamped her teeth into it. She couldn't get herself to look away, and the longer she stared into his violet eyes, the brighter they seemed to burn. His passion was so enticing, Sima almost believed he truly did want her. "Have you seen…my memories?"

His face softened. "Not all from this incarnation, but quite a few, yes." Sostene lifted her hand and pressed a gentle kiss against her fingers.

She studied his dangerously handsome face and lingered on his lips, the shape a mirror to Enzo's. Sostene wore the mask of a perfect lover well, but something about him both drew her in and repulsed her. "I want to go home."

His eyebrow twitched. "You want to go home?"

"Yes, I want you to take me back to the palace I grew up in, the one from my memories."

A smile blossomed across his lips. "That can be arranged, *Esti*. Your grandmother built it for Moira far outside of the Eternal Kingdom, but I can take you there." Sostene brushed one more kiss across her hand before he released her and stood up. "I understand why you are eager to return. The memories I have yet to restore are leaving you homesick. How are you faring with the adjustments?"

Sima shrank slightly in her chair. "It has been interesting." When he crumbled the barriers inside her brain, she devoured the overflow, sifting through her own mind like a treasure trove with discoveries waiting to be made. Alongside it, a strange ancient sensation slumbered beside her soul, though she would not mention that detail to him. "Can you return my memories to before Ehses captured me?"

Sostene frowned and cleared his throat. "I will in time. That is not an advantageous move at this moment, my little star, but soon, I will show you your past and galaxies more." He stretched out his hand. Sima took it and rose from her seat. He brought her as close as she would allow and stared into her eyes. "We are going to be moving with dizzying speed, so you will have to hold on tight to me, darling girl. I don't know that I could bear to lose you in the cosmic river."

"Don't let it go to your head," she said as she inched closer to him. She looked away as he pulled her against his body and tucked his head into her neck. His violet aura grew, engulfing her inside it. The thrum of his heart sent pulses of his power through her. Sima tensed, hating the way it filled her with ghostly pleasure. She pressed her hands into his chest, desperate to push him off her. "Sostene—"

"Sima," he breathed against her skin, sending charged waves of goosebumps across her body. "Feel how your magic dances beneath my touch."

Cosima wanted to protest, but she blinked, and the world disappeared.

Home.

The word was somehow foreign, as if all the time away had begun to erode her sense of belonging, making her feel like a stranger, even as she stepped onto the dirt of the Ombra District. Johanna held onto Ivo's shoulder as she exited the portal, pulling Isolde by the hand behind her.

"Well, here we are," Ivo murmured. "Do you have any idea where the pendant might be?"

Isolde reached into her pocket and pulled free a small notebook. She flipped it open and used her finger to skim down the pages until she spotted what she was looking for. "From our research, we've uncovered two ritual songs we believe are associated with the pendant located on this planet. The first mentions the line: 'down deep, a drop too steep, beneath sediment and stone, find the wings where they flutter alone.'"

"Does any of this sound familiar to you?" Johanna asked.

Ivo chewed her lip. "That sounds like the underground tunnels, either in Aeria or here in this District. I don't know much about the ones in this District, but I know the ones in the Archipelago like the back of my hand. The problem is getting back there."

She craned her neck to get a glimpse at the islands where she had spent decades in servitude to the king. From where she stood, it appeared no different.

"Ah, I recognize this place from your memories," Johanna said, tapping her finger against her lip. "The pendant may be there, but the Sacred Brother that inhabited the palace would surely have found it. With the butterfly so close, he would not be able to ignore its magic aura."

"Underground tunnels here, then," Ivo said, placing her hands on her hips. "I believe the entrance is in a town to the south. My sisters returned to this District once they were free of the king, and if we are lucky, we might be able to find a familiar face."

"Lead the way," Isolde said.

"Right," Ivo said.

She found the sun and oriented herself south, struggling to remember the path to the city Speranza from the portale del regno stellare. There was nothing but dirt, cacti, and rocks as far as her eyes could see. The heat was mild enough to signal mid-morning, and Ivo waved her two strange companions forward.

"This way, I'm sure of it."

The walk was quiet at first, with no one daring a word, until Isolde broke and began to ramble. "Johanna and I haven't always gotten along, you know. I'm sure you think we are the best of friends, but it wasn't that way in the beginning. We hated each other, couldn't agree on anything, but pure blooded Adenyeh Gaide are rare, so I kept finding myself at her doorstep with every new piece of information that came my way."

Isolde cleared her throat. "I am supposed to bring this information to our king, but the countess is the only one who understands, truly. Our allegiance to stopping the brothers of the Sacred Twelve came when the brother we stole the pendant from came to our planet. Through his memories, we could see how his…horrible siblings had destroyed planets for fun, hopping to another when they grew bored. I knew our world could not succumb to the same, so we worked together in secret."

Ivo wiped sweat from her brow as the afternoon approached. "If you are so powerful, why do you submit to your king? If he won't do what is best for the people, then you should fight back."

Johanna huffed. "It is simple to say when you do not understand his power. We are Adenyeh Gaide, but what we have not told you is the reason it is rare to find another pureblood. The king is Oretzen, a being with magic strong enough to permeate outside of our world and into the darkness of hell. They come from a realm filled with demons, and they have taken up residence in our world."

"How could you stop a brother of the Sacred Twelve, but not the Oretzen king?" Ivo asked.

"We did not stop the Sacred Brother. We merely touched his memories before he was slain by another. We are not weak to the mind magic the brothers possess, but we are incredibly weak to the black magic the king and his men wield against us. Our people were created to tackle the knots and frayed threads of the Weave, something that works heavily against the motives of the Oretzens." Johanna tipped her chin up. "We fought back as we could, but it grew clear our people would be wiped out completely if we did not surrender. So, we gave in, complied with the laws of the kingdom, all to protect what little we had. That was nearly fifty years ago."

"In that time," Isolde said, "we have been able to uncover much about the pendant, and the history obtained through other visitors of our world reaffirms that there are three pendants. The one on this planet is either green or purple."

Ivo nodded. "You are not the first, nor the last group of people who will be forced into submission by a man drunk with power. At least you have maintained your vision."

Isolde offered a small smile. "As have you. Your memories reveal you are a woman of courage. It is not easy for a mortal such as yourself to survive such dangerous circumstances."

"It isn't," Ivo admitted, "but I don't have another choice. I have to try my best to save my people. Cosima is brave and putting her life on the line, and I figured, why can't I? I know that there were close calls while hunting Carmine and Dario, but I have always known what was at stake. The Scouts…" Ivo trailed off.

She shook her head, unable to remember the Scouts clearly. She knew Merit, Earnest, and Horacio had been there, but her mind refused to fill in the details of the other Scout that had been tasked with monitoring Cosima. She initially thought she was mistaken, and that there had only been three, but something within told her there was someone else.

"I'm sorry," Ivo said. "I've forgotten what I was going to say."

"Don't worry," Isolde said, patting Ivo on the back. "You've had a rough go of things lately."

"Yeah." Ivo pressed her lips together, searching her mind for what tattered remnants of memories remained, only to come up short. "Maybe it wasn't important."

To pass the time, Isolde and Johanna meticulously offered information, recounting where they had obtained it from, how they thought it tied into the brothers, and what they planned to do with their knowledge. Ivo appreciated the thorough recount, but could not help the rising worry that she was not the proper person to take it on.

"What if you're making a mistake and I'm not the woman the Empress of Day told you about?" Ivo asked.

Johanna grinned. "That is not a possibility. Your power is quite strong, and if it wasn't for your vessel, others would feel its weight too. Your body conceals the greatness of your aura."

Ivo glanced down at her hands. "I don't feel like there is anything special about me."

Isolde scoffed. "If only you knew."

"What is that supposed to mean?"

The woman's eyes flicked to her and forward again. "The prophecy is not entirely stable, but it always regarded your power as something capable of spawning new eras. You have a significant part to play in what is to come."

Ivo didn't like the sound of that. "And what exactly is to come?"

Johanna frowned. "Don't worry about that for now, Ivo. We will prepare you as much as we can after we find the next pendant. Once we have two, we will be able to relinquish the blue one to you."

"Why the blue one?"

"It belongs to you," Isolde said. "However, our mission requires us to have another pendant as we must deliver it to the rightful owner. The Empress of the Day bound us in blood to the blue butterfly, and we will not be released by it until we have one of the others."

"It's mine?" Thoughts of the blue butterfly fluttered into her mind, and Ivo vaguely recalled a dream she'd had about the crystal. She also recalled the way her soul seemed to go peacefully silent when Johanna had shown her the pendant. If they gave her the blue one, she could use it to save Sima from Sostene.

Ivo looked ahead into the distance and felt her stomach lurch at the sight. A small settlement ahead confirmed they traveled the proper direction, with the buildings nearly identical to how they were before she was captured and taken to Aeria. "We should be able to stop and rest up ahead."

"I welcome rest," Isolde panted. "It is not quite so hot outside on our planet."

Johanna nodded her agreement. "I am interested in seeing more of your home. Where do you suggest we stop?"

"There is a small inn," Ivo said, "if it's still open, we should be able to find a friend of mine. She always told me if we were able to return home, she would come back to the city her mother had lived in. She ran the inn here, and perhaps she still does."

From what Ivo remembered, only a hundred people lived here, but the movement down the street suggested more had come to stay. Shadowtypes she had not seen in decades wandered by, causing her to stumble. Isolde caught her and placed her back on her feet.

"Are you alright?" Isolde asked.

"Yes, I just…missed this." Ivo spotted the inn, with a large sign spelling out *Itana's Inn*. "There." She pointed. "Let's wish for the best."

A bell chimed as Ivo pushed open the door. At the red stone table sat a Viipir with her feet kicked up, chatting with a witch who wore large, round frames with her deep purple bangs cascading over the sides of her glasses. Ivo could not believe her luck.

"Itana," Ivo exclaimed.

Not once during her time in the Eternal Kingdom had Ivo ever considered that her journey would lead her to an old friend from Ombra, one she had met long before becoming trapped in Aeria. Itana, who shared her mother's name, had always treated Ivo with unwavering kindness. Her heart raced, thoughts jumbling together as Itana whirled around, screeching when she saw Ivo. She tumbled into Ivo's arms and jumped up and down.

"What are you doing here?" Itana asked, fixing her glasses. "Where have you been?"

"It's a long story," Ivo said, "but we are only staying the night. Do you think your mother would allow us to stay? I don't have coin to offer."

"Oh, please," Itana waved. "Mama 'tana doesn't run the place anymore, and I don't take payments from friends. How many rooms do you need?"

"We need a room that sleeps three," Isolde said.

"Well, I have rooms with two beds. Those have enough space for two people to sleep together. Would that work?"

"Two of us will share," Isolde answered.

"Right, then," Itana said, clapping her hands. "Let me prepare those beds for you. In the meantime, feel free to wander over to the dining room and grab yourselves something for dinner, on the house, of course. I hear there is a roast with rice on the menu."

Itana winked at Ivo and disappeared. The dining room was half-full, and Ivo selected a quiet booth in the back corner for them to sit. Once they settled at the table, a member of the wait staff approached with a pitcher of water with condensation dripping down the sides. She placed it in the middle of the table and wiped her hands off on her apron.

"Hi, ladies, welcome in." The woman, whose name tag read Respelda, picked at the ends of her long, straight hair, readjusting how it lay against her uniform, and smiled at them. "The kitchen has a beef and vegetable roast, tomato soup, or fireplace-grilled chicken over rice."

"Do you have anything spicy?" Ivo asked.

Respelda smiled. "Something off the menu for you," she said, adding a wink. "And for you two?"

Isolde cleared her throat. "Chicken."

"Soup, and a slice of bread if you have it," Johanna said.

"Absolutely. I will be back with your meals."

When Respelda disappeared, Ivo poured herself a glass of water and savored its chill down her throat as she drank. She finished the entirety of its contents before she set it back down and met Isolde's gaze. Isolde lifted a brow, as if asking, "Everything alright?"

"I haven't exactly had a moment to rest, or eat, or…drink, lately."

"Ah," Isolde remarked. "Your vessel's mortal needs slipped my mind. The frequency with which you must replenish yourself must be exhausting."

Vessel? Ivo shook her head. "About that," she said. "You mentioned you are Adenyeh Gaide. Does this mean you are fully immortal?"

"Some believe so," Johanna said with a smirk. "We are immune to aging and have miraculous healing abilities, but we are not very resilient against illness. There have been many plagues across our people's history that spread rapidly and led to significant population decline. Our magic is unable to stop the progression of the sicknesses."

"Where does the sickness come from?" Ivo asked.

Isolde blew out a breath. "There are too many to count. Complete destruction of the corpse and all items they came into contact with became necessary. As you can imagine, this made it difficult for our people to defend against the king and his soldiers."

Ivo clenched her fists. "I can relate to being too weak and disorganized to fight back."

"Your people were also captives," Johanna said knowingly. "Your memories of your capture were particularly distressing."

"Tell me about it," Ivo said. "Anyway, the reason I ask is, what are your plans if we retrieve the next pendant? Are you sure keeping them in your possession is the best idea?"

Isolde looked away, and Johanna gave an uneasy smile before she spoke. "Due to your closeness to the brothers and their ability to manipulate your mind, it is probably best we do not disclose our plans in detail to you."

"You've told me other stuff!" Ivo protested.

Johanna pressed her lips flat and took a breath. "Yes, but…It is unwise, Ivo, you must understand. We have spent decades preparing this plan, and you were our divine piece missing from the puzzle to locate another pendant, allowing us to move forward. I can tell you only that we wish to find the final pendant, and you are vital to that plan."

"To keep them for yourselves?" Ivo asked. "If I were the missing piece, then how can you also say I am not to be trusted? How do I know you two can be trusted with them? Maybe you plan to wipe out your evil king and all his people, using it for selfish reasons."

Isolde grimaced, and Johanna scoffed.

"We were entrusted by powers high above with this task, and through our awakenings we developed a connection too devout to betray." Isolde sighed. "We told you we found it by accident, but that is not the truth."

"Isolde," Johanna hissed. "You must not."

"No, she has a point. She brought us here, and every step has brought us closer to the pendant. I know we can both feel it. Why would *she* have given us the signs so long before Ivo's arrival if we were not to have faith in her? She is a child of our savior as well," Isolde said to Johanna. She flicked her gaze to Ivo. "The Empress of the Day has blessed our journey, saving both the countess and myself from the throes of death, granting us more time with a purpose greater than we could have imagined. It is the Empress who connected us, and who told us to carry out our research in secret, so we may evade discovery. It is the Empress who foretold of your appearance in our land, describing your eyes as blue as dense, frigid ice and hair as deep as the sky without stars. I knew who you were immediately, but I needed to confirm with Johanna. The Empress told us you would come to us when the time came for us to collect all three pendants. Your magic is necessary in locating the remaining two."

Empress of the Day? What does she want with me? Ivo sucked in a breath, unsure of what to make of their claims. "You knew I would find you?"

Isolde nodded. "Believe us when we tell you we are the proper hands to hold these pendants."

"We are trying to save lives, not take them," Johanna said solemnly.

"Why does the Empress know who I am?"

Isolde and Johanna shared a look, and this time, Isolde was not forthcoming with the answer. "You will learn in time. Forgive us for the secrets we must hold."

Hushed, angry whispers came from the front counter, catching Ivo's attention. She stood up and wandered toward the heated discussion. Ivo peered through the archway toward the counter and spotted the Viipir who had been talking with Itana, now arguing with a broad-shouldered Rani woman.

"Yadira," Ivo said, rubbing her eyes.

"Ivo?" the Rani said, face slack with surprise. Yadira turned back to the Viipir. "I'll tell you one last time, if I find out this place is renting rooms to faeries, I will burn it to the ground." She walked toward Ivo and stared down at her. "What are you doing here? Are you alright? Where is Sima?"

Ivo frowned, unsure where to begin. She glanced back to Isolde and Johanna with their creepy, all-knowing smiles, recognizing Yadira from Ivo's memories. "Why don't you come sit? It's a painfully long story."

"Listen, I may not know what happened," Yadira said, placing her hand on Ivo's shoulder, "but remember: you are weary, but you are alive."

Ivo nodded, waving her hand dismissively, despite being secretly grateful for her reassurance. "For now."

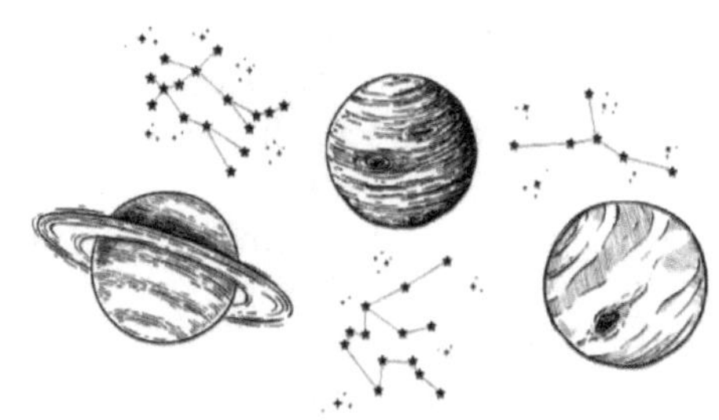

Chapter 47

Cosima

Sima did her best to maintain her composure as they hurtled through an empty black void, finding only speckles of light like distant stars in the sky. Sostene's embrace was tight around her, his smoky vanilla scent in her nose. After a minute, the void subsided, and they were thrust into a lush field with a palace. Sima recognized it the moment she laid eyes on it. She burst from his arms, and Sostene allowed her, trailing slowly behind her as she ran through toward the glimmering crystalline palace.

Clothed in a glimmering lavender gown from Sostene's magic, Cosima navigated through the towering blooming flowers, vines, and leaves snagging around her waist and scraping against the skin on her arms. She gathered the skirt of her dress and continued forward without waiting for Sostene. Her mind was locked so heavily on the goal of reaching it that she did not notice the dome of purple smoke surrounding the palace.

When she tumbled through it, she coughed, finding the smoke was thin enough to see through but was harsh enough to burn as she inhaled. For the first time, she turned back to see where Sostene was. He waltzed a few feet behind her, with his hands in his pockets as he followed.

"What is this?" she asked.

"A defense mechanism for the palace."

"Can it hurt me?"

He smiled. "Nothing can hurt you when I am near."

She rolled her eyes and turned forward, walking through the smoky quartz gates and into the courtyard. The interior of the courtyard had pristine serenity, a cleansing from the thoughtful architecture built to center the energy of those who entered. More crystals than she could identify were used to create the aesthetics, from garden statues spewing water in the pond to the jewels dangling from wind chimes that sounded like songbirds.

The stones hummed as they had on Haelos, but here, they were soothing. She spotted the main entrance on the opposite side of the courtyard. A small wooden bridge created a pathway over the pond, leading straight to the grand rose quartz doors. Dragonflies zipped through the air, their wings reflecting the sunlight in their iridescent wings.

"Can we go inside?" she asked, yearning for more.

"Of course, this is your home after all."

Sima laid her hand on an amethyst pillar and a memory surged through her, causing her body to fall limp into Sostene's arms.

"You know better than to interfere with the life cycle, little butterfly," Sima's mother hummed. "There is already a path for these creatures."

"But I don't want to watch them die," tiny Sima whined at the base of the pond. She had crumpled on the bank, cradling a dragonfly. She sat up slowly and carefully placed the dragonfly on the bank as its wings fluttered weakly.

"They are so beautiful, and the nighthawk has been killing them off one by one. It isn't fair."

"You are a Daughter of Fate. Your meddling disrupts the balance. Perhaps the clearing of the dragonflies will make way for better things to come."

"No, it won't," she said, crossing her arms and furrowing her brow. "I will never come to this pond again if they are gone."

Her mother chuckled, bending down to her level. She used a finger to tilt tiny Sima's chin upward. "But what of the lotus flowers? What of the smell after a good rain? What of the migration of the butterflies and the changing of the seasons? Won't you miss them?"

"Can't you change it, Anmah? Can't you keep them alive for me?"

"No, my dearest blessing, I cannot. It is forbidden for me to do so."

"But you said you had a special job of appointing Fate, just like—"

"Sima," she warned. "No. Anmah appoints the Fate of a chosen few. Your Hahlmon allows me to use my powers only as she directs."

Sima brightened. "Then I will ask her myself!"

The woman chuckled, picking Sima up and placing her on her hip.

"Come, then. We will have to devise a persuasive argument to save your beloved dragonflies, daughter."

"Anmah," young Sima said sheepishly, "will Hahlmon let me appoint Fate one

day too?"

Her mother beamed. "But of course. You are the brightest of our blood, and you will be an honorable leader."

Sima glanced back at the dragonfly, where it still rested on the bank. Its fluttering had ceased, and it was still with death. She sighed and rested her head on her mother's shoulders. "Maybe I won't be a good leader. I will try to save them all."

Her mother nuzzled her as she walked. "Your caring heart is not a weakness, it is more powerful than any magic. You will learn how to wield your empathy with wisdom and strength. For now, we will seek mercy for your beloved winged friends."

The memory subsided, and Sima sat up, finding herself inside a lounge room of the palace. The fabrics of the curtains and paint on the walls consisted of blue and gold hues, like sand and water in their simplicity. Sostene stood at the window, gazing out with a relaxed expression as he brought a glass to his lips and took a sip.

"Has this place been empty since my mother disappeared?" Cosima asked.

Sostene nodded. "In order to enter, you must have the approval of the owner, and not many do."

Sima's nose wrinkled. "Where is my mother?"

"I wish I knew," he replied. Something about his tone made her think he was being truthful, which only made her more suspicious.

"A Trine Scout told me that Alvize found her."

Annoyance flickered across his face. "Yes, it is quite unfortunate that my brother found her. If I knew where Alvize stashed her away, I would free her for you."

She shut her eyes, and behind her eyelids played images of her mother's face from her memories. If she had access to her magic, it would have swelled inside her as her emotions rose. *Where are you, Anmah?*

An explosion of vibrant energy tore through the room. Sima jumped to her feet as music played, and warm orange, red, and yellow lights flickered on like an inviting fireplace reflected off the walls. Doors flew open, and even the scent of cooking food drifted in, as if enticing her to venture deeper into her home. Sostene's brows were raised, and he made no moves forward. His magic had not done this, though he wore a satisfied grin.

"Why did you agree to bring me here?"

"I am trying to prove to you that you can trust me to take care of your heart. While you explore, I have the pleasure of spending time in your company, learning what I can of my future wife. I am not an inherently selfish man, little star. I can be possessive, I can be demanding, but I can equally be giving. Besides, it appears your home delights in your company."

Her lip tugged into a sneer at the word 'wife,' and although she did not know whether or not she trusted his words, the temptation to witness every inch of her home could not be quelled. She stepped through the doors of the lounge room and followed the smell of what she suspected to be her favorite spicy vegetable soup coming from down the hall. She ignored the smug grin on Sostene's face, knowing instinctively that he was as clueless as she was when it came to what they would find the deeper they explored. He moved, for the first time, without total confidence.

Something or someone is waiting for us within, Sima thought as she searched for the kitchen.

Cosima's nose led her directly to the kitchen, the scent of her favorite soup lingering in the air. Her neck swiveled as she took in the immaculate room, from the emerald green tiles lining the floor to the golden butterflies that littered the ceiling, twinkling with warm light. The kitchen was fully stocked, and simmering above a red flame was the dish she loved most in an iron pot. A wooden spoon spun within, as if the palace itself was preparing the meal, and beside it, a fresh pot of white rice steamed.

Sima glanced around, her eyes wide. "Is someone else here?"

Sostene cleared his throat, slowly strolling into the room. "I…am not sure."

She ran her fingertips over the white marble countertop, and a trail of sparkling energy appeared across it. Startled, she jerked her hand back. She looked up at Sostene, who had his back to her as he inspected a display of fine dinnerware. When she turned back to the counter, she found a small white bowl with piping hot soup inside it. She blinked, and a spoon appeared, along with a short stool for her to sit on.

This time, Sostene noticed the change. "You've poured yourself a bowl?"

Enzo would've gotten me a serving immediately, Sima thought. "I didn't do anything," she said. "It just appeared."

He raised a brow as he stared down at it. "Is this a meal you enjoy?"

"It's my favorite," she said, grabbing hold of the spoon and stirring the soup. "Do you think the palace remembers me?"

At that, he smiled. "I'd say it has never forgotten."

Sima could not resist any longer. Aged cabbage, mushrooms, and green onion swirled inside, chopped just the way she liked it. She lifted the spoon to her lips and took a tiny sip of the liquid. Her eyes fluttered shut as the spice hit her tongue. The soup was so perfectly made, she thought she might shed a tear over it as she went back for more. The sensation of the warm broth in her stomach made her smile, bringing her a familiar sense of comfort.

This is truly my home, Cosima thought. *I almost believed I'd never find where I belonged.*

"How is it?" Sostene asked, standing with his hands in his pockets.

She almost ignored him in favor of enjoying her meal in silence, but he continued to stare at her. "Delightful," she whispered, her voice dampened by the strange storm of emotions stirring inside.

"Why, then, are you sad, *Esti?*" Sostene asked, his eyes soft. "Shouldn't you be happy?"

Sima could not meet his gaze. "I have dreamed of the day I would return home, and I hate that it happened because of *you.* I hate that you're the one by my side and not Enzo, or my friends."

"Hate is a strong word," Sostene replied, cocking his head to the side.

"It is not strong enough," Sima snapped. "If you have deluded yourself into thinking I will happily obey, you have underestimated me the way all others before you have. At one time, I may have been pliable and timid, but that version of me is dead, because *I* was the one who killed her. I spent decades suffering in silence, surviving what I thought I could not. I did not put back together my own broken heart just to end up as your wife without a voice."

Sostene blinked a few times, considering her words. "I can understand why you may be resistant to me, little star, but I am not your enemy. I can give you as much power as you desire, so long as I know you will never betray me."

"But I will," Sima cried, tears bursting from her eyes. "I will stab you in the back at the first chance, I will bite the flesh you bring too close, and I will not rest until I am the reason you cease to exist. I will not go quietly." Her heart began to race, and the warmth from her first meal back in her true home ignited her strength, even if she was still without her powers. "Why does everyone believe they are allowed to make decisions on my behalf? Why does it not matter enough to you that my answer, Sostene, is 'no', and always will be?"

His eyes flamed a smoldering purple as he chewed his cheek. "I cannot accept that, *Esti*, you must understand. There are tethers tying us together, don't you see? I am the survivor, which means you and I are destined to not just be wed, but to be in love. You won't give me a chance. I have already glimpsed how this ends."

A chill ran through her. Something about the certainty in his voice made her want to flee. "I don't have to give you a chance. You don't even know the first thing about me. How can you claim we are somehow meant to be together? Do you know what love is?"

He scoffed. "Of course I know what love is."

"Do you? Do you know what it's like to trust someone even though you have every reason not to? Do you know what it is like to be drawn mercilessly to someone, to the point that you believe you are nearing madness? To have their face and their laugh burned into your mind? What Enzo and I have is not simply a comforting pastime or lust-filled desire—it is the natural outcome of a love too divine to contain."

Sostene's face twisted. "He cannot withstand the curse. Your union is hopeless, destined to fail."

"Then let it fail," Sima growled, curling her fists. "Anything is better than committing myself to an eternity by your side. I would rather mourn him than mourn my future."

He was quiet for a moment as he studied her. "Am I truly so awful?"

Her heart thudded loudly. "What?"

Sostene held her gaze. "I could give you everything you've ever wanted. The romance you crave, I will give you. The freedom you desire, I will create. Choosing my brother is a monumental mistake." He sighed, pressing two fingers to the bridge of his nose. "I wasn't going to tell you this yet, but I need you to see that I am not the monster you believe me to be."

"Nothing will change my mind," she said, crossing her arms.

"Perhaps not," Sostene said, "but either way you must know—Vincenzo is doomed, Cosima. There are pieces of the prophecy that only I know. Carmine was the closest to uncovering the full truth, but only I have the unrestricted details. The soul of the lastborn son of the Sacred Twelve is tethered to the Celestial Empress, Lethe. The deal my mother forged with Death required a sacrifice. It does not matter what order in which he dies, *Esti,* my youngest brother is cursed more thoroughly than the rest of us. He was never going to be the survivor."

Sima's heart pounded in her ears as she stared at him in disbelief. "T-that's not true. You're lying to me."

He shook his head solemnly. "I am not lying. I could show you…But it would require that I touch you again."

She trembled as she considered his offer. *Can he create false memories? If what he shows me is the truth, do I really want to know if Vincenzo is destined to die?* "What do you plan to show me exactly?"

He offered a soft smile. "The prophecy as I know it."

Sima stared at him for some time before she dipped her head, signaling to him that she approved. Sostene moved toward her slowly before he used his finger to tilt her chin up to look at him. He gazed at her with a haunting longing in his eyes before he touched her forehead with his fingertip, injecting her mind with a vision.

Sostene rubbed his shoulder as he sat inside the glittering green cave. Its ethereal glow further irritated his head, and the injury one of his brothers had given him pulsed with pain the longer he had to endure the light of the Oracle's aura. The woman had beautiful umber skin with her tightly coiled hair shaped into three peaks atop her head, each point decorated with marvelously detailed gold charms and chains. Her whole white eyes shifted back and forth as smoke toiled around her, creating a haze inside the cave as the Oracle's herbs continued to burn from the bowl at her feet. With a pulse of energy, she made her next selection, pointing toward the huddle of his kin.

One of his brothers, Amadeo, stepped forward, his black hair looming over his eyes as he stared down at the Oracle. She waved her hands slowly back and forth in front of her. "Oh, gracious mouthpiece for the cosmos," Amadeo sang gently, "grant me a glimpse into my greatness."

"Child..." the Oracle breathed. "One child."

Sostene shook his head as his spine went stick-straight. All ten of his siblings shared his surprise, stricken with silence as their mouths hung open. Their exact futures fluctuated by the second; however, something firm enough to be relayed by the Oracle had settled inside Amadeo's destiny. His brother would have one child before he was inevitably killed. Sostene didn't know what to make of the revelation.

"Are you certain?" Amadeo asked, his head bowed.

"There are no other threads," she replied, laying her hands in her lap.

"Does this mean he is the survivor?" Terzo asked, his face contorted with fury as his golden eyes flamed. "Or does he leave his child behind in death?"

The Oracle waved her hand, "The stars have hidden the final fate of all of you... except for one."

"Who is it?" Giancarlo asked, running a hand through his white hair.

The mystical woman smiled. "Twelve."

Sostene's lip curled. "There are only eleven of us."

"Twelve," she repeated.

"I've had enough of this," Matteo snapped, his burgundy eyes a shade darker than usual. "This is the third time this year we've been to this crook, and she never gives us anything worthwhile."

"You're impatient," Giancarlo replied, folding his arms over his chest. "She can only glimpse so much."

"She's just making shit up now." Nicolo rolled his eyes and huffed. "This is pointless."

Sostene studied Nicolo, from his wavy chestnut hair to the inky veins visible beneath the surface of his skin. Nicolo, along with Brio and Urso, had a difficult time adjusting to the stifling rise in their power. Sostene knew they would be among the first to shed their physical bonds and meet the ether.

"I'm done wasting my time." Matteo stormed out of the cave, knocking down a pillar adorned with gold beaded necklaces that sat near the entrance.

"Wait, brother." Giancarlo chased after Matteo, his blue eyes wide. "You can't go yet, you heard what mother said."

The Oracle blinked slowly but did not react otherwise. Sostene reached into his pocket and pulled a cigar free. He used his starlight to ignite the dried Lily of Demise flower buds, watching as his brothers, one by one, took off without so much as a 'thank you' for the Oracle that had channeled for them. Sostene scoffed and ashed his cigar in an empty shell that had once held a scent stick.

He crouched in front of the Oracle and took another drag. "Tell me about little twelve. Where has my mother hidden him?"

The Oracle's eyes widened as she inspired deeply. The breath came out at a deliberate, steady pace. "Among the Rani Guardians."

Sostene smiled. What fools his brothers were, leaving without prodding for more answers. "Interesting. What is his name?"

She ran a hand up her arm, her fingers gliding across her rich brown skin. "Vincenzo."

He raised a brow and absentmindedly puffed on his cigar. "What is his Fate?"

"Lethe requires his soul."

That sent a ripple of unease through him. "Why does Death call his name?"

The Oracle blinked. "There is a burden only he can bear. It is in his destiny to give his life for Lethe. His death will mark the beginning of a new era, and his offering to the cosmos will be his last breath."

"When will he die?" he asked, leaning forward in anticipation.

"His power will grow, igniting him from the inside out. When his fire has nothing left to burn, it will consume him instead." The Oracle raised her hands above her and spread them out as though collecting the future from the air around her. "One—the survivor— will whirl the wheel of favor through his connection to a loving bond. Twelve—the scythe—will rupture the curse over this realm as he sheds his skin and returns to Death's river. The Fateless daughter shall cleanse each of you, oh honorable and Sacred children, for the Weave honors your sacrifice. The end of all as we know it rests in your palms. As your lives conclude, the tides will turn, for metamorphosis requires souls to burn."

Sima gasped as the memory concluded. Sostene reached out to steady her, but she backed away, her mind and heart speeding too fast for her to breathe properly. What she had seen confirmed what Sostene had told her, but she was in denial, unable to accept that a Celestial Empress had cursed Vincenzo. Why did Lethe demand his soul and not the others? Why would the Empress reward the survivor of the Sacred Twelve, after all the chaos each of the men was fated to create?

"Don't you see? It was never going to be him. I am the one who lives, Cosima, and you are the woman destined to be by my side. Once Vincenzo dies, a new cycle will begin. I am not a monster, *Esti,* I am simply following my Fate as it was given to me."

Her thoughts were a blur, but one message consistently resurfaced.

If I am Fateless, then I am the one who dictates true destiny through my decisions.

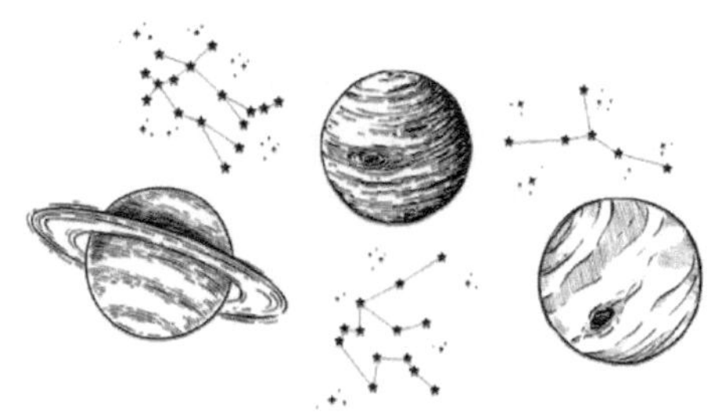

Chapter 48

Although his body powered forward, hurling magic as if it were balls of soft snow, his mind was immune to the horrors he enacted. The death, he knew, was wrong, but he could not bring himself to care as he cut down anyone willing to get between him and the future he deserved.

There must be a path lined with their blood, because they would have it no other way.

His clothes were soaked in blood, his shoes squeaking each time his feet touched the ground, before he swept into the air, never flying high enough to truly avoid detection or confrontation. In some ways, he craved the release, craved the fury and chaos that tunneled out of him, relieving his aching soul from centuries of torment. His lip twitched from the distant sensation of happiness each time another contender dared to challenge him.

"There he is," a man shouted from behind him.

Show the traitor who he has chosen to betray, his darkness laughed.

Enzo did not look back as his magic enveloped the man's mind and brought him to his knees, pressing his lips into the fluffy foundational cloud the Kingdom was built on. His mouth fumbled, failing to articulate the words he desired as Enzo forced him to kiss the ground, unable to resist the command. He bobbed up and down like a duck in fresh water, all while Enzo's powers squeezed his brain into a pulp, blood pouring from his nose and mouth.

As others who had sought to challenge Enzo grew dismayed at the sight, he drew their bodies into similar forms of demented worship until they collapsed, one by one.

"W-why?" a hoarse voice stammered.

Enzo's brow lifted, and he turned toward the source of the words. It was a man with sandy brown hair and a moderate aura of power, which had saved his brain from becoming slush. Somehow, it had not occurred to Enzo that the people he broke were Caelari, and the realization caused him to burst into laughter. Despite the haze of his own rage-filled delirium, he could see the poor god with such hilarious clarity.

"Why?" Enzo repeated. "This is what they want from me, isn't it? Isn't this who I am, deep down—aren't I what I was born to be? Sinful monsters willing to tear everything to the ground for what they want, isn't that all my brothers and I have ever been?"

Enzo shook as he spoke, his words harsher and more hateful than he had intended. He attempted to reel back his festering emotions, but his control over himself was waning, growing insufficient by the second as more of his power unleashed. He clenched his fist, hooking his mind on the devastatingly persuasive image of Cosima, reminding him there was a reason he was clearing a path before him.

The god's eyes sank to the ground. "You can repent."

Who is this small god to tell you anything? End this nameless fool, his curse snapped.

"Repent?" Enzo laughed alongside his dark companion. "So they may shackle my wrists again? Should I hold still as they bring the blade down on my neck?"

He turned his head away sharply, as if he could not bear to face Enzo. "That is what you deserve. The Divinity chose their successor, the sibling of yours best suited to rule us, and you—you killed him," he said, voice warbling. "You are not strong enough for what is to come."

Enzo lashed out, snatching the pathetic god by the chest plate of thin, decorative armor. "I was not before, but I am now." A hollow sensation like starving hunger pains echoed in his gut. "Nothing will stop me now, not your doubt, not your fear, not your disdain."

He released him, sending the god tumbling to the ground. The god choked as blood poured from his nose, the river covering the intricate designs hand-etched into his useless chest plate. At one time, he might have flinched at such callous violence, but in this moment, he felt nothing. Anyone who stood in his way would fall to their knees. Enzo turned his back and took to the air.

His connection to Cosima was intact and stronger than ever, allowing him to sense that she was not as far as he had once thought. He faithfully followed, finding solace in the familiarity of her warmth. His pursuit led him further into the Ethereal Realm outside of the Kingdom, the journey out an insignificant blip in his memory.

The hint of fatigue arose in his muscles, and Enzo absently rubbed his shoulder and bicep, registering none of what was happening around him. When a Scout or citizen aimed for him, he turned them on each other, synchronizing attacks like a choreographed dance that left everyone with broken necks in the end. It happened without his full attention because Enzo could feel her, could feel the sharpness of her fear in a way he had not noticed prior.

The fact strangled him, but his devotion would not allow him to give up on her, not when she was so near and her pain was so real. The bond was vague in its communication of Cosima's surroundings, but something in her emotions made his body move with urgency. His wings dragged him fast enough to make the realm around him a colorful blur. Each time he tugged on their connection, determined to learn all he could before he reached her, it communicated the waves of her panic and discomfort. He grimaced, wishing he could see through her eyes, but her shielding did more than keep him from accessing her mind. It meant if she were in the hands of Sostene, his brother would resort to desperate measures to sway her hand.

Witness your unstoppable nature, his darkness mused, *see how the winds of fortune propel you forward.*

His power had not depleted, the well seemingly infinite as he grew desperate and impatient. He growled, throwing his starlight in a fit of blind rage. A hole ripped through the space before him, creating a ragged portal, swirling a deep emerald green within. He tumbled through it, glancing back as it sealed after him, locking him in the river of space and time, at the mercy of its twists and turns.

When the galaxies themselves spat him out, he discovered he had transported himself a significant distance, ending up in a lavender field with a palace so grand that he felt unworthy of gazing at it for as long as he did. A pull on the bond to Cosima slapped him back to reality, and Enzo walked toward it, his wings folded flat against his back.

The palace hummed with an energy that was intimidating, but only because its strength seemed to mirror Enzo's, or perhaps eclipsed him entirely, he had not yet decided. He approached the gates, wary to find a magnificent structure unmanned. Not another soul was in sight, even as he poked his head into the courtyard, hands resting gently on a smoky quartz tower at the entrance. The stone responded to his touch, vibrating with an almost uncomfortable energy in his palms.

Enzo jerked his hands back and stepped fully into the courtyard. He closed his eyes and took in a heavy breath, letting it out in a ragged sigh. Cosima was not alone, and Sostene's aura washed over him, pungent and impenetrable. It was as if his brother's powers had tripled in magnitude as his own had. He shoved the thought from his mind, growing disoriented with Sima's grief.

He yanked open the door, hissing as it creaked loudly in response. He used his fingers to shut it gently behind him and took a step forward. A pulse of energy shoved him backward, pinning him against the door. Another wave washed over him, drenching him head to toe in a cloudy memory.

"Are you sure this is the right decision?" Moira asked, frowning as she brushed the full length of her hair, working out tangles. "If you make this choice, there is no taking it back. You are the decider of your destiny, so if this is truly what you want, then I will support you." She put the brush on the rose quartz vanity and chewed her lip. "But, be sure, child," she urged.

Cosima gave her mother a small lop-sided smile. Her features were soft from her young age, but she resembled her mother down to the curve of her nose. Her mother returned her own attempt at a smile and cupped Sima's face in her hand.

"I am sure, Anmah. I want to see the Kingdom." Her tiny brows pressed together. "Even if it is hard. I am brave!"

Moira grinned. "How can I say no to you?" She sighed. "Give me ten more years, Cosima. The Kingdom will need to be prepped for your arrival."

"No," she protested. "That will ruin it. I want the authentic experience. I need to know the truth about the people and the land I will someday rule." She wrinkled her nose. "I don't know why it has to be me and not you, Anmah, but I will wear my crown proudly."

She patted Sima on the top of her head. "It was always to be you. The honor of birthing the tidal wave of change is not lost on me. You were created for this purpose."

Cosima's eyes sparkled as she stared up at her mother. "Are you sure? I heard something the other day…"

Her mother's eyes narrowed. "You know better than to—"

"Please, listen."

Moira pressed her lips together and nodded.

"Those girls came back to the meadow, and they were discussing a curse. That a High Priestess did something forbidden and created her own army to overthrow the Divinity, and that her actions were too great to undo."

"That is true," Moira said tightly. "But have no fear, child, because you are what will save us. Your Hahlmon knew we would need your power one day. That is why she

bestowed it upon you. That is why you are so brave."

Sima's smile only reached one side of her face. "I know I can do this. I don't want other people to know who I am. I want them to treat me the same as they would treat anyone else. I need to see the problems with my own eyes. That starts now. Not in ten years. I need all the experience I can get if everyone is relying on me…"

Moira's eyes were sorrowful. "Strong daughter of mine…" She took a deep breath. "One year. Give me one year, and I will let you leave the palace and live in the Kingdom."

"Without arrangements?"

"Without prior arrangements, yes."

Sima squealed. "Thank you, Anmah."

As Sima ran away, the light in Moira's eyes dimmed. She picked at the skin around her nails with her hands folded in her lap. "I wish she did not have to sacrifice herself."

A black cloud appeared, and Kismet strolled out, her beautiful spring green dress lining the floor behind her. "She is a rare child of the cosmos, Moira. She is a gift. Let her fulfill her purpose. A little girl that not even the Hands of Fate can control is the only way to bring balance. Cosima will break the curse."

"I know, mother."

The memory faded, and the energy that pinned him disappeared. Enzo rubbed his eyes and walked forward, dazed by Cosima's past. It weighed on his heart to see a version of her so unmarred by the future to come, but more so, he thought of Kismet's last words. *"Cosima will break the curse."* It was almost impossible to imagine her freeing him from his dark companion.

Could this curse be broken? Enzo wondered. *Even as it thumps through my body?*

Outside of the entryway, there was a hallway, and the bond burned with recognition as he approached the rounded wood door with bright gold handles at the end. He reached for the handle, then stopped himself. The painful, demanding command of his power had finally quelled, as if his closeness to Cosima settled his storms, allowing him to see the truth. He trembled as he glanced down at himself, cringing at the frightfully bloody mess that greeted him. He was in ruins, but his job was not done. One brother remained, and he would not let go of that.

He swallowed hard and flung the door open, allowing him to witness for himself what had caused Sima's feelings of fear and discomfort. Sostene's hands encircled the top of Sima's scalp as he held his forehead against her, the energy wafting off his magic invasive and intimate. The intensity of her emotions pushed Enzo closer to the edge, his wrath already ignited by Sostene's grip on Cosima.

Burn away all of the flesh on his bones and grind what remains into dust, his curse snarled.

Enzo lunged forward, pulling Sostene off Sima and onto the ground.

Once more, his magic stormed within, hungry to kill another of his worthless siblings. Starlight poured from his palm, but Sostene deflected it with a shield containing a smoky glow. Enzo punched his brother repeatedly, allowing his curse to strengthen the blows, as blood smeared Sostene's face.

His brother threw himself forward and headbutted Enzo. The hit dazed him, but Enzo shook it off as Sostene rose to his feet. Enzo was prepared to react again when he caught sight of Cosima trembling from where she lay on a maroon sofa. Her eyes were rolled back, and what he could sense through the bond drove him to madness.

"What have you done to her?"

"I am only giving her what our mother took away," Sostene said, raising himself from the ground. He dusted himself off and grimaced. "Something you would never be able to do."

Enzo's lip curled, but he ignored his brother and reached for her. She flinched away, her eyes wholly white like orbs of snow. "Sima, it's me."

"Don't trust him," Sima whimpered, curling her body into a ball on the sofa. "Don't trust what you see."

"What?" Enzo stepped closer, but she moved away from him again. His breath hitched in his throat.

"*Don't* trust him, Enzo," she breathed. "He's been playing this game longer than we have."

"You should listen to her," Sostene replied. Enzo looked behind Sima and startled when his eyes met Sostene's. "How do you not realize it, even now?"

"What are you talking about?"

Sostene cracked his neck and smiled. "Absolutely everything has gone according to plan, except for one minor detail. That *bond* was not for you to initiate, you worthless runt. But since you were kind enough to take care of Alvize for me, I suppose I owe you a semblance of gratitude. You brought yourself here promptly, just as I knew you would, which will make the rest of this a breeze. When sweet Sima begged me to bring her home, my mouth started salivating, for I could not have picked a better backdrop for your permanent ruin, brother. Keeping Cosima busy with her memories means she will be *deliciously* distracted until the time is right for her to witness your demise."

"Run, Enzo," Sima said through her teeth, her white eyes ghostly. "Please, run."

Enzo's stomach flipped when he spotted black sparkling powder on the front of Sostene's violet suit. *Crystal powder, I'd recognize it anywhere.* He bit back his desire to scream. He should've known it would be impossible for his brother to ensnare her with mind manipulation alone. Like Aurelio,

Sostene had resorted to artificially amplifying his power. *You're getting desperate, Sostene. Why the rush?*

"She will forget about you, in time."

She loved you without knowing you, his curse reminded him. *He lies.*

Sostene's arrogance was spilling over the edge, provoking Enzo. With a desperate pulse of his magic, Enzo slammed against the magic in Sima's mind. To his surprise, his power shattered it almost instantaneously, leaving her gasping for air as she regained control over herself. His magic flooded in, creating a shield against further attacks from Sostene.

"How did you return her memories?" Enzo asked sharply. The one thing he knew for certain about the situation was his brother's self-absorption was the simplest route to distraction. Sostene was still too close to Cosima for him to properly separate the two, and Enzo would never put her at risk. "You're too weak to break her shields."

Especially with my help, Enzo thought.

Sostene's face twisted. "There was no need, you fool. Even our mother could only get so far in controlling her stubborn spirit, but the memories were merely blocked, hidden behind walls. They are easy to bring down if you know precisely where to look. A few of them had crumbled prior to my rooting around, so I brought down the rest."

"Her mind can't handle that," Enzo hissed, beginning to pace. He stopped near the open door. "You did this to her on purpose, didn't you? You knew she would try to stop you if you didn't find a way to keep her down. What happens if you scramble her brain? You know the risks."

Sostene feigned offense, but took the bait and stepped away from Sima, standing with his back to her. "You do not give her enough credit. She is strong enough to endure. There are…side effects, but nothing permanent."

Enzo sent more of his magic toward her, carefully controlling his facial expression as he watched it imbue her with energy. Sima's brows furrowed, and she stood with her fists clenched. Based on the defiant look in her eye, the woman he loved was already plotting. He could only hope that her plans somehow aligned with his. Enzo sent a pulse of reassurance through the bond, which reached her with unparalleled speed. She swayed on her feet as she blinked in her surprise. Somehow, more of his magic had gotten through to her, but Enzo did not have time to dwell on the discovery, despite how her heartbeat rang in his ears now.

"She is not some toy for you to manipulate." Enzo lifted his chin. A single beat of his heart thumped in his chest. "Do you know the first real thing about Cosima, or have you ascribed a fictitious mask you drape over her to keep from having to see the truth? Did you know that soft piano music can bring her to tears or that she prefers to bathe before bed, so the day gets washed away? Were you ever there through the nightmares or the panic attacks? Do you know where her favorite place to be kissed is and what she craves on a rainy afternoon? I have spent decades loving a woman you think you can win over with charm and lies."

The tether between him and Cosima was taut, allowing him to sense her pulse quickening as she listened to him speak. He caught a flash of Sima's onyx black hair moving. In between blinks, the palace shifted—the color of everything had darkened a shade, giving a moody tone to the room, soft orchestral music rang through the halls, and the ceiling sparkled with stars. Her energy blanketed the room and contorted their surrounding as if they were in a dream. Furniture flickered in and out of view, and artwork on the walls created moving images as they changed.

What are you up to? Enzo wondered.

Sostene's fists clenched as he looked around, violet tendrils of smoke wafting off him. "Gnaw at the chains around your soul if you must, you rabid animal, but nothing you say will save your life. Death has already laid claim to you, and your time to return has almost come. If you are destined to perish, then who will watch after our lovely Empress? You can see this burden from my perspective, can't you, brother? I am the survivor, and you are not. Her eternity was never meant for you. You must give your life in order to bless Cosima's and my union."

"I've had enough of you using my love for her to torment me. I'm going to rip your tongue out and let my starlight cook you from the inside out. Cosima is bound to me, and so long as that remains what she desires, I will do everything in my power to protect that tether. You will never know the mercy of her salvation; you will never know how sublime it feels to be loved by her."

He savored the way Sostene's eyes flamed a bright purple, swirling with anger. "Enjoy it while it lasts," his brother hollered. His wings unfurled, the color of his feathers so dark it seemed unnatural to Enzo. Sostene reached into his jacket pocket and pulled out a purple butterfly dangling from a thin gold chain, its aura magnifying his brother's harrowing energy.

Vincenzo smiled as his curse banged on his bones and scalded his marrow as it demanded release. "I can feel it, brother, how wrong you are to your core, how your body writhes with insanity, your tissue tainted with toxin. You slither beneath the light, too afraid to bear your flesh like it is silk and not skin. Your blood is full of scarlet shadows, and your every breath is an injustice. Fall so I may rise in your place. Crumble so I may taste the agony in your ashes."

Chapter 49

"Well," Ivo said, her voice warbling as she finished catching Yadira up to speed on everything that transpired after she and the others departed from the Eternal Kingdom. "That's everything. What do you think?"

Yadira had schooled her face into a neutral mask as soon as she sat down at the table. Johanna and Isolde were quiet, but accepting of Yadira's presence, both women keenly interested in any help that could bring them closer to the pendant.

"It is not what I was expecting to hear," Yadira murmured, her fingers pressed against her bottom lip. "Cosima and Vincenzo are both in great trouble. I will take you to Speranza, and we will find Vincenzo's contacts in the Depths. His absence affected the layout substantially, but it is still functional and packed with people. I guarantee someone there knows something about this missing pendant, especially if you believe Aurelio did not have it during his time here."

Ivo let out a breath. "Thank you, Yadira. It has been a lengthy journey already. We will arrive much faster with your aid." She chewed her lip. "If I may, how have things been since…"

"Good," Yadira said, pausing to clear her throat, "Aeria is manned currently by an Ambrosi Council with a couple members sent by the Eternal Kingdom to mitigate any conflict that might have arisen during the transfer of power. I have not been to the Archipelago since you three left."

"Why not?" Ivo asked.

Yadira glanced at Johanna and then away. "I do not yet believe Aeria is worthy of my trust. I feel safer here. Besides, we were fooled at one point into believing the people of these Districts were being cared for without verifying with our own eyes. At least with my feet on the ground, I can tend to those who need my help instead of waiting for a command to do so."

"They have not come looking for you?" Johanna asked.

Yadira frowned. "I did not say that. I think they have grown tired of fruitless chases, though. They have bigger messes to attend to than a rogue Guardian that could be as good as dead as far as they are aware."

"We have a room for the night," Ivo said, her eyelids growing heavy. "When would you like to leave for Speranza?"

"At dawn," Yadira replied. "I was heading that way already. I stopped to wrap up some loose ends with the inn in regard to a stash of crystals found after a guest left without checking out."

Isolde stiffened. "Crystals?"

"Not the kind you are searching for," Yadira said. "But they are nearly as dangerous, it seems. From what I know, there are three simple facts. One, the crystals are made with stolen life-force. Two, the bodies of those whose life force has been stolen become reanimated after death. Three, using the crystals has dangerous effects for those who use them with low tolerance."

"I see," Isolde said.

"I haven't had much exposure to them." Ivo rubbed her hands together. "Did you find who they belonged to?"

Yadira nodded. "Yes. I located a body west of the portal, and in his pocket was the inn key. I believe he meant to return before someone murdered him. I have not been able to uncover a solid reason, but my suspicions are that whoever killed him was in search of the crystals he left behind."

"What will you do with them?" Johanna asked.

"They are going somewhere safe, where they will be locked away. These should not fall into the wrong hands. Myself, and a few others, are committed to cleansing these lands of both the crystals and the criminals behind their construction. We shall go together and ask if those I seek wisdom from have seen signs of your pendant."

"I know you are the right person for this task," Ivo assured. "At dawn, then."

The room Itana arranged for them was spacious, with two large beds on either side of the room, and a modest wooden desk in between. Ivo walked in and plopped down on one of the beds, sighing as she sank into it. She glanced up and spotted Isolde staring at her strangely.

"What is it?" Ivo asked.

Isolde shook her head. "Nothing, I…nothing."

"Right," Ivo said. "Excuse me, ladies. If you don't mind, I would like to bathe before bed."

"Of course," Johanna said, pulling back the blanket on the opposite bed. "Take your time."

Ivo nodded and shut the bathing chamber door behind her. The chamber held a large basin at the center with a silver spout that conjured heated water, supplied by the witches within the settlement. As she filled the basin, Ivo wandered to the mirror and gazed at herself.

She did not look well, but she retained some life to her features, namely the redness of her cheeks and the brightness of her eyes. She sighed, using her fingers to comb her hair the best she could. She wandered to the basin and dunked her hair only, using some of the provided soaps to scrub free the dirt and grime of her adventures.

As she rinsed the soap out, she noticed something strange. A thick knot of dried blood matted her hair together along the base of her skull. She worked with the soap and warm water to untangle what she could, and as she grew curious if the blood was hers or someone else's, her temples pulsed with pain.

"Ah," Ivo hissed. "What in the…"

She drained the water from her clean hair and tied it up with a tan towel left by the inn. When she was upright again, she caught a glimpse of herself in the mirror, and Ivo gasped. She rushed forward and noticed the color of her eyes had changed from blue to a beautiful purple. Her magic coursed through her stronger than she had ever felt it, causing her to tremble.

Her finger pulled down her bottom eyelid as she inspected the change more closely. "Where have I seen this before?" Ivo mumbled. "So familiar…"

The pulsing headache returned with fury, this time causing her to suck in a breath as she willed herself through the agony. "Something is wrong," Ivo gasped, falling to her knees.

"Ivo?" Isolde yelled from outside the door. "Are you alright?"

"H-help," Ivo managed, though the pain was growing in severity. "Help."

The door burst open, and Isolde was at her side at once, lifting her by the arm from the ground. Isolde wrapped her arms around Ivo, hoisted her into her arms, and carried her back into the bedroom. Ivo's newest companions furrowed their brows as they helped lay her on the bed.

"Can you tell me what you feel, Ivo?" Isolde asked.

Ivo licked her lips, her tongue snagging on dry skin. "Bad headache. My eyes, are they different?"

Johanna raised a brow. "You appear the same as usual. Did you see something strange?"

"Yes," Ivo said. "I thought they had changed color, but…" She shook her head, the pain coming and going like waves against the shore. "It must be the exhaustion. My mind is telling me I am forgetting something."

Isolde swallowed tightly and looked away. "Perhaps you will remember after some sleep."

"Yeah, maybe you're right." Ivo rolled onto her side. Isolde lifted Ivo's legs and tugged the blanket out from beneath and then tossed it over her. "Thank you," Ivo murmured.

Within moments, she was asleep. Her dreams were the usual sort, quirky interactions with people who looked like those she knew but did not quite act the same way. Then, Ivo walked by a mirror, and instead of seeing her own reflection, she saw a taller woman with white hair and purple eyes.

For some reason, each beat of Ivo's heart felt like it snapped ligaments and tore tissue. She did not recognize the woman she saw, knowing she would never be able to forget her elegant face and mesmerizing wings. The woman watched Ivo with a glint of amusement before the image faded altogether.

Throughout Ivo's chaotic dreams, she encountered the mystery woman repeatedly, never growing closer to the answer behind who she was. At one instance, the woman appeared to be speaking to her, but no audible sound came from her lips.

When she woke at dawn, she found Isolde and Johanna gone from the room. Ivo pulled herself from the bed and padded over to the door, which she noticed was cracked open. Frost bit at Ivo's fingers, urging her forward. As she grew closer, their voices grew louder, allowing her to listen in on their hushed conversation.

"You should know better," Johanna hissed. "There are repercussions to meddling around like that. You know you are never supposed to keep them."

"I know," Isolde said, her jaw set tight. "I don't know what got over me, but I can't undo it now."

"Of course you can," Johanna hissed. "Or we may lose this chance entirely."

"I cannot," Isolde snapped.

"Isolde," Johanna warned. "You will undo your mistake, and you will do so promptly. Do not disobey this command."

"I cannot," Isolde repeated, this time weaker. "I destroyed it."

Johanna was quiet for a moment. "You create messes everywhere you go," she said harshly. "You are working against our purpose, not with it."

"I am well aware," Isolde replied.

"What of the Empress? How will she punish you when she finds out what you've done to her daughter?"

Isolde sighed. "I did what needed to be done to ensure our success. You are losing your edge. You used to be willing to do whatever it took to serve our Empress well. I simply did what you could not."

"My ruthless past does not apply here. We've spent decades preparing for her arrival, Isolde. She is not just another immortal like we're used to dealing with. If we aren't incredibly careful, we could end up harming her before she ever has the chance to fulfill the prophecy."

Ivo had an eerie hunch they were speaking about her, and her mouth went dry. *I have a feeling this prophecy is more significant than I first realized. What could a Celestial Empress possibly want with me?*

"I did her a favor; her emotions were so volatile, it's any wonder she didn't combust before I found her. You said it yourself, her vessel is weak."

Johanna clicked her tongue. "That doesn't mean you needed to destroy what ailed her."

"I'm sorry, Johanna, but we can't risk it. If she finds out what else *it* can do, she will take off running before we have a chance to finish this. The Empress needs the other one before it's too late. Please, see where I am coming from."

Johanna let out a puff of air. "I'll try to."

At the sound of their feet scuffling, Ivo scurried back into the bedroom and acted as though she had just awoken. She rubbed her eyes as she sat on the edge of the bed and smiled up at them. The two women responded with uneasy smiles.

"Thank you for letting me get some extra rest," Ivo said. "Shall we meet with Yadira?"

"Yes, let's be on our way," Johanna said.

Ivo led the way, though strange prickles trickled down her spine at having the two of them out of her sight. Their conversation had been strange, and Ivo had begun to second-guess her willingness to aid them. She knew if Sima were to stand a chance against Sostene and Ehses, she would need at least one of the pendants. Ivo just hoped she would get to her friend before it was too late. She had no clue what had become of Cosima and Enzo after Ivo was spit out on this new planet, but she prayed they were alright.

Ivo would feign ignorance as to their discussion for as long as she could. It didn't matter what the two strange women were talking about—she needed Isolde and Johanna until Cosima was safe. When she spotted Yadira waiting near the front counter, she let out a near-silent, shaky breath. She replaced her grim expression with one of appreciation and approached the Rani Guardian.

"Right on time," Yadira said, with an approving nod. "Is everyone ready to depart?"

"Yes, but, may I ask, how long is the journey to Speranza going to take?"

Yadira smiled. "Not long at all. If it is acceptable to the two of you, I have two Guardians venturing back with us today who would be more than capable of flying you to our destination."

Isolde lifted a brow. "That seems precarious."

"It's not as scary as you think," Ivo said. She did her best to keep her smile friendly as she attempted to shove away thoughts about Johanna and Isolde's secret conversation. "They won't drop you. Rani were made to carry multiple people at once if needed."

Isolde did not seem convinced and frowned. "I have never…it doesn't seem safe."

"My friends will be incredibly careful," Yadira said. "We could carry you through hellfire if needed."

Johanna's eyes flickered with an emotion Ivo could not pinpoint. "Right, then. I suppose it would get us there sooner, Isolde."

Isolde crossed her arms, looking ready to protest when footsteps clambered down the stairs. Ivo turned her head and spotted two Guardians with broad navy blue wings, blue eyes, and short white hair walking their way. The men shared a resemblance, save for the lengthy scar across the man on the left's lip, like a piercing made of lightning bolts. It had an unnatural glow, and Ivo could not tear her eyes away from it. Her power recoiled inside her, as if afraid of the man.

"This Yensa," Yadira said, gesturing to the man with the scar, who lifted a hand in greeting. "And this is Eeda."

Eeda bowed his head. "My brother and I are pleased to make your acquaintance, and we would be honored to join you on this journey."

Isolde glowered. "What happened to your face?"

"Mind your manners," Johanna hissed. "I apologize for her."

Yensa smiled, his teeth brilliant and perfectly aligned. "It is no matter. I do not often get to tell the story." He ran a finger along his jaw, stopping at his chin and moving upward over the scar. "This is the aftermath of the former king's blade, teeming with stolen energy."

"Under normal circumstances, it is quite rare for a Guardian to have scars," Eeda said, a hint of amusement in his tone. "But obviously, we are living in…unique times."

Ivo raised a brow. She knew Enzo had a scar, but he was not truly a Guardian. Yensa did not have the same otherworldly aura Vincenzo had, but something about the glowing scar made Ivo take a mental note regarding the Guardian.

"I'll go with him," Isolde said, gesturing to Yensa.

Yensa gave a slight bow. "Of course."

Ivo let out a breath, thankful she would be with Yadira instead.

***

The wind in her face gave her heart a rebellious sense of joy, as if this stolen moment would be taken if she were to fully indulge in the freedom flying granted her. Her heart panged, but she could not determine the reason for the intrusion. A lingering sensation of darkness plagued her from within.

Yadira glanced down at her, shifting Ivo slightly in her arms as she readjusted her grip. "Only half an hour more at most," she said.

Eeda and Johanna were to the left. The Countess remained composed but kept her eyes fixated on her hands in her lap as the Guardian cradled her. To the right, Yensa maintained pace and ignored Isolde staring intently at his lip with her nose wrinkled in disgust.

When the city grew close enough for Ivo to make out details, the Guardians placed them on the ground, allowing them to stretch their muscles. The architecture had changed greatly from what Ivo remembered. She sighed, wondering who she would have been if she had not spent much of her life imprisoned in the Palace.

At that, Ivo blinked, feeling as though she were forgetting something important. She struggled to recall it as Yadira entertained the group on their short walk into Speranza by speaking of the friendships she had garnered since Aurelio was murdered. It was strangely encouraging to hear that things had taken a turn for the better, even in her absence.

She had partially feared what she might find when she stepped through the portal, but it only inspired her to fight harder to save them. Ivo was again hit with a strange lingering sensation of something amiss. She slowed to a stop, falling out of formation with the group just as they reached the first rows of buildings.

"Ivo?" Yadira asked. "What is it?"

"I don't know. I feel like I am forgetting something important, like there is something I should have, but I don't. It comes and goes, but whenever I think of Sima and saving Haelos, my brain is screaming at me to remember."

Isolde grimaced, but the others remained neutral as they gazed at her.

"Maybe you are worried about your friend?" Yensa offered, crossing his arms in front of his chest.

Yadira stepped closer and ushered Ivo forward. "He is right. Perhaps it will come to you, but for now, we should focus on this. We can inquire about your…mission with Doc. If there is anyone who knows the answers you seek, it is him."

Ivo nodded, fighting the swirling unease lodged in her gut. "Yeah, let's go. It's nothing, I'm sure."

Inside the city, they walked several blocks before Yadira led them to an empty alleyway. At the end, a tall silver Viipir statue pulsed with power as they approached. Yadira approached it and pierced the statue with her starlight, causing it to recede and reveal a hidden entrance.

"Ladies," Yadira said, "down we go."

Yensa went first through the narrow opening and waited at the bottom with his arms outstretched. Her magic once again seemed to shy away from him, leaving her flushed with a warm discomfort. Ivo swallowed the lump in her throat and let her body drop through the hole.

Let it be his blood that awakens your true divine nature, his curse snarled, *and let his soul be the first you reap.*

Enzo narrowed his eyes at Sostene, humored by the pure audacity his brother possessed. In his hand, a purple butterfly breathed unfathomable energy. A mere few weeks ago, he might have been intimidated by its egregious power, but with his curse blurring the lines of reality, Enzo cracked a smile in the crystal's presence.

"As if that is enough to stop me," Enzo and his curse said in unison. "I am eternal, endless as time."

Cosima's magic continued to shift and contort the room. With every blink, more changes rippled, making the very foundation on which they stood quiver beneath the onslaught of snapping threads. Though he did not know for certain, Enzo perceived the intensity of her power to be proof that Cosima was shattering every bind, both on her spirit and her mind, whether his brother was aware of it or not. Their bond was taut, but steady as if it was her heart that beat in his chest, each alive if only because of their connection to the other.

Sostene lowered it, his gaze still sharp. "You underestimate it, brother. I have spent decades studying this crystal, and with time, I have garnered its trust and thus, the might of its strength. There is a new order coming and you will not be able to deter it."

A furious flame engulfed the whole of Vincenzo's body as he stepped forward. His emerald fire flickered as it burned brighter, boiling his skin and roasting his viscera. As his curse roared through his flesh, he found no need for restraint, even when his vessel began melting beneath its heat.

His brother's eyes grew wide, but he did not back away. Instead, Sostene tilted his head down as his purple gaze illuminated, locking into a harsh stare with Enzo. A tunnel of wind outside rattled the doors and windows as electricity charged the interior of the room like the fleeting seconds before lightning struck. Heavy rain slammed against the glass roof as the sky darkened and Enzo's viridian aura drenched him in holy rage.

Somewhere within the palace, Vincenzo's magic caught the scent of another entity. He blinked as he worked through the recognition that collided with his mind—Moira. *Has she been here with us all along?* Enzo wondered. *Does Cosima know she is here?* A plan formed in his mind, but first, he needed to remove the intruder from Cosima's home.

Give him the death he deserves, his curse laughed.

"I've grown tired of these games." Enzo snapped his fingers, and the palace cracked in two as the ground opened and swallowed the room whole.

As they plummeted into the cloudy foundation of the Ethereal Realm, Enzo formed a void to shove them within, grabbing his brother by the throat with a shadowy hand. He manipulated the space he created into a vortex of sharpened air and vicious speed, but it was not enough as Sostene shattered his cyclone. Enzo seethed, his vision blurring as he dropped Sostene into a magma-filled pit, the lava clinging to his brother's flesh as he screamed.

As his magma pit became an ocean of bubbling molten rock encompassing as far as he could see, something moved beneath the surface. Sostene emerged with a wide grin from the center, his body untouched, despite how Enzo had seen him howl with pain only seconds before. Sostene brushed his black hair out of his face as his violet aura flickered. Enzo crouched as he clapped his hands together in front of him, the force rippling outward as walls of sediment slammed into his brother.

A blast of rocks flew toward him as Sostene burst free, the purple butterfly around his neck humming with energy. It pulsed to the beat of his brother's heart as a force field clung to his skin. Enzo bared his teeth as he placed his hands in front of him with his wrists touching and his fingers pulled back. A beam of starlight consumed Sostene long enough for Enzo to shift the space beneath their feet, allowing him to appear behind his brother in an instant.

Shadowy hands emerged once more, this time digging their fingertips into the top of Sostene's forcefield, attempting to pry it open as wave after wave of Enzo's magic beat against it. Vincenzo unleashed his magic with reckless abandon, the void around them shivering as it struggled to contain the expenditure within it. Sparks of Enzo's energy created a spray of dazzling sparks, lighting up the room like a meteor shower.

A thin but vivid stream of galaxy light shot upward from Sostene and soared miles above them until it reached the bounds of Enzo's void. The second his brother's magic collided with the boundary, it crumbled, thrusting them back into the fluffy white depths of the Ethereal Realm. The two of them tangled in a dance of magic and fists, neither willing to relent, until they began to fall through space itself.

Stars flooded by their faces, burning and slicing their skin like hot blades. The unforgiving touch of the cosmos shredded through all of Enzo's attempts to shield himself from its ire with his magic. The two of them came to a screeching halt, suspended in a river of sparkling souls, before they were catapulted back through the confines of their realm.

Enzo grunted as he tumbled onto the floor of Cosima's home, this time finding himself back near the main entrance. His fingertips turned to ice as his magic burst through every wall in search of Sostene. He was startled when his power collided with Sima's essence before it reached his brother. His feet began moving before he understood fully that he was running toward her.

"Enzo," Sima cried out.

He could hardly see her through the haze of his delirious aura, but something was different about her. Her magic thumped nearly as loud as his own. At the end of the long hallway, she stood with an iridescent gown, bright like the stars that had torn at his flesh during his battle with his brother. Her raven black hair and a lavender field of energy swam around her body as her face contorted with confusion.

"My love," Enzo whispered as he moved forward. "Come to me."

Sima walked toward him, her steps slow and cautious. She came to a stop a few feet away from him and wrapped her arms around herself. "Your eyes, Enzo. Your magic…"

A flicker of shame made him pause. "Does it scare you?" His shining green eyes fell to the floor. "Do I?"

He shuddered as her hand touched his cheek. She gazed up at him, the corners of her lips upturned as she shook her head. "I see you, every part of you, and I am not afraid."

He did not know what to say, his mind empty as his heart pounded. Enzo reached into his pocket, pulled out two items, and shoved them into her free hand.

"Carmine's journal?" Sima raised a brow. "A key?"

"The key belonged to Alvize. Find Moira—she is somewhere here," Enzo choked out. His power continued to drain his attention, making it hard for him to stay grounded. A bloodthirsty desire to end his brother's life was taking precedence. He knew he was not thinking clearly with his curse ravaging his senses, but Enzo had one more thing to say. "I think I understand it now, Sima. You are connected to the prophecy because you were the only one capable of cleansing the poison of my bloodline. Everything I do, I do for you, because it is Fated to be so. You are unbound by destiny, and it is your greatest weapon. You are stepping into the power that has lurked inside you for centuries, and I will pave the way for you in blood. No matter what happens next, you bow to nothing and to no one."

A tear slipped down her cheek as the ground shook and paintings rattled on the walls. "You will lead by my side when this is over. It is you and me for eternity, Enzo. I won't do this without you."

Enzo smiled as he pressed a kiss to her forehead, feeling himself slip away. His curse submerged his consciousness in a black cloud. Sostene was growing closer, and the battle was far from over. "I am always with you. No matter what happens, don't forget that," he whispered. "My soul is tethered to yours, and not even death could keep me from you. I love you."

He stepped back as he used his last moments of clarity to contort the hallway, moving her as far away from him as possible before electricity seized him. The painful shock brought him to his knees, and Enzo laughed as tears poured from his eyes. Somewhere within, the old Vincenzo curled into a ball and died, severing his ties to his vessel, as what remained of him relinquished itself to his unimaginable divine power.

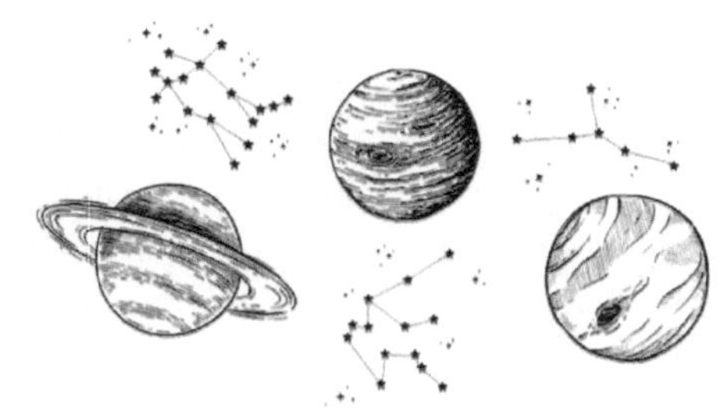

Chapter 50

Cosima

"I love you."

Before Cosima could respond to Vincenzo's words, the world around her faded, leaving her in pressurized silence and utter darkness. The air had a strange, almost artificial scent, and Sima found that her lack of vision left her unnervingly vulnerable. Enzo had told her that her mother was somewhere within the palace before he disappeared, meaning Moira had been there while Cosima was exploring with Sostene by her side. The fact nearly paralyzed her muscles, but magic flooded through her at such an intensity that her body seemed to vibrate with its energy. The waves of power made all her muscles ache as she collapsed onto the floor. Sima's anguish got the best of her, reducing her to tears and gasping breath, until some resilient piece of her resurfaced. That small piece begged her to keep moving.

I have survived the collapse of my world too many times to let it all end here, she thought. *This is the era of my rebirth, this is when the woman I've always been comes breaking through.*

She rested her back against the wall as she attempted to sift through her memories, finding it hard with the mess left behind by Sostene, restoring many of the recollections that had been locked away. Sima frowned as she remembered how quickly the situation had changed once she spotted her favorite room in the palace. She had thrown open the doors to the library with careless glee, enamored by the floor-to-ceiling shelves with dragonflies etched into the wood, each wing painted with expert hands. It was as though she had not had a demon in God form lurking behind her, but a familiar friend, as Sima basked in the room's comforting essence. Every book had appeared brand new to her, with no sign of age on any of the spines, as the scent of vanilla honey filled the room. However, one had caught her eye, drawing her in with its gold metal hardware on the cover.

Sima cringed, remembering how the moment her fingertips grazed it, a ravenous energy broke through her, stunning her mind as her legs gave out beneath her, and a vision shielded her eyes. There had not been a delightful memory that waited on the other side for her, but a vicious, clouded nightmare. One where she had been falling through space again, washing ashore on the bank outside the doors of those she was commanded to kill, to deter, or to erase. Aurelio's laughter had echoed in her ears, but it did not strike fear in her. Instead, she had found it sobering.

She had survived him. She had helped kill two more of his brothers.

She had become unstoppable.

Cosima let out a breath. She also recalled the sensation of Sostene's lips kissing her body as he unleashed her memories before Enzo appeared, saving her from his brother's grip. She was desperate to stay near him, but he was gone again, leaving her with only Carmine's notebook and a strange key that would supposedly lead her to her mother. Her hand wrapped tightly around the key as she rose to her feet. Even in the pitch darkness, Sima walked a path she knew intimately, knowledge she only had because Sostene had returned it to her in an attempt to overwhelm her mind.

As she made her way toward the second floor, she thought of the loving family her memories had shown. The grandmother and mother who adored her, intentionally stoking her fire and lifting her toward the stars. Her heart squeezed as she recalled how it felt to be wrapped in her mother's arms, how safe and naive she had been as a child.

She rounded a corner, now picturing her first experience inside the Eternal Kingdom. She had been young when she left her palace in favor of discovering the hidden secrets of the Kingdom she would rule, and her journey reflected this adolescent immaturity. She was horrified to find that the gods and goddesses of her realm were not the evolved, powerful souls Sima's mother had told her about.

Instead, they were shams, cheap recreations of the fortified souls they should have been. It had only grown worse, had only made her fury unbearable, when she learned of how the Kingdom treated new souls. Through the official word of the High Priestesses, the souls were treated with care, given only enough difficulty to grow. The souls watched over by Ambrosi and Rani Guardians were never to suffer more than was necessary to facilitate expansion, and yet, everywhere Sima turned, she only found one cruel violation after another.

She had been embarrassed, too heartbroken to return home and tell her mother the truth of what transpired beneath the Empire, that every bedtime story had been an unfortunate lie.

Sima found the stairs and stumbled on the first step. She caught herself on the railing and gripped it tightly as she ascended. More memories flooded by, including her first glimpse of Enzo. The behavior of others had discouraged her dreams of creating a better Kingdom, fearing the people did not share her heart or values.

Until she saw him.

It was his hair that caught her attention first, drawn in by the unique split of black and white. A curious moment between a frightened divine child and Vincenzo sparked a flame that only burned brighter the more she learned of him. Others passed by the child without concern for her wailing. When Enzo spotted her, he was by her side within moments, one knee planted on the ground as he spoke to her.

"Don't worry," Enzo had said. "You are not alone. I will help you."

He and Sima did not meet for some time after. She could not deny her desire to see him again, and though she kept her distance, she watched him. Enzo had been an ordinary Rani Guardian, moving as he was commanded, training until he dropped, drunk with fatigue, into the clouds below. But when the moment had presented itself, he did what others did not.

He had acted with kindness.

Other Rani Guardians did precisely what they were commanded and nothing more. She had witnessed every soul, evolved or otherwise, fail when presented with the same opportunities to do good without pressure. Ambrosi, Gods, Trine Scouts. All immortals faltered, none the wiser of how their ambivalence toward one another devalued the Empire as a whole.

She smiled as she reached the second floor, her lack of vision allowing her to picture Enzo's face crisply, alight with a familiar gentleness the first time he laid eyes on her. She made no mention of the intense aura he held that others seemed to ignore. Sima had known he was a divine being instantly, despite being raised as a Rani Guardian. Her finger slid over the key he gave her before vanishing, her mind putting the pieces together as she traced its familiar shape.

A long, thin table sat against the wall of the hallway, and Sima's hip bumped against the corner. She hissed and created a larger gap between her body and the wall as she used it for a guide. She found the room she had been searching for with ease, her hand wrapping around the handle with relief. At first, she was confused when Enzo had given her the key, but now, she knew instinctively that it would unlock a hidden door inside her old bedroom.

She pushed open the door and ventured inside, pleased to find the layout matched her previous memories. Despite her disappearance from the Eternal Kingdom, her mother appeared not to have moved the furniture, as Sima navigated around it without sight. She carefully made her way to the wall on the left side of her bed and pulled a tapestry out of the way. Her fingers slid across a keyhole, and she placed the key inside and turned.

The hinges groaned as the concealed door swung open. As she stepped inside, the sounds of movement caught her ear. She held her breath and paused, listening for more. What she thought was a gasp or hushed exclamation came next, and Sima cocked her head to the side.

"Hello?" Sima waited, but no response came. The noise ceased, and after a moment of silence, she wondered if she had imagined the sounds altogether. She bumped into something metal she had not expected to find, causing her to nearly lose her balance.

"Who are you?" a soft, feminine voice asked.

Sima jumped back and swallowed a shriek. "Who is there?"

"You tell me first," the voice said. "I can't see your face."

"What are you doing in my mother's home?" Sima asked instead.

It was quiet for a few tense seconds before the voice said, "Cosima?"

"How do you know who I am?"

"I'm sorry I didn't recognize my own daughter's voice. It has been so long. Am I dreaming?"

Sima froze, and her heart pounded in her chest. It could not be her mother, she reasoned. It could not, because that would mean her mother had been locked away inside the palace, all the while Sima had been exploring with ignorant glee.

"What are you doing in here?" Sima asked, her voice trembling.

"I have been here quite a while, child," her mother answered warily. "This is where he left me."

"Who?"

Her mother did not reply. Sima cautiously stepped forward until the bars of the large metal enclosure touched her hands. They extended higher than she could reach and were bolted deep into the stone flooring. Sima's mind whirled, struggling to comprehend how the secret room where she had stashed her most prized possessions had been cleared out and turned into a prison cell.

"It is dark in here," her mother said at last. "Ignite the light so I may see you."

Sima swallowed. She found her way to the left of the secret entrance and slid her hand against the wall until she discovered the sconce. As her finger found the switch, the flash of light allowed Sima to make out no more than the shadowy outline of shapes.

"Daughter," her mother whispered. "Your eyes. Come to me."

Sima sank to her knees, unwilling to close the short distance. "I can't see you. I don't know if you're real." She shook her head. "I don't know what is real anymore."

"I am here with you."

A hand touched Sima's, and she jerked back, startled by the unexpected action. It was not until her vision began to clear that Sima realized what her mother had done. The white barrier over her eyes disintegrated, allowing her to see her mother's face at last.

She was beautiful, her aura weeping serenity, despite the dire circumstances. Sima's heart exploded into furious beats as she recognized herself in her mother's features, from her full lips to her delicate, hooded eyes. Seeing the palace where she had grown up, Sostene returned all of her memories, meeting Kismet—none could compare to the relief this encounter brought her.

"It…it is you, isn't it?" Sima asked. She crawled closer and reached through the bars. "Anmah?"

Vincenzo did not have to search long for his brother, as Sostene came barreling out of the darkness only seconds after he pushed Sima away with his spatial manipulation powers. His brother moved with incredible speed, battering his core with hits before Enzo could manage to swing once. His curse flooded into his bloodstream, and his eyes dilated as time slowed.

The genesis that spawns in your wake will vindicate you of your crimes, his dark companion mused.

With a flurry of movements, Enzo launched his own attack, starting with explosions of sharp stone and metal shards that blew holes into Sostene's body. A thin slice of quartz ripped through his brother's cheek, taking off enough skin to reveal the bone below. Sostene did not let up, and as violet indigo magic funneled out of him, ghostly opponents shimmered into view. Each was more deformed than the last, his brother's army packed full of twisted alterations to the immortal form. They all resembled people in one way or another, despite their mangled bodies.

Enzo shot forward, a blade appearing in his hand as he swung. He sliced through one of the creature's stomachs, causing entrails to spill out onto the floor. Enzo hacked through the creature and threw himself at two more, taking their heads off with ease. A being with five enlarged hearts beating beneath thin, translucent skin slammed into him, sending Enzo flying backward. He rolled back onto his feet and gritted his teeth.

Blossom beneath sanguine skies, his curse sang, and *bring the last of a dozen's demise.*

Sostene stitched his body back together, congealing his flesh beneath his clothing in an attempt to repair Enzo's damage, all while he loosed a ghastly, sick laugh. Enzo had administered a great deal of damage to his brother, marring his body badly enough to slow him to a critical level, and he was not keen on letting Sostene undo his hard work. Enzo's electricity buzzed as it spiraled through the air, narrowly missing his brother.

Two more sacks of poorly stitched together flesh sprang from the ground, growing with size by the second. The being to the left had ten mouths spread across its arms and chest, each one expelling blood-curdling screams and expletives. Some of them begged for death while others taunted him.

"Kill me, please," one mouth whispered. "I pray for the mercy of Oblivion, detach me from this miserable existence, please."

"The twelfth moon is setting on the horizon," another screamed. "The violet sun is rising."

"I can't take it anymore," whined one along its shoulder. "All I feel is pain. My suffering is eternal."

The mouth in the center of the creature's chest grinned as it spoke. "Bastard child. Unwanted brat. Filthy fucking insect. Useless waste of power. Lonely little rat."

With haste, Enzo gave two merciful swings of his blade and sliced off the creature's arms. The other enormous being that accompanied the talkative creature seized its opening and latched onto him with its wide jaws. Enzo cried out as his skin burned, the creature's saliva digesting him as its mouth closed around him. His starlight bore a hole through the creature, causing its stomach acid to spill over his boots.

"Delirious weakling," the mouth on the remaining creature's chest hissed. "Unfortunate mistake. Cowardly little crybaby. Miserable, spineless failure."

Enzo snarled as he threw his sword directly through the being's chest, ending the spillage of words as its body fell onto the floor. The word *failure* echoed in his mind as he pulled his sword free and stabbed the creature again. Enzo was growing impatient; he desperately craved the moment he reaped his brother's soul.

Your peregrine soul summoned you to the riverbeds of the cosmos in search of a home, his curse whispered. *Shed your skin as you ascend to your rightful throne, twin of Darkness.*

His brother smiled as he wiped a droplet of blood off his suit. Half of Sostene's renewed flesh was a ghostly white, with violet energy pulsing beneath. "Think it truly ends with me?" A black and purple flash of light illuminated from the remaining holes in his tattered body. The air vibrated as his brother healed his wounds, the color returning to his skin. "This goes far beyond us, runt."

More of Sostene's globs of obedient tissue rolled from the shadows, which Enzo crushed with jaws of iron emerging from marble floors as his own team of creatures took turns ripping the stragglers to shreds. Power was palpable with every beat of his heart, marking his forehead slick with sweat, his eyes blazing black. The magic was consuming larger pieces of himself, and Enzo could not be more pleased with his mounting power. He could not hold back. His curse demanded more, would not stop until it was satisfied.

Blades spilled from Enzo's hands as he swung toward Sostene, slicing through the air with patient ease. "You thought you could take her from me," he growled. "I won't make the mistake of letting you get away. I'm not running anymore."

Enzo locked onto the silent beat of Sostene's movement as his brother dodged. The world slowed as Enzo dropped them into one of his voids. Never-ending black stretched in all directions, and viridian energy pulsed around them in the form of coalescing geometric shapes as they stood on a glass floor. Each time their bodies connected, the color of the energy changed, creating a cycling rainbow of light as they stepped through their deadly dance.

Sostene punched Enzo in the jaw before he kicked him in the ribs. Enzo swallowed both hits with ease, his body humming as trails of light followed his fists as he jabbed back. His brother ducked and followed through with a tackle. He wrapped his arms around Enzo's waist and threw him to the ground, causing the glass floor to crack. Enzo swiped his brother's arms out from under him and flipped Sostene onto his back. The cracks grew larger as Enzo beat in his brother's face, matting his black hair with blood.

Sostene's starlight scorched the skin on his abdomen, but Enzo grit his teeth and continued to hammer into his smug face. Enzo blinked, and his fist slammed into the glass. He growled and looked around for his brother. Sostene's midnight wings flashed as violet indigo magic tore through his void in destructive bursts. Enzo shot into the air and rallied his power until it was thrumming with such intensity, Enzo thought it might knock him out.

Their power clashed, fighting for dominance as Enzo erupted into laughter. "I can applaud your arrogant attempt to woo Cosima with your laudatory manipulation, if only because you have been a worthy opponent." His emerald ripples grew into soaring waves, forcing Sostene's magic back several feet. "Your savage fervor brings me closer to enlightenment."

Dull gray tissue bubbled from beneath them as lackluster muscle spread above, encapsulating them. The chamber flexed, and a scarlet sea swept Enzo off his feet. He flailed his arms as he fought to keep the blood from drowning him, all while Sostene rose to the top of the chamber. His hands shot out on either side of him as purple electricity shocked the muscle, causing it to tremor out of control.

Enzo held his breath as the discordant pulse sent him toppling through the crimson ocean. His magic speared through the muscular maze of tissue, morphing it into a masterpiece of Enzo's making. From atrium to axon, the space shifted into a neural fortress. As Enzo's feet peddled across the neurons, his energy sent rhythmic waves of emerald electricity into them, sending signals through them. The current collided with Sostene, and his brother's eyes rolled back as it coursed through him.

"I balked before my purpose, trembled as I witnessed my own enormity." Enzo's eyes flickered between green and black. "I incarnated tangled in responsibility with the power of Oblivion singing inside my veins, and though I long resented my burdensome accolade, I now wield it with pride. What an honor it is to be the one who will eviscerate you."

Sostene fought off Enzo's power, striking him with a sizzling shadow-like projectile. It lodged itself in his shoulder, and as the smoky shadows dissipated, pain echoed through Enzo's quiet insides. Sostene's magic festered inside his wound as his skin transformed. Enzo's left arm turned to ash, leaving him with the phantom sensation of his tissue dissolving. He glanced down as he watched the remnants of his appendage float away.

"I know the truth of your destiny," Sostene snarled. "You were always meant to perish by my hand. That force you feel clawing its way out of you has already done half the work. Your pathetic vessel is decomposing as we speak. When was the last time you felt your heart beat? Do you want to force sweet Sima to love a dead man?"

"I couldn't cope," Enzo said, blinking off his haze, the only pulse inside him coming from Cosima through the bond. "When I met Cosima for the first time, the mere sight of her almost did me in. I was fine spending my eternal life getting my teeth kicked into the mud. I didn't need direction or deliverance, I was addicted to the slow erosion of my being." More of his energy arced through the neurons, creating a resonance of his electricity, vibrating the void. "I thought my tarnished soul would wander without welcome until she found me. Her magnanimous love dissolved my ceaseless self-loathing, allowing me to see the knots in my threads as blessings and my power as a righteous blade. I let my devotion to her brand me, drench me in its benevolent direction. I'm willing to give my life in her name."

Sostene brushed back his black hair with his fingers, still matted with his own blood, as he stared down Enzo. "I can understand the obsession, brother. I can't tell you how many times I've already tipped over the edge with her name on my lips when I'm alone. Fate is generous for making my other-half unreasonably delectable. It won't take long to scrub your existence off her after you're gone. Once she is bound to me, I will have direct insight into her soul, and I will court Cosima with unflinching precision."

Enzo lashed out, and a viridian coffin of electricity encapsulated Sostene, shocking his brother until his teeth chattered and his hair singed. "If you manage to kill me, one truth above all others will haunt you—I've had her in a way you *never* will," he snapped as his gaze flamed, his phantom fist clenching. An unhinged hunger ate at his insides, begging for blood. "She chose me without any knowledge of the prophecy, and I didn't need to resort to strategic lies to get what I desired. We are bound together, not because of my thirst for the throne, but because she trusted me enough to fall for me. In the ruins of my soul, I crafted a home for her, one built of unwavering faith and endless adoration. The echo of her essence will rest there for eternity, even if I end up drifting in the ether. What has formed between Cosima and me can never be destroyed—it is relentless and everlasting."

Sostene laughed as Enzo's void disintegrated, leaving them once again standing in Cosima's home, right outside of the grand library. "Or so you thought, brother."

Chapter 51

Cosima

"Anmah?"

Cosima's heart beat with such intensity she thought it might burst through her ribs. Moira's arms trembled as they wrapped around her, the two embracing around the thick metal bars, which seemed to evaporate for a merciful moment as Sima sank into her arms and buried her face in her hair. Sima caught the familiar comforting scent of her mother beneath the smell of stale air and dust, causing tears to stream down her face.

Moira pulled back and studied Sima intently as she held her by the shoulders. "We must leave. I don't know when Alvize will come back, but I know we don't have much time."

"Alvize is the one who trapped you," Sima said with her eyes wide. "Why did he lock you in here?"

"In hopes you would come back...He told me our connection as mother and daughter is strong enough to fulfill the prophecy. In his mind, the only way to do so is by killing all of his brothers and then initiating a bond by tying your soul threads together. The bond requires that *you* feel immense love when it is initiated, but it does not have to be romantic in nature."

Sima took a breath. *Did Sostene only return my memories so he could attempt the same ritual as Alvize?* "Can the bond be broken once it is formed?"

Moira's gaze fell. "I do not know for certain. What I know of the prophecy is the limited information Kismet has granted me and the bits I have pulled from Alvize, but the bond is the most important piece, Cosima. You are a Fateless daughter. The Sacred Brothers may try to force you into the tether, but you can resist, you can bend Fate at your will."

Sima glanced down at her empty hands as her cheeks grew hot. "Anmah, my powers do not work as they should. I was unable to alter the threads of one of Alvize's brothers, Aurelio, and I feel my magic growing in magnitude inside me, but I cannot access it the way I desire."

Her mother nodded. "I understand. There is a light between the clouds, yet, daughter. You are powerful beyond measure, your well of magic is infinite in magnitude. Do you know why that is?"

"No," Sima answered.

"Because your grandmother's power was bestowed upon you when you were born, blessing you with strength far beyond those within this Kingdom. You were always intended to lead the Empire, just as she has. The Divinity may handle the details, but the Celestial Empresses rule with totality in this realm, as none are strong enough to defy them. The inability to utilize your magic as you intend is a curse upon your mind, casting doubt and obscuring the truth."

Moira cupped Sima's face and gazed at her with motherly adoration. "The only way they can truly stop you is through illusion and manipulation. You are not simply in touch with the Weave, able to command and change it as you see fit. You are *one* with the Weave."

"But I've tried to push beyond my limits without success," Sima replied, sinking into her mother's touch.

"They are only limits because you understand them as such. Become in touch with your intuition, listen to that guidance above all else, especially when using your magic. The way to alter what you wish is possible, but only if you expand your mind and allow the path to manifest before you."

Had the answer been there all along? Had Cosima only experienced limitations because she had believed the barriers to be true? Sima blinked away the water from her eyes, willing herself to build strength where there had once been hopelessness.

"I looked for you," Moira said. "Every single day. I told you I wouldn't watch you as you maneuvered through the Kingdom, but I did, and when I lost track of you, I knew something had happened."

Her chest ached. "How did you end up here?"

"I am not gifted with strength or magic as you and your grandmother are. I refused to stop searching for you, despite the risks. I came upon a glowing blue pond outside the Kingdom walls, and like a fool, I touched the surface. I fell into a deep sleep…" She cleared her throat. "And after I awoke, I was greeted by Alvize. He mistakenly believed I could be used to circumvent the prophecy as I am the Celestial Empress's real daughter, but it is you who carries her power and legacy. He has kept me hostage for years."

Sima's features twisted in fury, and her fingertips burned hot. Lavender magic sparked from her hands as she grabbed the bars of her mother's cruel cage and willed the bars to bend. She could feel a thread unspooling from somewhere in the grander universe as the metal gave way.

An astonished gasp escaped her lips, but before she could register the miracle, she grabbed Moira by the wrist and pulled her free. Sima ran, holding her Anmah's hand tightly as they fled. All other thoughts left her mind. She was locked onto her mission, committed to saving the mother Sima's homesick heart had been searching for all along.

Cosima and Moira approached the final set of stairs as the palace grew eerily quiet. The two paused, and Sima looked around, silently praying Vincenzo was still conscious. Although she had seen his power magnify, Sostene's power was devastatingly strong. Somehow, he had managed to grasp Cosima's mind in a way none of the others had been able to, despite her shielding. It terrified her, but even her own magic was rising to levels she hardly comprehended.

A strange sensation overtook Cosima, causing her to stumble down the last few steps of the stairs. Her mother lent a steadying hand as Sima struggled to get a grip on her breathing. Her mind spun, reminiscent of the times Aurelio forced her to ingest drugs, but this time, her vision was clear, and she retained control over her body. Instead, it was as if something had been fundamentally altered inside her. There was an unshakeable hollow feeling inside her, and she wondered if her heart had stopped. She placed a hand over her chest and gasped, surprised to find it beating.

"What's the matter?" her mother asked, Moira's eyes wide.

"Something is wrong," Sima managed to say.

An eruption from somewhere inside the palace shook the floor beneath them. Cosima's eyes locked on the front entrance door, and she pulled her mother forward, fighting through the overwhelming urge to collapse. Cosima ran straight up to it and threw the door open, ushering Moira through without a second wasted. They ran through the brilliant courtyard she had passed through with Sostene and approached the gate, standing just feet from the swirling purple smoke dome over the palace.

"We have to get you out of here," Cosima said, taking a step toward it.

"I'm not sure…" Moira shook her head as she backed up. "I haven't— I've only been here. I can't remember the last time I left the palace, and

I'm…not sure."

Sima's hollow chest panged. She knew this struggle intimately. "I am here with you." She faced her mother and placed her beautiful face in her hands with a gentle touch. "You can do this. The unknown lurks on the other side, that is true, but so does a life worth living. You have so much left to experience, and it can't happen if you're standing here. Don't you want to know what comes next?"

Her mother smiled as a tear slipped down her cheek, and Sima wiped it away. "Yes, but I can't go without you, daughter, and I suspect your business here isn't finished."

"Why do you—" Sima started to ask, before it hit her. The feeling of icy dread exploded as the purple smoke barrier crystallized, the dome freezing solid. Sima stepped away from it, shivering as a cloud of her breath appeared. "I think, perhaps, you're right. I only wanted to get you to safety."

"I will stay out of harm's way, but you must resolve what lies within."

Sima nodded and gave her mother a tight hug. Moira pressed a kiss to the side of her head before Sima turned back toward the palace. She stepped through the door and found the interior of the palace to be warmer, but flooded with water that rose to her ankles. A haunting piano melody whispered down the hallway, and goosebumps covered her skin as she followed the sound.

The emptiness of her chest grew more bothersome the farther she walked, and Sima struggled to keep her head held high. Her home was in tattered ruins around her, but somehow still stood, even with evidence of Sostene and Enzo's battle in nearly every direction. Something slid across the floor behind her, and Sima jumped, but found nothing there. She let out a small breath before she faced forward again and kept walking.

The music was coming from inside a ballroom Cosima had had visions of in the past. The ballroom was a desolate husk of the lively space from her memories. Although plunged in darkness, there was a faint glow coming from above in the middle of the dance floor. Her footsteps echoed as she moved toward the center of the room, spinning slowly as the music grew louder.

"Empress."

Cosima's heart skipped at the sound of Sostene's voice, and she whirled around to face him. Sostene's eyes were bright like purple suns, and his black shoes clicked as he waltzed in. "As I said before, I won't stop until you're mine, *Esti,* and nothing will stand between us and our magnificent destiny."

Sima's heart pinched. "Where is he? Where is Enzo?"

"He'll be here, right in time for the show." Sostene surged forward as the music grew louder. He pulled her against him, wrapping one arm around her waist and leading her hand with the other. He spun her in a slow circle, and Sima pushed against his chest with her free hand. "I'm happy to see that you've regained your footing with such haste after I unleashed your memories. You are much stronger than I gave you credit for. We make the perfect pair. Enjoy yourself, I have quite the evening ahead of us."

"Get off of me," Sima said. She swallowed the urge to scream and reached for her magic. As the threads exploded through the air, Sima's blood ran cold. There were only a dozen or so different strings when she expected to see thousands. "What's happening?"

"We are reaching the grand finale, my darling." Sostene grinned as he swept a kiss across her cheek before he dipped her. Cosima's head hung upside down, her hair nearly touching the floor, when she spotted Enzo sitting in the shadows, his mouth gagged with a black cloth. "His time has come."

Cosima screamed as she jerked away from him, falling to the floor. She scrambled toward him as she attempted to slow time, only for Sostene to shatter through as he appeared directly in front of her, his arms outstretched. Sima slammed into his body as he pulled her close. Her magic betrayed her; there were no threads that led to a favorable outcome. All ties led back to Sostene.

"Now, now," Sostene said, "I will let you say your goodbyes, but you must play by the rules. It wasn't easy to subdue your little boyfriend, and we can't have him getting away." Amber light illuminated Enzo from above as Sostene stared down at her. "I told you I was not heartless. I understand my little brother means something dear to you, and if you agree to behave, you may speak with him."

Tears streamed down her cheeks as her eyes fell over the restrictive, glowing amethyst binds around Enzo's body. His left arm was gone, leaving charred skin around his shoulder. Vincenzo's emerald eyes were vibrant and filled with the same familiar warmth as always. She could practically hear his voice whispering her name. Sima took a slow breath as courage swelled in her gut. She would find a way to save Enzo, no matter the cost.

"Please," she choked out, unable to finish her request.

Sostene smiled, his purple eyes sparkling with delight. "This is as close as you'll get, *Esti*. Say what you must before I extinguish his erroneous soul."

She shoved Sostene away from her but did not move closer to Enzo. Instead, she sank to her knees, her palms touching the ballroom floor. "Thank you, Enzo, for the ways your love has changed me." Though she resisted the urge to scream in agony, she was helpless against the river of her tears, causing her vision to blur. "Thank you for not looking at me as someone who needed saving, but rather as someone who needed your unwavering acceptance. You embraced all the unsightly parts of me I was desperate to hide away, and even though there is more of me I wanted to share with you, you gave me the courage to be myself again. You have loved me so thoroughly that I've had no choice but to see the light you see in me.

"Not many people know how to be gentle with someone who has been through what I have, but the challenge never made you hesitate. You were patient with me, allowing me to dictate every step forward we took together. You showed me that I am not a mistake, that there is beauty in my sensitivity, and that nothing about me is unlovable. All of those dreams I shared with you only seem achievable because of the impact you've had on me."

Sima's stomach clenched as tears rained down Enzo's face. She wanted to hold him so closely that their spirits melded together, reuniting their homesick souls. His suffering was nearly unbearable through the bond, but she knew there was more she had left to say. "I never blamed you, Enzo." Her lip quivered. "For not rescuing me from Aurelio sooner. I was scared of him, too. I could never blame you for being different than him, for being softer than he could have ever been."

Enzo opened his mouth and screamed, the sound muffled. The chair beneath him rattled as Enzo thrashed against Sostene's binds, his magic creating sparks. Sostene tugged Cosima backward, half-dragging her away from Enzo. The Sacred Brother held out a hand, and black smoke toiled toward Enzo, tunneling through his nose. His dual-toned hair concealed his eyes from view as Sostene's power rampaged through him, causing his body to illuminate at his core. Amethyst light beamed through Enzo's clothing, allowing her to glimpse his still heart. She cried out his name over and over, her voice cracking, as she fought against Sostene's grip.

"Your theatrics are adorable, really," Sostene purred. "But your crush has reached his expiration date."

He pressed her head against his chest with one hand as the other held the butterfly pendant from before. The energy wafting off the stone made her bones tremble, and Sima grit her teeth as she struggled to adjust to its aura. Sostene grabbed her by the throat as he doused the room in violet light and kissed her. Sima wriggled her arms up and scratched at his skin, her cries muffled by his lips.

Her body froze as Sostene's magic flooded through her, infusing into her bloodstream. Somewhere in her mind, there was a distant banging as memories blinded her, ones that she reasoned could not be her own. She watched as images of her in the throes of lovemaking with Sostene's bare body against hers flashed through her mind. Sima's heart pounded with almost as much intensity as her fists beat against Sostene's chest. At last, his lips left hers, but her vision remained blinded by more of the Sacred Brother's sick fantasies.

Enzo's heartbreak was clear in her mind through the bond, and Cosima hated that she could not run to him. Her stomach turned as she clenched her jaw and willed herself to fend off Sostene's intrusion. With luck, she managed to push the false memories far enough that they remained only ghostly overlays to her somewhat blurry sight. She searched for Enzo and whimpered his name when her eyes fell on his tormented face.

Sostene dragged his finger down her chin as the butterfly continued to pulse with power. "I decided to give him the same glimpse into your future I gave you. I wanted him to see that you will be worshiped for the rest of your days, just not by him."

Enzo's body began to glow so brightly, Cosima could no longer make out his face.

"Child of mistaken roots with impure blood, the ending of your life comes with great change. Your last breath is the initiation of the end. A new dawn is breaking over the horizon, and I will be the first to bathe in its light."

Sima rammed her knee into Sostene's body and broke free. Her magic burned her fingertips as she ran, moving with a speed she had never had before. She collided with Enzo's body, the heat of his skin burning her as she clutched onto him. She touched his face just as Sostene tugged her away from him.

"You cannot save him," he screamed, his words making her flinch. "You refuse to accept the truth, but that won't keep him breathing. His curse has already ravaged him. Death calls him home, and not even your desperate hands can give him more time. He has reached the end of his thread, *Esti*."

Sostene smiled as the butterfly hummed, the frequency loud enough to hurt her ears. A burst of glowing black and purple light shot toward Vincenzo, striking him in the heart.

"No, no. Please," she pleaded.

Enzo convulsed as their bond burned and unbelievable agony sprouted in her core, as if she was being torn open. Cosima screamed as she dug her hands into Enzo's skin, refusing to release her grip.

"I won't let you go, Enzo. I won't give up on you. I love you, you hear me? I love *you*, Enzo."

Vincenzo's normally vibrant emerald stare was dull and faded. As his body seized with his suffering, he held her gaze, his eyes communicating everything he couldn't say. *I'm always with you.* The madness of it all drove

Cosima to the edge of her sanity, and even as her ear-splitting screams tore through her throat, she expected to wake up from her nightmare. Her magic tore through her home, making the entire palace tremble.

Sostene laughed. He placed a hand on her back. "Can you feel it happening? Can you feel the threads begin to fray?"

Enzo's song played in her ears, its presence quiet, but undeniable. He was trying to comfort her, in the only way he could, with what remained of their bond. "Don't leave me, I don't want to do this without you." Sima panted as her emotions grew unstable inside her. Every beat of her heart brought more pain as if her blood had turned to magma. "I need you, Enzo. What am I supposed to do without you?"

The same words brushed against her mind. *I'm always with you.* Sima grit her teeth as Sostene yanked on her once more. She kicked him away and crawled into Enzo's lap, draping herself across his chest as his eyes began to roll back in his head. When her fingers touched his cheek, he gasped and gazed at her. His emerald stare was now gray, and the furious pain in her chest made her body weak.

The only thing she could see in his eyes was the future that was stolen from them. A piece of Cosima died as the final threads snapped, the unbridled agony coursing through her enough to halt her breathing. She watched as the man she had devoted herself to began to fade into Oblivion—their Fate-defying romance of untethered proportions, cruelly cut short.

Time slowed, and Vincenzo's last breath escaped his lips.

"Vincenzo," she screamed, gripping his shirt as Sostene walked and stood behind him. "Wake up, please. Please don't go. Don't leave me."

"You fought honorably, brother." Sostene placed his hand on Enzo's shoulder, his purple eyes brighter than Cosima had ever seen them. He leaned forward, grinning as he stared at the side of Enzo's head. "But it still was not enough. I told you I would have her, and mine she is, at last. Thank you, brother, for the blood you gave for the future."

Chapter 52

Once inside the hidden passageway, there was an athletic woman in a tight black uniform waiting for them. She greeted Yadira with a hug, and the Guardian immediately launched into explaining Ivo's predicament to the woman. Although he did his best to hide it, Yensa appeared particularly interested in the conversation. Ivo shifted on her feet, unsure if she should speak up for herself. Before she got the chance, the group began to move further down the tunnels.

"The stone you speak of sounds familiar," the woman said to Yadira. She turned, her red hair narrowly avoiding Ivo's face. "We should ask Doc as soon as possible."

Ivo wrapped her arms around herself, feeling unsettled in the dimly lit stone passageways. She did not realize how much it would affect her to be reminded of her time in Aeria sneaking around the sky islands without permission. This underground city was not the Archipelago, she reminded herself as she followed a few steps behind Yadira.

As they got closer to their destination, metal panels lined the stone, and Ivo could feel the electricity humming from beyond the double doors Yadira and the red-haired woman stopped in front of. Yensa reached into his pocket and handed Yadira something, their hands moving too quickly for Ivo to get a closer look.

"I'll let him know you're here," the woman said, ducking inside.

"That is Calix, by the way," Yadira said. "She is a close friend of Vincenzo."

"Who isn't?" Yensa said with a shake of his head, adding a small smirk.

Ivo swallowed the urge to cringe. Yensa's energy continued to agitate something within her, but she pushed the discomfort away as Calix popped her head back out and tugged Yadira in by the arm. Yensa held the door open and motioned for Ivo to go through. She ducked her head as she passed through and held her breath as she took in the immaculate laboratory. Beyond the dozens of leather-bound books neatly arranged on the shelves, there were intricate glass tubes with colorful swirling concoctions inside. The entire room had a sophisticated, but experimental vibration to it, as if the Doc the others spoke of was a mythical man with an overwhelming magical aura. However, as Ivo studied him, he seemed no different than any other person she had met.

A man with slicked-back black hair was hunched over a notebook where he took meticulously tidy notes. His tiny handwriting was illegible from where she stood, but with every precise strike of his pen, he poured words at high speed, even as Yadira whispered into his ear. Something she said to him made him frown.

"I see," he murmured. "You know where they go."

Yadira nodded. "Yes, Doc. I'll be back in a moment. Boys? Doc wants the stuff in the usual spot."

Yensa and Eeda flocked to her side and followed Yadira out of the room. Calix folded her arms in front of her and leaned back against the table where the man worked. She looked Ivo up and down with a flat expression before moving on to Isolde and Johanna. She glanced down at the Doc and let out a soft yawn.

"You sure, Doc?" Calix asked.

Ivo's brows pinched together as she cocked her head to the side. The Doc had not said anything to Calix, but did give a slight nod of his head. The redhead shrugged her shoulders and pushed off the table. She walked over to a cabinet and began to rifle through it. Johanna and Isolde exchanged looks but did not add anything to the conversation. Once Calix had found what she was looking for, she handed it to Ivo.

Ivo glanced down at the stuffed file. "What is this?"

"Required reading." Calix placed a hand on her hip. "Tell the Doc what it is you're looking for again."

She opened the file a crack and peeked inside, her eyes lingering on the title plastered across the first page—'Adenyeh Gaide: Memory Devourers'. Ivo quickly shut it again and cleared her throat. "We are looking for an important artifact. A crystal pendant shaped like a butterfly."

"Yes," Isolde said, straightening her back. "It is essential that we recover it."

"Hm," Calix said. "Doesn't sound familiar to me. What about you, Doc?"

The air grew tight, and Ivo's pulse quickened. Doc stopped writing and laid down his pen. He sighed deeply and turned to Ivo, catching her gaze with mysterious smoke and fog seeping out of his eyes. Ivo blinked, and it was gone, but he remained staring at her. "Why do you need it?"

Ivo opened her mouth to speak, but Johanna interjected. "It is a divine mission."

"Ah, yes, well, life is not quite interesting until you devote yourself to a cause much larger than yourself. But I am afraid that doesn't answer my question," he replied, cocking his head to the side. "Why do you need it?"

"She told you already." Isolde ran her tongue over her teeth. "We were sent by the Empress to retrieve the pendant. It is vital that we take possession of it before a member of the Sacred Twelve gets their hands on it."

Calix examined her nails as she raised a brow. "Oh yeah? How did you get the one you already have?"

Isolde's cheeks grew pink as Johanna stuttered. "H-how did you…? We…"

The Doc picked up his pen and resumed writing. "I could sense it from miles away. You should be more careful. Handling it without something to dampen the energy is quite dangerous, and there is no telling whose attention you might garner with its aura."

Ivo clutched the file to her chest. "Does that you mean you have the other one? Cosima and Vincenzo are in great trouble. There are only a few of the Sacred brothers left, and the last time I saw them, they were going to be interviewed by the Eternal Kingdom."

Calix frowned. "Apparently, the Divinity plans to put Cosima on trial for a bunch of bogus crimes, and it isn't looking good for Enzo either, Doc."

"That may very well be true," Doc said, "but I highly doubt your company intends to allow you to use it for that purpose. I would guess they are uninterested in aiding Vincenzo."

Johanna shook her head. "That's not true. If you give us the pendant you have, we will give the one in our possession to Ivo, and she may use it as she wishes. It is not ours to keep."

"Why swap one for another?" Calix asked.

Isolde narrowed her eyes. "Each pendant contains different properties and thus, different abilities."

"You don't even know which one we have," Doc replied, still writing furiously in his notebook. "There are three of them in existence, right?"

"How did you know that?" Isolde said, clenching her fists. "Where are you from? Why can my power not sense your heritage?"

Doc smiled, but Calix answered for him. "Doc isn't from around here, but that's never bothered us. We are not, however, fond of those willing to do whatever it takes to please their Empress, even if it means hurting innocent people."

"We would never," Isolde snapped. "Do not insult us when you hardly understand our mission. If the Sacred Brothers get their hands on that pendant, our entire realm could be destroyed."

"We are trying to tip the scales in our realm's favor. Please listen," Johanna said, waving her hands in front of her. "The Empress of the Day forewarned us of what was to come. When the eleventh brother dies, the survivor will be infused with all the strength of his fallen kin, and when that happens, there will be nothing stopping him from altering the Devotionals."

Calix scoffed. "Been a long time since we heard about those pesky things, huh, Doc?"

"What are the Devotionals?" Ivo asked.

The two women she had arrived with refused to meet her eye. Calix offered the answer. "Think of them as a mix between a hardened rule and a prayer. Only the Celestial Empresses know exactly what each one requires, but the balance needed to sustain the realm is delicate and requires ever more energy. There is a reason souls are reincarnated—their evolution creates energy, and the more refined the resulting souls become after repeated cycling, the higher our realm ascends."

"If a realm fails to maintain a certain level of balance, the Devotionals will begin to crumble." Doc turned the page in his notebook and continued scribbling. "If that happens, our realm is not only at risk of collapse, but of imprisonment as well. Not all of the other realms are as pleasant as this one."

"Why would the survivor want to alter the Devotionals?" Ivo asked. "Are the Sacred Brothers trying to kill everyone?"

Isolde clenched her jaw. "They don't want to kill everyone, Ivo, they want to disrupt the balance enough that the Spirit Goddess and her surviving son can change the very way this realm operates. The refinement of souls, the powers held by Caelari, the trillions of lives spread through the universe, all of it will be modified to fit their agendas. There is no telling what horrid nightmare they wish to enact, but the Empress of Day sent us to make sure that never happens."

Johanna placed her hand over her heart. "Please, you must give us the pendant. We cannot allow the Sacred Brothers to get their hands on it."

"Well, I am afraid you can't have it, but we assure you it is in good hands." Calix gave Johanna a plain smile, her eyes begging for the women to press the issue. "You're trying to keep it away from Vincenzo, and while I am sure you've already rifled through Ivo's memories, you don't know the first thing about us. We are willing to die to defend that crystal."

Isolde growled. "You don't understand the mistake you're making." Her limbs trembled as pale blue energy flamed around her. "Vincenzo must be kept from the pendant at all costs."

Ivo's eyes widened as she slowly inched herself away from the Adenyeh Gaide women. Johanna's body went up in pale blue flames seconds later, drastically increasing the temperature inside Doc's laboratory. The Doc continued writing his notebook, not even lifting his head to look at the commotion. Calix pulled a small stick from behind her back and flicked her wrist. It expanded into a full-sized staff, and Calix aimed it at Isolde's nose.

"I promise this isn't going to work out the way you think it will," Calix purred.

Isolde lunged, her energy creating spiked balls that flew through the air. Calix dodged them and jumped onto the table, her feet inches from Doc's notebook. She ran across it and jumped off, slamming her staff into Isolde's chest. Isolde planted her feet as she slid back. Two more eyes opened up on her cheeks, and Ivo let out a squeal, running to hide behind a metal cabinet.

As Calix and the Adenyeh Gaide battled, Ivo summoned her magic. She held her hand in front of her, and before she could shout out her spell, it responded, sending a bolt of electricity at Isolde. It struck her, and Isolde convulsed as Johanna locked eyes with Ivo. Johanna ran toward Ivo while Calix subdued Isolde, leaving her with no choice but to launch another attack.

Once again, her magic responded without her using a spell, and this time, she shot out a web. Johanna cut right through it with her blue flames and snagged Ivo by the wrist. The door opened as Yadira and the two Rani Guardians entered.

"Help me," Ivo cried, trying to yank her arm free.

Johanna raised her hand and clenched it, causing a portal to rip through the air. "You're coming with us."

"She's not going anywhere with you," Yadira hollered, surging forward. Her starlight hit Johanna just below her collarbone, and she howled as she threw spiked spheres at the Guardians with her free hand. "Don't worry, Ivo, I won't let them take you."

Ivo's pulse was loud as she pressed her hand to Johanna's arm. Her magic scalded the woman's and at last, she released Ivo, before Yadira threw the woman to the ground. She panted, still holding the file from Calix as Johanna bucked against Yadira's grasp. Yensa helped Yadira keep Johanna pinned to the ground as the woman fought with all her might. The Guardian with the scar scowled as Johanna's magic stabbed through his thigh, the blue flames creating a dagger in her hand.

He lifted her slightly and slammed her back into the ground as Yadira held her wrists together. A bright orb of light exploded from Johanna's hands, stunning the Guardians. The Adenyeh Gaide woman wriggled free and tossed her body through the portal. Calix and Eeda worked to contain Isolde, but the four-eyed woman was moving with disturbing speed. She flitted through the room, evading capture until she got close enough to slip through the portal.

With both Adenyeh Gaide women gone, the portal sealed shut and vanished. Doc's once immaculate laboratory lay in tattered ruins. There were liquids of all different colors leaking from smashed glass tubes, and papers littered the floor. The Guardians caught their breath as Doc stood up from the table and clapped his hands together.

"It is not every day one encounters the fanatical devotees of Nyssa, but it can only be an omen of worse to come."

Cosima

The blinding sorrow that engulfed her soul was suffocating, inescapable. Cosima could hardly breathe as her magic reached new heights, amplified by her boundless misery. Sostene pulled her off Vincenzo's frightfully still body, and she gripped onto his suit. Her power surged through her palms into him as she lost herself in her rage.

"I'll kill you, Sostene. I'm going to make you regret every beat of your heart, you miserable excuse of a man."

He threw his head back and laughed. His magic slammed against hers, and to Cosima's surprise, their power melded. A sickening wave of pleasure washed through her, and the guilt that followed immediately after threatened to swallow her whole. Sima let go of him and withdrew her power with haste, doing her best to refrain from collapsing.

"I was made for you, sweet Sima. Our union was written into the stars, and though you resist me now, one day I will have your true devotion." Sostene stepped toward her. "Until then, I'll have to do my best to make you see things from my perspective."

"There is nothing you can do to get me to stop loving him. I don't need the bond to be tied to his soul." Sima peddled backward, her eyes flicking between Sostene and Enzo's body. Being asked to leave him behind to save herself felt like too big an ask from the universe when her heart still whispered his name with each pulse. "You disgust me, Sostene. I see you for what you really are—a heartless lunatic."

Sostene tipped his chin down as his purple eyes ignited. "Now, *Esti*, you don't mean that, do you?" The amethyst butterfly once again hummed with incomparable power, making her ears ring. "You've hardly given me a proper chance."

"How long can you keep up the act before you begin to crack, Sostene?" The hollow sensation coming from inside her was nearly unbearable. She could not keep herself from reaching for Enzo, and each time she came up empty, she grew one step closer to the edge. "Your pretty words aren't enough to hide the creature that lurks within you. Aurelio taught me everything I need to know about men like you. You're truly disturbed if you think you can ever replace Enzo."

"I don't mean to replace him, I mean to eclipse him entirely." Sostene vanished and reappeared right behind her. Sima spun around and smacked away the hand he raised toward her face. He moved with impossible speed, wrapping her into his arms once again. "I can show you how I feel about you—the unrestricted, unfiltered truth of my heart."

Before she could respond, his magic engulfed her. Her power reacted, bursting forward without her call, and a violet indigo halo encircled them as Sostene leaned his face closer to hers. The combination of their energy sent waves of traitorous pleasure through her body, and Sima shuddered. Sostene's nose brushed against hers as images peppered her mind, his midnight wings creating a cocoon around them.

This time, the flood was gentle. The memories did not come with dizzying speed or overlap. They came one at a time, depicting her time in the Eternal Kingdom prior to being kidnapped by Ehses—the precise moments she had asked him to return to her. His magic continued to intrude upon her, giving her blissful sensations she wished she could escape from. With each wave of pleasure she felt in response to Sostene's magic, the worse her suffocating shame became.

Cosima's body was conflicted, unsure whether to react to his intrusion or the immersive visions playing out in her mind. Her eyes were blinded by a memory of Vincenzo, one where the two of them had spent hours taking turns telling stories as they watched the clouds float by. Her heart ached at the sight of him, and her knees were weak. If Sostene had not been holding her upright, she would have become a puddle at his feet.

A strange, warm sensation sprouted in her chest as another memory played out. Her eyes were filled with visions of Vincenzo's glorious smile and sturdy presence, the reminders of his love causing tears to drip down her cheeks. Sostene's magic increased to an intensity she could not bear, but Sima was helpless as the opposing experiences muddled the line between reality and fiction.

Soon, it was Sostene's face she was seeing in her memories and not Vincenzo. His amethyst gaze dripped with adoration, disguising Enzo's emerald eyes from view. She trembled as Sostene's magic sent chills through her. The confusing whirlwind of passion, pleasure, and pain made her desperate for some sort of grounding. Sima clung to Sostene, the only constant in the storm, sobbing as his vanilla scent filled her nose.

Deep in her chest, a transformation erupted. The visions came to a sudden end as a new host of sensations blossomed, reverberating through her hollow core. Sima's eyes flew open, and she locked eyes with Sostene. A persistent pulse echoed in her mind, and despite her pain, her lonely longing vanished, replaced with a firm presence. It was unwavering, assured, and magnetic.

"What did you do?" Sima choked out, too broken to bother fighting back.

She already knew the answer.

A smile spread across Sostene's face, each brilliant white tooth sparkling as he brushed back his dark hair. "We are tethered, darling girl, from now until eternity." Sima's heart dropped, and he frowned. "Don't be so frightened. You will have time to adjust before we attend to our restructuring of the Eternal Kingdom. On top of the chaos I created when I rescued you, the runt kicked up quite a bit of dust when he took Alvize's life. While things settle down, you and I will finally get the private time we deserve."

The bond to Sostene was overwhelming, taking up a great deal of her attention as nonstop sensation flooded through it. She experienced his every emotion, from the manic high he got after killing Enzo to the arousal he felt with her body pressed against his. It was violating, and her face flushed as she wondered what of her inner world he felt. He snapped his fingers, and a shimmering violet portal appeared.

Sima sagged against him. "Where are you taking me?"

"I want to be alone with you, *Esti*." Sostene licked his lips. "We are going somewhere even the three Fates cannot reach."

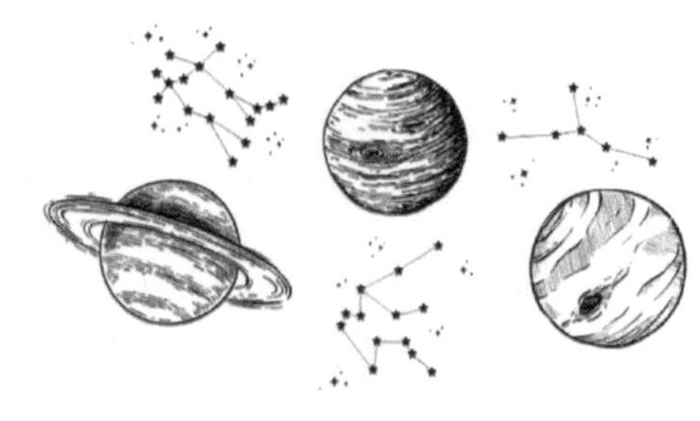

Chapter 53

Ivo

After Isolde and Johanna's abrupt departure, Calix and Yadira left to retrieve something for the Doc, leaving Ivo alone with him and Yensa. To keep from staring at the Guardian's scar, she had attempted to read through the research Doc had on Adenyeh Gaide. However, the words on the page seemed to blur together, and Ivo could not get herself to focus. She closed the files and looked up at the Doc, who was looking at a mushroom slice with a magnifying glass.

"How will we be able to find Cosima?" Ivo asked. "She needs our help. I don't know what has happened in the Eternal Kingdom since I left, but I am scared for her."

The Doc glanced up at her, peering over the top of his glasses. "I can open you a gateway to take you anywhere you need to go in the galaxy.

"Is there a way to track her?" Ivo asked, her gut twisting. "If she's not where she was last?"

"Not Cosima, but Enzo. I am surprised the boy has not already reached out for help. There is something not quite right with him. I can sense the fabric of the universe is reacting to his strangeness accordingly." Doc walked to a locked cabinet and inserted the key. He retrieved a small vial of glowing smoke. "Harnessed energy, given for emergencies. I will allow you to use it to bring the pendant to him. If he is not already with Cosima, I am sure he will be just as keen on finding her as you are."

Ivo did not know what Doc meant about something being wrong with Enzo, but she reassured herself she made the right choice in trusting his friends. Calix returned with a small leather sack and handed it to the Doc. He tugged it open and spilled the contents in his palm. Each slender gray stone had blue flashes, and Ivo recognized the type of crystal they were made from immediately—labradorite. Just as they had found on Carmine's planet. The Doc selected one with a white symbol carved into it and gave it to Calix.

"If things go wrong, don't hesitate to send a distress signal." The Doc held Calix's gaze. "If you can't find them, return with haste. Don't linger in the Eternal Kingdom—they are not fans of intruders—and be careful. I have a rather unpleasant feeling about this."

Calix nodded. "I hear you loud and clear, Doc." She turned to Ivo as she slipped the stone into a small bag attached to her belt. "Let's get you that pendant and get out of here."

When they arrived at the armory, two Rani Guardians at the door bowed their heads slightly toward Calix and opened the doors. Dozens of rows of weapons lined the walls, but they walked right by them until they reached a vault on the back wall. Calix held her palms in front of her and moved them in a slow formation, as if forming patterns in the air. A fiery red burst of energy left her palms and collided with the vault, causing it to unlock and swing open.

"Here we are," Calix said, strutting inside.

A powerful aura hit Ivo as soon as she entered, and she blinked rapidly as she attempted to adjust to the weight of the magic. Calix opened a drawer and pulled free a green crystal butterfly with mini rainbows trapped in its wings, making them iridescent. A sharp pain shot through her head, and Ivo winced, stumbling. Calix put the butterfly back and lent Ivo her arm to steady herself.

"I'm sorry," she murmured. "I forgot that these crystals can be intense for some mortals."

Ivo nodded as she backed up. "I didn't expect it to have such a profound effect on me like this. The one Johanna had didn't make me feel so…nauseous."

Calix sighed. "Either it's a fake or it's not as powerful as they think it is. This one is the real deal, and once we find Enzo, he will ensure it is properly utilized. I don't mind being the one to hold onto it. He put decades into keeping it safe. The least I could do is honor his desires by protecting it even in his absence."

Ivo's eyes widened. "Wait, Enzo knew it was here the whole time?"

Calix shrugged. "I doubt he knows what it is, if I am being honest. He never seemed to want to be around it, and he certainly didn't use it to usher in an era of destruction. Those memory eaters wanting to take it from him seem like all the more reason he should have it."

"Are they really that bad? I feel so stupid for trusting them."

"Don't," Calix said. "Not all of them are evil; in fact, many of them have good hearts. The problem is that they tip into obsession when they are given missions by Nyssa. They are willing to kill anyone standing in their way."

Ivo shuddered. "I can only hope they won't come back."

The walk back was quiet, but the butterfly in Calix's pocket continued to hum with energy, its presence leaving Ivo with an uneasy feeling. Outside of the Doc's laboratory, they found Yensa and Yadira resting against the wall, engaged in a hushed conversation that ended when they spotted Ivo and Calix. "Hey," Yadira said. "Got it?"

Ivo rubbed her shoulder. "Yes. Are you coming along?"

"Wouldn't miss it," Yadira replied. "Yensa is going to tag along, too. If there is need for further help, Calix will be able to get in touch with Doc."

Ivo's heart raced. "Let's find Sima, and fast."

"Absolutely," Calix said. Doc handed her a thin glass tube full of black smoke. She smashed it on the ground, and the portal ripped through the space above it, creating a jagged entrance of glimmering purple. "Ready to find Cosima?"

"More than you know," Ivo said, her fists shaking at her side.

"Remember your training," Doc warned as he held Calix's gaze. "No repeats of last time."

Calix beamed. "Oh, please, Doc, let a girl have a little fun. You know I'm ready for the end times."

The red-haired woman slipped her hand into Ivo's, and she tugged her across the threshold of the portal. Stepping through tore the breath from her lungs, but she did not feel the panic of breathlessness as the fabric of space held her tightly, relieving her of her mortal constraints and allowing her to indulge in a rare experience. Glimpses of distant universes flickered by, with colors that defied what her eyes could comprehend, expanding her mind and soul to accommodate the wisdom space provided as it transported them to Vincenzo's location. She reached out and let her hands slip across the stars, their energy biting at her fingertips.

Their arrival was abrupt, jerking Ivo out of her blissful respite and dropping her back into reality. She panted, catching her breath as Yadira and Calix did the same. They were in a dark, secluded courtyard, surrounded on all sides by intimidating slabs of crystal. It reminded Ivo of Aeria, and the hair on her arms stood up.

"He is nearby," Calix said, tying back her red hair into a tight bun. "No matter what, he is within a hundred feet of this spot." She marked an 'x' into the dirt with her foot. "Let's move."

Ivo followed, focusing on her breaths and remaining aware, while Yadira and Yensa guarded the rear of the group, lengthy twin blades at the ready. Calix marched with confidence, and Ivo did her best to keep up with her fast stride. When they reached the exit of the courtyard, Yadira used her starlight to break apart the lock, causing the door to slam inward.

Calix stepped through first and held her hand out for them to pause. A low groaning sound emanated from inside, and a twisted creature dove for her. Calix reached behind her, pulling a small stick from a hidden pocket along her spine. She flicked her wrist, and it expanded into a metal-tipped staff. In seconds, the creature with the beak of a bird and the body of a lynx lay twitching as its final tuft of air heaved from its chest. A strange sensation lurked inside Ivo's gut.

Something isn't right, Ivo thought.

"Come," Calix commanded.

Yadira nudged Ivo forward, and they stepped over the puzzling animal, tiptoeing around the blood seeping from it. The interior was concealed by shadows, save for half-circles of light every ten feet down the hallways to their left and right. Even in the dark conditions, it was clear a battle of some sort had taken place, rendering the entire palace unstable from within. As the structure trembled, Ivo bit her lip and took slow breaths. She was here for Cosima. She could not run yet.

"Which way?" Yadira asked. A pulse of energy caught their attention, and all three snapped their heads to the right.

"That way, I presume," Yensa murmured.

Another creature barreled from the shadows in front of them, narrowly missing Ivo as she ducked out of the way. It had long purple feathers and giant, ant-like feet. Yadira raised her hand to blast it with starlight, but the illumination caused the creature to cock its head to the side.

"Is it…looking at us?" Ivo asked.

At the sound of Ivo's voice, the creature jumped backward, disappearing into the shadows. They shared wary looks, but gathered themselves and plunged deeper with Yadira's light guiding them. From the edges of her light, creatures scattered and slithered by, but never came closer. At the end of the hallway, two obsidian doors slammed open, the thuds echoing far longer than should have been possible.

Her breath crystallized in front of her, shards of ice mystically forming from the cloud of heat exiting her lungs. Ivo gasped as the chilly display spread across the floor, responding to the environment in remarkable ways. Icicles manifested from the ground up and pooled on the ceiling. Yensa flailed his arms as his boots slid over a patch of ice, and Ivo swore his scar pulsed with white energy.

"Something unusual is occurring," Yadira noted.

"Oh, it absolutely is," Calix said as she tapped her foot.

A breathtaking pearl and onyx fox spirit twice their size cautiously toed out of the darkness, swishing its many tails back and forth as it circled them. The spirit was translucent and shimmering with a familiar aura. Ivo stared into its emerald eyes and shuddered as Yensa stiffened beside her. Yadira and Calix pressed closer, keeping Ivo between them, but something called her forward, and she pushed through them. She recognized this spirit.

"Ivo, don't," Yadira called.

"It's me," Ivo blurted, dropping to her knees in front of the giant fox.

Her heart pounded as she looked up at the spirit, silently praying she had not been mistaken. Its muzzle lowered and sniffed her head, its curious gaze dropping lower until it met hers.

"Vincenzo," she whispered, her heart aching. "Where is Sima?"

Cosima

Sostene tugged her through his portal, and Cosima stole one last look at Enzo's cold body before the palace she had grown up in disappeared. The cosmic roadway was gentle as they hurtled through it, as if the universe could sense her shattered heart and heavy soul. The stars flew by, creating streaks of light. When they reached their destination, space dissolved, leaving them standing in a luxurious garden, overflowing with roses.

"I dreamed of one day bringing you here," Sostene said, taking her hand. "I built this place for us so long ago that I started to doubt you'd ever see it for yourself."

Sima resisted the urge to burst into tears as she swayed on her feet. As her eyes ran over the gorgeous rose quartz statues, the glistening water pouring from the fountains, and the butterflies floating through the air, her body trembled with seething hatred. She did not want her misery to be smoothed over with idyllic scenery. She wanted Enzo back.

"Come, I have more to show you."

"No," Sima breathed, tugging her hand free.

Sostene cocked his head to the side. "I hate to see you like this, so drenched in sorrow. I can take your mind off the pain that sticks to you, if only you'll let me."

"This pain only exists because of you," she snapped.

The more she thought of Enzo, the closer she felt to pure insanity. Her magic soared, cutting off the air from her lungs as her lavender energy shoved Sostene back. Although her power did not keep Sostene from killing Enzo, it was her only defense against spending an eternity by his side.

Sima knew, somehow she would bring the man she loved back from the dead. She would pry new strings from the Weave of Fate demanded of it her. She would do whatever it took to reverse Sostene's mistake. If Enzo were truly gone, then she would only carry on with spiteful diligence. She would defy Sostene's every command until his lack of control over her drove him mad. If Sima were to be trapped for eternity with Sostene, then he would come to learn *he* was just as trapped.

The threads exploded from her core, and she reached for them. Her magic came in a calamitous wave, submerging her in darkness. She blinked, and color drenched her vision. Sima choked back a sob of disbelief as her surroundings had transformed. The stars twinkled in the sky above never-ending lavender fields, the moon too serene for the chaos inside her.

She stood in front of a worn path where feet had trampled the herbs. The air thrummed with mysterious power as she walked, lavender occasionally snagging on the sparkling stars hanging from the hem of her lilac dress. The moon glimmered, seemingly growing larger and smaller as though it were breathing. Her eyes rested on it until she came upon a pond. She knelt beside it and took in her reflection on the surface of the water. Ripples appeared over her face, and her eyes adjusted to view the shadows swimming inside. A small head popped up, and Sima gasped, nearly falling flat onto her bottom.

She collected herself and inspected the tiny being that sprouted from the water. She was delicate, with long, swooping lashes and blueberry colored hair that wisped around her ears. She had a short, plump nose with round cheeks, and she held a hand up, beckoning Sima within.

When she touched the water, the adorable being disappeared, and in seconds, the pond vanished as well, leaving Sima sitting alone in a barren patch of dirt. She got to her feet and walked forward, finding the path continued on the other side of the empty circle.

This time, she came upon a riverbank with a shadowy figure bathing in the center. He washed his hair dutifully in the rushing water, bobbing in and out as suds of soap drifted away. Sparkling pearl colored fish jumped out and spun, splashing as they returned to the river. Orbs of light drifted in the air around her as they sang. Their voices were effortlessly angelic, humming soothing harmonies.

"Oh, precious one," they sang, "come, at last, to save us."

Something about their presence was calming and inviting, as if Sima had been here a million times before. She held her arms out beside her as the orbs fluttered closer, and a cloud of light blocked out the river beyond and the man bathing inside it. It tickled her skin as they bumped against her, their song growing louder as they danced.

"There was a tiny Empress, with eyes like galaxies and strength like stars," the orbs sang in unison, lifting Sima off the ground.

"There was a tiny Empress," some of the orbs repeated, high-pitched and heavenly.

"With eyes like galaxies," some joined, humming low and deep.

"And strength like stars," the rest sang, full of life and a beckoning hope.

"Come, at last, to save us," they rejoiced in unison. "Come, at last, to save us."

When they set Sima on the ground, her dress from before had vanished, and now she wore a full-length, elegant gown in the dreamiest emerald green. She thought the color would break her heart in two, but no echoes of her torment and grief surfaced.

The orbs had dispersed enough for her to view the shadow in the river. A yelp of confusion and glee ripped from her throat, and Sima threw herself into the river. He turned toward her; his eyes as green as they had always been. Her arms wrapped around him, only to slip right through him. She stumbled, and the orbs caught her, setting her upright.

"What is happening?" Sima asked.

"My Empress," he replied, the warmth in his eyes causing crinkles around the edges. "Beacon of my mercy, how beautiful you are beneath the moonlight."

Her chest was too heavy for her to take a proper breath. "Don't tell me it's true. Don't tell me you're gone."

"I am always with you, Cosima," he said, his voice soft. "Nothing can keep us apart. Trust that this is not where we find our end."

"Where are we? Is this a dream?"

Enzo smiled. "Our spirits are in the Weave."

As he said the words, millions of iridescent threads surfaced, filling the sky. Her heart squeezed as her eyes fell back on him. "Can I stay here forever with you?"

"No, we both know that. You're not bound to this side the way I am." He pointed to the river. "There are things you came here to learn. I will find you."

Enzo vanished, and the soul-splitting pain threatened to drown her in the eternal river. She tore her eyes away from the empty space where he had been standing and focused on the water around her ankles and calves. The way it rippled was unnatural, the color not quite right. She stepped backward, and the water once again waved in random patterns. She walked through the river, her eyes glued to the mesmerizing designs that revealed as she waded through them. The sigils were unfamiliar to her, resembling interlocking circles, triangles, and even hexagons.

The orbs of light hovered above the surface of the water, further illuminating the dazzling patterns that left her feeling cross-eyed and confused. Sima pulled herself onto the bank along the river and examined the sight before her. The more she focused, the more she realized she recognized some of the designs from the sashes worn by the High Priestesses.

She was able to pinpoint the ones associated with Fria, Alena, Thera, and Keres—Goddesses of stability, strength, creation, and destruction. The river and lavender fields melted away, and she found herself in a serene temple with towering ceilings. The temple was empty save for thousands of strings that burst from the center of the room through the walls. The strings varied in color, creating a rainbow that vibrated with energy.

It drew her near, and Sima walked without thinking until her hand pressed fully against the threads. Energy shot through her palm, and a vision overtook her eyes.

A meeting had commenced amongst the Divinity, twelve High Priestesses with their assistants in tow, all sat around a golden and hollow circular table. The Goddesses sat with stone faces, waiting their turn to speak. First came Keres, who wore a nasty frown throughout the entirety of her speech.

"Sisters, I have gathered you all here today for matters of the utmost importance. As we have discussed previously, the banishment of one of our own, Ehses, has left us with an unfulfilled position. As such, this Kingdom cannot run optimally."

"Not this again," moaned Telma. "Can't we speak of something new?"

"No," Keres snapped, "not when this is unresolved."

"What is your suggestion?" Demi asked, her eyebrows raised. "I am curious."

"Replacing Ehses will be a time-consuming process, but there are options that do not involve waiting for our twelfth member. I suggest we divide her responsibilities among a select few."

"Doing so will also spread her power amongst those chosen," warned Sevasti. "Are you certain this is wise?"

"We cannot sit here and expect the realm to change without action." Keres drummed her fingers together. "If the situation is not improving, then we are responsible for forcing the renewal that this realm needs to flourish."

"We have never divided our power outside of emergency situations," Astraea said.

"I do not trust this plan."

Keres growled. *"You fear it because you fear change, favoring balance over all, Astraea. Do not let it blind you from making progress."*

Alessa, Goddess of protection, glowered. *"I do not know if I agree with your plan either. Sister Keres, have you considered the ramifications of long-term transfers of power? How might this ripple into the Kingdom if there has never been a case of only eleven High Priestesses in rule?"*

"As there has never before been a banished High Priestess, it is up to us to set the precedent. The Spirit Goddess held a vital role in this Kingdom. Without her, our people go without spiritual guidance, and we, as the Divinity, have lost our connection with the unknown. Can't you see that without her, we are already succumbing to the chaos of operating only within our own comfort zone? We must conquer this setback and take decisive action."

Demi chewed her cheek, then slammed her palm onto the tabletop. Heads snapped toward her. *"I agree with Keres. In the pursuit of eternal wisdom, we must continue to foster our relationship with the unknown. By the time we have fully trained and prepared Ehses' replacement, the damage may be too far-reaching to undo."*

Astraea sighed. *"Perhaps you have a point. If matters are unbalanced beyond what we can reverse, then it will be up to the Celestial Empress to balance what we cannot."*

"It is settled then," Keres said. *"We will divide Ehses' power amongst four of us, to properly distribute her duties."*

"How shall we decide how it is apportioned?" Demi asked.

Astraea tapped her fingers against the glass of water her attendant placed in front of her. *"It must be a vote. Only those interested in welcoming more duty shall be in the running. When we have our candidates, we will choose four to vote for."*

As the meeting drew to an end, Keres sat with a smug grin. Her gaze drifted over Thera, Alena, and Fria with a knowing twinkle in her eye. The four remained in the room long after the other Priestesses and their aides had left. Keres was the first to break the long silence with a drum of her long black nails against the golden tabletop.

"They are fools if they believe they can outrun this by following the rules," Keres hissed.

Thera rested her chin in her palm. *"If we didn't intervene, our sisters wouldn't realize how wrong they were until our realm came crashing down over our heads. We are making the right decision by moving on without them."*

Fria sighed. *"The Emperors from the Zolani realm sent more of their threats, but I managed to intercept them before they got to Demi. How long does Leilani have before the Zolani Emperors sense its vulnerabilities?"*

The room warmed as Keres erupted into flames. *"Our imbalance is growing worse by the year. The souls are taking longer to ascend, and the slower flow has left us without enough Trine Scouts or Rani Guardians. Our sisters have left us without a proper army to defend ourselves with should the Zolani Emperors decide they have tired of waiting.*

We cannot afford to put this off any longer."

Alena glowered. "I agree, Keres, but is it wise to target the Empresses? Ehses already has Kismet under her spell. Do we need to involve Nyssa and Lethe, too?"

"All three Celestial Empresses have hidden their descendants away," Thera said, crossing one leg over the other. "If we let them get away with this, there will be no chance for Ehses' chosen child to replace the hands of Fate. Their descendants are even more powerful than their predecessors. If we don't locate the remaining kin, it only leaves room for their family tree to expand. We can't spend an eternity hunting down the Fates' lineage."

"It's settled then," Keres said, lacing her fingers together. "Lethe and Nyssa will be incapacitated. I will be the one to channel Lethe's destructive power."

Alena let out a soft breath. "I suppose that means you will want me to absorb Nyssa's abilities."

"Indeed." Keres smiled. "Who else will make sure we have enough souls to go around?"

As the vision faded, Sima stepped away from the threads and cradled her hand against her chest. Her fingers continued to tingle with energy from touching the strings. She had deciphered the symbols for each of the four High Priestesses in the patterns of the water that inherited the Spirit Goddesses' powers. Sima thought back to Celestia, the High Priestess in training who aided her during her trial with the Divinity. She had not yet assumed power, meaning even now, those four Goddesses remained in possession of Ehses' power.

Slowly, pieces aligned in her mind, putting together a puzzle she hadn't known she was solving until this very moment. The picture was revealing, and Sima was becoming aware of corruption that far extended beyond Ehses and her sons. If Ehses suspected her plan for her sons might fail, then she saw no reason why the Spirit Goddess wouldn't have formed another one—without anyone in the Kingdom realizing.

Another vision swirled in the water, the memory so potent it paralyzed Cosima as it overtook her.

Chapter 54

Ivo

The fox spirit flickered in and out of view as it stared at them. Ivo's hands trembled as she stared into its vibrant, viridian eyes. The tremors coming from the crumbling palace were worsening by the second, but Ivo refused to leave without her best friend. The fox vanished, reappearing several feet away at the end of a hallway. Without waiting for the others, Ivo took off after it, jumping over rubble as she followed.

The spirit continued to lead her down a series of turns as the group from Haelos fought to catch up. When she approached a beautiful library with gilded glass doors, the fox appeared on the other side and pawed at the handle. Ivo held her breath as she opened the door and stepped inside. It slammed shut behind her, and Ivo gasped as glowing emerald energy sealed her friends outside of the library, leaving her alone with the spirit.

"Vincenzo," Ivo whispered. "What happened to Cosima?"

Somehow, the library had remained unscathed, the interior so breathtaking it nearly brought her to her knees. Once again, the fox faded out of view and reappeared near a row of bookshelves. She walked toward it, her footsteps echoing, as the spirit spun in a circle near a shelf with dragonflies carved into the sides. She ran her fingers along the details as she rounded the corner. Her eyes fell on a shadow crouching in the dark, and Ivo let out a scream.

Yadira and Calix pounded on the glass doors, their voices muffled, as the fox sat beside the crouched figure. With the subtle glow of the spirit, Ivo could make out facial features. The woman hiding in the library was not Cosima, but she shared such a strong resemblance to her best friend that Ivo's heart skipped. The fox rested its head on top of the woman's head and let out a soft huff.

"Who…who are you?" Ivo asked, holding her hands in front of her chest.

The woman sniffed lightly as the fox nudged her. She looked at Ivo, and a gasp escaped her. "You are a child of the Day, thank the threads. You will help us, won't you?"

A child of the Day? Ivo blinked and squatted down, bringing herself eye-level with the woman. The more Ivo studied her face, the more she understood who the woman was. "You're related to Cosima, right?"

Her eyes widened. "Yes, my name is Moira. You know my daughter?"

Ivo's lip tugged upward. "She's my best friend."

Moira jumped up from the ground and slammed into Ivo with a hug. "You will help me find her." She pulled back and looked at Ivo. "One of the Sacred Brothers has taken her and escaped."

Ivo's pulse raced. "What? No, that can't be true. We're here to save her. We can't be too late."

Moira's eyes filled with tears. "They left hours ago."

"What happened?" Ivo asked, doing her best to keep herself from shrieking.

The fox turned its head away, as if ashamed. Moira's gaze fell to the floor. "Cosima helped free me from the cage I was being kept in upstairs. She asked me to run, to leave her behind while she dealt with the chaos coming from within our home, but I couldn't do it. I hid instead, and when the sounds of destruction came to an end, all I could hear was Cosima screaming." Floods of tears poured from Moira's eyes. "I ran toward the ballrooms, but I was too late. Just as I arrived, a man with purple eyes pulled her through a portal." Her gaze flicked to the fox spirit. "That is also when I found his body."

Ivo focused on her breathing as she let the information settle over her. Not only had they been too late to help Cosima, Sostene had disappeared with her, vastly expanding the possible places she could be. Her magic bit at her fingertips as her anger surfaced, creating a flaming blue aura around her. Soft whimpers came from the fox as it hid its face with its paw.

"You need to come with me, Moira. We are going to find Cosima, but we need to move fast. There is no telling where he might have taken her, and we need all the help we can get." The fox's sad eyes made her rage stutter, reminding her that she wasn't the only one desperate to bring Cosima back. Ivo let out a harsh sigh as she placed her hands on her hips. "I don't know what happened in there, but it isn't your fault. You did your best to protect her, and we are going to find a way to undo this."

Its snout tipped downward a fraction. Ivo walked up to it and patted its head. "If…If I don't see you again…thank you. For everything you did for me, but also for everything you did for her. You gave her something no one else could—a safe place to bloom. I've watched her shine, even through the bloodshed, and I don't think that would've ever happened if your devotion didn't force her to acknowledge her own greatness. This isn't over, and I won't stop until we fix this. Until then…take care of yourself, Enzo."

The understanding in the fox's face made her heart pinch. Something about her grief was heavier than expected, and Ivo's body drooped as she took Moira's hand. The fox's form wavered for a second longer before it vanished completely, leaving the library feeling significantly more hollow without the weight of Enzo's energy. The library doors swung open, and as she led Moira out from behind the bookshelves, her friends poured in.

"Ivo," Yadira shouted, "are you alright?"

Calix froze once she got a glimpse of Moira. "Who is this?"

"This is Sima's mother, Moira." Ivo frowned. "She was held hostage here until Sima freed her."

The woman trembled as she offered a small wave. Ivo's stomach turned at the thought of how hard the situation must be for Moira. She had lost her daughter and been subjected to unjust imprisonment at the hands of a Sacred Brother, only for her liberation to end in heartbreak. It was now Ivo's responsibility to care for Moira until she could be reunited with Sima, and it was a role she accepted with honor.

"Where is Sima, then?" Yadira asked, deep lines forming in her forehead.

Yensa's jaw clenched as he stared at Sima's mother. Ivo pulled Moira closer and wrapped her arm around her shoulders. "Sostene has her. We don't know where they've gone."

"And the fox?" Calix asked. "T-that was Enzo? Is he…?"

"Yes," Ivo said, her voice barely above a whisper. "He's dead."

Calix pressed her lips together as she gave a small nod, her gaze distant with disbelief. "We…we need to get back to Haelos. The Doc will know what to do."

"What is Haelos?" Moira asked.

Yadira's expression softened. "It is our home and the planet where Cosima was held captive for half a century, until she killed the Sacred Brother responsible. You will be safe there, and there are many people who will lay down their lives if it means getting her back safely."

Moira choked back more tears, and Ivo hugged her tighter. "This is more than anyone should have to bear."

"You're right about that," Yensa said, finally breaking his silence. "This cruelty has to come to an end. We cannot let the remaining Sacred Brother lay claim to the Eternal Kingdom if this is the kind of destruction he leaves in his wake."

The ground trembled, and books from the shelves toppled onto the floor. Yadira reached for Ivo and Moira, steadying them as more of Sima's home began to give way. "Enough talking. We have overstayed our welcome."

Calix reached into her jacket and pulled free a vial full of glowing smoke that pulsated to an unspoken beat. Her palm illuminated as red beams of light burst from her eyes. The vial shattered, and a portal tore open, revealing Doc's laboratory on the other side. Calix ushered them through, and Ivo held her breath as she stepped into the portal.

Planets and stars flashed by at a mind-boggling speed, causing her eyes to cross as her skin was pulled tight. As quickly as it began, it ended, as if Calix had somehow managed to speed up their travel. It left Ivo queasy as she was spat out onto the floor of the lab, struggling to catch her breath. Doc rose from his chair and studied them with a disturbingly dark expression.

"Doc," Calix breathed, her face crumpled.

"Say it isn't so, firebird." Doc pinched the bridge of his nose. "Tell me you're mistaken."

"He's gone, Doc," Yensa said, his jaw flexing. "Sostene killed him."

Ivo tugged Moira toward the Doc. "He kidnapped Cosima and left her mother behind."

His eyes landed on Moira. "Did he happen to say anything to her before they disappeared?"

Moira nodded slowly. "I heard him say he was going to take her somewhere not even the three Fates could find them."

Doc frowned. "Not an auspicious sentiment, is it?"

"We have to do something." Calix reached into her jacket and pulled out the pendant. "It's time to stop playing by everyone else's rules, Doc."

He smiled as he took it from her. "About time you came around to the idea. The preparations will take time, though, Calix. We won't be able to find her or bring Enzo back overnight."

"Bring Enzo back?" Ivo's face flushed as she thought of her girlfriend, Ereyla, who had been killed by Aurelio. Ivo would've done anything to bring her back, and she knew Cosima would feel the same about Vincenzo. "There's a way to fix this?"

"Not in the way you might be thinking," Doc said, shaking his head.

"Enzo's spirit has been severed from his vessel, but because of how powerful he is, this is far from over." He looked to Calix. "He won't approve of this, you know. He made that very clear to us."

"I'm aware," Calix said with a smirk, "but he's not here to stop us, so what do I care?"

Yadira crossed her arms over her chest. "What plan are you two cooking up?"

Calix patted Yadira on the back. "Oh, my darling friend, we've been planning this for fifty years. Some might say everything we've ever done has been in anticipation of this moment."

"Why do I have a bad feeling about this?" Yadira asked.

"I take offense to your doubt," Doc said as he dropped the pendant into the pocket on the front of his buttoned shirt. "You know where to begin, Calix, but don't let the word get out. The people won't take well to learning of their hero's Fate."

Calix dipped her head. "Got it, Doc. Yadira, Yensa, let's move. I'll catch you up on the way to the pit." The two Guardians nodded and made for the door as the Doc whispered something in Calix's ear. She caught his gaze as she smiled brightly. "

"What about us?" Ivo asked, her throat dry.

"We've got spare rooms down here where the two of you can decompress from everything. Like Doc said, nothing is happening overnight, so for now, I want the two of you to focus on recovering. Then, when you're ready, Ivo, we will need your help, too."

"I understand, I'm willing to do whatever it takes."

"Good to hear. Follow me down the hall and I'll show you those rooms."

An electric buzzing overtook the lab, causing chaos as papers swirled in the air and glass vials fell from the shelves. Ivo's eyes widened as she clutched onto Moira. A navy blue portal appeared in the center of the lab, surrounded by giant arcs of blue light. A person tumbled through it, his arms flailing as he struggled to keep upright.

Ivo's jaw dropped. "Merit? What are you doing here?"

Cosima

Still tangled in the trillions of threads inside the Weave, Cosima fought to make sense of the images flashing behind her closed eyelids. Her heart thumped with a discordant rhythm as her trembling hands reached for the iridescent strings all around. Sima grit her teeth and slammed against the cataclysm of the past, tearing through her mind, willing her magic to bend the flow in her favor.

Her power soared to suffocating heights, bringing Cosima to her knees as a lavender current washed over her, drenching her in unbridled strength. Once again, she slammed against the intrusion of images, using her magic like armor to block out the untamed flow. The chaos simmered, reducing to a gentle reiteration of the past from a perspective Cosima did not understand. The three Celestial Empresses manifested in the endless black space behind her closed eyes, with such vibrancy that the real world paled in comparison.

"I don't know if I trust this," Nyssa said, her white skin more pale than usual as she toyed with the end of her braid. Hair as dark as the void fell just below her breasts, concealing much of the intricate silver detailing around the bodice of her dress. "How can you be sure that this is the proper resolution, sister?"

Kismet sighed, resting her head in her hands. Her eyes were rimmed in red and swollen, partially hidden behind the blanket of midnight her hair created. "We have avoided making a decision for far too long. The other realms are ascending at a rapid pace, leaving us far behind. If we don't do something now, balance will be restored as a cost we cannot reconcile with."

"We never thought it would come to this." Nyssa's icy gaze fell. "There have been quarrels amongst the Lanis before, but nothing near total devastation. How were we to anticipate the Zolani's drastic evolution? How were we to know that we would fall from the grace of heaven?"

Lethe frowned as she rubbed a scented oil made from meadow sage onto her arms and neck, the concoction making her luxurious brown skin shimmer. "It doesn't matter how we got to this point; we cannot go back and change the past. The imbalance over our realm rests on our shoulders, and we cannot sit by until our Kingdom becomes the pits of hell." Her eyes fell on Kismet. "I agree with you, my sister in spirit, we must restore balance with haste. You have already lost your daughter and grandchild. I will give my eternal son for yours."

"How could you?" Nyssa's face crumpled. "How could you hand him over with such little care?"

"He was never mine to own," Lethe snapped. "You may be too soft-hearted to sacrifice a sliver of your soul in favor of the greater good, but I am not, and it does not mean I do not care for him. We knew the knots we'd create when we had our children in secret. We knew there were risks to using the pendants in such a manner, but we did it anyway. After Cosima's birth roused Ehses' suspicion, I had no choice but to let the eternal river decide where he would incarnate. My son was carried in another's womb, listened to another's heartbeat as his vessel formed, and saw another's face through fresh eyes, only to be abandoned amongst the Rani like a malformed runt of the litter. I had no

choice but to comfort him from the shadows and cry for him in the dead of night. I have already watched my son suffer through the dawn of his incarnation. Now, he will rise as the harbinger of harmony. When my inevitable child takes his last breath, only then will the sins of those beneath our command be washed clean. In giving his life, balance will be restored and the wheel will once again begin to turn."

A tear fell down Nyssa's face, her blue eyes locked onto Lethe. "Is there no way to save him?"

Kismet pressed her lips together. "It is not a curse, Nyssa. She is liberating his soul. He was built with this purpose in mind; this was always his destiny. Ehses and her Sacred Sons have merely forced our hands."

Lethe placed her hand on top of Nyssa's. "The expulsion of energy that accompanies his departure from existence will fuel our ascension, yes, but it is his reincarnation that will truly save us. The clock begins to tick the moment he takes his last breath, for when he returns, all who disobeyed him will give their blood in the name of justice. The scales will be balanced, for he will make it so. See the honor in his sacrifice, sister."

Nyssa turned to Kismet. "What of your granddaughter? What of their bond?"

Kismet refused to meet her gaze. "I cannot pretend to understand her Fateless soul or how much heartbreak she can bear. Their bond is beyond our control and always has been. We have never encountered an untethered soul, and it is that very freedom our realm is depending on. Without threads for others to manipulate, Cosima cannot be stopped."

Lethe's jade eyes softened as she stared at Nyssa. "Cosima is transcendent, capable of traversing realms, and with Vincenzo's manifestation abilities, the possibilities are endless. Their union cannot be cleaved; they are as intertwined as space and time."

The vision faded, and Cosima blinked off her haze as the Weave transformed. The ethereal river disappeared, leaving her in a lavish grove of fragrant wisteria trees. The moon was high in the rosy pink sky, the stars twinkling like an exuberant audience beside it. Vincenzo stood with one hand tucked into his sapphire blue suit, his smile wide and welcoming.

Cosima strolled toward him, never taking her eyes off his. She placed her hands in his, and this time, he was solid beneath her touch. A familiar spark of electricity hummed through her body as he wrapped her in his arms and placed his head in the swoop of her neck.

"Empress," Vincenzo whispered against her skin. "I am your eternal protector, your unwavering blade. Wield me and witness the resonance we leave in our wake. Let my reverence adorn you, wear my heart as your impenetrable shield. Be the air that fills my lungs and give purpose to the blood inside my veins, for my soul is yours. I follow you even in death, you are my guide through the everlasting abyss of Oblivion."

He pulled back, and each breath was laborious as Cosima stared into his viridian eyes. "This isn't over, is it?"

"Far from it, my divine salvation." His hand brushed against her cheek, and somewhere far within, Cosima felt a tug. She let out a gasp, and Enzo grinned. "I know you still feel it, however faint it may be—your tether to me. Nothing can keep us apart."

Cosima bit her lip as she blinked back tears. "How? How can the bond still exist?"

"Sostene believes himself to be infallible and all-powerful, but what we have is ancient and undeniable. He does not have what it takes to truly fray our ties. You are mine, Cosima, and I am yours, because half my heart beats inside your chest and all of my blood sings your name."

"When will you come back to me?" she asked, her voice breaking near the end. "I'm scared I will never see you again."

"Only time will tell," he replied, his voice hushed. "Oblivion will welcome me when I wash away in the eternal river, but I will return, Cosima. A new era is upon us, and I see it now, the way the lines in my palms speak of the galaxies I will command. I ran from it, hid from it, denied it—all that is left is to accept it. I'm only sorry that it had to happen this way—that you had to watch my final exhale."

Sima shivered, and he pulled her closer. She leaned her head against his chest, the cavity within silent from his still heart. The helpless feeling taking root in her gut whispered gut-wrenching stories of her inability to save the man she loved most. "I saw the moment the Lethe decided your future, and although I understand that you were always going to have to give your life for this realm, I can't help but wish there was another way. What am I supposed to do without you? I don't know where Sostene has taken me or what he has planned. Am I supposed to try to stay alive with one eye on the horizon, awaiting your return?"

He pressed a kiss on top of her head. "Yes, Empress, but do not be afraid. Remember that it is your undecided future, your immeasurable free will, that liberates you. Your power speaks to you in a language only you can understand. Listen to that inner voice and know that it will lead to your ascension. While the Fates themselves cannot see precisely how your victory will come to be, they do know how it ends. With every breath, you alter the future timelines, but certain aspects remain fixed, immovable." He pulled back and cupped her face in his hands. "Our success is inevitable, Cosima. Live every day knowing the future you desire is already yours. You merely have to survive long enough to grasp it."

Tears streamed down her face. He was asking her to be strong, to hold on when she had no idea how to. It was something she had done an infinite number of times before, and though she resented the resilient pieces of her that refused to break, Sima believed in their future more than she trusted her fear.

"I am always with you," he whispered. "Look for me in everything and find my love is all around you, no matter how far I may be. Talk to the sky and let the wind whisper my devotion. Dance beneath the sun and let its rays kiss you where I cannot. Cry with the rain and let the thundering storms hold your rage." His brows furrowed, the ghost of a smile on his lips. "Don't lose hope, Sima, your faith is all I have left."

Her heart quivered, as if the organ couldn't decide whether to beat or seize. "I will wait for you forever, Enzo. I don't care how long it takes; my love for you will never die. No one could ever replace you."

"I love you, Cosima. When the valley of my absence begins to bloom," he whispered, his form beginning to flicker in and out of view, "know the petals speak of my reemergence. All that stands between us are the sands of time, my beloved."

He faded away entirely, and Sima crumpled in on herself, folding in half as she choked out a sob. The weight of her perilous journey had driven her to the brink of total collapse, and she struggled to rein in her grief as the Weave dissolved. Cosima hated every agonizing second of returning to her body, knowing there was only one person waiting for her on the other side.

Sostene.

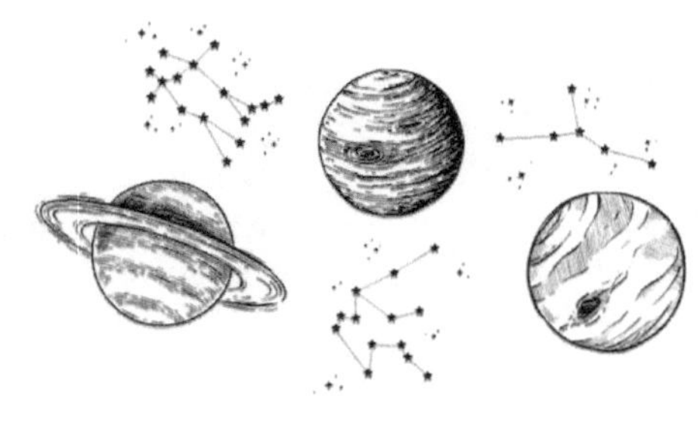

Chapter 55

Ivo

Ivo struggled to comprehend what had happened. In the middle of Doc's laboratory, a portal had opened up and spat Merit out on the other side. The navy haired Scout was grimacing as he adjusted his uniform. Calix and the two Guardians had their blades drawn, each of their faces full of sharp angles as they waited for him to make a move. Not willing to wait until someone stabbed her friend, Ivo rushed forward.

"Wait, I know him," she shouted.

Yadira's eyes flicked to her and back to Merit. "Who is he?"

Doc laughed. "He is very clearly a Trine Scout, and if that portal was any indication, he came here without permission. Tell us, boy, what trouble have you gotten yourself into?"

Merit's cheeks flushed, and his gaze fell to the floor. "I…betrayed my Kingdom and defied my oath."

Ivo gasped. "Why would you do that? What happened?"

His jaw flexed. "Cosima disappeared, and they were accusing her of violently escaping. When I heard what happened, I immediately went to check on Enzo, but it was too late. He had already killed Alvize and went to search for her. The Kingdom put a hefty bounty on each of their heads, and the Divinity ordered myself, and the others on the Sacred Twelve task force, to hunt them down." Merit sighed. "They wanted me to agree to kill Enzo and Sima, but I couldn't do it. Disobeying an order as a Trine Scout means certain death, so I…”

“So, you ran,” Ivo breathed.

Calix looked at Doc. “Should we be worried about the Kingdom coming to find him?”

Merit’s eyes widened. “No, they can’t, I made sure of it.” He rubbed the back of his head. “I have tracking abilities, but I can also shield my location. The portal I used only allows one person through, so I knew they wouldn’t be able to follow.”

Doc raised a brow. “Since when have Trine Scouts been able to manifest their own portals at will?”

“We usually can’t.” Merit shifted on his feet. “Unless we’ve had a drop of blood from an Empress.”

Ivo’s heart stuttered. “What?”

“I see,” Doc said, nodding slightly. “Are you sure you’re making the right decision? There might still be time to return before they notice you’re gone.”

Merit sniffed. “Oh, I’m almost positive they’ve already noticed.”

“Why do you say that?” Yadira asked, crossing her arms in front of her chest.

He reached into his pocket and pulled out a gold ring with a sizable berry colored gem. “I stole this from one of the High Priestesses. These rings help them channel their power; it is how they have a seemingly endless list of abilities. The gem inside this thing aligns the voltage of their energy to the proper levels for what they want to do. The Spirit Goddess used this planet as her testing grounds for more crystals in an attempt to create her own version of stones that the Divinity controls in the Eternal Kingdom.”

“How did you manage to take it?” Ivo asked, her mind reeling.

“We can talk about it later, but for now, we need to find a safe place to put it. Without it, the Priestess I took it from will be unable to perform her essential duties. Hopefully, it slows them down enough to buy us time to find Enzo and Sima.”

Ivo’s shoulders dropped. “About that…”

She did her best to recall the details with as much accuracy as she could, but she fell apart near the end. Explaining that Cosima had been kidnapped by Sostene after he killed Vincenzo was so difficult, Yadira had to take over for Ivo. Merit’s face crumpled, his grief multiplying her own. Unable to stomach reality any longer, Ivo excused herself.

Once inside the hallway, she leaned against the wall and tried to normalize her breathing. Merit’s arrival forced Ivo to face the fact that Cosima was truly gone, with no sign of where Sostene had taken her. She looked down at her hands, wondering how a mortal witch would ever be enough to save her best friend from the clutches of a wayward God. Calix emerged from the lab and gently offered to take Ivo somewhere she could rest. She agreed and wrapped her arms around herself as they walked down the hallway.

Calix stopped in front of one of the doors and pushed it open. Inside the bedroom, there was a small mattress on a white frame with burnt orange sheets and a red clay colored blanket on top. Calix disappeared for a moment and popped back in with a folded pile of clothing and towels. She gave Ivo a brief hug and promised to bring her a hot meal soon. Once Ivo shut the door behind her and locked it, her hands shook violently. She made her way to the bathing chamber and started the water for the bath before peeling off her clothes.

The tub was warm, the water forgiving as her sore muscles relaxed, releasing all stiffness. Once her body was in a state of peace, her mind wandered again as it had before traveling through the portal. This time, she only imagined the woman with wisteria eyes, forgetting all other details as she focused. The woman seemed so familiar, and Ivo wondered where she knew her face from. A disembodied voice floated through the room, its words indecipherable at first. The sound of it caused a cascading headache.

"No," Ivo said, resisting.

"Ivo," the voice whispered. *"Weakling,"* it mocked.

It was a feminine voice that she swore she recognized, but could not place. She paused, wondering if the tone was more light-hearted than she first interpreted it to be. At that, a sharp pain tore through her scalp, causing Ivo to hiss as her hands pressed into her tender skin. It was as if her mind could not reconcile the lack of information, as if it tormented her subconscious that she could not remember. She shook her head, intent on uncovering what her brain begged her to uncover. This woman, whoever she was, meant something to Ivo, and she could not understand how she could have forgotten.

Ivo sat up straight in the bath, her spine rigid. "Isolde," she said under her breath. "You stole from me. But why?"

She finished cleansing her body as quickly as she could, and when she emerged, she tugged on the slim black long-sleeve top and matching tactical pants Calix had brought. The pants hung loosely around Ivo's waist, and it was quite different from what she was used to wearing, but she found the ensemble to be comfortable.

In the mirror, Ivo's eyes caught sight of a pale white hand wrapping around her waist. Ivo jumped, but found nothing behind her. She let out a shaky breath and hesitantly looked in the mirror again. This time, a phantom hand trailed across her neck and down to her collarbone. She reached for it, her hand passing right through. Chills burst down her spine, and Ivo fled from the bathing chamber, diving beneath the covers of her bed with her hair still dripping wet. She waited for more hallucinations, but none came. After several minutes of waiting, her eyelids grew heavy.

Ivo let her eyes shut and sleep dragged her away with haste, thrusting her into a continuation of strange dreams, including the purple-eyed woman.

She was inside the Nuvola Palace on Aeria, sneaking around through the tunnels to avoid detection as the woman eyed her from around corners. She crept by Guardians and dodged Ambrosi, tucking items of interest into her pockets as purple eyes burned from the darkness.

The dream shifted, and Ivo found herself inside Aurelio's office, the walls covered in his self-given accolades. The king was nowhere in sight, but she was uneasy, finding herself unable to quell her panicked breaths. She fell to her knees, attempting to regain her breath, when the door creaked open.

She crawled beneath the desk and concealed herself within the shadows as two voices floated into the room.

"I have great faith in this plan," Aurelio said.

"And I, as well," replied a woman Ivo could not see. "All you must do is keep her occupied long enough for the others to be eliminated."

He laughed. "Easy enough. It has been some time since she bothered to fight back." Ivo held her breath as he sat down in the chair in front of the desk, ashing a cigar on the ground. "I have tried to use her to locate the artifact, but without giving her all the details, she cannot sniff it out."

"We will find it," the woman said simply. "I won't waste a moment believing otherwise. It is rightfully mine, and it will be returned to me when the time is right."

"Of course, mother," Aurelio replied.

Ivo froze, realizing that the woman he had in his office was the Spirit Goddess, Ehses. She clamped her hands over her mouth to keep from crying out.

The dream shifted again, and Ivo unfurled her body. This time, Ivo was running through tunnels she did not recognize, made of a strange blue and white stone that sparkled like diamonds despite the lack of light. Her hands ran along it until she reached an archway that revealed a sparkling fountain within.

The fountain resembled a waterfall with multiple tiers, with baby angels spitting water along the ledge of the pond at the base. The walls were covered in vines and thick green leaves, with light from the otherworldly stone shining through the gaps.

She approached the fountain and sat on the ledge beside one of the baby angels. It turned to her, but Ivo did not react to its movement. Instead, she merely watched as its tiny stone wings lifted it up and down as it smiled and spun in circles. The angel back-flipped and then flew right before her face and bopped her on the nose.

Ivo's hands flew to her nose, and the baby angel giggled before returning to its statuesque position on the fountain. She sighed and glanced down at the pond, letting her fingers create wakes in the clear blue water. A flash of purple light caught her attention, and Ivo submerged her hand, reaching for it.

When she pulled it back, a purple crystal butterfly sat in her palm. Ivo gasped, inspecting it closer to confirm it matched the pendants Isolde and Johanna had told her about. She blinked, and it was gone. Ivo spun around, searching for it, only to spot boots inside.

She dragged her gaze from the floor and made eye contact with the mysterious woman who had been haunting her conscience.

"Who are you?" Ivo asked.

"My name is not important," she said smoothly. "What is important is that you find this pendant." She leveled her wisteria gaze at Ivo and held up the pendant.

"Tell me where it is," Ivo pleaded.

"From ashes to winds of change," the woman whispered, "from slumber to vibrancy of life."

"What does that mean?"

The woman blinked. "Each pendant fulfills a duty," she said quietly, barely loud enough for Ivo to hear. "Nothingness. Resurrection. Death. Rebirth."

The pendant in the woman's hand pulsed with light energy, like a growing, hungry fire. Ivo innately understood what she was being told—the purple pendant could resurrect someone who had died. Before she could ask what the other pendants could do, she vanished. Leaving Ivo with only the hushed whisper of her name.

Nariah.

Ivo gasped, waking up in her bed alone. She had had her share of strange, cryptic dreams, but her intuition screamed at her to trust the moment of guidance she had been granted. She threw herself out of the bed and ran off to find the others, ready to uncover what Isolde and Johanna had tried so hard to keep from her.

Cosima

Cosima had held her breath when leaving the Weave, already dreading her arrival at her destination. As her spirit slipped through the fabric of space in search of her body, a memory occupied her mind.

"But I want to see my friends," tiny Sima protested.

Her mother shook her head with a firm frown from where she stood guarding the door. "For the last time, my little star. No."

"But you said we share a special connection, that we would share the Weave for eternity. You said we were going to be the best of friends. If that's the case, then why can't I meet them yet?"

She chuckled. "Because they must walk their paths just as you must. Each of you controls your own destiny, and as such, you three will cause more trouble than good if you go warping the realms with your magic."

Cosima rubbed her eyes as she sat up, finding herself draped across a fuzzy brown blanket in the grass. Sostene was beside her, his legs stretched out in front of him as he propped himself up on his elbows. His purple gaze was dripping with his amused curiosity, causing her heart rate to spike. His emotions bubbled to the surface through the wretched bond he had enacted between them, but somewhere lurking in the shadows was her thread to Enzo. It was faint, but intact.

"You were gone quite a while," he said, cocking his head to the side. "Quite inconvenient that your visits to the Weave cause your spirit to leave your physical body behind, isn't it?"

Sima rubbed her head as she stared out at the open sea in front of them. From where they sat on the grassy hill, the amethyst ocean seemed endless. The sun was setting, casting dreamy blues, purples, and pinks across the sky, reflecting off the deep, inky water. The sight nearly crushed her—despite how her world had been shattered, the universe moved on without Enzo, as if he never existed. "It doesn't happen all the time, only when I am diving beneath what appears on the surface of a person's threads. I wish I could've stayed there forever."

"I am impressed with the fluid nature with which you command your magic. You have uncovered quite a bit without proper direction, but there is more waiting for you."

She thought of Enzo's face again as a lump rose in her throat. He needed her to be strong. She could not give up yet. Until he returned to her, the only thing Cosima had to focus on was uncovering a way to stop Sostene. Discovering more of her powers would only benefit that cause. "What else could there be?"

Sostene chuckled as he snapped his fingers. A bowl of ripe strawberries appeared on the blanket in the space between time, and he took a bite of one. "As I said, your current skill set is admirable, but it is clear that you are thinking too small. You are considering your powers in the realm of what is possible for Caelari, but that is not what you are. You were built to create Weaves of your own, to wield pure, unfiltered destiny with your hands."

Sima let out a small breath. "How do I learn how to do that?"

"I will teach you, darling girl, one day at a time."

She raised a brow as he bit into another strawberry, pink juice dripping from his chin. "You know I will only use that power to stop you, correct?"

He swallowed and smiled at her. "I am a betting man, Cosima. I stand firm in my convictions—you will voluntarily offer me your heart. That being said, I did take into consideration that you perhaps would like to receive something from this relationship that my baby brother could never give you, to sweeten the deal. That is why I won't rest until you know your power more intimately than you know yourself. Not even the tapestry of time could contain you. Let me aid you as you emerge in your truest form, Empress."

"How do you expect to teach me something you don't even know?"

Sostene sat up fully. "You are not the only one who can alter the Weave."

Sima scowled. "What do you mean?"

"Three drops of Life, three drops of Death." He wagged his head back and forth. "Except for the runt, of course, I suspect he had more blood from Oblivion than he did from my mother."

"That's impossible. Why would two of the Celestial Empresses give you their blood?"

"Blood bestowing is a convoluted ritual for the Caelari. Giving a drop of their life force to the lesser immortals requires quite the preparation, not to mention the paperwork involved that the Kingdom must approve. However, Empresses are not bound by the same bureaucracy as the rest of us. They can easily offer their blood at will. They do not give it out freely, but it didn't take long for my mother to find a way around their stubborn denials."

He pulled the purple butterfly from his jacket pocket, its energy calling out to Cosima with resounding force. "Each of the High Priestesses was given a ring containing a gem called Exaltanite by the Celestial Empresses when their positions were created. Those rings allow the Divinity to access the full scope of their power. These butterflies perform, among many other things, a similar function for the three Fates. Though few can wield a stone with power of this magnitude, using it can…persuade an Empress to do as one desires."

Sima's fists clenched. "Ehses forced two Empresses to bestow their blood on each of you? Where are the Empresses now? Did she kill them?"

Sostene tipped his head back and laughed. "No one was forced. My mother found out about the pendants when you were a child and managed to steal the first from Kismet just after you settled into your immortality. She used its influence to convince Lethe and Nyssa to offer their blood to her child. At that time, the Empresses did not know we were of full God-blood; they believed us to be mere Ambrosi born of my mother's womb, with only a small percentage of her full power. The pendant hid our intimidating auras, and as she neared the birth of her final child, she acquired the remaining two butterflies."

As the sun grew smaller on the horizon, the sky became a painter's palette of magenta, sapphire, and indigo. Fireflies emerged, creating little trails of light behind them as they flew by. Sima wrapped her arms around herself, overwhelmed by the knowledge that Ehses' plans had formed when the Spirit Goddess had first laid eyes on her. "What did she do with them?"

His eyes scanned the darkening sky. "She gave one to Aurelio, one to me, and the last to another brother of ours, Giancarlo. I am sure it is unsurprising that both of my siblings lost their pendants. Although I had heard that Aurelio lost his, I was sure it would be found before we were down to half of our Sacred dozen."

Sima frowned. At one time, mentions of Aurelio would have sent ripples of apprehension through her. Beneath the blanket of her grief, she was numb to fear. "He never mentioned it to me."

"Why would he?" Sostene said, placing the butterfly back in his pocket. "If you got close enough to touch it, you would've used it to kill him, though I suppose the point was moot in the end."

Cosima said nothing as three fireflies swirled in the air a few feet in front of them. Disturbing sensations erupted across her body as Sostene slithered against their bond. She shuddered and scooted away from him, but he merely vanished and reappeared beside her, his arm draped over her shoulder.

"I think we've spoken enough about my family." He gazed into her eyes as his lips pulled into a smile. "I want to explore the enigmatic expanses of you until you're more familiar to me than the stars in the sky."

Sima shoved him off, but her action lacked the force she desired. Her internal smoldering left her with a perpetual ache, and Sostene's persistent flirtation made her pain intolerable.

"You're heartless, Sostene," she choked out. "You're asking to get to know me while you're still covered in his blood. Give me a fucking chance to breathe."

Surprise flickered through his brows. "*Esti*," Sostene said, his tone softer than before. "Why can't you see I am just eager to please you. A bit of distraction would do you well. I can feel the heaviness in your chest through the bond."

"There are things I can sense through it, too." Sima glared at him. "I can feel the parts of you that are withered and rotted. There are parts of yourself you wish to keep hidden, but you won't be able to now that you've tethered us together."

"I am not a perfect man," Sostene said through his teeth. "But, there is harmony to our power, Cosima. I was created for you, don't you understand? The Divinity cannot come where we are going, and no one else is capable of raising this realm's vibration to evade evisceration. It is you and I against the spark of creation itself." He cleared his throat and fixed his violet tie, slipping back into his usual poised mask. "Whatever we uncover about each other through the bond will only bring us closer. You are everything I crave and more. You will make a stunning bride."

His relentless badgering against her resolve reduced her to tears. Sima sobbed, unable to contain the flood any longer. Anguished cries and agonized moans escaped her mouth as she folded in on herself. Sostene moved closer and pulled her against him. "I hate you. I hate you," she screamed as she beat her fists against his chest, her vision blinded by sorrow.

Sostene shushed her softly as he held her tight enough to keep her moving. As she bucked against him, he slipped something over her finger. The metal band was cold against her skin, and the ring made bile streak against the back of her throat. Sostene wrapped one of his hands over hers, concealing it from view. "There, there, my little star. It is time to accept you're all mine now."

Sima sank into him as the fight drained out of her. She was hollow inside, but still the flame of faith flickered, singeing her viscera and heating her breath. A festering piece of Cosima would not allow her to surrender, even if the pain of losing Enzo was sharp enough to shatter her teeth. Despite how the Sacred Brothers and their mother had left her in ruins, Cosima intuitively understood that this was not the end of her journey.

When her breathing had returned to normal and her tears had dried, he finally released her. Something Cosima could not be bothered to turn and look at created a soft ringing noise behind them, catching Sostene's attention. He excused himself, granting her the elusive solitude she had been craving. The sun had fully set, leaving her drenched in moonlight as she sat on the grassy hill.

As she stared up at the pale green moon, the wind rustled her hair. She shut her eyes, letting its cool touch brush across her as she whispered his name. "Enzo." A faint buzz grew louder, prompting her to open her eyes. A brilliant emerald dragonfly hovered in front of her. Cosima put out her palm, and the creature landed in it, its legs crawling over the gold band around her ring finger.

"It's another shackle I can't escape," Sima whispered. "He has bound me to him."

You don't belong to anyone but me, Empress. Vincenzo's voice was crystal clear in her head, as if he were humming in her ear.

The dragonfly floated away, and Sima curled into a ball on the blanket as she watched the reflection of the moon on the surface of the amethyst sea. "Time is all that stands between us." Sima's eyelids grew heavy, her body begging for relief from reality. As she drifted off to sleep, his name escaped her lips once more. "Enzo."

"Cosima," Vincenzo called. "Echo of my spirit, mirror of my soul. Where are you, enlightenment incarnate?"

"I am here," she replied faithfully.

"I am here," he echoed.

A warmth spread across her being, igniting her soul with a sacred flame. She surrendered to its pull, allowing it to strip her of who she had been in favor of who she would become. She let the ravenous destruction clear the path for renewal, walking alone until footsteps appeared beside hers, the hint of a glimmer in the air. She held her hand up, tears flowing as his pressed into it.

"You can't see me, but I am here," he whispered. "Empress of the Stars."

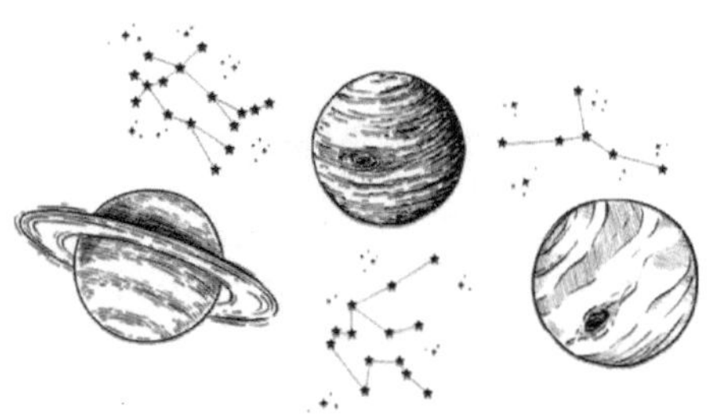

Epilogue

Vincenzo

Somewhere between nothing and everything, he lingered. Aware, mostly, but delirious with a madness no tonic could cure, equally. The gentle hands of the universe did not have to accept him, did not have to cradle him as it did now, but mercy was in his cards.

He drifted in the sea of souls, finding neither redemption nor reincarnation. There was no home for him, no resting place with his name on it to rest his weary bones—not here.

It was no matter, a rejected son would always search for a place to call his own, whether it ruined him in the process or not. If he were to float in eternity without finding belonging, his stubborn heart would wander still, persistent despite how he had been beaten down.

He had known a home once. He had been loved once.

He had been somebody once.

A ripple in the void consumed him, pulling him away from the valley of the dead and into the absence of all. His senses ceased, all connections that remained of his physical form vanished, leaving him with a deep sense of knowing.

Inevitable son—duality in harmony—your voyage has not been resolved. Wake, child.

"I cannot," he told it, speaking without sound, conveying without convoluted means required by existence, "I am lost."

Seek the other half of you, inevitable son. The Tenth is in need of you.

"I don't know where to go. There is no path before me."

Because you were made to forge, not follow. Crumble all that stands in your way.

"Destruction will only harm and maim."

Metamorphosis.

"What I do cannot be undone."

Do not fear your strength, inevitable son. It is unequivocally yours. Take without permission, but only because you are the scythe of destiny, and there is no start you cannot finish.

"It was given in error."

It was given in righteousness—ascend to your duty.

"I am flawed."

Forgive who you are for what you stand to gain, and allow your strength to grow from pain.

"I will lose who I am."

You already have.

"And if I am too cowardly to seize it?"

It would have already been written. Unleash what lurks within.

A snap of invisible energy thrust him from the space between the sprawl of eternity and the void of nothing. He resurfaced, on a plane hovering along the rim of reality, only to be submerged in the heavy weight of existence, forcing him to shed what no longer served his purpose.

He had been washed clean, renewed from the torment of a useless ego and fruitless fears. He embraced the shadows of his soul, no longer fighting the darkness within. The black of his inner being did not grapple with his light, his faith, or his divinity—it strengthened it, emboldened it to a blazing intensity.

He understood, at last, the mercy of a power so consuming and destructive. He was grateful, at last, to be the chosen son of Oblivion, to bear the weight of catastrophe on his shoulders as he paved the way for genesis. He would not escape the command of his devotion.

There was no Fated decree now that he had shed his constraints and erupted from the ashes, born again. Destiny was his to grasp, desolation his loyal servant. The cataclysm of his chaos knew nothing of bounds and limits. It sought rejuvenation, the renaissance of justice at its full capacity, acting in perpetuity.

He could not stand for another moment of depravity to go unpunished.

Vincenzo Atropos set forth on his divine mission—sculpting the way for a new era by whatever means necessary.

Books by Other Incredible Authors

Empire of the Void by Andrew Valenza (Science Fiction)

The Kimoni Legacy: Initiation by Omari Richards (Afro Fantasy)

Shadow Dance by C.K. Andersson (Portal Fantasy)

Paragon Exordium by Mikel Melwasul (Epic Fantasy)

Sweet Touch of Venom by Akita Sparks (Dark Romance)

Farodun Down by A.S. Miyasaki (Space Western)

The Maiden's Husband by Morgan Christensen (Dark Epic Fantasy)

Oceansong by C.W. Rose (Fantasy Romance)

Neon Flux by Ava Thorne (Cyber Punk)

Invoking the Blood by Kalista Neith (Dark Romantasy)

La Reina by J.D. Yanez (Gothic Horror)

Melanin by Dre Hill (Poetry)

The End!

Thank you for reading the second installment in the Frayed Threads Series.

This book pushed me to the absolute brink of insanity and because I hadn't had enough pain yet... just before I sent it off to my editor, I made the rash decision to rewrite 65% of it in just under two months (I'm aware that's insane. If you liked it then... it was worth it). I knew the draft I almost sent off to K.F. wasn't where it needed to be. I had to look myself in the mirror and ask, "would you rather it be done, or be done right?"

Well, it's not art if it doesn't make you question your entire life, so I rewrote it.

This story is the result of thousands of tears, endless hours in front of my computer, and more than a baker dozen's worth of mental breakdowns.

I quite literally took draft 4 of this book and chucked it at the wall while I cried to my husband about how it was never going to be done...

Anyway, guess all that panic was for nothing, right?

More works by this author...
Dragonfly Dynasty (New Series - Coming Soon)

Hierarchy Chart

Celestial Empresses - Isheori
(Kismet, Lethe, Nyssa)

High Priestesses - Goddesses
(Alala, Alena, Alessa, Astraea, Celestia, Demi, Fay, Fria, Keres, Telma, Thera, Sevasti)

Caelari - Gods and Goddesses

Trine Scouts - Celestial Guardians

Ambrosi - Immortal Citizens

Rani Guardians - Immortal Protectors

Souls - Creations of the Goddesses

Glossary
(May contain spoilers)

Adenyeh Gaide- immortal beings capable of reading memories of others through proximity and touch. They can erase memories at will, as well as take them to return at a later date. It takes seconds for them to view a lifetime.

Aeria Archipelago- a collection of three sky islands, home to the immortals and winged Guardians, on planet Haelos.

Ambrosi- Immortal beings with internal power, making them suitable for aiding the Kingdom. They have two primary pathways: they either remain in the Ethereal Realm and work for the Kingdom, or they are dispatched to distant planet. Their magic powers the Archipelago and allows them to care for people.

Aluyya trees- found inside of the Aluyya courtyard in Dileyna, these trees have a magical glow to their leaves and help channel the energy of prayers to Dario.

Aurelio- member of the Sacred Twelve and Cosima's former husband.

Butterfly Pendant- there are four butterfly pendants that contain crystallized souls from eternal beings. These helped the Empresses create the Weave and the Ethereal Realm. Each one has a unique power.

Caelari- the name given to Gods and Goddesses that reside inside of the Eternal Kingdom. They have special abilities and they are immortals that have received the highest amount of refinement possible for a soul.

Celestial Empress- title given to the three Fates. Although they are not blood related, they are sisters in spirit. Each has a different ability. One grants life, one apportions Fate, and one ends life.

Channeler- a special type of immortal gifted by one of Kismet's sisters, with the ability to harness the renewing powers of the Weave. They are skilled healers with a variety of ways to apply their magic inside of the Eternal Kingdom.

Defender of Dilenya- name given to Dario by the feline people on planet Yaailo.

Devotionals- somewhere between a Divine commandment and a ritualistic prayer, the Devotionals are used by the Celestial Empresses to maintain balance over the Ethereal Realm. The reincarnation of souls creates energy and helps the realm ascend. If balance is not maintained, the Devotionals will crumble and the realm will collapse.

Dilyena- city inhabited by feline people, located on planet Yaailo. Dileyna has high walls, keeping the citizens safe from roaming creatures.

Divinity- name given to the twelve High Priestesses that rule the Eternal Kingdom. They are beneath only the Celestial Empresses.

Domani- Vincenzo's father.

Drago- a large dragon creature residing in the In-Between. These creatures are tasked with defending the slumbering souls of those who have passed on, until it is time for them to be born again.

Ecliptic Court- the highest court in the Ethereal Realm, where the High Priestesses bestow their judgments.

Ehses (Spirit Goddess)- the creator of all the life on planet Haelos. She created the Faeries, Shadow-types, and humans. She did not, however, craft the physical planet. She was a High Priestess in the Ethereal Realm.

Empress of the Day- alternate name for Nyssa, the Celestial Empress.

Empress of the Night- alternate name for Lethe, the Celestial Empress.

Esti- means "little star". It is Sostene's pet name for Cosima.

Eternal Kingdom- a kingdom that resides in the Ethereal Realm. Here, there are twelve High Priestesses who rule the Kingdom and are responsible for creation of life in other realms. This is where Ambrosi come from, as well as where Rani Guardians are born and trained.

Ethereal Realm- realm where Goddesses, Ambrosi, Rani and more are born. Contains the Eternal Kingdom, as well as a multitude of other vast territories spreading through the Cosmos. At the very center is a giant lotus flower tower.

God of Terror- the name given to Carmine by the people on planet Paiturn.

Haelos- the planet where the Aeria Archipelago and Districts are contained. This planet contains many natural resources, including towering slabs of crystals.

Hand of Fate- nickname given to refer to Kismet specifically, but can also be applied more generally to any of the Celestial Empresses.

Helbrium- a divine element, best described as electrically charged air.

High Priestess- a set of twelve Goddesses who rule over the greater Eternal Kingdom, beneath Kismet only. This is a highly coveted position, allowing the ability to partake in the creation of new worlds and people.

Hyloten- a divine element, best described as water and gas.

In-Between- also known as tra paradiso e inferno (between heaven and hell). This is where slumbering souls rest until it is time for them to be reborn.

Isheori- Divine beings more powerful than even the High Priestesses. They have the ability to manipulate, create, and even destroy realms if not stopped. There are beings even above the Isheori in the highest realm.

Kismet- the Celestial Empress Isheori gifted with the power to apportion Fate to the creations of the High Priestesses. Even those in the Eternal Realm are endowed with predetermined lives. Kismet seeks balance above all else. She is more powerful than the High Priestesses. She is referred to as the Hand of Fate.

Lani- there are seven holy realms, one of which is the Ethereal Realm which holds the Eternal Kingdom. The other Lani include the Leilani and Zolani realms.

Life force- the magic power bestowed upon living beings by the High Priestesses. This power also allows the Goddesses to monitor or track their creations.

Lily of Demise- dried flower petals ground into fine powder and rolled tightly into cigars to be smoked. Gives users that can tolerate it the ability to tap into their spirit, heightening the energy inside of their body.

Lethe- the Isheori gifted with the power to breathe life into the creations of the High Priestesses. Without her kiss, the people created by the Divinity would lack a spirit, which is incompatible with existence.

Luciano- God of Light, tricked into being the father of eleven of the Sacred Twelve before he discovered Ehses' secret and revealed her plans.

Moira- Kismet's daughter. She is also an Isheori, but with limited magic.

Nuvola Palace- name of the palace on planet Haelos where Cosima was trapped for fifty years.

Nyssa- the Isheori gifted with the power to kill anyone and anything inside of the Ethereal realm.

Ohteha- a Riejj priest on planet Paiturn that prays over the bodies of the dead to keep them from rising.

Ombra- the Shadow District. The name translates to Shadow in reference of the large shadow cast across the District during the height of the day from the Archipelago blocking the sun. This District is primarily a barren desert, worsened by the shun from the Eternita District.

Oracle- in the Eternal Kingdom, they are Caelari blessed as Seers. They communicate with the Weave and read the threads to uncover the future. Oracles also exist on planets as immortal creations, with more limited capabilities than those in the Eternal Kingdom.

Oretzen- powerful immortal beings with magic strong enough to pierce outside of their home planet and into other realms.

Paiturn- Carmine's captured planet. Contains the city Riejj.

Pahyasa- breathable fabric exclusive to Riejj.

Raidnen- a divine element best described as smoke and flame.

Rani Guardian- the winged Guardians from the Eternal Kingdom tasked with protecting the Ambrosi and life-forms created by the High Priestesses on their assigned planet. They are raised together to form strong bonds, and the only way to kill one is by slicing off their wings.

Reijj- city inhabited by owl-like people on planet Paiturn.

Reygco- the first planet where the Spirit Goddesses plans disrupted the balance of the universe.

Sacred Twelve- the name for Aurelio and his eleven brothers. They are born from Ehses and Luciano, except for Vincenzo, who was born from Ehses and Domani. They were rumored to be Ambrosi, in an attempt to disguise their true heritage. Ehses created her sons in retaliation for being removed as a High Priestess by Celestial Empress, Kismet.

Salvatore- a large chicken-like creature that was named as the protector of the Riejj people on planet Paiturn. It was seen wearing a large crystal.

Scythe of Destiny- the name given by Oracles as the one who 'prevails'.

Seven- seven chosen members of Dileyna that are allowed to enter the temple with Dario.

Soul- the immortal true self or essence of a person that continues beyond physical death. It retains memories, personality, strong emotions, and accrued spiritual debt.

Spirit- the breath of the universe imbued in every living being. It is in some ways a spiritual connection the cosmos. Not to be confused with Life force.

Starlight- a magic power harnessed by the Rani Guardians, Trine Scouts, and Sacred Twelve. It is used in attacks and in practical ways such as disarming wards and altering a portal's destination. It physically looks like a galaxy, with small stars, planets, and empty space flooding through.

Survivor- the last living brother of the Sacred Twelve.

Trine Scouts- protectors from the Eternal Kingdom, occasionally tasked with "cleaning-up" the chaos on other planets.

Vinet- a creature found in the Eternal Kingdom that resembles a viper with no eyes and long fangs.

Void- a manifested space created between reality and the unknown. People enveloped inside of them vanish from the real world and appear inside of an endless black space. Wielders of the void can manipulate it as they please, manifesting attacks or defenses.

Weave- where all the strands of Fate originate from.

Wheel of Favor- found inside of the Weave, the Wheel grants favor through its turns. Some will rise and some will fall. The turning is a greater cosmic event, rather than an individual blessing.

Yaailo- Dario's captured planet. Contains the city Dileyna.

Zolani- one of seven holy realms. The Emperors from the Zolani realm are thought to be planning an attack on Leilani, AKA the Ethereal Realm.

Acknowledgments

I want to extend a huge thank you to all of the readers, fellow authors, and supporters of mine that have gotten me this far. This would not have happened if there weren't tons of people pressuring me to not set this manuscript on fire (I deeply considered it). Thank you to those who pledged through my Kickstarter campaign to fund the art work and publication of this novel! To everyone on Booktok and Bookstagram who shares my posts or makes their own, I adore you and I can't thank you enough. Expressing your support and showing up for me has made all the difference. Those who love my novel, please know, all the amazing people below contributed highly to getting this published:

Thank you to my sweet boys, **J. and A.** If it wasn't for you two, I don't know that I would be who I am today. You show me the true power of love and vulnerability. You show me that it is worth going through rain and mud if it means seeing your smiling faces at the end of it. To J., you have a heart filled with bravery and a mind filled with possibility. Each and every single day you make me proud. To A., your resilience and willingness to get out of your comfort zone can sometimes genuinely bring me to tears. Your tiny cuddles always make my bad days better. You both are the brightest lights in mommy's life and I love you, from now until forever.

Thank you to my incredible husband, **Rafael.** If there is one thing I am the most certain of after finishing this book, it's that you and I were meant to be together. When the world is crumbling around me, you hold me tight enough to make it all fade away. You wipe away my tears, give me the pep-talk I need, and make sure that I never give up. You're everything I have ever wanted in a partner and I thank the universe that we have each other. You have shown me that love is kind, soft, and reliable. You have shown me what it looks like to laugh on your worst days and what real happiness is like. You are so damn smart, empathetic, strong, brave, and you are, unfortunately, funnier than me (most of the time). I love you more with every breath I take.

Thank you to **Mom and Dad** for giving me life and buying me all those books as a pre-teen. You'd look at me, sigh, and say 'at least she's not sneaking out'. I love you both and I couldn't have made it this far without you. So much of what you've taught me throughout my life has helped me on this path to being an author.

Thank you to **Jinapher Hoffman** for the amazing cover images. You are a wonderful person and talented author. I feel so lucky all the time that you've made my covers for me because I am in awe of you all the time! I love seeing your posts on social media and I am always celebrating all of your wins.

Thank you to **K.F. Starfell** for doing the editing on this novel. You were so amazing to work with and if you hadn't told me "write your little heart out", I don't think the story would've came together the way it did. I reached out to you about a 160k manuscript and delivered you an almost 220k one. You deserve an award honestly.

Thank you to my watercolor artist, **Hope Garrity.** Girl. Your art is genuinely magic. You are so talented and I can't believe you've brought my characters to life. I can't tell you how much your art has changed my life. I get to show people my characters and look at them hanging on my wall whenever I want to give up. Thank you to **Rami fon Verg** for your absolutely stunning artwork of Cosima and Vincenzo. You are a magnificent artist and I can't wait to see more of my characters in your style.

Thank you to **C.K. Andersson.** Seriously, you are a life saver. So many times I came to you when I was struggling with self-doubt and you uplifted me through all of it. Whether we are talking about cozy gaming and keyboards, or crying about our books, our friendship is something I will always be thankful for. You have brought me so much sunshine and comfort and I adore you! You're a one-of-a-kind writer and I know you will go so far. I can't wait to be besties at the top!

Thank you to **Stevi Lynn** for alpha reading for me (but let's be honest, you did so much more than that). You have been there through all the ups and downs, all without blinking an eye when I come to you with my fears. You have shown me so much kindness and support, and you have the biggest heart. Your books are genuinely CRAZY GOOD and I can't wait for everyone to find out.

Thank you to **Rachel Lynn Hanks, Zaylan Flynn, Sara Crow, Alison Birks, Olga Ziminska, Erica Everett, and Emma Mortimer** for beta reading for me. Each of you are so dang important to me and I just want to tear up thinking about it. You guys saw this book in the early, scary days, and helped make it into what it is today with your feedback. You're incredible and I love you all!

Thank you to **Voice of Hel, Zack Rosenfeld, KJ Stewart** for all the amazing narration snippets you have done for me. Hel—you're everything anyone could want in a friend/narrator/person. You're funny, down-to-earth, sassy, and supremely talented. Each time I hear one of your snippets, I'm left gasping for breath. Zack—your range is impressive and your narration skills are jaw-dropping already. I know you will only soar higher in the future. KJ—you're someone so special, capable of capturing the tone of a scene with incredible accuracy. I am blown away by you all the time. You're all going to go so far.

Thank you to **Andrew Valenza.** Not only are you a magnificent writer, you are an even better friend. I swear that I think every author should want to be more like you. You inspire me all the time and I know if there every comes a day where I seriously consider giving up writing, you will come talk me off the edge in a heartbeat. You do so much for the indie community and I am thankful our paths have crossed.

Thank you to my girls: **Nicolette Andrews, Mariet Kay, Ava Thorne, Kalista Neith, Fleur DeVilliany, Kay Leyda, Aly Hollis, and Johnna Dee.** I would have never survived my first author events if it wasn't for all of you. Literally every single one of you are so uniquely talented, with beautiful souls. You all inspire me and push me to be a better author because you all work so hard, fight for what you want, and refuse to accept no for an answer. You're showing me what its like to believe in myself and pursue my dreams without waiting for the rest of the world to catch up. I hope all of you remember me when you're super famous.

Thank you to my accountability coven: **Stevi Lynn, Rachel Hanks, Anastasia Arellano, Lilybeth Schultz, C.A. Fray, Sareya, and Taylor Lust.** Publishing is hard enough already, but being alone can make it feel impossible. Thankfully, I had this amazing group to rely on. Our frequent check-ins, long paragraphs about our books, and life updates all made this journey so much easier. I am proud of all of you and I know each of you has your big moment coming soon.

Thank you to **Mikel Melwasul, River Seabrook, Kayla Falcone, Amy Tellez, Devon Perricelli, Omari Richards, Morgan Christensen, Cara Blaine, Hannah McGuire, Ashley Martin, Shelby Garner, Raven K. Storm, Ela Gordon, Kylee Smith, Kyra, Taylor Quick, Ellie Betts, and Sara Stokes** for your support. This path can be so daunting and lonely, but I feel stronger with you all by my side. You've all added to my life in priceless ways.

Lastly, THANK YOU to the person reading this. You're valuable, unique, and perfect just the way you are. The world is better because you exist.

About the Author

Jade Nioma currently resides deep in the Sonoran desert with her husband, their two boys, and their cats. She has worked in rehab facilities, lock-down psychiatric wards, and on a specialized crisis team for those experiencing psychosis. She has a bachelor's degree in psychology and prior to attending her first Master's level courses, Jade pivoted toward her life-long dream of writing. She is Korean-American and both of her parents immigrated to the US before she was born. She spent much of her childhood behind the counter of her parents' small business and attributes this upbringing to her desire for an independent career.

She is a keyboard enthusiast (with a collection that is taking over her house), a delusional DIY-er, and an avid computer gamer. When Jade isn't writing, you'll likely find her curled up with a book, journaling, or devouring anime. She is almost always listening to music (from Megan Thee Stallion to Sleep Token to Trance EDM) and loves to make people laugh. Close to Jade's heart is domestic violence awareness and mental health representation, especially after her own struggles with both.

Jade hopes her writing will inspire others and show those who are struggling that their story is not over.